Raves for *Faery Moon* and *Forest Moon Rising*:

"This third series outing for Frost's complex and quirky heroine reveals conflicts in her personal life and also in her relationship to the Citadel she has left behind. The author uses Las Vegas and its desert surroundings to good advantage, creating an atmosphere of affluence and decadence amid the stark beauty of ancient places."—*Library Journal*

"Finally! A female first-person narrative in which the main character does not believe she can take on the world all on her own, and using the people around her to assist her in her goals!"
—Night Owl Sci-Fi

"Tess is brave and resourceful as she copes with the traumas life his tossed at her. P. R. Frost has written a fabulous urban fantasy filled with danger, intrigue and heartache as Tess and Scrap bond into a powerful unit who symbiotically need one another to survive. Readers will stay up late enjoying this engaging magical tale."—*Midwest Book Review*

"This fantasy is campy and rather fun. With creative characterization, a deftly paced plot, and even some romance, this is a breezy novel meant for adult readers. *[Forest Moon Rising]* will find an audience especially with those who have their own favorite science fiction or fantasy conventions."
—*VOYA*

"Frost brings us another engaging novel that is action-packed from start to finish. Among the terror of the deranged villain the readers would find in this book wit, humor, and entertainment that will keep them flipping pages. The story pushes forward with fast-paced excitement as you follow Tess and her sidekick Scrap through the streets of Portland."
—Portland Book Review

"Fast pacing and startl ... a
touching (and startling ... *s*

P. R. Frost's
Tess Noncoiré Chronicles:

HOUNDING THE MOON
MOON IN THE MIRROR
FAERY MOON
FOREST MOON RISING

P. R. FROST

THE TESS NONCOIRÉ CHRONICLES

VOLUME TWO

FAERY MOON

FOREST MOON RISING

DAW BOOKS, INC.
DONALD A. WOLLHEIM, FOUNDER
375 Hudson Street, New York, NY 10014
ELIZABETH R. WOLLHEIM
SHEILA E. GILBERT
PUBLISHERS
www.dawbooks.com

Cover art courtesy of Shutterstock.

Cover design by G-Force Design.

DAW Book Collectors No. 1676.

DAW Books are distributed by Penguin Group (USA).

First Printing, December 2014
1 2 3 4 5 6 7 8 9

DAW TRADEMARK REGISTERED
U.S. PAT. OFF AND FOREIGN COUNTRIES
—MARCA REGISTRADA
HECHO EN U.S.A.

PRINTED IN THE U.S.A.

FAERY MOON

DEDICATION:

For all the mothers out there who dedicate themselves to raising their children to have manners and coping skills so they can go out there and achieve what they need to do to live life to the fullest.

In Memoriam
Miriam Elizabeth Bentley Radford

2/14/1915–8/28/2004

Acknowledgments

Many thanks to Gwen Knighton for permission to use the lyrics of her song "Fairytale" from her CD "Box of Fairies." Please visit her at www.gwenknighton.com for a full list of lyrics, more music, and a glimpse into her life as a harpist. Interesting how our lives have connected through this piece of music. Almost every song on the CD would have fit for Tess, Gollum, and Donovan and their journey. I had a hard time choosing. In the end, "My Fairytale" seemed the right choice.

I'm always amazed at how many memories I can trigger with just a snippet of a song. I hope you've enjoyed my trips backward in time with the featured songs in *Faery Moon.*

The history and full lyrics of "Mairzy Doats" can be found at en.wikipedia.org/wiki/Mairzy_Doats. I'm glad I looked up this interesting and favorite memory from my childhood.

And for "Three Little Fishes" and other camp songs, please visit www.backyardgardener.com/loowit/song/song193.html. Another favorite from Girl Scouts.

Many thanks to Deborah Dixon, her sister Pam, and niece Tonya for their gracious hospitality and help in researching the Las Vegas landscape and history. Without them, I might never have gotten it right. Any errors are mine, not theirs.

I highly recommend a side trip to the Valley of Fire Nevada State Park next time you happen to visit Las Vegas. The landscape is an awesome contrast to the city. The park employees patiently answered my questions and directed me to great research texts. And check out Cirque du Soleil's production of "Mystère" at the Treasure Island to find my inspiration for "Fairy Moon." I found "Las Vegas Trivia" by John Gollehon invaluable as a resource about the city and its culture.

My long-suffering and special friends who read early drafts of my feeble attempts at this book deserve a favored place in heaven. Without Lea Day, Deborah Dixon, and Jessica Groeller, I'd never have whipped those stumbling paragraphs into a real book. I cannot forget my editor Sheila Gilbert for her untiring excavation of my manuscript to separate the true gems from the dross and help me make them shine bright and true.

Last but not least, I need to thank my mom for . . . well for being My Mom.

Prologue

WHILE MY DAHLING Tess flies from here to there on a big mechanical machine that makes so much noise it hurts my tender little ears and smells too ripe, I'm wandering around the chat room looking for something to do.

The vast whiteness that stretches on and on, broken only by an occasional door to another dimension is strangely quiet today. I can't even find the demons that are supposed to be on guard duty. They keep beings inside their home dimension, only allowing passage to a privileged or wily few.

I'm one of the few. Imps may go anywhere. Convincing the guard demons of that is another issue altogether.

I stumble across a round stone door I haven't noticed before. It smells odd. My pug nose wiggles overtime trying to discover what lurks behind before I open it.

Stone, copper, dust, and sage.

I've smelled that before.

Instantly wary, I tug on the handle until it squeals in protest on rusty hinges.

I freeze—waiting, assessing.

No one comes to pummel me into submission or back where I came from.

So, like a good little imp, I poke my nose inside the scant inches between the round stone door and the arched stone jamb.

"Gargoyles!" I chortle. "Gargoyles in their natural form." Translucent spirits flit about. The smallest have hardly any features at all, just amorphous wispy forms. The larger ones begin to show signs of eyes, nose, and mouth. Nothing individual about any of them.

They all play tag with inanimate cutouts of demons, practicing pushing over bad guys with only the power of their aura. Some are better than others.

They are all good enough to keep me out. I can only watch from the doorway.

An old guy, his wrinkled and threadbare robes made of smoke sagging around his potbellied form, follows the youngsters about with a clipboard. He peers over half glasses at the antics of one particularly talented child. The twisted grimace on his face appears carved out of stone. He's lived long enough to develop features and a personality. A grim one from the way he frowns.

The kid he concentrates on can't be more than two or three centuries old. He won't stand still long enough to get a bead on his developing features. I get hints of bat wings.

"Report," the old guy barks, quill pen poised over his notes.

"Six Damiri lurking behind that pillar," the kid nods toward a Gothic column I hadn't seen before he pointed it out. Maybe it didn't exist before he mentioned it.

"Check. What else."

"Two Cthulhus in the moat, reluctant to come out. And a pair of Windago hunting innocents who enter the forest trying to find sanctuary."

"Very good. We have an emergency vacancy," the old guy intones. "You are young yet, but you are the best student we've had in three centuries. Go now. Replace the ancient one who fell asleep. His corner is a vitally strategic post. We need younger energy to fill the gap."

The kid salutes, bouncing up and down in his enthusiasm. Then his misty body trails off and escapes through the door I left partly open for my own escape.

The venerable gargoyle tutor makes a check mark on his clipboard and moves on to supervise another pupil.

The distinctive smell of stone, copper, dust, and sage shifts. Now I get granite, moss, and clay tiles.

So that's how they do it! The spirit form of the gargoyle inhabits the stone or metal body which gives them definition. Their magic exists only in their apotropaic ability to repel demons away from the edifice they protect.

Hmmm. I wonder if the kid's smell is unique to him, or

merely his type. I know that scent. I do not trust the man who cannot mask it behind a musky aftershave.

This is info my babe may need.

Time to check on her. She should have changed planes and started on the final leg of her journey.

Chapter 1

Gambling became legal in Nevada in 1931, the same year the divorce laws were relaxed.

"TESS, MY DARLING." Donovan Estevez cupped my face in his long-fingered hand. His thumbs rubbed circles against my cheekbones. The rasp of his calluses on my skin awakened nerve endings and sent flaring signals of welcome to my fevered brain. Then he traced my scar from temple to chin, trailing kisses along the ridge.

"I find this scar very sexy." He feathered more kisses behind his fingers' trail. "I can't see it, but I know it's there. Clouded with mystery and promises."

I waited, willing him to move closer, linger, and savor. Magnetic tingles drew our mouths closer. He held back.

"Are you certain?" he whispered. His warm breath drifted across me like the softest of spring breezes.

A new face appeared in my vision. Gollum peered at me from behind Donovan's shoulder, a stern frown of disapproval and . . . aching pain marring his lean face. He pushed his glasses up to hide his eyes.

I tried to banish the image of my friend and mentor; my Gollum. I could never think of him as Guilford Van der Hoyden-Smythe, PhD.

"Yes," I said to Donovan, doing my best to ignore my misgivings.

Our bodies pressed against each other in an explosion of

sensation, bonding us together. Our mouths blended and molded, opened. Our tongues entwined in an eternal dance, mimicking a more intimate joining.

Clothing disappeared without seeming to have ever been worn.

I stood on tiptoe, stretching to feel as much of him as I could. His hands ran the length of my back and lifted me higher by my bottom.

I nestled my face into his shoulder and inhaled his unique scent of copper, sage, and hot dust, enhanced by a dry cologne. A sigh rose, constricting my chest with anticipation. I belonged here. We fit. We were meant to be together.

"No, you don't," Gollum said, the erudite scholar, not a lover or a friend. "You belong with me."

A sharp pain in my neck wrenched me awake, out of my pretty dream. My head jerked forward and back against the airplane seat. The jet engine grated on my ears and my nerves. My balance skewed to the left.

I automatically keyed my laptop to save, and to back up to a flash drive.

One night. I'd had one wonderful, erotic, special night with Donovan.

Then I had three comfortable nights sleeping on Gollum's sofa, the only intimacies between us on the level of dear friends.

One friggin' night with Donovan. *Not enough,* part of me screamed.

Never again, my common sense replied. Not until he honestly told me of his past and his current agenda.

"Tess Noncoiré, you snore in a most unladylike manner," Mom said with a delicate sniff. Then she turned her lost and fragile gaze back to contemplating the agricultural patterns of the Midwest thirty-five thousand feet below us.

"Where are we?" I asked on a yawn. I scrubbed my face with my hands, trying desperately to banish the dream, the wanting, the need for a man I could not trust.

"We're somewhere south of Chicago," Mom replied. She played with her pearl necklace, more out of habit than nervousness.

Well, duh. I looked at my watch. An hour and a half after we'd lifted off from O'Hare. About another hour to Las Vegas.

A frisson of alarm suddenly clawed at my spine from tailbone to nape. I twitched in the too-narrow airplane seat, two seats side by side on our side of the aisle, three across the aisle. The tingles spread down my arms, making my fingers itch to hold a weapon.

The underlying smells of plastic and cleaning fluids combined with stale air, stale coffee, and stale bodies suddenly intensified. My nose is keen. My otherworldly imp's nose is better. Something was off here.

What?

Beside me, my mother glared at me, mentally ordering me to sit still, just like she used to do in church.

Nervously, I closed my laptop, secured it in the case, and shoved it beneath the seat in front of me. Then I unfastened my seat belt. Once free of my lifeline and slave driver of a novel, though little more existed than an outline and first chapter, I slid into the aisle, stretching and arching my back.

I used the innocuous movement to scan the other Las Vegas-bound passengers. Mostly couples in casual shirts and slacks headed out on vacation. They bubbled with excitement. A constant susurration of sound rose from their discussion of show tickets, excursions, and spa treatments. Discussion of the show "Fairy Moon" flew about more than any other. I hoped to get tickets for me and Mom to the hottest show in Vegas.

When excursions came up in the conversations, more than one mentioned the geological wonder of the Valley of Fire, only an hour north of Vegas. I'd have to think about that one if time allowed, with a full conference schedule and babysitting Mom.

Scattered throughout the nearly full coach seating, I spotted a few intense men and women flying solo. Their garb varied from business suits to jeans and Tees. They had the haunted look of addicts. Gamblers.

Then there were the business people. Suit jackets off, ties loosened, working furiously on their laptops.

No one person stood out in the crowd as different. No one person kept their gaze locked on me.

If I had a stalker, he wasn't going to be easy to spot. But then that's what stalkers do. They stay in the shadows and watch. Waiting for the opportunity to lunge. Like a crocodile.

Ambush predators.

I prefer fighting demons. At least with monsters from other dimensions, I know who I'm fighting and why.

"Mom, I'm walking back to the restroom." I spoke slowly and distinctly, making certain I had her attention before I touched her shoulder.

She nodded and drifted back into the tangled world of her nightmares. Last month she eloped with a demon: Darren Estevez. He was also the foster father of my former lover Donovan Estevez.

Fortunately, an escapee from a pan-universal prison had murdered him thirty-six hours later and Mom only had to endure one night of his inhuman attentions.

She coped. She went about each day's routine without protest. Darren had drained a vital quality from her. I'd never forgive him for that.

I had a few issues with him over the way he'd manipulated Donovan as well.

I hoped this five-day junket to Vegas would help Mom separate her mind from those horrible days of existing in demon thrall. I could stretch it to a week if I had to. Maybe some natural wonders out in the Valley of Fire would do the trick if all the glitz and neon of Las Vegas didn't.

A writers' conference was paying me and covering most of my expenses. For four days I had workshops to present. Up-and-coming writers wanted to pick my brain on breaking out of midlist into best sellers. New writers wanted my secret formula (there isn't one) for getting published. But that should only involve a few hours each of four days. The rest of the time I could show my mom the wonders of the oasis of light and noise and frivolity (not to be confused with *le frivolité* or tatted lace, a pile of which sat tangled and ignored in her lap).

Something, anything, to bring back the twinkle of mischief to her eyes. Normally, she delighted in playing the martyr—especially after Dad moved in with the love of his life, Bill Ikito. Mom had a right to feel used and abused since Darren and should revel in her martyrdom. Now, she lapsed into too-long sessions of silence and depression. No complaints. No trying to make me feel guilty for her problems.

What was worse, she no longer tried to play my sister

Cecilia and me against each other. Cecilia with her architect husband, her three children, her PTA meetings and garden clubs, no longer exemplified Mom's definition of a proper woman. I, the black sheep of the family, who fought demons and dressed up in costumes at Science Fiction/Fantasy conventions, was now her crutch and anchor in life.

No fair. I shouldn't have to take maternal responsibility for my mom. I was the baby of the family, the one all the others should take care of.

I took my time strolling along the aisle, nodding casually to anyone who looked up. Making myself as skinny as possible and plastering up against a seat back so the flight attendants could move about collecting drink and snack debris—no such thing as meals aboard anymore. Good thing I'd fed Mom in Chicago, not that she ate much.

Nothing out of the ordinary caught my attention. No suddenly averted glances or angry glares. Not even Scrap, my interdimensional imp, showed on my radar.

And now that I was moving about, the sense of danger and foreboding had vanished.

Just my imagination working overtime.

Yeah. Right.

While I was up and about, I might as well use the facilities.

"We'll be preparing to land soon, ma'am," an attendant in her prim gray jumper and white blouse, informed me. "The captain will ask you to resume your seat within minutes."

Sure enough, the floor had begun a gradual downward tilt.

"I won't be long," I reassured her.

The miniscule cubicle—barely enough room for me to turn around in—gave me just enough privacy to ask for other-dimensional help. Blue room smells dominated here, almost pleasant after the staleness of coach.

"Scrap?" I whispered into the ether. "You anywhere close, buddy?"

What? he answered querulously.

"Well, excuse me for interrupting your sojourn in the freeze-dried garbage dump of the universe." Scrap said he'd visit his mum while I flew south. He didn't like airplanes much.

A few mumbled grumbles passed through my mind. *What's up, babe?* he finally asked in an overly bright tone, like he was hiding something.

"Have I acquired a stalker?"

Not that I can tell from here. I'll let you know when you hit Vegas.

"And if that is too late?" This time I sent the mumbled grumbles his way. Mine were more specific and less polite.

No stalker worth his salt will cause an incident on a plane. No way to escape.

"And if it's a demon? Some demons can open the door and fly to safety." A Damiri demon, like Darren Estevez, took a bat form naturally.

I was pretty sure that Donovan Estevez, his foster son, could do the same, though I'd been told by semireliable sources he was now fully human. I didn't want to risk pushing him too hard, too far, too fast to force him into his natural form.

If you'd picked up a demon stalker I'd know, dahling. Trust me, the only danger you are in is from the fashion police. Faded jeans and stained golf shirts are for gardening, not flying to Las Vegas. And couldn't you do something else with your hair than cut it as short as a boy's? You look like a poodle.

Visions of short, fat, cranky dogs that yapped continuously flashed across my mind. I might have lost weight as part of the ritual that gave me Scrap—ten days of one-hundred-three-plus fever will do that to a body. But in my heart, I was always short, fat, and cranky.

"I thought you liked boys?" I needed to change the subject.

Boys, dahling, not girls looking like boys. I could almost smell the smoke from his favored black cherry cheroot.

I snorted as I washed my hands and checked my image in the wavery metal mirror. The mass of dirty-blonde kinky curls had brightened a bit over the last year thanks to a magical comb Scrap had given me. But the curls hadn't relaxed and I was tired of the tangles, so now I sported a bob that would have been cute if it didn't tend to stick out like an uneven afro.

Still feeling like a pair of eyes tracked my every move, I meandered back toward my seat, just in front of the wing.

A slender young man of no particular note in dress or form twitched as I passed. He looked pasty. His equally young companion, wearing an unremarkable suit, dozed in the center seat. At least I presumed they were together. Mr. Twitchy had both hands on the other man's arm.

An acrid scent whispered across my senses. Fear.

"Sit down, lady," Mr. Twitchy hissed at me.

"What?" I hadn't touched him, hadn't done anything to attract his attention other than walk past him.

"I said sit down! We're going to crash. I know it. I just know it." The smell of fear on stale sweat nearly overwhelmed me.

Chapter 2

The building of Boulder Dam (now Hoover Dam) in 1931 and the creation of Lake Mead behind it changed the economy of Las Vegas from an agricultural railroad town to a tourist destination.

MY HEART LEAPED to my throat. My balance tilted again. I had to grab the back of my seat to remain upright.

"Tsk," an older woman behind me clucked. "Flying is safer than walking across a street." Her hours-too-old perfume told a different story. Mr. Twitchy's fear began to infect her.

You might want to listen to the guy, Scrap said.

I didn't like his tone. Anxious. No sarcasm. No drawled "dahling," or affectionate "babe."

"Everybody sit down!" Mr. Twitchy moaned. "Please sit down before we crash."

I plopped back in my seat and fastened my seat belt. Then I made sure the laptop was secure under my feet and the flash drive clipped to a lanyard about my neck and safely tucked into my shirt pocket. I'd e-mailed the work in progress to myself from O'Hare. If both the computer and the flash drive trashed, I'd only lose about an hour's work.

I'm obsessive about backups. Or hadn't you noticed?

Of course, if the plane crashed hard enough to trash both the laptop and the flash drive, I'd be dead and wouldn't have to worry. The novel and its sequel became the problem of my agent, my editor, and my literary executor, all good friends of mine.

The plane bounced and plunged. I felt like I'd left my stomach a hundred feet above me.

Mom clutched my arm so tightly I knew she'd leave bruises. I don't bruise easily.

Yelps and gasps all around us. Mr. Twitchy moaned, "I knew it. I knew it. We're all going to die."

The canned air permeated with staleness became claustrophobic. More than one person tugged at a collar or neckline, seeking more air.

A steward emerged from behind the curtain separating us mere coach passengers from first class. He blanched as the plane banked right and then sharply left. He grabbed the curtain with both hands, nearly ripping it from its cable support.

Sweat poured off Mr. Twitchy's brow. He rocked forward and back, enduring his own private agony.

That's when I got scared. The guy had to be a sensitive. He knew things, bad things before they happened.

"Ladies and gentlemen," a reassuring male voice came over the intercom. "We are experiencing a bit of turbulence. The captain has turned on the seat belt sign. Please return to your seats immediately. We ask that you put away all carry-on items and secure your trays. Return your seats to an upright position."

All of the flight attendants disappeared to their own seats.

"In other words, prepare for a crash," I muttered. This was much more than the slight sideways jiggles we'd had off and on all the way south from Chicago.

The incandescent blue of Saint Elmo's fire shot around the wing tip.

"A bit of turbulence? I'd say that was an understatement." Mom sounded like her old self. Then the flash of fire in her eyes faded and she resumed staring out the window.

I followed her gaze. Weird, red rock formations flowed and twisted out of a gray-brown background below us. Splotches of black drizzled over the top. Like looking at the bottom of a seabed without the sea. The shadows promised mysteries. I'd hate to get lost in that trackless and waterless wilderness.

"The Valley of Fire," the man sitting behind me whispered. "It's awesome."

The plane lurched again. We lost more altitude. The gasps and cries of alarm grew louder. A small child wailed in distress.

We passed the Valley of Fire and approached volcanic formations. This landscape was born of fire and tumult; just as trackless and without water.

"Las Vegas has put us into a holding pattern. We're experiencing some severe crosswinds at this altitude. So please, ladies and gentlemen, sit back and relax. We'll keep you updated."

"Scrap, I could use some help here."

"Who are you talking to?" Mom whispered back at me.

"Myself."

"Fine time to start talking to yourself."

What's ya need, babe?

"A little information."

On my way, but I've got to fight my way through some pretty ugly energy in the chat room first.

Scrap always had to fight his way into or out of the chat room—that's the big white place with no sense of size or shape that exists between dimensions, giving access to all other dimensions. Some called it limbo.

I called it purgatory.

"Are these crosswinds normal?" I whispered, hoping Mom wouldn't hear me and get any bright ideas about ghosts or demons. Another encounter might tip her over the edge of sanity.

The plane banked again, smoothly. The jumping about ceased.

Everyone breathed a sigh of relief.

"Las Vegas informs us that we will be circling for about another fifteen minutes. We've climbed above the severe crosswinds," the copilot said, almost cheerily.

"They're coming back," Mr. Twitchy shouted. "We can't escape them. Not now, not ever! They're coming to get me. You all are just collateral damage."

Excited murmurs all around us.

I peered around Mom out the window. Plain old desert undulated beneath us like the bottom of a seabed. But the weird red-rock formations northeast of the city were coming into view again.

The plane took a nose dive. Bounced. Tilted. Climbed. Rocked. Dove. The wing tips moved a fraction of a second after each jolt.

Worse than a roller coaster.

Screams. Wailing cries. A miasma of unpleasant scents. Mom looked like she'd lose her lunch.

Mine wasn't sitting too well either.

Mr. Twitchy jumped up and ran toward the front. "We've got to get out of here. We're all going to die!"

I stuck out my leg.

He fell face first. Lay there pounding the deck.

More people got up. Some paced the aisle in agitation.

A steward tried desperately to push them back into their seats. The more he tried, the more people tried getting into the aisle.

Screams deafened me.

"Tess, you have to do something." Mom turned wild eyes on me. Her grip tightened on my arm.

"What can I do about crosswinds?" I returned.

"Are they truly crosswinds born of this Earth?" Her eyes took on an unearthly red glow. Demon thrall. Some*thing* other than my mother spoke with her voice.

I shuddered and leaned as far away from her as I could.

Are they otherworldly, Scrap? If so, there might be a rogue portal that bypassed the chat room hidden in the red-and-black shadows. I really hoped Scrap would catch my telepathic message. He didn't always. Our bond is not perfect. I couldn't risk Mom or anyone else hearing me talk to an imp that was transparent in this dimension except when he transformed into my choice of weapon.

I don't know! he wailed. *They're winds, but the source? I can't find the source.*

Where are they strongest?

Silence.

Another steward appeared from the rear and tried desperately to get people to sit down.

Mr. Twitchy pulled himself up, eyes wild. I saw the same panic reflected in the faces and cries of all those around us.

I unfastened my seat belt and pried Mom's hand off my

arm. Then I rose and hauled Mr. Twitchy to his feet from the deck. "Sit down and shut up. You are only making things worse."

"They're coming for me. Evil spirits use the winds to find their victims. We're all going to die!"

I edge my way toward the Earth portal in the chat room. New guardian demons have sprung up since I looked into the gargoyle nursery. Can't let these guys know where I'm really headed. A weird-looking demon I've never seen before tracks my every movement. He's all full of red scales and flits like a faery. He smacks me with the force of a fully loaded semi going seventy in a fifty-five speed zone. A little morphing and removal of the hard edges, this could be a faery on steroids dressed in unnatural neon colors of clashing orange and pink over the red scales and black hair, lips, and nails.

He smells of rancid tobacco and burning sewage.

This is not good.

From infancy, imps are schooled in many types of demons and their weak points. We have to know so that we can help our Warrior companions fight these guys.

If new demons are cropping up, then there's trouble brewing. The balance of the universe is going cattywhumpus.

What else is new?

The not-faery demon raises his hand for another blow. I duck underneath and scoot toward the wooden door with heavy iron crossbars. Iron doesn't bother me, but it should hold back a faery—even a not-faery—for long enough for me to open the door and duck back into reality.

Curses and taboos. The door sticks.

No, it's not stuck; the not-faery is holding it shut with his big hand resting on the iron. I smell flesh burning from the contact. My opponent doesn't care. A real faery would have flitted home whimpering and affronted by now.

I gulp.

My road back to Tess is rarely easy.

I still my inadequate wings for half a heartbeat. An endless time in the chat room where time is just another dimension. No way to know if the gargoyles I saw are in training now or a thousand years ago.

Then, with a mighty swoop, I push myself straight up and butt my knobby head right into the family jewels.

Mr. Stoic-pain-means-nothing jumps and howls and screams like a banshee deprived of robbing a soul and backs off.

I grab the door and am outta here.

Gray-brown desert with splashes of khaki plants is a welcome relief from the bare whiteness of the chat room that goes on and on and on without definition. Khaki is so not my color, but it's an improvement over white.

I look around, trying to orient myself. Shivers run up and down my spine so hard they almost shake loose the beautiful warts on my bum. I worked hard to earn those warts in battle; I won't lose them now to the creepy crawlies. No sirree.

I'm in the wrong place. I should have popped out on Tess' shoulder. She's near. But not close enough.

A plane cruises by thousands of feet above me. That's where Tess is. And she needs me. I sense the plane is in trouble. If it doesn't get out of the holding pattern that loops it through this space soon, the pilot will lose control and crash. The magnetic forces of this place are screwing up his instruments. The winds spiral up and assault the plane from every direction. The pilot can't steer clear or outrun them.

He's as lost as I am.

More shivers and portents of doom.

I'm surrounded by weird rock formations. Lots and lots of red, both broken and flowing. Something draws me here. Something that feels like death and liberation at the same time.

A mural of writhing petroglyphs dances across a rock face above me. I can't read the exact symbols of horned figures and broken lines, but I sense a human running, endlessly running in circles away from evil, only to confront it again at the next turn.

This area is a maze of dead ends, and caves, and winding canyons that lead right back to the starting point. Or off into another dimension.

My senses reel. I can barely tell up from down, north from south, good from evil.

Dust, drier than a mummy, clogs my nose.

I try to pop out of the here and now, through the chat room to go back to Tess. The magnet of this place keeps pulling me in.

This is too creepy even for me.

Not a gargoyle in sight to repel me.

Chapter 3

The oldest rocks in the Valley of Fire are only six hundred million years old, compared to four billion years for the oldest rocks on Earth.

"NO ONE'S GOING TO die. Not on my watch." I shoved and twisted Mr. Twitchy into the nearest seat. Then I clamped his seat belt closed.

He immediately reached for it as if it cut off his breathing.

"Stay there," I said in my teacher voice, the one no teen dared brook.

His emotions continued to infect the rest of the passengers. No one, it seemed, except Mom, was willing to remain seated.

The plane tilted again. And again.

Screams.

I longed for a strong dose of Mom's lavender sachets to counter the hideous air.

A good belt of single malt scotch wouldn't hurt either. I preferred Lagavulin, but I'd settle for Sheep Dip.

A man ran forward from the extreme rear, clawing his way past the rest. Three stewards couldn't hang on to him. His eyes wouldn't focus. "I've got to get to the captain. I've got to make him land. Right now."

A steward tried to follow him. Too many people blocked his way.

I couldn't let him get past me.

He outweighed me by a good one hundred pounds and stood nearly a foot taller than me. He looked like a fullback with the ball under his arm and the goalposts within easy reach. I didn't have a weapon. I didn't have enough mass to stop him. Especially since the plane nosed down again, giving him momentum and challenging my balance.

Some god or goddess must have been looking over my shoulder that day. Not that I believe in such things. A little kid, wailing like a banshee, trying to get away from her mom's too-tight hug, raced forward, between and beneath the maze of legs. She got ahead of Mr. Fullback.

I grabbed her up and held her so she could see my face.

"Mairzy doates and dozy doates and liddle lamzy divey," I sang in my brightest voice.

As if I'd conjured it, I caught a whiff of freshly laundered sheets, dried in a warm spring wind, and folded away with sprigs of lavender. Home, comfort. Safety.

The little girl blinked at me in amazement.

"A kiddley divey too, wooden shoe?" she whispered in the high lisping toddler monotone.

Then we giggled together. I raised my voice and continued the nonsense song.

"Mares eat oats
And does eat oats
And little lambs eat ivy
A kid'll eat ivy too
Wouldn't you."

Mr. Fullback stopped short, grabbing the seats on either side of him. He blinked in confusion. Like he didn't know where he was or how he got there.

The little girl and I sang the ditty again from the top. Cautiously, I eased back into my seat. Mom belted me in. Then she raised the arm between us and helped me shift the child to the more secure place. She joined us on the third round of song. Her strong contralto balanced my soprano nicely.

Mr. Twitchy picked up on the chorus, in his quivery tenor, fighting panic with every word.

Slowly, quiet and order prevailed. Soon the entire coach section was singing. And seated.

I tired of the nonsense words and started up an old campfire song.

"Down in the meadow
In an iddy biddy pool
Swam three little fishes
And a momma fishy, too!"

Mom picked up on it—she'd taught it to me after all. She gave me my first voice lessons in church choir, too.

The crowd around us took a few moments to catch on. Eventually, they sang the chorus with us.

"Boop Boop Diddim Daddum Waddum Choo!"

"Thanks," the hapless steward said quietly, touching my shoulder. "I'll take Jessie here back to her mama. And I owe you a drink when we get to Vegas."

"Make it Lagavulin, single malt."

He grinned at me and held up one thumb in agreement. Then he gathered up the little girl, both happily singing, and deposited her with a relieved mother.

"You did good," Mom said.

"We're entering final approach for landing, ladies and gentlemen. Thank you for your patience."

Ten minutes later we landed in Las Vegas. I could feel the sun beating on the outside of the airplane the moment we stopped at the gate. The whoosh of fresher air entering from the airport relieved much of the olfactory stress. I sat back, eyes closed, and soaked up the heat, letting it banish the anxiety of the last half hour. It felt like a week.

I let the other passengers scramble for their bags in the overhead and scurry for the exit. No sense in fighting them to get out first. I'd learned long ago that on airplanes and in airports the hurrier I go the behinder I get.

Mom seemed content to wait.

When I opened my eyes, Mr. Twitchy was still strapped in the seat across from me. The captain stalked back to lecture him firmly about the panic he'd caused. "We've added your name to *the* list," he warned. "Next incident and you're banned from flying again in this country, maybe arrested for causing an incident."

His angry presence blocked my easy exit.

When the aisle was clear, I looked over at the abashed Mr. Twitchy. He looked like he wanted to cry. "I can't help it," he said to no one in particular. "I'm clairvoyant."

"Not a great one. We ran into trouble, but we didn't crash, and no one got hurt—except for some bumps and bruises. And that wouldn't have happened if people hadn't reacted to your panic and started running about. If they'd stayed seated, nothing would have happened. You're also a projecting empath," I said. "You need to work with a competent psychic on controlling that talent."

"You're one, too," he said defensively.

I started to protest. The events of the flight replayed in my mind like a videotape on fast forward. "Maybe I am. I used it to calm people for a positive outcome. If I hadn't, Mr. Fullback, or even you, might have opened one of the exit doors, causing depressurization and sucking a lot of people out the door to their deaths. Think about that next time you have a vision."

I stood up and yanked my computer bag out from under the seat.

"You don't know that," Mr. Twitchy retorted.

"I know that if I hadn't stopped you, you might have made your 'vision' come true. A self-fulfilling prophecy."

"Listen to her, young man. She knows what she's talking about," Mom said. She handed me her overnight bag from beneath the seat, and marched down the long aisle to the exit, as full of majesty and determination as I'd ever seen her.

I whistled a jaunty tune and followed her, very happy to have my mom back.

"Took you long enough," I admonish Tess as she steps into the terminal from the long walkway off the plane. I flit around and around, then land on her shoulder. I have to hold on for dear life. Her life as well as mine. I do my best to disguise my tremors of fear as indignation. "You could have warned me you were going to be late getting off the plane."

Actually, I was the late one. I'd tugged and twisted and yanked myself away from those awful magnetic rocks with a great deal of difficulty. If Tess had gotten off the plane a moment earlier, I'd have some serious explaining to do.

And I will explain. Just as soon as I figure out what went on. Or if she treks out there on one of her mad excursions. Tess does love to explore when she visits new places.

You'd think she'd lose her fascination with rocks now that she's ditched the ghost of her geologist husband; and the demon construct made to look like the late and barely lamented Dillwyn Bailey Cooper. We'll see if the delights of Las Vegas keep her on the straight and narrow. I don't think we can fight whatever lurks out there in the desert. I don't think we need to.

Yet.

"You couldn't amuse yourself rigging the slot machines?" Tess rejoins, sotto voce. Her gaze goes to the bank of computerized one-armed bandits not ten feet away. A number of people exit the plane and make a beeline for the bright lights and clanging bells, eager to begin losing money.

"Come on, babe. Let's go shopping. I need a new feather boa, and you need a little glitz in your evening gown! We have an awards banquet to go to Saturday night!"

"Later. I've got show tickets to buy," Tess mutters angrily. Like she'd really rather go shopping with me but knows she has to come up with those tickets because it's the only thing Mom has asked for since Darren died.

Chapter 4

Most workers in Las Vegas make little more than minimum wage, even in the biggest and most impressive casinos. They rely upon tips to survive. Everyone in Vegas expects a tip, from the bellhop, to the dealer, to the massage therapist, to the bus driver.

"I'M HAVING A massage in half an hour," Mom announced as we checked in at The Crown Jewels Hotel and Convention Center. The noise from the casino ten paces away and down three steps from the narrow lobby nearly obscured her words. The writers' conference had opted for a small hotel/casino off the strip. Much more affordable for a gathering of under one thousand people.

Not able to compete with modern glitz and glitter, The Crown Jewels had gone for the genteel poverty look of an English manor. Dark wood wainscoting and hardwood floors, accented with deep red velvet drapes and upholstery, dim lighting from Tiffany style shades on floor lamps, and an abundance of potted palms and rubber trees gave welcome relief from the bright desert sun outside.

That and the air-conditioning. The red Oriental style carpets, and the upholstery had just the right touch of threadbare shabbiness. I thought it succeeded quite well in providing a comfortable and welcome ambience.

However, the sour reek of tobacco smoke drifting in from the casino and embedded in the upholstery spoiled the atmosphere.

I can smoke in here! Scrap chortled. *Everyone else does.*

Just what I needed. "You will not smoke around any of the conference people," I replied under my breath. "Offend one of them with your cigars, and I'll feed you to Gollum's cat." Scrap had a running feud with the long-haired white monster that owned my lodger back home.

I accepted our key cards and room assignment from the hotel desk clerk.

"You do realize, Mom, that you will have to remove *all* of your clothing for the massage." I tried to keep the surprise out of my voice.

"Not in public, Tess. They give you a bath sheet and keep it very discreet and professional. I'm not totally ignorant of the world." She hmfed and trotted off toward the elevator, leaving me to collect our bags. Again.

"I'm going to try again to get show tickets for tonight. If I do, we'll need to be at the theater by six," I called after her.

She waved an acknowledgment.

I flagged down a bellhop. Gone were the days when I could flit off to a weekend science fiction/fantasy convention with only a change of underwear and my toiletries crammed into a small backpack. I also found room in there for half a dozen books to be signed by the authors attending the same con. Now I traveled with professional clothes, banquet/party clothes, rugged clothes and hiking boots for excursions, a whole suitcase of my own books in case the convention dealers didn't have enough copies, and my trusty laptop with backup CD burner and flash drive. I also brought a cache of other people's books to read and to have signed.

While I sorted and organized my gear plus Mom's, Mr. Twitchy entered the hotel lobby and sidled up to the registration desk as if he didn't want to be seen. I saw no trace of his luggage or a bellhop in tow.

"Welcome back, Mr. Sancroix," said the perky desk clerk. She handed him a key card. He didn't fork over a credit card or sign a registration form like the rest of us had to. Even though the writers' conference paid for my room, I still had to leave a credit card number on file against incidental charges.

With barely a nod of acknowledgment, Mr. Sancroix marched toward a broad flight of stairs leading to the mezzanine.

I smell imp, Scrap wiggled his pug nose and slapped my back with his barbed tail in excitement. I could almost feel it.

"How can you smell anything over the stale cigarette smoke?"

Scrap alit from my shoulder and flitted around the lobby on stubby wings working his pug nose overtime. He honed in on Mr. Twitchy Sancroix.

"He a regular?" I asked the bellhop, jerking my head toward Mr. Twitchey's retreating back.

I betcha he's related to that last Sancroix guy we met. I just know it. I smell an imp. Scrap bounced from rubber tree to lamp to drapery pull.

I hoped he wouldn't break anything. Sometimes bits and pieces of him materialized in this dimension just enough to wreak havoc.

The bellhop pursed his lips and rubbed his thumb against his fingertips.

I sighed and slipped him a ten.

He looked at it with a frown, then back to me hopefully.

I stared him down.

This time he sighed. "Junior pops in and out a couple times a month for ten days at a time, practically lives here. His uncle has been here for the past three weeks solid, visiting."

"That would explain the lack of luggage, if he keeps clothes here. The uncle wouldn't have a first name of Breven would he?"

Betcha he does! Scrap chortled. *Just betcha. How much you wanna bet? This is Vegas, after all. They bet on everything here. How much, babe? How much you wanna bet?*

We'd met a Breven Sancroix briefly a few weeks ago. My Sisterhood had sent him to help me with a little demon problem. Only by the time he showed up, I'd solved the problem, or rather beaten it back to the otherworld. Breven and his dominant male imp Fortitude (Scrap called him Guts because the grumpy senior imp didn't return his affections) were the only Warriors of the Celestial Blade I'd met outside of a Citadel. We solitaries, or rogues, aren't too common.

For two of us to show up at the same off-Strip hotel in Las Vegas at the same time seemed too much of a coincidence. I don't believe in coincidence.

The bellhop stared at his empty hand.

"I'll find out myself." I smiled at him and trotted off to the elevator. "Scrap, what's appropriate to wear for the hottest show in Vegas?"

That little midnight-blue number with layered chiffon and just a touch of beads and sequins.

"I don't remember buying a dress like that."

Because you haven't bought it yet. I spotted it in the underground mall on the discount rack. Let's hurry before someone else snatches it!

"Sorry, ma'am, those tickets for 'Fairy Moon' have been sold out for months. I can get you two single seats, separated by half the theater in August."

I glared at the young man working in the box office for the show Mom had asked to see.

"Who in their right mind comes to Las Vegas in August? The heat . . ." No windows or clocks in any of the casinos to hint at the harsh sunlight outside. My eyes already hurt from the glare. Mid-April was bad enough in the desert. No way was I coming back in August.

"Ever heard of air-conditioning?" The attendant signaled the next person in line to move forward. The middle-aged blowsy bottle blonde wearing a bright orange tank top and green shorts three sizes too small shoved me out of the way.

"Psst, missy," a weak little voice whispered in my ear.

Back off, dude, Scrap hissed back.

I whirled, hands up, expecting Scrap to stretch and morph into my Celestial Blade.

He remained firmly attached to my left shoulder, leaning over and baring his multiple rows of teeth at the sharp face of a skinny man about my own height. Unusual to find a fully grown man as vertically challenged as myself.

"I got tickets." The little man looked around nervously, twitching his nose a lot like a weasel.

Don't trust him, babe, he smells funny. Scrap spat out his cigar only half smoked.

"I don't trust him. But if he's got tickets to 'Fairy Moon,' I'll listen." Two steps away from the ticket counter and I was close enough to smell something rancid on the man's breath, barely masked by an overly sweet and oily hair tonic.

No kidding he smelled funny.

He backed up with small mincing steps, subtly leading me toward an exit, a fire door nearly hidden behind a huge potted palm. We had privacy. I had him in the corner. He couldn't grab my money and run.

"Name?" I demanded of the scalper.

"Names aren't necessary between friends. And right now I'm your best friend with tickets. Two seats together. Not the best, but not the worst either." He smiled, revealing small, pointy teeth.

"Okay, Mr. Weasel." He smelled of very ripe musk.

He winced but didn't lose the smile.

"Scalping tickets isn't exactly legal. How much are we talking?"

"Five hundred apiece."

Ouch.

"Even my mom's heart's desire isn't worth that much. One hundred apiece or I call hotel security." Or I'd bash in his pointed nose myself.

"My boss will bite hard if I sell for less than four-fifty."

"Bite hard? What is he, a vampire?" I almost laughed. I can't believe in vampires. I may write fantasy fiction, but that is one topic I won't touch. No one comes back from the dead. I'd learned that the hard way with the ghost of my husband.

"Yes. She is a vampire. A very old and powerful vampire."

He really believed that. His eyes glittered in terror. His almost offensive aftershave intensified.

Best I play up to his fears.

Scrap trembled and flicked his barbed tail. *I don't think this guy is kidding, dahling.*

"Two hundred. Your boss will only make a light snack of you." I had that much in cash. Time enough to hit the ATM before the show.

"Three-fifty." His neck lost a bit of tension. He still looked around, constantly scanning the mingling crowds around the box office.

"Two-fifty." That would drain my wallet. About what I'd planned on having to spend on tickets after searching on line at home.

"Okay, okay. You're signing my death warrant, but I'll let them go for that."

I reached for my wallet inside my belt pack.

Not yet, babe. Make him prove he's got the tickets. I don't like the way he smells.

I trusted Scrap's nose, as long as it wasn't clogged by allergies from Gollum's cat Gandalf. Gollum might be one of my best friends and a convenient lodger, but his cat and my imp had periodic turf wars.

"Show me the tickets."

"Show me the money."

"How do I know they aren't forgeries?" I cocked my head to the side, giving Scrap a bit of room to do his thing if we needed to fight. My feet took an *en garde* stance automatically, right foot forward, left turned out at a ninety-degree angle, knees bent, balance centered.

"Now would I try to cheat a lady like you?" Mr. Weasel held out his hands palms up in a universal gesture of helplessness.

Helpless, my cute little bum. He's a were. *Knew I'd smelled that stench of rotten meat and musk before. You'd think these guys would learn to brush and floss!*

"You don't look like a werewolf, little man. Show me the tickets."

Not a werewolf, babe. A wereweasel. Much more dangerous. Sneaky little bastards. But tied to the moon just like their canine cousins.

"That's a new one. We haven't encountered weres before." Time for research.

"We?" Mr. Weasel gasped. His eyes turned yellow and the irises slitted vertically.

Uh-oh.

"We, as in my imp. Ever met a Warrior of the Celestial Blade before?" I held out my palm. Scrap hopped onto it and stretched his neck and bandy legs to make him look taller, ready to transform.

Except he remained firmly in his imp shape and only a pale pink. Normally Scrap became my weapon only in the face of a demon or someone impossibly evil. Then he flushed bright red and stretched easily.

Mr. Weasel's tanned and leathery skin, with a significant

brindled-brown five o'clock shadow, blanched. He shifted his weight to the balls of his feet, ready to run.

"Tell me true, Mr. Weasel," I pinned him with my gaze. "Are your tickets forgeries?"

"Y . . . yes."

"And I should fork over good money and risk embarrassing my mother when we are denied entrance to the theater—why?"

"Because Lady Lucia will kill me if I don't come up with a grand by midnight."

"Tell Lady Lucia that I don't care. And the next person in her employ who tries to cheat me will eat my Blade."

I spun on my heel and headed for the taxi stand.

Mom and I would have to settle for the lounge act in the casino of The Crown Jewels.

As I passed a blackjack table, a girl who didn't look older than fifteen, clad in layers of pastel chiffon, pushed a pile of gold chips toward the dealer. Stranger yet, she wore fairy wings in the shape of double oak leaves. I'd seen that girl and her costume on dozens of posters around town advertising the show "Fairy Moon."

Tacky of her to wear her costumes out in public. She even had the mottled pastel body makeup to match the pinks, greens, blues, and yellows of her costume. What was her producer thinking?

Chapter 5

Elvis Presley first played Vegas at the New Frontier Hotel in 1956. He closed after one week of a two week gig.

"I HAVE TO CHECK in with the conference people and get my schedule by five," I grumbled as I got out of the taxi at four thirty.

You will change your clothes, dahling, Scrap insisted.

No sign of Mom back at the room. She must still be with the massage therapist in the spa on the top floor.

"Of course. I'll even look professional." I shook out my layered maroon peasant skirt with the handkerchief hem and the light pink embroidered gauze blouse.

Scrap snorted. *That might look professional at a con, babe. But this is a* writers' *conference. Go for the navy blue suit.*

"Yuck. I didn't even pack it."

But I did!

Scrap's chortle made me cringe. The brat had too much control over my life.

Slacks, pale blue tuxedo front blouse, rope of gray fresh-water pearls, and your navy flats, he instructed, pointing to each item in the closet or on the bathroom vanity.

I growled at him, but obeyed. Like most of the gay men I knew, he had a better fashion sense than me. For that matter, most of the straight men I knew had a better fashion sense than me. I loved threadbare jeans and tees. Jeans are neutral. Color combinations didn't matter.

But I always felt better looking my best. Scrap took care of me in more ways than just in battle.

Conference Registration looked like chaos with only a hint of organization. That hint set it above and beyond the normal SF/F cons I attended. Along with the clothing people wore. Scrap was right. These people took professionalism to heart. Lots of suits. An occasional *pressed* golf shirt and khakis. No jeans at all.

At a con, I'd expect any one of these people to work for the hotel.

Tanya, the liaison for the pro writers nabbed me seconds after I stepped off the elevator on the mezzanine. She led me to a small room to our left, away from the knots of attendees waiting for their badges.

"We have a full house this weekend," Tanya bubbled. A tall and leggy woman with *café au lait* skin, she ate up the distance to the Green Room with ease. I had to work my hips almost painfully to keep up; either that or run. Most undignified and unprofessional.

"We sold every single spot three months ago," Tanya continued with hardly a breath for air. "We'd raised the rates to keep the attendance to pro and truly serious prepublished writers. I hope you don't mind that we added a second session of your 'Is It Love or Sex' workshop."

Inwardly I groaned. Outwardly I smiled. "That's fine." I got paid by the hour in the classroom with these people.

"While you're here, we have simple sandwich makings and veggie trays at lunchtime in the Green Room, cold cereals for breakfast, to cut down on your expenses. I understand your mother is with you?"

"Yes. She's prepared to foot her own bills."

"Oh, she's welcome in the Green Room, too. I know how writers have to struggle to stay above water in today's world."

Tanya had no way of knowing that Mom had inherited a considerable fortune from Darren Estevez. The wills he had drawn up at their elopement backfired. He didn't inherit my home (a highly contested piece of real estate among the Powers That Be from other dimensions).

The two hundred seventy five-year-old saltbox rambled with additions and renovations from succeeding generations. It also sat smack dab in the middle of two acres considered neutral since before people came to the area. The energy of the place made it possible to open a new demon portal there. The Powers That Be didn't want a Warrior of the Celestial Blade living on site. Nor did they want a demon turning it into a bed and breakfast retreat for others of his kind.

Darren thought Mom owned the house jointly with me. I owned it outright with no mortgage, thanks to my deceased husband's life insurance. Darren's plan was to murder me so that my half went to Mom, then murder Mom so that he'd inherit the house as sole owner.

Fortunately, an insane witch with a grudge and a criminal history murdered Darren before he could do the same to me and Mom.

"I'll pass on your invitation to Mom," I told Tanya politely.

"Since the conference doesn't officially begin until noon tomorrow, would you and your mother care to join the staff of *Writing Possibilities* for dinner? We and a few of the other professional writers thought we'd sit in the lounge adjacent to the casino. They serve food from the restaurant there and we can catch the first act at seven."

"Sounds like fun." It did, since Mom and I weren't hying off to see "Fairy Moon" tonight. Or ever most likely.

"Excuse me," Tanya stopped a cocktail waitress when she rose from her practiced dip to serve a drink to a spindly man in his mid-forties at the round table for ten.

They had a magnificent air filtration system. I hardly smelled the smoke in the casino at all.

"What can I get ya, sweetie?" the waitress, asked in a friendly drawl. Her accent might have started in Alabama, but decades in the west had given it an edge. She was made up and suitably coiffed for her job, but looked like a fit and firm sixty. Her body had filled out and begun to droop a bit, despite the bright red corset, off-the-shoulder peasant blouse, and short black skirt. The frilly white apron and cap made token reference to the hotel theme. But that corset—some twelve-year-old boy's idea of a wet dream.

"Don't stare, dear," Mom said. "This is like an old folks home for cocktail waitresses and dealers."

Sure enough, a quick glance around the casino showed that most of the staff moved at a reasonable pace and showed more gray hair and plumpness than allowed at the few places on the Strip I'd visited in search of show tickets. Most of the employees at The Crown Jewels Casino were treading water until they could collect Social Security.

"I thought a jazz combo played here tonight," Tanya said. She stared at the karaoke machine on a fold-out metal table at center stage.

"This ain't the Strip, honey. Groups like that get a better paying gig and they don't always bother tellin' us they won't show up for work. What'cha want to drink, dear?"

"Oh." Tanya looked really disappointed. "I guess I'll have a margarita. Can we order food from you, too?"

"Drinks only. I'll send over a gal from the restaurant."

"I'll have a glass of Riesling. What about you, Mom?" I asked as we sat down. I took the place next to Tanya. Mom sat between me and a tall woman in her mid-fifties.

"Whatever you're having, Tess," Mom replied. She busied herself settling the full skirt of her black dress and draping her knitted lace shawl just right. That way, she didn't have to speak to the other woman.

"Hi, I'm Jack Weaver. I write police procedural mysteries," Mr. Tall and Spindly leaned across the table with his hand extended.

I returned his firm handshake. "Tess Noncoiré. I write science fiction and fantasy. This is my mother, Genevieve Noncoiré." (I gave her the preferred Québécois pronunciation of Jahn-vee-ev.) Mom hadn't had time to change her name to Estevez before Darren's murder, so she never bothered.

"And I'm Jocelyn Jones, I used to write historical romance, got burned out, and now I'm ghosting Penny Worth's autobiography," the tall woman next to Mom said. She indicated a well-preserved older woman on her right as Penny Worth.

Ms. Worth took in each of us at the table with an assessing glance, smiled coyly. and said, "My name may be Penny Worth, but I'm valued much higher than that in select circles." She winked at me.

"Huh?" Mom whispered.

How did I tell my mother, a French-Canadian-Catholic-

June Cleaver, that Ms. Worth was a prostitute? From the glitter of tasteful diamonds on her hands, ears, and around her neck, I guessed she'd been a high-priced call girl in her day and invested her earnings wisely. She might even still work for the occasional long-term client.

"Penny?" Mom quizzed the other woman. "Penny Haydon, New York City, third-floor walk-up on Eighth in the Village?"

"Yes," Ms. Worth hesitated. "Ginny?"

They squealed in delight and half hugged across Jocelyn Jones. In seconds, Mom and the writer had switched places. The animated conversation changed Mom from quiet, mousy, and depressed, to a younger vibrant version of my mother I'd only glimpsed briefly when I was growing up.

I began talking shop with the two published writers and four unpublished writers, grateful I didn't have to stop and explain vocabulary to both Mom and Ms. Worth. After only half a drink, we busied ourselves with our food—sandwiches and salad, nothing fancy. The conversation lagged.

"Tess," Mom said to the table at large. "You sing. Why don't you try the karaoke machine?"

"Good idea," Tanya jumped in, looking relieved that her party might be saved after all.

Yeah, let's sing! Scrap chimed in. He bounced back to my shoulder from the top of a bank of slot machines halfway across the small casino. *They got any filk on it?*

Filk is the folk music of Science Fiction/Fantasy. A lot of it is parody to familiar tunes, some quite original tributes to favorite authors and characters.

He studied the back of the machine as if he really could operate it. Good trick since he's transparent and only partially in this dimension. Some things, he managed to touch and manipulate. Like his black cherry cheroots and feather boa. Most things he passed right through.

I gave the dreaded machine a long and distrustful stare. My delay earned me a sharp elbow in my ribs.

"Okay." I nervously approached the two steps up to the twelve-by-twelve stage flanked in black curtains. Singing my heart out in a filk circle at a con with twenty other people is one thing. Performing for this group something else entirely.

The last time I'd sung solo had been "Ave Maria" at the

wake of a dear friend; followed almost immediately by "There's A Bimbo On The Cover Of My Book," the greatest filk ever.

I studied the long list of songs, mostly from the fifties and sixties. I knew filk words to a lot of them, very few of the original. Would this audience appreciate the parody? I doubted it. Finally, I found one I thought I could vamp my way through as long as the machine gave me the words.

Not as much fun singing about a lonely outlaw with commitment issues when I'd rather tell the story of a popular car with design flaws. I may have slipped on one verse. Jack Weaver's muffled guffaw was my only clue.

Until Mom came up and grabbed the microphone from me. She rolled her eyes at me, then she spotted the song she wanted on the screen.

"Stormy weather," she crooned in her rich contralto. She caressed the words with a velvet tone that hinted at depths of passion.

Mom? Passionate?

Ms. Worth sat up and listened more closely. A hush fell over the tiny lounge. Even the noise from the casino seemed to mute.

You're a projecting empath, too! Junior Sancroix's words came back to me. So, apparently, was my mom.

I sat there, mouth agape in wonderment.

Knew it, knew it, knew it, Scrap giggled. He hung from a ceiling lamp and waggled his wart-bestrewed butt at me.

Settle down! How can you be drunk if I'm not drunk?

We're not drunk, babe, just high on life and music and—and Mom.

I flashed my gaze from Scrap's antics back to Mom. The strap of her little black dress slid slowly down her shoulder in a seductive invitation.

What happens in Vegas stays in Vegas. Whoo–ee, this is going to be fun.

"What happened to my annoying, conservative, fussy, control freak mother?"

Darren Estevez happened to Mom.

"Is she still in demon thrall?" Definitely unstable.

Darren, and his foster son Donovan, had the ability to reach into a mind and lull doubts, anger, and inhibitions. I'd seen Donovan quell a riot with a smile.

No answer. Scrap flitted from chandelier to chandelier, making the imitation flame light bulbs flicker among the faux crystal drips. The already dim lighting faded, making the spotlight on Mom more dominant.

I needed to get her off that stage and back to normal.

"Not yet, dear." Ms. Worth reached across the table and placed her hand atop mine. "Let her finish. She needs to do this."

"Stormy Weather" came to an end, but not my stormy temper. I sat there, alternately seething and applauding my mother as she sang sultry torch song after whimsical show tune after sweet ballad. Each piece ended to rounds of enthusiastic applause. The lounge filled and the casino emptied, just to listen to my mom.

"If she's still in demon thrall, then she's spreading it," I murmured.

"It's a happy thrall," Penny Worth said. "The best singers and working girls have it and know how to use it."

That got my attention.

Chapter 6

In 1967, Nevada passed a law allowing corporations to own casinos. Now it is extremely rare for an individual to own a casino lock, stock, and barrel.

"WHAT DO YOU KNOW about demons?" I whispered, wishing that Jocelyn Jones wasn't sitting between us. This conversation needed to be private.

"Oh, sweetie, all men are demons given the right incentive," she laughed, a soft trilling sound that sent shivers up my spine and raised goose bumps on my arms.

"Or she's a projecting empath, like you are," a new voice said quietly. A male voice, rough around the edges like he didn't use it much.

I turned away from the table to find Breven Sancroix standing just behind my left shoulder. In a lot of folklore, this is the place assigned to Death. That's Death as an entity rather than the state of nonbeing.

Fortitude, his huge imp, perched on *his* left shoulder. The nearly invisible beast lifted his long, fully formed wings in an elegant gesture that masked his shifting to a new more aggressive stance. The many warts on his spine and chest seemed to ripple and catch the briefest red glow from the candle lamp on the table. His skin had aged to a dusky patina.

I doubted that chubby Scrap with his stubby wings and bandy legs would ever reach this level of maturity and grace. He was just a scrap of an imp after all, a runt who should have died before his fiftieth birthday. Through sheer determination my imp now boasted a few warts earned in battle as well as nearly one hundred years of life. (Imp years. I had no idea how they converted to human years.)

My face lost heat. "Mr. Sancroix, what are you doing here?"

"My nephew lives here."

He pulled out Mom's chair and sat, careful to let Fortitude whip his tail and wing tips behind the back before settling.

Did the big imp weigh anything in this dimension? When Scrap rode my shoulder, he barely made an impression on my senses. Fortitude might prove a substantial burden, even on Breven Sancroix's broad shoulders.

"Just visiting, then?"

"I may move here. The climate soothes my arthritis. I sold my farm in Pennsylvania. We . . ." He glanced at the uninformed humans about the table. "I'm getting on in years and no longer wish to work the place alone. Junior would rather live and work here."

He didn't look arthritic to me. He moved with the power and suppleness of a much younger man. I found it hard to guess his age. Weathered skin from many years working out of doors, and a tightness about his mouth, suggested late middle age pushing sixty maybe. The scar running from temple to jaw that matched my own, looked old and faded. He'd been a Warrior of the Celestial Blade a long time. Looks can be deceiving, especially in us Warriors.

I stand five feet two inches and barely weigh in at one hundred ten pounds. Most people say I look tiny and frail. I've felled a dozen half-blood (Kajiri) Sasquatch demons twice my size. I've conquered full-blood (Midori) Windago. In a pinch, without any weapons but a set of car keys, I laid out two teenage muggers in a dark parking lot. I run nearly every day and fence three times a week when I'm home.

My scar still looks raw and angry to my eye after three years. So I cover it with makeup even though mundanes can't see it.

"What does your nephew do that he can afford to live in a hotel in Vegas?" I asked.

"He owns the hotel."

That stopped me cold. "He seems very young to own

such a . . . prime piece of real estate." Off the Strip, the buildings and businesses wouldn't command the same value as the major operations, but any casino and hotel in Vegas had to be worth a lot more than I could ever dream of making as a writer, even holding on to my place on the best seller lists.

The bellhop hadn't said anything about Junior owning the place. Was he protecting the man, or didn't he know?

"Long story short, he inherited a piece of it and managed to . . . acquire the remaining shares." Breven Sancroix looked almost embarrassed.

"Did he use his talent as a projecting empath to coerce the other owners into selling at a vastly deflated value?" I raised my eyebrows at him.

Breven Sancroix looked away.

"Better question, did Junior tell you about his little problem on the flight here from Chicago?"

Did I say that I don't believe in coincidence? The Sancroixs, uncle and nephew, began to look like the stalker I'd sensed.

"No, he didn't. What happened?"

"Your nephew has a problem." I scanned the bar for eavesdroppers. Every eye and ear concentrated on my mother as she reached into her repertoire for yet another steamy ballad of lust and betrayal.

This time Sancroix lifted his own eyebrows in question.

"This is a conversation best held in private."

"I'll keep an eye on your mom, sweetie," Penny Worth said. She patted my hand again. "She's safe with me."

Even Penny couldn't con Mom into getting into *too* much trouble. Maybe her worldly wisdom would counter Mom's naiveté. I had to trust my mom and her Catholic upbringing.

That trust did not extend to Breven Sancroix.

"There's another bar on the opposite side of the lobby. It's quiet there," Sancroix said. He took my elbow before I'd finished standing and kept me off-balance as we crossed the casino, dodging gamblers, waitresses, and a maze of slot machines. No straight lines and easy exits in a casino. They want you to stop and gamble.

Scrap scrambled to keep up, never getting close enough to alight on my shoulder.

Fortitude remained solidly in place, half asleep, ignoring the world.

"Another white wine?" Sancroix asked, nearly pushing me into the center stool of an unoccupied section around the bar.

I wanted something stronger. I needed my wits about me. "Ginger ale."

"Glenmorangie, straight up."

"A fine single malt scotch. I prefer Lagavulin," I almost smiled. The last time I'd drunk fine whiskey with a man—Gollum—I ended up sleeping with him. Actually sleeping on his couch with him curled up beside me, not making love.

"Anything is better than the homemade brew they served me in the Citadel."

"I spent a year in a Citadel with my Sisterhood. We had the same stuff. Reminiscent of the recipe in the Hammurabi Code. Needed a couple of filters and a less rusty fermentation tank."

We both laughed. A bit of my wariness crumbled.

Scrap dropped onto my shoulder and sank in his talons. I could barely feel his weight or the sharp impression on my skin, but a warning was there. *Don't get too comfortable, babe.*

"The Warriors of the Celestial Blade do take their Spartan living to the extreme," Sancroix said. He smiled, and the lines around his eyes crinkled nicely. He looked younger and less dangerous. "And I think the recipe is as old as the Code of Hammurabi, circa 1780 BC. We've been around a long time. Not a lot changes in the Citadels."

"We have a duty." I nodded. "For centuries, that duty centered around keeping demons from crossing into this dimension through limited access portals. Now the portals are changing. Demons are infiltrating everyday life. The Warriors need to change with the times." Sister Gert had thrown me out rather than accept change.

"Demons are getting more intelligent, gaining more and more human traits as they interbreed. Our duty has to expand into the world at large," he agreed with me.

"Is that why you left your Citadel?" I asked.

"Yes. You, too, I take it."

Our drinks came. No money exchanged hands.

"They kicked me out because I don't take orders well and asked too many questions."

He laughed long and loud, throwing his head back in genuine mirth. Fortitude shifted awkwardly to adjust to the change in balance.

"I bet you gave old Gert a comeupance." He mentioned the leader of the isolated fortress where I'd taken my training.

I'd stumbled on the isolated ravine in the Central Washington desert in a fever delirium. We call the disease the imp flu. Sister Serena, our physician, had to cut the infection out. That's how I got the scar on my face. But since the imp flu is other dimensional, so is the scar. Only other Warriors can see it.

Guilford Van der Hoyden-Smythe, Gollum to his friends, could see the scar: dear friend, researcher, companion, and owner of the dreaded white cat Gandalf.

"You know Sister Gert?"

"Knew. Haven't seen her in years. I think I fathered a child or two on her during shared midsummer festivals." Celebrated on the full moon closest to the Solstice. Demons are at their lowest power at the full moon. The only time it's safe to throw a party in a Citadel that sits atop a demon portal. "But as you know, men are not welcome to linger once the beer is drunk and the willing impregnated. Nor are women welcome to remain in a male Citadel."

"Another good reason to leave."

We clicked our glasses in silent toast. We had more in common than I thought.

"Gert retired last month. Gayla now leads my Citadel," I said.

"Gayla, I don't think I know her." He looked into his scotch as if the answer lay there.

"She's young, a relative newcomer. I pulled her in during a raging thunderstorm; her imp flu was in full fever and festering. She'd have died if I hadn't. Gert wanted to leave her outside, afraid of diminishing resources. Our physician had an injured hand from a demon tag. I cut the infection out of Gayla."

And our bond remained strong. "She's one of the few I can reach through meditation and telepathy when she doesn't answer the telephone she had installed two months ago."

"So, what has Junior been up to?" Sancroix asked after a long pause and one sip of his scotch.

"We hit some bad turbulence while circling Las Vegas. He panicked and nearly caused a riot by projecting his fear into everyone else. He's on a watch list now. Another incident, and Homeland Security won't let him fly again. Ever."

"Damn."

"He needs training to control his talent. Before he panics again and kills innocents."

"I doubt you and your mother had training. It's an isolated incident."

"Mom and I have never caused a near riot aboard an airplane twenty thousand feet in the air. Junior nearly got us all killed."

"I'll speak to him. Where did this happen?"

I shrugged. "We were circling in a holding pattern waiting to land. But he got twitchy and nervous on our first approach."

"The Valley of Fire," he said quietly, gulping a mouthful of the potent scotch.

"What's so special about the Valley of Fire?"

"Local geological wonder. Northeast of town. Worth a day trip. Just don't get caught out there at night. And leave your imp at home."

He rose and left abruptly.

Chapter 7

Average humidity in Las Vegas is 29%.

"WAS THAT A CHALLENGE?" I asked Scrap.

"Believe him, lady," the bartender whispered. "Valley of Fire is no place to be after the sun sets. Lots of unexplained stuff. Crosswinds with no source, compasses going berserk. Hoodoos. Even the Indians won't go there after dark unless they are on a vision quest." He looked like he might have some Indian blood in him, a hint of copper in his black skin, thick straight black hair cropped short, and an almost occipital fold around his brown eyes.

"You sound familiar with the place. Is there a tour bus, or should I rent a car?"

"Stay in town and gamble your money away. It's safer." He turned to answer the hail of another customer.

"Scrap, what do you think?"

I like slot machines. I may have figured out how to guarantee a win. He flitted off, strangely subdued.

Time to check on Mom.

I braced myself for the clang and jangle of casino noise. Near silence greeted my ears as I crossed the hotel lobby. Only a few dedicated gamblers maintained possession of preferred places at the slots or a blackjack table. I pushed and shoved my way through the crowd to the table I'd left half empty a short time ago. Three men in their sixties, wearing western-cut suits with bolo ties and huge chunks of turquoise filled my chair, Mom's, and one other. They sat forward, gazes glued to the stage and their mouths half open.

People had dragged stools in from the slot machines to fill the other tables to overflowing. A lot of people stood in every available space around and between tables. The waitresses hopped about with new energy and speed, filling orders, stuffing tips in their cleavages—their cloth bags attached to waistbands all bulged to overflowing.

Penny Worth sat back in her chair appraising the crowd, a small smile on her face.

My eyes followed the gaze of every person in the room. Mom stood spotlighted on the stage. She closed her eyes and stilled her entire being. The last lingering note of a ballad drifted into the shadows, more than a memory, less than audible sound.

Then she opened her eyes, animation and life returning to her face. She broke the spell with her smile—or continued it. I couldn't tell for sure.

"Magic," Penny Worth whispered. "She's absolute magic. I don't think she had that touch when we shared a flat in New York."

Mom in New York? When? She'd married Dad when she was only eighteen.

Without a word, Mom replaced the microphone into the karaoke machine and executed a deep, sweeping bow worthy of presentation at a royal court.

"More!" shouted the man with the biggest chunk of turquoise embedded in his string tie.

"More, more, more," the crowd picked up the chant.

Mom shook her head, gracing them with a huge smile.

"More, more, more." Feet stomped, and the applause took on the rhythm of the repeated demand.

Mom shook her head again. This time she glided the two steps to the edge of the stage. A strong hand reached up to guide her down the single step. She placed her hand atop it and descended with the grace and aplomb of a beauty queen.

"Your mama had good training. Shame to waste it on a karaoke machine," Ms. Worth said.

I barely heard her. All my attention focused tightly on the man who led my mother back to her chair.

Breven Sancroix.

He looked strangely off-balance until I realized Fortitude no longer rode his shoulder.

Scrap, too, had taken a powder.

I couldn't find either of them in any of the usual spots, i.e., hanging from the chandeliers or crouched on the wooden rail rafters. Like cats, imps prefer to perch high and study the surroundings.

Then my gaze lighted on a less welcome sight. A tall man with long black hair caught in a tight braid halfway down his back and shafts of white at his temples surveyed the entire room in one swift glance.

I forgot to breathe as his eyes unerringly found mine.

"No." I think I spoke. I must have because Penny Worth swiveled around and looked in the same direction.

I couldn't move. Couldn't think. Only drink in the superb fitness, grace, and beauty of the man.

Legally, I guess Donovan was my stepbrother. In my blood he was more. So much more.

Not in this lifetime.

No way, no how would I succumb to the power of his charisma. Again.

But that didn't mean I couldn't feast my eyes on him while he hastened to my side as if his life depended upon holding me in his arms.

I longed to hear him tell me how he'd found a way to reveal the truth of his past and his future agenda to me without breaking his covenant with the Powers That Be.

"My, my, my, what do we have here?" Ms. Worth tracked Donovan's progress across the nearly deserted casino as avidly as I did. "He yours, honey?"

"I sure hope not," Jocelyn Jones said. She straightened her back and smoothed her hair, like a predatory bird preening.

Donovan's smile of welcome turned to a fierce scowl.

Shatter one fantasy.

Oh, wait, he did that months ago.

I think I actually backed away from him. As much as Mom's adoring audience would allow me.

"Well, that explains where Scrap disappeared to," I snapped at the man.

"Not my fault the runt can't come near me. Do you know how much trouble I've had tracking you down!"

"Well, excuse me, I didn't know I was supposed to file my schedule with your secretary."

He broke eye contact and ran his fingers through that fabulously silky black hair. Not fair that a man should have prettier hair than I do. He had more than enough assets to get away with one little flaw.

"Sorry, Tess, that didn't come out right. I have some papers for your mother to sign. It's rather urgent." Then he lifted his gaze to meet mine again.

By that time I'd managed to "gird my loins" so to speak and resist the mind-fogging miasma of beauty he projected.

"Just because you are the executor of your father's estate, doesn't give you the right to stalk me or my mother." That didn't come out right either, but I let it stand. "Can't it wait till we get home on Monday?"

"No. And he was my *foster* father. No blood relation at all."

I'd heard that one before. Over and over again. So how come Donovan looked so much like his half-blood Damiri demon *foster* father and had so much in common with him? Like the ability to stop barroom brawls before they started and lull the inhibitions of the unwary?

"Donovan!" Mom cried. She broke free of her own enthrallment with Sancroix and rushed toward us. She rose up on tiptoe to kiss his cheek. "What brings you to Vegas, dear? Have you been eating right? You look tired. Did you sleep last night?"

"Estate business, Genevieve." He kissed her cheek with genuine affection.

I expected Mom to wince at the Americanized pronunciation of her name.

She surprised me again by patting his broad chest with affection. "I suppose I must do this. You will excuse me." She nodded graciously and vaguely toward me and Sancroix. "Do you have a room, Donovan, or will you be charging off again on the next plane out?"

"I got a room. I have other business in town. But the estate stuff is urgent. I can file the papers with the bank by fax first thing in the morning. I've got the hotel owner waiting to witness your signature in his office." They wandered off together.

"So that's Donovan Estevez," Sancroix whistled through his teeth.

"You know of him?"

"He's famous outside the Citadels."

I raised my eyebrows in question.

"Someone to watch. He has dubious contacts." Meaning with Kajiri demons. I knew that already.

Someone to avoid, Scrap snarled settling back on my shoulder where he belonged. Fortitude joined us as well.

"Do all the imps have a problem staying within ten yards of him?"

"Not all."

Clearly I wasn't getting any more information from him tonight.

A yawn escaped my lungs. "I've had a long day. And tomorrow looks very busy. I think I'll turn in."

"Let me escort you to your room." Sancroix offered me his arm.

"Uh—no, thanks. It's not as if I can't defend myself." I tilted my head to the right where Scrap perched.

"Las Vegas is home to creatures they never taught us about in the Citadels."

"Like wereweasels and vampires?" I joked.

"Precisely."

"Moisturize, moisturize, moisturize," I told myself as I smoothed lotion on my face, hands, and legs beneath my cotton nightie. "One day in the desert and I already feel like a prune."

So I sucked greedily on the bottled water I'd picked up in the convenience store two blocks up the street from the hotel. I predicted I'd go through at least another case before the end of the conference.

A knock on the door interrupted my attempts to mitigate the effects of seven percent humidity aggravated by canned air. Scrap would have a lot of trouble finding any mold, his favored food, anywhere, even in the air conditioners.

Quietly, I crept to the door and peered through the spy hole.

"Tess, I know you're in there," Donovan said. He held up a big bouquet of mixed spring flowers. "I come bearing peace offerings."

"Okay." I opened the door but stood firmly in the doorway, denying him entrance.

"Please accept my apology for my surly mood earlier," he said sweetly, thrusting the bulky bouquet at me, complete with cut glass vase.

I buried my nose in their delicate fragrance. Daisies, and an exotic lily I easily identified. The others I could only guess at the names.

"Can I come in and talk to you?" Donovan looked a bit lost and helpless.

How could I resist him in that mood?

I clamped down on my hormones and backed up enough to let him come in to the modest room with two queen beds, an entertainment center, a worktable—already filled with my laptop, notes, and cell phone charger. Some conferences could afford to give me suites. "Stretching Your Writing Wings" was too new to feel comfortable spending that kind of money.

"What do you want to talk about, and where is my mother?" I set the flowers down on the nightstand between the two beds. Nope, might give him ideas. I switched them to the worktable.

"Genevieve is back at the karaoke machine. A Ms. Penny Worth is keeping an eye on her, making sure none of her adoring fans gets too fresh."

I shook my head in bewilderment. This was so not like my mom. But if singing helped her cope with the posttraumatic stress of Darren, let her keep it up.

I wondered if Breven Sancroix stood among the adoring fans.

And had Mr. Twitchy Junior Sancroix tried to con Mom and Donovan out of anything with his empathic talent.

"What do you need to talk about?"

"This." He gathered me into his arms and lowered his head to capture my lips with his own.

My blood sang. My limbs melted. My mind turned to oatmeal.

For three endless heartbeats I welcomed his touch, gloried in the way our bodies molded together, invited his hands to explore my back and ribs and beneath my breasts.

His callused hands awakened nerve endings. I wanted more. His clothes and my nightgown put too thick a barrier between my skin and his.

His aftershave enticed me with hints of sage and copper.

Whoa, girl. Some tiny niggle of sanity sparked to life. It wiggled to the front of my brain and spread.

Reluctantly, I broke the kiss and pushed him away. I felt cold, empty, and incomplete with three inches of space separating us.

"Tess?" he sounded plaintive and hurt.

"You know my conditions. 'Fess up or get out of my life."

"I have four tickets to 'Fairy Moon' for tomorrow night. VIP circle." He held up four pieces of printed card stock with the whimsical logo of a fairy touching a crescent moon with a magic wand.

He offered me the sun and stars and the universe to go with it.

"Are they real?"

"Only the best for my girl. Think your mother can find a date for the fourth ticket?"

"I'm sure she can." Penny Worth came to mind, not Breven Sancroix. Eagerly, I grabbed the tickets and examined them closely. They looked real enough, heavy paper, printing on both sides; section, row, and seat clearly marked as well as date and time. Embossed logo. Tomorrow night, the seven o'clock show. Thursday night, no obligations to the conference.

Donovan waited expectantly while I scrutinized the gold I held in my hand.

"Thank you."

We looked at each other through a long moment of silence. New heat and awareness rose from my toes to my crown. The invisible scar on my face throbbed.

"Tess," he said with longing.

"Donovan, I . . . you know I want you . . ."

"But . . ." He took a deep breath. Pain flitted across his face. Then a spark of something deeper.

"What happens in Vegas stays in Vegas," I quipped. Goddess, I hadn't had a man in a long time. A very long time.

Not since Donovan and I had fallen together last October. And before that? No one since my husband Dill died in an awful motel fire three years ago.

"I need you, Tess." Both our gazes flicked toward the nearest bed. The bed closest to the window I'd staked claim to.

"My mom . . ."

"Will be hours yet. She's found something special she needs to cling to. Like I need to cling to you."

"What the hell."

"No commitment, no guilt, no regrets."

"And no assumptions of a repeat performance." I closed the aching distance between us and kissed him hard, as I'd yearned to do for a very long time.

Chapter 8

The Golden Nugget has the largest nugget of gold in the world on display. It weighs sixty-two pounds and is heavily guarded.

A LONG TIME later I fell asleep with Donovan's body wrapped protectively around me and his heavy arm draped across me, anchoring me against him.

There is something incredibly intimate about falling asleep with another person. More so than the act of sex. It becomes a mingling of minds and dreams.

Air rushed around me, pummeling me from all directions as I fell. I could see no bottom, no place to land, nothing to cushion my fall. My wings refused to work.

Half a thought reassured me that this was one of Scrap's adventures. The reality of truly falling took over.

A blast of anger, outrage, and unrelenting disappointment followed me down, down, and down some more.

"I don't deserve this!" I cried. At the same time, disappointing the one who'd thrown me down weighed heavily on me, almost like guilt.

"It's not my fault!"

My heart leaped into my throat. Dread formed a tight knot in my belly. The sheer walls of a deep and twisting shaft sped past me. No handholds. No ledges.

Only the debris of my former body falling looked real.

The anger behind me propelled me around all the convoluted spirals.

Nothing between me and a painful landing that meant the end of my existence.

Something glistened below me. Perhaps, just perhaps I might find enough water down there to absorb my plunge and spit me back out again.

The tiny shimmer grew brighter, more solid. Hard, unforgiving glass. My body and my soul would shatter at the same time as that window into the chamber of the Powers That Be.

This was the end. No recovery. No forgiveness. I had failed in my duty. My own inexperience and cockiness made me reckless to the point of ineptitude. I was the weakness in the wall of defense. Because of me a lot of people died.

I sobbed. Choked on my grief. My heart nearly broke.

Just when I gave myself up to an inevitable and very painful death, something soft and gentle cradled me from behind. It slowed my descent.

The sheer stone walls of a well became tall trees with feathery branches. The hard glass beneath me dissolved into a hidden mountain lake. Grass, moss, and ferns formed a soothing bed that awaited me.

My feet touched down. My knees buckled with relief and strain, unused to supporting my suddenly solid body. Arms encircled me.

"You must still face the Powers That Be for the damage you allowed to happen. But for now you may rest. I will keep you safe. I will teach you what you need to know."

I knew that voice. Dillwyn Bailey Cooper. My beloved Dill. The man I had met at a con and married four days later. Then he had died three months after that in a motel fire set by Darren Estevez and an unknown compatriot. Three short months. All I had with the love of my life was three short months.

My sobs renewed because I knew I must live through the agony of losing him all over again.

He touched my face and wiped away my tears. "This is a true dream. But not yours. Live and thrive in your new self."

And then I woke to the sound of the hotel room door opening.

I was alone in the bed.

"Who brought you flowers?" Mom asked as she breezed in, turning on all the lights and filling the room with vibrancy and the scent of stale tobacco smoke. At three in the morning.

"Huh?" I blinked my eyes in confusion, unsure if this was reality or the horrible dream with the puzzling ending.

I'd fallen asleep with Donovan's arms around my naked body. We'd curled up like two spoons, his breath warm and reassuring against my neck. Now he was gone. And I had dreamed.

This is a true dream. But not yours.

If not mine, was it his? I shuddered at the thought of what he had endured.

He must have left while I slept. I felt his absence more keenly than I wanted to admit.

"Oh, there's a card." Mom dug a tiny white envelope out of the depths of the bouquet and handed it to me. "You read it, I don't have my glasses on."

At home she wore them on a long chain around her neck. Tonight, only her inevitable strand of pearls accented her ample cleavage in her little black dress.

She looked happy and fulfilled for the first time in . . . well . . . forever.

As much as I appreciated the changes, I didn't think I'd ever get used to this mom. The Vegas Mom, more alive than I'd ever known her. Dad had left her for Bill when I was twelve. She was barely thirty-seven then. He'd been unhappy with Mom for a long time before that. She'd been nervous and edgy, afraid of the day he'd leave her. She showed a false and brittle brightness during the two and a half days of her marriage to Darren, a product of his demon glamour rather than true happiness.

"I had such a nice chat with Mr. Sancroix," she mused as she fussed with her toiletry bag.

"Breven or Junior?"

"Both, actually. Junior isn't nearly as nervous as I thought he'd be. Quite charming if a bit immature. Breven says he knows you. Another charming man in a rustic sort of way. I envy him the energy to work a farm all by himself after his wife left him. He raised Junior, you know. I never did quite find out what happened to the boy's parents. But his Uncle Breven is the only father he's ever known."

I let her prattle.

Silently, I read the card, carefully keeping the sheet and light blanket over my shoulders, masking my nudity. I didn't think Mom, even the new Mom, would understand why my prim little nightgown lay in a wadded ball beneath the discarded coverlet.

Did Donovan remember to flush the condoms? Yes, that's plural. Three of them in two hours. The man had stamina, and then some.

My innards tightened in memory of how well, and often, he'd filled me, pushing me to one exploding climax after another.

I yanked my focus back to the card.

"My apologies for trespassing on the goodwill of an honorable Warrior. I hope the four enclosed tickets ensure future good relations. Contessa Lucia Maria Continelli."

The manipulative, cheating, lying bastard!

Chapter 9

Built in the mid 1950s, the fifteen-story Fremont Hotel was the first highrise in downtown Las Vegas.

THE HOUSE LIGHTS BLINKED twice, signaling that "Fairy Moon" was about to begin. I sat between Donovan and Mom. Penny Worth sat beyond her. Donovan made a hunkily handsome man in a fine charcoal suit with a silky, silvery shirt and subtle blue, gray, and silver tie. I didn't want my hormones jumping so high I couldn't concentrate on the show.

Mom's happy smiles and bouncing enthusiasm had convinced me to forgive Donovan. Almost.

That and the limo and the champagne he ordered to transport us to the show. Even Penny Worth seemed impressed, commenting that the champagne was excellent, even if the flutes were plastic—good quality plastic, though.

Can't have everything.

She and Mom had spent a good part of the afternoon talking on the telephone, recounting adventures in New York—I still hadn't figured out when that could have taken place—and shopping for just the right dress for tonight's outing. I was surprised at their joint taste and subdued elegance.

"How'd they do that?" Mom breathed in awe.

An aerial dancer clad in pastel draperies and fairy wings swooped over the audience without visible support. She swung up into the top row, around the full horseshoe of seats and back onto the stage to settle on dainty feet and execute a cute pirouette. The lights made her garb—and her makeup—shift colors randomly. The rainbow morphed around her in time to the live, New Age music. For half a heartbeat I caught a glimpse of bright autumnal rust and green in the mix. Then it faded to softer spring colors.

On a higher level, upstage and beyond the spotlights more bits of action swirled and paused. Costumed beings climbed the walls; fog oozed up from the pit area.

A whisper of something floral drifted past me.

"They look just like real fairies," Mom said, her hand flat on her chest as if trying to calm her heart rate.

"Yeah, they do," I said, more a question to Scrap than a real answer.

My imp pranced around the upper levels of the theater, shadowing the dancers as they flew past him. He couldn't get any closer to me than that with Donovan next to me.

A male dancer took off from the circle of fairies dancing around a huge mock mushroom. A caterpillar smoking a hookah perched on top of the stage prop. That was another, very earthbound dancer in a long green body stocking covered in orange spots. The flying dancer took a different route from the previous one, turning cartwheels in midair and playing loop the loop with Scrap.

Or was Scrap playing loop the loop with the fairy? A human dancer shouldn't be able to see Scrap, let alone play with him.

A few weeks ago, during that dustup with Mom's briefly second husband, I'd heard a few interdimensional rumors that all was not well in Faery, the dimension that centered and anchored a good portion of the rest of the Universe.

More coincidences that weren't really coincidence?

Where were the wires supporting the dancers? How did the lights make this dancer's pastel costume shift colors in a different pattern from the female?

I didn't really care. Awe and wonder filled me, almost—but not quite—dampening my constant bump of curiosity.

Closer inspection of the dancers on stage showed that each was dressed differently, and their colors changed in different patterns, still keeping in rhythm with the music.

Scrap soon tired of flying around the audience. He settled at the feet of the musicians on a balcony projecting over the stage. They, too, wore similar costumes to the fairy dancers, but I hadn't noticed their colors shifting or their wings flapping.

"No wonder this is the hottest show in town," I said to Mom. "The special effects are fabulous."

"Thank you for sharing the tickets, Donovan," Mom replied. She reached across me to pat his hand, then quickly returned her attention to the stage where individual fairies lifted out of the round dance and dropped back down in an intricate pattern.

I allowed myself to believe that Mom just might recover from her disastrous marriage to Darren.

We gave the fairies a standing ovation as the tinkling music faded along with the stage lights. House lights grew brighter, like a dawning. Mom turned to discuss the show with Penny, her new best friend.

From their animation I guessed that this near stranger—or long lost acquaintance—was dearer to Mom than any of her garden club or church choir friends.

"You going to tell me how you got the flowers and tickets from Lady Lucia?" I whispered to Donovan.

"How did you . . . ?"

"There was a card."

"Oops."

"You bet your sweet ass, oops." A very nicely shaped and tightly muscled ass it was, too. "You're busted. Now tell me." I fixed him with a stern glare.

"Would you believe I encountered the messenger at the concierge's desk and assumed the duty to deliver them."

I hmfed. "Was he overly pale with blood-red lips and wearing a long black cape?"

"No. She wore faded jeans and a T-shirt with a rock band logo."

"Then Lady Lucia and her minions aren't really vampires."

"How do you know Lady Lucia?" Penny Worth asked. She looked upset, the first strong emotion, other than humor, I'd seen in her.

"Her name came up in conversation," I hedged.

"Don't mess with her. Ever. She's dangerous. People who work with her or socialize with her disappear."

"Have you . . . ?"

"Only once. When I was very young and new to the business. I left before *she* made an appearance at the party at midnight. I didn't like the taste of the drinks."

I didn't dare ask her if Lady Lucia drank blood and shunned daylight.

"Is there a better place for a vampire to hide than Vegas?" Donovan asked. A smile tugged at the corners of his mouth.

"Maybe it's just someone who wants us to think she's a vampire," I said. That's what I wanted to believe. Something creepy shook my convictions, though.

"Think about it. This town operates twenty-four seven. Who questions people who choose to work graveyard shift and sleep all day with the curtains and blinds pulled tight? Who questions their choice of beverage: *Bloody* Marys." Donovan's smile grew bigger.

"Not a good subject to tease me about." I shifted uneasily, fussing with the chiffon layers of my midnight-blue dress that glittered in the colored lights of the theater. Scrap had found the perfect dress for both the theater and the awards banquet.

As the lights dimmed for the next act, Scrap took off from his perch and flew circles around an area behind us. He trailed a new black-and-silver feather boa behind him like a seductive snake. I did my best to ignore his antics. He was such a queen showing off.

Another, larger imp flew up to join him. Fortitude flapped his wings in long, slow, majestic strokes. The two males contrasted like a pert jay harassing a black swan.

They seemed to converse on a wavelength I could not hear.

If Fortitude was here, then so was Sancroix, and possibly his twitchy nephew. I don't believe in coincidence.

Chapter 10

Topless dancers became a Las Vegas trademark in 1957 at The Dunes.

I DIDN'T DARE TRUST Sancroix, even if he did carry an imp on his shoulder.

In other circumstances I might count him as a potential friend. We had a lot in common, we conversed easily about our lives as Warriors and our experiences in the Citadels.

So why did he stalk me? I had no doubts left that Junior had flown from Chicago to Vegas on my flight just to watch me.

I was as leery of them as I was of Donovan.

Trust has to be earned, Scrap warned me as he settled back with the musicians where he could watch the show and keep an eye on me as well.

"You learn anything from Fortitude?" I asked under the mask of blotting my nose with a tissue.

Not one damn thing. That imp is more closemouthed than any I've ever met, including my eldest brother who barely said three words his first one hundred years.

Scrap rarely talked about his life before he came to me. Oblique references only. Just enough to tweak my curiosity, never enough to satisfy me. Yet I knew I could trust him with my life and my soul.

I also trusted Gollum—Guilford Van der Hoyden-

Smythe PhD—with my life and friendship. He, too, had a shadowy past, but I never caught him actually lying to me.

I trusted Donovan with my life. We'd fought demons together twice, and he'd guarded my back admirably. His lies and half truths kept me from trusting him with my heart. The flowers and tickets were just one of many lies.

Didn't stop me from enjoying last night and longing for more. There is something incredibly satisfying about hot monkey sex. Not satisfying enough to go the distance in a relationship.

In that moment I made the decision to contact my Citadel. If they sent Breven Sancroix to help me with Darren, (even if he did arrive too late) they must know something about him.

"How are they going to top the first act finale?" Mom asked. "For dramatic purposes, you end Act One with your second-best piece, saving the best for the Grand Finale."

Hidden depths kept coming out of her mouth. Did I have her demon husband to thank for that, or just time and a growing closeness between us.

Then, too, if Darren hadn't slammed into our lives, would we have torn down some barriers so that we could grow closer?

The house lights blinked once, twice, then doused completely.

The New Age synthesizer music started up on a long slow throb with a light wooden flute flirting with the descant above it. Perfect music to make love to.

Stop that, I admonished myself.

Donovan seemed to have the same idea. He traced sensuous circles along the back of my hand with his thumb.

I jerked it away from him.

A spotlight led our eyes around the perimeter of the theater. A dozen fairy dancers hovered above the audience, disappearing as the light moved on to the next. When each had been highlighted, they converged on silent wings in the center.

I craned my neck to look up to the middle of their circle. They swayed back and forth, hands joined, faces blank and empty. I wondered why, and when, the joy of flying and dancing to beautiful music had drained out of them. They performed by rote, perfectly coordinated in time to the music. Not a flaw revealed itself to me. Except for the total lack of . . . life.

They looked like Mom had when the enormity of Darren's death and his life finally hit her.

The music shifted, became urgent, almost menacing. The fairies broke apart, skittering around the rafters in manic movements.

The light floral scent that had drifted behind them became sharper, spicier with anticipation.

Abruptly everything stopped. Music and dancers. The lights blinked and flashed red.

Movement on stage in the semidarkness drew our eyes. A hint of yellow, suggestive of dawn, brightened the outer edges, partially blocked by a huge set piece that nearly filled the stage.

One by one the fairies converged around the blockage. Moment by moment more details emerged. The set took on the texture of twisted and weathered red rock. Cave openings, big enough for the fairies to enter and disappear, looked like facial features, definition of arms. I stared at a writhing goblin frozen in stone and time.

The dance continued, sometimes sweet, sometimes agonized. Always the intent to enter one of the caves in order to get home. No words. Just the dance and that intense longing.

I didn't have to be an empath to feel the heartbreak of exile.

When the dancers moved above the audience their faces had taken on animation. Anger. Loneliness. Bewilderment.

Maybe the total lack of expression earlier was part of the story.

Their costumes and makeup became uniformly grayer. A trick of the lights. I had to keep reminding myself this was just a story and didn't involve me.

A resounding thunderclap startled us all. Gasps all around. I jumped and found my hand firmly captured by Donovan's. Mom and Penny reached for each other.

Then sighs of relief as the audience realized this, too, was just part of the story.

The thud of raindrops on hard desert sandstone erupted all around the rock formation. A cool breeze wafted through the theater refreshing us. I hadn't noticed how warm the room had become until that tiny chill of sweat drying in the wind.

Lightning zigzagged across the stage. One of the caves, a little one almost invisible in the fold of the goblin's arm, showed a different texture behind the opening.

The clouds thinned and a diffuse glimmer of moonlight—I couldn't tell which quarter—highlighted the opening some more.

The fairies saw it at the same moment I did. They paused for a heartbeat. "Home," they whispered.

Did they really say it aloud or did I imagine it?

Before I could decide, they rose as one into the air on a level with the opening, formed a straight-as-an-arrow line and flitted in. Quickly. The lights changed again. The hint of moonlight was directly behind the opening, then passed on its eternal pathway. The portal darkened, started to close. One last lone fairy had stopped to pluck a fragile desert bloom. The last in line, lagging behind just a bit.

Too late. She'd wasted too many precious moments gathering that lovely memento, the only bright spot in her exile from home. She slammed into the rock wall and dropped like a stone toward the stage.

I gasped in dismay and sadness. The rest of the audience joined in. I felt like that horrible moment near the end of *Peter Pan* when Tinker Bell has drunk the poisoned milk and lies dying in Peter's hand.

Did I begin the slow clap of hands? Someone did. We all did. We clapped as if our lives depended upon it. The fairy's life did depend upon it.

"I believe in fairies," I chanted.

Mom took up the litany. In a heartbeat, twelve hundred voices told the Universe that we believed.

The dancer lying crumpled on the stage slowly changed from dull gray to white to palest pink. As the noise rose to a driving demand, a single yellow arm snaked out of the opening, grabbed the fallen fairy, and yanked her through the portal.

She waved a thank you to the audience and smiled. The entire stage seemed brightened by that tiny uplift of mouth and eyes. Layers of chiffon trailed after her, turning hot and vibrant pink.

We leaped to our feet, rejoicing with our applause and our shouts of "Bravo!" and "Encore!"

I had to wipe a tear from my eye, amazed at the cultural icons at play here. I could use these images, this feeling, the sharing of common goals and desires through the medium of story.

"She made it," Mom sighed. "I'm so glad she made it home safely."

"So am I."

I glanced over to Donovan, to somehow draw him into this wonderful warmth and joy. He stared off at the portal that was now just a shadow on a stage set. His faced creased in some internal pain I could not share.

"I can't ever go home," he whispered. "Never. I'm more in exile than they are."

Chapter 11

Las Vegas averages three thousand weddings on Valentine's Day weekend.

"YOU'RE VERY QUIET," I said to Donovan as we picked our way out of the theater. I wasn't used to seeing his face devoid of animation. It scared me.

Mom and Penny walked a few paces ahead of us, chattering gaily about the magnificent performance.

"I . . . old memories," he stammered. His gaze kept returning to the stage, now in deep shadow, the rock goblin only a vague outline.

It reminded me of the brooding presence of a gargoyle on a cathedral I'd seen in England.

"Sometimes shared pain is lesser pain," I coaxed.

"The fairy falling and crumpling a wing . . ." He shook his head, reached for his cell phone, and busied himself turning it back on.

I needed to pursue this. Donovan actually talking about his past was too rare and important.

Jostling crowds and a line waiting for taxis outside the hotel interrupted any opportunity to speak and expect to be heard, or not overheard.

Donovan's phone chirped discreetly as we pushed out into the cooling night air. He barked something into it, then cursed.

"The limousine got T-boned at an intersection. We'll have to take a taxi and bill them for the inconvenience," he explained mildly.

"Oh, dear," Mom sighed. "I really need to get back to The Crown Jewels. I'm singing again tonight."

"When did that happen?" I asked. Something akin to disapproval wanted to burst forth. I couldn't express that to Mom. I needed to support her now, help her regain her life after Donovan's foster father had nearly destroyed it.

"Excuse me for buttin' in here," a tall man in his sixties, wearing a white Stetson and an impeccable gray western-cut suit edged between me and my mother. "Name's Ed Stetson, like the hat." He tipped it. "I got a limo heading out to The Crown Jewels. Heard there's this hot new act there." He winked at Mom. "Saw her last night and just have to go back."

"Well, I'll be. Ed Stetson from Austin," Penny said. She hooked her arm through his. "If I remember correctly, and I always do, you drink Bushmills, smoke Cubans, and love strawberries dipped in dark chocolate."

"Only Oregon strawberries in season, sweeter than the California berries. Something about the cold winters sending the plants to sleep. They wake up refreshed and full of sweetness. Like you. How you doing, Penny?" He bent to kiss her cheek.

The conversation went downhill from there. Or uphill. Mom and Penny joined Ed in his big white stretch Cadillac. "He's harmless and rich as a Texan ought to be," Penny reassured me just before the driver closed the wide white door on the dim interior. "Your mama is safe with us."

"Want some supper? I know this lovely place at The Venetian. It's only a few blocks from here." Donovan smiled down at me. He didn't have to say, "Alone at last." It showed in his reinvigorated posture and the way he gazed at me.

A shiver of delight coursed through me. "Let's walk."

Blocks in Vegas can be irrelevant. Some of the bigger venues stretch for half a mile or more. I set a brisk pace, partly to keep warm now that the sun had set. More out of impatience.

Donovan's long legs kept pace with me easily.

Traffic on the sidewalks and streets grew heavier the closer we came to the Strip. We jostled other walkers constantly.

Donovan threaded his fingers through mine to keep me close. I enjoyed the warmth and tingles shooting from his palm to mine. He cast an aura of protectiveness around me. For once I let it stand, easing away my need for independence in favor of cultivating his semi-loquacious mood.

The massive facade of The Venetian loomed before us. The ever-present sound system played a synthesized version of a bouncy Italian tune I couldn't name. Its ever-so-slightly off-key rendition—no electronic medium could do it justice—irritated me. I inched closer to Donovan, shying away from the noise.

Inside, the rich carpets, faux marble walls, and pseudo-classical statuary muted the music enough that I relaxed. Our shoulders brushed, and I let my hand linger in his.

We followed the signs around the edge of the smoky casino toward the Grand Canal. The last half flight of stairs opened up into . . .

"Wow!" I stopped short, amazed by the lovely blue sky and fluffy white clouds above an open plaza flanked by quaint buildings. The broad painted sky looked too real and gave the impression of a long horizon beyond the rooftops. Nothing felt closed in. A hint of pink just above the roofline suggested we neared sunset. But outside, in Vegas the sky had gone full dark.

A Venetian piazza opened before us with shops and trees and jovial crowds. A group of Renaissance costumed singers performed while a Pierrot clown on stilts in traditional baggy white costume with black-and-white domino makeup manipulated a dancer/puppet in jester green, purple, and red playing the marionette.

I caught a hint of sweet citrus and sharp olive on the warm and gentle breeze, a full ten degrees warmer than the desert chill we'd left behind, but cooler than the hot and crowded casino.

"Have we zipped through the chat room and transported to Italy?"

"Not quite," Donovan chuckled. "Shall we take a gondola ride before we eat?"

"Why not?" I kept turning circles trying to take it all in at once. "I think I need to set my next book in Venice so I can go there for research. If it's half this nice, it will be wonderful."

"The real canal smells of sewage and brine instead of chlorine," he whispered conspiratorially.

"I don't care." I turned in a circle, trying to absorb it all, while still following him toward the canal. My heels caught on a crack in the tiled pavement.

Donovan caught me as I tilted downward. With a laugh, he held me close to his side.

I grinned goofily.

"It will all be here on the way back," he chuckled, tucking my hand into the crook of his arm. "And it will still be just before sunset, no matter what time it is outside."

Comfortably close, we made our way across the arched bridge over the artificial waterway. The incredibly clear, blue water and pristine white stonework sparkled with an invitation to follow it along its twisted pathway, alternately narrow and private and open and jovial.

I resisted the urge to lay my head against Donovan's chest. Even in three-inch heels I couldn't reach that special place on a man's shoulder meant for snuggling.

"Watch your step, my dear." A gentle tug on my hand and I paid enough attention to my feet to walk down the seven white steps lapped by blue water to a waiting boat. A fancy white one with gold trim.

Donovan stepped in first, then held my hand while the gondolier steadied the craft. At the last moment, just before I put both feet firmly on the deck, it rocked and threw me off-balance. Donovan caught me and we tumbled onto the seats laughing and clinging to each other.

The boatman pushed off from his mooring with a long pole. He wore the traditional black knee pants, striped shirt, and flat-crowned skimmer hat. He sang a soft ballad in Italian as he guided us into the center of the narrow waterway.

The subdued lighting caught the shimmer of sequins on my dress. They might have been stars in a midnight-blue sky.

"Thank you for this evening, L'Akita," Donovan said, kissing the back of my hand. His lips lingered and nibbled up my wrist. Then he turned our hands over and kissed my palm.

Delicious flashes of electricity wandered up my arm. Memories of last night came back with renewed intensity.

Coherent thought fled.

"After eight hundred years of watching silently, I need to take action, do things, follow through." His mouth shifted to my brow, my nose, my lips.

Oh, yeah, I was supposed to ask him about those eight hundred years before he became human fifty years ago, though he only looked forty—tops. And a very fit and vibrant forty at that.

The primal energy we shared deepened.

He bent down, reaching beneath the seat, while somehow never removing his mouth from my face. Velvety flower petals trailed along my scar after his caresses.

I managed to look down as the softness met my chin. A single red rosebud, absolutely perfect, with a bit of dew still on it. A matching red ribbon dangled a bright and shiny object from the stem.

A huge, honking, square-cut diamond in an antique gold filigree. The most beautiful and enticing piece of jewelry I'd ever seen.

The diamond flashed. I caught a brief glimpse of a jagged lightning crack in reality.

The ring called to me, begged me to wear it. Forever. If I but touched it, I could rule the Universe.

My heart skipped a beat. Three beats. I forgot to breathe.

"L'Akita, Tess, will you marry me?"

Huh?

I opened my eyes to find myself looking into the dark chocolate depths of his own. Fire sang through my blood.

I wanted to say yes.

Well, my hormones wanted me to say yes.

The ring demanded I say yes.

My brain stretched and snapped awake.

That was the biggest diamond I'd ever seen outside the crown jewels in the Tower of London. Greed reared its nasty head.

"I know I've messed up since we met." He had the grace to look sheepish. "But I figured it out. Well, most of it. And I want things right between us. Will you marry me?"

"You sure did mess up. Like knocking up the wicked little witch who murdered your father right after I refused to have your children without the commitment of marriage."

And he never said the crucial words: "I love you."

"Well, yeah. I really wanted you to be the mother of that child, our child. I want to fill your house with our children. WindScribe was, I don't know, I was just so very angry with you at the moment. I don't love her."

"Good thing since she's locked up in a mental hospital for the rest of her life." And my Aunt MoonFeather, the most honorable person and witch I knew was under orders from the prison warden of the universe to gain custody of that child by hook or by crook.

She'd filed suit in the mundane courts as soon as Wind-Scribe's doctors confirmed her pregnancy. Donovan had countersued. I couldn't help but think that marriage to me might help his case.

He'd seemed obsessed with having children since I met him last autumn.

Children to fill my house. *My house*! The rambling monstrosity on Cape Cod sat smack dab in the middle of neutral ground. A place where peace treaties could be signed in safety. A place where neither demon nor magic ruled.

But a neutral place that lay vulnerable to those seeking to open a new and rogue portal between dimensions.

The most valuable plot of land in Human space to those who knew what it was and how to manipulate it.

Donovan didn't want me. He wanted my children and my house.

My body calmed down and began listening to my head.

The gondolier listened raptly to our conversation as well. Did Scrap?

I suddenly missed his acerbic comments.

"Why can't Scrap come near you? You have to know that I can't marry you until that little issue is resolved." Scrap and I were bound together by magical ties that stretched through several dimensions and the chat room. If he died, I died. If Donovan came between us, I think I'd shrivel up into a mere shadow of myself.

Come to think on it, I hadn't seen Scrap since theater intermission.

Where are you?

Busy.

I felt like a door had slammed in my face.

A wave of loneliness washed over me, chilling any lingering ardor.

"What do you know of Scrap's past?" Donovan asked, so quietly I didn't think our boatman could hear.

"More than I do of yours." Not a whole lot more.

"If the imp is repelled by me, then there must be a darkness in his soul."

"And there isn't in yours? You fell from something. I know that much." And now I also knew he'd been a silent watcher for eight hundred years before that fall.

"What did you fall from? Grace? If that's the case, you have a darkness in your past worse than Scrap's."

His face went still as stone. Redness spread across his cheeks, making them seem sharper than ever and highlighting the faint copper coloring.

"Gondolier, I'm getting out." I stood. The boat rocked.

Donovan steadied me. I slapped his hand away.

"Sorry, ma'am. You have to wait until we reach a landing."

I looked up and down the artificial canal. Tall walls flanked us as we approached a miniature Bridge of Sighs.

"Can't wait that long. *Ciao.*" Oblivious to stares and shouts from people watching—including Donovan—I stepped onto the seat with one foot and launched myself upward. I clung to the smooth white faux marble of the bridge and swung one leg up to the railing.

The gondolier kept poling the pretty white-and-gold boat along.

The wedding boat.

All the others were plain black. Donovan had planned well. Too bad I couldn't go along with his plans.

"Tess. Wait," he shouted, half standing on the wobbling gondola.

The boat passed beyond me. He couldn't follow.

Anonymous hands reached down to help me. I scrambled onto the bridge, having flashed only a little too much leg in my precipitous escape. Good thing Scrap color coordinates my undies.

"Thanks, folks." I called and waved to my helpers.

Head high and shoulders straight, I marched for the nearest exit.

Scrap settled on my shoulder and wiggled his tail, lashing my back with its barb. Right where he belonged. Where I belonged.

You didn't ask if your first husband was Damiri demon like Donovan's foster father, he chided me.

"Next time. Want to tell me about the darkness in your soul?"

Next time, babe. I've got unfinished business in Imp Haven.

He disappeared again.

"Damn," I said as I hailed a taxi.

Chapter 12

Slot machines need a complete change of circuit board to affect the percentage of wins.

I HATE LYING to Tess. I had imp business—but not in Imp Haven.

Fortitude bugs me. He's too silent. Too big. Sure he's bonded to a rogue Warrior, but that's no excuse for shunning another imp. I'm bonded to a rogue, too.

Rogue means working outside the confines of a Citadel, not mean or bad or anything like that. I've heard rumors that more and more Warriors of the Celestial Blade are leaving the Citadels.

The portals to other dimensions aren't stable. We need Warriors out in the world, continuing what the secret fraternities and sororities have been doing for centuries in solitude.

Fortitude acts like that's top secret information and I'm not good enough to have access.

Well, I've got my sources, too.

Gayla's imp Ginkgo likes to chat. I think I'll skip through the chat room and over to the Citadel. It's only a thousand miles or so, almost due north. That's a much easier journey than through time. Done that once or twice, don't want to have to do it again.

Since I'm not hopping dimensions, I slip into the big white room without definition. I close one layer of eyelids to concentrate and visualize my destination. Gotta keep the other three layers open to make sure the scaly faeries on duty don't notice me. Then I slide back into the same dimension but at a different location. Easy as pie.

Except . . .

"Let go of my tail!"

A huge and hairy hand with four digits and an opposable thumb hangs on tight.

This is going to cost me a wart or two.

I twist and yank and send my wings into overtime.

Big fat on steroids laughs, a deep and foreboding expulsion of air that has little to do with humor and a lot to define evil.

I ache to transform. Tess is not here to command me.

What to do? What to do?

I stretch anyway, becoming thinner and sharper. My tail slices the demon's hand.

"Ouch, that hurts," it pouts, sucking dark green blood from its palm.

"That's what you get for detaining an imp on an honest mission," I snarl back. Can't let the beast know how scared I am. That blood was so dark it was almost black.

Faery blood is bright pink or maybe cerulean, never dark. If he's a mutated faery, we're all in trouble. Faeries are the bright and joyful balance of air sprites for the entire universe. They have the only dimension with three demon ghettos because their power of light is so strong. (That's a big secret, so don't tell anyone). Every other dimension has one race of light and one race of dark. (We keep demons in ghettos for a reason. They eat anything and everything in their path). Faeries can flit into many dimensions. Almost as good as imps.

The universe needs faeries.

An imbalance in their domain shakes up the balance across the entire universe.

Humans are weird, though. They don't need a demon ghetto. They kill themselves frequently and with unnatural glee. They are their own victims.

I think maybe I need to take a look in Faery after I talk to Ginkgo. We need more faeries, but not the kind on guard duty in the chat room lately.

"Are we anywhere near the Dragon and St. George?" I asked the skinny taxi driver. I'd come out of The Venetian at a different door and got disoriented.

"Thought you wanted to go to The Crown Jewels," the driver muttered. A longer drive, bigger fare, bigger tip. He looked like one of the many starving performers in town who worked at anything between gigs and tips. I thought I'd seen him before, but who remembers taxi drivers?

"I do. Later. But first I'd like to check on something."

"Tickets to 'Fairy Moon' are scarce as hen's teeth, lady. I know a guy . . ."

"I saw the show earlier this evening."

The muted roar of traffic on the Strip at the other side of the hotel filled the cab as he thought of ways to milk more money out of me.

I took a chance. "Lady Lucia sent me the tickets."

His eyes sparked with interest. And fear. He took a long, assessing look at me through the rearview mirror. I thought his gaze lingered on my scar. Maybe I'm paranoid.

"You a friend of Lady Lucia, you tell her Mickey Mallone take you anywhere in Vegas you want to go." A strange name for a guy with distinct Mediterranean coloring and broken English. "No charge. I wait for you to finish business at the Dragon, then take you to Crown. Anything for a friend of Lady Lucia." He put the car into gear and screeched the tires as he merged into traffic, as if he owned the street.

"I've never met her. She sent me the tickets as a professional courtesy." So I wouldn't go vampire hunting?

My imagination sped into overdrive. I hadn't done enough writing on this trip to control it.

Vampires were myths. No one comes back from the dead. No one.

Not even my husband Dill.

"No one meets Lady Lucia. I gotta go around a couple of blocks to approach the Dragon from the right." The barest flick of the turn signal and we were careening around a corner.

I decided to buckle up.

He pulled into the porte cochere of the Dragon less than ten minutes later, despite bumper-to-bumper traffic on and off the Strip. This hotel had grown up three blocks (each the size of a small city) away from the main action in a slightly less desirable neighborhood. It didn't have the cachet of a Strip hotel until "Fairy Moon" brought it to the attention of the masses. Now neon and glitter had engulfed it.

"I may be a while, Mickey. Get another fare." I climbed out of the taxi, pressing a ten into his hands.

"No charge, lady. I said no charge for a friend of . . . you know."

"A tip. Mickey."

He shrugged. The bill disappeared into his jeans pocket. "You got cell phone? Call me. I come back for you. You wait for me." He scrawled something on a fast food bag that smelled of fried fish, tore off the scrap, and gave it back to me. "You call. Mickey take you anywhere in Vegas."

"What about the Valley of Fire?"

He gulped and looked away. "Okay," he said reluctantly.

"What if I rent a car and you drive me?"

A huge smile creased his face. His blindingly white teeth shone in the dim interior. "That I can do. Forty, fifty miles each way. Good museum in Overton. When you want to go?"

I had a morning full of classes for the conference. "Pack a picnic basket and meet me at The Crown at noon sharp. I'll have you back in time for the evening shift." I slammed the door.

"Call Mickey when you ready," he returned as an overweight, mid-thirties couple wearing matching turquoise shorts and flowered shirts pushed into the taxi from the other side. They yelled something at each other and then to Mickey. He took off at a more sedate pace.

These people obviously were not friends of Lady Lucia.

No clocks anywhere inside. I checked the one on my cell phone, forty-five minutes to the next performance of "Fairy Moon." I hadn't spent as much time with Donovan as I thought. The fiasco felt like a lifetime.

Damn. I'd screwed up as much as he had. I wished I'd taken a better look at the ring. Sure, my inborn avarice wanted to own it, wear it, flaunt it. The ring offered me a sense of power and well-being. It needed to grace my hand.

I shook off that notion in a hurry.

The ring looked like it cost as much as my last advance on a two-book contract. If it was real. My first glance gave me the impression of an antique. The cut and setting might give me some clues to where and when Donovan acquired it.

His finances had undergone many ups and downs over the last year. I didn't think he'd recovered enough to buy that ring on the open market.

I edged around the casino, scanning the ranks of slot machines. The metallic music and constant clanking noises set my teeth on edge more than Donovan's proposal. My stomach growled for sustenance. My nerves rejected the idea of food.

Halfway around the small casino I spotted drifting pastel chiffon behind a knot of cocktail waitresses and suited people with discreet gold hotel name badges.

I took a stool at a slot machine between the fairy dancer and the madly whispering staff. I still couldn't understand why the hotel allowed the dancers out in public in costume. This young man's wings drooped and a layer of grime ringed his ragged knee pants and the cuffs of his elbow-length sleeves.

The flowing green, lavender, and blue of his costume looked pale, verging on the gray of the final act. As I watched him slide a gold chip into the machine, the colors of his garb shifted to brighter hues. Then when the rollers came up with another loss, the colors faded again.

This was no trick of the lights.

I looked closer. Narrow exquisite face, pointed ears, delicate grace. A fragile beauty on the verge of shattering.

"I don't understand how anyone could be skimming," one of the staff whispered to his colleagues. Anger made his voice grow louder than he'd intended. "The owners can't sell the hotel out from under us for a little discrepancy in the books."

The faery didn't look or appear to overhear the intense conversation right next to him.

I carefully avoided glancing in either direction. If I wanted to engage the faery or listen in on a private conversation I had to have a reason to linger. The only reason for staying in this section more than half a minute was the slots.

Reluctantly, I dragged my wallet out of my bra—I have to give myself cleavage some way. Cell phone on the left, wallet on the right and I actually look like I have boobs.

When the wasting fever of the imp flu peeled forty-seven pounds off my body and sped up my metabolism to burn every calorie I ingested, I think it took thirty-seven of those pounds off my chest. That's about the only regret I have from that awful experience. After all, the flu gave me Scrap and a whole new purpose in life.

I placed three quarters in the slot and pulled the arm. No mechanical resistance or click, just the smooth engagement of a computer.

The boxes rolled around and around, settling one by one. One double cherry. Two, and then three stalled in front of me. Clangs and whistles. A flashing light. A long shower of quarters dropped into my lap.

"Let me get you a bucket for those," one of the waitresses said, smiling hugely. "And can I get you a drink while I'm at it?"

"Single malt. Straight up. And can I get a turkey sandwich with that?" She moved off.

The knot of staff backed away to the end of the row, almost into the emergency fire exit.

"Lucky you," muttered the faery in a strangely stilted accent. Like he worked to pronounce each word individually and precisely. "My luck has deserted me."

"I'm sorry. Here. Share some of mine." I handed him a fist full of quarters.

He examined the coins as if looking for counterfeit.

"Are these real money?" he asked. "They are not gold. How can they be money?"

Uh-oh. What had I stumbled on to?

Did I say I don't believe in coincidence?

Chapter 13

Slot machines are negative expectation machines: the longer you play, the more likely you are to lose.

"THISTLE, YOU HAVE TO come now," a girl faery hissed at my puzzled companion. She had the same stilted accent and the same delicate features.

I'd heard that accent before. Where?

"You know what Lord Gregbaum will do to us if you're late again." Her flowing draperies had a dominant pale green beneath a film of grimy gray. At the mention of Lord Gregbaum, the gray became dominant and the green the barest hint.

Gregbaum? I'd heard that name before.

Thistle handed the quarters back to me. "Thank you, gracious lady." He bowed formally. "Faery is in your debt. Mint, wait for me."

Neither one of them touched ground as they hastened through the maze of slot machines.

I gulped.

Anyone but me would dismiss it all as delusion born of stress, drink, the extra oxygen pumped in so gamblers got an artificial high, the never ending noise and smoke in the casino, anything but challenge reality with the notion that faeries could be real.

The waitress appeared with my bucket and sandwich. I

dumped my quarters, handed her the bucket, and grabbed the tray.

"Hey, I'm not supposed to serve you if you aren't gambling."

"Keep the quarters. They'll cover the cost." I lifted the scotch in toast and took a quick sip. One does not ever, under any circumstance, waste good single malt scotch, or even mediocre blends, by gulping.

The fragrance opened my senses. A first taste rolled around my mouth with just a hint of a bite. I swallowed and the fire exploded on the back of my tongue and through every nerve ending in my body. "Ah, Lagavulin. The fire of the gods wrapped in velvet." Nothing but the best for a winning gambler. Got to keep them happy and gambling so they eventually lose everything they won and then some.

Another sip, then two more just so I didn't waste the water of life.

Fortified, I turned to dash after the dancers, sandwich and glass in hand. I have my priorities and never miss a chance to eat and drink. With my schedule, the next meal might disappear as fast as faery dust.

"That's the real trouble with this casino. Everyone is obsessed with that stupid show instead of gambling," the waitress muttered. "Except those blasted dancers. They gamble all the time."

"Is that why the casino is being sold?" I came to a screeching halt. "I mean this place is full to overflowing with people. Why sell a profitable resort?"

"Yeah, maybe." She looked embarrassed as she counted the quarters, stuffing every other dollar's worth into her tip bag at her hip.

"What happens to the show if the Dragon and St. George sells? Will the producer move it to another casino?" Judging by the difficulty getting tickets, another hotel should jump at the chance to host a winning show.

"Look, lady, I don't know anything. I'm just a waitress trying to hang on to my job. But if it means so much to you, most times a hotel sells, they implode it—selling tickets to *that* show—and rebuild, bigger and glitzier. And everyone who works there is out of a job until it reopens, two maybe three years down the road. As for the show? That's up to the producer." She finished counting the money and hurried away.

I tried to find the dancers. They, of course, had disappeared, probably into the maze of back corridors that serviced the entire hotel/casino/resort.

My spine tingled. Someone watched me. Again.

"Scrap, where are you?"

Silence.

I imagined hidden monsters behind potted plants and rows of gambling machines following my progress across the floor. I'd fought my fair share of monsters. But I needed help to do it.

"Scrap?"

A hazy stirring in the back of my mind.

"What are you doing sleeping on the job?"

Scrap never slept, except right after a fight. He needed rest then to recover from the difficult and draining process of transforming into the Celestial Blade.

I whipped out my cell phone and called Mickey. As I waited in the busy porte cochere, full of lights and people, I read the twice life-sized digital poster screen advertising "Fairy Moon."

Produced by Gary Gregbaum.

So who made him a lord?

"Who is Gary Gregbaum?" I asked Mickey as he pulled into traffic.

"Bad news."

"Anyone in Vegas who isn't bad news?"

Mickey flashed me his brilliant grin. "Me."

"How'd Gregbaum get a rep like that if he's now the hottest producer of the hottest show in town?"

"He used to be Lady Lucia's lover. Bad blood between those two." He gulped. "I mean . . ."

"Lady Lucia's supposed to be a vampire. There is no bad blood to a vampire." I grinned back at him. This town was getting spooky. Wereweasels, vampires. Faery lords. Someone stalking me.

"Yeah. She threw Gregbaum out on his ear. He's got a grudge. She's got her fangs in a twist 'cause he made a success of the show even after she pulled her financing. Rumor has it that someone else is working with Gregbaum behind the scenes. No one knows who. Maybe another vampire cutting into Lady Lucia's territory. Maybe someone or something else."

"How come you know so much?" I asked suspiciously.

"People talk in cabs. They do not expect the driver to listen. They do not expect driver with broken English to be smart enough to put together stray pieces of information. No one remembers cab drivers." He flashed me a wide grin through the rearview mirror.

Except me. I know I'd seen him before tonight. "So why tell it all to me?"

"Professional courtesy," he mimicked my words in describing Lady Lucia's gift of tickets. He nodded his head in an imitation bow or salute.

I mulled that over for a moment. Any information was better than none. I'd sort out the veracity later.

"What do you hear about the Dragon and St. George being up for sale? Lady Lucia leveraging a buyout so she can close him down?"

"You said it, lady. I didn't."

"My name's Tess."

"Lady Tess."

I rolled my eyes.

"Are you an escapee from Faery, too?"

"Where's Faery? Bulgaria my home." His accent suddenly thickened.

"Okay, so how does Gregbaum treat his dancers?" The look of terror on Mint's face came from somewhere. And she'd said, "You know what he'll do to *us* if you are late again."

"No word. No gossip. None of his dancers speak English. They live in a dormitory in basement of hotel. Never leave building." Mickey sounded bitter.

But they did speak English. Or at least I understood them to speak English.

"How come you know so much?"

"I auditioned and got rejected. Asked around. I'm a good dancer and gymnast. One of the best. They should have hired me. But no, Gregbaum hires each one personally. Brought in the entire cast from somewhere else. Should be some loyalty to people who already live here," he grumbled. His accent grew thicker.

I missed the flash of white teeth in his smile.

"So you are stuck driving a taxi instead of dancing."

"Yeah. Driving taxi for prettiest lady in Las Vegas. You still want to see Valley of Fire tomorrow?"

Did I? Was I connecting dots or following red herrings here. Maybe I needed to wait on that and check out Gary Gregbaum and Lady Lucia instead.

Maybe I needed help.

"Let's wait on that, Mickey. I'll call you."

"No problem. But you really should see the Valley of Fire before you leave. Is most spectacular at sunrise and sunset."

The times of transition in folklore. The times when magic is strongest. When portals to other dimensions open . . . ?

"Two days from now, when the quarter moon is rising and the sun setting. Mickey take you."

A waxing quarter moon, when demons most often breach their portals and invade our dimension.

Whooee! Time travel is such a rush. Back and forth to the Citadel twice without Tess or Ginkgo being aware that I've been gone for *hours* drains me. I really need some beer and OJ. Some mold would be better. Not easily found in the desert. Vegas is drier than the Citadel, if you can believe that. Not given to mold. In Vegas, they have tons of air conditioners that breed my favorite restorative in abundance.

But I don't dare leave Ginkgo while he sleeps off our heavy exertions. Now that he realizes he really likes boys better than girls, I must cement our relationship.

At last I have found the perfect lover. He's younger than I by a good fifty years, and already full sized. Such strength and stamina!

I could wax poetic on my lover's attributes for, like forever. Unfortunately duty calls. Duty in the form of Tess, my beloved Warrior.

Life in the Citadel stifled her. But now that Ginkgo and I are an item, (ooh, I like the sound of that) I wish Tess would visit more often. I'll have to suggest a refresher course in being a Warrior of the Celestial Blade.

"Psst, Ginkgo." I rouse my stud from his snoring slumber. An imp snoring is a beautiful song of love and life affirmation. Yet I must regrettably end it.

"Ginkgo, have you spoken to Gayla?" Gayla is his Warrior.

"Gayla." He smiles dreamily.

"Did you ask her to call Gollum?" Someone has to make use of that telephone she installed at great cost and near rebellion from the ranks of traditionalists. I mean, really, they use very modern pickup trucks to run into town for supplies and make lightning raids on rogue portals. You'd think they'd wake up to changing times and get some electricity and indoor plumbing out here!

"My Gayla made the call. This Gollum person wings his way toward your Tess, though how he can fly in one of those mechanical contraptions I do not understand. Now where were we?" He reaches for me.

He draws circles around the warts on my bum with his talons. Blood wells in the tracks of his tracing. I wrap my tail around his neck. Not quite domination, not quite subjugation with my backside in his face.

I'll check out Faery in a bit.

My cell phone chirped a phrase from "A Night on Bald Mountain," just as I entered the casino across from Mom's stage. The blame thing changed ring tones on its own every day or two. I tried for a discreet and anonymous chirp. The universe wanted to summon me with music geared to the weird.

I glanced at the caller ID and smiled. "Gollum, what's up?" Ten o'clock here. One AM at home on Cape Cod.

"I am. Or I will be in about fifteen minutes."

"Huh?"

"I'm in Chicago, on my way to Vegas."

"Huh? Don't you have classes?"

"None on Friday. Remember, we set up my schedule with the community college so I could have weekends to take you to cons when you need company."

"Oh, yeah. Listen, I'm glad you're coming. I hope you have your laptop with all your interesting databases."

"I figured you might need your archivist when Gayla called me and told me you needed help."

"Gayla?" Either I was missing something or all the smoke and noise of the casinos had fried my brain.

Off to my left, Donovan shuffled in by another door. His eyes looked heavy and his shoulders slumped. He'd been drinking.

Well, what did I expect. I'd be drunk, too, if he'd done to me what I just did to him. I turned my back on him, not ready to deal with that little problem just yet.

That little movement put me in line of sight to Mom crooning her way through "Foggy Day In London Town." No sign of Penny and Ed Stetson.

But Sancroix stood on the fringes of her audience staring at her in fascination.

Or was he studying her like a cat studies its prey? His big imp sat heavily on the man's shoulder. Fortitude had folded his wings, covering his head in sleep.

Except that imps rarely slept.

Was that an imp eye peering out surreptitiously spying on the room for Sancroix? Why the subterfuge if I was the only one in the room who could see the imp?

Because I was the only one in the room who could see the imp.

Junior sat at a table beside him, twisting a paper napkin to shreds. Still nervous and twitchy. A squarely built woman sat beside him, back to me. Something in the angle of her head looked familiar.

I pushed aside the images of stalker and prey. Sancroix had to be one of the good guys, or his imp wouldn't stay with him; Gayla wouldn't have sent him to assist me last month against a little problem with my mother's half-blood Damiri demon husband and a grieving widowed Windago—there was that crazy book title that kept haunting me. Next book. I had two newly under contract already.

"I'll book a room for you here at The Crown Jewels," I told Gollum.

"Already done, love. Don't wait up for me. I'll see you in the morning." He made a kissing sound.

Huh?

Gollum? Guilford Van der Hoyden-Smythe the pedantic professor. My dear friend and archivist. My confidant and the one I trusted almost more than myself.

I really had missed something.

Donovan sloshed up to the bar.

"I'm glad Gollum is coming. He can provide a buffer between me and my ex-stepbrother," I said to myself. I kept reminding myself of all the reasons why I had rejected Donovan. I had to. Otherwise, my hormones and my greed for that diamond might make me do something even more stupid than sleeping with him last night.

Chapter 14

Las Vegas means "The Meadows" in Spanish. The name appears on maps as early as the 1830s. Las Vegas was officially founded in 1905 when the railroad came to town.

MOM ENTERTAINED A LARGE crowd in the lounge with a vibrant rendition of "Seventy-Six Trombones." The song provided a nice balance to the moody torch songs. The audience sang along on the chorus. Some even got up and marched around their tables. She knew how to work an audience.

"Amazing! When did she learn to do that?"

Barely ten thirty. She'd keep them going for hours yet.

I took my cell phone back to our room. No signal.

Back to the lobby. No signal.

Outside in the parking lot. No signal.

I growled something very impolite.

"Is there a problem, Ms. Noncoiré?" a shaky tenor voice asked from behind me.

I whirled about, automatically *en garde*. No sign of Scrap. I sent out a mental call for help.

"Oh, it's you. Junior Sancroix."

He still twitched nervously, his gaze darting right and left, across the street, and back to my feet. Not my eyes. He looked firmly at the pavement.

"Is there a problem?" He grimaced like he should be embarrassed by my language, but wasn't.

"No cell service."

"That happens sometimes." He shrugged. "You can always use the hotel landlines." His smile turned greedy.

"And pay exorbitant connection fees as well as inflated long-distance charges." I wondered if he had magnets or something inside the building to block service. Or maybe he used his empathic talent to convince people they had no signal when they did. I wouldn't put it past him. He didn't have an imp to lull my distrust.

"Such is life in Vegas." He shrugged again.

"I'm curious. How'd a man in his early thirties come to own a hotel, casino, and convention center?"

"I have connections." He grinned at me. For half a moment in the glaring lights on tall poles his eye teeth looked elongated and extra sharp, his eyes tilted up and his ears pointed on the upward lobes.

"Connections to Lady Lucia?"

"Where'd you hear that name?" Immediately, he clamped his mouth shut, hunched his shoulders defensively, and scanned the skies as well as the parking lot. His hands twitched, and so did his neck.

"The Contessa befriended me with tickets to 'Fairy Moon.' I saw you and your uncle there tonight."

"You will have a full signal on your cell phone by morning." He turned on his heel and fairly ran back into the safety of the casino. He ran as if a vampire followed on his heels.

Stop that! I nearly slapped my face to shake off the imagery. I really needed to get back to work and channel my overactive imagination into my books.

But first, I had another way of contacting my Citadel for information about Breven Sancroix and his nervous nephew.

Too many lights and distractions in my room. I headed to the one place I might find quiet and privacy in this town. The roof.

I didn't obey the "Employees Only" signs on the doors or the chain and padlock across the last bit of stairway. My legs were too short to easily climb over it, but I was limber enough to duck under, even in a fancy dress and heels.

Huge, humming barrel units on the nearly flat roof ran the air-conditioning. I found a shadowed place between two of them, letting their constant and monotonous drone mask the roar of traffic that never ended on the streets. When

Scrap decided to come home, he'd find me here, right next to his favorite feeding ground.

I had to clear a space of gravel bits and blown debris before trusting the fine layers of my skirt to the dirty surface. It tilted just a little toward a gutter and filter system to drain the infrequent but heavy rainfall. I suspected somewhere in the maze one of these barrel units contained a cistern for maintaining the extensive landscaping.

Then I sat cross-legged, wiggling a bit to find maximum comfort.

Meditation is not my strong suit. Restlessness and muscles that need to keep moving plagued me as I tried to find an inner stillness. I could almost hear Gollum's voice in my ear, whispering "Breathe. Breathe deeply. Concentrate on breathing."

I smiled inwardly that he was winging his way to me even now. But I didn't let that tiny bit of joy distract me. Instead, I used it to conjure images in my mind of the good times I'd had at the Citadel. There weren't many. But a few.

Sister Serena, laughing with me as she made jokes about our scars. Sister Paige saluting me the first time I felled her in arms practice. Sister Gayla's exuberant shout as she and three pickup loads of Warriors joined me in battle against a band of Sasquatch. We fought for possession of an ancient native artifact, an unfinished blanket that held honor, dignity, honesty, justice, and a few other noble characteristics for all mankind woven into its design.

We Warriors of the Celestial Blade did some good.

My thoughts traveled all the way north to my Citadel and my friends. I imagined a tiny bit of candle flame sparking a light inside any receptive mind within the high stone walls in that hidden ravine between here and there, 'twixt light and shadow, only a part in this dimension and partly in the next.

I felt a connection, another mind rousing from slumber to acknowledge the brush of my thoughts. Serena, always the most sensitive to communication from near or far. She slept lightly, a requirement for a physician.

But this was not a medical emergency and Serena was tired. Her sisters had fought long and hard against another incursion from the Sasquatch trying to open a new portal.

I let her sleep. My questions would wait.

Something awakens me. I'm too groggy to recognize the weak call not directed to anyone in particular.

My Tess.

Duty calls. Duty calls. I can sense Tess getting anxious about me being gone so long. I'm so tired I don't dare manipulate time to return to her earlier in the day.

I can't linger any longer though I want to stay. Sleeping next to my lover has to be one of the greatest joys in life. I cannot imagine such intimacy with any other than my soul mate.

I crawl away from Ginkgo's bed, limp and sated. My legs feel heavy. At the same time, my wings keep carrying me higher and higher.

First, I need to check out Faery. What I left Tess to do in the first place. My visit to Ginkgo and his Warrior Gayla was supposed to be just a quick side trip. But then Ginkgo started throwing pheromones at me like there was no tomorrow.

And for most of the night and half the day, there was no tomorrow. Only us.

Ahhhh!

I duck into the chat room and pause by the doorway back to Earth.

I can see the portal to Faery, just two doors down. A little thing with a haze in front of it. One of the easier barriers to breach, if you know how or have enough willpower. Which I do.

The big, red-scaled monster faeries are still on duty. What is this? The guards are supposed to change every day. Different demon tribes rotate the watches to keep everyone in their proper dimension.

Three days running I've had to dodge these guys.

Maybe, if I make myself real small and keep close to the edge, I can avoid detection. One step. Then two. A third and a flit and I'm right in front of the door I need.

A quick peek inside. The stream that chuckles down the hillside runs clear and clean again. The grass is vividly green and the flowers splash brilliant color. Just like it's supposed to.

Last month, when faeries disputed the succession of their king and that king's murderer still ran loose around Earth, Faery did not look so lovely.

But what is this? The big oak tree with clumps of mistletoe has fallen. The grass beneath its rotting trunk is brown. The upper branches are damming the creek. Water backs up behind it and floods the meadow.

I set my wings in motion to carry me through the portal for further investigation.

And bounce right back into the path of the ugly demons on duty.

"Faery is closed," an ugly male says. "No imps in Faery. No imps outside Imp Haven." He reaches a hairy paw with an opposable thumb for my neck.

Demons with opposable thumbs? Gods and Goddesses, what is this universe coming to? Next thing you know the Powers That Be will give opposable thumbs to cats.

Cats, the most cunning, malicious, and evil of all demons!

I dodge the monster and dive right back to Earth. I need to tell someone about this. But who? Who can help? Who can restore the balance to Faery?

And the balance must be restored. Something is draining energy from Faery. That energy is building up somewhere, raw power an unscrupulous being can tap and manipulate for evil.

Chapter 15

"The Strip" is actually Las Vegas Boulevard, a section of US Highway 91.

A LOT OF THE "WORK" of a conference takes place at the breakfast buffet or in the bar. Since Mom had the main bar tied up most of the evening, writers, agents, and editors congregated in the small dining area adjacent to the casino. Everything is adjacent to or connected to the casino even in small hotels that cater to conventions and conferences.

I'd just settled next to the mystery writer Jack Weaver with a plate full of waffles with strawberries and whipped cream, scrambled eggs, hash browns, bacon, juice, and the watery brown stuff they called coffee in this town when Junior Sancroix elbowed a romance editor aside to take the chair on the opposite side.

Damn. I wanted to talk to that editor. I had some ideas about a contemporary paranormal romance I wanted to discuss with her.

"You're that ringer the conference brought in to draw more people," he announced to the table at large.

"I'm a published writer who has had some success," I corrected him. "So's Mr. Weaver here."

"I want to write a book," Junior said quietly. He looked directly at me.

"The only way to write a book is to write it," I replied.

"Hear, hear!" Jack raised his glass of juice in toast.

Everyone else at the table joined him in the salute, including the editor.

"There's lots of weird things that happen in Vegas, a lot of connections that don't make sense until you start unraveling them, take them back to the source. I need to write about them," Junior insisted. He picked up a stray knife from a cutlery set and began tapping the table with it.

"Then write about them." I tried to ignore him.

"I've never written before. I'll need help. But I think I'll make it a romance. That can't be too hard. After all, bored housewives do it for fun. And make a lot of money at it." He flipped the knife to balance between two fingers and waggled it back and forth.

The temperature around the table dropped below freezing.

"Try it Mr. Sancroix. Just try it and see how 'easy' writing anything is. Romance is one of the hardest to make real and believable." Did I say how annoying this nervous little guy was?

"I'm going to sit in on your classes."

"I believe all my workshops are full. You need to talk to the conference organizers." Pass the buck whenever possible.

"I own this hotel, I can join any damn class I want." He rose abruptly and left. His chair teetered on its rear legs a few seconds before regaining its balance and bumping back to a correct position.

"What was that all about?" the editor asked me.

"I have no idea." But Junior had emphasized "connections." After last night's conversation I suspected he meant Lady Lucia. Or possibly Gregbaum.

I checked my cell phone. Sure enough, I had full signal and a text from Gollum. He'd arrived in the middle of the night and would find me at lunch.

At least one thing in my life was solid and certain. Gollum.

"Why does every fantasy novel have a medieval setting?" a student in my morning workshop asked. She looked like she was approaching her fifties reluctantly, with a too-short sundress, starved-to-thinness body, and expensively dyed auburn hair. The lines around her eyes and at the corners of her perpetual frown gave her away.

"How many fantasies have you read, MaryLynn?" I asked, seeking the name she'd printed in tiny letters on her sticky name tag. Last-minute registration. Those of us who had signed up ahead of time had printed cards slipped into a badge holder.

"Not many. Every one I pick up is the same as all the others." She pouted prettily, like a twenty year old.

I'd had experience with women who used that kind of pout to manipulate people.

"I prefer modern romances. I've sold five and am considering diversifying." She'd mentioned those five novels in every comment she'd made in the last hour and a half.

"Seems like you've had bad luck in picking fantasies. The ones I've read in just the last month have settings in prehistory, outer space, and contemporary cities. But the medieval castle is a trope you find quite often, especially in historical romances. Any theories before I give my explanation—which is only an opinion."

A forest of hands shot up. This was a workshop on making genre fiction unique while keeping it sellable. One of the harder topics I had tackled at writer conferences. Registration for this class was supposed to be limited to those who'd sold at least one short story, preferably a novel.

Unpublished Mr. Twitchy cowered in a back corner. He didn't appear to be taking notes, contenting himself with glaring at me.

I turned the discussion toward the longing for older, simpler times when honor and valor could be measured, the romance of historical costumes, the "glamour" of hobnobbing with lords and ladies. Someone also brought up the influence of the Society For Creative Anachronism—the clubs that re-created their own version of the Middle Ages every weekend, the way olden times should have been—where everyone is a lord or lady, and the popularity of Renaissance Faires.

"We could also look at an anthropological explanation," I said. "Some theorize that when an industrialized society is cut off from communication and resources, they will revert to a Medieval level of technology within two generations. A monarchy or oligarchy flows out of that kind of society—strong leaders protecting average people from predatory animals or human enemies—or in some fantasies, alien beings or fantastical creatures like orcs or trolls. If resources are extremely limited, they will fall back to tribal level hunter-gatherers within another three to four generations."

At the moment the words flowed from my mouth, my resident anthropologist, Guilford Van der Hoyden-Smythe, PhD, ducked into the back of the room. About time. The digital clock on my cell phone showed the noon break approaching fast.

He looked freshly showered and shaved in his neat khakis and emerald-green golf shirt. For once his wire-rimmed glasses sat firmly on the bridge of his nose, masking his mild blue eyes. Every silver-gilt hair lay in place.

His professor guise effectively masked the breadth of his shoulders on his tall and lanky frame. I'd sparred with him, rock climbed with him, had him carry me off the field of battle. I knew the strength and power he could deliver.

Thankfully, he sat between me and Mr. Twitchy, blocking the other man's line of sight to me.

Gollum nodded approval of my statement. My heart shimmied for just a second. The windowless conference room seemed a bit brighter and less confined. Mr. Twitchy paled to insignificance.

My real students scribbled notes rapidly. Except for MaryLynn. I had a feeling she really only wanted to rest on the laurels of her five short contemporary romances. A good beginning to a career. But I'd learned early on, languishing in midlist, that building a career requires a new book every year. And each book has to be different, even those written in series. Now that I'd hit a few best seller lists with a new series based upon my time in the Citadel but set in a post-apocalyptic Earth, I had to work harder to constantly improve my prose and keep my readers happy with new adventures and varied settings within the context.

And the next novel was stalled at an outline and three chapters.

Last night I'd fallen asleep over the laptop without writing a word. Mom had put me to bed at two. Then I'd overslept.

No time to call the Citadel. Barely time to grab my notes.

A monitor appeared in the doorway with a five-minute sign.

"Good discussion, people. Any last comments before we break for lunch?"

"What's your next workshop?"

I'd already done two today. "Nine AM tomorrow. I'm spending this afternoon writing. The only way a book gets written is if I apply butt to chair and fingers to keyboard. Conferences are great learning tools, and can jump-start your enthusiasm, but you still have to write the book and I'm on deadline."

"A selling writer is always on deadline," Gollum said quietly when the room had cleared of all but the two of us. Mr. Twitchy was the first to scuttle away.

My friend hugged me lightly and kissed my cheek.

"Tell me about it." That greeting, while not inappropriate between close friends, felt different. Strange. Like I wasn't ready to deal with him after last night's fiasco with Donovan.

And the night before . . .

"What are you doing for lunch?" Gollum asked.

"Talking to you about some weird things happening in Las Vegas."

"What about Las Vegas isn't weird?" he chuckled. "I caught the tail end of Genevieve's set last night in the lounge. Took me a while to realize that was really her on stage wearing a red cocktail dress and spike heels. The pearls gave her away, though. I've never seen your mother without them."

"A wedding gift from her mother-in-law. I think they've been in Dad's family for several generations. They go to the person in the bloodline who is supposed to have them. Sometimes I think Mom sleeps with them." I took his arm and led him out of the conference center, a big block of rooms that had once been part of the casino. "The buffet still has breakfast items. Let's eat and then find a private place to talk."

"I love a woman with a healthy appetite."

"What's healthy about waffles with strawberries and whipped cream? And a ton of coffee."

"You don't add chocolate chips to the mess. I'll have an egg white omelet, thank you." He almost shuddered at my food choices. "I did bring you some freshly ground coffee from your favorite kiosk on Cape Cod. We can make a couple of pots in the hotel room machines."

"Bless you, Gollum. How did you know the watered-down dark roast they call coffee here would leave me a walking zombie?"

"Have you thought about buying a syringe and mainlining caffeine?"

"Wouldn't work. The stuff they serve here is too weak to jump-start my heart."

"I'll take on that job," he said so quietly I almost didn't hear.

I let that pass. "So what did you think of Mom's new career? The hotel manager is talking about giving her a contract and hiring her a band." After only two nights.

I still reeled at the idea of my *mother* as a torch singer. In Vegas.

"Would that be a bad thing?"

I had to think about that while we went through the buffet line. I decided to try their prime rib, fried shrimp, skip the macaroni and cheese to leave room for desert, and the endless salad bar.

"They make a really good cheese cake here," I said when I'd found us a booth near the kitchen door. I hoped the noise and constant traffic would hide our conversation.

The location didn't hide us. MaryLynn walked past to the adjacent booth. She sniffed in my direction. "Second man I've seen her with in as many days. And neither one is registered for the conference." She didn't try to keep her gossip secret.

Gollum's glasses slid down his nose, and he peered at me over the tops. "Who else have you been flirting with?"

I'd hoped to avoid that topic. No way to lie to Gollum when he looked at me like that. "Donovan came to town. He needed Mom's signature on some papers urgently. While he's here, he accompanied us to a show last night." I kept my eyes on cutting the fat off the prime rib.

"Did you get tickets for 'Fairy Moon'? I'd like to see it, too. I'm hearing wonderful things about it on the Internet."

"Good luck getting tickets. Mine came from an unusual source." Okay. Good way to divert attention away from what I had and hadn't done with Donovan in the last forty-eight hours.

"How unusual?"

I tried his egg-white-and-vegetable omelet without looking at it. I wished I hadn't. It tasted as disgusting and inadequate as it looked.

"Ever hear of Lady Lucia?"

He thought a moment. "I have a vague recollection of some kind of organized crime connection. I'd have to look it up, though."

"Spend your afternoon tracking her down. She may be important to another bit of weirdness."

"Oh? Like what?"

"Not here." I looked over my shoulder at MaryLynn and her companion, a stout woman wearing a respectable suit and a preprinted name tag. I knew her from the formal luncheon yesterday. One of the teaching pros, a romance writer breaking into mainstream and on the verge of hitting a major best seller list. She didn't look too happy at MaryLynn's constant stream of negative gossip about the other conference goers.

"Let's take a walk along the Strip. I'll call a taxi as soon as we finish eating."

"You going back for cheesecake?"

"I don't think so. It doesn't sound as good today. I had a bit of tummy upset yesterday afternoon. I wonder if Scrap's lactose intolerance is catching."

"Wouldn't surprise me. Is he here?"

"No. I haven't seen much of him at all since I got here."

"That's unusual. He shouldn't be able to get too far away from you for any length of time."

"That's beginning to worry me." Especially since Fortitude flitted in ahead of Breven Sancroix. Mom had one arm laced with his and the other with Donovan's.

"Let's go. We can slip out this side door."

"Avoiding your mother again? You really need to talk to her about her new career. Maybe she's decided that making friends and trying new things is good. What could happen to her that's worse than marrying a half demon?"

Chapter 16

The intersection of Flamingo Road and the Strip mark perfect compass points. A bend in the road at the Venetian moves the Strip off true north-south orientation and confuses the unwary.

MICKEY DROPPED US off at the corner of Tropicana and Las Vegas Boulevard—the Strip. I needed some exercise. The one mile plus of walking north to the Dragon and St. George should stretch my legs and give me time to talk privately with Gollum. With so much noise and confusion crowding the sidewalks, I doubted even the most avid eavesdropper could overhear us. If they could find us among the thousands of people jostling for position away from the bumper-to-bumper cars.

"They should close off traffic to all but taxis and tour buses," Gollum grumbled as we dodged six cars running a red light at the intersection.

"They did that down on Freemont, the downtown area. I think they roofed part of it, too. I haven't gotten there yet." I had to turn sideways to avoid being crushed by a phalanx of Asians dripping camera equipment. My breasts crushed up against Gollum's arm.

Without a word, he wrapped the arm around my shoulders and kept me close. For protection, I told myself.

Nothing remotely resembling sexual tension between us. But, oh, it felt good to snuggle next to him and let him guide us through the maze. Standing fourteen inches taller than me, he could see a path blocked to my view of chests and backs.

We goggled and gawked as much as any normal tourist. Each hotel spread out and up, grander than the last monstrosity. Each unique in theme, spectacle, and canned advertisements broadcast to the masses.

"It's much bigger than I thought," Gollum said. "Brighter and happier, too." He turned us in a circle so he could see the miniature Eiffel Tower in the distance and get another look at the sphinxes behind us.

I didn't think they were miniature. And then there was the pyramid.

"I'm told the light shooting out of the top of the pyramid is visible from space as well. When the aliens invade, they'll probably land in Las Vegas, summoned by that beacon," he laughed. "In fact, the elevators are actually inclinators rising at a twenty-nine-degree angle to accommodate the architecture."

I rolled my eyes. Leave it to Gollum to come up with esoteric facts and figures.

A particularly loud advertisement blared at us from one of the animated signs.

"It's a false happiness. It grates on my nerves," I replied, shivering in the desert heat.

"You need to relax and enjoy the carefree spirit of the place." He squeezed my shoulder, pulling me closer yet to his side.

"I need earplugs." We approached the curving bridges, wandering canal, and graceful balconies of The Venetian. I pulled Gollum past the quarter-mile-long hotel front, not wanting to think about my gondola ride last night.

"If you wore earplugs, we couldn't talk. So what do we need to talk about?" he asked. He had to nearly shout for me to hear over the blare of car horns and tinny music blasting out of an old strip mall that had become a tourist gizmo haven.

"Hey, do you want to take a gondola ride? It's not that expensive." He urged me toward the outside portion of the waterway.

I diverted him with the tale of Lady Lucia's wereweasel and her apology of flowers and tickets. I didn't tell him that Donovan had pretended they came from him. Then I told him about the faery at the slot machines and references to *Lord* Gregbaum.

"Hmmmm."

"That's it? No long-winded lectures on the origin of vampire legends? No extended theories on why the dancers never leave the building, and why they wear their costumes into the casino? And, by the way, the costumes look like they need about six sessions at the dry cleaners or complete replacement. What's wrong with you, Gollum?"

"Just thinking. I'll run some questions by my folklore colleagues and Gramps when I get back to the hotel. For now, I think we need to check out the Dragon and St. George. I want to see these gambling faeries myself. Did you know there is a tradition that faeries will bet on anything? Being nearly immortal, they've developed gambling to a fine art, just to pass the time . . ."

Now that's the Gollum I knew and . . . loved. In a way. Best friends. Really.

"I don't believe for a moment that Lady Lucia is a vampire, but if she were, she'd operate on the same principle," I added. "Manipulate us poor mortals into doing her bidding while betting how long it takes us to figure out what she wants."

"By George, I think she's got it!" Gollum laughed, mimicking a British accent.

Speaking of accents . . . "Mr. Master Linguist, where do you think Mickey is from?"

"The cab driver?"

I nodded while trying not to jostle a teenager on a skateboard with a mega cup of soda pop. All I needed was for him to spill it all over my good clothes.

"Couldn't place his accent."

"He says Bulgaria."

"Nope."

"What do you mean. 'Nope'? You speak what, five living languages and read at least three dead ones. Haven't you heard a Bulgarian accent before?"

"You wouldn't have asked me if you honestly believed he was from Bulgaria. I've heard plenty of accents from Bulgaria, Romania, Serbo-Croatia. He's not from there. Trust me on this."

"Okay. Why would he lie while he's trying to be so helpful? Specifically, trying to please Lady Lucia."

"I'll let you know when I know more about Lady Lucia."

We negotiated the sidewalks for the remaining distance to the Dragon and St. George. Once we got off the Strip, traffic lightened a modicum. Then it picked up again around the theater entrance of the hotel.

A lot of people turned away from the desk, shaking their heads in disappointment. Those who picked up previously booked tickets waved them in triumph.

A discreet hand beckoned the next disappointed one from the isolated potted palm near the fire exit.

"I'll try a single ticket. Might be easier than a pair," Gollum said, finally releasing me from his protective grip.

"You stand in line, I see someone I need to talk to." I approached a young couple, probably early twenties. He wore smart casual slacks and a shirt. She wore a graceful sun dress that fell a discreet two inches below the knee. She held her left hand up, flashing an expensive wedding ring and solitaire. Honeymooners. Professionals with some money.

"Never buy a ticket from a guy hiding behind a palm tree. If his tickets are real, he can only legally sell them through a licensed kiosk," I warned the couple.

They wandered off, shaking their heads.

"We'll try for one of the other shows on the Strip," the young man said, kissing his wife's temple.

The wereweasel tried to sidle to the opposite side of the palm and the exit. I reached behind the plant and grabbed his collar.

"You're still selling forged tickets to innocents," I snarled at him.

"What do you care, lady? Without your imp, you're just another tourist," he sneered back. Only his words came out on a strange lisp. His crooked mustache concealed a barely healed harelip scar. He looked as if he hadn't shaved since I saw him last. Come to think on it, he had the same two-day growth two-days ago.

Weird compounded upon strange.

"Scrap is never far away," I countered. I sure hoped so anyway.

Right here, babe. Scrap settled on my shoulder, the barest hint of dandelion fluff in weight.

The weasely man's eyes grew large. He really did have a

vertical pupil instead of round. He must be wearing contacts to give that illusion. I'd seen costumers at cons do the same. And the harelip and mustache could be faked just as easily.

I settled down. No more weird than a Science Fiction/ Fantasy convention or con. All of Vegas was a con in a way.

"Tell your mistress I thank her for the flowers and the tickets. Professional courtesy. I respect her territory as long as she stays away from me and mine." That sounded like something I'd write. Therefore, it sounded like what these pretenders expected.

You might want to reconsider that, dahling. We could bet on it. Wanna make a bet. Scrap chomped on a cigar, a big fat one, not his usual black cherry cheroots. He wrapped his tail around my neck. The barbed end had a strange luster to it. So did the rest of him. I was surprised the others in line couldn't see him.

The weasel sure could.

His mouth opened and closed, making strange gasping noises. "Don't feed me to the imp. Please don't feed me to the imp. Say, neat trick with the gondola last night. But you really should have accepted Donovan's proposal. He's one of the good guys."

"Coming from you, that's not a compliment. Sheesh, does the entire town know about last night?"

"Pretty much. Did you get a good look at the size of that ring? That would buy back my marker from Lady Lucia and then some. You really should have said yes."

I rolled my eyes upward in disgust. Or despair. Had I made that big a mistake in turning down Donovan? No way to know now.

"I'll let you go this time, Weasel. But if I ever hear of you scalping forged tickets again, I'll return your head to your mistress, minus your body."

"That's a bit harder than you think, bitch . . ."

"Tell that to the widowed Windago I slew last month." I dropped my grip on his collar.

He stumbled and slinked off. I watched him for a moment to make sure he left the building. When the closest doors whooshed closed on his backside, I returned to Gollum's side.

"Haven't you got anything? Even standing room at the

back of the balcony?" my friend asked. He sounded more desperate than disappointed.

"Sold that two months ago. Sorry. The show is sold out for the next six months."

"What about the single tickets in August you had day before yesterday?" I asked.

"Sold those on line right after . . . Oh, it's you. Why didn't you say you were with her?" He reached below his counter and came up with a heavy parchment envelope, the kind wedding invitations come in. He handed it to me. "With Lady Lucia's compliments. Next."

Startled, I slid my finger beneath the envelope's flap and pulled out a piece of notepaper in the same heavy parchment. Gold embossing at the top spelled out "Contessa Lucia Maria Continelli."

"Step aside, ma'am. I've got other people to serve. Please," the clerk said softly. Almost respectfully.

I backed up three steps.

Gollum paced me. "What does it say?" he asked.

"This note will gain you seats tomorrow afternoon at three to a special performance that will be filmed for the upcoming DVD of 'Fairy Moon.' My apologies that I cannot gain you access to the VIP circle. That area will be filled with technical equipment. Respectfully, Contessa Lucia Maria Continelli."

"Wow."

"Wow is right. So why do I feel like I've just been manipulated by the resident vampire crime boss?"

Chapter 17

Poker has the best odds in Vegas as the players play against the skills of each other rather than random spins of a wheel, throw of dice, or computer generated slots. The House still takes a percentage of the pots.

"IF YOU FEEL LIKE you are being manipulated, maybe you are," Gollum said. He took the note paper from me and read it himself. "Interesting handwriting. You don't see the flowing decorations around the capitals much anymore, except in formal calligraphy. But this looks like normal handwriting, not a studied execution of an antique alphabet."

"Scrap, is the weasel anywhere near?" I searched the crowds for signs of Lady Lucia's minion.

Weasel has left the building, he said trying to sound like Elvis. He blew a smoke ring in my face.

I waved it away, choking on the fumes, almost as thick as in the casino.

"What's your schedule tomorrow?" Gollum asked.

I had to stop and think. "Tomorrow's Saturday. Right?" Days tended to run together on the road.

Gollum nodded.

I found my PDA in my belt pack and scanned it. "Critique session nine to eleven. Workshop on adding sensuality to fiction eleven to noon. Formal lunch until two. Awards banquet at six thirty."

"So the only time you have free is late afternoon. Three to five. The exact time of the special performance of 'Fairy Moon.' "

"I've had the feeling of being watched ever since I got here. Do you suppose Contessa Lucia is keeping tabs on me?"

"Possible."

"Let's find Weasel and make him take us to her. Right now."

"It's still daylight, Tess. He couldn't get us in to see Lady Lucia if he wanted to," Gollum said. He looked most professorial as he tugged on his chin.

"Only if she wants us to think she's a vampire."

Both Gollum and Scrap stared at me in silence.

"So we wait until tonight to try to find the lady. For now, we can scout the casino for signs of faery dancers." I marched toward the center of the hotel so fast, Scrap and Gollum had to hurry to catch up.

"Think about it, Tess. What better place for a vampire to hide, than in Vegas?"

"I've heard that argument before. You've said it yourself. No one, absolutely no one, comes back from the dead."

If I believed someone could, I might have gone with the pseudo ghost of my first husband. Turns out I was lucky I did believe no one escapes death's clutches once he's touched you. The ghost turned out to be a demon construct sent to lure me away from my vows as a Warrior of the Celestial Blade and separate me from Scrap.

That would have been the true and final death for both of us. And freed my home from the decidedly non-neutral presence of a Warrior.

The Powers That Be really wanted my home back in neutral hands. Badly.

"Look at all these people," Gollum said. He stared in fascination at the wide variety of sizes, shapes, ages, and clothing. "All economic classes and degrees of education come here to gamble. There is the constant allure of instant wealth, even to the wealthy. The risk, the excitement. I've read some studies . . ." He droned on.

There must be a psychology degree in the alphabet soup that followed his name.

"What's the moon phase?" I asked, trying to bring him back to our topic and mission.

"Waxing new moon," he said, barely pausing in his musing about the human need to gamble. "There must be something in the kinetic connection to the arm of the slot machine. The energy applied and transferred to the gods of chance."

"We're headed toward the waxing quarter moon, the time of greatest demon strength. Are faeries classed as demons in this dimension since they are out of their own universe? Would humans be classed as demons if we entered one of the other worlds?"

"Possibly. Demons are usually classed as violent tribes needing the blood of other sentient beings to nourish themselves." He still didn't look at me, just at the chains of people wandering through the broken aisles—no way to walk a straight line without bumping into an opportunity to lose your money—and those fixated in one spot with card games, dice, or the ubiquitous slot machines.

Not exactly, Scrap said around his cigar. He let go of my ear and my hair to bounce up to a chandelier and peer down at a vacant slot machine. *This one's going to blow, it's primed and ready to pay out. Bet something, Tess. I just know you're gonna win.*

"If portals weaken and demons gain strength at this time of the month allowing crossovers, then the faeries might have growing strength now, too," I said, ignoring Scrap's half correction of my theory.

Screw that idea, Scrap said. He returned to me in disgust. Someone else had sat at the machine, plugged in a bunch a quarters, and lost.

"I wonder if I could win at poker simply by studying the body language and psychology of my opponents," Gollum mused, also ignoring me.

I could fly around and peek at the other player's cards! Scrap lifted off my shoulder and flew spiraling circles around us.

"Not on your life, Guilford." I yanked on his arm, trying to break his thrall. "We're supposed to be looking for faery dancers."

"Oh. Yes. Certainly." He shoved his glasses back up to the bridge of his nose. "I detect a bit of pastel chiffon over by the bar."

"Which bar? There are six of them."

"The one on our far left. I believe it has a medieval milieu. The bartenders wear tunics and tights. The barmaids have most fetching peasant blouses and bodices with extremely short shirts." He fixed his gaze on a deep cleavage exposed by one of those off-the-shoulder peasant blouses.

Love the way those tights mold to the bartenders' figures. Scrap nearly fell off my shoulder leering at the men when they stepped out from behind their barriers and revealed tunics that barely reached their hips.

I wondered if the guys padded their tights the way women stuffed foam into their bras.

"Totally inaccurate costuming," I said. Though they did present some interesting eye candy for women, and men of Scrap's persuasion. "And the bar specializes in flaming drinks ignited by the mechanical fire-breathing dragon in a cage behind the bar." I sighed. Gimmicks. "The whole town is nothing but one big gimmick."

"The faeries must feel at home here. It has the feel of a Renaissance Faire," Gollum said. His attention kept drifting toward the partially closed off poker rooms.

"Only in this dimension do faeries visit Renaissance Faires," I reminded him sharply. "Let's go see if we can talk to one of them."

I latched a proprietary hand on Gollum's elbow, guiding him toward that hint of pink chiffon. His eyes strayed toward the blackjack tables, then they flicked over one of the cocktail waitresses.

Which bothered me the most?

No time to think. Pink was on the move.

I walked faster.

Ever hear of sightseeing, babe? Scrap grumbled. He wrapped his strangely lustrous tail tighter about my neck to keep him from bouncing off my shoulder. His wings lifted slightly to gather enough air for balance. They looked longer and fuller than they had last time I saw him.

He reminded me of . . . of . . . of me right after Donavon and I had played our own jousting game in bed.

I almost burst out laughing. "Scrap, did you get laid?" I asked under my breath.

And what if I did? He preened, showing off his warts and the extra half inch of wing.

"Just wondering. May I ask who?"

Only if I can ask back.

I didn't want to admit that I'd succumbed to my hormones with the man who kept Scrap away from me with some kind of force field.

Thought so. Obviously not our dear friend Gollum or he'd be looking at you and not that tempting wench bending over the low table inside the bar.

"I think they make those tables that low just so the gals have to flash their cleavage," I said aloud. "It's all padding," I reminded Gollum.

"Oh, yeah. Right. There's our pink chiffon." He bobbed his chin at a bank of slots with whimsical dragon and unicorn décor.

Bells jangled and whistled shrilly. I cringed. So did Scrap.

Off pitch, babe, he grumbled.

"A pitch to make dogs howl."

Bright giggles erupted from one of the unicorn machines. "Sounds like one of our faeries won for a change."

"No such luck. Our winner is just a normal human girl," Gollum stalled our progress.

"Looks like a birthday girl celebrating her twenty-first." I pointed to the bouquet of shiny Mylar above her head and the platoon of "best" friends squealing and clapping their hands around the winner. They all wore similar pastel sundresses in layers of ruffled floral prints.

"So what do we do now?" Gollum asked. His eyes strayed toward a closed poker room.

"We find Mickey and figure out how to get an audience with Lady Lucia."

"Hadn't we better wait until after we see the show tomorrow?"

"Afraid I'll tick her off and she'll rescind the tickets?"

"Yes."

He's got your number, babe. Scrap nearly fell off my shoulder laughing.

They had a point. I did have a temper, easily roused in the face of evil manipulating people.

"Okay. Let's get out of here and put the word out on the

street that I want an interview with Lady Lucia at midnight tomorrow. After the awards banquet."

Done. And done.

"How?" I looked at Scrap to make sure he was still with me.

Just a word in the right ear.

Chapter 18

Due to racial prejudice, when Sammy Davis Jr. first played Vegas, he had to enter and leave the hotel by the back entrance through the kitchen.

WE MADE IT OUT of the casino into the theater lobby, aiming for the exit nearest there.

Suddenly, two big men grabbed my elbows from behind and turned me back toward the now closed and empty theater area. I saw muscle on candy-cane-red skin and black leather and not much else.

"Scrap, what is happening?"

You sure you want to know? He spat out his cigar. The faint glow left his skin as he stretched and thinned.

Uh-oh. Time to gear up for a fight.

"Tess, I don't like this," Gollum warned, too late. "Too much of a coincidence that these guys show up so soon after we request an interview . . ."

"Shaddup," growled one of the brutes.

Strangely, Gollum did. First time I'd known that to happen.

We passed under the archway to the theater lobby. A black curtain swooshed across the opening, giving us the illusion of privacy.

Then a steel gate slid across on well-oiled tracks, sealing us in. I heard the lock close in an ominous clack and clang. At the same time, the quadruple doors into the theater opened outward slowly, by unseen hands. A phalanx of human figures stood in the dark portal, none of them touching the doors. It looked like it opened into another world.

How'd they do that?

Hidden electronics must open and close doors and gates and curtains. Had to be remote controls.

The bad guys pulled so hard on my arms, my feet left the floor.

I relaxed my shoulders. My arms flew up and my feet flew down. The polished tile blocks, each a yard square, in a discreet and sophisticated green swirl imitation marble, had no traction. My professional-looking wedge-heeled pumps slid like an onion through sizzling butter in a fry pan.

The brutes tightened their grips on my arms, fighting to keep me under their control. I kept sliding, letting go of my balance, further separating me from my captors.

A rough spot in the tiles. My feet found traction. I threw myself forward, leaving the big and uglies behind.

"Scrap, to me!"

He landed heavily on my right hand, already halfway through his transformation.

Two of the leather-clad guys still held Gollum in grips that might break his upper arms. My two stalked forward intent on recapturing me. Three more hung around the edges, making sure none of us escaped.

Gulp. They all wore long broadswords in plain black leather scabbards to match their knickers and vests. Their exposed skin looked like fresh blood over muscles layered upon muscles. Just barely, I noted pointy ears and a flash of energy across their backs that might have been wings they left behind in their home dimension.

Faeries on steroids, Scrap whispered as he continued to change. *I've met these guys before.*

"At least they don't have bat wings," I grumbled as I twirled the staff that Scrap had become. The centrifugal force helped him elongate. His ears grew together and curved, becoming a half-moon blade. His bandy legs and tail became its twin blade at the other end. Each blade extruded long, hair-fine spikes on the outside curve, mimicking the star and Milky Way configuration of the Goddess of the Celestial Blade Warriors.

I drew strength from my memories of seeing the Goddess rise in the sky, of the unity with the universe, and the power pulsing from the heavens into me.

The brutes drew their swords. Seven against one. If they were just normal demons, I'd say the odds were even. But they had those monstrous long swords that must weigh ten pounds apiece. Even wielding the Celestial Blade like a sword, they had me on reach alone.

I kicked off my shoes. "Shit!" A string of more violent curses exploded from my gut. I'd worn knee-high nylons. Worse traction. No time to find the shoes and slip back into them.

"Okay, guys. Who's first?" I shifted my grip and swung the blade over my head, at knee level, and straight ahead, keeping it constantly in motion in no particular pattern.

They looked at my twirling blade, then at each other.

"Drop the blade, or we kill your boyfriend," a quiet voice said from the direction of the theater.

I chanced a glance in Gollum's direction. His two captors both held the tips of their swords at his throat.

"Fuck!"

"Don't listen to him, Tess. I can take care of myself," Gollum said quietly.

Right. That coming from the most nonviolent person I'd ever met.

Still, I did have a vague memory of waking up from a tazer-induced coma to find three Marines down with bruises on their throats and Gollum leaning protectively over me.

"What do you want, Gregbaum?" I asked the newcomer. He had to be the producer. No one else had authority in this area.

"I want you to leave Las Vegas on the next plane."

"No can do." I slashed at the goon edging over to my left side. He backed off. "I'm contracted to the writers' conference. I'm also sworn to protect the innocent from demons. These guys look like demons, and you are holding a dance troupe of innocent faeries hostage."

I parried a sword that crept too close. Without thinking, I slid into a long lunge and aimed for my attacker's bare chest. He yelped and arched away from the tip of the curved blade, sword held off to the side.

My feet continued sliding forward. My thighs burned and pulled. I flipped the blade and raked him with the tines.

A dozen parallel scratches oozed dark green, almost black blood—it matched their clothes.

At the same moment, Gollum's attackers flew across the lobby and bounced against the ticket desk. Their heads hit the edge with matching resounding cracks. They slid to the ground, mouths open in surprise as their eyes closed and bodies grew limp.

Gollum went to his knees. His face twisted in agony. He mewled something incomprehensible and buried his head in his hands.

The remaining four monsters backed off, taking up positions between me and Gregbaum. I recovered forward from the lunge, not sure my inner thigh muscles hadn't separated from the bone. They screamed at me. A groin pull. One of the hardest injuries to recover from, and I'd done it to myself.

Stupid, stupid, stupid.

"Get out of here, Guilford." I used his real name to break through whatever emotions tangled his mind in that awful grimace.

"I . . . can't . . . leave . . . you," he choked.

"Sure you can. You just get to your feet and walk out the fire exit." I edged closer to my enemies. I had to finish this quick before real pain set in and kept me anchored in place.

The guy I'd nicked still bled. Rivulets streamed down his chest to disappear beneath his pants.

"The alarms will sound if you open that door," Gregbaum said.

"And your point would be?"

For the first time, I got a good look at the hottest producer in Las Vegas. Medium height and build, he looked like the slime lord of lounge lizards: slick sharkskin suit and a black shirt open nearly to the waist, revealing a bit of a hairy paunch. Five gold chains of varying length encircled his neck and another his right wrist. The left wrist sported a watch nearly the size of the school clocks in Paul Revere Elementary, where I'd attended kindergarten through sixth grade.

The kicker was the diamond pinky ring. It looked like a miniature version of the one Donovan offered with his proposal.

What in the hell was going on here?

"You may stay until your scheduled flight home. But do not enter my theater again. Do not, under penalty of death, try to contact any of my employees."

"Agreed, as long as you do nothing to harm any of the dancers." Just because I couldn't complete this mission didn't mean I couldn't pass it off to another Warrior. Breven Sancroix had taken the same vows I had.

"The blade." Gregbaum snapped his fingers

"Scrap has tasted blood. He can retract as soon as I'm clear." I jerked my chin toward the steel gate and black curtain.

Gregbaum waved his hand. The lock clicked open and the gate withdrew about eighteen inches; just enough for Gollum and me to slip through.

"How'd you open that?" I asked, turning back toward Gregbaum.

He and his minions faded into the theater darkness. Concealing fog swirled around them. The doors closed quickly but silently.

On the last breath of air before the portal sealed, I heard a whisper. "Get back to the Valley of Fire. We can't let her near the place."

Nasty, nasty, nasty. Those brutes taste like they just crawled out of a toxic waste dump. Come to think on it, maybe they did.

But where is that dump and who put what into it to spawn these ugly thugs? Stolen energy from Faery for sure. But what else?

Imps used to offer a bounty on identification of new monsters not assigned a ghetto. Lots of credit with the Powers That Be and prestige all over the universes. I could parlay that into a new artifact of power for my dahling Tess.

Or break through the barrier between me and Donovan.

Gonna take some homework to figure out if these guys are mutated faeries or something entirely new. Their connection to Gregbaum and the "Fairy Moon" show means something.

If the dancers are real faeries . . . hmmmmm.

I'll have a nice long chat about this with my babe and Gollum. Later.

Right now I have to rest. And eat. The air conditioner atop

this casino is jammed full of mold. That will sustain me long enough to follow Tess back to our hotel. She'll order OJ and beer for me. Then I can sleep.

Maybe. I shrink back to my normal cute self (Hey, there's a new wart on my chest!) as Tess begins limping toward the exit. Gollum drags himself out of his own inner misery and supports her with an arm about her waist.

They look like lovers, but this is not an intimate embrace. This is one friend helping another.

Oh, no! My babe hurts. I can't leave her. But this is no ordinary wound that I can make all better with a bit of imp spit to counter demon venom and infection. This is something deep inside her muscles.

Sharp burning pains run up and down my legs in sympathy. My back aches, and my wings are numb. I need to curl up into a fetal ball and nurse my hurts. I can't. I have to stay close to Tess. I have to help her. But I can't. I must eat. NOW.

Useless. I feel so useless. Just a scrap of an imp who can't help his Warrior. And I'm so tired.

What to do? What to do? I can't even run home to Mum and Imp Haven. The freeze-dried-garbage-dump-of-the-universe offers me no comfort. No love. No sanctuary.

Tess drops into Mickey's taxi. Gollum follows. I can only fall into her lap and hope my body heat helps her pain.

Her pain is my pain. I can't heal myself because I cannot heal her. I cannot recover from the strain of transformation because I cannot leave her while she hurts.

We are more than vulnerable.

Chapter 19

A High Roller Suite at the MGM Grand has three thouand square feet and comes with a private butler and chef.

THANK THE GODDESS FOR ELEVATORS. My normal bouncing up eight flights of stairs in lieu of jogging five miles every morning would have done permanent damage to my groin muscles. Gollum acting as a crutch helped some. Still I fell facedown through the door of my room and onto the closest bed.

Mom's bed. Full of clothes. My face tangled with dirty underclothes inside her suitcase.

Ewww! Enough to push me to a sitting position. "Ice," I croaked to Gollum.

He left with the ice bucket and my key card.

"Mom, what are you doing? We don't go home until Monday morning." I held my injured right leg up with both hands while she extricated her red party dress from beneath me.

"I'm not going home." She tsked as she surveyed a crease in the georgette draperies.

"What?"

"You used to be more articulate, dear."

"Can't you see I'm suffering? Words elude me when I'm in pain."

"What did you do this time?"

"Fencing. Long lunge." I sank back onto her pillows.

"Would you call room service and order me two beers and two glasses of orange juice?"

Scrap sighed from his fetal ball in the crook of my arm. I couldn't tell if he slumbered or had gone comatose.

That sounded good to me right now. A couple of ibuprofen and about twenty-four hours of sleep ought to help.

Gotta keep movin 'r it'll stiff up, Scrap mumbled. His mental speech came through slurred. He was in worse shape than I.

"I told you years ago that you'd get hurt in a most unladylike manner with that horrible sport."

Now that was the mother I knew and loved.

"Let me see, dear." She held up my leg and probed gently. "Hmmm. Big knot forming. Might just be a strain instead of a true pull. I'll order you an immediate massage. That will keep the blood flowing and prevent it from stiffening."

Huh?

"You still didn't answer my question. If you aren't going home, why are you packing?"

"I've signed a contract to sing at the hotel Wednesday through Sunday nights. They're hiring me a band and giving me a wardrobe allowance, not that I need one. I'm moving in with Penny."

"Uh, Mom, you do know that she's a hooker."

"Not anymore. We had a long talk. She's retired. That Joyce woman is writing her memoirs. Pretty steamy stuff." She waggled her eyebrows.

"How can you be sure she's retired. She seemed pretty tight with that Stetson fellow."

"Penny is tired. Flirting is second nature with her. Always has been. But she's no longer serious. And she needs my help."

"You? Mom, you've barely stepped off Cape Cod for fifteen years or more. Your life is the Garden Club and church choir—and picking up after me." I gave Mom room and board in the mother-in-law apartment attached to the house. I didn't think she'd survive on her own. She barely knew how to balance a checkbook or pay her bills. Dad and I did that for her.

"Penny made a bunch of money, but she didn't keep it. Her jewelry is paste and her very small two-bedroom house is heavily mortgaged. She really needs money from that tell-all book. I can at least give her a little something extra each month for the mortgage payment."

"Mom, what is going on? This isn't you. You've always been suspicious of strangers. Disapproved of new friends. And I still don't believe you ever spent time in New York." No more stalling. Looked like this was the time to talk to her, even if I didn't really want to.

"But it is me, Teresa. This is the me I dreamed of being when I was in high school." She sat on the edge of the bed and gave me a long soulful look.

"I've never heard this story." I scooched over to make room for her. Girl chat, like I had with my friend Allie back home. Never with my mom.

Unthinkable with the old mom. Quite natural with this vibrant woman with the whole world opening before her.

"Your Grandmother Maria forbade us to talk about it." She caressed the silky fabric of the dress she held.

"Was it Grandma Maria or Grandpa Al who forbade you to talk about wanting to sing for a living?" Feisty and forgetful Grandma Maria was the only family member who cheered me on when I launched into the risky career of a professional novelist.

I hadn't known my grandfather well. He died when I was six. Either that or he left town. No one talked much about him. And I hadn't found a headstone for him in the local cemetery, at least nowhere near his parents.

"I thought I was ready to tackle New York my senior year in high school." Mom fumbled with her pearls, an old and comforting habit. "I ran away at the end of January, right after my eighteenth birthday, with a few hundred dollars I'd been saving since . . . since grade school. But I wasn't ready for New York. The competition, the dirt, the noise, the scathing critiques from really nasty people." Tears flooded her eyes. She turned her head away.

"That's when you met Penny!"

She nodded. "We shared a flat for a short time. We met at an audition and hit it off. Sometimes I think she was the only person in all of New York who had a kind word for me."

I pulled her down into a hug. "I know how bad rejection from strangers can be. When my first short story was rejected, I thought my writing career had ended before it started. The editor told me I should forget about ever putting pen to paper again. It wasn't even a professional level magazine. Just a paid-in-copies low-budget rag. Thank goodness my friend Bob . . ."

Here I had to pause. Bob had died last autumn while helping me on my first mission as a Warrior of the Celestial Blade.

"Bob convinced me to send the story to professional publications until it sold. He nagged me if I let a rejected copy sit on my desk more than twenty-four hours before mailing it to the next editor. You didn't have friends in the city to encourage and support you."

"I had Penny. Even she wasn't enough. I was so energetic and full of hope. But it didn't last long. You had a few positive rejections right off the bat. 'Good writing but not right for us. What else do you have?' I had only 'Get off the stage. Next.' "

"Friends make all the difference when you try something new." My thoughts turned to Bob, and then to Gollum and Allie, and yes, even to Donovan. Most of all I had Scrap. No matter how bad things got, I'd never be alone.

"And look at you now. On the best seller lists and making good money. You have done with your life what I wanted to do with mine. Instead, I crawled home with my tail between my legs and accepted a marriage to your father that my father arranged. A nice Catholic man with a good job as an accountant. And we all know what a disaster that turned out to be. I didn't even finish high school."

My father hadn't married by the age of twenty-six, very late for a good Catholic man from a French Canadian family. He accepted the arranged marriage under pressure from his parents. He'd needed another fifteen years to come to terms with his alternative sexual preferences.

"Was the whole marriage a disaster?" I know Dad had hurt Mom terribly when he moved in with Bill. Looking back, that was just one more rejection in Mom's life. One more person telling her she wasn't good enough at anything she tried.

I knew I couldn't be the next person to tell her not to bother trying because she would fail. She couldn't know she'd failed until she tried.

I had to let her do this.

"My marriage wasn't all bad. We had some good times. I

have three wonderful children, even though your brother Stephen lives in Chicago and rarely calls home."

I talked to Steve more often than he talked to either of our parents.

"What will I do without you, Mom? I mean, you organize my house and my life. You keep me fed when I forget to eat because I'm on deadline . . ."

"You'll manage, dear. You'll manage because you have to. And because you have friends. I can't be your crutch forever." Mom gave me a wicked wink, like she knew how Dad and I took care of her because she let us.

Then she straightened up and began pulling more outfits out of the closet. Mostly cocktail dresses. I didn't remember her packing so many. She must have gone shopping. "You have Gollum living in the cottage, and your father and Bill close by. And Allie. Best friends are more valuable than gold. Though I wish she'd find some nice man and give up being a policewoman. Most unladylike."

We both laughed at the idea of my best friend doing anything but be a cop. She'd saved my ass a couple of times when the going got tough with demons and escapees from the prison warden of the universe.

"And don't forget MoonFeather."

"Yes. Your father's sister does seem to have more in common with you than my side of the family. I don't approve of her being a witch, or living with Josh without the benefit of marriage, or her three divorces, but she is a good friend to you."

Wow. A compliment about MoonFeather. That was almost more than I could imagine. Mom really had undergone a major attitude adjustment.

"I worry about you, Mom. This is a big step. Something totally different from what you are used to."

"I know. Isn't it exciting!" She gave a little girl laugh. Then she sobered. "Marrying Darren was a disaster that taught me I have to live every day as if it were my last. When I found out that he only married me to get to you, and something weird about inheriting your house, I thought I'd never recover. I thought about killing myself. But that would only have given him what he wanted. Now I'm doing what *I* want to do for the first time in a very long time. I need to do this."

"If it doesn't work out," and I couldn't see how it could, "you can always come home. I'll keep a spare bed for you. I'm only a phone call away." We hugged again. "Now about that contract . . ."

"Don't worry. I had Donovan look it over. He's good about that sort of thing. But he seemed upset. Did you two have another fight?"

Gulp. "Yeah, sorta."

"You going to tell me about it?"

"No."

"Make it up soon. I don't like my kids fighting."

"He's not . . ."

"Yes, he is. He's my stepson and I care for him. He needs a mother. He's also executor of Darren's estate. Now I updated my will before we left home. I've left lump sums for Cecilia and Stephen, the rest goes to you. You gave me a home when no one else would. You took care of me when I should have taken care of you. If anything happens to me, you'll have to work with Donovan on the estate business. So apologize and get back to being friends. That's an order."

"Nothing is going to happen to you, Mom. You're still young and healthy . . ."

"Oh, good, Gollum is back with your ice. He can carry my bags down to the lobby. I'll order your massage through the concierge. Are you sure all you want is beer and orange juice? You've got my cell phone number and I've left Penny's number and address on the notepad by the phone. Call me." She bustled out, organized and efficient and in charge of her life.

I wish I could say the same for myself.

I dozed off and on for the rest of the afternoon. So did Scrap. The beer and OJ arrived. We slurped it down. I added some ibuprofen to mine, and nodded off again.

Gollum stayed with me, changing ice packs, coming up with a heating pad to alternate with them, taking phone calls from my mom, declining offers to dine with other writers from the conference, rejecting a last-minute request for me to critique a manuscript.

How many times in the past few months had he camped out in my hotel room helping me cope with a mission?

Around five, Gollum stuck a room service menu in front of me. "You have to eat to keep your strength up. Protein to rebuild muscle tissue."

"The chicken Alfredo is the only thing that looks good," I mumbled.

"Are you sure? You said at lunch that you thought you might have acquired Scrap's lactose intolerance." He frowned at me.

"I was only joking. Buffet cheesecake probably sat out a little too long. Honestly, I don't feel much like eating. Must be the beer and OJ. But the chicken Alfredo sounds good. And coffee. The coffee you brought me, not the watered-down generic beans they serve in this town."

"Okay. If you say so." He placed the order.

Food arrived nearly an hour later. The aroma of garlic and chicken woke up my appetite. My leg felt a lot better. Even Scrap roused enough to pop out in search of mold.

"You have a massage scheduled for seven," Gollum said, setting a tray on my lap. I hadn't moved from where I'd collapsed on the bed.

We ate companionably, chatting and rehashing what I'd seen and done since arriving. A music station played something soft on the television.

The chicken Alfredo didn't sit well. Maybe I ate too much. Maybe the pain pills had upset my digestion. I rarely take them. Since surviving the imp flu, my body doesn't succumb to viruses and disease. I heal quickly from wounds, and react strangely to any kind of drugs. Maybe my nerves had finally caught up with me after refusing Donovan's proposal.

Had I done the right thing?

Of course I had. How could I marry a man I didn't trust?

Donovan had sunk too much time, money, and energy into establishing a homeland for Kajiri demons—half-bloods. Any man with that much sympathy for beings that existed only to breed and eat—and eat anything including human flesh and blood—needed careful watching. I'd seen some of Donovan's buddies in the Sasquatch tribe do just that.

On the other hand, I had met a few Kajiri who truly wanted only to blend in and let their human genetics dominate. Their demon relatives cast them out. And heaven help them in the human world if any of their demon characteristics showed through, even for a moment.

No easy answers.

If I questioned the rightness of the match, then it wasn't right. I couldn't imagine sharing the emotional intimacy of friendship with Donovan like I did with Gollum.

Walking to the elevator and then to the hotel spa on the top floor wasn't easy. "Thanks for being my crutch," I said to Gollum when he left me at the door.

"That's what I'm here for. I'll get on the Internet while you're here and follow up on some research." He kissed my cheek and ducked back into the elevator.

"Gollum, can you do a background check on Sancroix?" I finally remembered my failed attempt to contact the Citadel.

He waved to acknowledge that he heard me. The doors closed on him and whisked him away. I sighed. He helped me more than he knew just by being my friend.

Massages are the best thing ever invented by humans. Maybe they were invented by the gods and passed down to us in heavenly visions. I don't know.

Raoul knew precisely how to manipulate, rotate, and stretch my injury, all the while applying proper compression. It was merely a strain and not a pull. Because I got treatment right away, it shouldn't bother me for too long. But it needed rest tonight and tomorrow. He worked my entire body to get everything back into line and balanced.

I came out of the spa feeling fifty percent back to normal. I could put weight on my right leg without wincing. It carried me all the way down to the room—via the elevator. I'm not stubborn enough or dumb enough to tackle stairs at this stage.

Two feet inside my door, I dashed to the bathroom and lost my lovely chicken Alfredo to the porcelain throne.

You don't want to know the details.

"Lactose intolerance," Gollum muttered through the closed door. "I'll get you some dry toast and tea."

"Yuck."

"It will help. I promise. And some acidophilus."

"And I've got some oceanfront property for sale, only two blocks from here."

I brushed my teeth and took a quick shower. Much better.

When I emerged from the bathroom in my royal blue terry robe, I found Mickey, in the doorway, with the door wide open. He and Gollum stared at each other in bewilderment.

Was that Junior scuttling toward the elevator, head down, fists clenched, looking about furtively?

Mickey carried a huge bouquet of white roses. His swarthy face looked as pale as the flowers.

"What?" I demanded.

He handed me a thick parchment envelope bearing Lady Lucia's crest.

I read the note inside, holding my breath. "The bearer will escort you to a rendezvous point at nine of the clock this evening."

"Crap." I felt like it, too.

Chapter 20

El Rancho Vegas was the first hotel/casino built on the Strip in 1941. The venerable hotel and its trademark windmill burned to the ground in 1960. The lot across from the Sahara, in the shadow of the Stratosphere, remains empty, and, some say, haunted.

"SO, WHAT DO WE KNOW?" I asked Gollum at eight thirty. My tummy had recovered enough that I could eat a roast beef sandwich and a ginger ale. I had some persistent bloating, like the day before my period, only worse.

Familiarity with Scrap's lactose intolerance led me to hope I wouldn't let loose the bloating at an inappropriate moment.

The groin pull still presented problems. I could walk with only a little limp, stand if I had to with my weight off it. Moving was better than standing. I hoped I wouldn't have to fight.

Scrap was still out of it. That meant mundane weapons at best. Should I steal a wooden kabob skewer from the kitchen? Or was it silver vampires were sensitive to? No, that's werewolves. I definitely needed a wooden stake, if for no other reason than intimidation.

I gazed at Scrap fondly. Usually he made his recovery elsewhere. Because of my injury, he couldn't get very far from me. For the first time I understood Gollum's attachment to his wretched cat. Having Scrap's body, insubstantial as it was, curled up beside me comforted me, reassured me that I wasn't alone.

"We know that a Contessa Lucia Maria Continelli, wife of Italian Count Antonio Bertrand Continelli died in 1818 along with her husband and small son. Their fortified Tuscan villa was burned to the ground. The count was not liked. Hints of taking prisoners during the Napoleonic invasions for the sole purpose of torture. He didn't discriminate as to which side they fought for."

I gulped. This sounded very like the blood-and-gore stories surrounding Vlad the Impaler.

"No modern driver's license, Social Security number, or telephone listing for Lucia." Gollum peered at his computer screen over the top of his glasses. Which had slid to the end of his nose, as usual.

I wanted to grab a miniature screwdriver kit and tighten the frames.

"So, whoever this woman is, she's maintaining a profile that would fit a vampire," I mused.

"Folklore around the ancestral estate in Italy claims she was repeatedly milked by a local vampire. A long wasting illness that prevented her from appearing in public during the sunlight hours. The villagers didn't trust her. I'm guessing she was foreign to them at the time of the marriage. Never discount the value of folklore."

"She's a charlatan. I bet we find she ran away from a farm in Iowa twenty years ago and has manipulated a mini empire based on a kinky reputation."

"The elastic bandage will help support the thigh muscles, and will be invisible under slacks," he added.

I'd learned months ago to blink and then try to follow the rapid twists and turns of his mind.

"Should I show up with a wooden stake tucked in my pocket?"

No answer. Gollum, at least, had the grace to almost blush.

"As for Gregbaum, he started as a stage magician, working small clubs and bars. Mostly for tips. Never made it big. Hung around the fringes of legitimate stage productions. Then, suddenly, two years ago he shows up with enormous backing for a real show. Launches it almost overnight, no auditions, already has sets and costumes. He signs a contract one day with a hotel on the skids. Puts up a few fliers around town the next, and opens 'Fairy Moon' on the third. Instantly, the Dragon and St. George is saved from forced sale and implosion."

"Where'd he get the money?" I thought back on the rumor that the hotel was on the verge of selling again. Apparently, "Fairy Moon" wasn't enough to bail the owners out of whatever hole they'd dug themselves into.

"I find no list of investors."

"He had to come up with it somewhere. That is not a cheap show to put on, even if he isn't paying his dancers and is keeping them locked in a dormitory in the basement, as if they were white slaves."

"Interesting simile."

"Why." I gave up trying to get my hair to do something sophisticated. The total lack of humidity kept it from frizzing, but that's the best I can say about it. I limped over to his station in the armchair by the windows, laptop perched on his long thighs, big feet propped on the table.

"There is an arrest record, no conviction, for Gary Gregbaum: illegally importing underage girls from Eastern Bloc nations for immoral purposes."

"What? Why wasn't he convicted?"

"Court records do not say. His lawyer of record is Gerard Moncrieff."

I whistled. "Very expensive bastard."

"Very tricky bastard. He wins all his cases on technical errors rather than on the evidence. I'm guessing the DA dismissed shaky charges rather than face Moncrieff in court."

A discreet knock on the door.

I looked at Gollum to see if he'd walk all the way across the room to answer it.

He continued to stare at his laptop, an occasional key stroke occupied all of his attention. "Nothing on Sancroix yet."

I sighed and limped over to find Mickey quaking in the hallway.

"You ready?" he asked, wringing his hands. He looked incredibly young, with his skinny shoulders and lean frame. Then he raised his eyes to me. He had big brown eyes that held an eternity of sorrow and grief. Age and frown lines radiated out from those soulful orbs, belying his youthful countenance.

"I'm ready." As ready as I'd ever be. I'd gone for classy casual (the same tone as the conference) with dove-gray slacks and a pink knit top, black lace-up shoes not much more substantial than sneakers but with good traction. A cable knit sweater in gray with pink flecks thrown over my shoulders completed the outfit. Scrap had, of course, picked it out and coordinated it for me.

"Gollum?"

"This is a scouting mission, you can handle it." He waved at me, never taking his eyes off his computer.

"Like hell, I can. Get your ass out of *my* armchair." A long-standing argument approaching joke status. "I need backup. I need you to listen to accents. I need you to whisper advice in the face of an unknown enemy." I was a schoolteacher before I began writing full time. I'd handled reluctant teenagers and quarrelsome five year olds alike.

Gollum responded to the same authoritative voice.

"Of course." He blinked at me as if seeing me for the first time.

"What about me?" Mickey asked. He kept his eyes on the carpet. He'd dropped the phony Slavic accent.

"No need to risk yourself."

"One such as you must know that I have to go." He didn't look happy about it.

"Do I get to ask why?"

"Not yet." He looked up finally and flashed me a winsome grin. For half a moment I caught an afterimage of pointed ears peeking through his jaw-length straight hair. Then it was gone.

"Did you bring the comb? I think you're going to need it," Gollum said. He referred to a magical artifact that allowed me to see through demon glamour and decipher auras. I hated wearing it as it turned bits and pieces of my hair crystal clear and brittle. It also gave me headaches.

"No."

I'll get it. Scrap surged up from his sleeping ball looking refreshed and eager. He popped out. Three eye blinks later, he dropped onto my shoulder, the precious antique gold filigree piece in his chubby hand.

Mickey followed his movements unerringly.

"You aren't from Bulgaria, are you?"

"My guess, he's from Faery." Gollum yawned and held the door open for us.

I held my breath and my temper for about as long as you'd expect. Exactly half of one heartbeat.

"And just when did you plan to share this information with me?" I was surprised steam didn't roil out my ears.

"When you needed to know." Gollum smiled.

"Which is when?"

"About three seconds after I figured it out."

"Oh." My righteous indignation drained out of me, like a slow leak in a hot air balloon. "Is this true, Mickey?"

"I am not allowed to say, but if a human figures it out, I do not have to deny it. That is the rule of the Powers That Be."

Hmmm. Something to consider when dealing with Donovan. Now I just had to figure out what he was hiding.

"I noticed the moment he stopped faking an accent that certain inflections reminded me of the speech patterns of the coven of witches that went missing to Faery for twenty-eight years . . ." Gollum droned on about nuances of accents and how much difference could occur in relatively small geographic distances all the way down the elevator and into Mickey's taxi.

The portal to Faery is closed, Scrap said. He leaned on top of my head to peer closely at Mickey. *Ask him when and how he got here. He might be a spy for the other side.*

I asked.

"Closed?" Mickey looked truly bewildered and frightened. "No one can get in or out of Faery?" A single tear leaked out of the corner of his eye.

"That's what Scrap says."

"I came through the chat room right after we noticed the dancers missing. A brightness and a luster vanished from our lives; from the goodness that is Faery. A trail of energy followed them and continued to leak. The Powers That Be must have sealed it off to prevent further leakage. I have to get my people back home soon!"

"I know you do. We'll help," I promised.

"May I take out my colored contacts now?" Mickey asked as he settled behind the wheel.

"As long as you don't need them to see clearly . . ."

"I see better without them. Necessary for disguise." He

bent his head and pressed fingertips to eye corners. When he looked up again the bright lights of the hotel porte cochere revealed the greenest irises I'd ever seen.

"Faery green," I breathed.

Mickey nodded and smiled shyly. "Too distinctive for blending in with humans."

Gollum and I rode in the back, as if we were paying passengers. I took the opportunity to test the comb. My hair tangled around it instantly, like iron filings reaching for a magnet.

Gollum looked his usual pensive self with layers and layers of energy radiating out from him; every color imaginable, some warm and inviting, others cold and calculated, even a few dark and brooding—or guilty.

We all have our secrets.

He kept talking.

Mickey, on the other hand, appeared royal blue with wings and pointed ears shadowing his body. I caught a hint of gold around his brow, then it vanished.

Ah-ha! Our spy from Faery had royal connections. Not just any normal volunteer for a do-or-die mission. I hoped no one had to die.

Part of me wanted to reach out and hug him in reassurance.

"He always this verbose?" Mickey asked as he pulled into traffic.

His words shattered my musing. So I snagged the comb out of my hair, pulling several crystalline strands with it. My scalp hurt where it had lodged.

I liked his new accent, his real accent. Some of his words came out with an almost Latin inflection, as in Classic Latin rather than Latino, and he tended to clip off the last sound.

"Get enough single malt scotch into Gollum and he spouts in tongues. But he always spouts," I laughed.

Gollum glared at me over the top of his glasses.

Mickey wound through traffic, right and left, left and right, circling buildings, and returning to the Strip in different locations. We passed the vacant lot where the El Rancho Vegas had burned. No one ever built on that lot, prime real estate though it was. I got a creepy feeling there.

Ghosts, Scrap whispered to me. *Not happy ones.*

We passed it by, almost glad that the raucous noise and

glaring lights of the Stratosphere drew our attention away from the dark shadows.

After a half hour Mickey cruised into an underground parking garage and jerked to a stop beside a long black hearse with tinted windows.

"Why the convoluted route to get us beneath the Dragon and St. George?" I asked before touching the door handle. I wasn't getting in that dark monster of a deathmobile.

"Just following orders," Mickey said. He looked abashed as he held up a page of printed instructions. He sounded defiant. Quite an actor this guy. No telling what he really felt.

"Probably to disorient you," Gollum said. He opened his door and unfolded his long limbs.

"Whoever gave you the directions didn't count on Scrap." My buddy preened. "I can't get lost as long as he's with me."

Gollum froze halfway to standing.

Instantly, I looked for danger.

"Mickey," Gollum said with deep seriousness. "Did you choose the route?" He snatched the printed directions from Mickey's hand almost too quickly to follow.

I think if I'd still worn the comb I would have seen a strange energy pattern follow his arm in both directions.

"I . . . I . . ." Mickey blushed and looked down.

"Ritual maze," Gollum muttered and threw the directions back at Mickey. "What kind of magic did we just weave?"

"The . . . the pattern will bind Lady Tess to the mission of rescuing the dancers from Faery," he whispered.

"What else?" Gollum pushed up his glasses and peered around us, examining each and every shadow minutely.

"Nothing. I swear."

Gollum fixed his gaze firmly upon Mickey, glasses slipping, nothing between his eyes and his prey.

I shuddered at the image of nonviolent Gollum unleashing his pent-up energy.

"I wove protection for Lady Tess around the edges," Mickey said after a long silence, as if compelled by Gollum.

"Good. She needs it. She's too reckless," Gollum said, almost casually as he unfolded himself completely and got out of the car. "She'd complete the mission without the spell. She's stubborn like that."

I took umbrage and started to spout a protest. There's a difference between dedication and stubbornness. Not much, but a difference.

"We appreciate the protection. Did you know she can't get lost as long as Scrap is with her?"

"I did. But don't tell that, or the ritual route to Lady Lucia. You need some secrets to come out of this alive," Mickey warned. "The Lady said to get you lost. Not how I was to go about it."

Gregbaum hangs out at this hotel. Is he involved in Lady Lucia picking this place for a meet up?

Tess described Donovan's little love token to me. If it does match Gregbaum's pinky ring, then the two are connected in some way. Near twin rings of antique design and great value are no coincidence.

I'm not going to comment on keeping Tess informed of where and when we are and which way is north. I'm good at that. Have to be to get around the chat room and other dimensions. I've got anchors all over the place that help me orient myself.

Except for those awful moments in the Valley of Fire. The magnetics there screwed up every one of my senses and blocked access to my pole points. For a bit, I couldn't even get back to the chat room.

I think I'm going to squash all ideas about Tess going there. Can't take a chance on either or both of us getting lost.

Now let's see what Lady Lucia has in store for us.

"The hearse is clean, babe. A bit morose, but a great bit of atmosphere. This fake countessa has a wonderful sense for stage management. Maybe she helped design the 'Fairy Moon' sets."

Chapter 21

Las Vegas has no mosquitoes. Due to the dry climate, there are no stagnant pools of water for them to breed.

WE APPROACHED THE HEARSE cautiously. I kept my senses open, listening to any sound behind our footfalls. My training at the Citadel had taught me not to stare at any one point for very long.

"Keep your eyes moving. Memorize every detail and note things that have moved or change on the next pass," I heard Sister Gert's words in my mind.

And I saw her off in a corner, shadowed by support pillars and classy cars.

I shook my head. Looked again. She was gone. A figment of my imagination?

I smell imp, Scrap said. His attention riveted toward the same corner. *Gone now. Running away. They know we are here, but don't want to say hello. How rude.*

An uneasy feeling crept up my spine.

The driver's side window of the hearse slid open an inch.

"My orders say only the Warrior," an androgynous voice said from the region of the driver's seat. It could have come from a male tenor or a husky female alto. Either one had been darkened by smoke and harsh whiskey.

"I bring my advisers or I don't come," I replied.

A moment of silence. I got the feeling from the shape of

the shadow within a shadow behind the glass that the driver consulted on a cell phone.

"They may come." A passenger door behind the driver opened by unseen hands. Or remote control.

I was getting tired of the special effects.

Gollum held the door open for me. I looked around carefully, making note of where Mickey had parked.

A flicker of movement over by the elevator bank drew my gaze like a compass homing in on magnetic north. Fortitude flew a wide loop around the lot, just above the roofs of the parked cars. Breven Sancroix whistled sharply and held out his arm, like a falconer calling his bird.

Junior stood beside him, tapping his foot. He and Fortitude exchanged a long silent gaze, like they communicated, excluding Breven, Fortitude's Warrior. "We have to get out of here before someone sees us," he hissed.

"What?" Breven looked around hastily, eyes gliding right over us as if he didn't notice a party of three and an imp hanging around a hearse.

Junior assumed a more relaxed pose and disengaged his attention from Fortitude, and us. "Mom's going to kill us if she doesn't get in to see the show. She can't get in without my pass."

How come they got tickets two nights running? He said pass, not tickets. That meant he had an important relationship to Gregbaum. And who was his mother? I thought he was an orphan. Or did Breven want the world to think Junior was an orphan to hide his parentage?

A bright pop of intuition lit my mind. I thought I'd seen Gert. Breven admitted to a long-standing relationship with her.

Could Junior be theirs? If so, why hide it?

Curiouser and curiouser.

The elevator came, and the two figures disappeared into its maw. Where had the third gone?

No more time to puzzle on it. The driver tapped his steering wheel impatiently.

I climbed into the hearse and sank onto wide red velvet seats, two and two facing each other. Real silk velvet, not upholstery velour. A single red rose rested in a gold vase attached to the panel between the windows. A magnum of champagne rested in an ice bucket on the console between the seats. A single crystal flute awaited the touch of wine. Real crystal, not the plastic Donovan provided in his limo.

I inspected the label. It looked expensive. I don't know wine. With single malt scotch, I could tell if I should be impressed.

Gollum whistled silently and raised his eyebrows. His glasses nearly slid off his nose.

Mickey reached for the glass. "We can share," he said. He looked like he needed a drink.

"No." Gollum stayed his hand. "Rules of hospitality. Same here as in Faery. Once you accept food or drink from an otherworldly creature you are bound to them. By obligation or magic. Depends on the realm."

Mickey sat back, arms crossed. His eyes kept straying to the wine.

We drove for over an hour. A dark partition separated us from the driver. Another from the long bed where a coffin could sit. Dark windows separated us from reality. The bright lights of the Strip disappeared quickly. So did ordinary streetlights. Traffic thinned to an occasional car coming form the other direction across a wide divide. Our speed felt freeway fast.

I began feeling closed in, suffocated, as if the hearse was a coffin instead of the conveyance for one. And my stomach hurt.

Gollum pulled my feet into his lap and placed the ice bucket against my inner thigh. "Might as well get some use out of it." He grinned and began massaging my calves.

I was too tense to appreciate how good his long fingers felt.

"He's taking us out into the desert. To dump us?" I tried to assess my resources. Could I walk out if we suddenly found ourselves in the middle of nowhere?

That idea made the closed stuffiness of the hearse feel less confining, more protective.

Maybe Scrap could whisk us through the chat room and back to civilization. If he'd recovered enough from transforming. He loves to fight, but the change process drains him terribly.

"I doubt it. Lady Lucia sent the champagne and the rose as a peace offering," Mickey said. He sat with his back to the driver, facing me. "She only does that if she intends to let you live. Otherwise, why waste the money?"

"To lull my suspicions. Scrap, can you get a bead on who or what is driving us?"

Human. Male. Deliciously male in tight black leather and a snap brim cap. Good pecs under the jacket. He works out.

I translated the important part. Scrap must be feeling back to normal if he bothered to size up the man's attractive qualities.

We fell into silence, not knowing if Lady Lucia had planted listening bugs or not.

Eventually, a swath of light cut through the desert blackness.

Looks like a town. Just a little place, tractor dealer, feed store, and a huge resort. Ooh, they have a pool with waterfalls and palm trees. Looks like an oasis.

"Pinyon," Mickey muttered without waiting for translation. Had he heard Scrap? "Fifty miles or so northeast of Vegas."

"Not far from the Valley of Fire," I mused, imagining the local map in my head.

"Side road fifteen miles behind us," Mickey confirmed.

"The resort is now the prime employer in this area," Gollum chimed in. "Agriculture is drying up—along with the underground lake and artesian springs that water this entire area. They have to drill deeper every year and import more water from other sources to provide enough for the city. Less and less for the farms. I've read estimates that Vegas will run out of water in as little as fifty years. Other so-called experts estimate one hundred fifty. The city has instituted state-of-the-art recycling systems—the most advanced in the world—to forestall the inevitable. Either way, the city is floating on borrowed water."

Our hearse glided to a stop, and our doors opened. Again by remote control. I peered out before exiting.

"We're at the back entrance to the spa rather than the front door of the resort."

"The contessa doesn't want to attract undue attention," Gollum muttered. "Let's see what the lady wants." He climbed out first and reached back to help me. Like a fine gentleman. Someone in his past had drilled manners into him until they came naturally.

I always felt like Donovan's courtesies were forced. Just a second's delay as if he had to pause and think about what he should do. Same way with his emotions. He had to think about what he was feeling, examine it from all angles, never truly understanding what was going on.

As I stood, the lactose-intolerance–induced bloating released. Not pleasant.

"Feel better?" Gollum grinned.

"Actually I do. Not so much pressure on my injury."

Our driver remained inside and unseen by any but Scrap. The door into the spa opened, inviting us in. Again, untended by human hands.

Scrap clung to my shoulder, stretching a bit, his nose twitching and his tail swishing across my back.

I don't like this place. Beneath the chlorine and antiseptic, it smells of blood. Human blood. He turned pink, and his talons pierced my top almost to my skin.

Nothing downstairs but two massages, a blow job, and a pedicure that's going to get kinky real fast. Wanna watch, babe? Scrap retracted his talons and flitted through the heavy fire door on the ground floor and back out again.

His normal gray/green translucency returned. The blood was no threat to us.

That didn't mean I had to like it.

"I vote we go upstairs," I replied—the only other egress from the landing just inside the exterior door.

You might learn something for when you finally decide to seduce Gollum. Not that he needs much seducing, dahling. If you know what I mean. Scrap waggled his unlit cigar at me.

"Sounds like a party up there," Gollum muttered. "Maybe we should look for an elevator." He stared me in the eyes as if daring me to walk up those stairs.

I glanced from him to the stairs and back again.

Watch da birdie in da camera, babe. Scrap pointed to a miniscule red light at the first turn of the stairs.

"I don't want to get trapped in an enclosed box at the mercy of electronics and the whims of Murphy's Law," I told Gollum, gesturing slightly with my head toward the camera.

He knew me well enough to catch on quickly and nodded. "Would you care to take the point?" He gestured me up the stair ahead of him. "We'll watch your back."

"You'd better." I jammed the comb back into my hair. Then I took my time, judging each step carefully, trying not to limp obviously or lean too heavily on the banister. If I showed any signs of weakness at this point, I made myself vulnerable.

When I hurt, Scrap hurt. He might not be able to transform.

True to his word, Gollum stayed one step below me. Close enough to give me a boost up if I needed it, or catch me if I fell.

Mickey came behind him, turning around and around, keeping everything in sight at once.

Eventually, we mastered the two sets of thirteen steps. I wondered who had a hand in designing that little bit of bad luck. The fire door stood propped wide open by a skull with the top hacked off raggedly and a black candle stub jammed inside. It gave off a creepy light, creating more shadows than it banished. It looked like real bone. I kept telling myself it had to be ceramic or good quality plastic. It just had to be. I refused to think about the possibility of it being a real skull, from a real human being.

"Dramatic Halloween nonsense I can do without," I muttered.

"Effective atmosphere if you're feeling vulnerable, though," Gollum replied.

"I'm feeling vulnerable," Mickey whispered.

"Don't show it," I hissed back.

He shrugged his shoulders and settled his back before putting on a brave, and totally false, smile.

I muttered something more and stepped across the threshold of the local lady vampire mob boss.

I had a fleeting impression of sparse and graceful furniture in pale wood and muted upholstery with far too many bodies vying for the few seats. More bodies stood around in listless, muted conversation. Black candles—mostly in antique brass-and-silver candelabra rather than skulls—barely lit the room. High ceilings robbed the lower reaches of light. I almost had the feeling of being out of doors.

How to tell if the room had tasteful appointments or impoverished scarcity?

This was how people lived in the "good old days" before electricity. They couldn't see anything after sunset unless they spent a fortune on smelly fish oil lamps or candles. They huddled together in the immediate circle of light cast by clusters of fixtures leaving the rest of the world in spooky shadow.

"Andiamo," a sultry feminine voice called. A lovely blonde in her early forties floated forward. A few streaks of white highlighted her hair nicely. She either paid someone a lot of money for those highlights or she had fantastic genes.

She linked her arm in mine and drew me deeper into the room.

A bevy of pale hangers-on edged closer to us. No sign of the wereweasel.

The magical comb I'd stuck in my short hair showed me nothing special in the auras. Just ordinary people.

Except Lady Lucia had no radiant energy at all. That scared me more than if she took bat form.

If you haven't heard already, I have a thing about bats. I'll fight a dozen Sasquatch and Windago any day before I'll face down even one little insect-eating bat.

Gollum looked like he wanted to take notes. Mickey looked numb and overwhelmed. They followed close on my heels.

"Nice gown, Lady Lucia," I said, taking in the delicate cream-and-terra-cotta silk that looked like it walked off a costume rack labeled 1835. Something about the cut and clean lines suggested a Florentine designer.

Her guests at least had kept up with the times with a preponderance of black silky fabrics and tight jeans.

"Introduce me to your friends, Signora Tess," she said with a frown. Her accent sounded thick, as if her English was newly learned.

I raised an eyebrow to Gollum. He shrugged, still studying cadence and inflection.

"Contessa, allow me to present Dr. Guilford Van der Hoyden-Smythe and Mickey Mallone, our local guide and driver." I thought I'd be polite and formal, play along with her game a bit before I decided to expose her.

From the looks of her cleavage, it wouldn't take much to expose a lot more of her than acceptable in polite society. But then, this was Vegas, or the outskirts thereof. Who knew what was acceptable.

Even as I thought about it, a hint of dusky skin peeked

above her tightly corseted décolletage, the same shade as the terra cotta in said gown's trim.

Gollum's eyes riveted right where she'd intended.

Okay. Gloves off. I was tired of being polite.

"You'd think someone who'd left Tuscany almost two hundred years ago, and who had prided herself on keeping up with the height of fashion would update her dress occasionally," I said. "Your headlights are showing and it's not a good look in mixed company."

She scowled at me, keeping her mouth firmly closed.

"Oh, and the accent is too thick." I thought fast and furious about what Gollum had said about how rapidly accents mutated. The details had gone in one ear and out the other eye.

"Tess . . ." Gollum warned.

I shrugged. "If she's really a vampire, you'd think she'd keep up with the times, try to blend in, stay under the radar. But then she'd have established a legal identity as Lady Lucia."

This time the lady sneered, revealing two very long and pointed eye teeth. Still no aura. She could have been masking it. Some people can do that—Donovan among them, just another reason not to trust him. But anger cracks any mask, and some energy should have leaked out.

"I've seen better implants and prosthetics at every con I've attended." I almost yawned. Then decided that reaction was too over the top.

A short lad drifted forward carrying a tray filled with silver goblets, brimming with dry ice mist. My height—which isn't saying much—he looked to be about twelve. Until he got close and the frown lines around his mouth and eyes added a couple of decades, or centuries, to his face.

He didn't have an aura either.

This was getting spooky.

"We party tonight, Signora Tess," Lucia said. Some of the accent faded, some—not all. "Time for word games and shadow boxing later. When we know what we both want." She lifted one of the goblets from the tray and handed it to me. "The specialty of the house. Goats from my beloved Tuscany contributed the milk. The blood came from a different donor. Whipped together into a froth with secret spices." She flashed more of the elongated teeth.

"We call it 'Smoothie Mary,' " the lad said with an evil grin that showed the same orthodontia as the Contessa.

"Um, thanks to Mary, whomever she may be, but no thanks. I'm allergic to milk. The animal casein." I trotted out an old high school biology lesson. The guy I'd dated my sophomore year had that allergy. Not just intolerant, allergic. He couldn't have cheese or cream or butter. Eggs were out of the question as well. "I think the blood falls into the same category as the goat milk."

I put the drink cup back on the tray. The icy stem burned my fingers. I wanted my hands fully functioning in case I had to fight my way out of here.

Scrap had remained strangely silent. I spotted him sitting on a chandelier, hanging almost upside down and spying on one of the men in jeans so tight they had to cut off circulation to vital parts. So far no comments about the legitimacy of our hostess' claims to being a vampire.

If she were truly evil, he'd have turned bright red and stretched halfway into transformation by now.

Wouldn't he?

"Tell me, Lady Lucia, are vampires in the same classification as demons? And if so, which ghetto did you escape from?"

The entire room went utterly still. Not even the candle flames flickered.

Chapter 22

The inland sea that covered much of SW North America began to recede 200 million years ago.

"SIR, TESS," GOLLUM STAMMERED. He hastily scanned the room for signs of trouble.

I'd already sized up the mass of bodies and dismissed them as useless wannabes.

Lady Lucia presented the only real threat. And maybe the pseudo child with the tray of drinks.

"Actually, vampires can't be classed as demons in this dimension," I blathered on. "Earth is their home world. Or is death a home world? If so, they'd be demons, if you use the 'out of dimension' definition, but I'm told that's not accurate." Gee I sounded a lot like Gollum there. I hate it when I babble. "So, what remains is the question of which dimensional ghetto did vampires crawl out of?"

At least Scrap diverted his attention back to me for about two heartbeats. Then he returned to ogling the shirtless males in black jeans that outlined every crack and protrusion on their bodies. Ordinary males. From the way their auras fluctuated, I guessed they found other men as attractive as females.

"Anyway, a vampire by definition is evil," I continued seemingly oblivious to the way the hangers-on pressed closer. "So if, Lady Lucia really is a vampire, then Scrap would have transformed the moment we walked in the door, I'd have killed her and we'd be on our way home."

A gasp of outrage ran around the room. I saw a lot of teeth in my peripheral vision. My attention remained on Lady Lucia.

She threw back her head and laughed long and loud. More of her bosom escaped the corset and lace. "Very good logic, *cara mía* Signora Tess. Very good indeed. However, your little friend cannot react to my inherent evil, because I offer no evil intentions toward you. Tonight." She looked long and hard at Scrap.

He flashed her a toothy grin. He had longer and sharper ones than she did. And a lot more of them.

And his were real.

How could she see him?

"I can see your imp, Signora Tess, because I can see the aura of blackness about him. He has many secrets, this one."

Now I felt more than a little uneasy. Did I really begin edging toward the door?

If I did, she came right along with me, and five of her minions slid between me and Gollum. Mickey stood isolated by another group of five to my left.

I couldn't leave them. They were defenseless, mostly. I was not.

"You brought me here for a reason, Lady Lucia. I want to know what it is."

"Is my little party not enough for you?" She reached out and grabbed by her leather vest a listless and anemic looking girl in her early twenties. She wasn't wearing anything beneath the vest except a micromini leather skirt that shifted upward to reveal wisps of blonde pubic hair.

She had an aura, barely. Mostly she'd been drained of so much energy—or blood—there wasn't a lot left to show.

The twin puncture wounds on her neck, right over the jugular, grabbed my attention.

Gollum looked a little sick. Mickey more so.

"This is Mary," Lady Lucia continued. "You may thank her for mixing the drinks tonight."

I gulped. "Um, thanks, Mary. I'm sure they were delish." I tried looking away. I really did.

Mary lifted her mouth in a feeble attempt at a smile.

"What's your point, Lady Lucia?" I still couldn't look away from Mary. Call it fascinated horror.

It felt a lot like fear.

Lady Lucia had taken my preconceived notions and juggled them, keeping them all in the air at the same time.

"My point is, that I have a lot of power in this region. I have many followers, many who will do my bidding without question. But I cannot bring down Gary Gregbaum."

"You have my attention. I do not like what that man is doing."

"His show is lovely, isn't it?" Lady Lucia dropped her grip on Mary and pushed her away. She stumbled toward a chair and fell into it like the rag doll she had become.

"Lovely. And disturbing," I said. "Tell me, does the audience clap for the dying faery at every performance? That has become a tradition in our world, to bring Tinker Bell back to life."

"No. You began that tradition for 'Fairy Moon.' Amazing that the performance touched you so deeply, you who are so jaded and contemptuous of that which you do not understand." She glided toward the center of the room.

My feet followed her of their own volition. The crowd shifted around us. I noticed the knots of people around Mickey and Gollum also moved, keeping the same distance between us.

Directly beneath Scrap's chandelier, Lady Lucia took the stage, bathed in gentle candlelight from the fifty or more flames above her head. One of them threatened Scrap's tail. I wondered when, or if, he'd notice.

"You, *cara mia* Tess, have the power to do what I cannot," Lady Lucia pronounced.

"Which is?"

"Free the faery dancers and ruin Gary Gregbaum."

"And how am I supposed to do that?"

"You must go where I and my kind cannot. You must find the portal in the Valley of Fire and lead the faeries to it."

No way no how, Babe. I am not going to the Valley of Fire. Never again. Not in this lifetime or any other. It will be the death of me. And that means it's the death of you, too.

When I die, you die. When you die, I die.

You aren't going there either. Much too dangerous. Mountains of iron-laden sandstone with twisted and looping canyons screw with the senses and challenge the balance of life.

Get Mr. Holier Than Thou Breven Sancroix and snooty Fortitude to do it.

Or get Mr. Stinky Donovan Estevez to do it.

Anyone but you and me, babe. Abso-fucking-lutely anyone but us.

"Glad to see something could grab your attention, Scrap," I muttered. The more I heard about this Valley of Fire, the more curious I became. And the more scared.

Scrap's aura sparked, or maybe that was just his tail catching fire. Normally, I couldn't detect his aura at all. I didn't need to. His body color told me what I needed to know of his emotions. Right now he was so pale, even I had trouble seeing him.

And I never detected the darkness Lady Lucia claimed to see around him. The king of the Orculli Trolls had told me about that darkness, too.

I looked to Gollum for inspiration. His eyes had glazed over in his need to get on the Internet and do some research.

"What do I get out of this venture?" I asked Lady Lucia. "I'm figuring it's as dangerous for me as for you."

A moment of silence as she looked me up and down, assessing, weighing her options. And mine.

"You fulfill your vows as a Warrior of the Celestial Blade, you restore balance to the dimensions. But you must hurry. My sources tell me the rogue portal is unstable and will close within days. If that happens, then Faery is forever damaged. The good energy that flows there, balancing many evils, will be lost to the universe." She looked serious. "You will gain much credit with the Powers That Be. Something you will need if you ever hope to survive outside a Citadel."

Believe her, babe. The good energy in Faery already turns bad. Think about those mutant faeries on steroids that Gregbaum employs.

"Okay, and what do you get, Lady Lucia?"

"I see Gary Gregbaum writhe in disgrace and poverty."

"If the portal closes, can't we get the faeries back to their homeland through the chat room?" I looked to Scrap for confirmation. He claimed to know the chat room as well as anyone.

Not a good idea, dahling. It's one thing for me to slip you in and out upon occasion when the demons on guard are particularly dumb. Quite another to take an entire troupe through. Besides, last time I flitted through, the door to Faery was sealed. Both directions.

"You need to know that I have purchased the Dragon and St. George," Lady Lucia continued. "My first act upon taking over in four days will be to fire all the managers who are skimming gambling profits and implode the hotel. Gregbaum will never produce another show in Las Vegas, no matter who has the audacity to back him. I will see to that."

There is nothing so great as the wrath of a woman scorned.

The skinny lad without an aura tugged on the flounce at the end of her three-quarter sleeve. "Do not forget the curse."

"Do I want to know?"

More bad news, babe. This does not look good, or like fun. We're gonna need help, maybe of the Donovan kind.

"Gregbaum has placed a curse upon his dancers. If any one of them leaves the building, they all become living torches."

Mickey nodded, confirming the existence of the curse.

"You must break the curse and lead the faeries to freedom before I take possession and the portal closes. I cannot be responsible for what will become of this world should you fail," Lucia continued.

Mickey fainted.

Chapter 23

Boulder City is the only town in Nevada where gambling is not legal.

NOW I RECOGNIZE Mickey! With his defenses down, his real self shines through like a beacon in the dark. That's what Faery should be and has lost.

Let me back up just a tad—like a month or two our time. See there's this psycho chick named WindScribe. She's one of the coven that went missing twenty-eight years ago, only they think they were only in Faery about a month. Got news for them. Time runs different in Faery.

Anyway, WindScribe got caught doing something more than a little naugty and very very dangerous. She tried setting free a bunch of Cthulhu demons from their ghetto in the back of Faery.

Naturally, the king of Faery was pissed. WindScribe snapped his neck. Now this little escapade led to all kinds of trouble that Tess and I dealt with already.

But back in Faery, life didn't return to normal. There was a big fight between our boy Mickey, who's something like the crown prince of Faery, and his stepmom the queen. Queeny won and now rules Faery. But there's a whole lot of things wrong. So wrong the chat room portal is closed until they get things right.

Mickey must be here to get back the faery dancers who got

kidnapped while no one was in charge and life was chaotic. Until he does that, Faery can't heal.

He's a true prince. He should be ruling.

"Time to get our boy home," Gollum said. He broke through his guards and Mickey's to crouch beside him. He tested Mickey's pulse and touched his brow with the back of his hand.

"Is he okay?" I asked, elbowing my way over to them.

Scrap descended to my shoulder like a good little imp. He'd gained a little color, back to his normal gray/green with just a hint of yellow concern. Not a bit of pink or red on him. We were still safe.

But for how long?

"Hard to tell what's okay for him," Gollum whispered. "Pulse too rapid and skin too cold and clammy."

Not good, Scrap said. He shifted to the top of my head, claws grasping the comb. I didn't know if he used its powers or merely kept it in place. *Faeries have a higher heart rate than humans, but that makes their skin warmer.*

I shook my head at Gollum, hoping he'd understand that we had to get him out of here. No sense in betraying his origins to Lady Lucia and her gang if we didn't have to.

Mickey's eyes fluttered. Again, I got the impression of something off in their tilt and placement in his pinched and narrow face. He moaned and tried to roll over.

Gollum steadied his movements. "Catch your bearings, boy, before you try to stand."

"I'll have you know I am no 'boy,' " Mickey sneered with the disdain of a true aristocrat. All traces of the bouncy youth vanished.

Then the familiar Mickey returned in a flash. "I'm okay. Just get me out of here. The heat, and the candles, and too much perfume overcame me."

Yeah, right.

I'd seen his eyes roll up the moment Lady Lucia mentioned the consequences of Gregbaum's curse. If any of the faery dancers left the building, they'd go up in flames. A horrible death for anyone. Might be especially tormenting to faeries.

"Lady Lucia." I turned and faced our hostess-cum-ally-cum-adversary. "May we trouble you for the use of your car for our return to the city?"

"Of course." She snapped her fingers.

The lad scuttled out. Then I heard footsteps clattering on a staircase at the opposite end of the building from our entrance.

"The car will meet you out front. It will take a few minutes to retrieve it from the garage. If you come this way, you may walk by the pool and wander the hotel gift shop for a moment. Feel free to gamble." She ushered us out of the party room, down a short hallway.

We passed a tiny kitchenette, a bath nearly as large a my hotel room. The luxurious tub had water jets, deep enough for ten to swim in. Three partially closed doors looked like they might be guest rooms, smaller than the bath. Couples were engaged in heavy make out sessions there, mostly unclothed and oblivious to us.

Then the hallway ended. To our left lay the master (or mistress) bedroom with a huge circular bed, sitting area, and access to another bath. I couldn't see the details but guessed it to be more utilitarian. To our right a broad green marble staircase curved downward.

But it was the painting on the end wall that grabbed my attention. A masterful oil portrait of Lady Lucia in her late teens. She wore a white gown, of the late Napoleonic period, with a full, flowing mantilla of white chantilly lace—very rare and costly; chantilly is usually black silk. She could have been pregnant, hard to tell in those high-waisted gowns. The painted image displayed her left hand quite prominently. On her heart finger, she wore a gold filigree ring with a huge square-cut diamond.

I'd seen that ring before, tied to a rose stem as Donovan offered it to me with his proposal.

Gary Gregbaum wore a duplicate on his pinky finger.

I checked. Lady Lucia did not wear that ring; several other very expensive ones, but not that one.

Who had the original? Donovan or Gregbaum? And how did they come to possess such a valuable and cherished antique?

I'm off to Mum's for a nice little chat about how to trace that ring. I'm surprised it didn't end up in Mum's front yard, the freeze-dried-garbage-dump-of-the-universe. That's where I found Tess' comb, and the brooch that signifies leadership of all the Sisterhoods of the Celestial Blade—maybe Brotherhoods, too. We'll see when she's defeated her thirteen enemies and earned a precious stone for each of the settings in the brooch. I also found a dragon skull there that now sits atop Tess' back door. No one ever uses the front door and it's sealed during bad weather. That skull works better than any stone gargoyle for repelling nasties from the house. And since it's from a real dragon and not a gargoyle, it doesn't keep me out.

No one special guarding the chat room tonight. Guess Gregbaum has called in all of his faeries on steroids for some other project. Just some giant fleas hanging around jumping hither, thither, and yon, biting at the air. They look like tiny dots against the endless white that stretches on and on and on forever. No color, no break in the vastness except an occasional doorway. Those fleas all seem to be congregating around the black splotch in front of Faery.

That used to be a clear opening, inviting any and all to share in the hospitality, the peace, and the joy of living. Anyone could get into Faery, if they could find their way into the chat room. Now Faery is closed to all until the balance is restored. Uh-oh! The seal used to be a perfect circle. Now it's distorted and ugly.

Things are getting worse, and time is running out. I've got to get to Mum's quick.

I slide toward the leather curtain that covers Imp Haven. A single flea nips at my tail. Ow, that itches. At least it didn't take off any of my warts. I worked hard to earn those beauty spots, I'm not giving them up to some *flea*!

Mum stands in front of her hovel, broom in hand. The broom has seen better days. Pretty useless now as a broom, still effective at swatting my cute little tush—now covered in six, count 'em six, lovely warts. She frowns the moment I come into view.

I drop down in front of her in an almost graceful flight just like a good little imp. Her frown deepens.

"What are you doing here?" she shouts. "I thought for sure somewhat would have killed you by now."

"Wishful thinking, Mum?" I bow, just like Tess taught me.

Always good to be respectful of one's elders. Especially if you want something from them.

"Get out, ungrateful, thieving, murdering runt!" She swipes with her broom.

I flit out of reach, ever so grateful my wings have grown enough to do that. "Mum, wait, please, before you kick me out on my own again; I need to know how to track the magical trail of an artifact of power."

"If you don't know how to do that by now, you are even more useless than when you left the first time." Another swat with the broom.

Ow! That hurt. And it, sniff, cost me the wart on the tip of my tail!

I hope it was the broom that took it off and not the flea. Too, too humiliating to lose it to a flea.

Chapter 24

The Desert Inn opened in 1950 with a color scheme of Bermuda pink and emerald green that carried onto the golf course with green grass and pink flags.

MICKEY LED THE WAY out of Lady Lucia's apartment, hastening down the green marble steps with reckless speed.

Some of his need to be away from this place, and our hostess, infected me.

Before I could comment on the ring, or the portrait for that matter, Gollum grabbed my arm and ushered me down the sweeping stairway. "Watch your step," he said quietly. "The marble may be slick."

I braced myself between him and the banister. Not until I tried to take the first step down on my right leg, did I realize how tired and aching that strained muscle had become.

Lady Lucia remained at the top, watching us through narrowed and speculative eyes.

I used my limping pace to give me time to survey as much of the area as possible, wondering why a formal entrance to the suite above opened into the bedrooms, and the back way gave access to the salon.

"The place is bass-ackwards," I muttered when we finally reached a fenced-in covered patio at the side of the building. Pale flagstones floored the area. Terra cotta tubs overflowed with flowering vines. A single circular table and lounge chair were placed at the center with an umbrella for additional shade. A four-foot-high split log fence and a hedge of some spiky desert plant offered scant separation from the rest of the resort. From the chair, one could watch the waterfall cascade down the artificial volcano at the center of the oddly shaped pool. Ah, Lady Lucia's private garden, protected from the desert sun.

Mickey held open a rough plank gate reminiscent of a rustic ranch. His feet twitched, and his hands clenched spasmodically.

Without saying a word, we followed a meandering path through the oasis-styled gardens, along back corridors of the hotel, with more than a few hints of Morocco in the décor—including some flamingo pink and desert green decorative tiles, to the front porte cochère. No telling who was listening.

A black, full-sized Hummer awaited us, the driver already secreted behind the wheel. Thank the Goddess it wasn't the hearse. I wasn't in the mood for mind games.

I crammed myself in the middle of the back seat, with Gollum on the right, stretching his long legs, and Mickey on my left, huddled in on himself, still fidgeting nervously. No discreet panel separating us from the front seat this time. None of us seemed inclined to talk anyway.

My leg wanted to curl up, but it cramped when I pulled my feet onto the seat and wrapped my arms about my legs. So I stretched them out again and lolled my head back against the seat. Eyes closed, I blanked the drive through the desert night, thinking furiously.

The rings. Donovan. Gregbaum. Lady Lucia. All connected. Maybe Sancroix and his nephew, too. All wanting different and conflicting things from me.

Danger lurked in following any course of action. How could I decide until I had more information?

I trusted Gollum to research Lady Lucia, now that we had a vital clue. As the new owner of the Dragon and St. George, she had to have a corporate registry somewhere, funding, investors, something.

Only I could approach Donovan and find out about that ring.

Could I trust Mickey to investigate the faery dancers and the curse upon them?

At last we stopped next to Mickey's taxi in the underground parking lot.

"What time is it?" I asked, coming out of my meditation with nothing resolved. "There aren't any clocks anywhere in this town."

"Past midnight," Gollum said, checking his illuminated watch with more dials and functions than I could count.

Eighteen minutes past, Scrap corrected him. He'd popped out for a few moments on the long ride home. Now he was back.

"Tonight's show is over. I need to talk to those dancers," I mumbled.

"Not tonight." Gollum forcefully steered me into the taxi. "You are in no shape to defend yourself."

Enough said. I knew he was right.

Mickey still hadn't said a word. He expertly pulled into the nighttime traffic on the Strip, no less dense than at noon. The Strip didn't need noon sunshine. Enough neon flashed, blinked, and scrolled to keep it bright twenty-four/seven.

"Mickey, what do you know about magic?"

"Not enough," he muttered. "I know faery magic. I do not know Gregbaum's. I sensed the spell around the building. I can go in and out. It must contain only the lost dancers. I came on the scene later and so it does not stretch to me, or any other faery. Only the dancers."

"Can you find out what kind of spell he's used?" I leaned forward and squeezed his shoulder, hoping to offer comfort and support.

He flinched away from my touch, as if it burned his skin through his light shirt.

"I have to. You may go home now, Lady Tess. I know what I must do. You cannot help me." His words came out tight and strained.

"Mickey, you bound me to the mission. My vows to my Sisterhood bind me to the mission. I'm not leaving."

"We'll talk about this tomorrow, when we've all had a chance to rest and do some research. Do you understand, Mickey?" Gollum asked in his sternest schoolteacher voice. "You will do nothing without consulting us. We have skills and knowledge you don't."

Mickey seemed to collapse in on himself, as if only his

anger, or his fear, had kept him upright. "I understand. I will wait to rescue my people until I talk to you."

He paused then looked at me through the mirror, engaging my gaze. "Lady Tess, I am not sorry I wove magic around your mother to help her sing. I needed you to feel safe leaving her alone to help me. I saw you at the airport. I recognized your scar and your imp. I watched you take the shuttle to The Crown Jewels and followed."

"You may have done Mom a tremendous favor, Mickey. Don't apologize for that. I need to see the show again," I said decisively. "We'll use Lady Lucia's letter to get us in to the special performance tomorrow afternoon. There are clues there. I know it."

You bet there are! The whole show is a road map, Scrap added solemnly. *I wish it led somewhere else.*

"If I may, I would like to accompany you, Lady Tess. I may recognize something you do not."

"We'll all go. But for now, we rest. Mickey, pick us up tomorrow at two thirty." Gollum put an end to any arguments at the same moment Mickey drew his cab to a stop outside The Crown Jewels.

"Scrap, keep an eye on Mickey. Make sure he doesn't do anything stupid," Tess whispered as soon as she was out of the taxi.

Babe, you're hurt, I can't . . .

"I'm going to bed. You can scout around until I fall out of bed ten minutes before my first conference session in the morning."

Gotcha, babe. Rest, secure in the knowledge . . .

"Yadda, yadda, yadda. Get going. Mickey's already three blocks away and burning rubber."

I mark Mickey with an anchor that leads back to the chat room. He won't get far without me knowing.

I can get from where I'm going back to Mickey or over to Tess and they won't know how long I've really been gone.

Time, after all, is just another dimension. If you know how to use it. And, thanks to my babe and her adventures, I'm getting better and better at manipulating that dimension.

There are nuances to the chat room not everyone knows. Imps learn some of them at their mum's knee.

Me, I had to listen to other imps whispering in corners when they thought I wasn't around.

Being only a scrap of an imp, I wasn't supposed to survive my first fifty years. I did. My siblings attacked me for my audacity.

I survived that, too. Though some of them didn't. Mum has never forgiven me. I don't care. I have never forgiven them.

Survival of the fittest. I may not be the biggest imp ever, or the most dignified. But I'm clever, and because of my small size, I can get in and out of places unseen and unheard that my bigger comrades overlook.

Like the side corridor off the chat room. It's hard to see. Harder to fit through. Only those flea demons can follow me. Well maybe a j'appel dragon can. They are only palm-sized until you call their true name. Then they grow and grow and grow to fill the chat room with smelly scales and sulfur-ridden breath.

Easy to avoid using a j'appel dragon's real name, you think? Not if they change it every hour. Not if they choose names like "Because" or "Help" as their true name.

Anyway, they avoid this tiny little corridor because if they suddenly grow to full size in there, they'll suffocate or get squeezed to death.

I skip along the dimensionless white that stretches into infinity. Good idea to trail my fingers along one wall, just to keep my bearings. Easy to get lost in here without landmarks. Even for an imp.

Ah, there, that's what I need. That magic ring Gregbaum wears so proudly bulges through the walls like the inside of a pimple. I told you it isn't firmly set in any one dimension. Therefore, part of it is always in the chat room.

Mum said I should know how to track it. I guess this is the right place. I stand on tiptoe and peer at the gold filigree and that beautiful, perfect diamond with just a hint of yellow in the coloration, or maybe a reflection of the gold setting. I could get lost in that stone, staring into its depths, seeing the tiny black spot in the middle that is an echo of the blackness in my own soul.

Back out. Back out. Can't afford to do that. If I look too closely, I might regret some of the things I've done in order to stay alive and grow big enough to companion my dahling Tess.

I memorize every twist and scroll and how the metal cradles

the stone. Now I know I can pick this ring out anywhere. So all I have to do is track it back in time.

Where is the energy signature? An object this powerful always wants to go back to its origins. Just like me. I always want to go back to Mum even when she hates me.

A wisp of smoke, almost clear, hard to see except for that very faint yellow tinge. Now I've got it. Follow the trail. Don't take any side turns. Just follow it back, back, back, nearly back to the beginning of time.

At least to the beginning of Faery.

Chapter 25

Casino floor layouts deliberately route customers past slot machines on the way to showrooms, restaurants, and other attractions.

REST WAS NOT in the cards, or the dice, or the slots, for me that night. At least not yet.

Mom finished another torch song on a lingering, wistful note, just as we walked into the casino. (We had to go through the casino to get anywhere in the hotel.)

"Ladies and gentlemen, let me introduce you to my daughter, a better nightingale than me!" she crooned into her mike.

The packed audience erupted in applause.

"Come up here, Tess, and join me in a song," Mom invited. She wore emerald green that sparkled and draped her full figure admirably. I don't think it was all faery glamour. My mom showed through, a bright, vibrant woman who'd finally found fulfillment of a youthful dream.

If I wasn't mistaken, she'd lost more than a few pounds since the fiasco of her brief marriage to Donovan's foster father. Either that or she wore a tightly laced corset that would make Lady Lucia's look baggy.

I went limp inside, too tired to sing, too tired to fight my mom. In her current enthusiasm, I'd not best her with arguments. Faster to give in, sing one song, and retreat.

But when I stood beside my mother, she handed me the mike and withdrew.

What to sing?

I looked to the lanky man with ebony skin and long black hair slicked into a tight ponytail who sat at an electric keyboard with an impressive array of controls.

Then it came to me. I knew precisely the song that fit my mood and the situation. I'd first heard Gwen Knighten perform her whimsical song solo with a harp at a science fiction convention. She kept us laughing and crying at the same time.

"Vamp along with something light and harpish," I told the musician quietly, giving him the rhythm and key. "This piece is called 'My Fairytale.' It sort of says it all."

"Oh, the day is warm, and sunlight is streaming
Through slotted windows on the battlements today
And the stone walls are holding so fast
But they always seem sturdy when you are away.
The spring flags are flying, the merry maidens dance,
The portents in magicland point to romance,
And it was a day like today, not so very long ago,
I lived in this castle, and you were my beau.
Or was that the time when I lived in the forest,
And you met me halfway to grandmother's place?
I forget, I forget; it all runs together,
But open the storybook, put on that face."

As I started in on the chorus, I spotted Donovan off to the side of the room. He was trying to blend in with a pillar, but my heart could find him anywhere. This song was as much for him as it was for me, or my mom, or all of us together.

"Take me in, yes, I'll be your victim,
I'll be the matchgirl, and you be the wind.
Take me in, yes, I'll be your victim,
I'll be Red Riding Hood, you be the wolf.
I'll be the girl who gets burned in the oven,
and you'll be the baker who serves me for pie.
I won't expect any boring old woodcutters
coming to save me at the end of the day—
In the end, yes, I'll be your victim
You'll be my frog and I won't be a princess.

In the end, no curtain, no laughter,
no pumpkin, no coachman, no happily ever after."

That got a round of laughter from the audience, including Gollum. It only earned a deep frown from Donovan. He wasn't about to forgive me. I didn't know how I was going to approach him with questions about the ring. But I had to. If not tonight, then tomorrow.

"Oh, the woods are deep, and yet it's still sunny,
The birds are all singing along with me now
As I walk on my way—don't know where I'm going,
But wherever it is, I'll end up villain-chow.
Oh, what's that behind me, that scurry, that scamper,
That rustle of movement just under the trees?
It's a bird, it's a pigeon, it's eating my breadcrumbs
Don't know my way home; now I feel ill at ease.
Is this the one where you're the fox in the suitcoat
Who spellbinds me, then carves me up for a snack?
I don't know, I don't know; but these plots never vary,
So I'll skip on along while you plan your attack."

This time the audience joined me in the chorus—at Gollum's prompting—just like a filk session at an SF con. My mood brightened, and I added a little gusto to the music.

"Oh, the night is dark, and my neck is aching:
The prince climbing up my hair is pulling too hard,
And I can't move an inch! This position is painful,
But I don't want my head to be down in the yard.
When you reach the window, your boots on the stonework,
You lean up to kiss me, I'm gasping for air,
And you shake your head sharply, say, 'Sorry, wrong tower,'
Then slide down while pulling out half of my hair.
I think you're supposed to be charming and handsome,
I think I'm supposed to be winsome and sweet,
But it all gets confusing, and right now I'm cursing—
I can't get these glass slippers onto my feet."

This time I ventured out among the audience, belting the

chorus, and getting them to clap along with me in rhythm. Using the song as a cover, I wound my way to where Donovan still clung to his pillar. His forlorn expression almost tugged at my heartstrings.

Almost.

I knew some of the blackness deep inside him. He wouldn't hurt for long. I was sure he'd already lined up a bedmate for tonight.

"I need to talk to you," I whispered while catching my breath for the next line."

"We have nothing to talk about." He tried turning his back on me.

Oh, how I longed to reach out and smooth the strain away from his well muscled shoulders.

"What about Lady Lucia's heirloom ring?"

I ambled back to the center of the room, still singing.

"Now it's just before dawn, and you know I'm not sleeping,
For you stuck that pea way down under my bed.
I would never have said that I'd go through with this one
If that damned poisoned apple weren't clouding my head.
Oh, you'll be the spindle that pricks the girl's finger,
And I'll be asleep for the next hundred years,
And while you're out riding your horse on the wold,
I'm stuck here spinning this flax into gold.
And when you struck me dumb and then made me knit sweaters
Of nettles for seven boys turned into swans,
Oh, I thought I would kill you; I did, but I couldn't,
We both know that I fall for all of your cons."

One last round of the chorus as I returned to the stage, ready to hand the mike back to Mom and make my escape. I didn't need to worry about Donovan. I could feel him heading toward the elevators.

"Take me in, yes, I'll be your victim,
I'll be Red Riding Hood, you be the wolf."

Please, oh please, don't let that part of the story be true this time.

But Donovan wasn't waiting for me at the elevators, or at the door to my room.

I dialed his room and was told he had checked out.

Now what?

Um, Tess?

"Now what?" I snapped at Scrap.

I can't find Mickey.

What do you mean? You've got instant radar. You can find anything or anyone." Anxiety began burning up from my gut to my throat.

He's dropped off the radar. Fortitude can't find him either.

"Where did you see him last?"

Three blocks from here. He just—vanished.

I called Gollum's cell phone. "We have to find Mickey before he kills Gregbaum."

"Wait . . . what . . ." he stammered. I hadn't even given him a chance to say hello.

So I told him what Scrap reported. "If he kills Gregbaum, the curse will die with him. That's what Mickey's going to do. And he'll get killed in trying!"

"Ask Scrap if he can find Gregbaum."

"Good idea." I shouted into the ether.

Yeah, he's in his penthouse wining and dining. Looking for a new home for "Fairy Moon." Scrap yawned, sounding bored.

"Is Mickey with Gregbaum?" Gollum asked.

I relayed the question, hating the delays.

Nope. I checked that first thing Mickey went missing. I'm not stupid.

"The curse may not die with the magician," Gollum said. He yawned himself.

I loosed my own. This sleepiness was catching. Well, it was almost two in the morning.

"Mickey has to investigate the spell before he does anything," Gollum continued.

"Is he smart enough to calm down and take the time to do that?" I wouldn't. I'd have charged right in with blade swirling.

"Mickey knows a lot more about magic than we do."

"I'm not so sure . . ." I heard a brief knock on the door. Before I could get up to answer it, Gollum let himself in with my spare keycard.

He folded his phone and spoke to me directly. "He's

from Faery. He knows magic. He knows the limitations. Trust me, Tess. Mickey is not a fool."

"Scrap, where are the dancers?" If Mickey was going to try a rescue, he might just go there directly.

All tucked up in their little beds, fast asleep. A bit of a pause. *Tess, they've cried themselves to sleep. I've got to go in there and give them some hope.* He sounded as if he wanted to cry, too.

My heart nearly broke. I'd never known Scrap to care for anything so deeply, except for himself—and me.

"Stop him, Tess," Gollum shouted, looking up as if he might espy Scrap. "If the dancers perform as if they have hope, Gregbaum will get wise to us and change his spell."

Ooops! Scrap bounced out of the air into my lap with a whoosh and a thud. For half a heartbeat he took solid form.

"Damn, but you are heavy." I started to shove Scrap away when he faded to his normal insubstantial translucence.

Gollum stared gape-jawed at the space where Scrap appeared.

Sorry, babe. Rebounded off Gregbaum's protections.

"Must be a strong web of interdimensional weaving around the dancers' dormitory," Gollum mused.

"Wait, did you hear Scrap as well as see him?" A spell strong enough to do that really scared me.

"I just heard bits of his words. Enough to piece together what happened. Then he faded. We're up against some pretty powerful stuff here, Tess. We need help."

"What kind of help?" I thought I knew where he was headed with this and didn't like it. "MoonFeather?" My aunt was a witch of the Wicca variety and knew more about real magic than I wanted to admit.

Gollum shook his head. "Donovan. He's got connections in all kinds of strange places."

"Including to Lady Lucia *and* to Gregbaum."

Gollum's glasses slid to the end of his nose.

I ordered a bottle of single malt scotch from room service. The price made me blanch. "What about a blend?"

The waiter rattled off a list and their prices.

"I think we'll try the Muirhead." That scotch had a decent reputation and they used to sponsor a top notch bagpipe band.

"Ma'am, if price is your consideration, I've got a bottle of Sheep Dip I can't give away. I'll let you have the whole bottle for half the price of the Muirhead," the waiter said.

"Sold."

I'd heard stories about that scotch. Farmers in England used to deduct it from their taxes as necessary agricultural supplies.

"Let's hope it tastes better than its namesake."

Chapter 26

Some of the best educated people in Las Vegas work as bartenders. The tips are better than schoolteacher salaries.

IF TESS IS GOING TO SPEND TIME with Mr. Stinky Man, I've got to get out of here. Might as well use the time to my advantage.

I zip into the side corridor of the chat room, noting that Mickey's beacon is blinking again. He's brooding in a tiny one-room apartment. Okay to leave him for a while.

I stand in front of a window into the past. The beings flitting about on the other side of the glass pane, or deep inside like a TV, I can't tell for sure, are faeries. Or the distant ancestors of them. I see subtle differences, more pointed ears, longer noses that almost resemble animal snouts. And they are bigger.

They frown more, too. Not since WindScribe killed the last king of the faeries and tried to loose a whole horde of full-blooded demons on all the dimensions, has anyone, I mean *anyone*, in living memory seen a faery frown. But here they stand in a big circle around a forge. They have linked hands to seal whatever is inside. No one escapes a circle of faery magic.

A very large human smith pounds his hammer against an anvil. He works a strip of gold thinner and thinner.

A dwarf, sitting at a tall bench beside the brightly burning hearth, chips away at a rock.

Bound in braided ropes of holly, mistletoe, and ivy sits an imp at the exact center of the circle. My heart reels in shock. The knots and twists in those ropes have turned three innocuous plants into imp's bane, the most dreaded form of punishment for my kind. At least the poor prisoner won't care what they do to him, until they do it. He's powerless, has no judgment, and cannot connect to those who love him. Worse of all, he can't duck into the chat room or through any portal to escape.

If you haven't guessed already, I've spent some time under the influence of imp's bane. Last autumn, when Sasquatch, masquerading as terrorists, kidnapped my Tess and filled their headquarters with imp's bane. I spent the entire time swinging from the rafters, making friends with a bat, and disconnected from Tess. If she hadn't discovered the purpose of the imp's bane and started burning it bit by bit, we would have died from the separation.

And I couldn't hop into the chat room for relief. The arcane knots anchored me in one dimension. Most beings can only get into one or two dimensions, if they can get beyond the demons in the chat room. Imps can go anywhere. We have to in order to do our jobs as Celestial Blades. We have to catalog as many demon forms we can. Can't fight them if you don't know what they are.

Then I noticed that this is no ordinary imp. He's big. The biggest imp I've ever seen. Which means he's old. And cranky. Imps change color to reflect their mood. Normally we're sort of gray-green, go blue with pleasure, purple with desire, yellow with laughter, green with curiosity. Vermilion just before we transform into a weapon.

This imp, beneath his deep orange anger—I'd be angry, too, with that much imp's bane coiled around me, and sick with it, too—is black. I have never seen a black imp before. His bat-wing ears are shaped wrong, too, more like pointy rat ears. And there's not a single wart to soften his ugliness.

The tap, tap, tap of the dwarf's tools changes to a softer, more hesitant rhythm.

I see the precious stone emerge from the rock. Little tiny chips fly away, revealing the biggest diamond I've ever seen. A few more taps of the chisel and he begins shaping the jewel, adding facets—lots of them—polishing it.

By this time, the smith has done something to the gold to turn it into wire. He hands it off to a lady faery who wears a gold filigree crown. She shapes and twists the wire into a ring to match her crown.

Much chanting and dancing in circles. Then, finally, the diamond is ready to mate with the gold.

And a true mating it is. For the ring that is born of both gold and diamond becomes something more, something special.

I can't see what they are doing; they close ranks and block my view. But I can smell the magic. Strong magic. Not black and evil, but not entirely white and healing either. Something more sinister than normal Faery Blessings.

The faeries back away. The imp is gone. The ropes of imp's bane lie limp and withering on the bright green grass.

The faery queen holds the ring up for all to see, The dark flaw at the very center of the diamond is no imperfection. It is the imp, imprisoned forever. Forced to stare at his own black reflection for eternity. No flaw or crack in the diamond for the black imp to communicate with the outside world. The faery magic keeps him from opening a portal to the chat room.

He can only open a portal under the direction of the ring wearer. This ring will open the portal to Faery so we can send the dancers home.

Then Queenie slips the ring on the thumb of her left hand.

I nearly faint with shock.

There is only one ring. Not two, as we thought. The ring flexes to fit the hand of the wearer.

But if Gregbaum just got the ring, and Donovan had it only days ago, how did he get the dancers over to Earth?

I move on. More to learn. I just hope I can get back to Tess before she needs me. These windows in time distort my senses and I'm not certain when I was when I entered the chat room.

I filled the water glass from the bathroom with scotch and handed it to Gollum. "Drink it down, language guy."

He stared at the amber liquid. "A terrible waste of good scotch to just drink it."

"I know. But this is necessary. And not necessarily good scotch," I busied myself fishing a tiny digital recorder out of my computer bag. The memory chip was empty. I hadn't had a single idea for the novel to record since leaving Providence on Wednesday morning.

Gollum closed his eyes and drank. A grimace almost formed on his face. "Tastes like burned butterscotch filtered through Groundskeeper Willie's moth-eaten kilt." He took another gulp. "You aren't joining me?"

"You bet your sweet ass I am. I'm not wasting all of that water of life on your ability to speak in tongues when you're drunk." I poured myself a healthy belt and topped off his glass.

"What legend am I supposed to channel this time?" He settled into the armchair and put his big feet up on the side of the bed. This could take some time.

Time I felt pressing close against my chest like a two-hundred-pound imp.

"I don't know what's going to come out of your subconscious or the ether. But last time you did this, you pointed us in the right direction based on local legends. Let's see what local spirits choose your brain as a vehicle to enlighten me." I sat cross-legged on the bed and stuffed pillows behind my back. Nope, the strained muscles in my thigh didn't like that. So I stretched out, my feet atop his ankles. A small connection. A familiar and comfortable connection.

The recorder sat on the table next to Gollum's left elbow. He took another deep swallow, grimaced at the burn, and turned on the gadget.

"If I have to guzzle alcohol, beer would go down easier." He took another belt. This time his face twisted only a little bit. He already grew a bit numb.

"Beer isn't strong enough. It would take too long." I sipped my own glass, respecting the miracle of decent whiskey as it should be. I don't know about filtering through a moth-eaten kilt, but I caught the burned butterscotch and the essence of heather in the blend. "And if you have to get stone-cold drunk, you might as well have the water of life." I saluted him with my glass.

He refilled his to the brim.

"And *if* I recite some obscure legend in an ancient and unspeakable tongue, who will translate for you while I sleep off the drunk? Presuming, of course, I could figure it out."

"I have my sources. Now drink up. It's getting late, and I'd like to get a little sleep tonight."

He downed his glass. His hands shook as he reached for the bottle. I took it from him and poured a steady stream. No sense in slopping good whiskey on the table.

One more glassful—I was still on my first, and he tipped

his head back. His eyes crossed and he smiled while his glasses slipped all the way off his hawk nose into his lap.

"Did I ever tell you how much I love you, Tess?" he mumbled.

"Um . . . not in so many words." What had I done to him? This was not my Gollum. But maybe it was. I took a long drink of my scotch. A new set of possibilities opened in my liquor-loosened brain.

What would it be like to have his long-fingered hands caress me with intimate care.

Shivers of delight ran up and down my spine, further numbing my mind.

Before I could pursue those thoughts, Gollum mumbled something I couldn't understand.

Anxiously, I leaned forward and held the recorder close to his mouth. I had to catch every word and nuance.

Without warning, he sat up straight, planting his feet firmly on the floor. I had to roll for balance as he dislodged my feet. His empty glass dangled from his hand.

His abrupt movement knocked the recorder out of my hand. He kept talking. Nonsense syllables to my ear. But I'm not a linguist.

"Shit! I hope we get all this." I fumbled around on the floor until I found the recorder under the lion's claw table leg support. Carefully I positioned it close to his mouth.

He stopped talking. His head rolled to the side, and he let out a snore.

Chapter 27

The highest recorded dealer tip in Las Vegas was $120,000 out of a $2 million pot.

I LEFT GOLLUM sprawled on the armchair, head lolling, drunken snores erupting from his mouth. I paused a moment to look back at him fondly.

Seemed like I was always postponing things with Gollum. Always the press of time on our missions when our emotions surged to the surface. On a normal day we walked politely around each other, careful not to tread on each other's toes or turf.

With the digital recorder in hand, I sought the bartender in the quiet bar on the opposite side of the lobby from the lounge. He looked up from polishing the bar as I entered.

Only one patron here at this late hour. The noise from the casino had dulled but kept going. With its convention-oriented customer base, this hotel did slow down in the wee small hours of the morning, unlike the bigger hotels closer to the Strip.

"I'm just going off shift, ma'am. My replacement will serve you in a moment." He looked tired, as if his night had been as long and fraught with emergencies as mine.

"Actually, I need to talk to you."

His eyebrows perked up, and he lost some of the look of fatigue.

"You said the other night that only local Native Americans venture into the Valley of Fire at night when they are on vision quest . . ."

"Yes," he replied slowly. A wall grew up between us, almost visible in the way his face lost all animation and his gaze found other places to rest away from me.

"I'm guessing you are at least part Native American."

He nodded.

"Do you speak or understand any of the local dialects?"

The relief bartender sidled into place beside him. "What can I get you ma'am?" she asked politely.

"We're just leaving. Together," my bartender said. He stashed his polishing towel and slid beneath a bar that blocked an opening between patrons and servers. "I'm not fluent. But I can at least recognize if it's Modoc or Paiute."

"Can you listen to a recording? It may be a local dialect or possibly something older." I held up the digital gadget.

He took it from me as he led me to a bench seat behind a potted palm in the lobby. "I'm not supposed to fraternize with customers, so let's keep this short and discreet." He looked around, barely acknowledging the sleepy desk clerks.

He turned on the recorder. Gollum's voice came out sounding strangely soft and lilting.

"I'm missing part of it," my bartender shook his head. Then he listened again.

"Please. This could be very important."

"It's very old. The language my great-grandfather used when he told the ancient legends of my people. He was the last full-blooded Paiute in my family."

"Do you recognize it?"

"Yeah. Even with the missing part in the middle."

I waited expectantly.

"You aren't a member of the tribe. You have no right to be in the places where you might have heard this."

"Believe me. I came by it legitimately. It's important."

"I'm guessing you aren't the normal Las Vegas tourist out for a weekend of fun and games."

"No, I'm not. I have connections in places you would not believe. Spiritual places." Dared I say more?

He nodded. "I won't give you my name, and I won't ask yours. This is between Warriors, though I've never met your kind before."

I nodded agreement. "I'll not repeat this to anyone who doesn't absolutely have to know in order to save their lives."

"Okay. It's a kind of riddle. I don't know the meaning. Only that it's connected to the vision quest my great-grandfather had when he became a man." He paused and gulped. "It translates loosely—very loosely as there are no modern equivalent words to a lot of it."

"Does it makes sense in English?" It wouldn't do me a lot of good if it only made sense in archaic Paiute.

"Maybe to you. It says: The moon awakes from a little sleep. It becomes a key held in the arm of a . . . a Guardian who is also a monster. That word is really not right, but it's the closest I can come."

"What does this moon key open?" A portal. It had to be a clue to a portal.

"It opens a path to twilight lands of peace and plenty, lands that a Warrior may glimpse but never enter. Only one Warrior will rise above the ties that bind him to this earth to walk between." He sat back and closed his eyes. The look of exhaustion returned, as if he'd channeled that bit of information instead of repeating a memory.

"Anything else?"

"Yeah. This recording cuts off before the end. My great-grandfather said that this key only works once in ten lifetimes."

I touched his hand briefly in thanks, and sympathy. "This was your vision quest, too, wasn't it."

"Yeah. Does it mean anything to you?"

"Not yet. But it will. The Powers that Be will let me know when I need to know."

"The Powers That Be?" he mused more than asked. "Do you fight alongside Breven Sancroix?"

Something in his guarded expression made me wary. "We trained in the same tradition, but I have never fought beside him."

"My instincts tell me that he is not to be trusted." He kept his eyes lowered to the recorder in his hands.

"Even though his nephew owns this hotel?"

"Especially because his nephew owns this hotel. He did not come by the majority shares honestly. He . . . he is not normal. His . . . you white folks call it an aura . . . his aura is not fully human."

He only confirmed my suspicions.

My informant lowered his voice further. "He doesn't talk about it, but I believe there is another stockholder. One who does not walk before twilight."

Abruptly, he dropped the recorder into my lap and left without looking back."

Gollum had left my room by the time I returned. I noticed he'd taken four bottles of water from the case in the bathroom. The best hangover remedy I've discovered is lots of cool clear water and as many aspirin as my tummy will handle, followed by orange juice or tomato juice in the morning.

As enticing as my bed looked, I couldn't rest yet. Still one more chore.

I tried Donovan's cell phone with another shot of scotch courage in me—the last of the bottle.

"What?" he growled.

"Sorry if I woke you. We need to talk."

"I have nothing to say to you. You've made it quite clear what you think of me."

"Don't hang up," I begged hastily. "Please. It's about the ring." I let that hang between us a moment, hoping he'd think I meant a possible engagement so he'd pause long enough to let me continue.

"What about it?"

"I saw the same ring in Lady Lucia's wedding portrait." I still hadn't convinced myself she really was a vampire and had lived during the Napoleonic Wars.

"You sure it's the same ring?" He sounded interested. Or suspicious.

"Pretty sure. It looked a lot like Gregbaum's pinky ring."

"You still at the hotel?" he asked.

I heard a rustle of clothing in the background and tried hard to rid my mind of the image of Donovan in the nude. Such a beautiful man on the outside. Why couldn't he be as beautiful on the inside? Or at least trustworthy where my heart was concerned.

"In my room."

"Alone? You don't need to answer that. The nerd is

there, too. Harder to separate you from him than it is from that imp of yours."

I didn't want to think about those implications. "Actually, I am alone."

Seconds later Donovan tapped at my door.

"You didn't check out of the hotel after all," I greeted him. "You just bribed the front desk to divert your calls."

"Nice to see you too, Tess." He bent to kiss my cheek as he pushed past me into the room. "What's this all about, and why do you have anything to do with Lady Lucia? She's more dangerous to you than you can imagine."

I swallowed my defensiveness. As long as Donovan had information I needed, I couldn't let my emotions lead us into another fight.

"Lady Lucia summoned us."

"Not good." Donovan took Gollum's place in the armchair. "Start at the beginning," he ordered me.

"You already know the part about the flowers and the tickets to 'Fairy Moon.' "

"But not why she sent them." I suspected a lie there. He knew, or at least knew part of it. I could tell by the narrowing of his pupils. "Talk, Tess."

My back bristled at his orders. I wanted to slap him. Or kiss him. I didn't know which. So I stood with my back to him and stared out at the lights of Las Vegas. After too many long moments I told him everything, from the beginning, from my first encounter with the wereweasel to Mickey disappearing.

"He's gone back to Faery for more information," Donovan muttered.

"Scrap says the entrance to Faery from the chat room is closed."

"Then how are you supposed to get the dancers back home?"

"Apparently there's a rogue portal in the Valley of Fire. Gregbaum's goons are guarding it. Lady Lucia thinks I can find it." And the nameless bartender had given me clues if I only knew how to follow them.

"You may be the only *human* who can find it," Donovan mused. He stared longingly at the empty bottle of scotch.

"Are you implying that Gregbaum isn't human?" I shuddered. Kajiri demons could transform into a human body in this dimension. Midori, or full-blood demons, could only shape-change in their home dimension.

"I didn't think Gregbaum was Kajiri, but from the way you describe him, he might be," Donovan mused. "How else does he have the strength to cast true magic?"

"What's his other half?"

Donovan shrugged.

"What about the ring?" I asked. "Does it have any special significance?"

"According to Tuscan legends, the Continelli family are magicians. But that talent died out around the time of Lady Lucia's 'death,' " Donovan said. "Perhaps the ring gave them the powers, and she took it with her when she um . . . left."

"Lady Lucia died. The family castle was burned to the ground in 1818, the entire family trapped inside. This lady is a fraud," I insisted.

"Are you sure about that, Tess?" Donovan asked. "Did they ever find *all* the bodies?"

"What do you know?" I rounded on him.

"Too much and not enough."

"Where'd you get the ring, Donovan? Why'd you choose that ring to propose to me with?"

"Marry me, and I'll tell you all I know." Donovan fixed me with a steady glare, daring me to refuse.

"You cheating bastard, that's blackmail!" I suppressed the excitement that warred with my anger.

Now what did I do?

Chapter 28

The Strip became the nickname of Las Vegas Boulevard because all the glitzy neon signs reminded a casino owner of Sunset Boulevard, also known as Sunset Strip.

"DON'T DO IT, TESS. Don't give in. I can tell you want the ring. It calls to you. You lust after it more than you lust after Mr. Stinky. And that is saying a lot." I call to her from my perch outside her door. I got back from my investigations just in time.

I can tell the ring must come to my Tess; if for no other reason than she could help me free the trapped imp from his diamond prison.

His fate scares me more than Mum does. I can't let him stay there any longer than necessary.

"Scrap, is the ring my next artifact of power?" she asks on a tight mental connection that Donovan will never intercept.

"Maybe, babe," I hedge. "Maybe not. Too soon to tell."

But I know. I know faery magic will make it fit her hand perfectly. I know it will safely guide her wherever she needs to go.

I don't know its history well enough to guess further. I only know it was meant for Tess.

But if she gives in to Donovan, he will be the death of me.

When I die, Tess dies.

I cannot let that happen. But how can I protect her when Donovan's presence pushes me away from my babe with a stronger spell than the protective web around the faery dancers?

I must find a way to separate Tess from Donovan. Maybe Lady Lucia can help. She wants the ring, too. She seems to favor Tess.

Hmmmm, I wonder why.

"If I married you tonight, what's to keep me from filing for annulment on grounds of coercion the moment you tell me everything?" I asked. Try as I might, I couldn't keep my face and voice bland.

There was more to this ring business than either Donovan or Scrap wanted to tell me.

"You have too much honor bred into you, Tess, to ever do that to me. And if you did plan on that, I'd still have a night in which to persuade you that you and I are meant to be together." Donovan stood up in one smooth movement. A step brought him to my side.

He didn't touch me. Yet he was so close, his warmth enfolded me in an aura that blotted out the rest of the world. His breath on my neck tingled all the way to my toes. My body tensed in anticipation of something wild and wonderful.

"You're right. I won't go through another quicky marriage in a drive-by wedding chapel. When I marry again, I'll do it right, in a church, with flowers and music, and hundreds of guests and a huge reception that costs the earth."

I had to step away from him. My head already spun with desire. I needed all my strength of will to keep from wrapping my arms around him and kissing his socks off.

"You'll never find out what you need to know . . ."

"I'll just have to ask Lady Lucia."

"Tess, no. She's dangerous. Even if she weren't a vampire, she controls criminal elements in this town that won't hesitate to eliminate those who get too curious." He reached a hand out to me.

I skipped away, as fearful of him as I was of any horde of demons.

Demons, I knew how to fight.

"The rules still stand. I can't marry you until I trust you. I can't trust you until I know the truth about what you are."

"I am a man."

"Now. What were you fifty years ago when you 'fell'?"

"How'd you . . . ?"

"King Scazzy, the prison warden of the universe, told me that you fell. What did you fall from?" That oh-so-real dream when I lay cradled in his arms rushed through me faster than I/we fell in that dream.

Something . . .

And Dill. What did my deceased husband have to do with his fall?

"A believer falls from grace," he offered, holding his hands out, palms up, in a universal gesture of supplication.

"That sounds close, but not the truth. Maybe you fell . . .

A flash of inspiration or memory or something very like a vision rocked me. Maybe something from the dream. The half-remembered sensation of wings falling off, the debris of a solid body shattering, the rush of fear and joy at the first sensation of movement after ever so long sitting and watching. Ever watching, never doing.

Failing in my/his/our mission because I/he/we couldn't move, could only sit and watch and let other powers overwhelm me/him/us.

And then another memory. This one was really mine. I had to grab hold of the entertainment cabinet to remain upright.

An autumnal rain in the middle of the high desert of central Washington State. I stood in the central yard of the Citadel surrounded by my Sisters of the Celestial Blade. A dedication ceremony for the newly repaired roof of the refectory. A line of copper-and-stone gargoyles on the edges, spouting streams of rain onto carefully placed plant groupings. One missing gargoyle failed to channel water off the roof. Instead, the empty place dumped a river of water onto Sister Gert's head. The rest of the Sisterhood had to suppress our giggles. Even then, three years ago, Sister Gert barely held on to the reins of leadership.

The broken gargoyle had been a bat.

The second time I'd seen Donovan, before we officially met, he'd been with a family group at a convention. All of them dressed very realistically as bats.

I shuddered in revulsion. Anything but a bat.

Donovan's foster father, my short-lived stepfather, had been a Damiri demon who took bat form.

Donovan had told me once that he was given to Darren for fostering because of a resemblance.

Dear Goddess, anything but a bat.

"Gargoyles are more than decorative rain spouts," I whispered.

Donovan blanched.

That told me all I needed to know.

"Which cathedral did you fall from?" I asked in fascinated horror.

"In a strange coincidence, Lincoln Cathedral, the home of the iconic depiction of all imps. I'll have to take you there sometime to show you the statue of Scrap's distant ancestor."

"Gargoyles are supposed to repel evil spirits. But you came to sympathize with them. You let them overwhelm you and invade a vital place!"

"I didn't consciously allow enemies into a sacred place. I was too young and inexperienced when I took the job. Gargoyles don't grow and change and learn after they assume a solid body."

"Is that why you are so dedicated to providing the Kajiri with a homeland? Because you sympathize with them, want to be one of them?" I really shuddered then. My teeth chattered with the ice that spread from my belly outward.

"No. I have other reasons for providing refuge to Kajiri."

"A refuge? A place where they can take their natural forms without prejudice. A place where they can eat what they need to sustain their lives—including human blood."

Blood drained from my head. Now I had to sit down. I wrapped my arms around myself and rocked back and forth on the edge of the bed.

How could I ever have thought I could have a future with this man?

How could I have ever let him touch me?

"You fell, all right. Fell from a noble calling, from honor and dignity. You have betrayed the very purpose of your creation! You have defiled your mission in life."

"I was ugly and reviled. Just like the ones I was supposed to banish."

"So the Powers That Be gave you physical beauty to teach you that there are things more important." I shifted so I didn't have to look at him. "How does Dill fit into this?

I shared your dream of falling, only to be caught by Dillwyn Bailey Cooper."

"You shared my dream? Do you know how rare that is? How special? Doesn't that tell you that we belong together?"

"Answer my question, Donovan."

He sighed and ran his hands through his hair. The braid loosened and softened the lines around his face. I had to look away or get caught in his mesmerizing trap again.

"Dill was there, an innocent who observed my fall, because he was attuned to changes in atmosphere and dimensional distortions. He transformed and rose up through a natural surrounding into a well of souls to catch me before I crashed. He sheltered me; gave me my first lessons in what it's like to be human. He and his family wanted desperately to foster me. But Darren Estevez got to the Powers That Be first. He convinced them that his stern chastisement was a better education for me than love and nurture."

I gasped and thought my heart would break. We'd waltzed all around the issue of Dill for months. I'd suspected his Kajiri origins but never had them confirmed. I still held out hope that this was just one more lie of Donovan's. That hope was mighty thin and fragile at this moment.

"Were . . . were you with Darren when he started the fire in our motel room that killed Dill? You owned the motel and profited from over-insurance." I knew Darren was guilty. Scrap had helped me travel through time to relive those awful moments. I'd watched Darren pull Dill back into the heart of the fire and knock him unconscious just as he was about to escape. But I couldn't identify Darren's shadowy companion.

If Donovan had been involved, I'd kill him right here and now. With or without Scrap's help.

"No. I was not a part of that conspiracy. Dill chose that motel because he knew I owned it. He wanted to spend some time with me before moving permanently to Cape Cod with you. Darren followed him there without my knowledge or consent."

I didn't believe him.

"Tess, I loved Dill like a brother. He and his family were the only bright spots in my life. Their love and friendship, even after Darren took me, gave me the courage to continue living; the courage to want to live as a human rather than a demon."

"Dill denied his demon ancestry," I said, as much to convince myself as Donovan. "He moved to Cape Cod with me to get away from his family, away from everything they stood for. Why can't you honor that part of his memory?"

"Because I watched him get physically ill, feverish, and aching in every joint when he refused to transform. Kajiri need to change on the night of the waxing quarter moon. It's a natural and necessary biological imperative with them if they have a demon ancestor within ten generations. But Dill wouldn't do it. He never felt safe doing it. He loved being human and loving a human woman. You. I want to build a sanctuary for mixed-blood demons so they don't have to make themselves ill denying who and what they truly are. Even the ones whose demon ancestry is so diluted they are barely aware of it. They *need* what I can give them."

"Dill risked everything to catch you in your fall."

"Out in the deep forest of Mount Hood. He was backpacking in the wilderness, collecting rock samples. No one around for miles. He could briefly transform and save me, or watch me die. He risked transformation."

The lights of Las Vegas blurred as I blinked away tears. That was my Dill. He took a small risk to save a stranger. He took a much bigger risk to save me during that fire.

"Tess, don't shut me out." Donovan knelt in front of me. He tried to take my hands.

I slapped him away.

"Go," I croaked.

"I suppose you're going to call Van der Hoyden-Smythe to comfort you in this new knowledge," he sneered.

"Just go."

I rocked and rocked some more, trapped in my own revulsion of him.

I barely heard the door snick closed behind him.

My mom wasn't there to help me through the tears.

Shaking with the knowledge of the power within the ring, and the horror of trapping an imp inside it for all time, I sneak back to the chat room.

There is a blackness within me. I could so easily have shared a similar fate with the black imp.

TRAPPED, held hostage, no way out. Forced to face his crimes day in and day out without respite.

With that much imp's bane in his system, and the magic of the diamond holding it in him, he'd probably forgotten how to open a portal even if he broke through. He has to be directed by the wearer of the ring.

If I had not found Tess and guided her to the Citadel, the one place that could save us both, I would have been banished from impkind, maybe given to the faeries so they could trap me, too.

I saved Tess from grief at the untimely death (murder) of her beloved husband Dill. Her anguish bordered on suicide.

She saved me from punishment for doing what I had to do to survive. According to imp law, I had no right to survive.

I probe deeper into the side corridor of the chat room.

The next window the ring takes me to is Earth. Medieval France to be specific. Another blacksmith. But this is no ordinary blacksmith. He plays with metal combinations and chemical formulae, seeking the Philosopher's Stone—that which will turn iron into gold, that which will answer all the questions of the Universe. Had he taken the route of a cleric and book learning, they'd have called him an alchemist.

By either name, he seeks to remove impurities from the ordinary to make it divine.

But he does not believe in the Church's teaching. He believes he can find God within iron and turn it to gold.

At this time and place, faith and religion are not separated. So they call him Noncoiré, the unbeliever.

I know all this the moment I see him. His blood sings with the essence of Tess. I read him as well as I read my dahling.

What is this? He gathers arcane herbs in the woodland, seeking poisons that will eat away at the metal, alter it, purify it, force it to transmute. In his primitive learning he believes that gold is pure. Iron is not. The concept of elements (the periodic table kind, not Earth, Air, Fire, and Water) has not surfaced.

His cat—a black male of course—that has become his familiar, stalks insects, tiny lizards, and mice. It bounds back to him with each new treasure. Monsieur Noncoiré exclaims with pleasure and caresses the cat with long and firm strokes.

I hate that cat already. I know it will do something awful. I just know it. Cats are only capable of inflicting horrible torture on other beings. And they purr while they do it.

But this is no ordinary woodland. The colors are a little too bright. Outlines and images just a bit too well defined.

I smell Faery.

Sure enough, just as this blacksmith yanks a mandrake out of the dirt by its roots, the plant screams. The preternatural screech obscures the sound of a faery popping into this dimension.

I don't need to hear it. I can smell it. Like cinnamon and lavender and warm comfort.

The cat smells it also and pounces. It comes up with a tiny white-and-gold faery in its mouth.

"Now, now, Balthazar," the man says in his ancient French. "Let the poor beastie go. You won't like the taste of him."

Gently, he pries the cat's mouth open and catches the wounded faery as it tumbles free.

"Well, well, well, what do we have here?"

"You have a king of the faeries, and I command you to release me!" the imperious little squirt says. He makes a big show of straightening his expensive clothes. They look a bit ragged and slimy from the ravages of the cat's mouth.

"I could let you go, inside my hungry cat."

"No, no, no. You don't want to do that." Kingy sounds scared. He's probably new to the job and hasn't learned how to outsmart a cat. (It ain't easy, friend.)

"Or I could let you go where you can get safely back to your own home before the cat nabs you."

Ah, Noncoiré is smart, or he's had dealings with faeries before. He knows how to bargain with them.

"I'd prefer the latter, sir." Kingy sounds scared.

"But my cat is hungry and I've naught to feed him. Except you."

The cat looks very sleek and well fed to me. Good thing there is a barrier of time between it and me, or I'd be sneezing my tail off by now. Funny how well-fed cats give off more allergens than skinny, stinky, mangy ones. At least for imps.

"Um . . . I could give you something valuable. You could sell it to *buy* food for the monster."

"Well, that would be nice. But even the village idiot knows that faery gold turns to dross the moment it leaves faery hands. No, no, I'd better just feed you to the cat."

"I have something else. Something more valuable than all the gold in France." Kingy is desperate now.

"And what would that be? I'll have to see it, hold it, and know it's not going to disappear before I can let you go."

Kingy frowns and drops his head. Then slowly he draws a ring from his finger and drops it into Noncoiré's hand. It grows to human size as it falls, landing solidly against the palm.

The stone winks and scintillates in the dappled sunshine. I hear a tiny crack in the Universe. The transfer of ownership of the ring has created a flaw in the diamond. A bit of the black imp's essence sends out a greedy probe.

Noncoiré gasps and opens his palm a bit to get a better look. A cunning smile replaces his astonishment. The power within the ring calls to him. But he doesn't know how to use it.

The faery flits away—on a drunken path because his wings are a bit torn—then pops back into Faery a whisker's width away from the cat's nose. He's lost the ring, he can't go anywhere but home, and only by the portal he came in on.

Maybe he didn't know the power of the ring. A long time has passed since its making. I'm thinking Kingy thought it was a symbol of his authority, sort of like the crown. Just part of the regalia.

So now the ring is in human hands. And no one knows what it can do.

And then I hear something else, the tiniest of sounds. Like a crack in the Universe opening. Just a little one. But enough for me to hear the black imp's scream of mental anguish. I must save him.

Chapter 29

As of 2000, because of the buffet, Circus Circus serves more meals than any other hotel in the world, 13,000 per day.

AFTER DONOVAN LEFT, I made my way back to the quiet bar and drank three more Scotches. The alcohol barely made a dent in my inner pain and turmoil.

At some point I must have moved on autopilot to brush my teeth, change to a nightgown, and crawl into bed. Scrap nudged me awake in time to shower and gather my supplies for classes and workshops.

By the time I joined my fellow writers at the breakfast buffet, I'd recovered enough to smile and reply politely to random comments. Mostly, I was numb. Numb in body and mind. Not even a hangover.

Gollum showed up as I pushed my scrambled eggs and ham around the plate, pretending to eat. He pulled an extra chair up to the round table filled with eager conference attendees. He straddled it and grabbed my toast off my plate.

"I had a productive evening after I left you," he said quietly. "Answers to a bunch of queries. You find anything interesting?"

"Oh, are you a writer, too?" one of the perky and eager writers at the table gushed. I'd forgotten her name. She had a couple of short fiction credits and her entry in the critique workshop for a full-length fantasy novel showed promise.

"Only academic papers," Gollum replied seriously. "Very boring stuff. Mostly I do research for Tess."

This set off a discussion on the value of research to the writer. I let the conversation flow around me, still avoiding thinking, avoiding eating, avoiding the fact that sooner or later I'd have to face Donovan again.

"Would you check to see if any gargoyles broke or fell from Lincoln Cathedral about fifty years ago?" I whispered.

Gollum's eyebrows shot nearly to his hairline.

Miss Perky heard me. "Oooooh, are you going to have gargoyles in your next book?"

"Maybe the book after the current work in progress." I hadn't thought about it, but yes, I could work gargoyles into my post apocalyptic fantasy novels involving a version of the Sisterhood of the Celestial Blade Warriors.

My best writing happens when my life sucks. I work through my inner pain by pushing it all onto my characters. That way I can examine it from all sides, find a compromise, dismiss it, whatever I need to do. Yes, I needed to work some very nasty gargoyles into my fiction.

Feeling began to return to my mind and my body. Good feeling, a need to work and be active again.

Maybe it was the fourth cup of coffee.

"Gramps got a line on the ring," Gollum said. "Go do your classes. I'll meet you in the lobby at two." He pulled out his ever-present laptop and logged onto the Internet.

"Any word from Mickey?"

"Not yet. But I think he'll be on time. He really wants to see that show." He let out a low whistle and clicked through several links.

"What have you found?"

"No record of a gargoyle falling at Lincoln Cathedral."

"Hmm, so he told another lie."

"Who?"

"Donovan." I had to change the subject here and now before my table mates asked too many awkward questions. "Any legends about the Valley of Fire and vision quests show up on your radar?"

No, Tess. Don't do it. Don't even think about going there. Scrap jumped off his perch on top of my head and flew an agitated pattern from one light fixture to the next.

"Strangely enough, very little. Mostly academic explanations of the petroglyphs. Very PC and mundane. If there are local legends of a more spiritual nature, no one repeats them to outsiders," Gollum said, following his gargoyle links around the Internet.

"Keep looking." I shoved my chair back and collected my folders of papers.

"Mind if I finish your breakfast first?" Gollum asked, only half joking.

"Be my guest."

"Never known you to turn away from food before," he muttered, grabbing clean cutlery from an empty table.

I grumbled something and left him to my leavings.

A thought hit me square in the middle of my chest, strong enough to rob me of breath. Gollum deserved better.

His tongue loosened by alcohol, he'd confessed to loving me.

He deserved more of me than just friendship.

My first husband had died over three years ago, after a whirlwind courtship of four days and three months of marriage. I'd banished his ghost for good last month. Part of me knew I needed to move on. Part of me still felt attached to Dill.

A part of my heart had broken off last night when I sent Donovan packing. I felt betrayed; leery of trusting my heart again.

Was there anything left for Gollum? Could I give him, or any man, more than friendship right now?

I really needed to talk to my mom.

Strange, I'd never wanted to turn to her with my emotional problems when she hovered around me like an overprotective mother hen. For nearly two decades she'd tried to live her life through me. But now that she'd flown the coop to find a life of her own, the one person who'd understand my dilemma wasn't there. Talking to her by phone wasn't enough.

Junior showed up at my morning class. "Is It Love Or Just Sex" was about the very fine line dividing a sensuous romance from erotica, and keeping either from slipping into porn. If Junior did indeed want to write a romance involving the inner workings of Las Vegas, he might need this workshop.

I spent a lot of time emphasizing verbs and emotions. A couple of men in the group wanted more graphic details. I pointed out the difference between experiencing love and reading an engineering text. I had more than a few memories of my night with Donovan to remind me.

"Some people get off on observing from a distance," I said, toward the end of the two-hour period. That idea came from my visualization of Donovan as a hideous bat gargoyle sitting silently and watching the sordid details of life for eight hundred years.

"The modern reader of genre fiction," and Donovan too, "wants to experience the emotions as well as the sensations. If we just want anatomical details, we can get a vibrator and rent some porn."

Donovan had the experiencing sensations down pat. I doubted he had mastered allowing emotions into the equations. One or the other, but not both at the same time. His humanity was incomplete. He hadn't spent enough time with Dill.

Neither had I.

Feeling better about myself and a lot of other things from this weekend, I dismissed the class to their lunches.

Junior lingered behind, grabbing me as I passed him to leave the room. I stared at his tight grip on my upper arm with all of the disdain I could muster.

Scrap landed on top of my head, glowing hot pink. He blew smoke into Mr. Twitchy's face.

Belatedly, Junior removed his hand, wiping it on his slacks as if stained or soiled. Maybe just sweaty. He looked as nervous as ever.

Let me at him, Tess. Let me give him a taste of his own violence.

I muttered something.

Scrap faded, still pink, still grumbling, but less ready to transform.

"I've got a couple of chapters of my book ready for you to look over," Junior said.

"I never agreed . . ."

"Doesn't matter what you agreed to . . ."

"Junior, mind your manners," Mom said, coming up behind him.

Only Mom could make this guy think about anything but his own self. Yeah for Mom.

"No one invited you, demon whore."

Mom gasped and reached for her pearls, a talisman.

Scrap turned vermilion and stretched.

Before Junior finished the phrase, I had my hands around his throat and his back against the wall. I didn't need Scrap for this. I wanted to inflict violence myself.

His skin paled to near perfect sculpted marble, his ears elongated to a point and the slant of his eyes shifted. The exquisite beauty had twisted to something terrible, angry, vengeful, more frightening than Gregbaum's mutant faeries. And as with those blood-red goons in black leather, I caught an energy signature of wings.

Changeling, Scrap gasped.

An old legend. Faeries are near immortal and rarely have children of their own. But their desire to raise a child and experience the joy of seeing it grow and learn approaches desperation. So they will, upon occasion, substitute one of their own, shape-changed into an infant—for a human child.

I can taste his magic. He set the spell around the faery dancers!

And I bet he was extremely bitter about his exile from Faery. He had to have arranged the kidnapping of the dancers and the enlistment of the mutants. Gregbaum, the *mortal* magician with no talent was Junior's puppet and front man.

That was why he had a pass to the show for himself, Breven and . . . and Sister Gert, the woman he *called* Mom.

As if he'd heard Scrap, Junior snapped back to normal mortal appearance.

"Apologize to my mother, you slimy worm," I said through gritted teeth. My mind spun with implications. He must be the shadow investor in the show.

"It's what she is," he whined. His eyes darted back and forth, lighted briefly above me on Scrap, then returned to face me with something akin to bravado.

"Despite your *opinion,* which I do not value at all, my

mother brings a lot of customers into this establishment. You should at least respect the money she makes for you and keep your mouth shut!"

He gulped and I felt his Adam's apple bob beneath my hands.

"Now, are you going to apologize or do I squeeze the life out of your miserable hide."

This guy needs to go back to Faery, fast, Scrap decided. *Too bad the portal is closed. You and I could zip him through the chat room faster than he can think.*

"Genevieve signed a contract. I don't have to . . ."

I squeezed harder until he barely breathed. "Her name is pronounced Jahn-vee-ev."

Couldn't do better myself, Scrap chortled. He blew more smoke, making Junior's breathing even more difficult.

"Tess, you can remember your manners as well. You, at least, had the advantage of a loving mother to beat some sense into you," Mom said mildly. Almost too much calm in her voice. If she'd been me, I'd start looking for a place to hide.

"His mother abandoned him to relatives when he was a baby," she continued. "That's no excuse I realize, but . . . no daughter of mine will stoop to his level of boorishness."

Now that was the mother I knew and loved. And respected.

"Remember, Junior, verbal abuse is grounds to invalidate that contract. Also grounds to sue you for your shares of stock in this hotel. I think about now that your silent partner would be more than happy to get rid of you." I eased up on my grip, but kept him pinned with my malevolent gaze.

I'm surprised a silent partner has put up with him this long..

"If you could just get me in to see Lady Lucia . . ."

"If she's your partner, why do *I* have to get you in to see her?"

"She stopped taking my calls months ago. She's trying to leverage me out."

"Then I'd think you'd bend over backward to be polite to my mother, the woman who is bringing in extra revenue and solidifying your position. And me, since Lady Lucia provided me with VIP tickets to sold-out 'Fairy Moon,' invited me to a private party, and *wants* me to see the show again."

I shook my hands and then wiped them on my slacks.

"She's waiting for that apology."

Junior's gaze darted about again, looking for an escape, from me as well as the apology.

Scrap and I hemmed him in. I took one step closer, hands raised.

He looked like he'd vomit.

"I . . . I apologize, Ms. Noncoiré, for repeating the opinion of others without thinking."

"That will do for now," I sighed. "Want to have lunch, Mom? Junior's buying."

I might even put up with his presence just to find out who dripped the venom of that opinion and why he got tickets to "Fairy Moon" for his mother if she deserted him when he was a baby, leaving him with Breven Sancroix to drag him through childhood any way he could.

I wondered if Breven knew he'd raised a changeling. And what happened to his real child?

Scrap, if we send Junior back to Faery, will his other self be returned?

How in the six hundred sixty-six hells am I supposed to know? That's a faery secret and they have never talked to anyone about it. Ever.

One more thing to talk to Mickey about.

Chapter 30

Prostitution is legal, and highly taxed, in much of Nevada; however, it is not legal in Las Vegas.

IF LADY LUCIA is Junior's silent partner, then I need to know what she plans. I zip through the chat room, barely lingering long enough to flutter my wings twice let alone get noticed by whoever is on guard duty today.

I come out in Lucia's parlor. It's deserted and totally tidy. I smell pine cleaner, the same brand Mom uses—used—on Tess' house. The place is silent, so I prowl, keeping to the ceiling—no one ever looks up.

The ageless and ancient lad servant sleeps like the dead in one of the little interior, windowless rooms. His bed is a coffin with a handful of dirt from his native land scattered on the bottom. Maybe he really is a vampire. I can't be sure since I've never met one before or had them confirmed in imp demon chronicles.

The sound of water gently lapping against tile draws me to the central bathroom and that huge hot tub meant for six. But only two occupy it this morning.

Donovan and Lucia.

Not a stitch of clothing on them. Her sun-deprived whiter-than-white skin is firm and smooth with only a little acceptance of gravity on her lovely, rose-tipped breasts. She's so beautiful she could almost tempt me to start loving females.

His muscles ripple sleekly beneath his nearly hairless coppery skin. A magnificent reminder of why I find men so enticing.

They make a couple that look good together. I bet their personalities fit, too—opposing strengths, weaknesses, and tempers.

The bubbling chlorine-filled water that reflects the deep blue tile in the tub can't mask the scent of their recent joining. The musk lingers in the air like a gentle aftertaste.

They are both pushing out hot and heavy pheromones that tell me there is more to come.

I'm quite happy to hang around the outside of the open door and watch.

But their conversation is what draws me as close as I can get.

"You don't seem so weary of your humanity now as you did at dawn," Lucia whispers. She runs a big toe up his inner thigh, letting it caress him in his most sensitive parts.

"I don't know, Contessa. The delights of a body, or your body aside, I just don't know what I'm doing right and what I'm doing wrong. It's all so confusing." He grabs her foot and brings it up to his mouth, sucking on each of her toes. His free hand drifts toward her ample breast, just barely breaking the water's surface.

"You are doing that precisely right," she gasps, very near to coming. "What is so confusing about enjoying every sensation the Universe inflicts upon us? The good as well as the pain." She purrs in response to his tugs on her toes followed by a vicious little bite.

"The emotions," he sighs. "There is no logic. I don't know if I feel anger, or fear, or jealousy, or love. I don't know *how* I'm supposed to feel when, or with whom."

Lady Lucia throws back her head and laughs loudly. "Welcome to being human, my lovely Donovan. No one can figure out emotions. That's what makes life so delicious."

"As delicious as you." His hands move around her breasts, nipping and kneading fiercely.

"If you are truly ready to give up all this . . ." She scoots closer to him, pulling her foot free from his mouth and draping her leg across his lap. Her hand caresses between his legs and gains instant and elegant response. "The Powers That Be owe me a few favors, or they will when I right the balances in Las Vegas. I can get you returned to your hideous gargoyle existence. You can sit and watch and do your job silently rather than have to figure out how to properly interact."

"I'm not that much of a coward," he growls. He's responding to her ministrations with enthusiasm.

"You wouldn't have to go back to that boring old Citadel and the copper body of a bat. I'd get you a new position, a prized one at Notre Dame de Paris. Perhaps somewhere in Florence and a dragon body beckons you more?"

What!

Donovan was previously a copper bat overlooking a Citadel?

I grow faint with this discovery.

No wonder he makes his human home on Half Moon Lake in Central Washington State. His magnificent glass-and-cedar house that lets him look out on the world from a private island is only twenty-five miles from the place where he looked out and watched the world from the refectory roof of my babe's Citadel.

This is too rich to keep secret. But now is not the time to tell Tess. Maybe later, when it's all over, she'll appreciate the irony.

I leave them to their activities that begin to grow violent. He bites her nipple hard. She shoves his face away with a fierce grasp of his chin. He pulls her hair back. She pinions his hands against the pool.

"Again, so soon?" she laughs as she yanks him up and onto his back on the tile floor with more than human strength.

"I'm never satisfied. Not even by you." Then he whispers or broadcasts telepathically, I'm not sure which. I have to strain to listen. "Except by Tess."

He flips Lucia over, capturing both her hands in one of his as he prepares to enter her most vigorously.

"Don't tell her that," Lucia giggles. Her ears are better than mine; that makes her otherworldly if not a vampire. "If you do, she'll never let you off her leash long enough for you come back to me or any of your other companions."

He seems most determined to banish his frustrations in this act. I hope it works and keeps him away from my babe for a while.

This would be fun to watch if I had the patience. Maybe I'll just nip over to that Citadel and enjoy a little of these dominance games with my own Ginkgo.

At five minutes to three, Gollum, Mickey, and I entered the Dragon and St. George and headed directly toward the theater.

Watch your back, babe, Scrap nearly screamed in my ear as he darted up to the ceiling of the adjacent casino. *Mr. Stinky is in the building.*

Sure enough, Donovan stood tall and steadfast in front of the curtain separating the casino from the theater entrance.

"You can't keep calling him Mr. Stinky, Scrap. We know what he is now, so he doesn't smell wrong. He smells of what he was, combined with what he is," I replied.

Whatever. I still say he stinks.

"What are you doing here?" Gollum snarled at his rival.

Mickey hung back, hollow-eyed and silent, as he'd been since he picked us up at The Crown Jewels twenty minutes ago.

"Lady Lucia's orders," Donovan spat back. He turned and threw the curtain to one side.

"Since when do you take orders from anyone?" I asked, squeezing through the slight opening in the metal gate.

Donovan muttered something. His face remained dark and resentful. His five o'clock shadow had expired and reached well beyond the wee hours of the morning.

How long since he'd slept, eaten, or shaved?

Too long by the angry set of his shoulders and clenching fists. Maybe Scrap was right. He did carry a certain unwashed quality.

I didn't need the magical comb, which lay hidden in my pocket, to know he hurt deeply.

My heart skipped a beat in the knowledge that my rejection of him had brought him this low.

It's all an act, dahling. Believe me, he's not as depressed as he wants you to think.

I had to remind myself that he had *betrayed* his life mission and his creator. He'd been *condemned* to being human raised by a Kajiri demon for his crimes.

Would he have turned out more complete, less ruthless, with a different purpose in life if my Dill had raised him instead of Darren Estevez?

He might have more morals, Scrap laughed, reading my thoughts.

I'd never know.

The curtain dropped behind us, shutting out the clang and clatter of the casino. The sudden silence and dim lighting of the theater lobby distorted my perceptions. I instinctively took up an *en garde* position. Only a little pull on my thigh warned me I hadn't completely healed yet.

At least I'd worn decent shoes this time.

But I had no weapon today. Scrap was exiled a good ten yards from me as long as Donovan was anywhere near. Or until overwhelming demon evil threatened me.

Did Lady Lucia know that when she ordered Donovan here?

More important, what sort of blackmail had she used against him? Nothing less would coerce him into doing something he didn't want to do, or didn't earn him a great advantage, or a great deal of money.

A phalanx of six mutant faeries in black leather greeted us. I jammed the comb into my hair, letting the tight curls grab hold of it.

Instantly a dark mist enveloped the faeries. I saw the energy signature of wings on their backs; great leathery and ragged-edged things. Normal eyes couldn't see them. They used up a lot of energy concealing those wings. I had a small advantage in that knowledge.

If these guys weren't evil, I didn't know what was. Scrap should be able to break through Donovan's force field if things got nasty. Or is that nastier?

Not until they threaten you, babe.

Then Gregbaum emerged from the center of his palace guard, dwarfed by them, but radiating a confidence that diminished them.

My gaze zeroed in on his pinky ring.

Gollum followed the track of my eyes and raised his eyebrows in question.

"It's a fake," I said dismissively. At least it didn't radiate an aura of magic as I expected. It just sat on his finger, but something . . . pulled at me, demanded I take the ring from him, use it as it was intended.

Gregbaum didn't have the power or talent to activate whatever it was. It wanted me, knew I'd use it to its full capacity.

I don't know if it existed entirely in this dimension.

Looking at the producer's pudgy fingers, I judged it could be the same size as the ring Donovan offered me. Was it the same ring, a duplicate, or just a fake?

There are no coincidences, Scrap reminded me from his perch atop the curtain rod behind me. *That ring keeps cropping up. You may need it to finish this adventure.*

Gregbaum bristled.

"He's a fake. No wonder Lady Lucia dominates him," I added with a derisive smile. I needed to keep him slightly off-balance.

"Tess, don't," Donovan warned.

"You have your agenda, Donovan. I have mine. Right now I want to see the show. I have Lady Lucia's private invitation for me and my entourage. Are you part of that?" With a slight gesture, I drew Gollum and Mickey closer.

"Lady Lucia called me an hour ago to inform me that I let you in or face her wrath. I admit you with extreme prejudice and reluctance." Gregbaum stepped aside a half step. His guards remained sternly in place.

"Noted. I won't engage a weapon unless they do," I stated the terms of this temporary truce.

A brief nod from Gregbaum and a narrow passage opened for us into the theater.

My skin crawled as I passed through the ranks of dumb muscle. Gollum and Mickey kept as close to me as they could without actually sharing the same skin. Donovan entered the theater a distant fourth.

Inside, the VIP circle was filled with cameras, lights, sound equipment, and crews. More of the same had taken up positions on the musicians' ledge and the varied levels of the stage. A quality production.

If Lady Lucia closed down the show in three more days, Gregbaum still had a money maker in the DVD.

Three days to negate any spells the smarmy producer and Junior had placed on the dancers, find the portal, and return them to Faery.

"This isn't your fight, Tess Noncoiré," Gregbaum said.

"If not my fight, then whose?"

But Gregbaum had already disappeared into the bowels of the backstage.

I wanted a different perspective from my first viewing of

the show. So I took a seat in the third row to the left of the cameras.

Mickey and Gollum sat on either side of me. Donovan pointedly walked around to the opposite side, where he could watch me as well as the show.

Scrap breathed a sigh of relief and flitted back to me.

Within seconds the cameras began rolling and the music came up. Once more the story, the dance, the music, and the magic of "Fairy Moon" sucked me in. My hair comb revealed the special magic of Faery shining through the performance, giving me glimpses of laughter, beauty, kindness, and joy. Qualities all the other dimensions needed to share.

If the human dimension had twisted Junior to the polar opposite of true Faery, then Donovan was right. We didn't need a demon ghetto to balance our goodness and light. We were often our own demons.

For endless moments I became a part of it all. I knew that if even a small amount of Faery's brightness dimmed, all the dimensions became poorer. The Juniors and the mutants would have a free rein to wreak havoc.

The action never stopped for camera or lights or tech problems. A true performance from beginning to end.

About halfway into the first act I jolted back to reality. The faces of the dancers were absolutely blank. They performed by rote.

My attention wandered to the set; an open garden, an oasis set in the middle of a forbidding desert, complete with tinkling fountains and false gaiety. A metaphor for the city of Las Vegas. The caterpillar on the mushroom reminded me of the hookah-smoking character in *Alice in Wonderland*. Another metaphor for the addiction of gambling, bright lights, glamorous shows, and more gambling.

The full moon set on the action as the lights faded for the end of the first act. My attention pricked. Full moon was the time demons' strength waned and portals closed.

We waited a scant ten minutes for the dancers to rest and gulp gallons of water. They lounged about the stage, watching the set and lights change. Gregbaum stalked around, shouting orders, growing angrier by the minute. Change this, adjust that.

"No," the dancers said as one. They flowed upright and

into position between Gregbaum and the set piece of the rock goblin. "We dance as before or we do not dance at all."

Mickey tensed beside me. "Gregbaum does not want you to see the truth within the set," he whispered.

Across from me, I watched Donovan jerk out of his slouch. He, too, noted that something was up.

More shouts. Some dancers slunk off stage. Others held their ground.

Scrap flitted about, invisibly tweaking hair and blowing cigar smoke in the faces of the stagehands who stood about in indecision.

"This theater is haunted," one of the hands said, waving smoke out of his nose. He made the sign of the cross and looked around nervously.

Gregbaum threw up his hands and contented himself with shifting camera angles. The DVD probably would show very vague impressions of the set rather than details.

"I've got to get closer," I whispered to Gollum.

He stayed me with a hand on my knee. "He'll notice and use that as an excuse to throw us out."

"I'm not on his radar," Mickey whispered. As he spoke, he slithered down to crawl along the narrow aisle between rows of high-backed seats. He really did have acrobatic talents. Quickly, he disappeared into the shadows. A hint of movement at the edge of the pit showed his progress.

The theater grew black.

Music drifted to life on a slow eerie flute note. Lights came up on the stage. Cameras fixed on the red rock goblin. Faeries crept out of holes in the stage.

A waxing quarter moon rose behind them all. The time when the walls between worlds thinned and portals could be unlocked. If you had a key.

Only at that time did the Celestial Goddess reveal herself in the heavens: the quarter moon defined her cheek, starscapes became her eyes and mouth, the Milky Way streamed away from her as hair blown in the celestial wind. When Scrap became my blade, he mimicked that configuration.

Everything glittered in the coruscated light. My eyes refused to focus, trying to follow the randomly blinking and scattered lights rather then settle on any one object. A blank spot appeared beneath the goblin's arm. That tiny circle absorbed the light rather than reflecting it so that it appeared a black hole.

"Gollum, what's the moon phase?" I gripped his hand tightly where it rested on my knee.

Waxing quarter on Monday night, Scrap answered for him.

This was Saturday. Not much time. A lot to do before then. I could only lead the faeries to safety on Monday night when the moon revealed the portal within the rocks.

I still needed Donovan to complete the task.

Chapter 31

A fire raced through the MGM Grand on November 21, 1980, claiming eighty-five lives.

TOO SOON, we reached the climax of the show. I held my breath as the little girl faery paused one last moment to drink in the awesome majesty of the desert embodied in one tiny yellow flower; so different from her home and yet so very beautiful in its own right.

As the portal grew smaller and smaller, I wanted to shout to her to hurry. My heart nearly broke when she tried to fly through and hit solid rock.

Once more I *had* to stand and clap, slowly, methodically. I had to let the world know that I believed in faeries and my belief gave them life. Gollum rose beside me, tall and determined. He increased the pulse of our clapping. Then Mickey added his own applause from the pit area, and Donovan, and the camera men, and the stage crew. We all made this a truly live performance for those who would only share the magic by DVD.

At long last, the portal opened a fraction and one long arm reached through to help the lost faery go home.

One huge group sigh of relief and it was over. I felt restored by the show. At the same time I knew sadness because it was the last time I would see it live. There could only be a few more performances before the show closed forever, and the dancers either died or I led them home.

I knew what I had to do next.

"Mickey, can you examine the spell on the dormitory and somehow find its weak spots?" He nodded. "Gollum, rent us a car, probably something with four wheel drive. Noon tomorrow. We're going to the Valley Of Fire."

"What are you going to do?"

"Besides the awards banquet tonight and my final class tomorrow morning?" I smiled sweetly.

They exited the theater ahead of me, heads bent in consultation.

I hung back, fading into the shadows beside the exit.

Sometimes I can become a chameleon. With a shift in facial muscles and posture, and a tug on clothing to alter its shape, I lose my distinctiveness. With Scrap's help, I can even adjust the shade of my clothes.

No Scrap this time. I set him to watch from the musicians' ledge.

"You can't hide from me, Tess," Donovan said as he came abreast of me.

"I don't want to hide, I just didn't want you to notice me until you were too close to avoid me." I took his arm possessively and walked beside him into the lobby. He didn't pull away from my grasp. Good. I knew he could. He had lots of honed muscle beneath his black polo shirt. He'd bested me more than once on the fencing strip.

He paused in the center. "What do you want?"

"I don't suppose you'd let me borrow that ring?" I tried to look innocent.

He scowled. "Why?" He wasn't going to make it easy on me.

"It has properties I need to complete my mission." I turned to face him, keeping my hand in the crook of his elbow.

"I don't have it anymore."

Damn!

"Then I'll just have to tell Lady Lucia you lost her treasured wedding ring." I stepped back and withdrew the slight connection of my hand on his arm.

"Lady Lucia!" he exploded. "I bought that ring in Paris last December. From a reputable antique dealer. I have provenance back to 1850."

Interesting. He had the ring a month ago when I refused to mother his children without love and marriage first. He had it when he ran from my rejection into bed with Wind-Scribe, who now carried his child.

"Did you give the ring to Gregbaum after I refused your proposal?"

"I sold it to him. At a handsome profit."

"He used to be close to Lady Lucia, possibly intimate with her. He had to have seen her portrait wearing that ring and recognized it," I mused out loud. "What made you buy that particular ring besides its beauty and value? There must have been others offered in the auction."

"There were. But I knew at first glance that ring was special. I catch glimpses of power in it, but I can't access it. Can you?"

I shrugged. "I only know that it begs me to wear it."

"If I thought he'd give it up, I'd buy it back and give it to Lady Lucia." Donovan turned as if to leave.

I grabbed his arm once more. "Please, Donovan, buy it back. I'll reimburse the money. I'll give it to Lady Lucia when I'm done with it. Please. I really need the ring to save the faeries."

"How? How does it work?"

"I don't know yet. I only know I need it."

Scrap, talk to me, tell me everything you've found out! I knew he'd been investigating, not how far he'd ranged in doing so.

Donovan stood there, challenging me to say more.

I met him glare for glare, equal in stubbornness and determination.

We stood there so long, Gregbaum slithered out of the theater, stopping short within a yard of us.

"Why are you still here?" he snarled. His face grew red. A sure symptom of high blood pressure. Maybe he'd keel over with a heart attack and I could just grab the ring off his hand.

"Sell me the ring, Gregbaum," I demanded.

"No. Why should I?"

Because it is an artifact of power. It only partially exists in this dimension. You can't control it. If you try, it will burn you up. That last was just a guess. But I couldn't say any of that out loud.

"Because I'll tell Lady Lucia you have it if you don't sell it to me or let me borrow it," I said. "She might even invent a new drink in your honor: Bloody Gary. Or do you prefer Gregbaum smoothie?"

The pudgy man blanched beneath his high color.

"I don't have to keep it from Lady Lucia. I might even make a present of it to her. With the proviso that you never get your hands on it." He folded his arms across his chest, calm again, face a more normal shade.

"What if I tell Junior Sancroix you have it?" I smiled sweetly.

He grew white again but held firm. "Go ahead. He can't do anything more to me once Lucia closes down my show."

"Can't he?" I tried to raise one eyebrow and only succeeded in twisting my face into a grimace.

Donovan quirked his left eyebrow up. I'm sure he did it just to best me. He was in that kind of mood.

"Fifty thousand, cash. Now. Otherwise I'll bury it out in the desert where you'll never find it."

I blanched this time. I might be able to lay my hands on that kind of cash given a week to liquidate some savings and stocks. A lot of stocks. Maybe raid my IRA.

"That's twice what I sold it to you for," Donovan snarled.

"Fifty large is half what it's worth," Gregbaum returned.

"I'll give you thirty in an hour. That's five grand in profit in two days. I'd say a pretty good return on your money," Donovan snapped back.

Thank you, I mouthed.

"I'm not doing it for you. I want credit with Lady Lucia for giving it back to her. It's a whole lot safer for her to owe me favors than the other way around." He stalked off, leaving me to face Gregbaum on my own.

If I could get it back to Lucia, she just might let me borrow it Monday night. She wanted me to rescue the faery dancers.

"You'll never get your hands on this little treasure now. I know Donovan. In fact, I may just let him have it for the twenty-five grand I bought it for. Just so's he'll let me open a new show in his new casino up in Half Moon Lake."

"He abandoned plans for a casino and is building a much smaller spa." I'd witnessed his signature (in blood) on the refinancing after his original casino building collapsed into a rogue portal when I closed it last autumn.

"Did he? I hear he's in Vegas looking for new investors.

Why do you think he's talking to Lady Lucia? She doesn't care who—or rather *what*—patronizes his 'spa,'" Gregbaum tossed over his shoulder as he turned to leave.

"You can't open a new show without new dancers," I called after him.

"I've got access to dozens more." His disembodied voice echoed ominously around the tile and marble lobby.

I need to do more research on that ring. Tess won't need me at the awards banquet, though I do love to watch her glow with satisfaction when she wins.

Maybe I'd better postpone my trip until I help her get all gussied up. She is absolutely helpless when it comes to clothes. She'll mix gold with silver jewelry, cover her shoulders with a shawl that clashes with her gown, and put on mismatched shoes. She's even been known to forget to brush her hair. A total fashion disaster.

Once she's set, I'll flit off to track that ring from Tess' ancestors to Lady Lucia. Then I'll find a way to get it back to her.

Hmmm, if it's only partially in this dimension, maybe I can grab it right off of Gregbaum's hand from inside the chat room.

After I know more. Can't drop it in Tess' lap and have it burn her up because she doesn't know how to use it.

Now for some fun dressing dahling Tess. That midnight blue number will have to do. No time to shop for something new and it is quite suitable for the occasion. the strappy black sandals with two inch heels—she's never comfortable in anything higher—will set it off and not strain her pulled muscle. Silver jewelry, I think. And I might be able to add some more sparkle to the chiffon. She lost some of the original sequins and beads climbing out of the gondola and the remainder are too subtle and already dimming in luster.

Yes! Silver glitter. Too bad I can't get back into Faery for some sparkle. Who else has some?

Pixies?

Tricky. They aren't as giving as faeries. There's always a cost and hidden condition with a pixie. I'll have to call in some favors and make promises with my fingers crossed. Might even have to let them tie my tail in a knot.

But my Tess is worth every bit of it. She'll look marvelous tonight.

She'll look even better when I get that ring for her.

So how did it get from the Noncoiré family of blacksmiths to Lady Lucia?

Once more I stand looking through a window in time. We've moved forward a lot of centuries to eighteen fourteen. The same remote village, on the slopes of the French Alps where the first Noncoiré tricked a faery out of the ring. Italy is just over the pass of the mountain visible in the distance. I bet the local language has as much Italian as French in it.

My lock on the ring takes me back to the same woodland. Another Noncoiré blacksmith reclines against a tree, powerful legs stretched out into the grass.

And he's naked. Magnificently, rawly naked except for the ring on a leather lacing around his neck. Oh, my. I have to mop up a little drool. This youth's muscles ripple cleanly beneath his sleek skin. And the way he stretches promises much prolonged delight. His blond curls look like gold in the dappled sunshine.

He glows with health and energy and optimism. He should. A young Lucia nestles beside him, equally naked. Her skin is smooth with pampering. No ugly calluses on her hands or feet. She doesn't work, or walk much, and her shoes must be custom made. Her black hair is sleek and tossed up into a casual do that probably took her maid hours to achieve.

Hey, isn't she a blonde now? Oohh, the secrets only her hairdresser knows for sure.

Nearby, an elegant palfrey nibbles at the greenery. She rides everywhere. Must have some noble blood and money in the family.

So this is an illicit love affair. The daughter of the local lord slipping out to tryst with a commoner. And not a bit of protection between them. Doesn't she know the consequences?

She whispers sweet nothings into the blacksmith's ear. As she speaks, she wiggles her body along his, enticing him to new—um—lengths of passion.

She is well practiced in these arts and probably not a virgin for all of her maybe fifteen years. At least that's how young she looks. I'm beginning to believe that looks are deceiving.

I notice that she speaks good French, hardly a hint of the thick Italian accent she affects in modern society.

Our young man responds with enthusiasm if not exactly gentleness.

Lucia matches him in passion and eagerness. I could watch these two lovers all day. Their passion is raw, not violent like she indulges with Donovan now. They remind me of my precious moments with Ginkgo.

When they finally finish and lie back all sweaty, panting, and satisfied—me, too, for that matter—Lucia dallies with the ring on its chain.

"A good luck charm. Been wit' me family for generations," the young man explains. His accent is thick, local and uneducated.

"Does it bring you luck?" she asks coyly. Her long dark hair dangles across his chest, tickling him.

He wraps a curl around his finger and tugs gently until her mouth reaches his. They kiss, openmouthed, devouring each other for endless moments.

I sigh. Young love is so sweet.

But I'm not convinced Lucia is entirely sweet. Her left hand has never left the ring.

"I call it luck that you favor me," young Noncoiré says. He's breathing hard again.

Oh, the stamina of the young. I may get another show.

"This ring should be a token of our love. As long as we have it, we can find ways to be together," she replies. "This ring is special. Magic."

"I'm off to war soon. Emperor Napoleon needs all Frenchmen to rally for his next campaign. France will rule the world again." He sounds as if he believes that claptrap.

How else can ambitious generals con men into following them into hell and death?

"I hate the thought of you leaving me! You could be captured. You could die. And I'd never see you again." She pouts prettily, a practiced look. Her hand clamps tighter around the ring.

If he takes the ring with him and dies, she's lost more than just a lover. And she knows it.

"That's the cost of bringing France back to her rightful place on top of the world."

I snort in derision.

"Perhaps I'd better keep the ring for you. Just in case." She clasps the ring tightly, keeping her hand and her body in close contact with him.

Deep in my mind I hear a chortle of triumph. That is a new voice, neither Lucia or the young blacksmith.

"*Oui*, ma sweet. It is my gift to you, so that you never forget me." He slips the leather thong from his neck and places it around hers.

Gods and Goddesses! It's the imp within the ring. He's using the tiny crack from the last transfer of ownership to leak power and enticement. He needs Lucia to own the ring because . . . I'm not sure why. But she offers him more hope than the peasant blacksmith.

Again she holds it tightly, covetously.

A tiny niggle of doubt wiggles into my mind. I'm not as sure as I was before that I should release that imp.

And then they are at it again. Their hands and mouths explore, nip, pinch, taste, and stroke. I watch them avidly, forgetting all about the black imp and the ring.

Their world goes transparent on me. I have nothing else to learn here.

Except in my last quick glimpse, I know that Lucia will never forget her strong blacksmith. Her first true love. The father of her child.

Does she know that Tess includes the son of that blacksmith in her family tree?

I bet she does. The name alone should give away the connection. No wonder she favors Tess with flowers and tickets to "Fairy Moon." I bet she also knows all about the Sisterhood of the Celestial Blade. She knows about me. She knows that Tess and I are the only ones who can rescue the faery dancers.

But we need the ring to do it.

Chapter 32

Downtown Las Vegas (Freemont Street as opposed to the Strip) is sometimes called Glitter Gulch because of the proliferation of big neon signs.

GOLLUM MET ME at the elevator on the convention floor. His dark blue suit with the crisp white shirt fit him perfectly. For once, his glasses sat firmly on his nose, where they belonged. He'd even combed his soft blond hair. The only mar on his perfect demeanor was the blinding tie filled with cartoon space aliens.

"I've gotta have some fun," he said, blushing.

"I like it. Sometimes these award ceremonies get a little too tense: as if they are more important than the books they honor."

He nodded. "Academic stuff is a lot more pretentious. The competition cutthroat. You look wonderful by the way."

I twirled in my sparkling cocktail dress. Who knows where Scrap found the extra glitter, or how he affixed it to the chiffon,(I'd lost more than a few sequins climbing out of the gondola and over the bridge at the Venetian) but it added just that extra dimension that made me feel special.

Gollum offered me his arm in escort.

Shyly, I took it, acutely aware of his masculine scent, his lean body, and a new layer we added to our friendship.

He stood a foot taller than me, even with heels. Still, we managed to match our strides and fit together.

For once I didn't want to talk about our mission. I just wanted to spend time with my friend.

We took our places at a round table for ten. A female mystery editor I didn't know and a male agent who specialized in Romance fiction already sat there. She was into her third drink and fidgeting anxiously, looking longingly into her purse. Probably at a pack of cigarettes.

She pulled out a cell phone and stared at the screen, willing it to ring.

So much for clichés. I wondered if she had a sick child at home and needed to check in with the family.

The male agent might not look like a romantic hero with his spindly frame, balding head, and ill-fitting suit, but he certainly knew how to market them.

I expected the other six places to fill up rapidly with conference attendees who wanted a chance to chat with our table mates.

Within moments, my mother floated in, looking elegant in a cream-and-gold outfit, with gold clips in her graying blonde hair—which had new highlights. Behind her walked her housemate Penny and the tall man with a Stetson we'd encountered outside the theater a few nights ago. The agent and editor looked grateful when I introduced them. They'd probably been inundated all weekend with unpublished writers seeking an "in" in the publishing industry.

"I wanted to share a moment of triumph with you, Tess," Mom said kissing my cheek. "I haven't supported you very well in your career."

"You kept house for me for three years so I could get on with the work." I kissed her back. "That was more help than you can imagine."

"But I didn't give you the emotional support. Now I understand the necessity of that. I want to be the first to hug you when you win this award." She preened a bit as if my triumph was all her doing.

"I haven't won yet." I didn't go on to say that this regional writers conference award didn't carry a lot of prestige. Yet. If they continued to put on a top quality conference like this weekend, it would gain in importance.

"Who's your competition, Tess?" Penny asked. Her eyes moved constantly, weighing and assessing everyone in the noisy crowd. She looked a little more careworn and dowdy than the first time I met her, more like the aging woman with more bills than income that Mom had described.

"A mystery writer and a historical romance writer," I replied, pointing out the man and woman in question at different tables.

"Lightweight stuff," Gollum muttered.

I tilted my head in silent question.

"I read them both. You're a shoo-in."

"When did you read them?" I asked. He hadn't known he was coming until Thursday.

"On the plane Thursday night. I read yours, of course, when it first came out. Got my first edition hardcover autographed, too." He cocked me a grin that warmed my heart.

And suddenly I knew that I loved him. My heart seemed to swell until surely it would burst. My gaze locked on his, and the room faded to insignificance.

I just knew that my heart was safe with Gollum. Donovan could back me up in a fight, to keep me from physical harm. But Gollum protected *me.*

I squeezed his hand beneath the table, promising . . . I didn't know what precisely I promised, only that we would talk.

My heart skipped a beat. But not from Gollum's gentle caress of his thumb across my palm.

My body knew before my mind did, that Donovan walked into the room.

He looked magnificent, as always, freshly showered and shaved, wearing a custom tailored black suit, gray shirt, and silvery tie. The white slashes at his temples added distinction to his already noble profile. Every woman in the room, and quite a few men, riveted their attention on him as he wove through the tables. Quiet and calm followed in his wake.

Gollum immediately withdrew his hand from mine. He seemed to shrink inside himself as well.

I grew cold inside.

Mom didn't need to wave to catch Donovan's attention. He zeroed in on us—or me—the moment he passed through the door.

I heard a few sighs of disappointment as he bent to hug my mother with one arm. "You look lovely, Genevieve. I hope I get to hear you sing later." His eyes met mine above her head. Cold, yet burning with resentment.

Penny and her date shifted to allow Donovan to sit next to Mom. At least I didn't have to look at him across the table. Or feel his body heat beside me.

Instinctively, I edged my chair closer to Gollum so that our thighs touched. Our hands found each other again like magnets to iron.

Only two places left to fill at our table. The pretentious romance writer who wanted to rest on her laurels claimed the seat next to the agent. "I'm thinking of changing agents for my next project. Are you interested?" she demanded before she finished sitting.

"Talk about rude," Penny said, rolling her eyes.

The writer didn't seem to hear anything but the agent's mumbled comments about needing a formal query and proposal.

"I'm an established writer. You need only look at my previous success," she humphed and shifted her chair.

"In this business you are only as good as the next book," the agent insisted and turned his attention to a writer at the table behind him.

The editor waved over Jack Weaver, the gentleman I'd met the first night who wrote police procedural mysteries. Obviously a friend, or client.

Did we have enough critical mass to overcome the negative vibes coming off Donovan and the romance writer?

Any further discussion was interrupted by waiters in formal livery bringing salads and taking drink orders.

Fortitude flew in, scouting the room. I didn't dare follow his progress by turning my head and looking up. No one else could see him.

But I did check out the door, a normal action. Both Sancroix men stood, waiting and assessing. They wore suits that needed pressing with their ties loosened. From the flush on Junior's face, I wondered if he'd been drinking.

Then I spotted a squarely built woman behind them. She wore an ill-fitting and dated gray taffeta dress that matched her bluntly cut short hair.

Sister Gert. Sancroix had suggested an old relationship with her. I thought I'd seen her in the distance at the St. George and Dragon. Something was up. Something strange.

And Scrap wasn't around to scout for me.

Gert's imp, Juniper, remained firmly on her shoulder. Maybe it was just the shadows but he looked darker than I remembered.

"I'd go greet Breven and his new wife, but I really don't want to talk to Junior," Mom whispered.

"New wife?" I nearly choked.

"At first I thought he was courting me, very attentive. Then I realized he was merely making me more comfortable singing in Junior's hotel."

"Hey, Tess, you going to sing tonight?" Jack Weaver interrupted. "I really enjoyed that victim song."

His question distracted me from the newcomers. They took seats in the corner, their backs defensively to the walls. The two imps took up positions near the ceiling, two dark smudges against the white-and-gold scrollwork decorations.

"*My Fairytale*," I corrected Jack, forcing my attention to my immediate companions. I gave him enough information to find the CD on-line.

"Yeah. That was really fun. I've been doing some web searches. I may have to change genres just so I can go to SF conventions and do more filk."

"Actually," his editor interrupted. "We're starting a new imprint of SF/F mysteries. If you could set one of your usual styled stories on a space station and extrapolate forward some forensics gadgets, we might be able to open you to a new market and keep the old one."

"I've been wanting to try out a scanner that would pick up from an eyeball the last thing a victim saw . . ." Jack mused. "I'd have to find a way to prove it's reliable. Then I could get someone to screw with the settings or implant the wrong image . . ."

"SF readers tend to be pretty omnivorous," I added. "Once they discover you, they are likely to cross over and read your backlist."

"Then I can legitimately go to cons and enjoy more filk!"

Gollum took up the thread. He had a nice light baritone and filked with me at cons.

Donovan, however, avoided the free-for-all song fests. Though we'd met at High Desert Con last autumn, and he professed to be a fan, I'd only seen him at one other, in the Bay area when he and a family group dressed as bats.

At that fateful con in the high desert, my best friend from college had died tragically and unnecessarily. Gollum had stayed with me and helped me deal with the aftermath. Donovan had gone off to coddle and hide the children of some half-demon clients who had actually struck the killing blow on my friend.

I was better off with Donovan out of my life.

But I still needed his help getting that ring, and maybe the extra body to rescue the dancers.

The rest of the evening passed in a blur of animated conversation and decent food. It was an awards banquet, after all. The food was standard fare, but nicely prepared and not overcooked.

Then Tanya, the organizer, took her place behind the podium. A nervous hush fell over the crowd. After the usual speeches and introductions, the guest editors began handing out the awards: cover art, short fiction, small press fiction, and lastly "Best Genre Book of the Year."

Mom took my hand and held on tight.

Gollum took my other hand and pointedly kissed my palm.

Donovan continued to glower.

I lost to the historical romance writer. This was largely a romance-oriented crowd after all. Resignation rather than disappointment filled me. Fatigue crept up my spine.

"Well, now I can get back to work," I muttered. I flicked my gaze to both Donovan and Gollum, so they'd know which job I intended to get back to.

They both nodded.

"After I listen to my mom sing, of course," I added.

We all laughed and adjourned to the lounge.

Tess has settled in with Gollum. I am so happy. He's the man she belongs with, not Mr. Stinky who never has smelled right, even for a fallen gargoyle. Stone and copper and desert sage and something rotten at the core don't add up. I knew those scents never came from Lincoln Cathedral like he claimed. Now I know they come from the Citadel. There is more. Much, much more to learn.

I'd also like to know what Fortitude and Juniper are up to. Somehow, they don't belong here, and not together.

The next window in time I find in the chat room, only a few years have passed since Lucia bartered sex for the ring. As I look over an ancient villa in Tuscany, I sense that the young blacksmith is no longer in the picture, either as far as the ring is concerned, or in Lady Lucia's life.

I zero in on a walled garden. A gnarled old tree props up the western wall. Graceful benches of sunwashed stone rest beneath the shady boughs. A central fountain shows a nude nymph pouring water from an urn.

Long shadows fill the garden as the sun drops behind the western hills.

Lady Lucia, now a more mature and full-figured woman (she's about twenty now by my calculations) plays with a blond toddler, probably a boy. A strand of pearls graces her neck—a typical wedding gift. Most pearls look alike to me, I haven't studied them like I have that diamond on her hand. Something in this strand whispers to me that I should recognize them.

The little boy screams in delight and chases dandelion fluff she has blown for him. I guess he might be three. I do not know human children. They grow more quickly than imps. But they die sooner than we do, too. Unless the imp faces a murderous sibling. Then we die quite young.

Or should, if the murder goes as planned and doesn't backfire.

But I digress.

A very angry count paces the garden. His dark hair and olive skin have little or nothing in common with the child. He's at least forty, maybe older.

Lucia seems very unconcerned for the amount of rage pouring out of her husband.

"Send the child away. I will not look on him."

"I prefer to keep your son close." Lucia brings the child into a tight hug that ends in a tickle. He laughs delightedly, finding much joy in life and in his mama.

Oh, that I had ever known such joy and love!

"That is not *my* son," the count spits. He is in a towering rage now. Spittle forms at the corners of his mouth. His swarthy skin takes on red hues from too much blood. He looks like he could stroke out at any moment.

"You acknowledged the boy at his birth," Lucy reminds him.

"I did not know then what I know now. Who is his father?"

"I have slept with no man since our marriage," Lucia spits back. I think she's actually telling the truth. "Not that you have taken me to your bed very often. You seem to find the boys in the scullery more to your taste!" Now she's mad, too.

Ah, he's a man after my own heart, but a bit too long in the tooth for me. I like my men young and firm and strong. He might have been a soldier once, but now he's had too many years of soft living and frequent loving. His belly sags and his jowls flop when he walks.

The babe senses the anger and begins to cry. Both parents ignore him. He runs to his mama and beats on her lap, demanding she fix this upset.

"But what of before our marriage?" the count yells. "You pushed for a quick wedding after your father and I agreed on the marriage contract."

"I will not dignify this discussion by answering you." She rises gracefully and gathers the child to her bosom. He cries pitifully against her shoulder.

"The villagers already whisper that I am cuckold," the count sneers.

"Better a live cuckold than a dead vampire. They also whisper of that. They compare you to some ancient Carpathian who dined on the blood of his enemies."

The count has the grace to grow pale with fear. " 'Tis not me they call vampire—but you. You and the changeling child!"

"Only because you feed their fears and direct them away from yourself toward me."

Before he can respond, angry shouts from the front gates spill into the closed courtyard. There is only one escape from here, through the villa. While they argue, the sun sets and the quarter moon rises.

I smell fire. Fire within and fire without. The villagers surround the villa. The walls may be of stone, but the floors and ceilings are old wood. Rotting wood. The once rich furnishings are brittle with age. One torch thrown through a window left open to catch the evening breeze begins an inferno.

The count tries climbing a wall.

The villagers catch him and drive a stake through his heart. Then they pour over the wall in search of his mate.

Lady Lucia twists the diamond-and-filigree ring on her finger. She twists and twists as she prays for deliverance.

A door opens in the air. She does not question it, does not look back. She takes with her only the clothes on her back, the pearls around her neck, and the child in her arms.

And just before she steps through, I see the pointed ears, elongated teeth and folds of bat wings beneath her arms.

Some distant, very distant, ancestor of hers was a Damiri demon; the same as Donovan's foster father Darren, and apparently Tess' husband Dill.

Chapter 33

Even though summer temperatures soar to 110F for days on end, the average daily temperature in Las Vegas is only 66.3F degrees, due to relatively cool winters.

THE AWARDS CEREMONY seemed to adjourn *en masse* to the lounge. The winner and her friends needed to celebrate. The losers and their friends needed to commiserate. Drinks flowed fast and furious.

Mom ran through a series of upbeat show tunes before crooning a trilogy of bluesy torch songs. Once again, she managed to make her last note a long, haunting, melancholy memory. This was more than faery magic. It was Mom magic. My mom.

Her audience seemed almost in shock, on the verge of poignant tears. They'd go home with that note lingering in their minds for a long time.

I wished I knew how to do that with words at the end of a novel.

While Mom took a breath and a sip of water, my table mates pushed me toward the stage. "What do I sing?" I asked Gollum.

"'Bimbo.' What else?" We both laughed. The crowd was well populated with book people. They'd appreciate the greatest filk song ever written.

Easy enough to get Mom's accompanist to play "She'll Be Coming 'Round the Mountain." Looks of puzzlement passed around the crowd.

And then I sang, soft and jazzy, imitating my mother's caress of the microphone, "There's a bimbo on the cover of my book."

A slow ripple of laughter beginning with Gollum and Jack Weaver spread outward in ever wider ripples.

By the time I got to the verse about a rocket ship on the cover that isn't in the book, I had them all laughing and clapping.

Good thing the audience picked up the chorus for me. I nearly choked at the sight of Lady Lucia, resplendent in a fringed red sheath straight out of the Roaring Twenties. She sparkled and glittered, the waving fronds of her dress shifting like waves on the sand. Her entourage of pale young things in black leather faded into the background. Lucia's fangs gleamed in the spotty light almost as bright as the long strand of pearls dangling from her neck.

But those modern cultured pearls couldn't hold a candle to the luster of the shorter strand of older, Mediterranean pearls on my mother's throat, about an inch and a half from Lucia's mouth.

In three steps I was at my mother's side, thrusting the mike into her hands and pushing her back to the stage, away from the red menace.

"Stay away from my mother," I snarled. "She's innocent and off-limits to your games."

"What about you, *cara mia*? Are you off-limits, too? What about your boyfriend?" Her gaze lingered on the angry pulse in Gollum's throat.

"I'll complete your mission on time. Then we are done."

"If thinking that makes it easier for you to do as I requested, then go ahead and believe it." Lucia pouted prettily and left abruptly. Her followers had to hastily down their drinks, or place them unfinished on tables to keep up with her aggressive stride.

"How have you managed to avoid getting killed in a car accident?" I asked Gollum as I clung to the hand rest above the passenger door of the SUV he'd rented.

"What do you mean? I've never had a ticket. I'm a good driver!" he said as he drifted across the center line of the northbound freeway to the accompaniment of honking horns and flipping fingers.

"When you pay attention and don't speed." This relationship might go nowhere fast if he got us both killed. "Scrap's not around to whisk me out if you crash this thing."

"Oh, okay." Dutifully, Gollum checked his mirrors, put on his turn signal and crossed over to the righthand lane of I 15. Within a few minutes his speed had crept back up to fifteen miles an hour over the speed limit.

I sighed and made sure my seat belt was snug.

"You can come back anytime, Scrap. Donovan's not with us," I called into the ether.

Um, babe, how badly do you want that ring?

"Why? What did you find out?" I translated for Gollum.

Um, only that it's yours by right of inheritance according to some very ancient laws. Lady Lucia had no right to sell the ring to feed herself and her child.

"Scrap, if she was totally broke and starving, I think that's an excellent excuse to sell the ring, especially to feed her child."

"Wait, a minute, did he say Lucia had a baby? Vampires can't have children," Gollum interjected.

"Depends on the timing," I said. "If she had the child before she became a vampire."

"Scrap, did you find out if the ring will help me complete this mission?"

No answer.

"What did he say?" Gollum asked. This time he slowed down to half turn toward me.

"Nothing. He's gone again."

"The turnoff to the Valley of Fire is just up here. Scrap's view of the place would really be helpful."

I sat in silence, gawking at the undulating landscape. At one time, something like two hundred million years ago—you'd have to ask my deceased husband the geologist for more exact details—this entire area had been under an inland sea that cut the North American continent in two. Gently rounded layers of multicolored sandstone flowed up and down with ripples revealing ancient tidal and current action. Mostly creams and yellows with occasional hints of rust and brown didn't show the promise of the fiery landscape I expected. Some of the hilltops and mountain peaks twisted into jagged outcroppings born of volcanic action and earthquake upthrust.

Towering clouds built up from the south, casting it all in weird yellowish light. I picked out sharp details on one rock formation and lost the next in shadow.

"I didn't expect so much plant life in the desert." I shifted back and forth looking at new green foliage and bright yellow, pink, and red flowers.

"End of April. Two-week window for wildflowers when the winter rains are balanced with the increasing spring sunshine. Not that there's that much sunlight today. We might get some rain out of those clouds," he muttered as he slowed to a crawl onto the access road. The narrow two-lane (more like one and a half in places, no shoulder) pavement wandered around following a natural depression.

"Look at all those cairns! Stop, I want to take a picture." I was out of the car, camera in hand, almost before he finished pulling up the emergency brake.

This was a scouting expedition, after all; never know when something weird that attracts my attention might turn out useful.

I knelt before a two-foot-high pile of stones. Someone had carefully balanced each rock atop another into a kind of memorial. I'd read about rock cairns in Celtic lands many times, marking the location of the death of a loved one, a special romantic tryst, a sacred spring, or even an ancient peace treaty.

"I wonder if Scottish sheepherders brought the custom with them?" Snap, snap. A bunch of pictures loaded onto the memory chip. Strange, the automatic flash came on for one but not the next.

"According to my source, the locals call them Hoodoos," Gollum said. Of course he'd read all he could about this area before coming with me. He was an anthropologist. He'd left me at the door to my room last night with just a gentle peck on the cheek so that he could bone up on this place. "No one will tell me what the cairns are for or why they call them Hoodoos. It's possible they trap evil spirits, or ward against them. Perhaps they commemorate successful vision quests. There are certainly a lot of them."

Long lines of rock piles, ranging from tiny to several feet high, marched off into the distance, mostly lining the road.

"I like to think some of them at least mark the moment a couple fell in love. Some of the ones in Britain do that." I sighed, remembering fondly each and every one of the men I'd loved, from Bobby Smith in third grade up to my husband Dill, and then, in a strange erotic needful way, Donovan.

And now . . .

"I like that tradition."

Quickly, Gollum wrapped an arm around my waist and drew me close. His mouth hovered over mine.

I held my breath, savoring the quick intensity of the moment.

And then I rose up on tiptoe, he bent his head, and we met in an explosive kiss that chilled and warmed me from crown to heel. We melted together, arms and bodies entwined. Our lips melded, then parted to allow tongues a more intimate exploration.

"Wow," I whispered several long minutes later.

"I've wanted to do that since the moment I met you, back on that hillside in Alder Hill in the aftermath of an attack on adolescents by a hell hound last September." His breath brushed my cheek.

Passion flared in me again. The two inches that separated us was too much. We kissed again, slower this time, sweetly and gently, exploring possibilities.

Chapter 34

Card counting, while not illegal, is highly frowned upon. Not many casinos use fewer than three decks to discourage the practice.

TESS NEEDS THAT RING to open the portal for the faery dancers. I'm the only one who can get it for her. Once she's completed this mission, I have to find a way to free the imp inside. No creatures, no matter how bad they are, no matter what crimes against the universe they have committed, should be trapped forever inside a diamond prison.

The facets reflect only that imp's image. He must examine his crimes over and over again until he goes insane or repents. Even then there is no escape.

Only more insanity.

He calls to me through the cracks in the diamond. He tells me of his agony. I share it. I have to free him.

Since I'm already in the chat room, tracing the ring, I'll just pop along to see where it is now.

Gregbaum still has it on his pinky finger. He hasn't sold it back to Donovan, nor has he given it to Lady Lucia.

For once the slimy lounge lizard is alone. Actually he's sitting on the john, just like any normal human being. PeeeUUuuuuu. He stinks worse than I do. Wonder if he knows about milk and what it does to a sensitive tummy. He probably doesn't care. He's so angry at the world he must think his indigestion is the result of a conspiracy against him fostered by Lady Lucia.

The ring bulges through the fabric of time and dimension,

as much in the chat room as it is on his hand. That's because of the imp inside. Now if I can just wiggle my body into that translucent fabric of woven energy, sort of half merge with it as if I'm about to pop into that stinky bathroom with Gregbaum.

I have to stay right on top of the ring and slide my talons around it.

Nope, that won't work. It slips out of my grasp, moving partially into another dimension of time and space.

Hmmmm.

I catch my claws into the elaborate filigree, making my energy part and parcel with it.

YES!

Now I just wiggle it downward, ever so slowly, pausing at the swollen knuckle. A second talon pulling on the other side of the ring activates the bit of faery magic in the metal. Inside Faery, everyone is the same size. So I have to let the ring know it needs to change size to fit the next recipient.

Gregbaum gives off another smelly grunt. He clenches his fists.

Ugh. This is one of the most unpleasant jobs I've ever done. I'll take Mum's freeze-dried dump any day. Nothing smells when frozen that deeply.

Oooh, ahhh, I kind of grunt along with Gregbaum to encourage him.

At last he relaxes his fingers and the ring pops off his hand and into mine.

Before he can notice it's gone, I'm fully back into the chat room in firm possession of the key to any dimension.

Oh, crap. Which rhymes with Scrap. My claws scratched Gregbaum and drew blood and smeared the ring. Now—if he knows how—he can track me or the ring through any dimension.

I'm betting that Junior knows how.

No time to think, or gloat. I've got to get this thing to Tess, the rightful owner now. It's hers, both as a descendant of the first Noncoiré and a descendant of Lady Lucia's son. I've checked the family tree Tess' sister Cecilia keeps. The first Noncoiré to leave France for Quebec was indeed the fair-haired boy. Somehow, Lucia must have taken him back to his grandparents where he grew up not knowing his true heritage—human or demon.

Tess isn't going to like that little bit of information. I can only hope that the demon in her is so diluted with human blood that she can't accidentally transform into a bat under extreme duress or anger. I don't think Lucia knew her own heritage when she escaped Tuscany. If she did, then she would have transformed and flown over the wall and out of harm's way.

Tess' blood is almost two hundred years more dilute. She should be safe. I hope. She's never ached to transform at the quarter waxing moon like other mixed bloods.

I think Lucia knows her connection to Tess. The name is not common. And she has this fondness for my babe. If she knows, then I doubt she'll harm her descendant. After all, she went to great lengths to protect her child. The family ties are blood ties. Tess' blood calls to her great, great, multigreat grandmother.

Not harming Tess doesn't mean she will go out of her way to protect Tess.

I pray my babe is safe.

I can't smell any demon in her, and I bonded with her like any good imp will bond with a human Warrior. Never heard even a whisper of imp and Kajiri pairing up.

So let's just keep that a secret from her for now. She really hates bats. Fears them, too.

Cecilia has a lot to answer for. It was she who scared three-year-old Tess out of her wits in a bat Halloween costume. Scared her so much that she quakes in fear and goes all sweaty at the mere mention of a bat.

Gulp. Maybe her phobia really stems from knowing deep in her hind brain that part of her wants to take on the natural bat form of a Damiri demon.

Later. I'll deal with all that later.

Right now, I'm going to drop this ring in her lap just to see how she reacts.

Now, where is Tess?

A sharp wind swirled around us.

"That storm is likely to dump rain soon. We'd best get going," Gollum said, sounding as reluctant to separate from our kiss as I.

"The sooner we see what we need to see, the sooner we can return to the hotel." I swallowed my smile. We both knew what would happen back at the hotel. Tingles ran all through me like champagne bubbles in my blood.

"Right." He kept looking into my eyes, almost reading my mind.

Well, my thoughts were pretty close to the surface.

Before he could tug me back to the car, I bent and placed two loose stones together, the little one atop the other. "Ours."

Laughing and holding hands, we climbed back aboard the huge SUV.

"What do you think the Hoodoos are for?"

"I don't know. No one wants to talk folklore about this place, though they'll talk forever about the stories depicted in the rock paintings," Gollum rambled on, much as Gollum was wont to ramble about favored subjects. Just one of the things I love about him. He's a wellspring of information.

"There's one string of images of a steam train and a trestle that depicts an actual wreck in the late 1800s. Another very ancient one shows a tragic fall of a young man from a high place and the ordeal he and his father went through getting him back home. The obvious truth behind these incidents leads anthropologists to think the others are more than random graffiti."

"I'd like to see some of those paintings. Maybe they'll give us some insight, or directions."

"First stop is the Visitor Center. The best petroglyphs are beyond it."

The road climbed a slight hill and turned a corner . . .

"Oh, my God!" My mouth fell open. Towering walls of red filled the valley below. Single weathered rock formations stood out in a barren plain of brown. Clusters of rocks nestled together in fanciful outlines. Tall mountains with rounded slopes and sheer cliffs. Cave openings, arches, everywhere signs of time's slow erosion.

All red.

As if the rocks themselves burned with an unholy fire.

Chapter 35

No reliable dating process exists for petroglyphs. In cases where the images were created by scraping off the black patina, regrowth of a new patina suggests approximate time spans.

GOLLUM DRONED ON ABOUT iron in the rock. I didn't care. I twisted and turned, afraid I'd miss something.

"We've got to find the Goblin Rock. Just like the one in the show," I said over and over.

"This valley stretches for miles. There are side roads and trails. People get lost hiking around here. And there's no water."

"Then look for activity of the mutant faery on steroids kind. I'm sure Gregbaum has set them to guard his private portal."

"Maps at the Visitor Center. And photos. We'll find the goblin, but it's going to take some time."

"We only have today. Waxing quarter moon tomorrow night."

"And a fierce storm building. Looks like enough water in those clouds to cause flash flooding." Gollum sped up, taking the twisting road a little too fast for my taste. But he got us to the Visitor Center in only a few moments.

Inside, native art, sculpture, and baskets tempted me. CDs of music and books made my fingers itch and my credit card burn. Lots and lots of books. I needed to examine each and every one. I needed to talk to the people who worked here. If only I had the time to totally immerse myself in the magic of this beautiful valley.

"Have you ever seen a rock formation that looks like a goblin?" I finally asked one of the guides.

"Um. Describing a particular formation is very subjective." The young woman wearing the gray-green ranger uniform cast a wary glance at a large group of people milling around. With jet-black hair pulled into a ponytail and a coppery cast to her skin, I guessed that more than one indigenous aboriginal lurked in her family tree.

All the people in the group she indicated wore badges that boasted a large cross in each corner with barely enough room for the name in the center.

How politically correct of her. Don't use the goblin word in front of church-going tourists.

Gnashing my teeth, I turned my attention to a rack of postcards. Lots of different views naming the rocks innocuous things like "Lion" or "Turtle."

"I've got a line on some petroglyphs that might help us," Gollum said. He tugged on my arm and handed me a stack of maps, books, fliers, postcards.

"Spend your entire expense account?"

"Not quite. But I may come back for some of those baskets worked around deer horns. Magnificent examples of symbolism for my classes."

I liked the way he placed a firm hand at the small of my back and leaned close to speak to me. He radiated clear signals that we belonged together. I envisioned us going on together like this, working closely, sharing ideas and careers and goals, for a long, long time.

Funny I never had thought of a distant future with Donovan, only a passion-filled present.

Hot monkey sex isn't everything.

"I don't suppose you fence?" I asked as we climbed back into the car.

"I know the principles and can quote the rule book, but no, I do not engage in that violent sport." He looked sad.

I wanted to reach out to him comfortingly. "Oh, well, we'll find other things to do together." Damn, I was hoping to replace Donovan as a sparring partner.

The next stop in our quest was an area called "Mouse's Tank." We drove north from the Visitor Center along a two-lane paved track imitating a road. Buses and cars filled the tiny parking lot. As we drove in, three buses hastily loaded their passengers, all of them anxiously looking at the sky.

Luminous white clouds with black underbellies roiled higher and higher. Rain soon. I hoped we had time. An intense storm could wash out the roads. Good thing we'd opted for four-wheel drive.

"Late 1800s, an outlaw Indian hid out here for months. It's the only reliable water source at the surface in the entire valley," Gollum paraphrased the pamphlet he read. "It's rich in petroglyphs."

"And there's an interpretive sign." I pointed at a large set of drawings covered in plexiglass and mounted at eye level.

Gollum opened the back hatch and retrieved a hefty looking backpack.

"What?"

"Two years in the African bush. I learned to never venture into an unknown area without supplies." He clamped his mouth closed.

"The two years you spent in the Peace Corps?" Those years had come into question before—by Homeland Security and the Marines no less. I wondered what secrets he guarded regarding the dark continent.

"Yeah, the Peace Corps." He slung his arms through the pack straps, and walked to the sign.

He looked over the top of his glasses at drawings and nicely lettered translations. "Some of these are okay. Some of them have been whitewashed to make them politically correct—but no one will admit that. We'll be better off taking a bunch of digitals and downloading them into the laptop. Then we can interpret them ourselves." He set off down the marked path with long strides, too absorbed in the anthropological treasure to remember me.

I shrugged and followed. Good thing I run five miles most mornings when I'm at home. I had to pump my legs double time to catch up with his long strides. A sharpness in the stretch of my inner thigh reminded me I'd hurt myself, badly, only a few days ago.

If we did indeed become a couple, would my life be one long catch-up with his brain and his long legs?

"The footing is tricky here." He paused at a slight drop-off, holding out his hand to me with a grin.

He hadn't forgotten me after all. I clasped his fingers. My world brightened far more than the gloomy cloud cover should have allowed. The three metal stairs installed by the parks department—or whoever maintained the trail—were covered in sand and looked a bit rickety. The jumble of rocks beside them didn't look any steadier. We balanced each other and jumped to safety.

We walked about one hundred yards hand in hand, comfortable together. We fell into a rhythm of steps that almost matched.

"This place is truly ancient," I whispered. "I feel like an intruder into sacred space."

"Me, too. It's something akin to the atmosphere inside a cathedral. Something waiting and observing."

Like a gargoyle. Like Donovan.

I looked around anxiously. No sign of anything *visible*.

"We won't linger," Gollum reassured me. He wrapped an arm about my shoulders. "And remember, we're here to learn, not to desecrate."

"Every place is sacred. It's the actions of people that desecrate it," I quoted a half-remembered book.

More people returned to their cars than traveled in our direction. The twisting canyon channeled a chill wind. I was glad I'd worn a sweater over my jeans and T-shirt.

"I thought this area was supposed to be covered in rock art," Gollum said. He looked all around him with a puzzled frown.

I searched, too. "Look up." I pointed.

"How come I didn't see that?" he gasped, taking in the black on red, or beige on black handprints, stick figures, and squiggly lines that marched across the rock face twenty or more feet above us.

"Because you're too tall. You have to look down to keep from stepping on other people. I have to look up to see around you."

"Being five foot nothing has its advantages." He peered down at me. Then closed the difference in our heights for a quick kiss. Sweet and affectionate.

It ended too soon.

"That's five foot two," I countered, still gazing fondly into his eyes. "Grandma Maria is five foot nothing."

"Camera?" He broke the moment.

I hauled it out of my pocket, one-handed, reluctant to let go of him with the other.

Between the two of us, we snapped over one hundred photos. A growing awareness of isolation and the freshening wind drew us closer together. We progressed along the trail more rapidly than we expected.

"That looks like a family dancing together," I whispered, pointing to a line of stick figures holding hands. Snap, snap.

"I think that one next to them is a shaman, see the antlers on his head?"

"The squiggle lines could be water. See there's a break where they spread out, a river crossing."

"I'd almost bet the single squiggle is the course of a journey, each bend could represent a day's travel."

My eyes kept returning to the groups of human figures dancing in a circle. Faint smudges, an almost round "head" with triangular shoulders and long body trailing off, above them looked ominous. But they could be just smudges, not necessarily spirits or predators.

My vision tilted and rocked. For half a moment the images and symbols came alive. "Guardians protecting an important shaman," I whispered. "Worshipers coming here in respect, offering food and water to the spirits. Another man who doesn't respect anyone, not even himself, is cast out."

The world reeled around me clockwise, then reversed and halted back at the beginning, bringing me back into myself, in the here and now.

"Interesting idea," Gollum mused. He took more pictures.

"What about the cross—recent Christian missionaries?" I asked, pointing to another image near the family.

"Judging from the patina that has regrown, I think it's older. More likely it represents the four directions. See how the top doesn't point straight up? It goes off to the side a bit; could be aimed at true north. Hard to tell. My sense of direction is twisted around."

"Mine, too." I stopped for a moment and closed my eyes, trying to feel the tug of the north pole, just like Scrap taught me. The increasing wind tugged at me from all directions. I had no sense of where I was. Or when I was.

"Scrap?" I called, hoping he'd help me out.

Silence.

Swallows chirping and swooping about signaled water. We searched further. The trail ended.

The birds showed us the recess that held a miniature reservoir. Hidden beneath another of the ubiquitous arches, I had to lean precariously over the top of a boulder to catch a glimpse of the clear pool. If Gollum hadn't steadied my balance, I might have fallen in. The air inside the chamber—roofed to slow evaporation, and open on two sides and part of a third—smelled damp, but not rank. I guessed the sandstone filtered the water clear as it seeped from above.

"Easy to get trapped in there." I shuddered and withdrew quickly. Drowning in the desert seemed a particularly horrible way to go. I was certain some villain in my next book would meet his justly deserved end that way.

"No wonder Mouse was able to hide out for months. Unless you know this 'tank' is here, you'd never find it," Gollum said. His voice echoed in the water chamber as he took his own turn looking in.

"We'd better start back. That storm is getting closer. This trail looks like a flood channel and I don't want to get caught here when the rain hits," I warned.

We spotted more petroglyphs and arched caves on the way back, taking yet more pictures.

The parking lot was empty by the time we reached our car.

Something ominous crawled up my back.

"I don't like this," I said. "Something smells wrong."

"It's just the electricity in the air. Extra ozone. We'll get thunder and a lightning show before long," Gollum reassured me, stowing the backpack.

"If Scrap were here, he could scout ahead for us."

"Where is he?"

"I don't know. He refused to come. Something about weird magnetics among the rocks scare him." I saw again the drawing of the disrespectful man being cast out of the valley.

"I don't like the sound of that. Let's start back. Keep your eyes peeled."

We headed back the way we'd come. Having learned my lesson with the rock symbols, I looked up as well as all around.

"There!" I pointed to some unusually large birds circling an area south of the road, west of the Visitor Center. They flew an ever-changing spiral, moving west and then south, never getting too far off one central point. The silhouettes were wrong, proportions distorted. Nothing sleek and aerodynamic about those airborne beasts.

Once more, I thought of gargoyles watching and waiting.

"I don't think those are birds," I said.

"But they are predators," Gollum agreed.

A flash of lightning left black spots in my vision and strange afterimages. But I'd seen the distinctive ragged bat shape of the wings of Gregbaum's mutant faeries.

Chapter 36

Rock, one of the hardest substances in nature is gently shaped and molded by water, one of the most pliable and flexible substances.

THE RING BURNS HOT and heavy in my hand. I've got to drop it. But I can't. Tess is nowhere near. She has to have it on her finger to invoke universal laws of possession.

I seek in a wider and wider circle for her. We are so tightly bonded I should be able to just follow the threads of love tinged with her unique colors of gold and yellow and topaz. They are faint. Something masks them from my perceptions.

There is only one place that I know of that can do that.

The Valley of Fire.

My blood runs cold with fear.

She needs me. Trouble looms on her horizon. The mutant faeries circle and swarm. Their flight plan brings them closer and closer to her. They draw their swords and fold their wings to dive.

I have to go to Tess. Now.

Cautiously, I circle her essence, avoiding the flea demons on guard in the chat room. They nip at me, over and over, never satisfied with just a little bit of blood. Always needing more. Just like a vampire. Or a demon.

Then, at last, I find a faint echo of my Warrior. That tentative signature is weaker than the ring when it bulged through the dimensions.

I have to trust my instincts and my love for Tess to break through the barriers. With a deep breath, I close my eyes and plunge.

I fall and fall through time and space. I keep falling until I sense air around my wings. At the last instant they snap open and slow my descent to Tess' shoulders.

I rub my cheek against her hair, grateful to be back with her. I am complete now. We have a mission.

She commands me to her hand, needing me to transform and fight those awful red-and-black faeries.

My blood runs hot now. I flash from fog to flamingo to poppy in an instant. I stretch and thin. My ears start to curve into one blade, my tail sharpens into the other.

Before I lose it, I drop the ring onto her finger.

And then, just as I am almost complete, Tess twirling me like a baton to help me, something reaches out and grabs my essence.

I am yanked away from my Tess into blackness.

"What!" I screeched. Scrap was here, in my hands, fast becoming a weapon to fight those horrible beasts. And then he disappeared. Just winked out . . . no, more like continued to stretch wire-thin and rush through the air to someplace . . .

Someplace like that towering rock formation about a half mile from the small parking lot and picnic ground where we've pulled over. A boulder on top looked like a round hay bale resting on its side. Below it a tower with protrusions and arches and openings just like . . .

"Gollum, look at those rocks."

"Which rocks? There are dozens of them." Again he focused at foot- and eye-level as he shrugged into his backpack and pulled a collapsible walking stick from a side pouch.

"Look *up*. And out."

And then he spotted it and his jaw dropped. There, in the near distance was the side profile of the Goblin Rock we sought.

"Why didn't we see it on the way in?"

"Because the angle and the light were wrong. The sun

was behind the clouds. Now it's below them, coming at us sideways."

I took off running. I had to see more of that rock, test it, probe it, make certain this was the one we wanted and that a portal truly did exist.

Eight winged forms, with blood-red scaly skin, wearing black leather knickers and vests to match their wings, alit between me and the formation. The last remnants of sunlight glinted on the blue-black steel of their broadswords.

"What better signal that this is what I'm looking for than you guys guarding it," I sneered at them.

Where in the hell was Scrap when I truly needed him?

"Tess, catch," Gollum called. I reached up, only half daring to turn.

His aim was true. The walking stick sailed into my hand, fully extended. It had a cork knob on one end, and a small point on the other.

Not exactly a Celestial Blade, but something. I grasped it like a quarterstaff and faced my opponents.

Gollum's ragged breathing sounded in my ear. Crap. Now I'd have to protect him as well as myself and get us out of here.

"I'll watch your back," he said.

I didn't have time to snort. The first of the mob lunged at me with his four-foot blade.

I blocked it with the staff, heavy metal ringing against lightweight metal. The staff bent but didn't break.

A quick series of attacks and parries. My ears clanged from the noise.

Movement on my periphery. Scrap? Please, oh, please, let it be Scrap.

No such luck. Just the bad guys trying to circle us.

I kept the attacker in my center focus, trying to maneuver him around so I only had to battle on one front. Gollum's body warmth against my back didn't reassure me much.

Then a whoosh of air and a black-and-red form slammed against a small outcropping five yards away. Air rushed out of his lungs and his neck bent unnaturally.

"What?"

"Aikido. I used his own energy against him. Quite an interesting phenomenon . . ."

"Not now, Gollum. Just get me his sword."

"Oh. Yes. Of course."

The bad guys backed off a bit, suddenly wary of us. Easy prey had turned into nasty cats. I was madder than a wet cat—mad at Scrap for disappearing and mad at myself for dashing into this situation.

Mad made me mean. I'm not proud of it, but it is a fact.

I swung the staff like a club, aiming for the gut of my nearest opponent. He skipped back, confused.

These guys weren't terribly bright, didn't know how to think on their feet.

A fat raindrop hit my forehead with a splat. Then another. The dry sandy soil sopped up the first drops thirstily. But it came too fast, drenching me in seconds. The ground beneath my feet became a slurry.

Once more, I faced these guys with treacherous footing.

Shit! Actually I said something a lot stronger and less polite.

But if I had trouble finding traction in hiking boots, they weren't doing any better in bare feet.

The next thing I knew Gollum slid a sword grip into my left hand. I'd been too busy watching red-faced bad faeries watch me to notice how he got it.

"I'll love you forever for getting this," I whispered, dropping the staff as I gripped the sword.

"I'll hold you to that."

Using both hands on the big grip, I lifted it high over my head. Not exactly a fourteen-ounce fencing foil. But thanks to my training with the Sisterhood of the Celestial Blade, I knew how to use it.

My shoulders groaned. I'd skipped weight training over the last few months.

My closest opponent opened his eyes wide. I saw fear reflected there.

I swung the blade and felt it connect with muscle and bone.

An unearthly screech pierced my eardrums. I didn't dare cover them to block out some of the pain.

Another, more daring (or desperate) bad guy jumped toward me, using his wings to get him close. Too close.

He should have read the rule book. If you are close enough to kiss, you are too close to fence.

I wasn't fencing. I was fighting for my life.

An upper cut of the sword connected between his legs and bounced back. Damn, he must have been wearing a cup.

He grinned at me, showing far too many razor-sharp teeth, not unlike Scrap's multiple rows.

A quick spin and I backkicked into his gut.

He doubled over with a whoosh. I used my momentum to get the sword up and slashed his neck. The rain turned his black blood gray. It joined the small river forming at my feet and disappeared downslope—into the base of the goblin rock.

I smelled sulfur and rotting garbage tinged with black licorice.

They'd had enough. With another unearthly screech, they all lifted into the air, grabbed their fallen comrades, and sped off to the south, trying to outrun the storm.

I tracked them as they disappeared into the lowering clouds. For the first time in my life I wished I had bat wings to help me fly after them.

"Tess, we've got to get out of here." Gollum sounded frantic. "We're standing in the middle of a wash. It's going to flood!"

As if to emphasize his words, lightning seared across the sky. Thunder boomed before the jagged fork had completely disappeared. For half an instant everything in my path showed sharp and clear in the too bright light.

Afterimages nearly blinded me.

Still holding the sword—don't ask me why I didn't throw down the extra weight—I grabbed his outstretched hand. He scooped up the backpack by one strap with the other and we dragged each other uphill, toward the SUV.

Another flash and boom. This time I spotted a black winged image at the lower edge of the clouds. One of the black faeries pointed his sword toward us. The next bolt of lightning channeled down the blue-black blade directly into the gas tank of the SUV.

Flames and heat erupted in a tower of black smoke. The blast sent me reeling backward. I lost my balance and fell into a gush of water at the edge of the wash.

Where am I?

I want to choke and sob in fear. I can't find my body.

Total blackness surrounds me, robs me of all my senses. No smell, no sight, not even a hint of a taste on my forked tongue.

Do I still have a tongue?

Tess! I scream with my mind. The words echo back to me, without sound.

Okay, officially time to panic.

Tess, help me!

Nothing.

I am nothing.

My Tess will die because I am nothing.

Chapter 37

Rain is scarce in the Valley of Fire, but when it comes, it can cause torrential flash floods that alter the landscape in a moment.

"OFF YOUR ASS, sweetheart. We've got to get to higher ground." Gollum hauled me to my feet, one-handed. The muscles in his arm strained and stood out.

A sudden deep lethargy washed through me, stronger than the waters swirling at my feet, reaching for my knees.

Sharp pain on my cheek.

"Snap out of it, Tess. This is no time to go all weak and girlie on me."

"What? How dare you!" Anger heated my blood. I still felt heavy, but enough strength trickled through me to follow Gollum. As long as he held my hand.

I felt like a psychic vampire, feeding off his energy just to stay alive.

We scrambled and reached. Stepped and slid. Eventually, he hauled me over the lip of a rock into a cave opening. This time he needed both arms to get me up.

"Is it safe?" I choked out through chattering teeth. My wet underwear clung to me like a second skin of snow. Jeans and sweaters did little to ward off the chill.

"As safe as anywhere. Water formed the cave, trickling through here over aeons. I don't think we'll get inundated. The walls are still pretty thick.

I checked them out skeptically.

"Trust me on this, Tess. I know how to survive in the bush."

"You also know some pretty esoteric martial arts." Memory of the battle returned to me. Memories of waking to find U.S. Marines passed out on the floor with bruises on their throats chilled me more than the rain.

"Well, yes. I had to switch from some more aggressive and lethal forms after I took a vow of nonviolence. But that was before I met you and learned I might need to more actively defend myself upon occasion." He chattered on, filling the cave with calm words as nature raged outside.

A fierce wind howled through the canyons, adding its voice to the thunder, the pounding rain, and the rushing floods.

"Nonviolence?" I had to back up a bit, having lost my thoughts while he pulled a tiny camp stove out of his pack and lit it. The acrid scent of canned fuel burning sharpened my wandering focus. "Is that part of the Peace Corps?"

"Well, not exactly. I wasn't in the Peace Corps. Or at least, not what you think of as the Peace Corps. But we did keep the peace in a way."

"You're rambling, Gollum. Covering the truth with so many words I can't find the lie. You're very good at that."

I left hanging my primary, and frequently vocalized, objection to Donovan: the fact that he lied, often, glibly, and with convincing acting.

"Well, um, I guess I have to tell you the truth, don't I?"

"If we want to build on that kiss we shared, yes, you do. My life is an open book to you. About time you shared a bit of yours."

By this time, he'd filled a pot with rainwater and set it on the stove to boil. Packets of instant coffee came out of the pack next, along with sugar. Lots and lots of sugar.

"No, cream. Sorry. But then you shouldn't have real cream anymore."

"You're stalling." I dug into the pack myself this time. Meals Ready to Eat. A silvery space blanket. A sleeping bag. First aid kit. And more. The thing must have weighed fifty pounds, and he hauled it around like I did my purse.

"I ran away from home and became a mercenary for two years."

Something? Anything is better than this nothingness. Sort of like having five full-sized imps jump me and land on my chest. Then one gets off to beat me in the face. Still a pressure choking the life from me but not quite so heavy.

A ray of hope. Who said that as long as there is hope, there is life?

Now that the deep oppression has eased, my panic lessens as well.

Now I can think beyond gibbering.

Now I must face the darkness within me as well as without.

I need a cigar.

"A mercenary? I just don't see it," I said, sitting cross-legged in front of Gollum's stove. Its tiny warmth wasn't enough (I was almost surprised I felt no trace of the muscle pull). Chills made my entire body shake and tremble.

"Get out of those wet clothes and wrap the space blanket around you," Gollum ordered. He began peeling off his own sweatshirt and polo shirt.

We both looked at his clothes as they came away in pieces.

"Wait." I cast aside my drenched sweater. Too bad it was acrylic and not wool. Wool would have insulated me wet or dry. "Where did that cut come from?" I tentatively ran my hands across a long bloody slash that started in his left bicep—a very nicely formed and firm bicep at that—and continued down his chest to disappear beneath the belt of his jeans.

"Oh." He stared at the blood oozing out of the cut. It looked raw and angry, ripe for infection. His face paled and his glasses slipped off.

I caught them before they hit the ground and smashed.

"Scrap, get your ass back here. We've got a demon wound."

Nothing.

"Imp spit won't help this," Gollum muttered, just barely remaining upright. "It's a sword cut, not a demon bite."

"Good thing you brought a first aid kit and started water

to heat. I'll need to clean the wound. Lie down on the blanket while I patch you up."

"I'm fine."

"No, you aren't. If you were fine, you'd still be sitting and not falling over." A gentle shove to his good shoulder got him flat on his back.

During my years as a schoolteacher I'd learned basic first aid. I'd helped Sister Serena in the clinic back at the Citadel. I wished she was here to help. She'd know if the wound was deep enough to need stitches.

After basic cleaning with soapy water—he'd brought along one of those miniature bars you get in hotel bathrooms—and a liberal dose of basic antiseptic, I used every adhesive strip and gauze pad I could ferret out of the kit. I was about to start ripping up his T-shirt (the same dark maroon as the polo) when he stayed my hand.

"I'll be fine. I wasn't even aware that the demon managed to slash me. It was just the shock of seeing my own blood. Heaven knows I've seen enough of other people's and demon blood to numb my sensibilities." He placed his glasses firmly back on his nose and struggled to sit.

I got a shoulder under him and heaved.

"Speaking of which, I still don't see you as a mercenary in Africa." I draped the space blanket around his shoulders and set about reading the directions on the MREs. He needed food and liquid to heal the wound and fight infection.

"You have to understand, I suffered a great deal of rage at the time."

"You?"

"I'd just turned twenty-one. I'd graduated from Yale at nineteen, completed the course work at Columbia for my first masters and was halfway through the research for my thesis. Yet I was still reduced to working for the company that handles my mother's family finances. Entire financial empires built on lies, deceit, manipulation, and beating down the competition at any cost. I lived in New York and hated every minute of it."

Okay. I knew he was smart and that his family had money. This sounded like three or four steps above what I'd imagined.

I sat back and listened, hoping that once he got started,

he wouldn't stop until I'd learned everything I could about him.

"Then my dad died and a bunch of other crap happened. Gramps was the only one I could talk to, and then he had a heart attack. Mother ordered me not to upset him with my trivial problems. I left New York and didn't stop for a long time. Somewhere in my head I had the idea I'd become a Warrior of the Celestial Blade, if I could only find a Citadel and an imp. Africa seemed as good a place as any. The army wouldn't take me because of my vision. Mercenary companies aren't quite so picky."

He swallowed the barely warm coffee I handed him. His eyes remained focused on the inside of the empty cup.

"I made it through basic still angry. Then my sergeant handed me a uniform, a gun, and a backpack." He fell into a deep contemplative silence.

"Surely your rage ran out before two years," I whispered.

"It did. But I'd signed a contract. The day it was up, I went home. I didn't know what I was going to do, only I wasn't going back to the financial firm. My first night back in New York, some kid tried to mug me for thirty-five bucks in my wallet."

Another long silence.

I knew I couldn't break it. He had to speak on his own. The hurt on his face told me more than words.

"I killed him with my bare hands. Then I looked at him, really looked at him. He was a runaway, literally starving to death. I'd seen enough starving kids in Africa to know what it looks like. He needed my few bucks to buy food."

I pulled his head down into my lap, caressing his fine silver-gilt hair and let him sob out his guilt and grief.

"At that moment, I took a vow of nonviolence. I intend to keep it, Tess," he finally said into the darkness. "I will defend myself, and you, to a point. But I will never kill again."

Chapter 38

Little evidence exists to indicate any group of people have lived permanently in the Valley of Fire.

"CAN YOU EVER FORGIVE ME for killing an innocent?" Gollum asked quietly in the darkness. The cave shrouded us and muffled the sound of the rain outside. We might be the only two people in the world.

"I'm probably the one person in the world who understands," I said quietly.

"Those kids who mugged you last month." A glimmer of hope came through his voice.

"They weren't starving, but they were so young. They had their whole lives ahead of them. Except I broke the boy's trachea. And I enjoyed the release of all my pent-up frustrations and anger and aggression."

This time I fell into a silence only I could break. The vivid image of the feel of the boy's throat beneath my fingers. The satisfying crunch as I slammed my hand into him.

Then the horrifying knowledge that I'd killed him. With my bare hands.

"If Allie and her partner hadn't showed up when they did, if Joe hadn't known how to perform a tracheotomy in the field, I'd have murdered a fifteen-year-old child."

He squeezed my hand and sat up. "We'd better get some hot food into us, and cold clothes off of us."

We set about getting ourselves fed and warm. Gollum

proved quite skilled at survival camping. In moments I had the sleeping bag wrapped around my nearly naked body and my hands wrapped around a steaming cup of sweet coffee. He wore the space blanket like a toga, his long limbs sticking out awkwardly. Only he wasn't awkward or nerdy now. He was magnificently alpha male taking care of me.

Somehow I always knew he'd be a plaid boxer shorts kind of guy. Nothing pretentious about him. Unlike Donovan who wore black and tight and trendy.

Finally, I had time to worry about insurance for the rental car, worry about my mom, worry about the book I needed to write, worry about how to save the faery dancers, worry about Scrap.

I lifted the cup to my mouth, avoiding the hard thinking with the anticipation of the hot liquid trickling down my throat into my tummy and spreading out from there.

Something glistened in the dim firelight. I stopped and stared.

"Gollum, where did this come from?" I couldn't look away from the diamond-and-gold filigree that adorned my right hand. It had no weight, fit me as if made for my hand, and acted as if it had been with me for a lifetime.

"Gregbaum has fat hands. Even his pinky finger is bigger than my thumb. Lady Lucia is taller than me, she has bigger hands. How come this fits so well when it was made for her?"

"We already know it's no ordinary ring." Gollum took my hand and twisted it to better catch the light. "It belongs to you now, it fits you. It suits you." He kissed my fingers. "I wish I could offer you something quite so fine."

"I think you'll manage, once we get back to civilization." His kiss warmed me more than coffee and food ever could.

"The rain is letting up. We really should do something about getting out of here." He didn't look anxious to return to reality. Our little cave seemed quite snug and comfortable.

"I think I lost my cell phone in the fight." As good an excuse as any. I'd look to make sure. Later. Much, much later.

"And mine got drowned in the rain. It needs to dry out. Maybe get a new battery before it will work again."

As if we needed excuses.

"Scrap's been gone a long time. He must have given me the ring before he took off again. I've never known him to run from a fight before."

"Maybe he knew you didn't need a lot of help this time. Imp business has always been a mystery." He looked like he might say more, but didn't.

I remembered the time I asked Gollum if he ever turned off the professorial lectures. He replied, "When I make love to a beautiful woman."

He wasn't talking now. He turned my hand over and kissed the palm. Then the wrist. When his lips met my elbow, I thought I'd jump through the cave ceiling from the intensity.

"Scrap knows enough to give me privacy when I need it," I reassured us both. "But are you sure you're not too injured for this?"

His mouth reaching the hollow at the top of my shoulder was answer enough. Every muscle in my body turned to liquid. The sleeping bag fell away.

"Still wearing red underwear, I see," he murmured on a chuckle.

I couldn't comment on the habit developed during my year at the Citadel. Red reminded us of the blood demons spilled and we needed to avenge.

My thoughts skittered far, far away from that time.

We both came to our knees, hands and mouths exploring skin textures and tastes. I tangled my fingers in the light hair of his chest that spread out at the waist band of his shorts. I followed the enticing arrow down and down, relishing every inch of him, smooth and rough. Salty and sweet.

Then, finally, we could contain ourselves no longer. His mouth latched onto mine, open with a tentatively questing tongue.

I responded, like to like. We molded and blended together.

The last remnants of our clothing fell away. We needed no blankets. We made our own heat.

Slowly, tenderly, we touched again. Fire followed his fingertips as they traced my nipples. I nipped at his. His tongue circled my belly button.

I arched my back, willing him lower.

"Not yet, my love," he whispered. "Time. Tonight we've got time."

We took our time, learning each other's bodies, drinking in each new sensation. Dimly I noted as I covered him with a condom (smart men always have one, or a couple, in their wallet) that he'd been circumcised. Neither Donovan nor my husband had. It made no difference in the end.

At last, skin tingling, heat filling us, every nerve ending on fire, we came together in an explosion of passion. I'd never known such completeness; such a feeling of rightness.

I saw stars and knew we must have burst into a million pieces that unified the Universe. I didn't know where I left off and he began.

We affirmed life.

All too soon, the chill night and our growling stomachs brought us back to the mundane realities. I wanted nothing more than to nestle alongside my love; my one true love.

Why are you still alive? The booming voice echoed and rattled around my empty skull.

"Why indeed?"

You should not have survived.

"Tell me about it. Snatching me right out of my Warrior's hand at the moment of transformation hurt."

You dared trespass.

"So?"

Silence. Just when I thought something might show me a way out, it disappears again.

"Why am I here?" I shout into the nothingness.

You know.

"No, I don't! I was trying to do my job. A job I do very well by the way, helping my Warrior of the Celestial Blade send some nasty demons back where they belong. We restore the balance."

Small atonement for the balance you destroyed.

Oops.

I cover for my deep guilt by imagining the euphoria of tobacco smoke, hot and raw in my throat, then the rush of pleasure in my brain. Almost as good as sex.

Now how am I going to explain to Ginkgo why I didn't make our next rendezvous?

You should think instead on why you will not return to your Warrior. As long as you live here, she will live. But she will not fight demons again with the Celestial Blade.

"Now wait just one minute . . ."

We have waited many millennia. We can wait longer. But can you?

Gulp.

I really need that cigar.

We ask again, why are you alive?

"I'm alive because my Warrior needs me."

You have lied to your Warrior.

"No, I haven't. I'm always truthful with Tess."

You commit the lie of omission. Your silence puts her in danger.

"She doesn't need to know everything about me!"

You neglected to inform her when you learned the truth of the Fallen One; long before she discovered it on her own.

Ouch. That experience was so humiliating I blocked it from my memory. I actually lost a wart in a mud puddle when the gargoyles of York Minster cast me out.

More silence, a deepening of the oppressive blackness. That fifth imp is back on top of my chest.

"I'm alive because I was more cunning than my siblings."

Imp law required your death.

"Imp law is unfair! So what if I'm a runt? So what if I'm half the size I should be? I'm cunning and I'm smart. I'm the best imp for Tess. We fit together well. We work together well. Together we have taken out a tribe of rogue Sasquatch. We have battled vengeful Windago who broke the rules of King Scazzy. We've subdued those mutant faeries on steroids. Show me any other full-sized imp who has done that much and lived to tell about it."

Another silence. I get the feeling whoever or whatever judges me is thinking about that.

You survived those who were sent to murder you—to carry out imp justice. But you did not stop there.

Now I'm in real trouble.

I watched the dawn burst above the horizon. No lingering glimmer while the birds woke up. I'd grown used to a gradual lighting further north. But here, in the desert with a long, long horizon, one moment a bare hint of sun, then the fiery orb appeared and filled the valley outside our cave with morning freshness.

The floods had passed. A few droplets sparkled on plant leaves, then evaporated in the desert air.

I sat fully dressed and cross-legged on the lip of the cave, rocking back and forth. Only a tiny pull on my inner thigh remained of my previous injury.

"Where are you, Scrap?" I whispered, not wanting to wake Gollum.

"Hasn't he returned?" Gollum asked. He propped himself up on one elbow and blinked at me.

I handed him his glasses. They'd gotten buried in the jumble of his discarded clothing. Wonderful memories of last night wanted to settle peacefully all through me. Worry pushed them aside.

"He's never been gone this long. I think he's in trouble." I returned to my vigil at the cave mouth.

"He's clever . . ."

"Something has gone terribly wrong. I can feel it." My eyes kept returning to the Goblin Rock fifty yards away. Long shadows made it look black, robbing it of dimension and texture. Only its distinct silhouette stood out.

"Park rangers will be coming around soon. We should be out by the car when they arrive," Gollum said. He set about folding up our camp and returning it to his backpack. "You should eat."

"I can't."

He sat beside me. I had to scooch over to make room for him in the narrow opening.

"Something is terribly wrong if you can't eat. Let me at least make you coffee."

"Whatever. I'm going to hunt for my cell phone and get a better look at that rock."

Without waiting for him, I slid down the five-feet-high cliff face. Finding Scrap was something I had to do on my own. That goblin cave looked like the best place to start.

Over and over I heard Scrap whisper in my ear. *If you die, I die. If I die, you die.*

Back at the Citadel we'd sat death watch over a Sister. Her imp, Tulip, had taken a demon tag to protect her. Sister Jenny suffered no injury, yet she died by inches because her imp suffered. Neither one would let the other go. Finally, Tulip had succumbed and Sister Jenny died with a sigh of relief.

I suspected Scrap had delivered a *coup de grâce* for them. Who would do that for us?

I hoped that Gollum loved me enough to break through his vow of nonviolence for that one last mercy.

Chapter 39

In 1935 the Valley of Fire became Nevada's first state park.

WE ARE THE GUARDIANS of this sacred place. We cannot allow your murderous ways to desecrate our valley.

"Self-defense is not murder." This could get dicey. I have to choose my words carefully or lose everything.

If I die, Tess dies. I cannot allow that to happen to my babe. She's mine and deserves the best imp possible.

That's me. One way or another, I'm going to get back to her.

"I killed those who attacked me. That is allowed."

They had a lawful warrant for your execution.

"They didn't tell me that. They just jumped me. I fought back the only way I could, as would you, or any self-respecting imp."

You did not stop there.

A cigar would really help me think right now. When did I ever let that stop me?

"Good imps have to give in to the bloodlust. That's how we continue to fight demons when all looks lost."

Bloodlust must be controlled.

"But that goes against the definition of bloodlust. We lose control and keep swinging until there is no one left to swing at."

Even the innocent?

There's that "I" word. Gods, I hate it when people throw that at me.

"When I am the Celestial Blade, Tess controls me. I can only kill those she decides must die."

You had not yet bonded with your Warrior when you murdered five innocent imps, three of them your siblings.

"Yeah, well, they were standing around watching, and cheering on my vicious siblings with their compounded bloodlust. One brother with a grudge fed his hate to another and another. They let that anger compound, bouncing back and forth until it became a living entity that would not rest until they killed someone. The watchers fed that bloodlust as well. They weren't totally innocent."

Silence.

This is it. This is the moment when these Guardians decide my fate.

"Tess, no, you can't climb that rock." Gollum lifted me down from where I clung to the sandstone precariously. The soft surface crumbled when I put my weight on it.

"I've got to. Can't you see, that's Scrap's face up there." I pointed at the round hay bale that had taken on a full face twisted into a grimace, more than just the suggestion of eyes, nose, and mouth. Intelligence dimmed by pain peeked out from those cavernous eyes.

"I don't know Scrap like you do, Tess. All I see is eroded red sandstone. I can't let you risk yourself on a treacherous climb. If the rangers find you up there, we'll be in big trouble. Bigger trouble than from the burned-out car and staying past closing. Maybe in jail so we can't make tonight's deadline with the moon." He sounded so practical, and so very concerned.

I knew he stopped me because it was the best thing. But if Scrap were somehow trapped inside that formation . . .

I collapsed in a heap at the base, sobbing and pounding out my frustration. I could not banish the emptiness in my gut where Scrap used to be. That annoying, preening, sarcastic, cigar-smoking brat! Not even Gollum's love could fill that void.

"Come back to me, Scrap. Please come back to me."

Do you consider the deaths of the bystanders necessary?

"Well, when you put it that way . . . in a way, yeah. I needed to teach all of Imp Haven that I'm not just a useless runt. I'm someone to contend with. I count. I'm just as important as they are."

Did you not prove that when you killed your attackers?

"Well, yeah. I guess."

Can you bring yourself to regret those deaths?

"Can I have a cigar while I think about it?"

Instantly, the darkness grows thicker. I feel my cute little bottom sagging deeper and deeper into the hell this nothingness becomes. My hearts slow. My thoughts drift.

Who knows how long I've been here. Who knows how long I must stay. No light, no sound. This is worse than the diamond prison of the rogue imp.

Tess must be worried. I ache all over that my actions cause her pain. I regret that if I die, she must die. She deserves better.

"I do regret that I needlessly killed." Maybe not for the reasons these Guardians wanted to hear, but if in any way I have done something that will come back to hurt my dahling Tess, then yes, I do regret it.

For once I keep my thoughts to myself and my voice silent. I owe Tess that much.

You have much left to give. You and your Warrior have a destiny to fulfill. Remember the darkness within you and learn from it.

The imp within the diamond didn't have that chance.

"Tess, someone's coming. I can see a dust trail on the road. We have to flag them down or we'll never get out of here in time to rescue the faery dancers." Gollum tugged at my shoulder.

He could have picked me up and carried me. I think he knew that I had to come of my own volition. Abandoning Scrap had to be my decision alone.

I wasn't ready to do that. But I had to. I had to trust that if he ever broke free, he'd find me.

Maybe when I came back to open the portal, I could get him out.

The rising sun glimmered against the diamond in the ring.

I twisted it, trying to get it off. I hated it. I hated that it was the last artifact of power Scrap gave me. Perhaps stealing it from Gregbaum had caused him to get trapped here in the Valley of Fire.

The ring wouldn't come off. It just kept turning around and around my finger.

I glanced up, looking for inspiration.

Elongated streams of smoke with oval, faceless heads and triangular bodies that trailed off into thin wisps seeped from the rock. Just like in the petroglyphs. They flew around and around me, swooping to include me in their widening spiral around the Goblin Rock.

I ducked, but kept staring at them, entranced by their awesome beauty.

Then in clouds of black, copper, sage, and deep purple they separated to the far corners of the park.

Or was that just dawn light catching a mist?

Hiya, babe. Miss me? Scrap landed on my shoulder with a poof of displaced air.

"You've got some explaining to do, young man." My tremendous relief came out in anger. I couldn't help it.

Later, babe. Right now you've got some explaining to do to those rangers looking over the mess of a car. What'd you do to it anyway?

"Those black faeries channeled lightning into it because you weren't here to help me defeat them." I scrambled to my feet and hastened after Gollum.

Don't suppose he's got a cigar in that backpack . . .

I rolled my eyes. The almost sensation of Scrap on my shoulder felt good. I wanted to hug him, smother him in kisses, and spank his bottom all at the same time.

"Say, how come you lost all your warts?"

He hung his head in humiliation and faded until all I could see of him was his little pug nose and the outline of his bat-wing ears.

"You'll have plenty of opportunity to earn them back. Maybe tonight," I reassured him.

He brightened at that.

"You can go get a cigar if you want."

Nah, not yet. I don't want to leave you in this valley alone. There's all kinds of nasties hanging around.

"Like those forms that preceded you out of the rock formation?"

He looked back over his shoulder, wrapping his tail around my neck in a near choke hold.

Actually those are the good guys. The Guardians of all that is sacred within the valley.

I didn't quite hear him mutter something else. Something like "I'm one of the bad guys."

By the time I caught up with Gollum, he'd already explained with heated gestures how we got trapped in the park overnight.

"A gang of five teens were climbing the rocks. We stopped to explain to them why they shouldn't and they took offense. They torched the car! And then the storm hit and the few streetlights went out. We were trapped here. All night."

"You really need better security," I added. A trick I'd learned from schoolchildren when I taught: always make the accuser look guiltier than you are.

"Cell phones?" the fair-haired young man asked. His tanned skin flushed and he looked embarrassed.

"Out here?" I pulled mine out of my pocket and showed him the half-full battery and no bars of signal. Actually, I was a bit surprised to find it intact.

"I hope you took full insurance on the rental," said the second ranger, the same dark-haired woman I'd talked to at the Visitor Center yesterday. She nodded her head slightly in the direction of the Goblin Rock, acknowledging that I'd found it.

She probably knew something about it. And maybe something about the misty forms that had streamed out and away from it.

"Of course," Gollum replied to the insurance question, pretending affront. From the glint in his eye, I guessed he enjoyed playing this role.

A forest green SUV pulled up behind the beige park service pickup. Breven Sancroix leaned out of the driver's side window. "Thought you two might need a ride when you didn't show last night. Flash floods closed a bunch of roads. I came as soon as they bulldozed them free of debris."

I saw no sign of Fortitude. Scrap's pug nose worked overtime, seeking the big imp.

Now that's one of the bad guys. Fortitude is so bad he doesn't dare enter the valley, Scrap said. He shifted around so that his back was to the newcomer. *I dare you to ask Mr. Holier Than Thou Sancroix why his dark-skinned imp is waiting for him, safely back at the entrance.*

Chapter 40

There is a one in thirty-five chance that rain will fall in Las Vegas on any given day.

"HOW DID YOU KNOW we needed a ride?" I asked Sancroix as soon as he put his truck in gear and headed toward Las Vegas. Scrap occupied my right shoulder, looking out the window and away from our driver.

Gollum and his monster backpack stretched across the back seat. He half reclined with his feet up and the backpack in his lap, as if he didn't trust it in the rear compartment.

"Fortitude told me you were in trouble." Sancroix stared straight ahead, seemingly concentrating on the road.

Small construction vehicles with front loaders scooped gravel and sand from the pavement where washes and arroyos had overflowed their banks. We might not have been able to get out of the park last night, even with four wheel drive.

A mountain of paperwork awaited us, from both the rental agency and the park.

"I hope you have a story to tell the rental agency," Sancroix said.

"Did Fortitude tell you about our battle?"

"Yeah. He also told me your imp deserted you. No wonder you two had to go rogue. I'm surprised the imps let him live to adulthood."

Angry words of defense jumped to my lips. I swallowed them. No sense aggravating this man when he'd come to our rescue.

"How'd the imp allow your mother to marry a demon?" he asked when we reached the freeway and he could engage cruise control. "That should have brought a full herd of them down on you."

I looked over my shoulder to Gollum in the back seat. No comment from him, just a shrug of his shoulders.

"I didn't let her do anything. She eloped. I don't know how you work, but we aren't in Citadels. We have to appear to work within the law. Darren Estevez was a prominent and wealthy citizen. He paid taxes and, as far as I know, voted regularly. I couldn't just kill him and leave the body for someone else to clean up. As it was, I spent most of a day in jail, accused of his murder." And missed an important combat challenge because of it.

"How'd you know about Estevez?" Gollum finally asked. He sounded as if he didn't really care. I could tell by the way his eyes flicked about behind his glasses, that he thought furiously, weighing and assessing information.

"What he really wants to know is why you don't have an archivist assigned to you," I added.

"Had one. Didn't like the guy." Sancroix closed his mouth with a snap. No more discussion on that subject.

I looked to Gollum again for more information.

Another shrug. He didn't know any more about that than I did. Then he froze, mouth half open. "Gramps' brother," he mouthed.

His grimace told me that man had not died comfortably in bed, at home, surrounded by his loved ones.

"Mom's marriage to Darren only lasted thirty-six hours. He's dead now. We don't have to worry about it anymore."

"Don't we? Do you know how much damage a Damiri demon can do in thirty-six hours?"

I had a good idea. For weeks I wondered if Mom would ever recover. She seemed to have found her feet along with her new career. With a little help from a faery. I figured I owed Mickey and his clan a lot, even if my vows to the Sisterhood didn't compel me to rescue the dancers.

Somehow we filled the hour-long drive with boring and

mundane conversation. Mostly about the storm and power outages in the city.

First thing I did back at the hotel was book the room for three extra nights. Gollum winked at me and did not engage his room beyond noon.

"Do we have time for a shower?" I asked.

"A quick one. We've got to connect with Mickey and you have to have a long conversation with Scrap about that ring."

And a longer conversation with my mom. Just to talk and share and make sure she was all right off on her own. But it wasn't even ten in the morning. She sang last night until after two, so she wouldn't be up yet.

I'd take that shower first.

Well, I can see I'm not needed for a few moments—make that an hour. I've got some errands to run. Mickey needs to know where and when to find us.

I need to know if Lady Lucia knows that Tess is her great, great, multi-great granddaughter. And if she does, is she going to tell Tess?

If she does know, there is more than a little bit of kink in her, screwing Donovan, the same man who lusts after her descendant. (I'm tired of figuring the number of greats in that relationship.)

I can't allow that. I may have atoned for some of the darkness in my soul. But when it comes to my babe, I'll kill and kill again to protect her. Even from her own ancestor.

I pop in on Lady Lucia's parlor. Empty. Dirty glasses, spilled snack trays, scattered used napkins all over the place. Cleaning services haven't arrived yet.

So I creep silently, and as invisibly as possible, toward the back of the suite. At the top of the marble stairs, I hear muted voices. A quick check leads me down to the covered patio.

The contessa wears a black caftan that covers her from neck to ankle. Only the very tips of her fingers reach beyond the heavily embroidered sleeves. A huge black straw hat with a cartwheel of a brim shelters her head and face. Smoky dark glasses with lenses that cover her from above her sculpted eyebrows to her cheekbone add to the protection.

I can smell sunscreen with an spf of about 200 on her. It almost masks the odor of stale blood. She fed last night.

The bored driver of the hearse, not the wizened boy who served drinks at the party—he's asleep in his coffin—attends her at her elbow, placing sheaves of papers on the round table before her. He's as covered as she is, and the table's umbrella shades them both.

I don't think I could pick up an aura on either of them from the numbers of layers between them and the sun. But something is leaking from Lady Lucia. Something warm and gentle that seems totally alien to her vampire image.

I sneak a little closer, very slowly, keeping to the darkest of the numerous shadows. At last, I'm on top of the hat and peek at the framed drawing that captures nearly all of Lucia's attention. Her fingers trace the image of a child's face. A blond child dressed in antique breeches, shirt, and short coat. Her son.

More than that, I see an image of a very young Tess creeping through the pencil lines.

Oh, yeah, Lucia knows that Tess is her relative. She knows and she cherishes.

Feeling good and safe from her, I flit off to my other errands.

The shower took longer than we planned since we took it together. By the light of day we delighted in relearning each other's body through the exquisite mediums of soap and water. For the first time in a long time, I felt cherished and protected without any agenda except mutual affection. I nestled my head in the hollow of his chest and just listened to the rhythm of his heart while hot water poured over us.

By the time we finished, room service had arrived with full breakfasts for us both, including beer and OJ for Scrap. He really did know how to leave us alone when we needed privacy.

Caught up with Mickey, he announced around a huge cigar. He flicked ash out the open window where he perched.

"What does Mickey have to say?" I ground out the cigar and pointed him toward nourishment.

Strangely obedient, he refrained from complaining about his lost cigar.

I stared at him, wondering what had brought about this abrupt attitude adjustment.

Mickey says that Gregbaum's magic net around the dormitory is pretty strong hoodoo. Partly faery in origin—which explains Junior's participation—partly something else he can't figure out. No way to break it without knowing everything Gregbaum and Junior know about magic. But he thinks you can break the spell around the hotel with the ring. Scrap slurped up half his breakfast in one long pull on a straw.

I relayed that message to Gollum. He dressed and munched bacon while he thought long and hard. "I need to call Gramps. I also need to get someone to cover my classes tomorrow. Do you suppose MoonFeather would talk about something Wiccan that can pass as Anthro 101?" He fished in his overnight bag. "Damn, I don't have any spare batteries for the cell phone."

I tossed him mine. He took it to his laptop to look up phone numbers, still working on breakfast and pulling on his shirt at the same time.

Easily, we fell into a familiar routine. I had my tasks, he had his. We worked comfortably together.

Between my cell phone and the hotel's exorbitant long-distance charges, we managed to cover some of the bases.

"Ask Scrap about the ring," Gollum said between calls.

The imp snoozed on my shoulder, clinging to my hair. At the sound of his name, he roused. *Yeah, wadda ya want*, he growled in his Chicago gangster voice. He leaned away, clinging to my hair for balance to grab his cigar from the windowsill.

"Ow, I felt that," I complained, reclaiming possession of my hair with a tug.

Time to close the window and turn on the AC. A proper imp can only take so much, ya know. The clear blue sky was rapidly paling to white in the desert heat.

"Nice to see some of your spark and disrespect has returned," I replied. I don't think I'd know how to work with a docile and obedient imp.

Mickey's at the door.

I got up to answer it before I heard the knock. "We need to know about the ring," I reminded Scrap.

Um—It opens any portal into any dimension. He lapsed

into silence as Mickey entered the room and we all exchanged pleasantries.

"Something is wrong with Scrap," Mickey whispered.

Hey, I heard ya! I'm right here. He still hadn't moved from my shoulder. His insubstantial tail tightened on my throat again.

Strange. I shouldn't be able to feel that much of him. Was he more in this dimension than before, or was he more intense in his need to stay with me?

"I need to know how the ring works to be able to use it," I said to Scrap.

No, you don't. You just have to twist it, round and round your finger, willing a doorway to appear. Oh, yeah, and it helps if you twist it widdershins, toward the thumb.

"What aren't you telling me, Scrap?" Anger tinged my voice, masking my deep concern.

Ask Mr Bloody Sancroix and his black imp. He popped out with a whoosh of cigar smoke.

Twenty minutes later we wandered the outer aisles of the Dragon and St. George Casino, searching for access to the backstage.

"How are we going to get twenty dancers out to the Valley of Fire?" I asked. "Supposing we can get them out of here alive."

"Can't they fly?" Gollum asked. His glasses slid as he looked up from examining the lock on a fire door.

I thought the door should lead where we wanted to go even though it stated in plain letters across it: "Fire Exit. Alarm will sound if opened." My sense of direction faltered under the barrage of flashing lights, loud music, and animated shouts from gamblers.

Something about the assault on my senses made me want to let the machines make decisions for me. I should plug in some quarters and gamble. . . .

Scrap was of little help. He kept dangling over the slot machines, still trying to figure out how to hack into one.

"The dancers may be too weak to fly that distance," I argued. "They are fading from too long a separation from Faery."

"I will get a bus," Mickey affirmed. "From the taxi company." He looked grim. His leaf-green eyes looked dull.

His time in this dimension also stretched too long.

"Scrap, get your ass back here."

Have I told you today how beautiful you look with the glow of love about you? He waggled his cigar at me in a poor imitation of Groucho Marx. Then he circled above me, relishing the stretch of his wings.

"Can the crap, Scrap. What's on the other side of this door?"

Your wish is my command, babe. He popped out, leaving me wreathed in cigar smoke.

I coughed and waved the noxious fumes out of my face.

Mickey laughed. Mickey laughing worked better and thought more clearly than grim and frightened Mickey.

At least Scrap was good for something.

It's just a long corridor. Scrap whooshed back in. He tangled my hair in his talons and buried his nose against my scalp.

"I just washed my hair, it's clean, I promise." This clinginess, alternating with distraction was getting annoying. "Now tell me where that long corridor leads and does it really have an alarm on it?"

You didn't ask that, Scrap pouted.

I rolled my eyes. He was worse than a kindergartener on the first day of school.

Three doors off the corridor going left, back toward the theater. One goes down. One goes up, and one zigzags around to the dressing rooms, he sighed. He must have noticed my lack of patience. *And yes, this door is wired with alarms.*

"I wish you'd go back to being your normal sarcastic self," I muttered under my breath.

He heard me. I knew he did because he blew a smoke ring that completely circled my head, like a halo drifting down and tilting.

I'd seen that cartoon too many times.

Mickey and Gollum, at least, thought it funny.

"Upward staircase must lead to the theater control booth," Gollum mused when I'd translated Scrap's report.

"Down goes to the dormitory," Mickey added.

"Scrap, is there an exit to the outside at the end of that corridor?"

Yes, dahling. And it is also wired into the alarm system.

"Alarms can be cut or hacked." I looked hopefully toward Gollum.

But it was Mickey who nodded with a grin. "This I know how to do."

Scrap twisted my curls around his claws some more. *I'm thinking we grab the dancers backstage and take them out that exit.*

"I'm thinking the same thing. But there's no show tonight. We'll have to gather them up from the casino and the dormitory. Now how do we negate the magic around the building that keeps the dancers from igniting into faery torches?"

We all looked at each other blankly.

Gollum led us back to the center of the casino action. "We don't want anyone to notice us hanging out in any one location too long," he whispered.

"So, Mr. Professor-who-knows-everything, how do we break that spell?"

"We ask Lady Lucia. She set us onto the project. She must have some idea how Gregbaum works."

"It's not even noon. She won't be up yet."

I think she can be roused. Try her telephone. Scrap bounced a bit, like he was excited. I couldn't see him to tell what color he'd turned.

"And where do I find her telephone number?"

Scrap rattled off a string of numbers. Gollum already had out his new super-duper cell phone that does everything but breathe and entered the number.

"How'd you get the number, Scrap?" Maybe he'd actually been scouting around while AWOL.

I memorized it when I visited. She's got a nice blood-red landline phone next to her bed.

"That is also the number listed on the incorporation documents registered with the escrow office handling the sale of this casino," Gollum mused as he dialed.

Chapter 41

There are more churches per capita in Las Vegas than any other US city representing some sixty-five faiths and denominations.

"OKAY, SCRAP, WE'VE GOT AN HOUR to kill before we can meet Lady Lucia at her office," Tess says. She hangs on to my tail just so. I can't fade out of her grip or escape to the chat room when she does that.

I'm as trapped here as I was in the Goblin Rock by the Guardians. This is a little less unpleasant though.

We're in a back corner booth of a café on the end of a horseshoe-shaped strip mall. Lucia's office is in the center of the long block. This place serves breakfast twenty-four/seven. Gollum and Mickey are slurping coffee like it's going out of style. Tess toys with her second breakfast of pancakes with fresh strawberries. No more whipped cream for either of us.

She lets her coffee sit. A sure sign that she means business. Even if she is sitting so close to Gollum they might as well be one person.

About time. I've known all along that Gollum is her soul mate. But no, she had to dally with Donovan because he's beautiful. She had to succumb to lust that clouded her good sense.

Now she knows better. She's distracted with the newness of their love. Maybe I can get her all the way off the subject of Lady Lucia and the ring long enough for her to let go of my tail.

"I'm hungry." Being trapped in sensory deprivation will do

that to a body. "There's no mold in this town, even after a rain. If you don't mind letting go of my tail, I'll just pop back home, check on MoonFeather and your dad and grab some mold from around the washing machine in the basement."

"Nope. Not until you tell me everything you know about the ring and how to use it." Her grip becomes firmer.

My tummy growls.

She doesn't listen to it.

"You want to eat, you've got to talk first."

"Ask him the origins of the ring," Gollum says. He's peering at me like he can almost see me. Now that he and Tess have gotten so close, maybe he can. He can see her scar and it comes from the same place I do.

"The faeries made it," I admit.

Mickey brightens. "I know how to use faery magic."

"Not this magic. Your ancestors forgot its essence a long time ago. That's why they lost it," I growl back at him.

Then I have to unfold the story of how alchemist/blacksmith Noncoiré got the ring.

"So it really is mine by inheritance." Tess stared at the ring on her right hand as if diving into the diamond.

"Um . . . Tess, I wouldn't do that if I were you." I can feel the black imp leaking power, manipulating, urging Tess to meld her mind to his, give him a way to slip through the crack that got bigger when I stole the ring from Gregbaum.

"Do what?" She's still mesmerized and going deeper.

"Don't get lost in that diamond." I yank on her hair.

"What's in there that's so dangerous?" Mickey asks. He sounds really stern . . . like maybe he has an idea what lurks within those facets.

"A rogue imp," I admit quietly. I hope that only Mickey hears me. I should know better. Tess is attuned to me and my thought patterns. "An imp so evil he's turned black."

Maybe that will get her thinking about Fortitude instead of the ring.

"An imp can go anywhere," she breathes.

Nope, my ruse didn't work.

"What could an imp do that the faeries imprisoned him like that. Was it voluntary or is it being punished?" Gollum asks.

"I don't know. I only saw that his skin had turned black from his misdeeds." I emphasize the black to make sure she hears it this time.

"Your skin changes color with your emotions," Tess offers. Small comfort.

"I cannot turn black."

"Have you ever been as completely enraged, hopeless, and helpless as that imp?" she asks. I know she's trying to help.

"Yes." I cannot say more. I look her dead in the eye, begging her not to pursue it.

"Tess, when this is all done, I have to free that imp. I cannot condemn him to that bleak existence that is no existence. Not any longer than he's already endured."

"Scrap," Gollum addresses me directly once Tess has relayed my words. "Scrap, after all these millennia, that imp has to have gone completely insane. If he was black and rogue before, he will be more so now. You don't dare loose him."

"I have to!"

"We'll discuss this later. Tell me how Lady Lucia got the ring."

"She stole it from one of your ancestors, then he went off to Napoleon's war and got killed." That's all Tess really needs to know. I can't tell her that the young blond blacksmith with the godlike beautiful body fathered Lucia's child. So I fall into storytelling mode and make that final scene in the Continelli garden as exciting as possible, adding a few nuances to make the count the villain of the piece—maybe a vampire—and how Lucia used the ring to escape with her child. I also suggest that she might be a Kajiri demon rather than a vampire.

"We know sometime after that escape Lucia sold the ring. From that point, it's traceable to the auction house in Paris last December when Donovan bought it," Tess muses. If she noticed that I left out some bits, she doesn't push the issue.

"Then Donovan sold it to Gregbaum," Gollum adds.

"So how did you get it back for me, Scrap?"

"I stole it, like any self-respecting imp."

They all laugh at that.

"Can I go find some real food now?"

Tess lets go of my tail and I'm off before I have to reveal any more secrets.

Something rattled around my hind brain, demanding attention but sliding away whenever I tried to get close to it. It would hit me when I really needed it.

"For a woman wealthy enough to own the Pinyon outright, and be sole stockholder of the corporation buying the Dragon and St. George, you'd think she could afford an office in a more prestigious part of town," Gollum muttered.

We sat in that back café booth staring across the parking lot at the plain glass door. It was tucked between two storefronts in a strip mall at the corner of a residential intersection. A coffee shop that served only specialty coffee and pastries stood to the left of her door and had a constant stream of patrons. A hair salon occupied a large space on the right. For a Monday just after noon both places seemed very active.

"You'd think she'd have one of those mansions out in the hills overlooking the city instead of living in an apartment above the spa at the Pinyon," Mickey added. "She'd have more privacy out there."

"It's two minutes to one. Let's go in." I slid out of the booth. Scrap returned to my shoulder and burped. I was suddenly enfolded in a cloud of damp, musty air. He'd only been gone a minute. Long enough to gorge on his favored food. He'd also grabbed his new black-and-silver boa on the trip. He tossed it over his shoulder dramatically.

Gollum threw some money down. He's good about that. We approached the office door slowly, looking all around and taking note of those who took note of us.

At the last minute I slipped the ring off my hand and onto a key chain in my belt pack. I didn't want Lucia to know I had it yet. If the time came when I needed a major bribe, I'd tell her.

A thick layer of paint on the inside of the glass blocked any chance that daylight might filter in.

"We're being watched. I can feel it," Mickey whispered.

"From inside or out?" Gollum asked, also peering around.

Mickey shrugged.

Camera above the door. Scrap preened and mugged, flashing the boa in front of the lens.

"Scrap says we're safe." I replied.

Gollum opened the door and ushered me in with a gentle hand at my waist. Have I mentioned how much I enjoyed his little courtesies that come so naturally?

A dim electric bulb gave off enough light to see a narrow

landing and a staircase leading up. No space between the stairs and the walls. No way to get behind the stairs. I couldn't see if maybe the coffee shop and salon jutted into the area behind.

"At least there's no place for an attacker to hide," Mickey added. He twitched and started as a heavy truck drove past on the through street.

"Scrap, please scout ahead."

Do I have ta?

I rolled my eyes. "You can leave me alone for ten seconds."

That's a long time in demonland. Time enough to get us both killed.

"Scrap, stop stalling and scout ahead."

He popped out. Two seconds later he landed on my shoulder again, flapping the boa in my face. *All clear for us, dahling, but there's a fierce argument going on behind closed doors.* He sang the last phrase, only slightly off key.

"Remind me not to ask you to join in next time Mom drags me up to the stage."

He blew a smoke ring in my face.

I coughed and waved it away. But I didn't need to. The air-conditioning sucked the smoke away so fast I almost didn't see it.

"What does this place smell like, Scrap?"

Car air freshener. Pine. Fading. He wrinkled his snub nose in distaste. *No character at all.*

"Would the air conditioner at the Pinyon account for Lady Lucia's lack of demon odor?"

"Shouldn't," Gollum answered for the imp.

Something clicked in my mind. Then it slid away again.

"I'm thinking, that if Lucia has been poor, so poor she sold a valuable and treasured heirloom, that maybe the habit of saving money is how she gained so much. She doesn't spend where she doesn't have to."

"And she doesn't share. I couldn't find a single list of stockholders in any of the multitude of shadow corporations. Layers and Layers of secrecy."

"Just like Darren Estevez," I added.

Damiri demons are all richer than Bill Gates, Scrap laughed.

"No one is richer than Bill Gates."

Wanna make a bet? Lucia's got assets upon assets that no one knows about. Darren, too, but not as many. That's why his kids are fighting so hard to get your Mom's half of the fortune.

"Hmmmmm." I had to think a moment and paused on the last step, one foot in the air. "The estate is tied up in probate. Mom's getting an allowance from his liquid assets. Donovan can't cash in on the capital yet, except the exorbitant fees he collects as executor of the estate."

That's when I heard the raised voices behind the closed wooden door to the left of the landing. Fancy scrollwork detailed the door, avoiding the traditional cross-shaped reinforcing panels. The wall straight ahead and to the right was cement blocks painted a boring and unobtrusive gray.

"I have to own at least fifty-one percent!" Donovan nearly screamed. "A haven for the Kajiri is useless if I don't control it!"

"I will not invest in your great enterprise. But I will own one haven and pay you to manage it," Lucia replied, a little too loudly for the sweetness in her tone to be convincing. "I'm thinking an entire town built around a resort. No one lives there unless they work there and we screen all employees to make certain they contain at least one drop of demon blood in their veins."

"You, of all people, should recognize the wisdom of diversifying. You own too much in and around Vegas. The SEC and the IRS are going to start investigating your corporations sooner or later. Experience tells me the haven should be elsewhere."

"Like Half Moon Lake, Washington?" Lucia lowered her voice enough that I almost couldn't hear her through the thick door.

"Precisely. Invest the forty percent I need to start building, and I'll either buy you out in five years or you'll start earning handsome dividends." I recognized the subtle magic of Donovan's ability to persuade creeping into his voice.

"I do not like dividends. I like profits. I control the entire enterprise or it does not happen." Lucia bit each word off precisely, adding steel to her determination.

I sensed they'd reached a major impasse. They'd repeated these arguments over and over and gotten nowhere.

"I can go elsewhere for the money." Donovan slammed something, maybe his fist, against the desk. He had a temper, worse than mine. I'd been on the receiving end of it when he let his emotions get the better of his good sense during a fencing match. I still bore the scar on my right forearm. It would heal eventually. Not soon enough to my mind.

"Where?" Lucia asked sweetly. "I have made certain that no one in Las Vegas will lend you anything."

"Gary Gregbaum owes me. Therefore, his silent partner Junior Sancroix also owes me. I'll give them a theater designed for the show. Junior doesn't have to compromise The Crown Jewels and his financial arrangements with you. We'll attract people away from Vegas just to see the show, let alone every Kajiri in Vegas just trying to blend in. I'm helping him move his dancers tonight."

Mickey, Gollum, and I shared frightened glances at that. "We have to get the dancers first," I mouthed.

They nodded.

"Gregbaum wouldn't dare," Lucia hissed.

"What has he got to lose?"

In the moment of silence that followed, I decided to knock on the door. It was already five past one.

"Enter!" Lucia ordered.

"I'll be leaving you to your other business," Donovan said angrily. "This discussion is not over yet."

"You will stay," Lucia replied. "This discussion requires your cooperation. I will owe you a favor. Perhaps a forty percent favor. Perhaps less."

I pushed open the door to find Donovan leaning over a massive ebony desk, both fists planted on the glossy top. Lady Lucia sat across from him in a high-backed chair that molded to her frame. Today she wore a long red skirt and a black silk shirt. A red suede blazer was draped across one end of the massive desk.

Every one of the six windows in the wall behind her had been painted black. The only illumination came from wall sconces with electrified candles that flickered like real flame.

As I walked across the ten feet that separated us, I expected Scrap to disappear. He remained firmly on my shoulder, tail wrapped around my neck, in Donovan's presence.

"Either Lucia's evil overcomes Donovan's power to push you away, or you've overcome some darkness in your soul so that gargoyles don't repel you any longer," I whispered to my buddy.

You got that right, babe. Almost worth the price of my warts to know you and me can take this cheater down together. He's sleeping with Lucia by the way.

"Tell me something I didn't already suspect. He's not picky about his bed partners."

Chapter 42

Gambling debts are now legally enforceable in all states.

DONOVAN CURSED LOUDLY and fluently when he saw me enter the room. He slammed his fist into the desk again, this time leaving a dent.

"Tsk, tsk," Lucia clucked. "Temper, temper."

Donovan jerked upright. "I'm outta here."

"No," Lucia ordered.

Everyone in the room stilled, even Scrap.

"You will stay, Donovan. You will listen, and in the end, if you want any help with your great enterprise, you will assist me in any way I deem appropriate." Her accent slid toward French and away from Italian. Natural, I guess since I now knew it to be her birth language. Like my mother. I knew the inflections and the tendency to emphasize the last syllable well.

Funny, my mom hadn't lapsed into her own baby talk version of Québécois since coming to Vegas. She'd found herself on this journey. She no longer needed to cling to a past she couldn't reclaim. At least some part of this trip was a success.

Thinking about my mom, I wondered at Lucia's interest in her the other night.

The lady flashed a bit of fang at Donovan. I figured I'd probably confront her in private. Later. Mom wasn't singing tonight, so Lucia couldn't approach her in the lounge.

"You aren't taking the dancers tonight, Donovan," I said crisply. I braced my feet and held my hands loosely at my sides ready to command Scrap into weapon form.

I sensed Gollum and Mickey moving behind and beside me, to give me space and watch my back if necessary.

"Who's going to stop me?" Donovan sneered.

"I am. Because I'm taking them back to Faery tonight." I wished Scrap would turn red as a precursor to transforming.

Instead, he moved to the top of my head and hissed. A lot of good that would do. But also a signal that neither Donovan nor Lucia posed a serious threat to me at this moment.

"Good one, Tess. In case you didn't get the memo, Faery is closed until they restore the balance within." Donovan threw back his head and laughed.

"The only way to restore the balance is to return the dancers to their home. While they are here, they drain energy and faery gold into this dimension."

"Faery gold?" Lucia asked.

"They gamble with it," Gollum said.

"The gold remains gold as long as it is inside the building. But it turns to dross the moment it leaves." Mickey quirked a mischievous smile at our hostess.

Now it was her turn to laugh. "So that is why the accounting is always short. The managers aren't skimming and the owners are losing money at gaming because they host 'Fairy Moon,' drawing ticket holders away from the slots." Lucia almost wept with mirth. "They didn't have to sell. They merely needed to cancel the show and evict Gregbaum."

"That doesn't change anything. The faeries can't get home," Donovan said. "That's the Powers That Be wielding their power for power's sake and not thinking through the consequences. They're good at that."

"You'd enjoy making the Powers That Be look foolish, wouldn't you, Donovan," I said. I almost smiled, too, but didn't want to play my ace too quickly.

"Damned right I would. They haven't done me any favors lately." He began to pace, a sure sign of his discomfort. He had an amazing quality of stillness when he needed it; a leftover from the centuries he'd spent watching the world pass by. Most of the time he made up for those centuries of watching and waiting with vigorous action, pacing when there was nothing else he could do.

"I've got news for you." I smiled as sweetly as I could. "There's a back way in. But I'm the only one who can find it. Help me tonight, and I'm sure the Powers That Be will make note in their scorekeeping."

"I'm not going to help you do anything." Donovan aimed his restless steps toward the door.

"You will help her," Lucia insisted. Her quiet voice filled the room with authority. She half stood and leaned forward, revealing just a hint of fang. In the uncertain light, the white streaks of hair at her temples showed clearly—like a hereditary birthmark among the Damiri. Except those were artificial sun streaks in blonde hair. Weren't they?

Scrap, explain.

Expensive dye job. Underneath, her hair is as black as Donovan's heart or Fortitude's skin.

Donovan had those wings of silver hair, as did his foster father Darren. My deceased husband Dill had the beginnings of white at his temples. But then, he was a lot younger than Donovan.

But the Damiri always give their children names that began with D and usually ended with N. I sent that thought to Scrap.

Dunno. He lit up a new black cherry cheroot with a bit of flame at the tip of his finger. *The demon blood is pretty much diluted in her. Maybe her folks didn't know.*

Or maybe it's a more modern custom.

I felt a shrug from Scrap. Maybe, maybe not.

"Why do I have to help? You've already turned me down on financing." Donovan faced her, fists clenched, shoulders hunched. I half expected him to lift his arms and spread bat wings.

Quickly, I banished that image from my mind before it made me curl into a fetal ball in a corner gibbering in panic.

"With this new proposition on the table, financing can be renegotiated." She sat again, the atmosphere around her fading from menace to sweetness and possibilities.

"Sixty-forty split, we build in Half Moon Lake, and the new corporation is in the name of my choosing," he spat back at her.

"Gaming laws?" she countered.

"Nominal tribal affiliation on the spa. This is an extension of that project."

"Have your lawyer call my lawyer. They will draw up the contracts. Usual signature practices." Meaning they signed in blood. If either of them broke faith with the contract their blood would burn in their bodies, as if the contracts burned, too.

"Can we get back to the dancers?" I interrupted.

"Easy. I drive the bus. You three ambush us and take the dancers to the destination of your choice." Donovan dismissed us.

"What about his soldiers? What about the magic net around the Dragon and St. George? What's to keep him from extending that net to include the bus?"

"What magic net?" Donovan asked.

I looked to Lucia. She seemed disinclined to meet anyone's gaze. Okay. So she knew about the net, but she didn't want to talk about it.

Why?

So I told Donovan about the spell that would immolate the faery dancers the moment they left the building, and about the stronger one around the dormitory.

"You've got to be kidding. No one in this dimension can work that kind of magic. Other dimensions, yes. But the energy fields are all wrong on Earth."

"Are they? Are you forgetting about the energy leaks out of Faery?" I asked. A wave of weariness washed through me. The better part of valor seemed to be for me to take the visitor's chair resting at an odd angle across from Lucia. It looked like Donovan had thrust it out of the way, hard, at some point in the earlier argument.

Good move, babe. Puts you in a position of authority. Scrap chuckled. He hopped onto the desk and waggled his ears at Lucia.

She didn't seem to notice him. I hoped she couldn't see his disrespectful strutting. We still didn't know the extent of her power or her deadliness.

"You know how the net was set," I addressed Lucia.

"How would I know such a thing?" She gestured expansively, reverting to her fake Italian accent.

"You were intimate with Gregbaum at the time he

started the show. I suspect you financed him as part of the relationship. He did something to split you up, now you want revenge, to destroy him. The thing he values most is that show. You have to close it."

The ring in my belt pack nearly burned with the need to be back on my hand. Or I lusted to show off that diamond. I don't know which.

"I may have watched Gregbaum dance around the building, setting candles and chanting strange words that Junior Sancroix dictated," she conceded.

"I think you know more than that." Somewhere in horror fiction I'd read that one must never give a vampire control by engaging their gaze. I ignored it. All vampire fiction anyway.

Lucia squirmed. "How would I know anything of magic?"

"Because when you escaped from the fire that destroyed Castello Continelli, you ran to Faery." That had to be the default setting on the ring. Faeries made it for a reason. A way to always return home no matter where they were trapped.

"How did you . . ."

I smiled sweetly and gestured toward Scrap. The brat continued to prance and make ugly faces at her.

She didn't get my meaning. So Scrap blew smoke in her face. She choked and waved it away.

"The imp," she said matter-of-factly.

"The imp," I confirmed. "Imps can go anywhere, anywhen. He watched you. Learned something of your history."

"Something but not all?" she asked archly.

"This is all fascinating, but it's getting us nowhere," Donovan interrupted.

"Oh, but it is," I replied. "I have something you want, Lady Lucia. Something you want very badly. In return, you will give Gollum and Mickey a detailed account of the setting of the spell so that they can find a way to reverse it."

I toyed with my key chain. The ring was half hidden between my car key and my house key.

Lucia leaned forward a bit. A spark gave life to her overly dilated eyes. She truly was quite beautiful when she wasn't playing vampire crime boss. Lustrous hair and flawless skin, and a face with symmetrical features and high cheekbones. In human terms she'd reached her prime. In demon terms . . . well I didn't know what Kajiri considered prime.

"Where did you find it?" Lucia asked breathlessly.

"Do you know the most recent history of the . . . um . . . artifact?"

She shook her head, still leaning forward. If she pushed her reach to the fullest extent, she could snatch the ring from my hand.

I shoved my chair back two inches.

Gollum moved to stand behind me, one hand on my shoulder. More importantly, he stood between me and Donovan. Two days ago I thought Donovan could swat Gollum aside like a pesky fly. Now I wasn't so sure. Gollum had pushed those mutant faeries a goodly distance with his esoteric martial arts. Donovan coiled enough energy within him, that if used against him, it might knock him through those painted glass panes.

"Donovan, please leave the room," I said.

"That is not necessary," Lucia dismissed my request.

"Can you control him when he loses his temper?" I looked only to Lucia.

"How'd you get it?" Donovan snarled, half angry, half amazed. He looked like he wanted to grab the ring, taking my arm off at the shoulder if he had to. His perpetual anger rose off him in hot waves. But he had to go through Gollum to get to me.

I sat back easily, unworried.

"Professional secret. Can you control him?" I repeated.

"Donovan will remain calm." Lucia sent him to the far corner of the office with a glimpse of her pointed teeth.

"You must understand that this artifact will be returned to you only when the faeries are back home and I have survived the mission," I hedged. Something deep inside me did not want to share the ring. It kept shouting in my mind that it was *MINE*.

I tried to believe the imp inside was still coherent enough to understand that Scrap would try to free it. That could only happen if the ring remained in my possession.

If Scrap was bloodthirsty, irreverent, and sarcastic, the trapped imp must be completely evil and insane by this time.

Lucia looked disappointed, but she nodded.

Reluctantly, I flipped the keys so that they nestled in my palm, the ring between them. It caught each nuance of the flickering light and reflected it in a dozen colored shafts. The entire office seemed filled with dancing rainbows.

Lucia's hand reached for it.

I closed my fist.

She sat back sighing in disappointment. A wistful look of longing and nostalgia crossed her face. (More evidence to me that she wasn't a vampire. She showed too much emotion for the soulless undead.) "You know it is genuine?" she asked.

"It damned well better be. How'd you get it away from Gregbaum?" Donovan snarled.

"Gary Gregbaum had it all this time?" Feral hunger snarled from her lips.

"Gregbaum only had it a few days. Donovan bought it at auction last December in Paris. He claims to have provenance back to 1850." Something about the date bothered me.

Scrap had said that Lucia sold the ring to buy food for her child. But the child had been about three in 1819 when she escaped Tuscany to Faery. In human years he'd have been an adult by 1850. Maybe they spent a couple of decades in Faery. Time runs differently there.

"Donovan sold the ring to Gregbaum on Friday, I believe. Or possibly Thursday night," I returned to the topic at hand. I left out the interlude when the ring could have been mine in the rocking gondola at The Venetian Hotel. No need to revisit that fiasco.

"And you acquired it . . . how?" Lucia asked more politely.

Donovan started pacing again.

He made me nervous. I clasped the ring tightly, then returned it to the inside pouch of the pack.

"I claim the ring by right of inheritance. It belonged to the Noncoiré family for many generations before it came to you, Lady Lucia."

"How much of that . . . um . . . episode do you know?" she asked arching an eyebrow.

I shrugged. "Only what Scrap told me. That you seduced my ancestor just to get the ring, then hightailed it over the border to marry Continelli, while your lover went off to Napoleon's war and got himself killed."

She looked squarely at Scrap. He turned his back to me and some silent communication passed between them.

Instant jealousy rose up in me.

"Very well. You know that the ring was a gift of love; honorable, and genuine."

I nodded.

"It was mine to keep or sell as I needed."

"Yes."

"Gregbaum doesn't have enough power in him to retain the ring," Lucia said, glaring at Donovan. "I declare it Tess' rightful possession for the time being. Spoils of war. When this is all over, Tess will return it to me as a gesture of thanks for my help."

"Agreed," Donovan sighed.

"Before the alchemist tricked a faery king to gain possession of the ring, it belonged to my people. It should come to me," Mickey insisted. For the first time he looked avaricious, bordering on turning into one of the black-and-red faeries if thwarted.

Time to end this.

"Lady Lucia, you have only to give Mickey and Gollum a detailed account of Gregbaum setting the spell and order Donovan to assist me tonight in getting the faeries home. Then the ring is yours."

"You've got to sign a promissory note to help finance *my* casino before I'll help Tess do anything," Donovan said. His color ran high, and his muscles tensed. His temper rode very close to the surface.

Gollum's new phone chirped an airy waltz. He glanced at the screen. All color drained out of his face. He looked a little unsteady on his feet. "Excuse me, I've got to take this."

He fled.

Donovan smiled wickedly. "Looks to me, Tess, like you might be on the receiving end of rejection this time."

"What are you talking about?"

"Let's just say, I've done my fair share of background checks. Made more than a few phone calls, too. You're in for quite a surprise. But that has nothing to do with our agreement for tonight. Just don't come running back to me afterward."

Chapter 43

In Spanish, Nevada means snowcapped.

I DON'T LIKE the clipped New York accent that slides into Gollum's words. He sounds terse and angry through the heavy door. He also sounds a bit sad.

This could be bad news for Tess.

So I slip away from her and hover around Gollum's left ear trying to hear both sides of his conversation.

Drat, I'm too late. He's closing the phone that does everything just as I pop through. I count to ten then ten more as he sucks in air and lets it out again verrrrrry slowly. That's his martial arts training. He's got to regain control over his emotions before he faces Tess again.

This does not bode well.

I never thought to probe his secrets before. He's so right for my dahling I figured he'd come clean honestly, without manipulation when the time was right. Tess says he did that last night when they were in that cave becoming a couple. A lasting and important couple.

Ouch, he nearly closes the door on my tail. Good thing I'm only partly in this dimension and can slide through the dense wood with little problem. Still it reminds me too much of the nothing place between here and there where the Guardians trapped me.

I do not like dark and dense anymore, even though it does

provide nice hiding places from the too-perceptive. I'll just have to be better at camouflage.

This may call for another feather boa, or some makeup.

First things first. Gollum's gearing up to say something.

"Tess, let's figure out this spell. Now. We haven't a lot of time and there's no repeat performance," Gollum ground out the moment he reentered Lady Lucia's office. His face was bland, but he bit off the last syllable of his words and his gaze would not meet mine.

"What's wrong?" I reached out to touch his hand.

He jerked away from me as if burned.

"Later. We'll talk later. I promise. Just not right now." Each of those last four words sounded like a separate sentence. Maybe even a full paragraph.

Something twisted in my belly. I'm not usually prescient. Gollum's tense shoulders and board stiff fingers—like he was afraid if he clenched them he'd smash his fist into something, or someone—told me more than I wanted to know.

Then there was Donovan's satisfied smirk marring his handsome face. If I ever doubted my decision to sever an intimate relationship with him, I didn't now. This man could be cruel.

The conversation turned to esoteric circles, pentagrams, incense, candle placement, and chants. My cursory reading in ceremonial magic for my books wasn't deep enough to fathom the importance of the details Gollum pried out of Lady Lucia's memory.

"I am certain that the black candles belonged in the center of each triangle that formed the points of the pentagram," she insisted for the third time. "The red ones went inside the pentagon at the center and the white ones between the points but inside the circle marking the pentangle."

That caught my attention. "In white magic, MoonFeather always places the white candles representing Air at the center, the red for Fire at the points, blue for Water goes between the points, and the black or brown for Earth outside the circle." My aunt always used multiple symbolism. I knew that in her pentagrams the white center represented purity of spirit. Any darkness that might creep into the spell had to remain outside the circle. Dark Earth also represented a grounding or anchor to reality.

She used a much lighter incense, blending the ingredients from her own herb garden as much as possible.

"This is not white magic," Lucia reminded me. "Gregbaum needed something very dark, but not truly black." Hence the heavy, artificial incense and the burning blood. He cut one of his mutant faeries to get that blood. He set plain incense smudge pots at the cardinal direction points around the building. The ones containing blood went around the dormitory in the basement of the building.

If MoonFeather needed blood, she'd use her own menstrual blood or take a little from a goat or chicken, but only an animal that was destined to die anyway to fill her table later.

"I think you should use green candles for Earth. Green the same color as Mickey's eyes, faery green."

Gollum nodded assent and made a note on his new cell phone that replaced his PDA and laptop.

"This is not like any magic I know of." Mickey shook his head. "We are creatures of the Air. Trapping the dancers in the basement, beneath the Earth is draining them of strength more than being away from home for so long."

"I know this as much as anyone," Lucia said proudly. She looked as if she intended to say more but bit off the last words.

"You designed the spell." I kept my voice matter-of-fact, avoiding any hint of accusation.

Her silence said it all.

"I advised Junior on some of the symbolism. How did you guess?" she asked sweetly.

"Because I don't think Gregbaum or Junior is smart enough to layer symbolism on top of symbolism and rearrange those symbols so subtly."

Lucia's smile grew bigger. She almost bared her fangs.

Did all Damiri have those fangs? I didn't think so. Darren hadn't, not when he was in human form anyway. Dill had never showed evidence of them, other than prominent eye teeth.

"You are correct." She nodded her head regally.

"If you set it, then you know how to reverse it," I said.

"That is just the point, my dear Tess. I do not know how

to reverse it. I planned it as a one-time trap, never needed again. Then Gregbaum betrayed me, and I severed our relationship. Now I need to finish severing every connection I ever had to the man."

Uh-oh. Gregbaum's blood is on the ring. When it goes back to Lucia, she'll be able to track him.

Huh?

Trust me, babe. She'll trace the scent through three dimensions before giving up. Even cleaning it with bleach won't help.

I didn't want to think about what Lady Lucia would consider betrayal.

Did Gregbaum take another to his bed? Eeewwwwww!

Or had the slimy lounge lizard deprived Lucia of a meal? Double eeewwwww!

I hoped, I really, really hoped, that he had just cheated her out of some money.

And to think, nine months ago I didn't believe in any of this crap. Now I easily envisioned Junior bent over a bowl of water, scrying our conversation through magic, tracing us through a drop of Gregbaum's blood in the water to call to the blood on the ring.

"We're out of here," I said. "Gollum, you and Mickey go back to the hotel and put your heads together on this."

"What are you going to do?" Gollum looked up, meeting my eyes for the first time since his phone call. He'd banished the strong emotions and now showed only a deep interest in something bizarre.

"What any self-respecting woman would do. I'm going to call my mom. And if that doesn't work, I'll contact the Citadel. Someone, somewhere has to know how to get those faeries back home."

Don't bet on it, dahling. Can't we go shopping instead?

"Tess, before we go to our separate tasks, I have to talk to you." Gollum didn't look happy about that. He didn't touch my back as he escorted me down the stairs, away from Lady Lucia.

"So talk."

"Alone." He looked pointedly at Mickey.

Oooh, one of those talks. I'll leave you to it while I check out the mall. Scrap popped out. I barely noticed.

"I'll drop you at The Crown Jewels. Then I'll check local magic shops for supplies while you talk," Mickey said distractedly.

"Thank you, Mickey. What are we going to do about the blood . . . ?" I didn't want to finish that thought.

"You may have some of mine," Mickey said proudly. "Good faery blood to balance the wrongness of the changed ones."

We said nothing more until Gollum closed the door of our hotel room. He went immediately to the long windows and stared at the mountains in the distance. A tiny bit of snow glistened on the high peaks, left over from last night's storm.

"So what is so important?" I asked, making myself comfortable on the bed with pillows propped behind my back. I had a bad feeling about this. Our relationship was so new, still fragile, I didn't want to risk it just yet. Give it time to grow and strengthen. Then we could weather any storm together.

As we had last night.

Inwardly, I smiled at the specialness of making love with Gollum.

"Tess . . . I . . ." He gulped and swallowed. Then he hung his head, reluctant to turn and meet my gaze.

"Spit it out. One sentence at a time, stripped bare of emotion." That's what I did in my books when I didn't quite know how to get from here to there.

He straightened and stared through the window. His eyes clouded and I knew he looked deeply into his past. A shadowy past I had not shared with him.

"Tess, I'm married."

The world went white. I grew hot with chill pricking the edges.

"How . . . why didn't you tell me last autumn when we first met? Why isn't *she* with you?" I could write a better *fictional* excuse to get out of a relationship.

My temper threatened to boil over.

I had to remind myself, this was Gollum, my Gollum.

Well, maybe he wasn't mine after all. Maybe I should listen more closely.

"We were very young. I was nineteen and had just finished the course work for my first masters. Julia had just graduated from high school. Our parents had known each other forever. They'd planned for us to marry since we were infants. And I do love her. I'll always love her. She's special. But in a different way from you. You are my soul mate. She's a sprite from my childhood."

He sank onto the edge of the bed opposite me. Finally, he dropped his eyes to mine.

"I know now that Julia and her mother never got along because they are both bipolar. Bridget—that's my mother-in-law—always saw raising a daughter as a competition. Almost a blood sport. She decided it was time for us to marry because she wanted to put on the social event of the season. I agreed because I thought I could rescue Julia from an emotionally abusive situation."

I gulped. Living on Cape Cod where some of the wealthiest people in the country had summer homes, I'd seen the same thing happen over and over. I'd even taught some of those girls in school.

"The wedding was a disaster, I take it?" I prodded.

"Yeah. Bridget couldn't allow Julia to outshine her. She even wore white and commandeered the photographer to follow her around, ignoring the bride and groom." He said that as if he was an observer and not the groom in question. He suddenly looked younger and more vulnerable. At the same time, his eyes became care-hardened. "My mother wasn't much better. She, at least, had the decency to wear ice blue—not quite white."

I thought I understood why he'd taken the job with the financial advisers in New York even though he hated the city. "What happened to send you off to Africa two years later?"

"Three miscarriages." He had to stop and blink rapidly. He took off his glasses and rubbed his eyes. "Julia grew more and more depressed. I got her to therapists, specialists, anyone who might help her. She flushed her meds, certain they'd caused her to lose our babies." He winced. "Maybe they did. Maybe she just wasn't healthy enough to carry a baby to term."

Damn, damn, damn.

"After the third one, her mother convinced her she was

a total failure as a human being. Julia tried to slit her wrists. Her doctors recommended a stay in a very expensive, very exclusive sanitarium." He recited each word methodically, without emotion. Just spitting it out.

"Like the one where we stashed WindScribe?" WindScribe, the witch who'd started the imbalance in Faery by killing the king. She'd also murdered Darren Estevez. Her violent tendencies and ravings about demons and beings from other worlds guaranteed she'd never convince the authorities she was sane enough to stand trial or ever earn release. If she'd just kept her mouth shut, Donovan might have married her just to gain custody of the child she carried.

"Actually, they are in the same facility, different wings. Julia isn't violent, but she does tend to wander. She's been there for fifteen years. That phone call . . . she escaped and jumped into the river. She . . . Oh, God, Tess, she can't swim."

"Did . . . did she drown?"

"No. Her nurse dragged her out in time." Another long pause.

I didn't know what to say or how to say it. He looked as if he'd reject any attempt to touch him. So I wrapped my arms around myself and held on tight. If I kept it up, maybe I could keep my heart from breaking.

"When she regained consciousness, she came back to reality, quite lucid and sane. She does that sometimes. The first thing she asks for is me. I'm her only anchor, her only link to happiness. She made the phone call. She wept and asked that I take her back home, to our apartment in New York."

"Are you going to do that?"

"I doubt her episode of clarity will last long enough to fill out the release papers. But I have to go see her."

"Yes, you do."

"I always thought that once I fell in love again, found the right woman, I'd just divorce Julia so I could remarry. Now that I've found you . . . now that I know that you and I could have a future together, this happens and I know I can't divorce her. I can't abandon her like that."

"And I'd be a complete heel to ask you to."

Chapter 44

Las Vegas receives on average 4.13 inches of rainfall a year. Their extensive water management program uses more recycled water than any other. Nothing is wasted.

AFTER SEVERAL LONG MOMENTS of absolute silence, Gollum left.

What could we say? Our emotions rode so close to the surface, any careless word or inflection could shatter us both. Irrevocably.

We both had chores to do before he could return to his wife. Before he could walk out of my life forever.

Maybe he didn't have to leave forever. Julia existed behind locked doors, incapable of leading a normal life with her husband.

Could I live with a married man, and continue to love him?

I did the only thing I was capable of doing. I went for a walk. The moment I stepped out into the afternoon heat I called my mom. Not that I could tell her anything over the phone. I just needed to connect to her, know that when I needed to talk, she'd be there for me.

"I'm not singing tonight, why don't we have dinner together," Mom said on a yawn.

"If it's early. I have a . . . a date tonight," I replied.

Off the Strip, Las Vegas was just another city. I walked past homes with desert landscaping—lots of crushed rock and succulent plants and cacti. An occasional cottonwood offered shade from the unrelenting sun. Nearly every corner had a convenience shop, drugstore, or small strip of shops. No different from any other residential neighborhood.

"I hope you and Donovan are finally getting together," Mom said showing more interest in the conversation than in her yawns.

Not bloody likely.

"He'll be there tonight. It's sort of a group thing. But I'm not dating him." Never again. After one night with Gollum I had little interest in Donovan. Even though . . .

Did I have to give up Gollum because of his youthful commitment to Julia? She need never know. Even if someone told her that her husband had chosen another, she might not understand in her few moments of sanity.

I knew what my mother would advise before she left New England. But this new mom, the Las Vegas mom, might have a different perspective on my love life.

My heart twisted with guilt.

"How early is early?" Mom asked.

There was something unusual in Mom's voice. But then nothing about this trip had been ordinary for her.

"Before sunset, like around five. Six at the latest."

"Sorry. I'm having brunch right now with friends. I won't be ready to eat that early. Call me in the morning or when you get back from your date. I'll be up until about two. That's my new schedule." I heard a doorbell ring in the background.

"Mom, last night you spoke with a woman in a red dress and a long strand of pearls," I continued before she could hang up.

"Oh, her. She wanted me to break my contract with Junior and sing at her club. I don't remember which one." The doorbell rang again in the background. "Tess, I've got to go . . ."

"Just tell me if she sounded in any way threatening."

"Threatening? I don't think so."

"She looked like she wanted to bite you."

"Oh, that," Mom laughed. "I think she's a lesbian. But it was awful noisy with the whole lounge singing along with you. She had to bend quite close so I could hear her."

"If you say so."

She hung up without saying good-bye.

Before I could decide what to do, the phone chirped out the opening phrase of "In The Hall Of The Mountain King."

"Mom?" I asked hopefully, not bothering to look at the caller ID.

"Have you lost your mother, Tess? I can't let you two out of my sight for a minute," said Allie Engstrom on a chuckle. She'd been my best friend since kindergarten.

"Not really lost her, just misplaced the Québécois June Cleaver and replaced her with Auntie Mame," I replied.

"Wow! That must be some weekend getaway."

"You wouldn't believe half of it." Well, maybe Allie would believe half of it. She'd helped me out with some pesky garden gnomes with teeth last month and knew about Darren being a demon. "What's up?"

"Do I still need to pick you up at midnight in Providence?"

"Gosh, Allie, sorry, I forgot, I'll be staying over an extra day or maybe two." Picture me pounding fist to forehead.

"What about your mom?"

"Well, actually, she's not coming home."

"Did you kill her?" Only half a joke. I'd threatened to strangle my mother upon occasion. She'd frustrated me beyond words until last Wednesday night when she broke free of her chrysalis.

"No, Mom has taken a job as a lounge singer. She's moved in with an ex-hooker, and I think she's found a new boyfriend."

"That's the premise of your next book, right?"

"No. That's what really happened."

"Wow! And what about you? How are you handling this?"

"I don't know yet. I'm happy for her, but I'm still processing the changes. Gollum is helping." I winced. After tonight Gollum might not be around to help. Too much unknown about *us* to tell at the moment.

"You finally did it!"

"Yeah, we did." I started melting a bit. I could talk about anything with Allie. We knew everything about each other, right down to the inflection of voice that said more than words.

I could cry with her and find a balance as well as exult with her over my one night of joy.

"How was it? Is he as gentle and caring as he comes across? Or is he secretly wild and abandoned?" she asked breathlessly.

"Both!"

We laughed out loud together. Remember the good times. Hold them close against the pain to come.

Make decisions when the emotions are under control.

"Maybe I need to come to Vegas to change my life," Allie finally said a bit wistfully.

"I really wish you were here right now." How could I convey the depth of my need for her friendship now. Telling her everything over a cell phone wasn't enough. Wasn't right. I needed her to hold my hand and offer her shoulder for me to cry on when the truth spilled out of me.

I needed her to help me work through the dilemma of Julia.

Scrap came back and rubbed his cheek against my hair. I'd never be truly alone. As much as I missed Gollum already, Scrap would comfort me. I slipped the ring off the key chain and back onto my hand where it belonged.

"Anything I can do to help, long distance?"

"Not really." I reached up and tweaked Scrap's tail affectionately. I didn't need to talk to him. He knew everything and understood my hurt.

I didn't dare tell Allie about Lady Lucia pretending to be a vampire. She'd be on the next plane. She loved vampire fiction and secretly longed to meet one.

"Say, remember last month when you asked me to do a background check on Breven Sancroix?"

I paused in the middle of the sidewalk. The sun beat down on my neck and head, reminding me I hadn't put on sunscreen or worn a hat. That's how stupid and distracted I was after Gollum's confession.

I moved to the shade of a cottonwood overhanging someone's yard. "Did you find anything unusual?"

"Not much. He's lived quietly for the most part on a farm in western Pennsylvania for about twenty years. The deed is held jointly by him and Gertrud—no e on the end—Sancroix née Jarwoski. What flagged my interest was that, before then, neither of them exists—she still doesn't. No birth records, no Social Security number, no driver's license. Nada. Nothing. And no one has ever seen her."

"You said he lived *mostly* quietly."

"Except for periodic reports of violence—taking apart a bar that didn't have his favorite beer, road rage, and shooting a trespasser on his land. Luckily, he didn't kill the teenager breaking into his barn. And since the kid was high on drugs, his parents got him into rehab and didn't press charges."

I shuddered. Would I become so used to killing demons with the Celestial Blade that I let it spill over into ordinary life?

For the first time I truly understood Gollum's vow of nonviolence.

Oh, God. Gollum!

"That's what made me think he had a prison record under a different name," Allie continued, unaware of my mental digression. "If you could get me a sample of his fingerprints I could cross-check."

"I'll see what I can do." We chatted a few more minutes and said our good-byes with promises of a long catch-up chat when I got home. My mind had already jumped ahead into more useful patterns than crying over my lost lover.

Breven Sancroix had an imp. Therefore, he had to have spent some time in a Citadel. And that's where his wife Gertrud Jarwoski had holed up for just as long. Hence the blank spot before the farm in Pennsylvania. His conversation led me to believe he'd lived in the Citadel quite a while. Longer than I had. Fortitude had a lot of warts earned in battle. Scrap kept losing his due to some strange law of impland so that I couldn't tell how many he was supposed to have, or if an imp gained some of those beauty marks in the normal aging process.

My deductions led me to believe that Sancroix had battled more than a few demons since living in the real world. (Citadel life is quite surreal.)

By this time I'd looped around the block and returned to the hotel. I hurried back to my room. Then I hid the ring inside my computer bag. I also turned on the shower and the television. I didn't want any eavesdroppers, mundane or magical.

I'll keep a lookout, Scrap promised and flew back out to the hallway.

With as much privacy as I could manage surrounding me, I hit my speed dial for Gayla, leader of my Sisterhood.

Chapter 45

Of the men who died building the Hoover Dam, the first and the last were father and son.

"SISTER SERENA?" I queried the voice that answered my call. I hadn't expected the Sisterhood's physician to pick up the landline.

"Tess, so good to hear from you," she cried. A moment of rapid exchange in the background. I could well imagine a half-dozen women gathering around for the thrill of an infrequent phone call. Those who chose the Citadel life didn't have much outside contact.

I made small talk for a few sentences, heard about this Sister's ailment, that Sister's retirement, and the ongoing pressure against the portal they guarded.

Tonight, of all nights, they needed to prepare for battle in a good mood, with reminders of what they fought for and why. The good times among themselves, and the innocents outside their walls.

Tonight, when the moon waxed one quarter full, demons were at their strongest and portals at their weakest.

Tonight, when I fought to get innocent faeries through a rogue portal, my Sisterhood would fight to keep a stable portal closed.

"But you do not call to gossip," Serena said quietly. "Our imps can pass that information back and forth."

"Yes." I wondered why Scrap hadn't acted as messenger

very often. But then, as the runt of the pack, and gay at that, he hadn't made friends among his kind. Until recently. I remembered a certain glow about him and the name Ginkgo on his mind.

"About a month ago I requested help from any other rogue Warrior you could contact."

"I remember that." Serena sounded thoughtful. "Did someone come?"

"He came too late to help. I managed on my own. With the help of some friends."

"Oh, Tess, you haven't violated your vow of secrecy," Serena said, disappointment dripping from her words.

"Not really. My friends are either involved in our lifestyle or figured it out when I got attacked in broad daylight by the Orculli trolls." I almost laughed at that. King Scazzy of the garden gnomes with teeth, was actually the prison warden of the universe. He'd been on a mission at the time. No one had thought to clue me in until after we'd exchanged blows and blood had been drawn. MoonFeather's blood. I was still hard-put to forgive Scazzy for that.

"I called to find out what you know about the rogue Warrior. Breven Sancroix is still hanging around."

"Sancroix?" Sister Serena paused a moment. She probably drummed her fingers on her thigh, a habitual gesture—she had to constantly work the fingers of her right hand to keep them supple after a demon tag. "Sancroix! I remember him from long ago. He and his Brotherhood visited one Summer Solstice. It was quite a party. I'd just come back from my residency. So I got to deliver a bunch of babies around the Vernal Equinox. Gert had a boy, I think, and sent it to Sancroix for raising once he'd been weaned."

Junior was too old to be that baby, perhaps thirty-five. No reason he couldn't be the child of a previous Solstice celebration, though. Unusual that Sancroix referred to his *nephew* as Junior.

"No wonder Sancroix remembers Sister Gert quite fondly," I prompted.

"Gert's not here at the moment, or I'd ask her."

"Where'd she get to?" As if I didn't know.

Sister Gert had a lot invested in maintaining the status quo. A status quo outdated about one hundred years ago.

"Um." Serena dropped her voice to a barely audible

whisper. "She's talking about going rogue, something about a farm in Pennsylvania."

Uh-oh.

Did I say I don't believe in coincidences?

I needed to keep an eye on Sancroix and Gert. The best way to do that was to include them in tonight's activities—let him burn off a little of his reported violence constructively. I had no doubt that Gregbaum had a dozen or more minions guarding both the dormitory and the portal at Goblin Rock. Two extra Celestial Blades would help.

I've got better ways to glean the truth from gossip. Time for a quick trip to visit my lover Ginkgo.

Imp memory goes back a long way.

He'll know everything there is to know about Juniper, companion to Sister Gert. If the good sister did give birth to a kid or two by Sancroix, then her imp probably loosed a couple of litters by Fortitude.

Once I know Fortitude's character, I'll know a lot about Breven Sancroix.

I don't trust either one of them. Interesting to find out if anyone else does.

More interesting to find out why Sancroix left his Citadel. Did he go voluntarily or was he kicked out?

Sunset came late, around seven thirty. Moonrise was scheduled for nine fifty-seven. Not a lot of time to break into the Dragon and St. George, free the dancers, get them on a bus, and drive them for a full hour out to the Valley Of Fire.

Timing was everything.

The moon awakes from a little sleep. It becomes a key held in the arm of a . . . a Guardian who is also a monster. The words of the Paiute bartender's vision quest came back to me.

That part had to refer to the waxing quarter moon rising behind the Rock Goblin.

It opens a path to twilight lands of peace and plenty, lands that a warrior may glimpse but never enter.

That part had to be Faery.

Only one warrior will rise above the ties that bind him to this earth to walk between.

And that meant me. And this happened only once in every ten generations.

Gulp. Tonight or never. In a few hours when the moon rose.

My hands trembled. I wiped sweaty palms on my jeans. This had to work. We only had one chance, one very small chance in a narrow margin of time.

The dancers did not perform on Monday or Tuesday night. By Wednesday when Lucia took over, no one would miss them.

Except Gregbaum.

Breven and Fortitude prowled the casino, gathering up any stray dancers. He refused to take Fortitude into the Valley Of Fire but seemed more than willing to help at this end of the operation.

Junior remained at The Crown Jewels, wringing his hands. I didn't want him broadcasting anxiety around me when stealth was the key to success. I suspected Lady Lucia kept an eye on him, though she didn't say where she'd be tonight.

Sister Gert supposedly had gone back to Pennsylvania. And if you believe that I have some oceanfront property in Arizona I'll sell you.

Gert and Juniper are giving Junior a serious talking to. She's really upset with him, Scrap said, flitting about, seeking shadows within shadows.

Fortitude has problems. Big problems. Don't trust him, Scrap continued curtly. *He listens to Junior more than to his Warrior. Junior is the one who dragged them down the current path of violence and total disregard for rules and the well-being of others. That's why Gert's giving him a hard time. Juniper is leaning toward Junior now, too.* He disappeared when I tried to get specifics from him.

Great. My allies were an angry faery changeling, a fellow rogue Warrior and his imp who had anger management problems, and a demon masquerading as a vampire crime boss.

Gollum and Mickey wandered around outside with a compass and GPS, setting tiny smudge pots at North, East,

South, and West. Candles got tucked into crevices in between the pots. They'd both been unnaturally quiet all afternoon.

Donovan drove around and around in an oversized van. A tight fit for our crew and the dancers, but the most inconspicuous vehicle he could find on short notice that suited us.

I was just as glad he kept his sullen countenance away from me.

Me? I stayed hidden between the deserted backstage and access to the dormitory. Scrap did my scouting for me.

"This is too easy," I whispered to Scrap. My internal clock told me the sun dipped below the horizon.

I can't find Gregbaum anywhere, babe, he growled, coming in for a landing on my shoulder.

"What about his guards?"

Missing in action as well.

"Do you think Donovan warned them about our operation?"

Scrap shrugged and took off again. *All twenty faeries present and accounted for in the dormitory.*

"Time to get this mission going.

My phone vibrated—no way I was taking a chance on a ring tone alerting the bad guys to my presence.

"The sun just hit the horizon. I'm lighting things up," Gollum hissed through the phone. "We've got to do this the exact opposite of when Lucia set the spell."

Sancroix came around the corner, looking tired. Fortitude looked like . . . well like Fortitude, gray-green skin darkened with age—more charcoal than green—wings held high, ready to flee in a heartbeat. He avoided looking at me or at Scrap.

Seconds later, Gollum and Mickey skidded to a stop in front of me.

"Is it working?" Gollum asked.

Nothing yet, Scrap replied.

"Try the dormitory, Scrap."

He mumbled and grumbled as he popped out and bounced right back in. *Still in place, babe.*

"What are we going to do?" I began absently turning the diamond ring on my right hand.

Mickey sniffed. "Something different . . ."

The magic smells different!

Fortitude nodded acknowledgment and spread his wings until they formed a curtain behind Sancroix. His skin grew darker, flushed with the barest hint of red. Sancroix winced as his imp's talons gripped his shoulder tighter.

Something was wrong between them. I could sense when Scrap did the same thing; he never hurt me.

Scrap flashed from gray to pink to red in an eye blink.

"Bad guys," I whispered to one and all.

"Where?" Sancroix turned in a circle, automatically extending his hand for Fortitude to land there and begin transforming.

I did the same for Scrap.

Scrap was still elongating when Fortitude's tail and ears curved into blades at opposite ends of a shaft.

I'd never seen an imp morph so quickly. He seemed a bit too eager to taste blood.

No time for questions. No time to think.

Fifteen black-and-red Faeries dropped from the flies above the stage, blued broadswords drawn and swinging.

Chapter 46

The Las Vegas Hard Rock Hotel & Casino uses only recycled metal, glass, and paper products.

"GOLLUM, MICKEY, GET the dancers out *now*!" I yelled.

Before Scrap had a chance to fully sharpen, I twirled the blade over my head, at the level of the black-and-red faeries' throats.

Flurries of movement all around me.

No rules. No confining fencing strip. No honor. We fought all out; to the death.

In the movies the bad guys politely wait to attack the hero one at a time. Real demons aren't so nice.

Fifteen armed bad guys against two Warriors of the Celestial Blade. "I've seen worse odds. Seen better ones too," I mused.

Scrap vibrated with agreement and a need to taste blood. The viler and blacker the better.

Sensing that my lack of height and reach made me the weaker prey, eight mutants descended on me, swords extended and slashing. Sancroix faced seven of the monsters.

I might be vertically challenged, but I'm fit and trained.

One opponent on my left caught the full curve of the blade across his middle. He stood staring and gasping as the wound gushed black blood. Before he could collapse, I'd taken out the guy on my opposite side with a backhand. He caught the tines of the outside curve in his throat.

Two down. Six to go. Sancroix had wounded but not taken out one of his attackers.

I didn't have time to gloat.

Three more black-and-red faeries landed between us.

Where were they hiding? Where did Gregbaum get so many goons to do his bidding?

I almost believed he recycled them back to life, like something in a science fiction novel.

We really needed some help.

Where the hell was Donovan when I needed him?

As if I'd conjured him with my thoughts, he burst onto the stage. In one swift movement he retrieved a sword from a fallen enemy and stabbed a black faery in the back.

Before he could recover his grip on the sword, he had five pressing him backward.

"To me," I called.

With barely a nod of acknowledgment, he sidestepped a blow and placed himself at my back.

"Just like old times, love," he said, almost gleefully.

I slashed at a goon that had sneaked under Donovan's guard in reply. His squirt of black blood covered my hands and made my grip slippery. A little heat and tingle, but my skin didn't burn like it would if these guys were truly demon-born and bred.

"Can we hurry this up? I'm double-parked," Donovan joked.

Slash, stab. Shift my grip, parry two blades, jump back from a third.

My shoulders ached. My thighs burned. The lingering groin injury flared back to life, feeling like a knife had ripped muscle. I kept changing my grip and the level of my blows to stave off fatigue. Fatigue that could get me killed.

The ring on my right hand twisted about my finger with every shift. Part of me registered fear that it slid too easily and I'd lose it before I really needed it at the Goblin Rock.

Presuming I survived that long.

And still they kept coming at us. Armed demons are ten times more deadly than unarmed. Worse, these guys had wings to lift them beyond my reach. No way we could even the odds.

"Tess, the magic net won't drop!" Gollum yelled from the corridor.

"Chant something. Light a candle." Damn, that blue-black blade almost cut me in two. I dodged and caught the tip on my upper arm. Blood dripped down to my hand, further threatening my hold on the shaft of my blade.

Scrap shuddered from within. He tired as much as I did.

"I've tried everything I know how."

"If we could just cut a door in the net rather than destroy it," Mickey said.

An imp can go anywhere, Scrap reminded me. His eyes blinked at me from the right-hand blade.

Imps open doors into any world. Could I break away from the fight long enough to slash through the magic?

Another faery came under my guard.

Donovan took him out with a swift stab to the solar plexus.

The ring twisted again on my finger.

I had a second imp trapped in the ring.

"Donovan, cover for me for two seconds." I kept twirling the Celestial Blade in my left hand, keeping at least one enemy at bay. All the while I ran my right hand up and down my leg, letting the rough fabric of my jeans turn the ring.

In my mind I pictured a door opening in front of the dormitory, and another to the outside. The image became so real I almost missed the black faery flying down onto my head, his leathery wings absolutely silent.

Just barely in time, I cut his hamstrings and he plopped into the middle of a phalanx of three of his buddies.

They went down like bowling pins.

I gulped air three times before I dove into the pig pile. Three of them died with a single blow. By the time I got to the fourth, Scrap began to dull and shorten.

My strength flagged.

We couldn't keep up this fight much longer.

"Hang in there." Donovan's voice came to me as if from a long distance.

I could barely lift my blade. He stepped in front of me and dispatched the last of the fallen foes. "The dancers are out. We've got to make sure they get away."

"I've got to go with them. They can't get home without me," I ground out. I lost my grip on the blade. It clattered to the stage and lay there inert for ten long loud heartbeats. I just stared at it, knowing I needed to do something, too tired to remember what.

The blade disappeared. Scrap crawled away to feed and rest.

My balance teetered.

Donovan grabbed me and braced me against his side.

I felt like I could stand there forever, letting him prop me up.

"I shouldn't admit this, but I feel an overwhelming need to watch over you and protect you," he whispered. His breath stirred my hair. "Put the ring on the other hand and we can make it official."

Something stirred within me. I couldn't decide if it was pleasure or terror.

"I owe it to Dill to take care of you, finish what he started."

Cold sweat broke out on my back.

A ruffling of black side curtains saved me from having to answer.

Without thinking, I grabbed the sword Donovan handled so lightly and leaped to the flurry of movement. One last spurt of adrenaline carried me the ten steps I needed to go.

Gregbaum tangled in the yards of thin black cloth.

I held the broadsword to his throat. "Talk."

"I . . . um . . . uf . . . eek!" The last squeal in response to a nick from the sword tip. He bled red just like any normal human.

"How many more of your mutants await us at the Goblin Rock?" I pressed a little harder.

His throat apple bobbed as he swallowed. "A dozen," he squeaked.

"Donovan. Find us a car. Fast."

"Take mine," Lucia purred from directly behind me.

I like to think I had enough presence of mind to accept her presence and not let her sudden appearance startle me.

Actually, I was just too tired to jump.

"What do I need to do to restore the balance in Faery?" I spat, still holding the sword at Gregbaum's throat.

"N . . . nothing much."

"That doesn't tell me anything."

The drop of blood on his throat turned into a little rivulet.

Lucia licked her lips.

Gregbaum's eyes grew wide in fascinated horror. His pupils fully dilated.

Lucia came up beside me. She drooled a bit as her lips opened to reveal her fangs.

"C . . . close the portal behind the last faery. Kill all the mutants or throw them through the portal. Make sure all of them go. The leak will stop. They'll rebalance on their own," Gregbaum babbled.

"Go. Fight your battle," Lucia urged me. "There is food and drink in the car to restore you. I even managed a bit of mold for the imp." She half laughed, shouldering me aside so that she faced Gregbaum directly.

"It's not wise to accept food and drink . . ."

"The food is safe. It carries no obligation of hospitality. Just my little part in restoring the balance of portals. I, too, need to score points with the Powers That Be."

I backed away, keeping the sword close to my side. No telling if I'd need it out in the Valley of Fire.

"Where's Sancroix?" I asked, sagging more than a little.

The only evidence I could find that he'd ever been there was a pile of mutilated bodies. Not just dead enemies, but hacked-off limbs, severed heads, ragged slashes, and guts spilling all over the place adding their stench to the miasma of sulfur rising from the other corpses. And black blood everywhere. Great pools of it.

I gagged and had to clamp my teeth shut to keep my bile from adding to the stench.

Sancroix had gone far beyond defending himself or helping the mission to restore the balance. He'd succumbed to a berserker's bloodlust.

"Sancroix lit out as soon as the last black faery fell." Donovan cleaned his sword of black blood on the vest of one of the dead ones. "We've got to go if we're going to catch up with the bus."

"You aren't going to leave me alone with her!" Gregbaum screamed. "She'll . . . she'll . . . tur . . ." He stopped in mid word mouth, moving but no sound coming out.

"Do not worry about the bodies. My crew will clean up," Lucia said. "Just remember to return the ring to me when you have finished." She opened her mouth wide and aimed her teeth at Gregbaum's throat.

He just stood there, frozen in horror, totally mesmerized by Lucia's exotic beauty and bloodthirst.

"You can't . . ." I was equally horrified.

Donovan grabbed me and dragged me away. "That is a confrontation long overdue. None of our business," he ground out.

"But . . . he's human!"

"None of our business how the lady takes her revenge for his deceit that jeopardized all the dimensions with imbalance and deadly consequences." With one arm around my middle, he pulled me backward toward the exit and the waiting black Hummer.

Chapter 47

In 2000 the Aladdin Hotel became the first hotel to be closed, imploded, and reopened without a name change.

"SHE TRULY IS A VAMPIRE," I whispered as Donovan maneuvered the powerful car in and out of congestion on the strip. "I thought she was Damiri, just pretending to be a vampire because humans might accept her better."

"She is. The demon in her needs blood just like a vampire. But vampires are much more socially acceptable than demons. There is power in the legends," he ground out, shaking his fist at a stretch limo that tried to cut him off from the freeway entrance.

"Has she pretended to live as a vampire so long that she believes her own lies?" I delved into the picnic basket—a real old-fashioned wicker one with folding handles and a top hinged in the middle that opened at either end—and produced rare roast beef sandwiches, cans of iced cola, and rich, dark chocolate bars. Sugar, caffeine, protein, and chocolate. All I needed.

In the very bottom was a jar of blue cheese that had gone moldy.

Or is that moldier?

I didn't care if it gave Scrap gas and an upset tummy as long as it helped him recover. I left it open in the basket. He could crawl in there to recover in private. "You've got an hour, buddy. Make the most of it."

Heaven, came his reply, weak and distant.

"As near as I can tell, she had no idea she might have demon blood in her until it took thirty years for her to age five. And she didn't know the value of the ring until many decades after she sold it." Donovan settled in for a long drive at fifteen miles above the speed limit. He drove competently with one hand, holding food with the other.

"An artifact of power of that magnitude must have left some kind of psychic trail," I mused. I thought of my lust for the ring.

Or was that the imp inside seeking an owner who might have the power to free him?

Got that in one, Scrap mumbled around a full mouth.

The headlights of an approaching car made the diamond on my right hand flash and sparkle.

"There are always rumors. Most of them false. When dormant, the ring doesn't betray its importance to any but the most sensitive. Lucia became sensitive enough to detect it after she investigated her demon ancestry. Her family always had an eccentric aunt or uncle who lived well beyond normal years and played with magic. They thought them witches and hid them." He downed half a cola in one gulp.

"If she didn't know, when did she start needing blood?"

"Once she'd tasted blood in her vampire act, she started craving it. The demon genes sort of leaped to life. That's one of the reasons Dill never allowed himself to indulge, even though he craved blood nutrition as much as he ached to transform." Donovan passed a line of cars only going five miles an hour over the limit in the left lane. His tires skidded on shoulder gravel, but he righted the car quickly and competently.

"Dill always did like his meat very rare." I dwelled briefly on a memory, then banished it as useless. I needed information about living demons. "When did Lucia leave Europe?"

"About forty years ago. The freewheeling hippie lifestyle in the States attracted her. She started speculating in real estate right off, in a small way. Built an empire in an amazingly short period of time. Most of her deals were cut at parties where she strewed just enough blood about to strike fear in the hearts of those with property to sell or develop. She can be up and about during the day when she has to. As long as she stays out of sunlight, she perpetuates the myth."

Hence the office with the painted windows and the covered patio below her bedroom. "You knew her then?"

"Yep."

"How well?"

"Not well enough for you to be jealous." He flashed me one of his anxiety-dampening smiles.

I did my best not to fall for it. Scrap said they were sleeping together now. I wasn't jealous. Not really.

"So, what exactly did Gregbaum do to Lucia to deserve . . ." I tried to banish the sight of her fangs sinking into the pudgy rolls of flesh on his neck.

"He lied to her about the dancers. She knew they were real faeries. But Gregbaum told her they wanted to escape the imbalances in their home, not that he'd kidnapped them. He told her the magic net was to keep out Clean Up Teams from the Powers That Be. She had no idea in the beginning the spell she designed with Junior's help was to keep them trapped in the building and enslaved. He lied to her about the origins of his goons, too."

"Which is?"

"Mutations caused by the imbalance when WindScribe killed the king of Faery and nearly set off a civil war in a dimension that had never known violence. Trickery, yes, but not the kind of rage and need to kill we found in those black-and-red monsters. Contrary to a lot of fiction and propaganda, vampires, demons, and witches do not seek violence for its own sake. But they have to get blood to survive somehow. Dill was the only Kajiri I've ever met who abstained. It nearly killed him at times."

He swallowed deeply, blinked his eyes rapidly, and reached for another cola to mask his emotions.

"Now that I think about it, Dill spiked a fever three times during the three months we were married. He ached all over and couldn't eat anything. I remember worrying about him, applying cold compresses, making chicken soup. I don't remember the timing to know if it happened on the night of the waxing quarter moon. But I'd have figured out a pattern eventually. He'd have had to tell me the truth."

"Reluctantly. He'd have put it off for a long time by

arranging to be out collecting rock samples alone on those nights."

He swallowed and cleared his throat. "Junior kept leading more and more good faeries through the toxic waste dump their primary river became. They came out the other side, twisted, angry, more than willing to follow him as long as Gregbaum let them kill."

"Lucia has a point. Any time there is an imbalance, or a lot of dead bodies piling up, the threat of exposure increases. Witch hunts, demon hunts, vampire hunts, all become bigger threats," I mused. Europe in the seventeenth century. Salem witch trials. Jewish pogroms and the Holocaust.

Anyone "different" became fair game for execution.

In a way, that strengthened the need for Donovan's secluded resort that catered to sorcerers, demons, and vampires, where they could indulge their needs without fear of exposure.

I didn't like it, but I understood it, a little.

"I'm helping you tonight because Lady Lucia's long-term goals suit me better than Gregbaum's quick money grab," Donovan said reaching for another cola from the basket.

"Can we still be friends? We seem to fall into the same . . . um . . . social circles and require each other's help. And I'm not jealous of Lucia, or WindScribe, or any of your other women." Having been raised by a Damiri—who are incredibly fertile—I don't think Donovan was capable of fidelity.

And I believe in monogamy once a commitment has been made.

Oh, God. Gollum and Julia! I think I just made my decision.

Anyway I looked at it, my relationship with Gollum was an unbalanced trio. Was I the third wheel? Or was Julia?

No way to naturally, or gracefully cut it down to two people.

One of us had to step away.

"We'll see. I take it Van der Hoyden-Smythe hasn't talked to you yet about that phone call."

I didn't like the feral satisfaction in the way he bared his teeth.

"Yes."

"Marry me, Tess. You and I are a better fit than you and him. I'll find a way to live with your imp, though I know you love him more than any man."

"I'll think about it." I twisted the ring again, wondering. Every time I tried to imagine myself committed to Donovan, I hit a blank wall that morphed into Gollum.

Shit!

"Is that our turnoff coming up?" Donovan wasn't the only one who knew how to change the subject without answering questions. I really didn't want to have to explain the sudden churning in my gut that had less to do with the three sandwiches and five cans of carbonated beverages than it did with the memory of all the color draining from Gollum's face when he recognized the caller ID on his phone.

We caught up with the van carrying the dancers as it careened around a sharp bend in the access road. Gollum had to be driving. Our headlights picked out few details.

The line of hoodoos appeared to be dancing families, frozen mid-step, hands stretching to join with another and failing. The one I'd put together to commemorate my first kiss with Gollum, was lost in the myriad of other ghostly forms.

Lost like our love.

As we crested the hill guarding the valley entrance the moon sent a shimmer of light along the eastern horizon. Not a lot of time left.

"Damnation!" Donovan spat as he pounded the steering wheel. "The gate's down."

"When has a little thing like a gate ever stopped you?" I dashed out of the car to raise the barrier, only to find it padlocked in place.

"A feeble attempt to cut down on vandalism, like we reported this morning," Gollum grumbled, coming up beside me. "This is a state park."

I wanted him to slip an arm about my waist, to reassure me that we'd find a way out of our dilemma.

He kept his hands to himself.

"It's at least a mile to Goblin Rock. Can we hike it before the moon lights the portal?" I asked surveying the landscape, what little of it I could see in the glow of the headlights.

"I think my friends are too far gone to walk that far," Mickey mused.

"Donovan, sword!" I commanded.

He emerged from the Hummer with the blue-black blade one of us had taken off the mutants. "Let me. I've got more strength." Before he'd finished speaking, he raised the sword and severed the hasp on the gate with one mighty blow. "Might have been easier to drive around, but that was more fun. And satisfying."

I held the gate open while they drove through, then closed it behind Donovan's vehicle. No sense alerting any passing rangers that we trespassed. They'd have to look close to note that the lock was gone.

Donovan pulled ahead of the van. He kept our speed reduced, compared to freeway excesses, but still faster than I would have driven the narrow road without streetlights.

We pulled into the gravel turnout. I checked on Scrap. He'd consumed the entire jar of moldy cheese.

Go away. I'm sleeping, he mumbled.

"You going to be up for a fight in a few minutes?"

Mft, phew, grl. Yeah, maybe. For you, babe.

At least the basket didn't smell like a toxic waste dump from his lactose intolerance. Yet. I'd hate to have to burn Lucia's gift.

"Moon coming up," Mickey said excitedly as he climbed out of the van.

Twenty faeries in varying shades of gray with mere hints of pastel in the folds of their wings and draperies tumbled out behind them. They twitched their noses eagerly, and as one turned to face the cave opening in the crook of the Goblin's "elbow."

"Home," they whispered breathlessly. "I smell home."

"No time to dawdle, folks," Gollum said. He began herding the dancers down the path, lighting the way with his flashlight. He had his backpack, stuffed with essentials.

"The Eagle Scout at work," Donovan sneered.

"That's why I love him," I said and followed along, taking the arms of two of the weaker faeries.

We made a great deal of noise coming down the path. No way to hide all those shuffling feet. The faeries might have been more silent if they could spread their wings and lift their feet more than half an inch. The desert chill on a clear night and near zero humidity didn't help them much.

Still we made good time on the hundred yards or so. We saw no signs of Gregbaum's guards.

"Is it too much to hope that when Lucia killed Gregbaum, his minions died, or reverted, or disappeared into the chat room and another dimension," I whispered to Donovan.

He paused while helping a male faery over a rough patch. The female he'd thrown over his shoulder.

I noticed Gollum had done the same thing.

"I don't think so. Once created, mutated, whatever, they take on lives of their own, separate from Gregbaum. They're here. I just can't tell where. Something about their Faery origins masks them from normal perceptions until they want to be seen."

"Scrap, can you smell any bad guys?"

Nope. He sounded a little more alert.

"You up to joining us yet."

Yeah, yeah, in a moment.

"Now, Scrap. You can doze on my shoulder as well as you can in that basket." I took ten long steps with faeries in tow before the imp roused himself long enough to pop onto my shoulder. He rested his head on my hair and wrapped his tail around my neck to keep himself in place.

"You aren't going to be much help if it comes to a fight, are you."

Mumble, mumble. Nothing coherent from him.

Great.

Good thing Donovan and I had brought swords along. He carried them across his back inside his shirt as a makeshift sheath.

"Moon coming into place," Gollum called the moment he reached the base of Goblin Rock.

"That's not the only thing in place." From my perspective ten yards back, with the moon just starting to glimmer behind the portal, I spotted the distinct shape of a bundle of dynamite jammed into the cave opening.

And three long wires trailing away behind the monolith. Some*thing* chuckled wickedly from the thorny shrubs in the near distance.

Chapter 48

The Apache was the first "high rise" hotel in Las Vegas with its own elevator. It towered three stories.

"BOMB!" I CALLED in my best schoolteacher voice. "Everyone freeze."

They obeyed.

"Gollum, can we cut the wires without setting that thing off?"

"You're asking the useless professor?" Donovan sneered.

"Not as useless as you may think. What do you know about explosives?"

"Um . . . a little bit of construction type demo."

"Not enough. Gollum, verdict?"

"Can't tell from here in this light." He edged closer, playing his light along the wires.

"Scrap, where are the bad guys?" I whispered.

Running for the hills like they're expecting the sky to rain down fire and brimstone, he replied on a yawn.

"We'll have to go after them."

Later, babe. Gotta get these faeries back home first. Close the portal, then black, red, and ugly are easy prey.

Tendrils of moonlight stretched through the opening portal in a dozen different directions, ethereal, wispy. And turning to black smoke as they traveled closer and closer to the fleeing forms.

"They're drawing energy continuously from Faery. Cut off their power and they lose strength," I mused.

"It's only about ten feet up. I think I can get to it," Mickey said. He closed his eyes a moment in concentration. Royal blue energy shot out of the portal to enfold him. It shimmered around him in a glorious aura. The glow coalesced into a pair of magnificent wings that stretched from above his head to his heels.

Transparent wings, without a lot of substance.

"My God, he really is the crown prince of Faery!" Donovan breathed.

"You expected less?" I replied. "A true prince risks everything to save his people."

I almost heard Donovan's argument that he had risked his financial empire time and again to provide a safe haven for his people.

Only they weren't truly his people. He was a gargoyle turned traitor, condemned to live as a human.

The wings weren't enough to lift Mickey to the portal. They only kept his steps light so that fragile sandstone didn't crumble beneath his feet.

"It's just resting there. I can move it," Mickey said. He reached his right arm to encircle the bundle.

"Mickey, no!" Gollum ran to stand directly beneath him. "It's on a timer and going to blow. Get out of there."

"The moon is rising. The portal's going to close," Donovan added.

"I can do this." Mickey pushed off from the rock face, the dynamite cradled against his chest.

"Everybody down!" Gollum yelled. "Drop it, Mickey. Drop it now!"

Blinding light. Deafening noise. A whoosh of air knocked me on my ass.

Fire and rock rained down us.

I crouched, my head down, arms forcing two faeries into tight fetal balls.

Hot rock burned my hands, ate through the synthetic fiber of my sweater. Not as much as I expected. I endured the brief pain.

"Mikhail," the dancers wailed as one.

I spread my wings over my Tess. Sparks bounce off them. Bigger embers scorch holes in my tender flesh. I endure. I have to protect my Warrior though the pain nearly drives me home to Mum.

Come to think on it, this pain is less than Mum's broom swatting my cute little bum.

If only I had a cigar to lessen the pain.

I've known worse. I will know worse still.

The fire threatens to engulf my soul.

I remember the Guardians and the black nothingness of their prison. This brief searing lessens.

I feel a wart or two breaking through on my spine. The pain is worth it to save Tess.

Are those elongated figures whipping through the smoke? They come to protect their valley. I am in no danger as long as I protect and serve.

Over the ringing in my ears, I heard a whump and a thud against the desert floor. "Mickey," I breathed and dashed to the fallen prince. Flying dust caught in my throat and burned my skin. I tasted grit and spat it out.

"Everybody up to the portal, now!" Gollum commanded. "You've got to get through before the moon moves and it closes again."

I sensed Donovan helping to herd the dancers toward their home. They kept trying to break free of his grip and return to their prince.

"Mickey?" I held a hand to his chest. He seemed intact, a little singed around the edges, but nothing severed or bleeding externally.

A faint whisper of air.

"He's breathing!" I told the assembly.

Vague forms scrambled up the rock face. As they neared the opening, they took on more color and definition. The gray of fatigue and separation washed away in a flood of benign light from home.

I tried to lift Mickey by the shoulders.

"Don't move him," Gollum said, coming up beside us. "He's bleeding internally from the fall. Probably concussed." As he spoke, the light from the portal began to close. "He must have thrown the bomb aside at the last second."

"Easy, Mickey, just keep breathing," I urged as I lay his head back down.

"Home? Did they make it home?" Prince Mikhail gasped for more air, painfully.

I almost didn't hear his words. Tears burned my eyes.

"Two more to go. They're going to make it, My Lord Mikhail," Gollum said with respect.

"I have served." Mickey closed his eyes. His breathing became fainter yet.

The light dimmed further.

"They're through, and the portal's closing," Donovan announced.

"You can't die. I won't let you die." I rubbed Mickey's face, willing him to open his eyes again.

"If he could get to Faery, he'd heal," Gollum mused.

"Too late," Donovan said.

An imp can go anywhere, anywhen, Scrap said.

"Scrap, can you take him home?"

Nope. But you can.

The ring near burned on my hand. I yanked it off and slipped it onto Mickey's thumb, making sure I twisted it.

"Mickey, I know you still live. You have to will yourself home. Think of home. Picture it in your mind."

A tiny glimmer of a smile lit his face. "Home."

"Yes. Think of home. Will yourself to go home." I twisted the ring again and again. "Just go home."

"I don't believe it," Donovan breathed. The portal's opening again. The moon has moved past, but it's opening again."

"Quick, help me carry Mickey up there." I kept twisting the ring, remembering bright flowers, a clear stream falling over a jumble of rocks, rainbow-colored beings flitting about in the sunshine. I'd seen it once before, the first time I entered the chat room in a fever dream years ago when the imp flu first possessed me.

Donovan slid his hands beneath Mickey's shoulders. Gollum took his ankles. I braced the faery prince beneath his back.

"On three," Donovan said.

We lifted in one smooth movement, keeping Mickey as level and still as possible. Desperately avoiding dropping him, we stumbled and slid the few yards to the base of Goblin Rock.

The monolith looked as if it sagged a bit. I didn't care. If we could just get Mickey up to the cave mouth . . .

Gollum pulled a coil of lightweight rope from his pack. Quickly, he fashioned a harness.

Donovan slid Mickey's legs through it and looped the length around his shoulders.

I placed Mickey's left hand over his right so that he could touch the ring.

By the time Donovan finished, Gollum had hauled himself up to the cave, the other end of the rope in his hands. He braced himself at the opening.

"Think of home," I reminded Mickey one more time, giving the ring a last twist.

"Oh, my," Gollum gasped, looking over his shoulder. "Even faded, it's beautiful. I think it's healing already."

"Home," Mickey whispered. His face twisted in pain.

"Tess, you've got to climb beside him, keep his body as level as possible," Donovan said. He scanned the height of the monolith. "The rock's too fragile to support my weight. You're the only one who can do this."

"I know. Okay, Scrap, it's you and me. You tell me where to grab and step so I can concentrate on Mickey."

Gotcha. The imp lifted free of my shoulder and flew back and forth. *Left hand here, right foot there,* he directed me.

Somehow we managed it. With one hand bracing Mickey so he didn't bang into the uneven rock, I held the picture of Faery in my mind. I let the others think through the climb for me.

Mickey gained enough strength and presence of mind to give the ring an occasional twist.

Gollum bless him, lifted a full-grown man smoothly.

Donovan boosted us from below, then directed the beam from the flashlight where I needed to be.

At last, sweating and breathless, I grasped the cave lip. With my shoulder under Mickey, Gollum hauled him the last few feet.

With the worst of the drag off me, I chanced a glance into the cave. About five feet high at the opening, it went back only a few feet.

But where a blank wall should define the end, the red rock dissolved and showed a distant view of light and color, like looking through the wrong end of a telescope. I couldn't move, couldn't think. I could only gaze with longing at the most beautiful of all the dimensions. I'd said the word "home" so often I almost believed that was where I needed to go.

Easy, dahling. Don't get lost. That is not home to you.

Gollum eased out of the cave to make room for Mickey's supine form. Together we pushed his feet, aiming his head toward the opening.

As we worked, the image at the end began to fade.

"Clap, Donovan," I called. My hands were too occupied with Mickey and keeping myself from falling.

"What?"

"Just do it. Like the end of 'Fairy Moon.' Clap as if Mickey's life depends upon it."

Strangely, he did. He brought his big hands together again and again. The willful slap of flesh against flesh resounded through the valley, picked up by the hills and bounced back to us. The sound doubled and doubled again, filling us with the resolve that this faery must live.

The lines of smoke and energy swirling around and around coalesced into vague outlines of beings with round heads and long triangular bodies that trailed off into wisps of energy. Red, black, gold, purple, and green, they gathered in a ritual circle around us. And they too clapped, continuing the magic through the dimensions. Helping us. Guiding us. Guarding us.

At the last second, two pairs of arms reached through from Faery and aided their prince home.

Just like the end of the dance.

Chapter 49

Ronald Reagan played Vegas in 1954 at the Last Frontier.

MY BABE LAUGHS AND CRIES as she and Gollum slide back to the safety of the ground. They hug joyously. Donovan joins them.

Each of the men vies with the other to kiss her. They both do.

I'd laugh, too, but my mind returns to the other side of the closed portal. Prince Mikhail has taken the ring with him. Now I'll never get a chance to free the black imp inside the diamond.

Is that such a bad thing? I feel for that imp. My fate could have been his. But would loosing him help maintain the balance among the dimensions?

I guess it's only fitting that the ring has returned to the faeries; they made it after all. They removed a violent imp from the universe for a reason. An imp too bloodthirsty to bond with a Warrior has no purpose in the grand scheme of things.

But still, I really, really needed to end the agony of that nameless imp. He calls to me across the dimensions through the cracks in the diamond.

Only my love for my dahling Tess saved me. I should rejoice with her.

A cigar and a big dose of beer and OJ will ease some of my pain.

Maybe Ginkgo will help remind me of the glory of life. I'll

just pop over to the Citadel for a bit and give Tess and Gollum a little privacy to celebrate on their own. They need this time together, to remind themselves of the importance of their lives together.

They can't let a little thing like the insane Julia come between them.

That would be just wrong.

They're already starting with a deep kiss across the center console of the Hummer.

If Tess is going to get laid, so am I!

Donovan's going to ditch the van registered to Gregbaum out in the desert somewhere. My babe and her love will meet up with him at a nearby freeway junction.

They'll work it out on their own. No one needs me right now.

"Hey, Scrap," Tess calls. "Good work, buddy. Get some sleep. You deserve it."

Ah, Tess. She does think of me.

Life is good.

Exuberance carried Gollum and me all the way to the door of *our* hotel room. We touched, held hands, kissed often. A couple. Together. No doubts, no encumbrances.

While he fumbled with the key card, I held his mouth captive with my own, frustrated that I couldn't get his shirt off until he shed the heavy backpack.

At last, the door swung open and we tumbled inside, too eager for each other to think.

The pack hit the floor with a thud. My boots followed. I pushed him backward onto the bed, jumping on top of him, mouth open, hungry for more kisses, more everything of my Gollum.

Something chirped. An annoying sound interfering with my celebration of a job well done and beautiful lives saved.

The chirp continued.

"Um . . . Tess," Gollum mumbled around my mouth. "Tess, that's the alarm on my watch. I have a plane to catch." He sounded disappointed.

"Can't it wait?" I slid my tongue along his cheek, down his neck, amazed at the fairness of his midnight stubble.

"I'm sorry. I have to go back to New York. Tonight. Now." He groaned. His fingers clung to my back fiercely.

Then he pushed me aside and rolled off the bed.

Instantly chilled and sober, I knew I had to face the questions I'd hidden from since that phone call this afternoon that sent him into a terse funk.

"Talk to me, Gollum. I need to know what you want from me." I think I knew.

But I also had to examine my own role in this threesome.

Methodically he set about packing his few clothes and toiletries into a small duffel, zipping a vinyl bag around his suit.

"Gollum?"

He wouldn't look at me.

"Gollum, I understand why you have to go to her."

Damn, damn, damn. I did understand.

"You understand?"

I nodded, unable to speak, unable to think. I just had to hold myself tight enough to keep my damned heart from shattering into a million pieces.

"Thank you. You know I love you. I'd do most anything for you. Except . . . she depends upon me. She's more like a much younger sister than a wife. But . . ." He stood and gathered the last of his things.

"It's all about balance. I'm the one that threw you and Julia out of balance."

"Julia and I were out of balance long ago. But I'm her only hope of ever recovering."

"Gollum?"

"Yes, Tess?" At least he didn't call me "Sweetheart" or "Darling" or any other endearment. I couldn't stand it if he did.

"Gollum, I can't be with you. Not as a loving couple. That's wrong. Wrong for me, for you, and for her. Until you and Julia can find a peaceful way out of your marriage, I can't be your lover."

"I . . . I know. But I will be there for you when next you need an archivist. I'll not desert you."

"Just go. Please, go now before I . . . before I can't let you go."

"Good-bye."

I turned and stared out into the night that was never quite night in this city.

Agony! Pressure in my chest. My heart beats erratically. I'm dying.

I curl up into a fetal ball.

"What ails you?" my beloved Ginkgo asks. He enfolds me in his arms, closing our bodies together with his tail.

"Not me," I wail. "It's Tess. My Warrior . . ."

I can't stay here wrapped in love any longer. Tess needs me.

This kind of pain speaks of personal disaster. What could go wrong? She and Gollum are so right for each other.

I pop out of Ginkgo's arms and into the chat room without a thought. I barely register the Cthulhu demon on guard. I'm not there long enough for the ponderous water monster to notice me.

Then I am on Tess' shoulder, smoothing her hair, rubbing my cheek against hers.

I wish I could become solid in her dimension so that I can hold her as she needs to be held.

I can only share her tears and her pain.

Her agony is my agony. Her life my life. Not even death can separate us.

Chapter 50

Las Vegas no longer caters to a primarily adult crowd. It offers water parks, amusement parks, G-rated entertainment, and other activities aimed at the entire family.

SOMEHOW, POURING MY GRIEF and anguish into words for Scrap helped me gain some perspective. Yes, I loved Gollum. Yes, he had betrayed me by his silence and oblique promise of a future. But he hadn't totally abandoned me.

He'd be back. We'd have to renegotiate our relationship and find a way back to the friendship we'd shared before this weekend.

Do you remember when you claimed Gollum as your mate before the Windago and King Scazzy? Scrap reminded me of an incident last month. In order to protect Gollum from the Windago's vengeance—I had killed her mate so she would kill mine—I had to stake a claim on him.

"I claimed him as a friend."

You implied that he was your mate.

"If the Windago and the prison warden of the universe interpreted my statement that way . . ."

You claimed him before witnesses. He's yours by the laws of the cosmos.

"That doesn't mean we can be together. Not while Julia lives."

He's yours. He'll be back. Scrap blew a wisp of black cherry cheroot smoke up to the corner away from my face.

A small courtesy I hadn't expected from him.

"What I need to do right now is call Mom."

Yeah, you need to restore the balance of your relationship. Let her be your mom and take care of you. You've been taking care of her too much.

"Balance. It's all been about balances. Junior upset a balance by projecting his fears on the plane."

Before that. The faeries upset the balance by exchanging him for a human child.

"And he twisted the change into a hated exile."

You restored the balance on the plane with your songs.

"WindScribe upset the balance by killing the king of Faery."

Leaving the universe open to plundering by the likes of Gregbaum and Junior.

"But we put things in motion to heal that breach." The image of Lady Lucia sinking her fangs into Gregbaum's throat threatened to overwhelm me.

"How did Gregbaum kidnap the faeries? He was human. I know he had Junior's help, but they'd both have trouble getting into the chat room let alone into Faery. Otherwise Junior would have gone back a long time ago."

Scrap let that one sink into my mind.

"He had help. Not Lucia. She thought the faeries had come willingly to escape the imbalance in their home. Donovan?"

He's human now, too. But he will make sure any remaining mutant faeries are dealt with.

The place where the diamond ring had rested on my finger burned with emptiness. "An imp can go anywhere. An imp can take his Warrior anywhere! Sancroix and Fortitude."

Scrap and I stared at each other in horror. The darkness of Fortitude's skin, almost black now, finally took on meaning. The imp had gone rogue and dragged Sancroix along with him.

Fortitude stopped listening to Sancroix and started working with Junior a long time ago. Sancroix may not have been involved.

"He had to have known even if he didn't participate. The bond between imp and human is too strong to hide something like that. He and Fortitude have become almost as evil as the imp imprisoned in the ring."

Junior started Fortitude on the path of darkness. Sancroix and Sister Gert believed him to be their son. They registered him as their orphaned nephew because of archaic prejudice against children born out of wedlock.

"Why'd they help me free the faeries?"

Because Fortitude likes killing things. Doesn't matter what side they're on, as long as he tastes blood. Just like the mutant faeries. Just like Junior. He gains pleasure vicariously when others kill.

They hadn't just killed the mutant faeries on the stage. They'd mutilated them with extreme violence even after they were all dead. Junior must have been watching from the wings.

Or maybe he diverted Gert away from the carnage, knowing she'd object.

A knock on my door. I dashed to open it, praying with every step, every rapid heartbeat that my Gollum had returned to me.

Lady Lucia stood before me in flowing red draperies from the Napoleonic era. The high-waisted gown, lace-trimmed scoop neck, and puffy sleeves suited her. She'd dressed her bleached locks in casual ringlets. More than a bit of her youthful beauty shone through her lustrous pale skin. The long strand of pearls, doubled and looped about her throat echoed the same luster.

"Invite me in," she demanded with almost no accent.

"Do I have to?"

"No. But you do not wish to discuss our business in public, and I may not enter without invitation." She tapped her foot impatiently.

More vampire mythology.

Don't do it, babe. She smells funny.

"For this one meeting I grant you permission to enter." Yeah, I'd read a bit of vampire fiction myself. I knew the rules.

She breezed past me and took up a position of command before the windows. The night lights of Vegas made a halo around her.

I didn't need my magical comb to recognize it for an illusion.

Scrap flitted about, trying to stay between us. I wanted to swat him away, but didn't dare betray his agitation to a potential enemy.

"The ring." Lucia held out her hand.

"No congratulations on a job well done? No questions about the disposition of the mutants? No polite 'Hello'?"

That's it, dahling, show no fear.

Lucia tapped her foot impatiently. "I know all of that. You promised me the ring. Now give it to me." Her eyes betrayed her. They shifted constantly, wary, only occasionally glancing at my neck.

If she could see Scrap, she didn't let her gaze linger on him.

Self-consciously, I shifted my shoulders so that the turtleneck of my sweater rose higher.

"I apologize, Lucia. I no longer possess the ring."

"What!" she screeched like a banshee. Her eyes turned funny. Not the vertically slitted yellow monstrosities portrayed on television. I can't describe it. They just looked strange.

Uh, oh. Pink flashed across Scrap's skin like a neon light on the fritz.

I shrugged. "I had to give up the ring to Prince Mikhail as part of the rescue operation." I tried for casual and dropped into a chair. My knees continued to tremble even after I took the weight off them.

Maybe it was just that groin injury making them weak.

Yeah. Right.

Anyway, I knew better than to engage her gaze. I stared at my ringless fingers instead.

Damn. Now I'd never wear Gollum's ring. The only one I truly wanted.

"What happened to *my* ring?" she ground out.

"I had to put it on Mickey's hand to keep the portal open long enough to get him through. He got hurt. Badly."

"This is not acceptable."

"Sorry. That's the way it is. There is nothing you or I can do about it now."

"You owe me that ring." She grabbed my collar and lifted me to my feet.

I didn't see her move. I swear it. One heartbeat she was five paces away. The next she was on top of me, holding me upright by one hand. Baring her fangs.

This close I could see the seam of artificial dentures.

In my peripheral vision I saw Scrap turn vermilion. He dropped to my hand, half extended.

"Uh, I wouldn't do that if I were you, Lucia."

"By the rules of the Powers That Be, I claim you as forfeit." She opened her mouth, aiming for my neck.

"Want a Celestial Blade embedded in your spine? You may have a few drops of Damiri demon in you, but I can end your shadow existence before you can break the surface of my skin." To make my point (pun intended) I let Scrap's sharpening tail caress her ribs.

She dropped me abruptly.

"We are not finished, Warrior. You owe me."

"I acknowledge that I owe you an *honorable* service at some time in the future." I'd figure out how to break this rule later. Right now, I needed my life intact.

She dropped me abruptly.

My knees wobbled, but I remained upright. Scrap shrunk back to his normal shape and size but remained bright red.

Lucia's nose wiggled. "I smell blood. Close. It smells like yours."

"I'm not bleeding." I checked to make sure.

"Not you. A relative." She aimed her rapid steps for the door.

"Mom!"

Call your mom, babe. I have a funny feeling. Scrap rubbed his very red belly.

I speed dialed her cell phone.

It went right to voice mail. She was either using it or had turned it off.

I called Penny's landline.

A sultry voice promised to call me back if I left a message.

"Where is she, Scrap? You've got to find her."

Parking lot. Now!

Elevator too slow. I pushed Lucia aside and fairly flew down the stairs, sliding on the banister when I could. Five flights. Ten landings. Too many.

"Time, Scrap."

Hurry!

"Go ahead. Do what you can."

My imp needed no other prodding. He popped out. Then

came back to me as I launched myself out the fire door into the parking lot. He glowed bright vermilion and stretched longer than I'd ever seen him.

I hit the pavement, feet *en garde* and shaft of my blade twirling. Lamps on tall poles lit the entire area as bright as day.

Breven Sancroix faced me. Fortitude lounged on his shoulder, cleaning his talons with a long forked tongue. His skin had darkened perceptibly.

Then I saw my mother's body lying neatly on the ground, hands crossed on her chest. Her eyes stared sightlessly at the stars, her mouth half open in a surprised "Oh." Six long bloody gashes spread upward from her belly to her throat. Her favorite plum-colored slacks and lavender blouse were ruined.

"What have you done to her?" I screamed. I longed to run to Mom, to force her heart to beat and her lungs to breathe.

I knew in my head it was too late. I'd wasted too much time with that bitchy pseudo vampire.

I hadn't been here for my mom when she needed me most.

"I did the world a favor," Sancroix defended himself. He sounded almost casual, as if murder were an everyday incident for him.

Maybe it was. Fortitude didn't look particularly troubled.

"She was an innocent!" A red mist rose before my eyes as my temper soared. She couldn't be dead. She just couldn't.

I had to go to her. But I had to go through him to get to her.

"She carried a demon baby. No woman who lies with a demon is innocent," he sneered.

That stopped me cold. "Darren. Her husband died less than two days after they married!"

"Makes no difference. The Damiri are incredibly fertile. They breed and breed and breed again with as many women as they can. We took care of the problem."

"You idiot. How stupid can you be? She's too old . . ."

"Not for a Damiri."

He made to step past me.

I blocked him with the shaft of my Celestial Blade.

"You have broken your most solemn vow of the Brotherhood. To protect the innocent. You should have done your research before you took the law into your own hands. But you killed your archivist, too. Because he got in your way."

"I watched her for five days. She picked at her food. Yet she glowed. She was pregnant. I had to dispose of the baby before it grew enough to take over her body and make her nearly invulnerable." His eyes became hard and cold.

"She glowed because she was happy, she'd finally found herself in her music. She picked at her food because she was trying to lose weight for her new career," I ground out, keeping my teeth clenched so that I didn't scream.

"That doesn't . . ."

"She had a complete hysterectomy right after I was born. She had no eggs to fertilize, no womb to nurture a fetus. You murdered an innocent woman. You murdered *my mother*."

He lost some of his self-righteous calm. His imp looked up from his grooming. Fortitude nudged him. They communicated silently.

Can you catch what they're saying, Scrap?

A strong sense of negative emanated from my Celestial Blade.

"Don't listen to her, Dad. She's lying," Junior said quietly from the shadows. His voice carried a similar calming magic to Donovan's.

"Your mother married a demon. She had to die," Sancroix affirmed.

"That's right. She had to die," Junior echoed.

"Did she?" Sister Gert sounded hesitant, from right beside her son. Her *changeling* son, I reminded myself.

"No, she didn't need to die. Your imp, goaded on by your changeling son, needed to taste innocent blood. They elected my mom. You've lost control of your imp, Sancroix. Lost him to the man you raised to be your son."

"Impossible."

"Look at his skin. Look at how dark he is. The last time a rogue imp turned black, the faeries imprisoned him in a diamond, forcing him to stare at himself and examine his sins from inside the facets for all eternity." I shifted my stance, ready to lash out the moment I had the right opportunity. The fact that Scrap remained in Blade form with no demons present meant we faced incredible evil.

Sancroix had to die. I should turn him over to the law. But with an imp to whisk him away through the chat room, no prison could contain him.

Did I have the courage to kill another human being, no matter how evil? Would I be stepping along the same rogue path he'd taken if I did?

"What have you done, Breven?" Gert asked from behind me.

"Have you gone rogue, too, Mrs. Sancroix?" I sneered.

"An innocent. You have killed an innocent," she said. Anguish colored her voice. She moved forward, knelt beside my mother's body. "You have changed beyond recognition, Breven. I turned a blind eye to your bloodlust when it came to demons. I let you fight the mutants tonight without me because I knew you needed to spill blood. No more. You must kill no more."

Then, quite unexpectedly she bowed her head as in prayer. Juniper, her imp, did the same.

Gert's hand covered my own in the only act of tenderness I'd ever seen from her. "Take care, Sister. You are needed outside the Citadel. Don't let the monsters make you one of them. Go back home often to renew yourself and your commitment."

Fortitude saw us as no threat. Not even a hint of pink on his wing tips. Just that unrelenting deep green that bordered on black. I'd seen him completely transform in a heartbeat.

Overconfidence led to stupidity. These two had already committed that blunder once tonight.

I knew what I had to do.

"You need to go back to a Citadel, Sancroix," I said.

"Those useless, hidebound . . ."

Before he could finish his thought; before I had time to think, Gert rose up and clamped a choke hold on her husband. Juniper keened long and loud. She rose up and landed on Fortitude's back, talons out, all three rows of her teeth clamped upon his throat.

The two imps tumbled and rolled, snapped wings open and shut. Fortitude flipped himself on top of the battle.

I stepped forward, ready to break it up.

Go to your mother, Tess, Scrap commanded me. In an eye

blink he'd morphed into a glowing white imp, far larger than I'd ever seen him.

"Stop it, Gert. They'll kill each other!" Sancroix screamed. He looked pale and sweating.

"Scrap?"

Imp business. Imp law. I must judge as a neutral party. Go to your mother.

A fake to the right, then Juniper sank her talons deep into Fortitude's spine.

At the same time his jaws clamped on her neck.

I heard bone crack.

"No!" Sancroix screamed, clutching his back in the exact same spot where Juniper hit Fortitude.

Gert gargled, releasing Sancroix to clutch at her throat with both hands.

The imps flashed into blade form even as death throes jerked them backward, toward the limp hands of their Warriors.

They all collapsed together onto their weapons. The tines of one penetrated Sancroix's heart, the blade of the other slit Gert's throat.

Scrap bowed his head, faded and shrank back to normal size. *So be it. I declare an end to this.*

I jerked out of my paralyzing horror and stumbled to my mother's side. Her hand already grew cold. A glaze covered her eyes.

She looked so peaceful, so relaxed.

All traces of the tense and waspish woman who'd raised me had vanished.

"Tess," she whispered.

I bent closer to catch those precious words.

"Tess, I love you. Tell Steph and Cecilia I love them. You are my baby. My last baby. I cherish you."

And she wilted, an almost smile frozen in place.

I wanted to believe the true woman, the *chanteuse* who empathically projected love, compassion, and joy through her music shone through.

For a few hours each night she had balanced some evil in the world with her songs.

I couldn't speak. The horror of my dead mother lying on the pavement choked me.

As sirens erupted around me, Lucia bounded out of the

fire door. She grabbed me beneath the shoulders and dragged me back inside the hotel.

"You can't be seen here. Let them believe this a love triangle gone wrong," she whispered. "But don't let them bury her with the pearls. You have to claim the pearls."

I nodded numbly. "Why?"

"No time to explain. They were mine once upon a time. Now they are yours. Guard them better than you did the ring."

"Junior?"

"I'll find him. He's finished in this town and he knows it. But I'll find him and bring him to the Powers That Be for justice. And you will help me. Later. Now you must flee."

Some morsel of self-preservation kicked in, and I followed her back up to my room.

Sister Gert's final words pounded into my brain. "I don't have the luxury of looking for a future, a normal life with Gollum, do I?" I said to no one in particular.

"If you stay with him, you will want a family. Your concerns will shift from fighting demons to protecting your children. Believe me. I know this." Lucia fixed me with her gaze.

Her sincerity penetrated my growing grief.

"I have to remain alone, focused and angry enough to complete the jobs the Universe hands me." That scared me more than a full pack of Midori, Windago, Sasquatch, and Damiri combined.

"Good-bye, Mom."

Epilogue

What happens in Vegas, stays in Vegas. Sometimes.

THE NIGHT BEFORE I took my mom home for her funeral and burial in the family plot on Cape Cod, I stood on the tiny stage of the lounge in The Crown Jewels Casino and Conference Center. I wore the midnight-blue dress spangled with pixie dust and my mother's pearls.

They caressed my neck with warmth and the memory of her love.

Donovan and Lady Lucia sat in the front row. Lucia had used her influence to end the investigation into Mom's death before it got started. She convinced high-powered lawyers and commissioners that the three bodies in the parking lot were a bizarre lovers' triangle gone sour with murder and suicide.

Everyone in Vegas and back home accepted that story as the truth.

I wanted to believe it.

Even more quietly, Lady Lucia bought out Junior's stock in The Crown Jewels. He disappeared. Even Scrap couldn't find him, and I know he looked long and hard.

Penny Worth and Mr. Stetson also sat in the front row. She wore a new wedding ring and had her heavily mortgaged house up for sale. She looked tired and resigned rather than a radiant bride.

Allie had come, too. That's what best friends do. They fly halfway across the country to hold your hand, help you make hard decisions, become a buffer between you and people who ask too many questions.

Gollum offered to come. I had to tell him no. Seeing him again this soon, while I was so fragile, would upset the tiny bit of balance I'd found within me.

"I'm dedicating this song to my mother," I said. No other words would come through the growing lump in my throat. I had to sing now or never.

"Take me in, yes, I'll be your victim,
I'll be the matchgirl, and you be the wind.
Take me in, yes, I'll be your victim,
I'll be Red Riding Hood, you be the wolf.
I'll be the girl who gets burned in the oven,
and you'll be the baker who serves me for pie.
I won't expect any boring old woodcutters
coming to save me at the end of the day—
In the end, yes I'll be your victim.
You'll be my frog and I won't be a princess.
In the end, no curtain, no laughter,
no pumpkin, no coachman, no happily ever after."

Gollum is standing behind a pillar where Tess can't see him. He clenches his fists and squeezes his eyes shut to keep the tears from leaking out.

He listens closely to Tess' music. In his heart he sings a different song, one that Mom sang often. A song from a different era.

A song people sang when they sent their lovers off to fight a war. "I'll be seeing you in all the old familiar places."

It ends, "I'll be looking at the moon, but I'll be seeing you."

FOREST MOON RISING

This book is dedicated to the armies of volunteers and professional foresters who work very hard at maintaining the treasure of green spaces in urban areas everywhere.

Acknowledgments

A lot of a writer's time is spent in isolation; our minds engaged in a fictional world, our thoughts shaped by the imaginary characters, and the impossible demands we put upon them. But no book is totally created in solitude. We need to come up for air upon occasion and take inspiration from reality (no matter how you define it), and from the people around us who graciously allow us time alone, the right to be cranky when the plot ties itself in knots, and rejoice with us when all the puzzle pieces fall into place.

So I must give hearty thanks to Tim Karr, my beloved husband of forty years. Without you I couldn't do any of this or be a complete person. My brainstorm crew of Deborah Dixon, Lea Day, Sara Mueller, Jessica Groeller, Lizzy Shannon, Maggie Bonham, Bob Brown, and Big Brother Ed deserve more thanks than just a mention here. These are also my first readers. They help lever my wandering prose into a story that is actually readable.

The lovely filk song "Heart's Path" by Chris Dickenson is printed here with her kind permission. A recording is available on the "Harmony Heifers" CD produced by Mystic Fig Studios, available at www.mysticfig.com or CD Baby.

Many years ago, ElizaBeth Gilligan and I sat in a filk circle at Orycon and crooned "Where Are All The Aliens." I thank her for the loan of the lyrics we compiled together.

And I can't forget Sheila Gilbert, editor extraordinaire, the best in the business.

Prologue

In the Chinook Jargon, Devil's Lake was called me-sah-chie-chuck which means evil water. There are many stories about malign spirits and creatures inhabiting the lake's clear turquoise waters.

"TESS NONCOIRÉ, Warrior of the Celestial Blade, you really don't want to do this," Scrap whispered.

In the chat room—that big, white, blank space between the dimensions with portals to all of them—my interdimensional imp had substance and size. He no longer fit on my shoulder or on top of my head. So he stood beside me. His potbelly looked thinner than usual and his bandy legs stronger—we'd been working too hard. A lovely scattering of warts decorated his chest and his bum. His tattered wings stretched from above his head to his heels. They fluttered in agitation.

His normally gray-green skin flashed between yellow and pink. He was scared and we were in danger.

I knew that. I was as scared as he. Maybe more so.

My scar, which ran from right temple to jaw, pulsed and burned, a clear warning that I needed to either fight my way clear or flee. Rapidly.

I couldn't accept either option.

"If this is such a bad idea, why'd you bring me this far?" I asked, trying to keep my teeth from chattering.

"I brought you here to scare you into going home."

Scrap's actual voice came through deeper than his normal telepathic communications.

I caught sight of the demons on guard duty in the distance. Their bright blue, stacked-tire bodies with pink feather ruffs at neck, wrists, and ankles loomed larger with each giant stride toward us. Think the Michelin man decked out for an Easter parade.

"B'Cartlins," Scrap whispered. "Their stupidity makes them more dangerous than their size. They need everything repeated six times before they understand."

"I think I want to hide." No shadows presented themselves in the limitless white. The B'Cartlins grew by the heartbeat as they approached. Without a thought, either of them could squash us to unidentified road pizza.

"No trespassing in the chat room," one of them boomed. Demons took seriously their duty to keep everyone in their home dimension.

I covered my ears against the cannon roar of sound.

"Imps go anywhere, anywhen," Scrap announced to them with authority and dignity.

"No imps outside Imp Haven. Those are the rules," they both repeated by rote.

Full blood, or Midori, demons aren't terribly bright.

"If we stay very quiet, maybe they'll forget we're here," I said quietly.

If we needed to remain quiet, why were we talking? It was either that or run away and leave this essential errand unfinished.

"I have to do this, Scrap."

"I know. This is going to cost me some warts. I worked hard to earn these!" He heaved a sigh that might provoke a hurricane. "You couldn't wait for backup?" He produced a black cherry cheroot out of nowhere and lit it from a flamelet atop his thumb.

"I don't have backup anymore."

"What about more information?"

"I dismissed my archivist." I would not think about Guilford Van der Hoyden-Smythe, PhD. I would not. I had to cut Gollum out of my life and my heart.

I did not like where this conversation was leading. So I took a couple of steps toward where I thought the proper portal should be.

Scrap grabbed my arm and steered me in the opposite direction. My frail human flesh began bruising beneath his solid, unrelenting grip.

"Are you sure this is the right way?" I asked, trying to peel his talons off my forearm.

"Unfortunately, I am." He led me at a ninety-degree angle to the guardian demons.

The burning along my scar flared higher. The B'Cartlins were the least of my problems.

In the blink of an eye, an elegant brass door with stained glass panels to either side loomed before us. It just showed up to block our way. No dark spot in the distance that grew larger as we approached. One minute nothing but white stretching on forever, misting to more white to hide corners and angles where floor or ceiling met wall. The next heartbeat the door became a solid barrier.

Or a chance at salvation.

A blob of mottled bile green and sulfurous yellow flesh pooled across the entrance, sort of growing out of the white on white.

"You know there's a reason Donovan told you that few beings who faced the Powers That Be have survived the encounter, and never a human," Scrap grumbled, eyeing the blob between the door and us.

"I can't trust anything the former gargoyle says. He betrayed his calling and his creation. For that he doesn't deserve to raise his daughter Lilly. He lies as easily as he breathes."

"He didn't lie about this."

"Then we'll just have to make sure we get what we want before they execute us."

"Today is a good day to die."

"As good as any," I replied, not sure I believed my own lies.

The blob stirred, raised a bulbous head with two intelligent eyes and a parrot beak. At least eight legs stretched outward, flicking their tips.

I recoiled before it could strangle me. Another eight or more legs kept it anchored to the suddenly shifting ground.

Or were those my knees shaking hard enough to upset my balance?

"Mind if we pay a visit?" I asked.

The beak snapped once, hard enough to break my body in two if it chose.

I accepted that as a yes, and stepped around the beast—I didn't want to chance it changing its mind and grabbing me with one or more of those tentacles. With one deep breath for false courage I grabbed the lion's head door knocker and let it drop. I wished I had some scotch to help with the courage thing. It didn't have to be single malt. A cheap blend would do better; I could drink more of it faster.

A loud bong resounded around the chat room, bouncing off walls that shouldn't exist, compounding with each repeat of sound. Tsunamis of noise built and echoed. The bong grew louder yet, more insistent.

I had to grab my ears. Then I collapsed to my knees and shrank within myself.

Still, the knocker flapped and boomed and let the entire Universe know that someone had the audacity to approach the Powers That Be without an invitation.

That's me, Tess Noncoiré, Warrior of the Celestial Blade, who bounds in where no one else dares, and bullies my way through.

Chapter 1

Forest Park in Portland, Oregon, was established in 1898, has 5156 acres, a hundred types of birds, sixty (known) species of animals, seventy miles of trails, and is the largest naturally forested area within the city limits of any municipality in the US. It is the third largest city park in the country.

STINKY, STINKY. I smell demon-inky.
Demon and baby poop.

If demons are breeding I need to follow my cute little nose and find them so my dahling Tess can wipe them out. After I find some bleach to clean up after them.

Screaming draws my attention along my line of smell. This is sounding ominous. My spine shivers and stretches. I need to transform into the Celestial Blade. Where is Tess when I need her?

Off to a fencing tournament so she can avoid work.

I'll gather information before I summon her to my side. Then the two of us can lash and lunge, slice and stab. Such a wonderful way to end the domination of a demon.

My nose leads me to a strange room within a hospital. Locked doors that need codes to get in or out. Triple locks on the drug stashes that are carefully disguised behind normal cupboard doors. Casually clad nurses dash about, converging on a gurney where a hysterical woman thrashes about, trying to push away the newborn baby on her tummy. But her hands are lashed to the sides of the portable bed with thick layers of bandage so she can't reject her child.

The child looks human. But it stinks of demon, demon laced with astringent pinesap.

A bit of scaly bark clings to the baby's feet. His (oh, yes, he is male) fingers look a bit like twigs, too long and skinny for such a tiny morsel of life.

Even as I watch the abnormalities fade along with the demon stink. Just an afterthought of pine cleaner, that might be part and parcel of a hospital, clings to him.

The woman still screams. A doctor in blue surgical scrubs approaches with a big syringe hidden behind his back. "Hold her arm, Nurse," he commands in that all too calm and soothing voice of one who has dealt with this before.

"Third case this year," the squarely built nurse with disastrous blunt cut hair mutters. She too wears blue scrubs. "This is looking like a new postpartum syndrome."

"Strange one. I wonder what triggers it," the doctor says as he stabs the patient with the syringe and depresses the plunger. "I think I need to research a new paper."

I've found our next mission. Tess isn't gonna like this. She has a thing about babies. She'll want to give the infant a chance to grow up normal and human, not letting me take it down until after its demon half inflicts unnamable horrors on humanity.

Portland, Oregon's Forest Park is a wonderful natural treasure. Most of the time.

Five thousand plus acres and over seventy miles of hiking and biking trails. One nasty little dark elf had lots of places to hide. Lots of places to ambush weary hikers, joggers, and mountain bikers. Too many victims had fallen into his traps lately. He probably ate the homeless pets that got dumped here too.

So why had he avoided me for over a year?

"Where are you little Nörglein?" I asked sweetly as I jogged slowly along the well-beaten path. "Tonight the moon will show a waxing quarter. That's the time of a demon's greatest power. You should be out trolling for victims."

Tonight was the time a goddess showed her face in the skies, the sickle moon defining her cheek like the scar on mine. The starscape behind the moon revealed her face and the Milky Way became her hair blowing in a celestial wind.

I'd seen the goddess a couple of times and felt her power infuse me with the strength to fight demon hordes.

Not tonight. Even a goddess can't break through the thick clouds and rain the weather service predicted.

"Scrap, do you smell anything that doesn't belong here?" I called to my otherworldly imp companion.

It's a forest, he shot back at me. *I smell green—trees, shrubs, and moss. That's what forest denizens smell like.*

"How do you know that?"

I'm an imp. I know these things.

"If you say so."

I do say so! Scrap landed on my shoulder with more clumsiness than usual. I barely felt his weight, just a bit of dandelion fluff. That's because he lives only partway in this dimension and is invisible to everyone but me, or another Warrior of the Celestial Blade.

"He won't come near me if you are this close," I complained. Only another mile to the trailhead. Another day wasted searching for our quarry.

This trail is too popular. A blind rat could find his way home.

I passed a couple hiking uphill with daypacks and water bottles slung on their belts. They wore sensible low cut boots, matching black shorts, and bright red Tees that complemented their chocolate and *café au lait* skin nicely. They also had black sweatshirts slung over their shoulders. The sunny Saturday morning in mid-September had warmed up, but this late in the year, the weather could turn wet and/or chilly with only a moment's notice. The equinox didn't have a lot to do with determining the actual season change in Portland. Next week could be bright and beautiful and ninety degrees.

Don't like the weather here? Wait a minute.

Don't like the forecast? Change the channel.

This is the Pacific North *Wet*, after all. Great coffee, wonderful microbrews, and frequent rains sweeping in from the Pacific Ocean.

The couple hurried a little faster than normal hikers out for a Saturday morning walk.

I sweated heavily from my five mile run—mostly

uphill—in my loose shorts and tank. My sweatshirt was tied around my waist and my light running shoes felt every imperfection in the dirt trail.

I felt naked without my mother's pearls around my neck. The strand was too short to hide beneath the tank top. Pearls while jogging? Even I knew that was a fashion disaster.

The hikers and I nodded in mute acknowledgment of fellow travelers in the wilderness. Never know when you might need help. Or if one of us turned up missing, we'd remember seeing each other and the basic location when searches began.

Too often in the last year solitary hikers got "lost," then walked out the next morning, dazed and mumbling about the ugly little guy who sheltered them overnight.

That shelter and directions came with a price.

The Nörglein had a bad reputation in the Italian and Swiss Alps. His reputation in the western hemisphere was nastier.

I looked to either side of the trail into the thick ferns, underbrush, and moss-covered fallen tree trunks crowding around tall Douglas firs. A million shades of green melded into each other, shifting with each breeze whispering through. Ripples and mounds showed just how uneven and precarious I'd find the footing off the beaten path.

I saw faces in the whorls of bark and moss. Images of the Green Man so popular in forest lore popped into my head. I shook myself to get rid of a fear that every plant and tree embodied a malicious creature peering out at me.

"High noon and not a lot of sunlight penetrating." I slowed to a walk. Time for a cool down.

Perfect for a dark elf.

Put the emphasis on dark in that description of the Nörglein. Nothing tall and elegant or beautiful in this critter. Nothing honorable or enchanting either. This was the real thing, not High Fantasy fiction.

Take that little game trail on your left.

"That's not a game trail, that's a runoff channel." It meandered down a really, really steep hill. Portland has built up from the river plain across numerous cinder cones and volcanic ridges. It was the only city I'd ever visited that you had to climb uphill both directions of any trip. Nothing was ever downhill for very long unless it was really steep and scary.

A light wind that smelled of salt and damp riffled the ferns to my right. A single frond continued to wave at me several seconds after the air had paused for breath. The scar on my face grew warm.

I veered off the trail onto a slight separation in the underbrush barely as wide as one of my size six shoes.

Scrap took himself off into the top of a Douglas fir two hundred feet up. His gray-green skin blended perfectly with the short evergreen needles. Even I couldn't see him. And we were so closely bonded I could find him anywhere. He could find me anywhen, across five dimensions.

He waggled his butt at me, showing off his seven warts. Imps won those—er—beauty marks in battle.

A tiny hint of pink on his wing tips told me that something less than nice lurked close by. My scar was a less accurate alarm system. Maybe he'd earn another wart today after all.

The sparse sunlight disappeared beneath a cloud. Uh oh. Maybe the weather critters on TV got it right for a change, predicting afternoon showers and a twenty-degree drop in temperature.

Autumn in the Pacific Northwest is rarely predictable. About the only certainty is the presence of good coffee on every other corner and a decent brew pub on the corners in between.

I could do with a drink of either about now. I gulped a long swig of water from my sports bottle hanging on my belt pack and took three more cautious steps.

Ten paces away a fern beckoned. Scrap turned hot pink in the tree directly above me, the same color as his favorite feather boa.

"I think we're on to something, buddy."

You got that right, babe.

"What's he look like?"

Woody skin and green beard, what do you expect a forest denizen to look like?

Okay, not easy to spot.

Buff-colored knickers and linen shirt, a dark green short jacket, and three-cornered hat are so last century, dahling. More like two centuries out of date.

That about summed it up.

With my eyes on the slowly advancing movement through the underbrush, I stepped forward and . . .

Snagged my foot on a blackberry vine stretched taut across my path. The spiked tendril came alive, coiling around my ankle and tugging.

My face met the dirt. I came to my knees spitting out crushed fern fronds and gagging on something sluglike.

Then the vine tugged again and I flailed forward.

A ragged, moss-covered stump caught me across the middle, taking my breath away.

I heard evil chuckles off to my left.

I yanked my left foot free of the entanglement and threw myself further off-balance.

Was that an alien hand pushing against my back?

Bracken and sword ferns crumbled beneath me as I rolled and tumbled downhill. I tried desperately to grab hold of something. Momentum pushed me faster and faster.

Sticks dug into me. Reaching shrubs scratched my face.

And still I rolled. The world twisted and spun. My eyes couldn't focus. Dizziness robbed me of any sense of direction.

Then with a back-numbing thump, I fetched up against the base of a tree.

Every inch of my body ached inside and out.

Each desperate attempt to draw breath met with knife sharp pain.

"Miss, miss!" A male voice inserted itself into my hearing.

"Hhuh," I mumbled, not yet comfortable with consciousness.

You can wake up now, babe. Bad guys have gone bye-bye, Scrap sneered at me.

I couldn't ignore my imp's mental jab. It felt somewhere between a migraine and a shrill whistle. Or maybe both at the same time.

With a wince and a groan, I opened my eyes and tried to raise myself to my elbows.

Wrong move.

Fire demons raced around and around my chest, pressing tighter and tighter.

"Lay still, miss. You might have broken ribs." That intrusive male voice again.

Nah, you're not broken, just bruised and sprained. Had the breath knocked out of you. Scrap landed on top of the jagged stump. He conjured a black cherry cheroot from the ether, lit it with a flame on his fingertip, and blew a smoke ring in my face.

I had to cough. I couldn't cough. Each breath hurt worse than the last.

The man I heard but couldn't see dribbled some water across my face. The urge to cough the smoke back at Scrap eased.

The impudent imp waggled his eyebrows at me. *See. If you'd broken something you wouldn't have coughed at all.*

Thanks a lot. I thought you were my friend.

"Easy now. I'm a paramedic. Let me see if we need to get a crew up here or if you'll be able to walk out." The man must have been crouched at my head, uphill and out of my line of sight.

He pressed gently on my ribs and neck with dark hands. Nothing hurt any worse.

"She's not walking on that ankle," a female said from behind him.

The man sucked in a whistling breath. He moved around to my side. I recognized him then as the African American who'd passed me going uphill a little while ago. Another shrill breath through a gap in his front teeth. "That needs an X-ray, miss."

"Scrap?"

No answer from my buddy.

"It's crap all right," the woman said. "Raquel Jones." She sort of offered me a hand to shake, then realized I'd have to sit up to reach it or she'd have to move downhill onto uncertain footing. So she looked at her hand as if at an alien being, then stuffed it into the pocket of her shorts.

"I'm Jordan Jones," the man said, putting his hands to better use assessing the damage to my left ankle. "JJ to most people."

"Tess Noncoiré," I said on a sharp inhale as he touched the rapidly swelling and bruising ankle. My lightweight shoes felt six sizes too small.

Raquel gasped. "Tess Noncoiré the writer? I've read all your books. What are you doing in Portland? Research?"

"I live here now," I ground out. What a horrible, ignominious way to meet a fan! I tried brushing twigs out of my short sandy blonde curls to fix *some* of the damage. "I bought a condo in John's Landing last year."

"I'm so proud to meet you. Oh." She put a hand over her mouth. "Sorry it has to be under these circumstances. I'm just glad JJ and I can help."

"It won't be comfortable with those bruised ribs, but I think I can carry you over my shoulder to the trailhead," JJ said, oblivious to his wife's gushing, fan girl chatter. "We'll drive you to the emergency room. It's only a few miles across the river." Middle height and wiry, he didn't look big enough to carry me two steps, let alone one hundred yards to the parking lot.

I'd fallen far enough downhill to almost meet the snaking path again. Could I crawl that far?

Not with those ribs, dahling. Scrap informed me.

Obviously, Raquel and JJ had no idea he was there.

"If you can just get me to my car, I'll drive myself," I replied to JJ. If Scrap said I hadn't broken anything, I believed him.

"Not a good idea, Tess." Raquel shook her head emphatically. "I'm a nurse and I can guarantee you'll feel dizzy and maybe nauseous from the pain. Then there's shock, which will set in as soon as the adrenaline wears off. How about if I follow you and JJ to the ER in your car? That way it'll be available when you can *safely* drive home." She efficiently relieved JJ of his daypack, placed it and her own on the path, then returned to help get me upright.

"You've had the breath knocked out of you," JJ said as he shoved one of his hands beneath my shoulders to heave, while Raquel grabbed my hands with her own to haul. "It's gonna hurt, but I promise you, things will look better once we get you back to the cars."

That was not fun. Nope. No way in hell.

About halfway up, balancing on my right foot, I passed out. As a tidal wave of blackness washed over me, I heard a demonic chuckle in the far distance.

Round one to the Nörglein.

Chapter 2

In February 2007 Fit Pregnancy Magazine named Portland the fourth best city to have a child.

"ARE YOU GOING TO BEHAVE YOURSELF and stay off that ankle for a few weeks, Tess?" Dr. Sean Connolly asked me. He looked maybe thirty, a year or two younger than me. Dark circles ringed his eyes like a raccoon and his white coat needed a good washing and pressing.

"You've been on duty too long, Sean," I replied. I banked on his longing for a shower and eight hours of sound sleep before his next shift. "Of course I'll take it easy," I lied.

"Good one, Tess. I don't want you in here again for at least two months. We've got to stop meeting like this."

I grumbled something. So I'd taken a few falls and fencing accidents this past year. It's not like I was stalking him.

"You'll have better luck putting her in a body cast and drugging her insensible for forty-eight hours," a familiar voice said from the doorway. "If you want to know why she winds up in the ER so often, read her books. She takes her research seriously."

"Steve!" I called to my brother. He was a taller copy of me with sandy hair that curled too tightly and a lanky build. But unlike me, he stood six feet tall, topping me by a good ten inches.

Not the voice I truly wanted to hear, (I'd probably never

hear again from the man my heart called to) but welcome nonetheless. "Aren't you supposed to be in Chicago?"

"Can't I come visit my baby sister?" He bent to kiss my cheek. "I have some good news to tell you and wanted to do it in person."

"You didn't call first. How do you know I'm not on deadline and therefore cranky and dedicated to solitude?" I scooched to sit a little higher on the hospital bed and winced at the pressure on my ribs and ankle.

"You're always on deadline," my best friend since kindergarten, Allie Engstrom, said coming around the corner. "Don't worry, Steve and I won't intrude on your precious privacy." She too kissed my cheek. When she straightened and caught Steve's gaze across the bed—they stood nearly eye to eye in height—something strange and wonderful clicked in my head.

"You two, together? You came all this way just to tell me you got together." I pointed first to Allie then to Steve. "When and how did that happen?"

"Long story short, you decamped from Cape Cod after your mom's funeral, leaving the family at loose ends. I picked up one of them," Allie said with a quirky grin that was half remorseful at Mom's tragic murder seventeen months ago and half full of the joy of new love.

My own heart sank. I'd never get that kind of happiness. The only man I loved and truly wanted had married another woman. I knew his heart belonged to me, but his loyalty and honor were legally tied to the woman his family had selected for him to marry when they were infants.

"More than just together. We're engaged," Steve added.

"Since it looks like you'll have family to look after you for a couple of days," Dr. Sean Connolly said, "I'll see about releasing you. After we put a cast on that ankle. I doubt an air cast will be enough to keep you down. There's a lot of soft tissue damage that might never heal properly if you don't *stay off it*." The doctor left, taking the x-rays with him.

"Anything broken?" Steve asked with a frown.

"No. Bruised ribs. The ankle's badly sprained and he's afraid I'll walk on it too soon and permanently damage things." I dismissed the diagnosis. Part of being a Warrior of the Celestial Blade was the ability to heal fast and clean.

"Even you will have to take a few days' rest," Allie said,

as if she'd read my mind. She knew my role in keeping a balance in this world between the humans who belonged here and the demons that didn't.

That nasty little Euro trash Nörglein from the Italian or Swiss Alps (they used to have a big range until tourists and industry civilized most of their habitat) didn't belong here. He didn't belong anywhere in my world.

I needed to get back out there and take care of the little bugger, not sit on my rear end nursing a sprained ankle.

"So how did you find me?" I finally asked.

"I pinged your cell phone's GPS," Allie said, still gazing fondly at my brother.

My eyes went to my fanny pack that rested on a corner chair along with my shoes. The phone pouch sagged emptily.

"It was in your car, Li'l Bit," Steve said on a chuckle. "If your car is in the ER parking lot, then you must be in the ER."

"And you have three missed calls from your sister-in-law, Doreen Cooper." Allie pulled the phone out of her pocket, checked the screen, and tucked it into my fanny pack.

"Doreen can wait." I'd put off meeting her for weeks. "How . . . ? Not just anyone can ping a cell phone."

"I'm a cop, Tess," Allie replied. "I have access to those sort of things."

"An off duty cop out of your jurisdiction. Way out, by three thousand miles." I have to admit I pouted a bit, envying these two their happiness in each other.

"Well, that's another long story." Allie dropped her gaze to her hands and fidgeted with the tasteful diamond on her left ring finger. A new diamond in a modern setting, not much more than a half carat. Quite a bit less gaudy than the three-carat antique I'd turned down in Vegas last year. Donovan Estevez had offered it, not the man I wanted to marry. I wanted the ring, not him.

No regret there. The ring had gone back to Faery where it belonged.

A nurse bustled in with a wheelchair and my chart.

"See if there's a way to put rebar in the cast so she can't saw it off," Steve stage-whispered to the nurse.

Nasty drugs they keep pumping into my Tess. Everything they give her they might as well shoot into me. We are tied by bonds of love and loyalty, blood and magic. What happens to her happens to me.

I'm too sleepy to keep up with the complex ins and outs of her family.

I trust Allie to take care of my babe. She's one of the good gals. Maybe if I scoot through the chat room and back to Cape Cod for a bit I can purge the drugs from my system.

Some people call the chat room limbo. To others it's purgatory.

Not just anyone can slip through the chat room from here to there or now to then. But I'm an imp. A special imp because I'm bonded to a Warrior of the Celestial Blade. I know ways around the guards the dumb beasts never thought of.

If the adrenaline rush of a quick trip through the chat room doesn't help cure me of the numb sleepies, then maybe I can take a bit of a nap with Ginkgo, my life mate. He and his warrior, Gayla, run the Citadel where Tess took her training.

Hmm, just a little nap with my lover to watch over me. Then I'll listen in on the gossip in Cape Cod. I promise.

"We have to ask her!" I heard Raquel's voice from a long way off as I swam up through layers of drug-induced sleep. Pain meds, my cotton ball stuffed mind sort of remembered. Just a little something to take the edge off while they twisted and folded my ankle before slapping a cast on it.

That "just a little something" became three increasingly strong doses as my body rejected the first one and most of the second. I have weird reactions to drugs.

"What can she do? She can't even stand on her own two feet," JJ snorted with disgust.

"There are rumors in the SciFi community that her books are based on a real-life Sisterhood of Warriors," Raquel whispered. "They fight demons all the time."

"We're not dealing with a demon. We're fighting a dark elf."

How did they know? Unless they'd had a child stolen.

"Same difference," I muttered. Oops. Not supposed to let on to civilians about that sort of stuff. Curse those drugs.

But the sleep felt so good. I wanted to drift away on worriless clouds.

I heard Scrap giggling in the background. He loved it when I stuck my foot in my mouth (figuratively of course) or fell flat on my face.

"See," Raquel said excitedly. She dragged her husband over to my bedside, back in the curtained cubicle in the ER after a stint in the X-Ray room and then the cast room.

I thought Steve and Allie were over at registration filling out reams of paperwork to spring me from the hospital. Takes longer to complete the forms than it does to treat the emergency.

I noted with some despair that my incredibly heavy left leg was propped up on a wedge shaped pillow. It was also decorated in pink and lavender swirls. Nothing discreet about that fiberglass cast. Dr. Sean meant business in keeping me off that foot. Allie must have picked out the colors.

Or Scrap. Did I mention his penchant for pink feather boas along with his black cherry cheroots? He's normally more tasteful in picking out my clothes and accessories.

Where was the brat anyway? He shouldn't be able to get very far from me when I'm hurt or sick or wounded.

"Can you help us?" Raquel asked desperately. As she leaned over me I caught a hint of a tummy bulge I wouldn't expect in a thirty-something woman as fit as she seemed to be.

Inspiration hit me like a two by four between the eyes. The Nörglein had victimized her, probably four or five months ago. So how come she *remembered?*

"I don't know if I can help, until I know the problem," I hedged. "I also seem to be in less than fighting shape at the moment." I tried lifting the leg with the cast but that was beyond my strength at this point. So I waved at it weakly.

"We didn't say we needed you to fight anything," JJ said sourly. He stood very upright on the other side of me.

More foot-in-the-mouth-itis.

"You were hunting that awful dark elf in Forest Park this morning, weren't you?" Raquel insisted.

"This isn't a Tolkien novel," I hedged.

"I've done some research," JJ said. He pulled a battered trade sized paperback book from the inside pocket of his black windbreaker.

I recognized the book. Guilford Van der Hoyden-Smythe

(Gollum to his friends), my once-upon-a-time archivist, short-time lover, and missing friend, kept one just like it in the glove box of his battered van. I had my own newer copy of the "*Field Guide to Gnomes, Trolls, and Ogres*." In fact, some of the green sticky note tabs on this book looked remarkably like the ones Gollum used.

And that illegible scrawl . . .

"Where did you get that?" I grabbed the book from JJ. Sure enough, it fell open to the page describing the Nörglein, complete with a drawing that looked like a copy of an antique woodcut. The black and white rendition showed the moss-covered Tyrolean jacket and three-cornered hat, fat bare feet covered in frondlike fur, full beard of more fern fronds beneath a long hooked nose, and strong body. It didn't show the deep red eyes or rows and rows of razor sharp teeth.

I was more interested in the notes scribbled in margins and on those sticky squares.

"I spoke with a folklorist at McLoughlin College. He loaned me the book." JJ snatched it back as if it were his most treasured possession.

My temper roiled up from the ache in my foot to the crick in my knee to my very empty stomach.

Calm down, babe. JJ and Raquel are victims not the source, Scrap reminded me on a deep yawn. He sounded far away.

"Did Dr. Van der Hoyden-Smythe tell you to look me up?" I ground out.

"No, he didn't. Say, how do you know . . ."

"I knew him a long time ago." A lifetime of memories crammed into two days and one night of loving each other. "Don't suppose you've got his phone number?" I'd deleted his cell phone from my speed dial. I didn't need the temptation to call him, just to hear his voice mail message.

"I have the number at home. I can call you later to give it to you," Raquel offered.

"Do that. I'm in the book."

"Does this mean you'll help us?"

"Not today." I waved at the cast again. "First tell me how you know about the Nörglein?"

"I—um—" Raquel blushed.

"We went hiking last spring. A thunderstorm blew in

suddenly. An unpredicted storm. We took shelter beneath a rocky overhang. Next thing we know, I'm tied up with blackberry vines and this ugly guy is raping my wife," JJ spat out.

"Crime of opportunity. No time for seduction or spells or whatever he uses to block memory," I mused.

"That about says it all," JJ said. "I called the police and they just looked at me blankly when I described the guy. They said I was delusional from the shock of spending a night in the cold."

Or they'd been blackmailed, coerced, bespelled, or bribed to consider reports of the Nörglein delusions.

"I want to kill the monster!" Raquel cried. "I just don't know how. I should have aborted the baby. But I couldn't kill it. I just couldn't."

"I promise you I will end that little monster's reign of terror before you deliver your baby."

That didn't give me a lot of time, considering I'd be out of action for six weeks at least.

Chapter 3

A climate survey in the 1890s revealed Portland's rainfall near equal to New York and Philadelphia. But more days of rain spread over six months, and more cloudy days give the impression of perpetual precipitation.

"WHO ARE YOU and why did you kidnap my friend?" Allie asked just inside the doorway of my third story condo on the Willamette River.

"I'm too tired to play head games with you, Allie," I muttered as I heaved myself up the last step on crutches, being careful not to let the cast on my left foot touch down. I had to stop, five steps short of my doorway. My lungs felt on fire and the wide elastic bandage around my ribs couldn't contain the bruises. I had to stop and breathe, carefully, shallowly, letting my heart rate calm.

And I was damp from the last onslaught of rain that blew down the river into my face the moment I lurched out of Steve's rental car. Copious sweat from the exertion of getting up the stairs didn't help.

Call you Miss Cranky Pants, Scrap taunted.

"Don't push, Steve," I pleaded as he applied gentle pressure to my lower back. "I can't go any farther yet."

"Want me to carry you this last little bit?"

"No. You're a computer geek, not a super hero. You'd drop me and then Allie would have to take us both back to the ER."

I hadn't experienced this kind of fatigue since I'd become a Warrior of the Celestial Blade, dropped fifty pounds, and taken up running and fencing as hobbies. Speaking of which, I needed to call my coach and explain why I wouldn't be in class tonight.

"This place is *clean!*" Allie protested. She stood in the open doorway, hands on hips, a scowl marring her strong face. "Not a single piece of dirty laundry or moldy coffee cup littering the place. No research books strewn across every flat surface. No piles of unanswered mail. I mean, Tess, this can't possibly be your home."

Not home. Just a temporary lodging. I didn't know where home was anymore.

My hand went to my throat. No pearls. My talisman, my last connection to my mom wasn't there.

"What did you do with all your furniture?" Steve asked as he peered inside at the same time he prodded me forward.

"I sold most of my stuff along with the house to Dad and Bill. They needed furnishings to open a Bed and Breakfast." The mahogany dining table and twelve chairs had come with the house when Dill, my deceased husband, and I bought the two-hundred-seventy-five-year-old monstrosity. The earnest money agreement included the appliances, the curtains, and the ghosts. I made sure Dad and his life partner bought them too.

Taking a deep breath, I muscled my wobbling way inside. Then I stopped again, more because I saw my condo as my brother and best friend did than because I couldn't take another step without rest.

"I guess it is kind of minimalistic," I half apologized.

"Not minimalistic. Stark," Steve clarified.

"Try stark naked," Allie added in disgust. She took the bag of groceries she carried toward the galley kitchen.

I usually ate at the countertop with barstools that separated the kitchen from the dining area and sunken living room. That eliminated the need for a table and chairs. The empty space spread wider than I remembered. The parquet floor was as new and unscuffed as the day I bought the place. A simple banister of Craftsman styled pale wood protected the upper level from the drop-off. Two steps near the entry hall and another two steps in the corner from the dining area were covered in the same textured carpet in mottled cream, seafoam green, and stone blue as the main floor.

A wall of windows overlooking the river and marina dominated the spacious living room, almost half the square footage of the apartment. A white stone chimney with a raised hearth and a gas log filled the adjacent wall. My one piece of good furniture, a comfortable sofa with foldout footrests, sat before a big screen HD TV with surround sound.

The kitchen at least got used more than the rest of the house. Even then a single sparkling wine glass occupied the hanging rack over the counter in a space for two dozen.

"You never watched TV much," Allie said cautiously. "Only two sets in the entire rambling house designed to house three generations." She rummaged around the kitchen, opening and closing every cupboard and drawer. She only paused when she stuck her head into the fridge. "And you never cooked much either. You've got all the makings for a dozen gourmet meals stockpiled."

"I have more time now that I'm not maintaining a colonial era house that sprawled in uneven levels and up three stories," I grunted. "Dad and Bill seem to be making a go of their B&B in the place though." I flopped onto the sofa and did some sprawling myself.

Allie creased her forehead and looked at me strangely. But she kept her mouth shut.

"What's going on here, Tess? This isn't like you." Steve crouched beside the sofa at my eye level.

I turned my head away.

"You have a right to be upset over Mom's death. My God, you were there when she was murdered. She died in your arms. I understand you wanting to get away from the house she shared with you. But you've always been the strong one in the family, Tess. The one we could rely on. Now you're falling apart."

"Not to mention you've pared down your skinny frame to a bony husk," Allie muttered. She carried a few pounds more than she wanted, but on her tall, long-limbed body you couldn't tell. "I'm heating up some of your homemade soup and making sandwiches. You need to eat in order to heal."

Listen to her, babe. Scrap sounded more alert now, but still far away. I knew he'd maintain a connection.

"You two can have my bedroom. I'll sleep here." I rolled over so I wouldn't have to look Steve in the eye.

Over my head Allie and Steve exchanged "The Look." You know, that weird silent communication two people have when they are thinking the same thing.

"Where's your cell phone, Tess?" Allie asked, all smart and businesslike.

"Why?"

"I'm calling Gollum."

"No, you aren't. I deleted his number right after he went back to his *wife.*" I sneered the last word. Not that Julia had been much of a wife to him over the past fifteen years. She'd been locked in an insane asylum for most of their marriage.

"Don't you remember the number?" she asked.

Of course I did.

Instead of answering I pulled a pillow over my head and pretended to sleep.

"That does it. If I can't get hold of Gollum, I'm calling your other boyfriend, Donovan Estevez."

"Not on your life!" I bolted up to prevent her from doing anything so drastic. Dumb me forgot about the pounds of fiberglass on my lower leg. Sharp pains shot, wiggled, and zigzagged in all directions.

With a muffled scream I lost my balance and fell back where I'd been. Panting through the pain, I couldn't prevent Allie from fishing my phone out of the fanny pack strapped around my waist.

"Donovan, this is Allie. Tess is hurt. We need you now!" she said and hung up. I presumed she spoke to his voice mail.

I wondered why the sexiest man alive, sort of my step-brother, champion of demon rights, and one-time suitor wasn't glued to his business number like his life and fortune depended on the next call. They usually did.

Dawn found me on my balcony cuddling a lidded travel cup of coffee with both hands, bracing myself on the crutches. I'd almost spilled the precious brew of life twice, even with the lid, when I'd stumbled out to watch the moon set and the sun rise.

But I had my pearls back on. I felt dressed even in my pajamas and robe.

I faced east, looking across the river as light gradually revealed lines of hills marching up to the base of Mt. Hood. The snowcapped peak towered majestically above the city. For about two seconds the low light sparkled against new snow. Then scudding low clouds raced across the lowlands and piled up against the mountain, blocking my view.

The Ross Island Bridge half a mile north had clogged with early morning Sunday traffic. People rushing to get out of town and enjoy the last of the mild weather. Cars on the Marquam Bridge, the double-decker freeway bridge next in line, still flowed freely. The mist obscured the other bridges that gave Portland one of its nicknames: Bridgetown.

Scrap perched precariously on the railing. Today his transparent body took on a shade of green content and he almost glowed. At least he'd gotten lucky recently. He faced south, upriver toward the Sellwood Bridge, in the direction of McLoughlin College, the small, exclusive, incredibly expensive institution of learning that was almost as old as the state.

"Did you know he was there?" I asked Scrap. We both knew I'd only speak of one "*he*."

I knew he was close. I didn't look to see how close.

"Why didn't you tell me?"

You didn't want to know.

"You're right."

What are you going to do about it?

"I don't know." Why had Gollum come to Oregon when his insane wife was locked up in an asylum outside of Boston? Surely if he were free of her, he'd look me up.

He'd said he would remain my friend, help me when I needed an archivist, just before the door closed on his retreating back.

"I don't need him."

If you truly believe that, I've got some Alpine cottages in Kansas I'll sell you, Scrap offered with a toothy grin.

The moisture-laden air carried an autumnal edge of chill. It smelled sharp and musky, of fallen leaves and ripening fruit. I caught a whiff of pumpkin spice from the bakery down the street. My mouth watered. My stomach growled with a hunger I hadn't felt since Gollum had left me and Mom had died at the hands of a rogue Warrior.

Those spiced muffins would make a perfect breakfast.

Maybe my soul was coming alive again after the deep grief. Maybe I could write again. My dwindling bank account sure would like me to finish the book that was more than a year overdue.

But I couldn't just dash out and grab a muffin to go with my excellent coffee while I pounded away at the keyboard. I was stuck in this apartment, chained to the crutches and the heavy cast.

"Tess, I'm fixing omelets," Allie called on a yawn.

I might not be able to dash out, but my brother could. "Send Steve to the bakery for pumpkin spice muffins!" I closed the lid on my cup and stuffed it in the pocket of my robe. Then I made the awkward turn on the crutches to go back inside. That wind seemed colder and wetter than it had a minute ago. Fat raindrops splattered on the edge of the balcony. I made it through the French doors half a breath ahead of the onslaught of the next shower.

Uh oh, Scrap said. He rose up from the railing on his stubby wings, large bat-wing ears flicking forward. His contented green flashed back and forth between angry orange and hot pink. Not complimentary colors.

Instantly on my guard, I balanced on my left crutch and prepared to swing the right.

"What?" I whispered so that only he could hear.

Tall, dark, and toxic has entered the building! He landed on my right shoulder, cocking his head, trying to figure a way for me to hold him while he stretched and solidified into the Celestial Blade.

"Donovan Estevez," I sighed.

Scrap really doesn't like Donovan. For the first year of our acquaintance, remnants of Donovan's gargoyle aura repelled Scrap completely. The only time the two could get within ten yards of each other was when the presence of a demon or tremendous evil overrode the repulsion.

Donovan spent about eight hundred years as a gargoyle, keeping demons and evil away from whatever structure he protected. Some of that apotropaic nature remained after his fall. He claims that he was inexperienced (gargoyles don't learn and grow after they are assigned a statue). Smarmy persuasion and vast numbers of demons overwhelmed him about fifty years ago. Whatever the cause, he was kicked out of the gargoyle business. A half-blood or Kajiri demon rescued him from his fall. I'd only recently learned the rescuer had been my deceased husband. That knowledge still ate at my gut.

I had a hard time convincing myself that a few family photos I'd accidentally tucked into a box of Dill's stuff I had sent his family were worth bringing back painful memories. His sister Doreen wanted to return them. I didn't want to have to think about all the people I'd lost in the last few years. Mom, my best friend Bob, Dill . . .

Those were just the ones who'd died.

After Donovan's fall, Dill had sheltered and nurtured him for a time before the Powers That Be passed sentence—condemned him to be fostered by Darren Estevez, a Kajiri of the Damiri tribe and nowhere near as nice and nurturing as my Dill.

Donovan claimed he hadn't been involved in Dill's murder at Darren's hand. I didn't believe him.

You see, Donovan developed sympathy for those he'd been charged to keep out of sacred space and now served as their human champion. Scrap had a darkness in his soul that made him and Donovan mutually repulsive, sort of like magnetic fields. Scrap overcame his problem. I'm not privy to the details of his time of trial.

Now the two can face each other and snarl.

I didn't like Donovan or approve of his mission to create a homeland for half-breed demons in human space—for that reason I had helped my aunt MoonFeather gain custody of Donovan's daughter, Lilly. The baby's mother certainly couldn't care for her in an asylum for the criminally insane.

But I trusted Donovan with my life. Several times we'd fought side by side and triumphed over some truly nasty Midori (full-blood) demons.

"What about Donovan?" Steve asked, emerging from the bedroom, blond hair scraggly—longer than he usually wore it and in need of a good cut—jeans zipped but not snapped, T-shirt half tucked in, feet stuffed into loafers, sans socks.

"He's approaching the front door," I said and flopped onto the sofa amidst the tangle of pillows and blankets that had made my bed. My hand automatically went to the strand of pearls.

"How?"

"Don't ask. Call me psychic like MoonFeather." Our father's sister was an avowed witch. We'd learned long ago not to question her powers of observation, intuition, and healing calmness. Who's to say I hadn't inherited her talents?

Allie, of course, knew about Scrap. She'd been deeply involved in one of our little escapades a while back. I hoped she'd kept that information secret.

Scrap flitted to the door, growling and gnashing his teeth, glowing an angry dark pink.

If he'd truly meant it, he'd turn deep red and stick himself to my right hand. If Scrap thought for an instant that Donovan threatened me in any way he'd have stretched and curved halfway through transformation into the Celestial Blade without my command.

A loud knock on the door and a simultaneous peal of the bell demanded attention.

"A bit impatient, isn't he?" Steve shuffled to the entry, peered through the spy hole, then unlatched the dead bolt and security chain. The door thrust open, nearly knocking him into the wall. He harrumphed and departed, presumably for the bakery and my requested pumpkin spice muffins.

"Good morning, Donovan. Have you visited your daughter lately? You look like you drove all night," I said, gluing my gaze to the weather report on the big screen TV. I didn't want to take in his lean, muscular frame, the high cheekbones and copper tone to his skin. His long black braid touched with silver at his temples could send me into paroxysms of joy when he tickled me with its silky ends.

Nope, not going to think about that, not one little bit.

"I'm flying out next week to testify on my custody appeal for Lilly. What's wrong with you?" He stalked over to stand between me and the map of the region with predicted high temperatures plastered over it. "Did a demon invade your dad's place and open a new portal? I can't believe you actually sold that very vulnerable piece of land to someone you love."

A memory flashed behind my eyes. My head reeled and my present location and condition reverted to an earlier time.

I lived again the gnawing fear that drove me to the most

dangerous portal of all in the chat room. Once more I stood before the tall elegant door with stained glass panels to the sides. I heard again the deep reverberations throughout the Universe when I dropped the knocker. Felt the vibrations as my pearls picked up the harmonics. I shuddered anew with the bone deep, burning cold of the doorknob when I finally screwed up my courage to open the damn door to the Powers That Be.

Seven beings from seven different dimensions sat in judgment of the entire Universe. Seven beings hidden and shadowed by long cloaks and deep hoods. I had no way of knowing who they were or where they came from. If any of them were human or had human sympathies they didn't betray them.

Chapter 4

Portland is sometimes called Bridgetown. Nine bridges cross the Willamette River that bisects the city: Sellwood, Ross Island, Hawthorne, Morrison, Burnside, Broadway, St. Johns, and the two double-decker freeway bridges, Marquam and Freemont.

THEN THE VISION WAS GONE as fast as it came.

Back in reality, I pointed to my pastel-swirled cast sticking out below my pajama bottoms. "I tangled with a Nörglein. Actually, I tangled with a blackberry vine trip wire he strung across my path."

"L'Akita," he said gently, sitting beside me and taking my hand. His thumb stroked my palm sensuously.

Part of me tried to melt into a puddle of desire. Been there. Done that. Didn't like the consequences. But, wow, did we have fun in the middle of it.

"You should have called me. I'd have helped you hunt the monster. What kind of demon is he?" His gaze met mine full on, without shying away. A sure sign he knew more than he implied. This man could lie more convincingly than most people told the truth.

I knew him too well to fall under his spell.

I jerked my hand away from him. "Nörglein are forest elves. Dark elves without conscience or a molecule of sympathy for others. They blur and change the paths before solitary travelers until they are thoroughly lost. Then they offer to show the way out in return for favors."

Donovan had the grace to look away.

"Sexual favors from women hikers, the demand of a night with the wives of males. Any children born of the liaison belong to the Nörglein after weaning." I coldly recited the *modus operandi* of the beasts, like reading a police blotter.

"I can't allow you to endanger yourself with this guy, Tess. I've heard about him before." Donovan took my hand again, lacing his fingers with mine.

Somehow I found the strength of will to reclaim my hand and my heart. There was a time when he could dissolve all my fears and reservations. Not any more. I loved someone else. I'd broken his power over me.

That was one of my problems with Donovan. I never knew if that intense desire and willingness to share my mind and body with him was true attraction or part of his magical glamour.

"How does the Nörglein get the wives of his male victims to cooperate?" Allie asked. She brought me a plate piled high with a veggie and cheese omelet and chunks of fried potatoes. The food smelled heavenly and I dug in without reservation.

For the past year and a half, I'd looked at food as fuel and picked at it only when necessary. Everything tasted like straw. I'd taken up exotic cooking in an attempt to find something, anything that appealed to me. I took more joy in the preparation process than the eating. My neighbors loved me for my leftovers.

Now it seemed the challenge of a demon quest had awakened my appetite as well as my mind.

Or maybe I'd finally worked through the seven stages of grief and could live again. About time.

"As near as I can tell, from hints in old legends and letters, the elf binds the lost man and then shape-changes into his form. He walks out, has a joyous reunion with his wife. During the night he slips away and releases his prisoner at the trailhead," I related between bites. "When a baby is born nine months later, the woman remembers who fathered it. Not unusual for her to have a complete nervous breakdown. Two years later, the husband takes their baby and turns it loose at a designated spot in the woods. That was in medieval times. Modern women aren't so obedient. If they fight giving their baby away, the Nörglein kidnaps it."

Donovan snarled angrily.

"Ew, does he eat the kids?" Allie looked as if she was about to gag on her own omelet.

"Unknown. If he dines on toddlers, you'd think he'd just prowl the city kidnapping them at will. No, he seems most particular in claiming children with his own DNA."

But Raquel remembered. The pattern was breaking down. Something had changed. I needed to know what in order to exploit his weakness.

"What's the plan, Tess? This guy needs to be taken out. Fast." Allie moved to the middle of the room, hands on hips, balance forward, outrage written on her grim face and aggressive posture. She pulled up the belt of her jeans as if hitching her utility belt full of weapons. Her fingers twitched, eager for the grip of a weapon.

"The plan is to watch and wait until I'm out of this friggin' cast and can fight again." I almost threw the now empty plate at her.

"If the Nörglein tripped you, then he probably spotted Scrap and knows who you are and the resources at your command," Donovan mused. Somehow my hand was back in his again. His gentle thumb caressing my palm and up my wrist was more an extension of his thought process than seduction.

"So I'll go in as bait. You two can follow at a discreet distance. Scrap can keep an eye on me and guide you to the lair. Easy." Allie looked as if she wanted to draw her gun. Once a cop, always a cop.

"Don't you have to go back to work?" I asked.

Allie looked away. "Steve should be back with your muffins by now." She marched to the door and opened it, leaning out into the open stairwell. "Couldn't you buy a condo with an elevator and interior corridor?"

"Limited access for bad guys following me. Corner unit with limited access to vulnerable neighbors. Metal stairs so I can hear anyone who approaches," I mumbled. "Allie, what's wrong with you and work?"

Steve appeared in the doorway. He kissed Allie and squeezed her shoulder. "She shot a man in the middle of a domestic dispute. She's on administrative leave until state authorities complete an investigation."

"I'm sure you'll be exonerated," I murmured. "You'll be called back soon."

"I'm not sure I want to go back to work." Allie kept looking at her feet.

"You love being a cop," I protested. "That's all you ever wanted to be from the first day we met in kindergarten."

"I hate dealing with men who beat their wives to death and then rape their thirteen-year-old daughters. I had to shoot him to keep him from coming after me with a baseball bat. I'm glad he died. Monsters like that shouldn't be allowed to live," she claimed righteously. Then her face fell and sadness clouded her eyes.

"I'd rather fight demons than my own kind who behave worse than demons." She looked up and glared at me defiantly.

"Huh?" Steve said, his mouth hung open and he held the bakery sack loosely.

"Okay, there's only one thing we can do." I struggled to my feet—or rather one foot and the crutches.

Donovan leaped up and offered to pull me. Or carry me. I batted him away.

"What can we do, Tess?" Allie asked. Wisely, she stayed out of the way and let me manage on my own.

"What I should have done when I first moved here."

"Find Gollum?" Allie offered hopefully.

"No."

Silence all around as they looked at me speculatively.

"Go buy some furniture from my sister-in-law."

Chapter 5

Portland has more microbreweries and brew pubs per capita than any other US city.

"This is a really bad idea, Tess," Donovan says as he drives his pretty cream-colored Mercedes across the top level of the Marquam Bridge. The rain-swollen Willamette River passes beneath us, muddy swirls catching on the bridge supports.

"If it's such a bad idea, why are you driving me out to Cooper's Furniture Emporium?" Tess asks from the backseat. She sits with her cast in Allie's lap. Steve is riding shotgun.

And I'm perched on the window ledge behind Tess. It's a pretty drive on a late Sunday morning. I don't have enough calm to add to the acid mixture upsetting my tummy to appreciate the scenery. Showers and broken sunlight offer different perspectives on lovely vistas at every turn.

"For once in your life, I think you should listen to him," I whisper to Tess. I've tried tugging her hair to make her pay attention to me.

She's ignoring both Donovan and me.

"I'm driving you so you don't go off on your own and get into more trouble." Donovan scowls. He does that beautifully. Too bad he's not gay. I could really go for him. But no, he's in love with Tess in his own twisted, selfish way. "You should meet Doreen on neutral territory, tell her what you need and have it delivered."

"How much trouble can the Coopers cause?" Tess asks. "We're customers. And they are Damiri. They like money almost as much as they like blood."

"Um . . . what's a Damiri?" Steve asks. He looks car sick. But I think it's the conversation.

"It's a tribe of demons," Allie supplies him the information. "The Coopers are half-breeds, otherwise they couldn't shapechange to human form in this dimension."

"Um . . ."

"Get used to it, Steve. Your baby sister has gotten involved with some really bizarre lifestyle groups," Tess tells him.

I almost laugh. But that would mean she's winning this argument. I can't have that. I need her to go home and nurse her hurts and spend some quality time with her brother and his lovely fiancée.

"More bizarre than the kids at science fiction conventions who dress up as demons?" Steve asks hopefully.

"Modern day demons hang out at those cons and win hall costume prizes, but they aren't really costumes," Tess says. "I found that out the hard way."

"Tess, is it legal to tell Steve the truth?" Allie asks. "I mean . . . didn't you take an oath of secrecy?"

"Too late now." Tess flashes them a grimace of a grin. "I'm out of the broom closet."

Oh, boy. We're all in trouble now. When she gets that determined look on her face, nothing can dissuade her.

What if I got sick? Imps don't vomit like humans do. We reject toxic food in other ways. If I blow enough flammable gas in her face she'll just open a window and throw me out.

What to do? What to do?

"The Coopers will recognize you, Tess. You married their son. Hell, they *know* me!" Donovan protested.

I rolled my eyes. I'd only met the Coopers twice. Right after I married Dill, then again at their son's funeral three months later. They'd avoided me through the entire painful procedure, barely recognizing my short time with Dill as a real marriage.

We'd reached a compromise on Dill's estate only after I threatened to take them to court with an ironclad will. They got his trust fund—or what was left of it after he liquidated it as a down payment on our house in Cape Cod, the one I sold to my father and his partner last year—and the income from his share in the mysterious furniture store on a back country road out in the middle of nowhere. I got the house and his life insurance—double indemnity for murder or accident.

Only Doreen seemed intent upon contacting me again, to return a few family photos of mine that got mixed up in Dill's stuff I couldn't bear to look at again. In the last month she'd become even more persistent in trying to arrange a meeting.

I'd driven by Cooper's dozens of times in the last year and never had the courage to stop. They didn't seem to keep normal business hours, or to have any customers. The open sign never changed to closed, even at two in the morning.

"I think I'll start with a dining table and chairs. Something simple, Craftsman design to match the railing. Lots of plain wood, light colored, to accent the parquet floor and kitchen cabinets," I replied. "And maybe some end tables and lamps." That is, if the Coopers had in stock anything but heavy, dark, gothic stuff for their fellow half-breed demons.

"She's serious, Donovan," Steve said. "I wish someone would fill me in. I'm a computer engineer, not a superhero." He flashed me a wry grin, parroting back my own protests.

So I told Steve all about the year I went missing after I buried Dillwyn Bailey Cooper.

"Only you, Tess, would find a Citadel hidden in a dry canyon in Central Washington that houses a Sisterhood of dedicated demon fighters. I thought you made that up for your books." Steve shook his head and frowned in disapproval. "Part of me dismisses this as illogical, the stupid wanderings of your imagination. But it explains a lot. And Allie believes you. She's hinted . . . I just thought her reading material had latched onto her mind a little too tightly."

"Where do you think I got the idea, Steve? I may be a bit crazy but I'm not delusional. You know me. I changed the situation in my books to a post-apocalyptic world to protect the guilty from witch-hunts. Last time that happened a lot of innocent women died horribly," I said nonchalantly, as if everyone should know about my secret life.

"So where's the imp?" he asked.

"You *have* read the books!"

"Only the ones you've had published, not the one that's a year overdue," he replied.

That was hitting below the belt. I had my reasons for not writing a word since Mom died and Gollum deserted me. But I had this mental block. Every time I sat down to write, the words evaporated. Nothing. Nada. And I was running out of money.

What would I do if I never wrote again? I felt like only half a person without stories and characters running rampant through my brain demanding I give them life through words.

My checking account was also growling like an empty stomach.

I could tap the money Mom left me. But that was blood money. I didn't feel like I had a right to it.

The rain evaporated and the clouds thinned. A bit of bright sunshine peeked through the tattered remnants of mist.

Donovan wove deftly through traffic headed east toward the mountain. Most of the cars turned off into the farm country, probably looking for corn mazes and harvest festivals. And don't forget the wineries and microbreweries.

Not once did Donovan ask for directions. He drove like he really knew his way around, getting into the proper lane on the freeway well before interchanges and exits.

"Did you drive all night from Half Moon Lake?" I asked when the conversation wound down and he turned uphill from the freeway toward the Mount Hood Parkway and took the quick left turn onto Elsewhere Avenue. This was the back way into Cooper's, not the simpler, but longer route offered by the road signs.

He'd been here before.

"I was in town already," he growled. "I have business and friends in this town other than you. I even have a new girlfriend. But I'll dump her in a minute if you take me back." He flashed me an almost sincere grin in the rearview mirror.

A hay wagon pulled out in front of him and crawled at twenty-five miles an hour in a forty-five zone. It shed bits of straw like a long-haired cat snoozing before the fire. Donovan backed off to avoid soiling his lovely car.

"Who is she? I want to give her my blessing, or warn her

about you. I'll have to meet her before I decide which," I riposted brightly. I didn't dare settle back in the luxurious seats. I might get too comfortable and let someone else make decisions for me.

Me, a control freak? You bet your sweet patootie I am. For a good reason.

"You'll meet when I decide you deserve to meet her. Mostly, I'm here on business." He clamped his mouth shut, a clear sign that he didn't want to talk about it.

"Halfling Computer Games business, family business, or Cooper's business?" I never know when to shut up.

"You work for Halfling Computer Games?" Steve asked in awe. "I love their games." Donovan might legally be described as our stepbrother. His adopted father married our mother then got himself murdered thirty-six hours later. I don't think Steve and Donovan had met any time other than Mom's funeral. Steve normally lives in Chicago, far enough away that our wacky family couldn't just drop in on him but close enough to get home in an emergency. Donovan only showed up to Mom's funeral because he was executor of the massive fortune Mom had inherited from his adopted father. Most of that money was supposed to come to me now.

I couldn't bring myself to touch one filthy dollar.

"I own Halfling," Donovan said proudly.

"Wow, if you ever need a beta tester, let me know," Steve replied eagerly. The two men rolled off into geek speak about various role-playing games and the logic puzzles of programming them.

I sighed. No more information coming from Donovan.

I let the luxury car cradle me and turned my attention to the autumnal colors beginning to show on the trees, mostly golden cottonwood and brown alder in the foothills, with just enough splashes of red vine maple to delight the eye. With the sunshine breaking through the broken cloud cover, those crimson leaves nearly glowed from within. They looked like something a faery would paint.

The last time Gollum and I had been together we'd helped some lost faeries get home.

Don't go there. Don't even think about those few magical days with Gollum.

"The place looks closed," Donovan said almost happily

as he pulled into the gravel parking area in front of the single story building. Blinds covered the multitude of windows beneath the flat roof. A big sign nearly filled one corner. CLOSED. No hours of operation. The brick house behind the store had plywood nailed to all the windows and doorframes. The door of the barn/garage sagged, showing three empty bays.

"If I didn't know better, I'd say this place had been deserted a long time," I said. "But I drove by two weeks ago. It was open and well kept."

Maybe it's not deserted, Scrap whispered to me. *I smell demon glamour. Like they knew you were coming and disguised the place. Like someone tipped them off.*

Someone like Donovan? I whispered back to him.

Someone like the Nörglein.

Chapter 6

Eighty-four waterfalls plunge off Mt. Hood along seventy-five miles of the Columbia River Gorge. The highest concentration of waterfalls in the world are in the fifteen miles between Ainsworth and Crown Point State Parks, including Multnomah, the highest double falls in the US, Wahkeena, Bridal Veil, Horsetail, Shepperds Dell, and Latourell Falls.

"STOP THE CAR, Donovan!"

"No." Gravel spewed out from his tires as he peeled out onto the road between a twenty-year-old tank of a sedan and a tailgating oversized pickup.

"Scrap smells the Nörglein. He's here. We have to stop." I leaned forward between the seats reaching for the steering wheel. Too far. I needed to put both feet down and push my body halfway through the gap.

"The man said no." Allie grabbed the back of my sweatshirt and yanked backward.

At the same time, Steve put his arm across the divide.

"But he's here! The Nörglein is here. He's disguised the place to keep me from finding him."

"What can you do about it, Tess?" Donovan asked calmly. He let the pickup pass with a flash of lights and a blaring horn. "This elf is tricky. He's smart. He's mean. And he's a shape-changer. For all we know he could be that big leaf maple tree ready to drop a thousand pound dead branch on us."

"I agree. We can come back when we have more information and you are fit again." Allie refastened my seat belt, and planted my cast back in her lap.

"You are in no condition to fight," Donovan continued. "I can't take this guy down with mundane weapons. And we have two humans on board who won't survive a confrontation with a dark elf. Especially one as nasty as this one."

"I beg your pardon. I know exactly how to fight a dark elf," Steve interjected. "I've made it through all six hundred sixty-six levels of *Halfling*. I know how to wield every weapon in the game arsenal."

Donovan and I both snorted in derision.

"It's not the same, Steve. Believe me," Donovan replied.

"Scrap . . ."

"Doesn't like me. And I don't like him. I can't and won't use him as my weapon." Donovan clamped his mouth shut and sped around the ambling old Dodge.

"You're going the wrong way." I couldn't let him get the last word.

"No, I'm not. We're going to drive until you calm down. Besides, you need to show Steve and Allie the sights, like a good hostess. How about a late lunch at Timberline Lodge, then we continue around the mountain and take in the waterfalls of the Columbia River Gorge? Maybe dinner at Multnomah Falls Lodge. I've got a camera in the glove box. We can take lots of fun pictures. Then email them to your father." He set his course.

"Tess," Allie said hesitantly once Donovan had turned onto the major highway again. "Maybe we should call Gollum. He'll know what to do."

"I hate to admit it, but I think she's right," Donovan agreed. He didn't look any happier than I did at the prospect. "Where is your boyfriend anyway?"

"He's not my boyfriend." But, oh, how I wished I had the right to claim him as mine.

Donovan raised his eyebrows at that and peered at me through the rearview mirror. "He was your boyfriend in Las Vegas last year."

Allie squeezed my knee in sympathy. She knew the whole story. Steve studied the autumnal colors, carefully avoiding eye contact with anyone. He must have learned about Gollum's loyalty to his crazy, fragile, dependent wife from Allie.

"Where is he, Tess?" Donovan demanded.

"I don't know."

"Yes, you do. I know you. You wouldn't let him disappear completely."

But I had. Until yesterday.

"Leave her alone, Donovan. Gollum gave me an emergency number before he left Cape Cod," Allie said. She whipped out her cell phone and pressed the first name on her speed dial. "Damn, no signal up here."

Scrap laughed. *Not yet, Allie. Not yet. I'll let you call later. But not yet.*

What was *he* up to?

Protecting your heart as well as your ass. With that, he winked out in a puff of black cherry smoke.

"Look, dahling, do you really want Allie, or worse, Donovan, to be the first one to call *your* Gollum?" Oh, the things I found out while Tess and clan were touring the grand sights. I got caught up in watching and forgot to go home until almost midnight.

Normally, I'd love to tag along on sight-seeing trips. There's something exhilarating about playing with the water gushing off our mountain and then tumbling over steep cliffs, spraying droplets hither, thither, and yon, moistening neon lichens or carving rivulets in rock. Then there are the ones that careen down broken inclines, twisting and turning through channels gouged over aeons. Always the same, ever changing. A philosophy of life. Sacred since time began.

Water droplets forming rainbows in the sunshine are perfect hiding places for imps. Gives me practice in changing colors at will to match the arcing prisms.

Sigh. Another time I'll wax poetic about waterfalls and bright leaves.

"What do you mean, Scrap?" Tess roused from her computer. Sunday night and she'd only written three new pages. But that's three more than she's written in ages and ages. This from a best-selling author who churned out a fat, fat, fat book every nine months or so until the dark side of life caught up with her.

I shouldn't interrupt her, but this is important too. I'm hoping that once she's talked to Mr. tall, lean, scholarly, and absent, she'll feel better. At least maybe that huge gaping hole in her soul will shrink a bit.

How can I find true and utter happiness with my Ginkgo when my warrior is so sad and empty?

How am I going to find the time to spend with my beloved if Tess isn't occupied with her writing? Her lack of a love life is putting a strain on mine.

"Letting Allie call him is the coward's way out." I feel like whispering because I know Steve and Allie are asleep in the next room. No sense waking them to share in this very private conversation.

"Calling him at all is the coward's way out." Tess plants her face in front of the computer screen and pretends to type.

I insert my cute little body behind the screen and peer out at her making funny faces.

She jerks away with a gasp. "Warn me next time you do that," she snarls.

"If I warn you, you wouldn't pay attention," I pout with just a perfect bit of jutting lower lip that Ginkgo finds irresistible. Then I waggle the tip of my black and silver boa in her face. Pink is fine for daytime wear, and my favorite. For evening calls the black and silver is proper attire.

"I can't do it, Scrap. I can't call him out of the blue. I don't know what he's doing, how he's coping, where he's living."

"What if I could show you?" I slip through the computer screen—these new flat pieces are more porous to my kind and it's easy.

"It's after midnight. He's probably sleeping. And I don't want to see who he's sleeping with."

"Not to worry. He's awake. I promise you we'll just take a quick peek from the chat room. If things get embarrassing, we'll dart back home so quick you won't have time to blush." I let the barbed tip of my tail glow a little, green with lust. I'd love to see what goes on in that household. If Tess knew what a voyeur I'd become she'd spank my bottom good and hard.

Oooooh, if only Ginkgo would do that!

"I hate the chat room. I'm in no condition to fight whoever is guarding it today . . ."

"So stop with the excuses. I've got a few tricks up my sleeve, dahling. I would never endanger you. I just wish I could lick that wound and make it better." I pout again. Imp spit works wonders on demon tags and infections. We have a natural antibiotic attuned to our warriors. Sprains, strains, and breaks are beyond our healing ability though.

Only the person who broke a heart can repair that kind of wound.

"Okay." She gives in reluctantly after a long silent pondering.

I bounce to her shoulder and whisk us through the dimensional portal and into the white nothingness of the chat room before she can change our mind. I spot a few doors here and there, some on the edges in neat rows; some randomly placed above, below, and in the middle. There are glass doors, brass doors, leather curtains, and painted screens. Little ones, human size ones, bigger ones, and giant openings with no visible cover at all. Pick a dimension, any dimension; the chat room opens to all of them, anywhere, anywhen.

Tess stands unsteadily on one foot blinking rapidly. Her cast has paled to a translucent echo of the real thing. Reality twists and fades in the chat room. It also grows big and fast and slams you in the face. You never know.

"Don't think about the cast, babe. In here you can put your foot down without danger. I can see the bruises and torn muscles. They are healing clean, but slowly."

"It's the dragon growing from butterfly size to nearly fill the room I'm scared of." She points needlessly to the bright blue and yellow scaled beastie.

"Oh, yeah, the J'appel dragons. That skinny Larper quaking on top of his closed portal must have stumbled on the guardian's real name."

For the uninitiated, Larper stands for Live Action Roll Playing gamer. They stumble into the chat room all the time without knowing how they got here. Most of them have enough sense to back out by the door they came in by. A few don't realize they are beyond reality and keep plowing forward, hoping to find Impland—the freeze-dried garbage dump of the Universe. Lots of magical artifacts end up there and are highly prized by critters more dangerous than the J'appel dragons. I've given a couple of those artifacts to Tess.

Tess stomps over to the Larper who's hunkered down with

his hands over his head. "What did you say to him?" she demands.

"I . . . I . . . said . . . hello."

"Crap. That's what the dragon changed his name to about a minute before you came through. Call his real name and he grows to dragon size until he decides to change his name again. Now get out of here." She pulls him off the splintery wooden door with chipped white paint and tarnished metal fittings, opens it, then shoves the poor mite back where he came from.

"Um . . . Tess," I call as I flit over to her shoulder. "I think we need to get out of here. We've attracted some unwanted attention."

"No kidding. Do we have to fight?" She takes up a stance *en garde.*

"Not here, babe. Just follow me." I lead the way around the perimeter of the room without true dimension. I'm an imp. I know how to use the chat room. I've learned a few tricks over the decades. I may be small but I'm tricky.

The dragon lowers his head, swinging it in a wide arc, sniffing. He's nearsighted. Great. Those are the most dangerous kind. He can smell Tess and me but he can't see us. So he's going to flame us just in case we don't belong here.

At the last possible second I drag Tess into a side corridor I discovered while doing research on that magical diamond Donovan tried to give her as an engagement ring. It's back in Faery now where it belongs, but, oh, it was a gorgeous ring. Both Tess and I lusted after it.

Dragon flames lick my hind end. "Stop that." I slap the beast's nose with my tail. His snout helps me beat the flames down to embers.

He backs off, looking hurt and confused, as if his mother had just reprimanded him for overcooking his dinner.

I'll have to remember that next time.

"Oh, my!" Tess covers her heart. A tear trickles down her cheek. She's looking through a little window into Gollum's home office. He's staring at his computer. An image of the Nörglein and a lot of text in Italian fill the twenty-four-inch screen. I think that's the language, though it looks a bit like German. He speaks and reads both—modern and medieval.

Tess half reaches out as if to caress his face, or run her fingers through his fine silver gilt hair.

Her hand lingers, fingers frozen half reaching for him. She forgets to breathe. The single tear gains sisters.

Her other hand clings to the pearls as if to a lifeline.

"I'd forgotten how tall he is," she whispers. "He needs to fix those glasses. They keep sliding down his nose."

His hand reaches for the phone.

I grab Tess and drop her back in her own office just as the first chirp comes from her landline.

She stares at the phone as if it's an alien being singing the "Halleluiah Chorus."

It might be.

Chapter 7

Gold Hill, Oregon, where balls roll uphill and people appear to stand sideways, is known as the Oregon Vortex.

THE CALLER ID SHOWED "PRIVATE NAME" and a number with a local area code and exchange.

It rang a second time.

I hesitated.

Pick up the damn phone, Scrap yelled into the middle of my mind.

Okay. I could do this.

A deep breath for courage.

A third ring.

One more and it would go to voice mail. I could return the call.

He might not leave a message.

I'd not hear his clipped tenor voice with hints of upstate New York mellowed by the dozen languages he spoke and read.

Desperate, I grabbed the phone in the middle of the fourth ring. "Hello." I tried to keep my voice from sounding breathless with anticipation. My heart raced and my teeth nearly chattered.

A long moment of dead air.

"Hello?" I tried again.

"Tess," he breathed.

"Who is this?" As if I didn't know.

"It's me, Guilford . . . um, Gollum." I could almost see him blushing.

"Good morning Dr. Van der Hoyden-Smythe. A little late to be calling."

"Tess, please. We need to talk. I've found some new information about your . . . um . . . problem." He rushed through that, as if afraid I might hang up on him.

I thought about it.

"What kind of information?"

"Not over an open line. We need to talk. In private. Before it gets any worse."

"How could it be worse? Seven women in less than a year."

"The problem is escalating. Please. Where can I meet you?"

"How did you get this number?" I'd changed it right after leaving Cape Cod.

"JJ and Raquel gave it to me. They said you're in the book."

Damn.

Yeah!

What did I really feel?

Anger certainly. Fear. Deep and abiding longing to keep this conversation going forever.

"Tess, where can I meet you? Neutral territory if you like."

"Do you know Bill's Café on Bancroft, right off Macadam?" Two blocks away. Surely I could manage to hobble two blocks on my crutches. No way I could drive my car with a stick shift. Maybe I could hotwire Steve's rental . . . No, he was leaving at zero dark thirty and returning the car. Allie was staying with me. I wouldn't ask her to drive.

"I'll find it. Eight-thirty tomorrow . . . this morning?"

"Why not earlier?" He'd always been an early riser, even after a late night of deep conversation and a bottle of single malt between us.

"I can't get away until eight when Julia's nurse is available. Then I have to be back at the college for a ten o'clock class."

"Back up. Julia? Your wife is with you and not locked up in an insane asylum?" I started shaking with chills that began in my gut and spread outward. My hands grew so cold I almost dropped the phone.

"She's had a remarkable breakthrough but I'm not comfortable leaving her alone . . ."

I dropped the phone back in its cradle, cutting him off.

The phone rang again.

I turned it off without answering.

Too angry to cry, too filled with loneliness to think, eyes too full of tears to see the computer screen, I hauled myself off to my sofa, hugging a pillow so tight I burst the seams. It spewed down feathers, like a snowstorm had vomited all over my living room.

I watched tiny specks of white flutter to the floor at the same speed as the tears dripping off my cheeks.

As dawn crept around the edges of the blinds I turned on the gas log in the fireplace and cleaned up the mess. I had to use a hand broom and dustpan while crawling. Scrap didn't help much, fluttering around, scattering clumps of feathers to the far corners.

I kept at my silent sweeping. No sense in letting Steve and Allie know how much I hurt.

Or Donovan.

At eight-thirty on the dot I swung up to the front door of Bill's Café, sweating and limp with fatigue. Manipulating crutches is hard work. I had to stop and breathe deeply before figuring out the awkward process of getting through the heavy swinging door.

A long arm reached from behind and above me to hold the door open.

I knew that hand. Long fingers, hairless knuckles, ink stains on the middle finger.

"Thank you, Gollum." I had to close my eyes and force air into my lungs.

"I wasn't sure you'd show up," he said softly.

I couldn't not show up.

He looked damp and a bit rumpled. His usual polo shirt and khakis had lost their crispness. I hoped I looked less battered by life than he.

Fat chance.

Bill, the café owner, bustled up and swung the door open further. Balding, middle-aged, once heavy but slimming down nicely from all the hard work of owning, managing, and cooking in his own place, Bill and I had struck up a friendship right after I moved into the neighborhood, a week after he opened.

"Tess, what happened?" He ushered me to a center table and pulled an extra chair over for me to prop my foot on.

"I tripped while jogging." I followed him very slowly.

"Tsk, tsk. You must be more careful. You're my best customer. I might have to close down if you stopped coming."

Fat chance of that. People filled the line of booths under the windows on two walls. The five tables in the middle of the long narrow room were mostly occupied as well.

Big windows offered a glimpse of the river between tall office buildings across the highway, and a good look at the state of the rain. I'd learned that in the Pacific Northwest people depend upon a lot of big windows to let as much light in as possible. We consider the sun a UFO.

Maybe that's why we have such excellent coffee, to brighten our moods when the sun can't do it.

"Nothing's broken. You won't get rid of me so easily," I quipped back.

"The regular, Tess?" he asked, helping me settle.

"Yeah, the regular. Black coffee and whole wheat toast with strawberry jam."

Gollum quirked a questioning eyebrow at me. Then he handed his menu back to Bill without looking at it or sitting. "Pancake sandwich. Eggs over medium, patty sausage. Blackberry syrup if you have it. Coffee with cream and sugar."

At least one of us hadn't changed appetites. And he hadn't tried to change my order to something more substantial. Donovan would have, in the name of taking care of me.

As I dropped into a seat ungracefully, Gollum gently raised my injured foot to rest upon the extra chair. "That should be more comfortable for you."

"You've talked to JJ and Raquel so you know what happened." I fingered the pearls nervously, wondering if I'd have had better luck in the forest if I'd worn them.

"Yes."

We stared at each other in uncomfortable silence.

"Do you still have Gandalf?" I asked about the long-haired white lump of a cat Gollum took everywhere.

"Of course. He's quite the elderly gentleman now. Spends more time sitting on the windowsill looking out than anything else. But he has become quite attached to Julia. She needs him."

"Oh." His wife again.

"What are you teaching this term?" I finally asked just to break the silence.

Bill brought us big eggplant-colored pottery mugs and an emerald thermal carafe of coffee—freshly ground beans, dark roast, the house specialty. A ceramic cream pitcher in Bill's colors and a clear sugar dispenser were already on the table along with cutlery wrapped in printed, paper napkins also in the same deep colors.

We fussed with the details of pouring and accessorizing our drinks.

"Oh, Tess, I almost forgot." Bill came back with a second pitcher, this one in beige plastic. "I laid in a supply of soy coffee creamer. You aren't my only lactose intolerant customer. Try it. If you don't like it I'll get you a fresh cup. Your orders will be up in just a minute."

He left us alone again, too busy to chat. Although with the six booths and three tables nearly full we weren't really alone. Not the best place to carry on a private conversation about otherworldly critters I needed to fight with the Celestial Blade.

Gollum took a sip of his coffee, smiled and nodded at the excellent brew, then answered my question. "McLoughlin College hired me to teach all levels of anthropology, including a class on the persistence of old folklore into modern urban myths."

"Your area of expertise."

He nodded, falling back into silence.

"Why McLoughlin? With your credentials you could go anywhere."

"When I knew for sure I'd have Julia with me, I needed more than adjunct work, a term here, a year there. I applied to fifty different colleges. McLoughlin was the only one to offer a tenure track position. And it's three thousand miles away from Julia's mother. And mine."

"So tell me about your wife's breakthrough." I had to know just how well she'd recovered after fifteen years of institutionalization. Maybe if I knew she was fully functioning in modern society I'd finally accept that Gollum was lost to me.

But if she were fully functional, why did she have a nurse? Why couldn't he leave her alone for more than a few minutes?

A small niggle of hope burned in my heart.

I squashed it.

"Julia's caregivers noticed years ago that on Wednesdays she was bright, cheerful, and coherent. Then on Thursdays her mother visited—blew in and took over. Within the hour Julia reverted to mute wandering, and refusing to acknowledge her surroundings, or other people. By the following Wednesday she was on the road to recovery again."

"Until her mother descended and convinced her she was useless, a hypochondriac, and a drain on her resources," I finished the thought.

My own relationship with my mother had been weird, but at the end we'd found rapport. Mostly I'd given up running my life in a futile attempt to win her approval. She'd never acknowledge that I could do anything right until . . . until after Donovan's foster father died. But she depended on me to take care of her, no matter what guise she put on her actions.

"How'd you get her mother to stop exerting control over Julia, keeping her dependent and useless?"

"Bridget found a new charity. She's turning vacant lots into mini parks, planting trees and community gardens, and commissioning murals on ugly walls. She doesn't have time to run up to Boston every week." He flashed a half smile. Just a brief glimpse of the warped sense of humor we shared.

"Are you well? Other than the bunged up ankle that is?" he asked before I could pursue the topic of his wife.

"Mostly."

We fell back into silence that lasted until Bill brought our plates. He fussed about for a moment, refilling coffee mugs, grabbing extra butter, and satisfying himself that we wouldn't starve in the next few moments if he left us to tend other patrons.

"I found a psychiatric nurse who works swing shift at the local hospital," Gollum blurted out between bites. "I give her room and board. She gives Julia companionship when I'm tied up at the college."

"Precautionary or necessary?" No polite way to ask that.

"Necessary. Julia had a couple of relapses early on, short-lived, but scary when they happen. Nothing serious for nearly three months now." He stared at his half finished meal.

I wanted to ditch my toast. Bill had put too much butter on it.

We both found solace in coffee.

"I'm not sharing her bed," Gollum finally said. He kept his mug close to his mouth, muffling his words.

My heart skipped a beat and my breath caught in my throat. I don't know why. I was the one who ended our affair. I couldn't carry on with a married man and I couldn't ask him to divorce the woman who always asked for him first during her moments of coherence.

"I'm sorry, Gollum, I can't do this. I need all of you or nothing." I knew that he was safe if not happy.

More than I could say for myself with the Nörglein preying on women in the hills above Portland.

I fumbled for my crutches and ended up losing my balance, banging my cast on the floor and nearly falling off my chair.

Gollum was right there helping me with a strong hand. He settled me on my feet and escorted me to the door after flinging money on the table. More than enough to cover the bill and a generous tip.

"Take this file, Tess. I printed out something that might help you. Call me if there's anything else. But please, I beg you, don't go deeper into this until you heal." He handed me a manila file folder from the folds of his leather jacket.

"I'm going to High Desert Con in three weeks. I should be mostly healed by then," I mentioned the science fiction convention in Pasco, Washington where we'd first gotten to know each other and begun our adventure with Sasquatch and hellhounds out of Indian legends. "I won't do anything about the Nörglein until after that."

"I'll hold you to that." He kissed my cheek and ran off into the rain, disappearing into the mist rising from the river. As substantial as a dream.

Chapter 8

Depression from too much rain and too many cloudy days in a row in western Oregon led to a diagnosis of SAD—Seasonal Affected Disorder or light deprivation depression—in 1872 by historian Frances Fuller Victor.

"I'M IN A HOLDING PATTERN," I told myself. "Just waiting. I can't do anything about the Nörglein until I'm fit and cast-free again." I repeated the mantra láter that week at dawn as I watched the sunrise behind Mt. Hood from my balcony. This morning I watched a lessening of the dark more than an increase in light.

Winter approached.

Maybe if I said the phrase often enough, I'd feel less frustrated and channel all my energy into writing. Two pages yesterday. That's all I managed.

But that's two more pages than you're used to doing, Scrap reminded me.

I cradled my hot cup of coffee in my hands and repeated my words.

"If I have to stay cooped up in this apartment I'll go crazy."

Crazier, Scrap commented from his perch on the railing.

"I need to do something, *anything.* What do you think about contacting Doreen Cooper to get those photos?"

You aren't going to Cooper's by yourself.

"No. I know I can't confront that nest of Damiri demons

on my own. What about neutral territory? I'll meet her for coffee at Bill's." I hadn't been back to my favorite café since meeting Gollum there. What better image to banish his association with the place than my wicked sister-in-law?

Scrap just shrugged. He shifted to straddle the railing and stare at the depths of the river. It ran swift and dark today, swollen by recent rain. He reminded me of a curious cat.

"See anything interesting out there?"

Not today. But soon. Something important is connected to that river. I just don't know what yet.

The cell phone in my pocket droned a phrase from "Dance Macabre." I'd changed it back to the *Star Wars* theme but somehow, no matter what phone I had, the ring tone changed daily to the weird and weirder.

"Speak of the demon." I recognized Doreen's private number on the screen. The ring tone fit. It always did.

"Why are you putting me off, Tess?" she asked without preamble.

"I'm not anymore." I gave her directions to Bill's.

"I'm in the area. I'll buy you breakfast. Twenty minutes."

"Make it thirty." The thought of the long trek on crutches didn't appeal to me in the least. Next week I'd get a boot over the cast or something so I could actually walk. Today, I was still handicapped.

You're building upper body strength, Scrap reminded me cheerfully as I dressed in navy blue sweats—the only slacks I could pull over the cast. *When you're fit again you'll be swinging the Celestial Blade around like a toy.*

I snorted something impolite.

One half minute before the appointed time I wrestled with the swinging door at my favorite café.

Donovan of all people jumped to help me.

"You? Why are you here?"

He shrugged and motioned me toward a booth in the back corner.

"How long before I can expect my favorite customer to manage the door on her own?" Bill asked from behind the prep counter.

"Soon. I miss this place. And you." I gave him a genuine smile.

"That's my girl. Coffee, of course. Something more substantial?"

"Don't know yet."

"Someone is waiting for you," Donovan reminded me.

"She commandeered the back corner booth like she owned the place," Bill whispered as I stumped past him. "He seems to be taking orders from her."

Totally unlike the Donovan I knew. My hackles rose. "Careful or they might leverage you out," I replied sotto voce.

"Is that worse than 'careful or I'll put you in my novel'?"

"About equal." This time I wasn't joking. More than one Kajiri demon had been embarrassed by a thinly disguised, not very flattering, version of themselves in one of my books. A few normals, too. Nothing I could get sued over though.

"I'll leave you two to talk. Call me when you're ready to leave, Doreen," Donovan said. He leaned over and gave her a gentle kiss on the top of her head.

Huh?

Doreen lifted her gaze from the depths of her coffee cup, black, no sugar or cream to add extra calories, and with a jerk of her head granted me permission to sit.

I did. Awkwardly. But I had a better vantage point to study her.

Her espresso-brown eyes tracked Donovan to the door and along the window line to his car in the back of the lot.

That was why I hadn't seen the distinctive vehicle before I entered the building. That, and being preoccupied with the cumbersome crutches.

Dill's sister had twisted her thick mane of black hair into an intricate knot on her nape. A white streak from each temple drew dramatic lines up and away from her full cheeks, making her face look thinner than it was.

Her elegantly cut black slacks and blazer over a pale pink blouse disguised her robust curves, bordering on Junoesque. Two-inch heels on her sensible pumps would add to her above normal height, furthering the illusion of slenderness.

She looked Damiri through and through.

Except for the pearls, so fine and translucent, they picked up hints of pink from her skin and her blouse. Her strand appeared to be a duplicate of my own. I touched mine through my sweatshirt just to make sure Doreen hadn't stolen them.

The hair on my nape rose and my Warrior scar throbbed.

"Oh," she said flatly as I scooted and shifted to find a comfortable position with the leg elevated. Her gaze remained fixed on my cheek. She could see the scar. That confirmed her demon ancestry.

Not all half-breed demons are menaces to normals. A lot of them want to blend in more than they want to highlight their otherness.

Scrap remained transparent. No hint of pink or red to warn of danger.

"Just, oh? No hello? No, 'how've you been for the last four years'? Just, oh?"

So much for family reunions. I noted that she no longer wore a wedding set on her left hand and wondered what had happened to the husband she clung to at Dill's funeral. I couldn't even remember his name or what he looked like. Just a vague shadow. But then I'd been so filled with grief, and the beginning of a raging fever, I barely remembered my own name at the time.

"I . . . I expected . . . I don't know. Maybe this was a mistake." She rose as if to leave.

"Not yet, Doreen." I blocked her exit from the booth with a crutch.

She settled back with her coffee.

Scrap took a seat on the back of Doreen's bench. He stuck his tongue out at her, then reclined, crooked his arm to support his head, and settled in to listen intently.

He faded so transparent and remained so still I had trouble seeing him. Clear evidence that I could forget his presence and we'd compare notes later.

Doreen offered me no threat.

Bill came over with my coffee and soy creamer. He helped me twist and leverage the cast onto the seat beside me. I thanked him and took a sip of his excellent brew.

"Can I get you ladies some biscotti, or pie? Maybe a late breakfast?" Bill hovered a little longer than necessary. A friend showing caution around an unknown.

"Nothing for me," Doreen said. She didn't have to look at her full hips. All Damiri developed weight problems in middle age. Only the most rigorous diet and exercise kept the pounds off.

When I'd known Dill, he'd still been young and active,

maintaining a slender and well-muscled body. A lovely body. And a keen mind.

I ached with missing him.

"I'll have the huckleberry pie." I loaded another spoonful of sugar into my coffee.

"You have pursued me, almost to the point of stalking for several months, Doreen. Why?"

"Donovan says I need to give you these." She handed me a large manila envelope. "I'm not your enemy, Tess, no matter what impression my parents have given you."

"They haven't done anything hostile, just ignored me; pretended my marriage to Dill never happened."

"I loved Dill. We were very close. Circumstances . . . I'm sorry we didn't get a chance to know each other when he was alive."

I accepted her apology with a nod. Then I peeked inside the envelope. Sure enough there were a couple of faded photos of me and Steve and our sister Cecilia from our teen years. As usual Cecilia managed to give the illusion she stood separate from Steve and me.

But there was also a picture of me and Dill, arms draped around each other, staring lovingly into each other's eyes. The rough, violently sculpted terrain behind us belonged in the high desert of central Washington State. I pulled it out and looked closer. Of our three months together, only one week had been spent rock hounding on the Columbia Basin Plateau. I wore my hair longer then, pulled back into a tight ponytail. A few unruly curls always escaped, framing my face in corkscrew tendrils. I hadn't Doreen's grace to disguise the fifty extra pounds I'd carried then.

Delicately I traced the line of Dill's jaw with my fingertip. Almost reverently I brushed the same finger over the few white hairs at his temples.

Then I closed my eyes against tears I thought I'd forgotten how to shed.

I recognized Dill's plaid shirt with the sleeves rolled up over tanned and muscular forearms.

My breath caught in my throat.

"You okay?" Doreen asked. She looked almost concerned.

I handed the photo back to her. "Where did you get this?"

"It was in the stack with the others."

"No, it wasn't. I've never seen this photo before. It was taken the day before Dill died. I don't remember posing for it. I don't remember anyone being around to snap it five miles from nowhere in a deep arroyo between gouged cliffs."

"Shit! That's why Donovan said you needed to see it."

"Shit is right. Who took this photo and why do you have it?"

"I don't know who took it. My guess . . . only a guess but based on other information . . . it was Darren Estevez. Probably through a high-powered telephoto lens."

"Donovan's foster father."

"Your stepfather."

I snorted at that. "Darren's marriage to my mother only last two and a half days before he was murdered. Now my mother is dead too. Donovan and I have no more connections. How'd the photo get mixed up with the others?"

"Planted among Dill's books and academic papers along with the legitimate photos. Darren needed us to know he was the one who set the fire."

"He had an accomplice."

"How . . . ?

"I was there." Actually, I didn't find that out until I went back. Imps can time travel if they have to. Scrap didn't want to do it, but he'd taken me back to that fateful night so I could see who had murdered my husband. I'd seen Darren clearly. His helper remained in the shadows behind him.

"I have no idea who worked with Darren then. Oh." She paused and put her hand over her mouth.

"What?"

"My guess in that area isn't as well-educated."

"Donovan comes to mind."

"No," she said emphatically. "More like his assistant, Quentin. His loyalty has always gone to the highest bidder. Darren could buy and sell Donovan twenty times over."

I spread the full contents of the envelope on the table. Two printouts from a Web site followed the photos. Duplicates of the information Gollum had given me about the Nörglein, including the critter's full name.

Names have power. Knowing it could be an advantage. If I chose to use it.

"Want to explain that?" We both knew this was why she'd pursued me so relentlessly. The photos were just an excuse, or a diversion.

"No. I suspect it's information you need. Donovan prepared the envelope."

I met her gaze with silence.

"Okay, he said you needed that information when I saw him using my computer and printer. He had the information on a flash drive. Is he," she tapped the printouts with a long fingernail painted pale pink to match her blouse, "the reason you're on crutches?"

"Yes."

"Then, I'm sorry. You can't help me. I need a Warrior capable of standing on her own two feet." She stood up and threw a ten dollar bill on the table. "Enjoy your pie. It's on me. I won't bother you again."

As she strode gracefully toward the door I detected a trace of moisture in the corner of her eye.

"Bother me. How and why are you connected to . . . this person?" I held up the printout.

"Not today." She exited with less grace than I'd expect from her. Donovan pulled into the parking lot after circling the block a couple of times. He got out and helped her into the passenger seat, fastening the seat belt for her.

"What do you make of this, Scrap?"

She's hurting. He's worried about her.

"Obvious."

Eat your pie. You've strength to regain before you clump back home again. I have a feeling life is going to get messy. Again.

Chapter 9

A 1978 survey in "The Oregonian" reported that most denizens of Oregon welcome the return of rain each autumn.

WHEN I FINALLY GOT HOME AGAIN, damp and exhausted, I flopped onto the sofa, foot propped up on three pillows. Allie brought me soup and crackers at about noon.

Days passed. I wrote a little. The manuscript grew slowly. Too slowly for my liking. When the words refused to budge out of my brain I retreated to the balcony. I had things to think about. Doreen left me more puzzled than informed. She needed help. From a Warrior of the Celestial Blade.

Why?

Her demon blood should make us natural enemies.

Only another interdimensional creature could threaten her. The Nörglein came to mind. Why else would she bring me information on how to banish the bastard?

I knew the dark elf had some kind of connection to Cooper's Furniture Emporium. What had he done that Doreen needed help getting rid of him?

The rain faded to a thick mist and the wind died down. A tug hauling three long barges headed north, toward the ports on the Columbia River. I followed it with my gaze as it disappeared into the thick air beyond the bridge.

Things lurked in the mist and shadows. Things more dangerous than gravel barges on the river.

I heard a car door slam. Nothing between me and the river but a public paved path and access to a marina. All the cars were parked on the other side of the building. Whoever disturbed the midday, mid-week quiet had packed some anger into the closing of the car for me to hear it so clearly.

Serious footsteps clanged on the exterior staircase; I felt the vibrations in the railing.

Knowing my neighbors and their routine visitors, I suspected I was the target of all that energy. With a sigh, I pivoted clumsily and wrestled with the French door that wanted to close too quickly in the increasing breeze at my back.

I had no idea if Allie had retreated to the bedroom or gone out to avoid my moody silence or not.

"Who is it, Scrap?"

Hrmf t hmmm grblt.

Since I was out of action Scrap spent more time with Ginkgo than he did with me.

Jealous? Scrap came through clearer.

"Get your ass back here. We've company of the unpleasant kind."

I hobbled over to the door, opening it at the first trace of a knock, before the visitor could pound it to smithereens.

"Why, Donovan, how good to see you. Would you like a cup of coffee?" I hadn't seen him since he'd dropped off and picked up Doreen from the café two weeks ago.

"How'd you do it, Tess?" he snarled. His fists clenched at his sides and his face darkened with suffused blood. The copper highlights in his skin grew dominant. His chocolate-colored eyes became deep holes of blackness.

The force of his emotions pushed me backward, almost physically. I raised my hand to the talisman of my pearls. They didn't help. This must have been what Scrap felt whenever he and Donovan were in the same room before Scrap overcame the darkness in his soul; the repellant force field of an active gargoyle.

He's human now, I reminded myself. *He's no longer a gargoyle.*

I turned away and fussed with the coffeemaker in the kitchen rather than face him. "How'd I do what?" I returned.

"I've just come from my appeal on the custody hearing for my daughter."

"I gather that it did not go well. MoonFeather retains custody." My aunt hadn't called in tears to tell me she'd lost the baby. Therefore, she hadn't been forced to turn Lilly over to Donovan.

I added soy creamer and sugar to my cup along with fresh coffee. Donovan's cup of black brew remained untouched on the counter.

"Your aunt has no right to my daughter. I'm Lilly's father." He moved closer, looming over me with barely controlled anger.

I had the crutches to fend him off if necessary.

"King Scazzy, prison warden of the Universe, ordered MoonFeather to raise WindScribe's child," I replied mildly.

"That has no bearing in mundane courts. Lilly is *my* daughter."

"So, what did I do to push the courts to honor MoonFeather's commitment to the baby? She is darling. Only nine months old and trying to walk already." My aunt emailed me pictures every week.

"My DNA test. How'd you get it altered? According to the lab my genes aren't even close to Lilly's." He wrapped his hand around the coffee mug like he wished it was my neck and he could strangle me.

"I did nothing. Perhaps Lilly isn't your daughter. Perhaps WindScribe slept with someone else." I shrugged and moved past him into the living room. If I had to defend myself I wanted space. "Rumor has it she seduced the king of Faery just before she killed him."

Scrap, I think I need you.

Coming. He popped into view behind Donovan's head, his wings beating wildly enough to create a draft. He bared his multiple rows of dagger-shaped teeth and made ugly faces. Then he turned his hind end toward our guest and farted so loud and noxiously I was sure Donovan could hear and smell it.

If Donovan did, he didn't let it divert him from stalking me.

Scrap landed on my shoulder, glowing pink. He prepared to turn into the blade and defend us. But he stayed pink, not vermilion. Donovan wanted to scare me, not hurt me.

"You and I both know that Lilly is mine."

"WindScribe did not name you as the father. She did

sign a paper requesting MoonFeather, her mentor and friend, adopt her child. The courts agreed."

"I am Lilly's father. How'd you alter my DNA test showing differently?"

"I didn't."

"You must have. No one else . . ."

"King Scazzamurieddu has more reason than I to keep you away from the baby."

"He wouldn't dare."

"Why not? What are you going to do, tattle on him to the Powers That Be?" My insides quaked in memory of my one and only interview with the board of seven beings, each from a different dimension, each with a different agenda, each shadowed deep within a robe's cowl, and unidentifiable.

"Why have you dared breach our portal?" I heard again the deep booming voice. A ten-foot tentacle stretched across the tall judicial bench toward my throat. "What are you prepared to offer in return for your audacity?"

Forcibly, I yanked myself away from that memory.

"Oh, God, they're still punishing me," Donovan gasped, dropping onto the sofa. He set the cup down and buried his face in his hands.

Scrap faded back to his normal gray-green. *Time for a snack, babe. We going out or eating in?*

I didn't answer him.

In. He popped out, probably to the laundry room in the basement where mold grew thick and deep behind the washing machines.

"Maybe they are ensuring Lilly is loved and cared for by the best person for her to learn about life, from both sides of the chat room. Maybe they need you to settle down and live a normal life with a wife and no more plans to create a homeland for half-breed demons before entrusting you with a precious child," I said soothingly.

"Marry me. Help me prove that I'm the best person to raise my daughter." He looked up, catching my gaze and holding it.

"Sorry. Wrong formula again." His third proposal and he still didn't get it that he needed to ask me because he wanted me, just me, to be the love of his life. He always put his agenda ahead of that, not realizing that if he loved me, and me him, then I'd gladly help him with anything he needed. "Why don't you discuss it with your girlfriend? I believe you are seeing Doreen."

"Doreen can't compare to you and what you and I have together, what we can do for each other. What's it going to take to convince you that we belong together? The other women are just diversions to distract me from you." He rose up to his full six feet of height, shoulders hunching upward in anger again.

"Figure out what I need and we might have something. Until then, I'm sorry you can't have Lilly. Maybe you should move to Cape Cod. Then you could at least visit her more often."

"If you're trying to get rid of me, I don't have to move three thousand miles away. Good-bye."

The doorframe shook for long seconds after he slammed it in his wake.

Allie hummed softly as she closed her cell phone.

"So, when's the wedding?" I asked casually. Since I'd discarded the crutches in favor of an ugly strap-on boot over the cast—Dr. Sean still refused the lighter air cast, wanting to keep me as immobile as possible—I'd retaken control of my kitchen. In a few minutes we'd have fish baked in a gentle lime and mango chutney sauce, brown rice pilaf, and a salad with a variety of fresh local produce from the farmers market.

At least I had an appetite again. My brain had only partially awakened along with my stomach. I'd added three chapters to my manuscript, enough to send to my editor as proof of my progress. That should buy another extension on the due date.

Unfortunately, I couldn't squeeze any more money out of them until I finished the book. Maybe my royalty statement next month could breathe some life into my checking account.

"We have to decide some things before we set a date," Allie said. Her dreamy-eyed gaze and humming halted abruptly. She began twisting her ring round and round her finger.

Until that moment, she'd looked happier and more relaxed than I'd seen her in a long time.

Uh oh, trouble in Lovesville, Scrap chomped down on his cigar. *Don't want to hear it. Don't want to deal with it.* He flew from his perch on the wine glass rack, which now held two glasses, through the closed French doors onto the patio.

"Decide what?" I hadn't asked why she lingered in my apartment a week after she'd been cleared of wrongdoing on her job, two weeks after Steve returned to his house and job in Illinois.

"If I want to go back to being a cop. Do we want to live in Chicago," she mumbled almost inaudibly. "Can I stand living in Cape Cod if I'm not a cop? Can Steve tolerate going home again? Can we find jobs out here?"

A long moment of silence. What did I say to that?

"Tess, I've wanted to leave home for a long time. But I didn't dare get too far away from The House without you there to guard it. How could you leave vulnerable a plot of neutral ground containing the right energies to open a rogue portal to a demon dimension? How could you leave your father and his life partner alone with no protection?"

"Your cop partner can guard it," I mumbled.

"Mike went back to Miami."

"Say again?" I'd heard her. I needed confirmation.

"Mike, the part water demon, went back to Miami now that Darren Estevez no longer holds his family hostage. The House is wide open to attack."

"Would you believe I took out some insurance before I left?"

"What kind of insurance?"

The scar on my face grew hot and knife fresh. I was surprised Allie couldn't see it glowing. "Insurance that cost me a lot."

I set my chin in an expression she had to know meant I would say no more.

I couldn't say more.

My hand shook as badly as it had when I held a very special onyx fountain pen. I felt it between my fingers, watched myself dip the nib in a pool of my own blood and sign my name. My full name that only my mother used: Teresa Louise Noncoiré. With each stroke my veins and arteries filled with searing warmth, a precursor to the flames that would consume the document and myself from within if I ever violated that contract of silence or returned to The House for more than five days at a stretch.

The House stood on neutral ground. It had to remain in neutral hands. As a Warrior of the Celestial Blade I was decidedly not neutral. My dad and his partner were.

Donovan had signed a similar oath about his past as a gargoyle after he fell. I'd had to figure out his "Big Secret" on my own.

Allie set her chin in a similar stubbornness to mine. "Tomorrow morning I'm going to make some calls, start looking for a new career." She pocketed her phone decisively and rose from her curled position on the end of the sofa.

"Doing what?"

She shrugged and began setting places for us on the bar.

"Allie, this isn't like you. You don't know how to not be a cop. I remember you breaking up a fistfight between two bullies when we were ten. You read them their rights!" I paused in scooping rice onto our plates. "I've driven patrol with you, helped close down bar fights. Being a cop is who you are."

"I know." Her eyes moistened. "Police work made me feel useful. I could protect ordinary people, make the streets a tad safer, bring a sense of order and balance into our chaotic world."

"But then life showed an ugly side you want to run away from." *Been there, done that. Just now crawling out from under my rock.*

"Yeah. I can't be a good cop if I'm looking at every teen as a potential drug addict, every poorly dressed female with a passel of children she can't afford to feed as a potential thief." She gulped and closed her eyes. "Every adult male as a potential child abuser and rapist." She bowed her head and turned her back on me.

Welcome to my world. Only I look for demons, not criminals. Same thing, I guess. There's a reason Earth has no demon ghetto. We are our own demons.

I gave her a couple of moments to master her emotions. "So what will you do?"

"Steve's not really happy in Chicago. So he's pursuing some leads in the job market in the Portland area."

"What about you?"

She shrugged again.

"Allie. You can hide from yourself, but you can't hide from me." Just like I'd tried a number of times to hide from myself, only to have her ferret out the truth.

"I got my masters in criminal justice while you were off getting yours in demon fighting. I'm looking into teaching at the Police Academy, maybe one of the community colleges." She finally looked me in the eye. "Gollum gave me some leads."

So that's what she'd been hiding. Not the change in career, but the source of her contacts.

Gollum was keeping tabs on me through my best friend.

"You're welcome to stay with me for a while," I said quietly. "I have really enjoyed having you here, appreciated your help while I recover. I still need you to drive me."

"Thanks, Tess. I'll repay you, someday, somehow."

"You'll earn your keep next week driving two hundred miles each way to High Desert Con."

"That's where you met Dill. Where your friend from college got killed."

"Yeah, I've got a lot of memories tied up with that Science Fiction convention. Time I stopped running away from them." And myself.

Chapter 10

English Ivy was imported by early settlers to remind them of home. It escaped and now threatens to strangle entire forests of native trees.

"TESS!" A FEMALE ALTO VOICE that bordered on a tenor called from across the hotel lobby.

I looked up from signing a registration form for Allie and me. Allie had driven me the two hundred miles east of Portland to Pasco, Washington, home of the High Desert Con.

"Squishy!" I called back, beckoning the squarely built, forty something woman with board straight hair dyed an impossible blonde. I knew no other name for her than the handle she used on-line and for con badges.

"I need to talk to you," my acquaintance said on an urgent whisper.

"Go have a cup of coffee. And put your foot up. I'll take the luggage to our room," Allie urged me toward the garden café in the middle of the hotel ground floor. She hoisted her overnight bag and dragged my wheeled suitcase toward one of the sprawling wings. The desk clerk had taken one look at my booted cast and walking staff and changed our room from the quiet third floor at the far end of the most inaccessible wing to a close handicap room on the ground floor.

I'd have to remember that trick next year. Might save me about three miles of walking each day.

Scrap turned bright yellow and popped out of my vision. He loved exploring conventions, sniffing out who wore a costume and who used costumes as an excuse to shape-change into demon form. Most of the attending demons were relatively benign, just trying to fit into modern society. A con gave them the chance to let their hair down, so to speak, and be themselves.

Donovan claimed that these were the Kajiri demons he worked to find a homeland for, the ones who were too human to live as a demon and too much a demon to truly live as human all of the time. They needed to shape-change at least once a month and take an occasional sip of blood.

Gave new meaning to "That time of the month."

I suspected from oblique conversations that Donovan really dealt with those Kajiri who used their human facade to prey upon the innocent. The closer to their demon roots they remained, the more they needed hot fresh blood to survive.

Lady Lucia Continelli actually lived as a vampire in Las Vegas, finding it a more socially acceptable way to drink blood than admitting her very dilute demon heritage. In fact, Lady Lucia hadn't craved blood until she tasted some as part of her facade. She worked hard at maintaining her image as the vampire crime boss of Sin City.

"What's up, Squishy?" I asked, stumping toward the café.

"Something weird I need advice on. But more important, what happened to you?" She claimed a booth just inside the arched entrance to the eating area.

Artificial shrubs and a chest-high brick wall gave the illusion of separating patrons from the mass of convention goers. Illusion only. We could check out and be checked out by all those who wandered around in search of old friends.

"I tripped over a blackberry vine while jogging," I muttered as I plopped into my seat and scooted toward the wall so I could stretch my leg sideways along the bench.

"You know that I'm a nurse. Anything I can do to help?"

"I guessed you were a healthcare professional from the detailed answers you give to research questions on our email list." I shifted and squirmed to get more comfortable. The four-hour drive in a small car had been a nightmare. Now my foot had swelled because I hadn't been able to elevate it.

"What did you break?" She peered at the redness of my exposed toes.

"Soft tissue damage. The doctor put the cast on to keep me off it and slow me down. He didn't trust me with an air cast. If I could figure a way to saw it off I would. At least I'm not still on crutches."

"Don't." She glared at me sternly. "And get some ice on your toes, soon."

Our coffee came and I dumped sugar into it, thought about indulging in the savory richness of real cream, and settled for packets of dry whitener I carried with me. I'd had one bout of lactose intolerance—inherited from my tight bond with Scrap—and studiously avoided all dairy products ever after.

"It hurts. I may have to do a bar con this year," I muttered.

"I've never known you to sit still long enough to let the con come to you in the bar, or the café," she laughed, more of a snort.

"So, what's so weird it couldn't wait?" I kept half an eye on the increasing crowd wandering the open area in and around the café. The con didn't officially start until noon the next day, but early arrivals were beginning the party already.

"First off, I brought a . . . er . . . friend to the con. It's her first. Her husband reads a lot of SF and attends the occasional con. She wants to understand the attraction and I'm trying . . ."

"You want to protect her from the weirdest of the weird."

"Yeah. She'll probably spend most of the con in the room reading or with costumers. But . . . um . . ."

"My word of honor I won't mention this conversation to you again except in deepest privacy. Now, what is so weird you have to talk to me about it?"

"Back to being a nurse: I've worked most every department at one time or another. So, even though I'm now in a specialty ward, when other departments get busy I fill in. Last month I did a stint in the ER. On the night of the full moon, a Tuesday I believe, I assisted in a slash and grab C-section. We didn't have time to get the mother to surgery. Didn't even have time to get an OB GYN resident out of bed. Except they were all busy in their ward with deliveries." Her ruddy complexion paled a bit and stress lines around her eyes and mouth deepened. That experience must not have been pretty.

"I hear that happens fairly frequently on the night of the full moon."

"It does. But not like this one."

"I'm a fantasy writer. Why do you need to talk to me about a medical problem?"

"The whole thing felt like something from one of your books." She studied her milky tea as if it held the answers to all universal mysteries. "Or one of my horror short stories. Not sure where to draw the line between horror and dark fantasy these days."

I'd never read her fiction. Maybe I should search it out.

"Describe the baby." I sat straighter, instantly alert. Scrap had told me about the scaly skin and wood scent of newborns with hysterical mothers. "You know that reality is often more horrific than fiction," I hedged. "Describe the baby."

Squishy dropped her gaze back into the depths of her tea. "When he first came out, breech, the skin looked dark. Mom is Caucasian. I hadn't met the father, but mixed couples aren't unusual any more, so I didn't question it. As more and more of him presented, the skin looked mottled, scaly, like bark. And he had one tuft of green hair that looked like moss. His cries were weak—he was about five weeks premature—sounded like tree limbs sawing together in the wind. But his eyes . . . red and very aware."

My gut sank. "What . . . what did you do?"

"The attending and I sort of stared at each other. I could tell he was thinking the same thing I was, some kind of terrible birth defect. We wondered if it would be kinder to everyone involved if we just sort of. . . . We'd never do it, but sometimes we think it might solve a lot of problems." She shook her head as if rousing from a nightmare.

I wondered if in the same situation I'd have the courage to go through with a mercy killing of a horribly deformed baby.

"Then, before we could decide to do anything about it, the baby took a deep breath and squalled like a normal infant and he just sort of morphed into a regular pink baby with a shock of dark brown hair on his head. The bark scales sloughed off. I saved them in a baggie but I haven't figured out how to get a DNA test and keep it anonymous."

"You're trying to tell yourself it was a trick of the light, but the image won't go away," I finished for her.

"Yeah."

"And the mom started screaming as if living a nightmare."

She nodded. "In the psych ward I'd seen another mother with the same reaction. The attending is researching to see if we have a new form of postpartum hysteria. I don't think it's from imbalanced hormones. I think there is something in the babies."

"So why talk to me about it? It was a trick of light. Mom had a stressful birth and was in a lot of pain."

"But . . ."

"Convince yourself it was a trick of the light. You'll be safer both physically and mentally. Burn the scales."

"The hysteria?"

"Uneducated women, or unemployed families subsisting on welfare, who barely know how to care for themselves let alone an infant."

"You're probably right."

"I am right. So why tell me about your nightmares? We're Internet and con acquaintances, not best friends."

"Word gets around. You have a reputation for stumbling into trouble and the explanations are a bit contrived. In this community, people believe in the stuff we write. Some other weird things have happened too. And I found that ER attending looking on the Internet for other 'woody' babies. I've begun to wonder just how blurred the boundaries between realities have become."

"Ground yourself in mundane details and you'll forget about it before long," I promised her. Actually I lied. I knew she'd never forget. I hadn't.

But then I had Scrap to remind me of my responsibilities to maintain a balance between dimensions.

Speaking of the brat, where had he gone?

Right here, babe. He flitted to my shoulder, an almost weight. He'd returned to his normal translucent gray-green. *Squishy's the nurse I saw in the psych ward with the first baby I noticed. You're safe with her.* He yawned.

Then, within another heartbeat he began to glow bright red.

Huh? Why the color of danger if I was safe with Squishy?

"There's another thing, Tess," Squishy set her chin and fixed my gaze. "There's a gang of kids here for the con."

"Three boys, two girls. Their costumes look an awful lot like that baby. They look too real to be latex. Woody skin, mossy hair, and red contact lenses." I described the phalanx of Nörglein flowing out from the glass corridor that led to the party wing. "Their jeans and T-shirts are brand new, fresh out of the package, never been washed. Since when do teens at cons look like store models?"

Yeah, that's what I was going to tell you.

A hush falls over the hotel lobby. Time seems to jerk into a new flow. The humans are moving slowly, like treading water. All light concentrates on the forest children and my Tess.

I smell rotting vegetables and putrid water. My body needs to stretch and sharpen.

Tess sits, wounded and inert. She cannot fight. We cannot fight here in a public place.

The compulsion to transform into the twin, half moon blades makes my every bone and muscle ache. My ears elongate and meld together above my head. My tail stretches and curves, flattens into half a scimitar.

Not yet.

I cannot go beyond this until Tess commands me. And yet the need is so powerful I wonder that I continue to live half in one state, half in another.

"Um . . . Tess, what's that red glob on your shoulder?" Squishy asks, pointing directly at me.

Apparently, the forest teens see me too. They stop short in their march around the central lobby. The youngest boy hesitates and half turns as if ready to retreat back up one of the arms of the hotel.

The girl next to him grabs his arm. "Don't even think about it!" she chides him. I hear a bit of German—or maybe it's old Italian—in her accent.

Yep, these kids were raised by a Nörglein.

I don't believe in coincidence. Our Nörglein sent them to deal with my Tess.

My body feels as if every joint will twist into a huge knot if Tess doesn't command my transformation this very instant.

The kids turn to their right and head toward the conference center where the gamers are setting up in one of the divided ballrooms.

They stop just shy of the double doors they seek. Donovan, dressed all in black, as usual, stands in their way. They exchange quiet words and the kids slink out into the parking lot. He starts to follow them, thinks better of it, and heads to the registration desk.

He has no luggage. We've never seen him carry any. But he always has clean, freshly pressed clothes.

Doreen joins him at the desk. She's pulling a full-sized rolling suitcase. And she looks angry. She and Donovan exchange a few words. Then he smiles that all too charming smile, kisses her cheek, and saunters off. Doreen clenches her teeth and leaves finger impressions in the handle of her rolling suitcase. She's pissed. Really pissed. At Donovan?

I don't know if Tess sees her or not. Her focus remains on the double doors that block her view of the forest children.

The grinding heat inside me tamps down to glowing embers. I fade to dark pink.

Tess relaxes, or is that collapses, against the banquette of her booth. Her grip on her walking staff loosens and her knuckles turn from frigid snow to warming spring pink.

Squishy shakes her head and mutters something. She sits back as if she only imagined me.

When I see Allie circle around the café looking for us, I know my dahling Tess will be safe for a few moments.

"See ya, babe. I need a smoke." And I flit off in the opposite direction in dire need of some mold to soothe my frazzled nerves and upset tummy.

The high desert of the Columbia River Basin is notoriously dry and mold free. But I know a few air conditioners that need cleaning.

Chapter 11

Dandelion seeds first crossed the Rocky Mountain in the 1830s, brought by fur trappers for garden sass at spring green up. The plant escaped to become a nuisance. Now, the rich saw-toothed leaves are highly prized by restaurants for Oregon Field Green salads and the flowers for dandelion wine.

ONE FORTY-FIVE AM ON SATURDAY I held down a sofa on the outer reaches of the bar, waiting. Small knots of people littered the coffee shop and the hallways, talking quietly. On the ground floor of wing two, parties continued at high volume. The gamers played on in their enclosed ballroom, oblivious to the passage of the sun.

The bartender polished the bar one last time. All his paying customers had left. He eyed me suspiciously.

Reluctantly, I made a move toward heaving myself out of the soft cushiness of the sofa.

My prey strolled past, head swinging right and left as he searched for someone. Not me.

I flipped the end of my staff in front of his knees.

He spotted it just before he fell flat on his face.

"Want to help me up, Donovan?" I tried to look pitiful.

He scowled. One of his more attractive expressions. Actually, I don't think he had an ugly one. Too bad I'd grown immune to his beauty and his charm.

"No."

"Will you help me up? This cast is more than a bit awkward, even with the boot."

He stuck out an arm. We clasped elbows and he heaved. I almost flew past him into the lobby.

Without apology he tried to push past me.

I blocked his way with the staff again, but this time I held the knobby end decorated in turquoise and knotted leather level with his groin. "Why are you here, Donovan?"

"This is a public gathering. I have every right to be here."

"But why did you come?"

"This is my home con. I live about an hour north of here. Why shouldn't I come?"

"Because you don't read science fiction or fantasy. You live it. So does your girlfriend. I saw her check in, but not since."

He shrugged as if disinterested. "It's none of your business."

"I'm making it my business."

"You threw me out. It's none of your business why I'm here or who I'm with. Jealous?" He flashed me a cocky grin.

"This con is my turf too. I intend to protect the normals that love this con and only came for a good time so they don't get mauled and maimed by your pet Kajiri. Like the ones who killed my friend, Bob."

"You're wasting your time and mine. I always come to this con to promote Halfling Games. You should have gone to bed hours ago. Do you need help getting to your room?"

"I'll take her," Squishy said from deep inside the bar.

I hadn't known she was there. Or why.

"Tess, you need ice on that foot again." Squishy wrapped an arm around my waist and propelled me in the direction of my wing. "I'm sticking close to you until I know more about those tree kids and what they're up to."

Donovan didn't follow us.

When I looked back he remained where we'd left him, a puzzled frown on his face.

"Is he one of the bad guys?" Squishy whispered when we were out of earshot.

"That changes from day to day, hour to hour," I replied.

"One of those," she snorted.

"What's that supposed to mean?"

"Read some of the gaming manuals from Halfling. Shape

shifters and tricksters. Sometimes they are your best ally, sometimes, your worst enemy. A roll of the dice says which. In real life we don't get a roll of the dice to tell us ahead of time which side they're on."

"I feel like a stalker," Allie whispered to me Saturday afternoon as we elbowed our way through the crowd in the wake of the only teens wearing store-fresh, stiff jeans and Tees.

"We are stalking prey," I replied. My ankle ached. I'd been on my feet all day. When my foot was swollen, the cast fit snugly. After icing and elevation, every time I stood up, the cast slid down, banging on the injured tissue. Each time felt like Scrap was playing tic tac toe on my foot with one of his lit black cherry cheroots. Today it had swollen up again. No more banging, but now the cast was too tight, threatening to cut off circulation to my toes.

"You should sit down. Better yet, go back to the room and take a nap. You look like a zombie. I know how to follow suspects discreetly," Allie continued.

As much as possible, we'd followed the Nörglein teens. I still hadn't fathomed why they'd come to the con since they spent the majority of their time in role-playing games, the tabletop variety, not the live action.

I wished I dared take Allie's advice and sit. Truth be told, this was the first time in a year and a half I felt a stirring of my old self. I'd grown into the science fiction/fantasy community through conventions. My first professional sales had been short stories to editors I met at cons. I loved playing with colors and textures to create my own costumes. I was at home among these seriously weird folk.

"If I look like a zombie then I should fit right in with the other costumes. I wonder why the kids haven't gone into dark elf mode. Not just the people competing in the Masquerade tonight are dressing up," I said.

To prove my point, a Green Man—he looked benign like the fanciful plaques and medallions for sale in the vendors' room rather than evil like the faces I'd seen in Forest Park—clothed in swaths of fake oak leaves and acorns strode past us toward the grand ballroom where the costume competition gathered. A hefty woman with dozens of black braids, wearing a bikini made of chain mail and rabbit fur that didn't cover near enough of her, scurried behind the Green Man. A troop of preschool girls in wispy pink and fairy wings added to the festive mood.

"Maybe the elves are behaving themselves because they have Donovan calling the shots," Allie said. From her perspective over the top of most of the crowd, she had a better view of the grand picture. At five foot two and hampered by the cast, I saw mostly the backs or chests of the increasing crowd.

Scrap was useless. He swung from chandeliers, nearly drunk on excitement and gorged on mold. I suspected he'd taken a side trip to the Citadel with his lover only a hundred miles north of here.

"Donovan's still here?" I craned my neck seeking a glimpse of the familiar black braid with silver slashes in the shape of wings at his temples. "Usually, he sticks to me as if he owns me. I haven't seen him at all since Friday night." More like Saturday morning. "But then he's got his girlfriend, Doreen, stashed in a room somewhere."

"I've seen him all over the con, usually not too far from the forest children." Allie angled our path to the right toward the gaming rooms instead of the ballroom.

And there he was, standing tall and grim at the head of a long library table filled with cards, miniature figures, oddly shaped dice, and other arcane equipment important to the players. I'd never indulged in gaming so I didn't know how to use those bits of junk. I knew more about my aunt's herbs and elemental symbols for ceremonial magic than this stuff.

Donovan kept his hands locked behind his back and his chin high, supervising initiates. As if he knew I watched, he turned and flashed me that magnificent smile that turned my bones to pudding and my will to thistledown blowing in the wind.

The elf children scurried into the room bearing nachos and pizza for a large group. They settled in with another group of teens. I wanted to back away from the thick odor of day old pizza, unwashed teen bodies, and spilled soft drinks.

"L'Akita, you should be resting before you jump into charades." Donovan flowed to my side and took my arm. Gently, he steered me away from his charges.

"You know my schedule better than I do," I replied, digging in my staff to balance against him. That cast wasn't moving until I willed it, which was my decision, not his.

"You are my priority here, Tess." A complete reversal of his previous attitude. Another reason not to trust him.

"I thought controlling the junior Nörglein was your prime purpose for being here. No, wait, you said you needed to promote Halfling Games. What is it you truly want, Donovan?"

He frowned. "Not so loud. They might hear you." He jerked his head toward the five forest children.

I couldn't tell if the greenish cast to their skin was natural or an aspect of the flickering fluorescent lights.

"So you did follow me here to supervise them."

"I don't need excuses to come to my local con."

Liar! Scrap proclaimed from the crystals dangling from the light fixture. *You'd only been to one con before meeting my babe—and that was dressed as a bat surrounded by cousins and nieces and nephews. You haven't been to a con since we battled the hellhound and lost a dear friend to a knife wielded by one of your Kajiri charges.*

I kept my face bland, pretending to believe Donovan.

"Are you going to challenge those children to a duel?" Donovan looked at my cast and staff with stern disapproval.

"If I have to. Or I may call for help." I forced myself to look away from his beautiful face and body and watch the five teens. This was the first time I'd been close enough to really study them. Three boys and two girls ranging in age from about twelve to fifteen. But being otherworldly in nature, they could have lived a hundred years to reach this level of maturity. I knew for certain that Donovan had "fallen" fifty years ago and gone to live with his foster family with the appearance of a teen. He could pass for late thirties, maybe forty now, even with the silver hair at his temples.

All of the junior elves had brown hair that tended to stick out in tufts, in shades ranging from cedar to oak bark. Their skin, minus typical teenage acne, was uniformly two shades lighter than the hair with just a hint of green. The girls had the appearance of short and slender saplings or sturdy vines. Their faces had angles and hollows, brown eyes tilted slightly up. The boys had more muscle mass similar to fast growing trees. Their noses and jaws were blunter and their heavy-lidded eyes barely opened.

"Tess." Allie dragged my attention away from the Nörglettes' quick and furtive glances as they wrapped their hands around their paper plates, protecting nachos and pizza from thieves. "Do you see how they're eating?"

"They are shoveling greasy junk food into their maws like they haven't eaten in a week and are afraid someone will take the food away before they get their fill."

"Yeah, I know a lot of teens have the manners of a troll. But these kids are really enjoying that food, as if they've never tasted anything like it. And they're smiling and talking to the other gamers."

"Your point would be?"

"They are redeemable. I deal with gang refugees all the time. These children need education and socialization, but there is hope for them." Allie sounded truly excited. Her face took on an expression of crusading glee.

I'd seen her in the same mode when she tried rehabilitating an aggressive pit bull rescued from a dog-fighting ring. Amazingly, she'd succeeded and found a home for the beast guarding chickens from coyotes on a farm. Rumor had it the dog babysat the children with loyal and gentle protectiveness.

I had little hope of convincing my friend of the inherent evil in the minions of the Nörglein until she watched them kill or rape. Even then she'd order therapy for them before going into battle.

"Donovan, the filk circle begins at nine in the executive meeting room. Bring them." I turned to retreat to the cooler and fresher smelling lobby.

"They won't want to come."

"You can make them listen to you. Do it. For me. I have a theory that might save them from their upbringing."

Chapter 12

Teasel thistle seeds were brought to western Oregon by Methodist missionaries to card wool in their mission mills. It escaped to become a prolific nuisance and impenetrable barrier in ditches.

THE NÖRGLETTES HAVE BARELY BEEN BACK to their room for two and a half days. While my babe entertains friends and fans on a panel discussion of etiquette for first contact with aliens, the forest children obsess over the gaming table. I'm going to check out their digs.

There's hair in the shower drain and on the bar of soap, so I guess they know about basic hygiene. The cute little triangle folded at the end of the TP roll by the maids has been mangled and the seat is up, so they know what a toilet is for. The two queen beds have not been slept in. Dirty underwear spreads across the floor in distinctive patterns. I'm reminded of a dog peeing to mark his territory. The guys are doing it with their discarded clothes. The girls too. Boxers in three of the piles, white cotton panties for the girls—high waisted and low legged preferred by older women, not the scanty and silky stuff of modern teen girls. No bras. Didn't notice if the two girl trees are well enough stacked to need them.

Fresh, unopened packages of underwear lay neatly in the dresser drawers. Five sets. I count two in each of the five piles on the floor. The kids are wearing a set. They plan on staying one more day. They'll leave the con when Tess does Sunday evening.

They haven't changed their jeans and Tees. The ones they are wearing begin to crumple enough to look normal.

Where'd they get the money for clothes and transportation, lodging and food? Someone in this family has a job or a trust fund. That could be the link to Cooper's Furniture Store.

Hmmm, if all these clothes are brand spankin' new, I wonder what they wear in the woods? Anything more than skin? Or do they live in bark?

I closed my eyes and let the words and music of a song flow from my heart.

There is no such thing as requited love
I have seen it enough to believe
It is not enough that I open my heart
A heart in love must receive.

I sat on a straight chair with my cast propped on a matching seat. Beside me a young man with a guitar strummed the chords of the song based upon a love triangle in a popular SciFi TV series. I wondered if I could manage to choke out the entire piece before breaking down. The semi-tragic fate of the two men and one woman mirrored my own situation with Gollum and Julia too well.

But I had to get the sentiment out of my system. My mother had used music as a catharsis. This wasn't a bar in Las Vegas with a karaoke machine. For me, it was better. It was a familiar venue among true friends.

And I had my mother's pearls to help me imitate her sultry command of the music.

I have watched you go; I have seen the change
Though my pledge to your side I will keep.
It is not enough to be who I am
And to savor your smiles in my sleep
He will tell you now that three is a crowd,
And you know that I leave with my heart
It is not enough to just take what is left.
So I'll love you and serve you apart
Follow your heart's path, in Valen's name.

Now it leads me away to defend
I will fight, I will die, I will be what you wish.
And my love for you will never end.

I bit my lip at the end, lost and alone, believing that Gollum heard my thoughts two hundred miles away. When I looked up again, Allie and several others scrubbed at their eyes, some openly, some surreptitiously.

Donovan stood against the far wall, the forest children in a line beside him. His chin quivered a bit. He brought a folding chair and set it beside me. I caught a glimpse of Doreen's back hastening down the corridor away from here.

"You don't sing that song for me, Tess," he said sadly.

I looked away from him, unable to answer. He'd used my name, not his pet endearment. I still don't know the true meaning of L'Akita, or its linguistic origins. I might have solved the mystery of Donovan's origins, but he had depths and secrets I didn't quite dare compare to mine.

Paul strummed the opening chord of a brighter and livelier tune. The crowd of about fifteen joined in on the chorus of a saga about never being able to leave the dealer's floor of a con.

"Life might be less complicated if I could love you, Donovan. But I don't. I can't order my heart."

"Do you have to love only one? I'll settle for being second best, if only you'd settle with me." He took my hand and kissed it with hope in his eyes.

"Not yet. My wounds are still too raw. You've found someone else who suits you better."

He dropped my hand like a burning ember. "What did you hope to accomplish with my charges?" He shifted his gaze to the five teens propping up the wall.

"The devil does not stay where music is."

"I don't know that quote."

"Martin Luther. If you stood guard over a cathedral . . ."

"Lutherans didn't attend my cathedral."

"Perhaps you are more familiar with Milton: Music doth soothe the savage breast."

"If you say so. It all sounds the same to me," he growled.

But the Nörglettes were tapping their feet. The two youngest, a boy and a girl joined a clapping game on the next round of nonsense songs based upon a goblin character from the gaming community.

"Maybe they are redeemable," I whispered, oblivious to Donovan's latest sensuous assault on my palm.

Then they started whooping and dancing—more like stomping and banging themselves against the wall.

I spoke too soon.

Squishy appeared out of nowhere. Deftly she grabbed the hands of the tallest of the Nörglettes and danced him out the door. The others followed, imitating her nimble hopping and sliding.

Scrap jigged above their heads, nearly drunk on their enthusiasm.

"I didn't know she could be so graceful," I whispered.

"Size and grace are not mutually exclusive," Allie snorted. She sidled after them. "You should be in bed. We'll keep an eye on the guests. I think they'll enjoy the dance and rock music more than this quiet interlude of song."

"She's right. May I escort you to your room?" Donovan stood up too. He offered me a hand.

He was back to being nice and charming; his usual seesaw between angry resentment toward me and trying to woo me into compliance.

I resisted, not trusting his charm any more than his anger.

"I can manage," I returned. Instead of taking the assistance I sorely needed, I grabbed my staff and leaned heavily on it as I levered myself upright. I'm perverse that way.

My staff seemed to have a mind of its own. The rubber tip slid along the vinyl flooring, nearly taking me with it.

Donovan moved with demon quickness to grab my elbow and slide his foot in front on my own skidding one.

I flailed wildly, trying desperately to right myself on my own.

"One of these days you will learn that you can't do everything by yourself," he growled.

"Pratfall practice is three doors down," the guy with the guitar called.

A general laugh went around the room.

Then he strummed "Old MacDonald Had A Farm" and sang:

Good ol' Tessie had a cane
Ei eye ei eye ouch
Without the cane she is quite lame
Ei eye ei eye ouch
With a yowl yowl here and a
Yowl yowl there
Here a fall, there a fall
Everywhere a pratfall
Good ol' Tessie had a cane
Someone throw her on the couch!

Somewhat steadier on my feet, half supported by Donovan, I sketched an awkward bow and stumped out to a round of wicked applause. My face burned with embarrassment.

Donovan's lips twitched with a half-suppressed smile.

"Don't start."

"Start what?" He opened his eyes in feigned innocence.

And then I lost it. Gales of laughter poured from the tips of my toes to the depth of my gut. I laughed at the ridiculousness of my grim approach to life these last eighteen months.

I laughed for the joy Mom had found in singing the last few days of her life.

I laughed for the freedom Julia had found away from her mother and her locked hospital room—were they symbolic of the same thing? Oh, my, I had a story in there somewhere.

I laughed at the idea of trying to tame five elven children.

And then I laughed at the wrong turn my depression had taken my book into and I knew how to write the next chapter properly.

"What's so funny?" Donovan asked. He looked bewildered.

"You. Me. Squishy dancing with the Nörglettes. Allie and my brother, Steve, engaged. I'm laughing at life. Come on, Scrap. I've got a book to write." I limped down the hallway, spine straighter and lighter than I'd felt in a long, long time.

"Let me help you." Donovan was at my side again, his hand under my elbow.

For half an instant I considered letting him take me back to my room to enjoy a few minutes of privacy . . .

Nah, we'd done that before and I always ended up distrusting him and hating him for his lies while thoroughly enjoying his sexy body. Even now I envisioned his sleek muscles sliding beneath his smooth skin, his braid draped over one shoulder caressing my breasts.

Gulp.

And then I remembered Doreen.

And I remembered the sweetness of Gollum's kiss.

Suddenly, Donovan wasn't so attractive. Or maybe I just didn't need him in the same way I needed Gollum.

How to get out of this gracefully?

A whiff of smoke drifted past my nose. I looked up to see if Scrap had broken the no smoking rule inside the hotel.

No sign of him or his cigar.

I sniffed cautiously. More than a bit of burning leaves outside. Only sharper, more acrid.

Trouble, babe. Scrap landed on my shoulder, glowing bright pink.

Donovan slammed his fist into the nearest fire alarm, grabbed me around the waist, and threw me over his shoulder as he ran for the nearest exit.

Isn't it amazing what runs through our minds when being rescued by a hunky male!

Tess keeps batting at her denim skirt so that it doesn't fly up and reveal her dark blue panties. I picked out this skirt for her ages ago, but she never wore it much because she lives in jeans, unless she's dressing up. She wears tailored slacks with a silk blouse and blazer when she needs to look professional. For parties and awards banquets—too few of either since Mom died—she lets me choose glitzy dresses with sparkles and drapes and interesting necklines.

But this skirt has proved perfect for her incarceration in the cast. Jeans don't slide over the bulky thing. This skirt hangs just below her calf and closes up the front with brass buttons. The eight inches of slit below the last button gives interesting peeks at her legs. It's casual enough for a con, but dressy enough to remind people that she is a professional writer.

Much more stylish than plain sweats.

"Why did you hit the alarm?" she yells at Mr. Toxic.

"Because there's a fire. Can't you smell it? It's the responsible thing to do." He continues carrying her across the courtyard, beyond the pool and hot tub.

I can tell by his pheromones that he's thinking about how sensuous a hot tub can be. Then he remembers my babe can't get the cast wet and his scent turns from lushly sweet to icky sour.

"Not at a con!" She slams her fists into his back. "Kids pull the fire alarms as pranks all the time. No one heeds them. Call 911. The kids will come out to see what the sirens are about. They won't even notice the alarm."

"Oh."

Well, duh. More proof that he doesn't hang out at cons like he claims.

"Hey, babe, my nose tells me that the fire is small. So far. But it's in some shrubbery near the back door to the vendors' room. No, not shrubbery. On the sidewalk. A planned fire, built of presto logs and newspapers."

I can't fly away from Tess. My instincts to stay with her override my need to know who started the fire and why.

I should not be able to smell moss and damp wood in the middle of the high desert. Even in October when rain does fall here, moss is not an option.

My instincts are always right. The who and the why have something to do with Donovan taking her as far away from the fire danger as possible. Right into more danger. Demon danger.

Heat builds inside of me, fueling my transformation into the Celestial Blade. This time I cannot, I will not wait for Tess' command. I stretch and stretch and sharpen. She grabs the shaft of my body with both hands. This is our destiny. This is why imps were created.

Tess is still draped over Donovan's back.

Chapter 13

The Tillamook Burn, in the Oregon Coast Range 1933, began in a logging camp. 400,000 acres of old growth forest burned in two days; ten days later, 250,000 acres still burned. Smoke rose eight miles high. Ash fell on ships 500 miles at sea.

"OUCH! THAT HURTS, TESS. What are you doing swinging your blade around?" Donovan squirmed and shifted, but he didn't put me down.

"Why in the hell is the blade out anyway?" he continued.

"Put me down and find out," I snarled. A dim shape that might have been a tree but was too stout and massive to be native to the high desert, moved toward us from the archway between two wings. Nothing but an abbreviated parking lot over there that abutted a dry and deserted lot devoid of anything bigger than a tumbleweed.

"Thank you for bringing me this woman," a deep voice echoed around the courtyard and swimming pool. I caught a whiff of pine. "I know she is attracted to you. I will need a moment to assume your shape. You will take possession of the item we discussed yesterday while I take care of this business."

The cool lights beneath the water only heightened the shadows and obscured details. Other than two arms, two legs, a head, and a stout body the size of a young black bear, I couldn't tell who or what addressed us. Then two red eyes opened and glowed with menace.

"Your reward, Donovan Estevez, is free passage back to where you came from. You have succeeded where my children have not. You have proved yourself a friend."

"You're a little out of your element here, Nörglein!" I yelled. I circled the Celestial Blade from my awkward position. "You have no power here, no trees to hide within, no paths to blur and confuse."

"Ouch!" Donovan yelped and jumped a little as the twin half moon blades with tines extruding from the outside curve brushed his calves.

"Put me down if you value your body parts, Donovan Estevez."

"If I put you down, will you try not to take off my head with that thing?"

"No guarantees."

"Look, I'm trying to save you. I had no idea he set the fire and waited for you to run out the opposite door. You can't fight in your condition."

"Wanna make a bet? How about the Mercedes if I turn him into firewood." I ignored, for now, the idea that Donovan knew of the plan.

Now, dahling. I need to taste demon blood now! Scrap reminded me that my blade was alive and hungry.

Donovan bent his knees and ducked beneath me. "Not bloody likely," he sneered.

I came up swinging.

The right hand blade met resistance, then flew free.

Yuck! He tastes like tree sap. And he's not a sugar maple.

Scrap doesn't usually have the energy to converse while in blade form.

Adrenaline is a marvelous drug. I forgot my fatigue, the aches and pains, my depression. Nothing existed but me, my blade, and the enemy. I spun in a slow circle, using my casted leg as an anchor and pivot, weaving my weapon up and down, back and forth.

The obscure form sulked behind the signpost that announced, "NO LIFEGUARD ON DUTY."

"Want another taste, Scrap?" I edged toward the elf in a kind of sliding lunge, right foot forward, slightly dragging the left.

"Estevez, you are to blame for this. I told you to deliver her subdued and rational. She is not like other women."

"You bet your gnarly ass I'm not like other women. I kill demons. I don't lie down and submit to rape by them." I stumbled on an imperfection in the dry grass. I needed a moment to center myself again. I lost track of my quarry. I sought movement in the shadows.

My blood still ran hot.

"All you have to do is say my name, Warrior," the Nörglein said sweetly from my right, the other side of the pool. "Say my name and I will disappear from your domain forever." He slid away from the metal pole.

"I know that. I even know your name, thanks to my friend, Gollum." That's what was in the file he gave me, as well as some details about cycles. The Nörglettes were nearly ready to go out on their own, find their own patches of forest to terrorize. That's why the attacks had increased in the last year. He needed a new batch of young to rear to his evil ways.

"But if I speak your name out loud so that you can hear it, you will disappear from my proximity, but not this dimension. You'll just find another patch of forest and continue your sexual predation upon innocent women." I flashed the blade and he ran around the hot tub.

With my weapon in my hands, I felt stronger, more confident, and less clumsy with the cast. I followed him, moving onto the cement walkway that encircled the expanses of water.

"No woman is innocent," Donovan snorted behind me. Wisely, he stayed out of my reach, or I just might have taken him out too for that remark. I'd been tempted before when I discovered his lies and treachery. But in a serious fight, I trusted him to protect my back better than anyone else. He'd saved me from Sasquatch, Windago, and mutant black faeries.

The big question remained: Would he protect me from demons he found useful?

Ask me again why I couldn't marry him.

"Modern women are no longer true women," the Nörglein whined.

"You mean because we think for ourselves and defend ourselves against monsters like you? You mean we are no longer property to be traded back and forth as favors by men?" My temper pushed me closer and closer to my prey.

Another few steps and I'd have him.

Most demons attack. This guy looked for a way to run. "Coward. Sneak. Pervert!" I yelled at him.

Maybe he just looked for a way to trip me up like he had a few weeks ago in Forest Park.

No blackberry vines here to twine across my path at his command.

"Precisely. I have to use all my strength changing into the form of the man she will accept. My children are born weak because of that."

"If your kind is so weak that they can only propagate by rape, then maybe they need to consider extinction." I lunged, all my weight on my stable right leg, the cast anchoring my back foot. Scrap tasted blood again. Just a little from a scrape across his potbelly though.

The demon ducked and ran. "Who will defend and nurture the forest if there are no Nörglein to protect it?" he called over his shoulder.

He ran back toward the hotel, growing taller and more humanlike with each step. His height, his gait, and the swinging braid down his back, looked exactly like Donovan.

If I hadn't known where Donovan stood, I couldn't have told the difference. Could the Donovan Doreen argued with at registration have been the Nörglein in disguise?

I was beginning to suspect as much.

They smell different, Scrap reminded me. *I know who is who. Now. Thursday's sighting is undecided.*

The demon favored his left arm. The one I'd cut with the Celestial Blade.

Donovan moved into my path, preventing me from following.

I ignored him and shifted my grip, bringing the shaft of the weapon to my shoulder for a javelin throw.

"I'm not part of this. I never agreed to help him. Just because he orders, doesn't mean I do his bidding. I would never harm you," Donovan pleaded. "You have to believe me on this, Tess. I'm not lying."

"Fool me once, shame on you. Fool me twice, shame on me. I'm not going to fall for that line of Blarney on your say so." I adjusted my grip.

"Father, what's going on? Everyone is leaving the games

and the clanging noises hurt our ears." A teen voice cracked up and down two octaves.

Suddenly, all five of the Nörglettes surrounded their sire and helped him into the sanctuary of the hotel. Dozens of people spilled out the doors—finally—in reaction to the fire alarm and the sirens in the distance. I couldn't follow my prey. I couldn't pursue this fight to the end.

My vows to the Sisterhood of the Celestial Blade demanded discretion in public. Protecting the innocent sometimes required keeping them ignorant of the nastier things that have invaded our dimension.

I slumped with exhaustion, hunger, and defeat. No more adrenaline to fuel me.

Scrap shrank back to his normal gray-green self.

"You okay, buddy?"

Yeah, babe. I tasted blood. We didn't win this fight, but we didn't lose it either. We've got the enemy on the run. I'll earn a wart for this. Now I need mold. And some sleep.

"Me, too."

I took my mold in the form of a B&B salad in the garden café. That's blue cheese and thin slices of rare roast beef on a bed of greens. Soft cheeses are not the best choice for lactose intolerance. Hard cheeses are better. But close to midnight after a frustrating confrontation with the Nörglein, I needed something special.

I'd pay for it in the wee small hours of the morning though. I didn't care while my tongue savored the creamy sweet and tart of the blue cheese.

"Nice to see your appetite has returned," Allie said, flopping onto the bench seat opposite me. She looked tired but in a happy sort of way. She'd enjoyed her first con. "We'll have you up to snuff in no time." She grabbed a hunk of beef slathered in blue cheese crumbles from my plate.

"What happened with the fire alarm?" I asked, then stuffed enough garlic toast into my mouth so I couldn't speak for a few moments, and also to keep her from stealing it. I was as bad as the Nörglettes.

"The Fire Marshal threatened everyone at the dance with jail time if he didn't get a confession from someone about who built the little campfire on the arse side of the building." She grabbed my second piece of toast.

I almost slapped her hand away. On second thought, I knew I was having trouble finishing my fourth meal. My appetite had returned but not full force. My stomach must have shrunk during my months of gloom and doom.

"Did anyone confess?"

"Two girls in our quintet of forest elves." She signaled the waitress for decaf coffee. She took hers black and strong enough to get up and walk off by itself. I think that's how all cops drink coffee.

"Decaf?"

"I want to sleep tonight. In case you don't remember, I'm driving two hundred miles tomorrow evening."

I shrugged and speared more lettuce and cheese into my mouth.

"What did the local boys in blue do with the girls?"

"A stern lecture and release to Donovan, who claimed to be their father."

"Was he favoring his left arm?"

"Yeah." She suddenly sounded very interested and wary.

"That was the dark elf. Who happens to be their genetic father. I left Donovan unharmed. Reluctantly."

"Let me guess, he's playing both sides against the middle."

I nodded, chasing the last crumb of blue cheese around the plate.

"Miss, may I speak with you?" The middle brother in height of the Nörglettes stood beside my table, twisting his hands together. I think I'd placed him eldest in the lineup.

"Since you asked politely, pull up a chair."

As he dragged a chair from a nearby table to the end of my booth, I laid the staff with the knobby end encased in blue leather with dangling bits of turquoise on knotted leather thongs along the table, within easy grasp.

Not a Celestial Blade, but still a weapon in trained hands.

The kid sat silently staring off into a distance I couldn't fathom.

"Speak up, umm . . . What is your name?"

"Oak," he replied automatically, still only half here.

"That makes sense. You have the coloring of an oak tree.

You're broad in the shoulder. Deep roots anchoring you to life too, I bet."

He roused a bit. "My brothers are Fir and Cedar. Taller, less stable, shallow root balls that spread wide but don't hold up in a fierce wind. My sisters are Blackberry and Salal."

"I'm surprised one isn't named Fern or Bracken."

He shrugged. "The next batch maybe."

"So what do you need to talk about, Oak?" I fiddled with the leather wrappings on my staff.

Allie shifted uneasily, as if she missed her utility belt with gun, taser, flashlight, and handcuffs.

"Our father is sorely injured. We must take him home tonight, before the gaming ends. He cannot heal in this dry land. Our home is the deep, damp forest on the other side of the mountain. He needs moss and lichen and mushrooms to bind the wound. We will miss the end of the gaming. We will never know who wins. I will never know what fascinates my father in the dealers' room."

I nodded. The sooner the dark elf left the better. I needed about another week off before I healed completely and could defeat him.

The Celestial Blade is one of the few substances in this dimension that can penetrate demon hide. I hoped he'd need longer to heal than I.

"We do not understand why you hurt him so dire." He looked up from studying his hands to capture my gaze.

I saw true perplexity there. This child was as much an innocent of my world as humans were of his.

"Do you understand how much he hurts his victims?"

"Victims?"

"The women he rapes to get more children."

"I do not know this word rape."

"It's the most heinous crime I know of." Allie leaned so that her face was only inches from his. "It's a violation of a woman's soul as well as her body and her dignity."

"I do not understand. Trees must spread their pollen."

"But trees allow their pollen to be carried by the wind or by insects. The fertilized seed lands where it may, grows without the helping hand of a parent. Our children must be reared carefully, with love, from the moment of conception," I tried to explain.

"Women have the choice to decide if they will accept a man's seed within their wombs. A woman has the right to choose the man who will plant a child within her body," Allie took up the litany.

Something in what we said landed on fertile ground within his brain. I saw a light of understanding. Maybe not complete comprehension, but something for him to think about.

"I chose not to accept your father as the sire of a child," I pressed him. "For him to force himself upon me is rape. If he tries it again I will kill him. Our laws will treat me lightly and not call his death much of a crime."

"Self-defense. Most courts wouldn't even order your arrest if you killed him during the act," Allie confirmed.

"Soon you will go out and find your own patch of forest to nurture. You must ask yourself if you will choose to force women to bear you children or if you will woo them and gain their consent first."

"But my father changes into the form of the man these women love."

"But he is not the man she loves. He will not stay with her and help her raise the child to adulthood."

That caught his attention. "Do you mean that your children have both a mother and a father past the time of weaning?"

"Got it in one."

"I cannot believe this. My father says that all creatures have only one parent. Look at the deer and bear. He would not lie to us." Oak pushed his chair back, preparing to leave.

"Look to the wolves. The entire pack raises the cubs. Deer fawns stay with their mother, but she has the help of her sisters and older daughters. They form a herd. We call them families. Your brothers and sisters are part of your family. But where are your mothers? Do the women who bore you not grieve for the loss of you?" I found my language growing more formal, settling into a similar cadence to his.

Maybe he'd appreciate the words better in a familiar form.

"My father does not lie." This time he shoved his chair so fiercely it tipped over.

"Oak, take my card. If you or your siblings ever need to

talk again, you can find me." I fished a business card out of my belt pack and stuffed it in his jeans pocket.

He grunted and fled, leaving the chair on the floor.

"That went well," Allie said sarcastically.

"We planted a seed. That's all we can hope for at this stage."

Chapter 14

The Oregon State rock is the thunderegg, actually a geode. It looks like an unassuming lump until you break it open to reveal marvelous agate or crystal cores.

SUNDAY MORNING I SAT on two writer oriented panels with fair attendance for the last day of a con. If the topic of discussion had been fan based, like "Are virgins the natural prey of dragons?" no one would have been awake. Unpublished and under-published writers are a different breed, even if they come out of fandom. I looked out on eager faces primed with notebooks or laptops, willing to drink deeply of my well of knowledge.

My brain wanted to follow the Nörglein home. Fortunately, three other published writers sat with me and carried much of the discussion.

"Tess, did the injury interrupt your career badly? How do you cope with personal problems that rob you of writing time?" About the only question I felt qualified to answer.

"Actually, the bad fall woke me out of a long depression. I'm happy to say I'm writing again, even if I am overdue on my deadline. I didn't cope with personal problems. I let them consume me. And my career suffered. So now I'm playing catch up."

Scrap had told me time and again I needed to get back to work. I didn't listen. I wallowed instead.

We went on to discuss ways to make time for writing around busy schedules, how to channel anger and frustration into characters, how to recognize the symptoms of clinical depression and when to seek help. Just as the audience members began comparing antidepressant prescriptions, Allie came to collect me.

"Is the car packed?" I asked, my mind already on strategies for removing the Nörglein from my neighborhood. How I'd deal with his children, I had no idea.

"Yeah, all packed up and checked out. I'd like to take one last cruise through the dealers' room first," Allie said. She adjusted her gait to match mine.

"What are you looking for?"

"A corset." She blushed. "It's white brocade with a lily of the valley pattern. I was thinking of my wedding night."

I swallowed my smile. "Okay. There's a rapier I'd like to fondle again. My collection is in mini storage and I'd like something trusty but inexpensive to keep in the house. I feel half naked without a backup weapon."

"Me, too," Allie said quietly. "Tomorrow morning, first thing, I'm going to buy a gun and get a carry permit. I feel so vulnerable without one. Last night . . ."

"A gun wouldn't have worked on demon hide, or bark, or whatever."

"But it will make humans stop and think twice about snatching your purse because you're in a cast and can't move fast." She slapped the hand of a grubby teenager (couldn't tell if it was male or female in generic jeans and a black Tee, with short hair gelled into hornlike spikes) away from my belt pack.

The kid slunk away grumbling about life not being fair.

"It's not just here. Most of the con community is well behaved. Out in the real world we are both in greater danger. I'll feel safer with a gun. I'm trained when to use one and when not to." Allie veered off to the costume racks of capes and corsets, hats and feathers.

Oooooh, Tessie, look at this! Scrap popped into view directly in front of me and led the way to a different table in the crowded room. Two dozen dealers with twice as many tables or racks lined the walls of the large ballroom. Another dozen filled in squares in the middle. Scrap zoomed in on a display of crystals in the back corner. Hanging sun catcher crystals, crystals in jewelry, candlestick dependents. And a crystal ball.

From twenty feet away I felt the power pulsating from it. A real crystal ball made of beryllium or goshenite, not blown glass or rock crystal. Three inches in diameter, it would fit nicely in the palm of my hand. Mineral traces made it a bit milky. As I approached, the imperfections seemed to swirl and coil, giving peeks at something beyond the here and now.

At least I now knew what fascinated the Nörglein père in the dealers' room. If the kids had broken away from the gaming long enough to look, they'd know too.

My pearls grew warm and my scar throbbed.

"What is it?" I asked Scrap out of the side of my mouth as he landed on my shoulder. He turned bright green with lust.

The real thing. If I didn't know better, I'd say it came from Mum's garbage dump—you know where I found your magic comb, the dragon skull gargoyle, and the Goddess brooch.

Imp Haven is cold. Nearly freeze-dry cold. Magical artifacts tend to get dumped there. No one other than imps and the occasional gamer goes there by choice. The cold preserves the magic but makes it inert. Otherwise, the power within would broadcast their location across every dimension. So they remain jumbled up with the rest of the Universe's garbage until someone like Scrap finds them and brings them out.

I understand Scrap lands in the middle of the dump frequently when his Mum swats him out of the house for being inadequate, a runt, or too smart for her to understand. He's lost more than one of his hard-earned warts to his mum's broom.

The merchant peeked out from behind her display boards filled with earrings and pendants.

"Starshine," I called to the familiar figure.

Like most dealers, she made the circuit of cons, Renaissance Faires, harvest festivals, small town celebrations, Highland Games, and pagan gatherings. We ran into each other frequently. Today she wore her usual uniform of long, gathered black skirt, pink peasant blouse, and laced gray bodice. She contained her springy black hair with a pink scarf worn Gypsy style. A few tendrils escaped showing traces of silver. She also displayed samples of her jewelry on her wrists, at her ears, around her neck, and dangling from the scarf. She sparkled in the artificial light. In full sunshine she'd near blind the unwary.

"Tess," she said brightly, immediately moving a tray of unset crystals toward me. In years past I'd made some of my own jewelry from her wares.

Much as I tried to find something interesting in the tray of aquamarine and morganite—colored forms of the goshenite—my eyes kept wandering toward the little ball anchoring a stack of silk handkerchiefs in a basket.

Starshine laid a possessive hand atop the polished crystal, covering it from view.

The power within it still vibrated on my own personal frequency. I think I could locate that ball anywhere in the Universe now.

I picked up a pair of drop earrings with rough heliodor beads. That's the greenish-yellow variety of beryl. Not my favorite color, but a useful distraction. Now if she had emeralds, the rarest and most precious of beryllium colors, I'd jump on the beads in a minute.

"Where are these from?" I asked.

"You know I can't tell you that. My rock hounds would skin me alive if I revealed their secrets." Her deep whiskey sour voice almost chanted. She bustled back behind her table.

Hmm, the ball no longer sat in the basket, and the top silk square—a red one—had gone with it. The silk dampened the crystal's aura but didn't entirely mask it.

I put down the beads. "Actually, I'm looking for something larger."

"Oh?" That almost tenor voice rose to an alto. She opened her eyes wide feigning innocence. "I have some crystals still in the rock matrix in the back. I didn't know you collected them."

"I don't. What about the crystal ball?"

"The what?"

"The crystal ball you had in the hankie basket."

"Oh, that old thing. You don't want that."

"I think I do. It speaks to me."

She froze in place; blinked several times; remembered to breathe again. "Do you hear it?"

"In my own way." Yeah, it was sort of like a distant chime calling me to Mass or reminding me of a banquet waiting.

Only the banquet wasn't of food. With that crystal ball I could eat and drink of spiritual journeys and quests. I could fill the empty places in my soul left by my mother's death and Gollum's desertion.

I needed that hunk of beryllium more than I needed food.

"It's not for sale."

"Everything is for sale." I mentally calculated the balance left on my credit card.

"Not for one thousand dollars."

I gulped and did some fast math in my head. I'd have to tap some of Mom's inheritance to cover it. "What about two?"

"Um."

Could I survive on salad and peanut butter until I conned Donovan into cutting me a check? "Two-five will cover all your table rentals and percentages for the next six months. Everything you sell will be gravy."

"Make it three."

I gulped.

Do it, babe. We'll find a way to pay for it later.

I hesitated, fingering the card in my belt pack.

With that ball, we can bypass the chat room.

"I can't. I just can't. That's too expensive." My credit card would bounce faster than Scrap caromed in and out of his mum's dump.

As I turned away from the table I hesitated. Starshine looked a bit stunned. "Here's my card in case you change your mind." I handed her the one I reserve for business contacts with landline and cell phone numbers as well as private email and Web site addresses, the same card I gave to Oak.

"You should have bought the rock," I tell my babe for the umpteenth time. She doesn't even look up from her computer screen.

So I slide inside and peer out at her, making faces until she acknowledges me.

Actually, she hit the delete key and that kicks me out of the system as fast as Mum's broom.

"Starshine wants too much for the crystal ball," she mutters and types another short paragraph.

"We'd have found a way to pay for it," I insist.

"I won't go crawling to Donovan for money."

"What about Gollum? He's got that mega trust fund for Warrior expenses while on quest."

"That crystal ball is not part of the current quest. Besides, I'd almost rather take money from Donovan than Gollum. And I won't call either one of them."

"But . . . but . . ."

"No buts about it. I can't afford a crystal ball. No matter how much you want it."

"But we *need* it!"

"How can you tell?"

"I just can. I'm an imp. With that ball we can spy on the forest elf and his band of juvenile delinquents."

"We can?"

"Yeah, and we can keep an eye on Donovan, and Gollum."

"No!" she screams at the top of her lungs. "Go do imp things and leave me alone. If I finish this book before the end of the year I just might be able to salvage my career and my credit balance."

"If you hadn't let Dad tie up so much of your money in retirement accounts . . ."

"Out!"

So out I go. Allie's no fun. She's making phone calls and pretending to read bride magazines, in between petting the matt-black revolver cradled in her lap. Now if she'd let me design her gown we could put together the wedding of the year on a budget. But no. She can't see or hear me, and Tess won't interpret for me. I settle for marking a page in a magazine on the bottom of the pile and move it to the top.

What's this? Allie's talking to the community college. They've got an opening for an instructor in the Criminal Justice Department. Woo Hoo! She and Steve are gonna move here. Tess needs that. She misses her family, though she won't admit it. She's been lonely for too long.

I can't help Allie write up her resume. But I can do something about the crystal ball. I know my babe needs that artifact of power. The Universe or the Powers That Be wouldn't have put it in her path if she didn't.

So I pop out to the chat room.

What? I can't see any demons on guard. Usually, they are visible as the only spots of color in the vast expanse of nothing.

(I'll tell you a secret. You know that white light people talk about when they have near death experiences? That's really just the chat room. Imps aren't allowed to know what happens after death. For us there is nothing. The end is the end. But some races and tribes get to start over again. To do that they have to wander through the chat room from one dimension to the next, or one life to the next. Whatever.)

Eeeeeek! It's the Politbutts. Big as trees, shaggy with a fur made of lies. See, a Politbutt can't tell the truth if you paid them to do it. And every time they tell a lie, it shows up as a long tendril of fur, some white, some black, some mixes of colors. The white guys are the worst. They make their lies sound so very believable.

This guy is white, barely discernible against the white-on-white room. It lumbers toward me. I scoot to the right, the opposite direction from where I need to go.

Politbutt anticipates me and snakes out an arm the size of a sewer pipe. It slams into me; I can't move fast enough to avoid something that big.

The breath whooshes out of me. My mouth tastes metallic—like copper. I hope it's not blood.

The blow shoots me straight across an acre or two of empty space, down a long corridor with windows into the past. I scream past glimpses of the crystal ball's origin and history.

I came here with the resonance of that ball in my mind. The windows show me what I'm looking for. But I have no control over my flight. I can't breathe. I can barely look at the scenes in the life of the Crystal.

I catch pieces of its discovery by a druid in Scotland. The ball changes hands dozens of times, from grandmother to grandson, to distant cousin. A clan of Romany takes it in trade for healing magic. The clan sells it in desperation during the Holocaust where they are hunted down with the same zeal as if they were Jewish. And then . . . and then . . . our Starshine finds it in a pile of junk at a flea market. She pays a pittance for it. I see another buyer, can't tell who it is, but she (?) finds it too late. Starshine doesn't know what it is; she just knows it is valuable. And powerful. She lusts after it with greed, not with understanding.

My Tess understands it. I can show her how to use it.

Then I smack into a solid door. My wings crumple. Pain lances like fire along the full length of every bone and cartilage. I sink down to the floor that suddenly goes squishy and starts to absorb me.

Revelation. Imps don't truly die or pass into nothingness. We, with our special powers that allow us to travel through the dimensions anywhere, anywhen, become the chat room. We don't need fixed portals, we make our own. My ancestors have become the walls of this transition place. We live forever, continuing our duty to the Universe in a new way.

Peace and warmth flood me with this knowledge. I can pass into this new existence with ease. It won't hurt.

Much.

Lingering stabs of fire remind me of who I am and what I am.

I've got to find some life deep within me to cling to.

If I die, Tess dies. It's not her time. She still has so much good she can do.

If she'd just bought the damn crystal ball I wouldn't have had to chase it through the chat room. I might live to become the Celestial Blade once more.

If I die, she dies.

The white envelops me. . . .

Chapter 15

The Beaver coin in $5 and $10 denominations was legal tender in the Oregon Country for one year before Territorial status was granted by the US in 1849. Beaver coins were melted down and reminted as the gold content was worth more than coin denominations. The few coins left command collectible prices ten to twenty times their face value.

THE COMPUTER SCREEN BLURRED. I blinked my eyes several times to regain my focus. How long had I been at work?

My vision cleared enough to check the time at the bottom of the screen. Six twenty-three. Was it morning or evening? Hints of dull, rain-washed light paled the sky. In late October, that could mean either sunrise or sunset.

Static filled my eyes. White static. I tried to shake my head to clear it of the fuzzy vision and scattered thoughts. My head was too heavy. So were my arms.

I needed to put my head down. The desktop seemed a league away and retreating.

Sleep. If only I could sleep a little.

I flopped back against the high back of my office chair, letting my head loll to the side. I closed my eyes.

Just for a couple of minutes. Allie would be calling me to dinner soon. I'd be okay with just a short nap.

"Tess, wake up. Tess?" Allie shook my shoulder vigorously.

I swam up through layers and layers of white mist, trying desperately to speak, hearing only a gargled croak.

"Tess, what's wrong?" Allie crouched before my chair. Her long fingers encircled my wrist, testing my pulse. She shook her head and moved her touch to my throat.

I think I breathed.

"You're alive. For a while there I wasn't sure." She stood up and glowered down at me from her superb height.

"Huh?"

"You scared me. What happened?"

"Wh . . ." I licked my dry lips and swallowed deeply. Then I tried again. "What happened?"

"That's what I asked you?" She ran the back of her hand across my brow the same way Mom used to check for fever.

"Time?" I blinked a couple of times, trying to focus my eyes. The room kept trying to spin away from me. After a couple of tries I found a scratch on my desk to focus on. Gradually, things stopped sliding away from me.

"It's after nine. Have you eaten anything? Have you even been to bed?"

"Nine in the morning!" More than just lamplight filtered into the room. Dull and gray outside, but still brighter than when I'd succumbed to sleep.

Or was it more than sleep?

"Scrap. Where's Scrap?" I shoved my chair back in panic. I had to find him. Something was wrong. Terribly, awfully wrong.

The room lurched right then left. I fell heavily against Allie.

"Easy, Tess. Take it easy. Let's get you to the kitchen and pour some coffee and food into you. I'm calling Gollum."

"No."

"Yes. Either him or Dr. Sean. You know he'll put you in the hospital and run a thousand expensive tests that will show nothing. You need help. So swallow your pride along with your coffee. We're calling Gollum." She slipped her arm around my waist and braced us both for the trip across the hall to the tall counter between the kitchen and living room.

I eyed the swivel barstool warily. I knew that if I tried climbing onto it, it would twist and fling me away.

Allie solved that problem with a heave and a push.

"I feel as helpless as a child."

"You are. Drink this and think about letting someone help *you* for a change. You don't have to do everything alone."

"Tell that to Scrap. He's alone somewhere and hurting. I need to find him."

"You need to regain some strength so he can. You two are bound so tight with magic and love and blood you're almost the same person."

I sat listlessly staring into the black depths of my coffee. Black and strong like a hungry black hole in space; bitter enough to etch the sugar spoon I stirred.

The whirlpools within the cup drew me deeper and deeper. If only I could see through the murkiness, I was sure I could find Scrap. I knew I had to find him before this terrible listlessness would dissolve.

I do not know this door that pushes so insistently at my back. I should know every door in the chat room, all six hundred sixty-six of them. This is one that has never revealed itself to me before. It wants me to rise up and push it open.

But I know if I do that, it will swallow me whole and I will leave my beloved Tess to drift into nothingness, neither alive, nor dead.

This is worse than the time the Guardians of the Valley of Fire trapped me within the Goblin Rock. They at least asked questions. They demanded I look deep within myself and find the source of the darkness in my soul. Only when I brought forth my guilt for allowing my bloodlust to extend beyond those who sought to kill me to the onlookers who cheered them on did I find a sliver of light within the darkness. Only when I admitted that I didn't need to kill them did I loosen the hold that guilt had upon me.

Only then could I stand within the same room as Donovan Estevez, the former gargoyle who still repelled those who would taint the sanctuary he had guarded for eight hundred years.

This solid and unmoving door reminded me of all that. Inspiration born of instinct tells me to get away from that door. Behind it lies a dimension from which I can never return.

Slowly I roll to my dimpled knees. The door tries to follow me, pressing against my bum like a lover.

Death stalks me like a lonely lover.

I crawl back the way I came. I cannot return Death's affection.

My wings sag over my shoulders. Tiny movements rock them with pins and needles of fire. I do not think them broken. Just sprained, like Tess' ankle.

The windows I passed on my way down the corridor of curiosity have closed. One shot. That's all you get on a search. One lousy look. The window decides how long you can peer through, taking note of details that might prove useful later. Then it slams closed, never to open to you again. I don't know if it will open to another searcher. I hope not. Otherwise, our enemies will know what we know.

Tess might come here and learn that the magic ring she gave back to the faeries connects her by blood to Lady Lucia, a demon masquerading as a vampire. But that's another story I'm not going to tell her.

Without landmarks I have no sense of time or distance. But with each painful slide forward the pressure from the door lessens and the floor becomes more solid. If I can just find the main room I'll be able to pop back to Tess. We can heal together.

While I languish in this half state of living so will she.

I woke up abruptly to the sounds of blue jays squabbling over a morsel of stolen food—blue jays always steal food and they always squabble—and the smell of stale coffee and burned toast. My own rather ripe and unwashed body added to the pungent mix.

"A hospital would smell better." I must have mumbled out loud. The sound of my own voice startled me. My throat felt as if I'd torn each word from a fixed position inside it.

"You're alive!" Gollum whispered. His hands encased one of my own, and his head rested on the side of my bed within the cradle of his arms. He looked up, blinking blearily at me without his glasses. For once I could truly see his emotions through the mild blue irises. He smiled a bit. "You're alive," he said somewhat louder.

I reached over and caressed his fair hair as if I had the right to touch him so intimately and lovingly.

"Did you say something?" Allie peeked in. She wore a maroon suit, complete with flared skirt, matching blazer, and a pink blouse.

"You look like me at a publisher's lunch," I said, somewhat surprised.

"Job interview. Welcome back to the land of the living. I've got to run, Gollum. You okay alone with her?"

"Of course." He removed one of his big hands from atop mine and fumbled for his glasses.

I found them next to my pillow and handed them back, though I'd miss the honesty of his expression without the disguising lenses.

"You shouldn't be here," I said, when he was safely hiding behind his glasses once more.

"Yes, I should." He raised my hand and kissed my fingertips.

"What about . . . Julia?" I couldn't bring myself to call her his wife.

"Pat is with her."

"The nurse?"

He nodded as he checked my brow for fever with the inside of his wrist.

"But Pat works nights and you've been here all night."

"Don't worry about me and mine. I need to know what happened to you. You've been in a kind of coma."

"I don't know. I think Scrap is hurt. My back aches like it's been hit with a two by four."

"How?"

"I don't know. I told him to leave me alone and let me work. So he left. Sometime later I couldn't keep my eyes open." I tried to recall those lost hours. "I think I dreamed about some Gypsies and a crystal ball."

"Why?"

"I . . ." After gulping and organizing my thoughts a bit I told him about the ball of beryllium.

He didn't question why I had refused the price.

"Try calling Scrap with your mind. He might respond to a direct order to return to your side."

"If he can."

Gollum raised his eyebrows in mute question.

"I think I also dreamed of death. Something about a big heavy door that leads to a dimension from which there is no return."

"Try calling him. You are alive and awake, therefore, he must be also."

Scrap, get your ass back here!

Yeah, yeah, I'm coming. Hold your horses. A perfect donut ring of cigar smoke preceded him. He poked his head through a crack in reality, wearing the ring like a lei.

"You can stop playing games now. I was worried about you."

You were worried? I was worried, he snarled sarcastically. *Catch me!* He popped through, landing on my belly with a whoosh.

My breath expelled explosively.

"You're heavy," I complained when I could breathe again. "You're heavy? You don't weigh anything in this dimension. How could you knock the breath out of me?" I reached to hug him.

Relief at his reappearance outweighed my discomfort.

He mumbled and grumbled and waddled around until his back was to me.

"Nice wart on your spine," I complimented him.

He humphed and grumphed.

"Oh, your wings are . . . a bit droopy." The cartilage on the upsweep had lost stiffness and the barbed joints looked a bit dull and twisted.

Droopy! Droopy? Is that all?

"Tell me about it," I soothed him. I ran a gentle hand along the outside of the wings, amazed that I could feel the suedelike texture.

"Good to see you in the flesh, buddy," Gollum said, peering at my usually invisible imp. "You've grown a bit since I last saw you. Got a few new warts too. What can I do to make you feel better?"

Mold. And lots of it. Scrap thought a minute. *And some beer and OJ. And could I please have my favorite pink boa?*

"You got it. Coffee for you, Tess?"

I nodded. "Hey, how come you can see *and* hear him?"

"Ask him while I get some fortification for both of you." He exited with his usual long stride.

"Talk, Scrap."

Don't wanna.

"Nothing to eat until you tell me why we both almost died."

I guess. He sounded like a recalcitrant teenager caught playing hooky or with a stash of marijuana.

"Talk. I won't judge you."

More mumbles and grumbles. And then the story of his time in the chat room with the Politbutts came out in one long burst with hardly a breath.

Gollum came back in with a tray of treats and drinks about the time Scrap speculated how the bodies and souls of dead imps made up the chat room. Professor Van der Hoyden-Smythe nodded sagely and reached for his everything in one cell phone to take notes. His glasses started slipping down his long nose.

The geek I fell in love with was back in true form.

"You going to get an academic paper out of this?" I asked.

Scrap finished his tale with his long slow crawl back home. Before the last word dribbled from his mouth, he scooped up a glob of mold—from the balcony baseboards judging by the color and texture—plucked out a tiny spider and swallowed it in one gulp. Then he chased his tidbit with a long slurp of beer mixed half and half with orange juice.

His skin turned bright orange and began to fade.

"Is he still here?" Gollum asked, staring right at Scrap. Or maybe staring through him.

"Of course. He must be feeling better to go transparent. I wonder why he was so visible when he was hurt."

"Probably an instinct thing. So you could care for him."

Hey, I'm still here. I can hear every word you say.

"We know that, Scrap. Why don't you take a nap. Your eyes look very heavy."

Stay with me. He waddled up to the spare pillow and curled up in a ball with his wings spread out over him. In seconds he began snoring.

"He's sleeping," I whispered. "I didn't know he did sleep."

"All creatures need sleep to heal." Gollum knelt beside the bed and captured my hand again. "I am very relieved that you are both safe now."

"Thank you for keeping vigil. I can't think of anyone I'd

rather have beside me if I died." My throat started to close. I had to look away, knowing what I had to do, no matter how much it hurt.

"I had to be here."

"And now that we are healing, you need to go."

"Tess, you can't keep on doing this by yourself. You've gotten hurt too many times this last year. You need backup. You need help."

"I do what I have to do, the way I have to do it." A stubborn wall of hurt pride rose up around me.

"Tess, I . . ."

"Go. Please, go now, while I can still release you to your obligations."

"We may not be able to be together as a couple, Tess. Not the way we want to. But I am your archivist. You are as much my responsibility as Julia. You need help. I am always available."

"But not to love. Just go. Before I make a fool of myself and both of us sorry you came at all." I turned my head to the wall so I wouldn't have to watch him leave. Again.

Chapter 16

Oregon's 1848 Territorial motto was Alis Volat Propriis—*"She flies with her own wings." It remained when statehood came in 1857. In 1957 patriotic citizens changed it to "The Union" to commemorate the upcoming centennial of the Civil War. In 1987 the legislature reverted to the original.*

THREE MORE DAYS I LINGERED, half awake, aching all over, gorging on any food Allie fixed or left in the fridge while she went about her business.

I noticed new smells with every turn of my head. Was my own sense increasingly sensitive? More likely, my bond with Scrap deepened as he glued himself to my shoulder. His thoughts became my thoughts. His hunger my hunger. His keen nose spilled over into my own.

During the day I wrote, reverting to older habits. When the going gets tough the tough keep writing. I'd been someone else in my depression, letting my frantic lack of accomplishment rule and push me into a self-defeating loop.

I stared out the windows toward the river a lot, absorbing the life and routine of passing barges, and the venturesome few who took out sailboats or tried water skiing this late in the year. The honking of migrating geese invaded my soul with a restlessness my body couldn't keep up with.

The damp grass and falling leaves smelled of sleep and quiet.

My thoughts wandered back over the events of my life.

What could I have changed? Did I make the right decisions? Where did I go from here?

Gollum's absence gnawed at me like a sore tooth.

A car backfired on Macadam Avenue. I jumped and crouched with my hands over my head.

Once more I was back in the chat room, reliving the reverberating door knocker on the portal that led to the Powers That Be.

"You ask a lot," a reedy voice intoned as I stood before the high judicial bench. I thought the voice came from the huge creature hovering behind the panel. It alone did not sit in a thronelike chair. Maybe it was just too big for the available furniture. An occasional questing tentacle reminded me of the Cthulu demon on guard outside.

Scrap kept a very low profile close to the door. He looked like he wanted to flee, but as long as I remained, he had to remain as well.

His nose twitched constantly, seeking a whiff of danger.

"I ask for no more than what you want," I told the court, forcing my fears down into a tight knot behind my heart. The same place where I bottled up my grief over my mother's murder. "My home on Cape Cod is on neutral ground. Sacred in its neutrality. It has always been neutral since before the coming of humans to that land. You want it to remain neutral."

"You are decidedly not neutral, Warrior of the Celestial Blade," the booming bass voice flowed out of the deep hood on my left.

"I propose a compromise."

Seven cowled heads turned toward each other, bent in some silent communication.

"Explain," said a new voice, definitely female, with musical undertones and an accent that might have originated in Faery. This being sat dead center, more senior than the others. Her vote weighed more than all the others as well.

I addressed her directly.

"My father and his partner wish to buy the house from me and turn it into a Bed and Breakfast, a kind of an inn. They are neutral. Neither Warrior nor demon. They are normal, without power or interest in rogue portals. "

The faery nodded in agreement. The others remained silent in their grim mysterious secrecy.

"But the energies around the house make it vulnerable to the opening of a rogue portal. It's a kind of vortex that attracts ghosts, faeries, and demons. I have no fear of the ghosts or faeries. I do fear the demons."

"Rightly so," boomed the one on the end.

"I want protection for my father and his partner. I want your guarantee that no one will use the land to open a new portal. That no other beings will try to take over the land. It must remain neutral."

"And what will you give in return? If we agree to this."

At that moment I knew why Scrap's nose twitched so incessantly. Danger didn't lurk here. Nothing lurked here. It was absolutely sterile. No dust, no mold, no growing things. Not even cleaning fluid invaded this chamber. No smell at all.

To my world filled with tiny odors and bad smells underlying the sweet scents of trees and grass and flowers and animal musk, this place smelled more dangerous than a charging black bear.

Or a lurking Nörglein.

Abruptly, I fell back into the present. I made the right choice going to the Powers That Be. I'd never had any doubts about that. Especially since I'd sent Gollum away and refused Donovan's proposal.

Things change, Tess. A year from now that might not be the right choice. Think about the victims of the Nörglein. Think of the upheaval in their lives. Think of the choices they don't have, Scrap reminded me.

"I think about that every day. No woman should have to give her child to a monster. Not me, and not the victims of that horrible dark elf."

I turned away from the churning, rain-swollen river that rushed toward the sea in its endless change that remained much the same.

"I've made the right choices. Now it's time to get on with my life. I need to call Raquel Jones and the other victims I know about. I wish I knew how to contact Squishy. She should know about other victims. They need to talk to each other, make plans and preparations. But first I need to get rid of this cast."

I'll find an email address for Squishy. You make an appointment with Dr. Sean. Scrap dove into the computer as if it were the familiar chat room.

"Does this hurt?" Dr. Sean asked as he gently rotated my left ankle.

After being in a cast so long my leg looked shrunken, wrinkled, and hairy.

"It's stiff but not painful," I replied. Yeah, there were a couple of twinges at the extreme end of each manipulation. Not enough to complain about and risk having the cast put back on.

As if he read my lie, the good doctor smiled and began massaging the weak muscles. He winked at me as if he shared the secret. "If you don't injure it again, you should be fine now. Ribs okay?"

"Never were much of a problem. Bruises heal faster than sprains and breaks," I replied. But the huge bruise on my spine that I shared with Scrap was taking longer to fade.

I needed to give the right answers to Dr. Sean so I could put on socks and shoes and *walk* out of the clinic. If the physician would just let go and stop that heavenly massage of my foot.

I could get used to this.

"You'll need physical therapy," the physician said. He paused his massage long enough to make a note on his order forms. "If you promise to follow up with that and do your exercises, I think we're done here." He placed my foot back on the exam table almost reluctantly. "I'll just sign off on your treatment and you cease to be my patient. Until the next time you do something self-destructive." He half grimaced as he applied pen to paper.

"Do you think I'm self-destructive?" I asked, suddenly alarmed.

"I think you've been depressed and not as careful as you should be. But I see improvement in the sparkle in your eye. It started the moment your brother and his fiancée walked into the ER."

Gollum's words came back to me. I couldn't do it all alone. I didn't have to. Was that part of the problem, just plain loneliness?

Dr. Sean cocked his head and looked at me with an appraising eye. "You do look a little pale though. Is your family feeding you right?" He ran a gentle finger down my cheek.

Anyone else and I'd have said he just wanted to feel the texture of my skin. My rational explanation was that he tested for fever and clamminess.

"I had a touch of . . . of a tummy bug earlier this week. It's gone now. I'm eating better." Easier to explain my near coma and Scrap's languish in the chat room as an illness rather than spill the very complicated truth.

"In fact, I'm eating better than I have for a year and a half." I smiled brilliantly knowing that I still was not eating as well, or as much as I should. As Scrap healed, his appetite ruled mine less and less.

"Good. Wouldn't hurt you to continue taking it easy for a few more weeks, rebuild the strength in that leg gradually. Use a cane if it helps. And do your exercises. Start with this one until you see the PT. Do it with both pointed toes and flexed foot." He rotated the ankle in a full circle left and right. Then he handed me some paperwork. "You are officially dismissed and no longer my patient."

That was the second time he'd used that phrase.

"Right." I took the papers and read them carefully. Lots of strange codes indicating what he'd done today—mostly removed the cast, took new X-rays, and examined them. There was an order for his receptionist to make an appointment for me with physical therapy. No mention of massaging my ankle.

"Right. Then how about we do something about your eating and go to dinner tomorrow night?" He quirked a full smile.

My heart panicked. He wasn't Gollum.

But I'd probably never see Gollum again. I needed to get out and . . . and . . .

Too soon.

"Okay." I overrode my own arguments.

"Pick you up at six?" He handed me the spare shoe and sock I'd brought with me.

"Fine." I pulled on the foot gear and lowered my pant leg to hide the ugly, shrunken, *hairy* leg. "My address and phone number are in your file."

"I memorized them a year ago."

What could I say to that? Instead of putting my foot in my mouth I let him help me down from the table and escort me all the way to the outside door of the clinic with his hand warming my elbow. "My receptionist will call you with the PT appointment. Don't let that slide, Tess. You'll be less likely to re-injure yourself if you work at strengthening and limbering those joints and muscles."

And the glass door swung shut between us.

Now what have you gotten yourself into? Scrap demanded

"I accepted a date with a handsome, intelligent man," I replied blithely.

He's mundane. He's got no part in your world of fighting demons.

I spotted Allie in the parked car. She'd been on her cell phone the whole time I'd been inside, talking to Steve and other people she wouldn't tell me about.

"True, Scrap. Maybe I need a strong dose of reality now and then. Especially after I host a meeting with Raquel and three others in my living room tonight. We need to stop at a bakery for dessert for them."

He's not Gollum, Scrap pouted, waving his cigar stub at me.

"No, he's not. And I think that's the point." I slid into the car next to Allie, not nearly as happy as I should be.

"So what's new with you and Steve?" I asked my friend, putting as much brightness into my voice as I could. Maybe if I pretended my heart wasn't breaking I'd eventually convince myself it wasn't and I could move on.

"Steve got a job offer in Hillsboro. I got a job offer at the community college not far from there. We're getting married at Christmas! We both start work right after the holidays." She whooped and threw her arms around me.

"I'm very happy for you. Do I get to be a bridesmaid?"

"Of course. I just wish you could find the right guy." She paused. "One who's unattached."

"We'll see. I have a date with a cute doctor tomorrow night."

"Way to go, Sister." She high-fived me.

"In two months you really will be my sister as well as my best friend," I said somewhat awed.

"So, let's go shopping for your matron of honor dress. Something lovely that you can wear again and again."

"Then we'd better let Scrap pick it out." Maybe that would brighten his mood. "Why aren't you torturing me with the ugliest gown ever designed that costs way too much? That's part of the ritual, sort of a test of how much I love you."

"I'm buying you something lovely because I want you to love me after the wedding."

Tomorrow I'd test that love to the limits by going off on my own, exercising my newfound freedom from the cast and do some investigative shopping.

Chapter 17

The International Rose Test Gardens in Portland were created in 1917 to preserve European hybrid roses that might be wiped out due to World War I devastation.

"NICE TO SEE YOU OUT OF THE CAST," Raquel Jones said upon entering my condo. She held a plate of cookies in one hand and half hugged me with the other.

"I'll be fit again very soon," I told her. "I have physical therapy tomorrow morning. You're the first here. Did you have any trouble convincing JJ to stay home?"

"He's downstairs walking the river path. Patrolling is more like it."

"This will be easier if we keep it girl talk. Less embarrassing that way. My friend Allie is hiding in my office. She's an ex-cop if we need her to talk about self-defense."

The clang of footsteps on the metal stairs alerted me to the arrival of more guests. Four more, all I could find in a hurry for this impromptu meeting of a potential support group. Two of the other women, like Raquel, were pregnant. The other two carried tiny infants, no more than two months old. Squishy had sent them.

Scrap flitted about cooing and making funny faces at the babies. Both of them reached tiny hands up to touch him. No one else could see him. Interesting. Did the dark elf blood in the children allow them to see the imp, or just their innocence?

Raquel took charge when we were all seated in the living room with coffee (decaf in consideration of the pregnancies and nursing babies) and small pieces of rich chocolate cake, homemade chocolate chip cookies, and trail mix with chocolate nuggets. Hard topics always go down easier with chocolate.

"I don't want my baby stolen," Michelle whispered a little later, clutching her tiny boy against her shoulder where he drowsed, wrapped in the cocoon of a brightly colored blanket. She barely looked old enough or large enough to have given birth. Her perky short hair and rounded cheeks gave her a cherubic look. She was the mother who'd delivered in the ER with Squishy assisting.

"None of us wants the Nörglein to steal any more babies," I affirmed. I passed around photocopies of the dark elf from the field guide.

Michelle and Annie, the two mothers, took one look at the woodcut picture and shuddered. Both dropped their papers, as if touching them was like touching the monster himself.

"I can't believe I actually let him make love to me," Annie said, burying her face in her daughter's blanket.

"I knew he wasn't my husband the moment he walked in the door," Caroline said. At six months along, she and Raquel must have been victimized about the same time.

"How?" I asked.

"It was like my husband rode on top of a new core body. I can't explain it any other way. He looked, talked and, moved just like Jeff. But, I don't know, something was off. Then he sort of solidified and I forgot what I saw." She shook her head.

Ask her what the guy smelled like, Scrap said, hovering in front of the athletic woman in her mid-thirties with stunning blonde hair and bright blue eyes.

I did.

"Smell . . . I never thought about that. But come to think on it, he smelled of pine. Jeff doesn't use that aftershave anymore. Not since I turned up allergic to evergreens. We can't have a real Christmas tree anymore because of it." She paused to gulp back tears. "My baby will never have a Christmas tree."

"But the Nörglein made you forget your allergies, made

you forget that something was wrong," I said. "He made you all forget that abortion is still a legal option for you."

"You make it sound like magic," Donna said. Clearly she didn't believe in magic. Dark hair, trendy dark-framed glasses, her designer maternity jeans and turtleneck proclaimed her professional social situation. Raquel said she was an accountant.

I needed her to believe in magic before the evening was over.

"It was magic," Raquel butted in. "I know our science oriented society, our churches, our *logic* tell us that magic and dark elves don't exist. We all have proof it does." She cupped her swollen belly for emphasis.

"I can't believe our doctors didn't put two and two together," Donna continued.

"Did any of you have the same doctor?" I asked.

They compared notes and shook their heads. Only two of them had even been in the same hospital. Squishy encountered one in the ER and the other in the psych ward. No connections except a bit of skin that sloughed off barklike scales. Allie was even now trying to track down the other postpartum hysteria patients.

"What can we do?" Michelle asked. "How do we fight magic?"

"You don't. I do," I replied.

Four sets of puzzled eyes riveted on me.

"Believe her," Raquel said. "She knows what to do."

I wish I did. "Michelle and Annie, are you in a position to uproot and move out of town? As far away as you can get."

"I can," Annie said. "I telecommute. I can work anywhere."

"What about your husband?" Caroline asked.

"I'm not married. I'll take a loss on my house if I sell now, but I can move. You think that will keep my baby safe?"

"I'm not certain. But I think so. The Nörglein seems desperate. That means he'll make a mistake. If he has to chase you halfway across the country, he's vulnerable. But he only takes the children after their second birthday. You've got a little time."

"My husband just lost his job. I suppose we could make an excuse to go live with my mom in LA," Michelle said.

"I'm not going anywhere. I intend to fight this guy," Raquel said. She sat straight, chin jutting in determination. "I've already started self-defense classes. As soon as I deliver I'm taking up martial arts. JJ is too. We're going after him every chance we get."

"Let's back up a moment." I needed to get away from the idea of these women aggressively hunting the monster. Danger lay on that course, for them, not the Nörglein. "Annie, you said you weren't married. How did the Nörglein trap you if he didn't impersonate a husband?"

"I was hiking, alone. I had a backpack with essentials, so I didn't panic when the paths just disappeared. I dug out my compass and headed downhill. But it rapidly became uphill and the damn compass started swinging round and round, never settling on a direction."

"Then you blacked out and didn't remember anything until you walked out at the trailhead the next morning," I prompted her.

"I thought I just slept in the lee of a hollow log. When I woke up, the path was back in place, straight and clear."

"What did you think when you turned up pregnant?" From the quivering chins and rapidly blinking eyes I knew I ventured into territory these women didn't want to remember. "I need to know, Annie. The Nörglein varied from his usual MO by taking an unmarried woman. He's from a different era and culture. He feels that what he does is okay because he has the enchanted coöperation of a husband."

"I . . . have a couple of boyfriends. I figured that when I got a little tipsy one night not long after my night in the woods I'd been indiscreet enough to overlook an essential condom." Annie flushed with embarrassment. "When I went looking for the one I thought I remembered, I discovered he'd left town two months before the . . . um . . . incident."

"Something is wrong for the dark elf to go out of pattern twice. Once with you and once with Raquel," I mused. "I need to do more research."

"And we need to arrange our next support group meeting. With the men in our lives. And we need to find the other victims. I'm certain we aren't the only ones." Raquel said.

They set about arranging it.

I decamped to the balcony to think. No moon peeking

through the clouds tonight to suggest a silver river that marked an ending and a beginning.

Why had the dark elf varied his pattern? A pattern that had worked well for centuries.

What had changed beyond women thinking for themselves and refusing to be treated as tradable property?

Chapter 18

In 1841 Ewing Young died without heirs or a will. The dilemma of how to handle his estate led to formation of the Provisional Government in 1843. An acorn planted over his grave is now a Heritage Oak Tree.

FIRST THING THE NEXT MORNING after my PT session, Allie went off to meet a realtor and look at houses closer to her new job.

"Alone at last," I sighed, sitting back on the reclining sofa with a cup of coffee and soft new age music on the satellite. I looped a huge rubber band around my foot and pushed against it until my leg straightened. I had to pause at ten and take a sip of coffee, then again at fifteen. Building up to fifty stretches was going to take some time.

"Good thing I am alone. I'd hate to have Allie see me sweating and panting after so little exertion."

You're never alone, dahling, Scrap reminded me. He perched on top of the flat screen, dangling his pink boa in front of it.

"You're leaking feathers, Scrap. Shall we go shopping for some new accessories?" I knew I needed to bribe him.

Only if you look for a necklace to go with the matron of honor dress. His skin brightened to pale green. He lusted after something at the mall.

I considered the route to my destination and picked a convenient shopping center for the ride home.

He fluttered up and down, exercising his still recovering wings. His skin took on an emerald green hue.

All the better. Whatever he wanted was really important to him. Almost as important as my true errand.

Engaging the clutch in my car was a little awkward at first. I jerked and stalled my way out of the condo parking lot until I found the right pressure with my weakened left foot. By the time I hit the freeway entrance half a mile up the road my muscle memory took over and I shifted smoothly.

But I did keep my speed down to the limit.

Hey! Why'd you turn off onto I84? Scrap bounced to the rear window, staring at I5 retreating in the distance. *You can't get to the mall from here.*

"On the way back," I reassured him.

Back from where?

"You'll see."

No, Tessie. Absolutely not. We can't go there alone. Scrap planted himself on the steering wheel, between me and the window. I could see the road perfectly well through him.

"You reminded me, not too long ago, that I'm never alone. I have you. You are my backup, the eyes in the back of my head, and my weapon of choice."

He sulked into an even more invisible white. He looked like the chat room walls.

"Are you okay? That color scares me!"

And well it should. This is more dangerous than you know. You aren't healed yet. Your leg is weak and your balance off.

"So? What else is new? This can't be any worse than entering Lady Lucia's lair when I had a groin pull. She was serving smoothie Marys that night. I hope Mary recovered after donating the blood for the drinks."

Half an hour later, I pulled into the graveled parking lot of Cooper's Furniture. The open sign was in the window, the blinds were up, and the house behind the store looked well maintained and occupied.

"They aren't expecting us," I whispered.

You wounded the Nörglein. Let's hope he's not back to work yet.

"You think he works here?"

Makes sense.

Scrap clung to my shoulder as we moved from the car to the shop. A cowbell the size of a ten gallon barrel bonged loudly when I opened the door. The clapper sounded again when I closed it behind me. No echoes or reverberations. The heavily padded sofas and recliners artfully arranged in conversation groups absorbed the sound.

I felt like I'd walked into an elite salon. Graceful lamps and silk flowers accented the expensive furniture. Highly polished woods reflected the light, making the interior of the building look much brighter than the gloomy exterior suggested.

The light made the sales floor appear three or four times as large as it should be.

Maybe it was.

A tall, dark-haired woman looking near my own age glided out of an office area, separated from the floor by walls of glass. She hesitated only half a heartbeat when she saw me, then continued forward. Doreen Cooper, my former sister-in-law. I guessed that naming girls in the Damiri tribe held true as for boys. Doreen, Dillwyn, Darren, Donovan, all started with D and ended with N.

Made for a lot of confusion when they all jokingly referred to each other as D.

The Coopers also held true within their family by giving all the children B middle initials. Which one of them was the infamous D.B. Cooper, the first to hijack a plane demanding ransom money? Back in the early '70s he became a kind of folk hero in the Pacific Northwest. Not really a Robin Hood, but he put the screws to a major corporation, exploiter of the masses, and got away with it. At least that was the feeling when it happened.

Distinctive white streaks at Doreen's temples, running the full length of her magnificent mane of hair down to her waist, stood out like beacons in the darkness.

She looked thinner, more drawn in the face than she had a few weeks ago.

Her tasteful red suit hung loosely. She'd lost weight recently. Not as much as she'd probably like, but her figure had more definition today, less flab.

Stress had aged her a bit. She looked forty instead of thirty. She'd undoubtedly lived several decades (or centuries) longer than I had.

Scrap had seen her at High Desert Con, arguing with Donovan. I hadn't noticed her, so I couldn't tell if the changes in her had taken place before or after that.

I still wondered if she'd actually argued with Donovan, or if the Nörglein had worn that form as a disguise.

"Doreen, just the person I need to see about some new furniture." I strode forward, hand outstretched in greeting, with more confidence than I truly felt.

"Oh?" she said with a superior sniff. "I see you're finally out of that hideous cast. Still weak though, Teresa?" She didn't offer to shake my hand. Her gaze lingered a little too long on my slight limp.

"Tess. Only my mother called me Teresa, and then only when she was really angry."

"Yes." A long, pregnant pause. "So, what does a Warrior of the Celestial Blade want with a known demon establishment? Come to murder us in broad daylight, like you did Dill?"

"Huh?" I'd held her brother in my arms as he gasped his last breath with fire riddled lungs. The fire started in the middle of the night while we slept. "Dill was murdered by one of your own. Darren Estevez had a heavy hand in that. You acknowledged that when we met a couple of weeks ago."

A pattern of selective memory loss, similar to what the Nörglein's victims suffered.

Her sharp inhale caught in her throat as color infused her face. She coughed, turning discreetly to the side. "So you killed Darren in revenge."

She clung to the implanted memories. I had to break through that barrier. For her sake as well as my own.

"No, I did not murder Darren Estevez. Donovan's girlfriend did that."

"Aren't you . . . ?"

"Nope. He sleeps with a lot of women. Including Lady Lucia, the vampire crime boss of Las Vegas. You too?"

She had the grace to blush. "I hadn't seen him in quite a while. Then he turned up again a few weeks ago. We fell into dating."

"WindScribe did the dirty deed against Darren. Then Donovan knocked her up. She's incarcerated in a heavy security insane asylum. My aunt is raising their daughter."

"Oh." Her mouth formed the word, but no sound emerged. Then she coughed again. "We were told differently." Understanding began to brighten her eyes.

I bet you were, sweetie. These guys embroider the truth with lots of twists and curlicues, Scrap added.

I noted he hadn't bothered to light his cigar.

"I've decided to refurnish my condo and thought of looking here first. Keep it in the family, so to speak." I broke eye contact with her and scanned the delicate Louis XVI style dining set.

Doreen's gaze shifted to my left shoulder where Scrap sat. He wrapped his tail around my throat tightly, only partly for balance. I sensed new heat coming from him as his skin pinked.

Oh, yeah, this woman was a demon, but so far not a threat to us.

"What exactly are you looking for?" she asked.

Double angled question

"This looks nice," I said, wandering over to an early American styled dining set in honey maple. Round table polished to a mellow gloss, four captain's chairs in the same wood. The price made me blanch.

Then I had a quick flashback to the kitchen nook furniture Dill and I had picked out for the house on Cape Cod. The extra leaves in the table allowed us to seat eight. We'd planned on having breakfast there with a whole passel of children. Mom and I had made seat pads, café curtains, and matching place mats in a delicate blue and brown calico.

Gone now. All gone. First Dill died in a fire. Then I'd burned the table and chairs and calico after being contaminated with Orculli troll blood. Then Mom had been murdered.

A wave of grief and loneliness nearly drowned me.

I must have staggered as I clutched a chair back. Doreen grabbed my elbow to steady me. "Dill selected that line of furniture for the store. It's one of our most popular," she said flatly. She fought as much emotion as I did. Dill was her brother. The humanity in their bloodline dominated when it came to family.

"Maybe something more Craftsman for my new place. I don't need reminders of what I lost every time I sit down to eat." Looking everywhere but at the table, I saw a basket of glass balls on a lamp table beside a more suitable sofa, loveseat, and wing backed chairs that would complement my parquet floors and simple wood railing.

Not just any glass balls. At least one of them had the milky swirls of true beryllium.

Power radiated from it. I'd tasted that power before.

Without thinking my feet marched over to the basket. I reached for the crystal ball, anxious to truly hold it, caress it, bond with it, make it my tool and my companion.

Scrap added a layer of green lust to his pastel pink. Not a good combination.

Doreen moved to intercept me. "Those are not for sale," she whispered. She kept a wary eye on my imp.

Who was she hiding that information from?

"Not for sale? Or not for sale to me?" My feet adjusted to *en garde* without thinking. I had to shift my weight forward into a half lunge, taking pressure off the newly freed and still weak left ankle. I caught a glimpse of my profile in a mirror on the far wall. The pose made me look more aggressive than I felt.

Doreen backed off, the crystal ball in her hand. The other bits of blown glass in the basket remained inert.

"You really, really don't want to push this, Tess," she hissed, still keeping her words quiet and private.

Ask her if she knows the history of the ball, Scrap ordered. He'd lost his cigar and poised on his hind legs, ready to jump to my hand and transform if I commanded.

Something crashed in the back room followed by a series of smaller thuds. It sounded like a bookcase turned over, spewing books to the far corners.

Then the angry stomp of heavy feet. Multiple heavy feet, like four or five sets of them.

"Doreen!" a shrill female voice screamed. "Get back here now."

Doreen paused, staring at the prized crystal. Her gaze rose to meet mine.

"A woman came in yesterday. She said she'd been threatened and needed to turn this over to them. They trashed her storeroom looking for it, broke a lot of stuff. She had a black eye, favored her ribs, and limped when she came in," Doreen explained, just as quietly as before.

"Starshine?"

"Maybe. I bought it from her for a fraction of its worth. One thousand. Mom doesn't know I spent that much. It was my own money."

"Doreen, where the hell are you? I need your help," the other woman screamed. "Get out, weed-ridden, tattooed vermin. Get out of my shop and my home."

Uh oh. I only knew of one tribe that fit that description and had the audacity to invade another demon's territory.

"Scrap!" I held out my right hand, ready to charge in and fight the Nörglettes.

"Take it!" Doreen thrust the treasure into my hand. "I freely gift it to you. Take it and get out. Never come back. Especially with the imp. This is not your fight. It's mine! I don't want or need your help." She dashed for the back room.

I gimped toward the opposite exit as fast as I could and still retain my balance.

That went well, Scrap mused, peering closely at the ball.

"Time to hit the mall and get you a new boa," I groused as I put the car in reverse and fled. The ball nestled safely in my jacket pocket, absorbing the warmth of my body and reflecting it back.

crystal ball almost burned, begging me to take it in my hands, gaze in wonder at the miracles it could reveal. "You ready for this, Scrap?"

As ready as I'll ever be. He crawled to my shoulder and wrapped his tail around my neck in a choke hold worthy of a professional cage fighter on steroids.

I cupped my hands around the ball. But I watched a drop of rain caught on a sword fern reflect a rainbow in a tentative beam of light. I hoped its invitation proved stronger than the clouds threatening to fill in the pockets of blue sky.

Look at it, Tess. We'll never know for sure what it is, what it can do, if we don't look. Scrap leaned forward, nearly falling off his perch, eyes glued to the crystal sphere. He was totally entranced.

"Okay." I drew in a deep breath and shifted my gaze to the milky swirls. I traced them, learned them, followed them in, deep, deep, deeper.

I caught a tendril of floating minerals and rode the trail with the power of a celestial wind in our light sail.

Light squeezes against me. I twist and slide, dragging Tess in my wake.

The strange mineral deposits inside the ball twine around us and drag us around and around. My head spins faster than my senses can keep up.

I need to close my eyes. The real estate inside the ball passes by so fast I'm getting dizzy.

But If I don't watch and memorize it, I may not be able to get us home.

"Where are we?" I ask Tess as we slide around and around.

"I'm not sure. In a way it smells a bit like the mutant faeries. A bit of rot overlaying something that used to be sweet and pure.

"Yeah, it does smell like that."

Strange that her nose is more sensitive than mine in here.

We come to a stop with a thump that jars my neck and gives me a headache. At least we have solid ground beneath our feet.

We turn around and around taking in the landscape. I recognize the winding creek as it chuckles over a three-foot waterfall. The spreading, patriarchal oak with mistletoe in the upper branches looks familiar too. But it's bassackwards.

"Am I still dizzy or is everything fuzzy around the edges, like it's not fully formed yet?" Tess asks.

"Fuzzy. That's what's wrong!"

"You sound happy, is that a good thing?"

"I have a theory. Close your eyes and think about what that tree should be like."

She does. "You mean like the oak in the front yard at home—in Cape Cod home, not Portland."

"The one with the swing," I remind her.

Sure enough, as her mind re-creates the beloved image of happy summer days lazing on the simple board swing dangling from a stout branch ten feet up, the tree firms up. The vague smudges of green resolve into sprays of broad leaves. Clumps of acorns tip the ends. The bark ripples and mottles into the appropriate shades of brown.

When the swing drops down from the upper branches, complete with the thick splice in the rope about five feet above the board, I nearly fall off Tess' shoulder.

While I flail for balance I notice the creek. The water takes on definition. It loses the artificial feel and smell of a computer generated painting where only a few things move.

A breeze springs up, completing the picture.

But it's still upside down or twisted right to left.

Left to right.

I hang upside down on Tess' shoulder and view it all from a different perspective.

"Um, babe?"

"Yes?" Tess is gazing around in wonder. As her eyes light upon a too-bright blue jay in the tree, it begins to move as if released from a spell that froze it in place. It scolds us angrily, then flies off.

Sounds begin to form, insects, birdsong in the distance, wind in the tree canopy.

"Tess, dahling, I think we need to go home. Like now. Right now, before we do any more damage."

"Damage? It's like we are creating the place just by being here."

"That's what I mean. We shouldn't be here. This dimension isn't ready for us yet."

"You mean it's a brand-new dimension?"

"Still forming."

"How?"

"Don't know yet. But I got a theory."

"Care to share it?"

"Not yet. I need to do a little research."

"You aren't going back to the chat room by yourself! Remember what happened last time."

"All too well, babe. There are other methods of research closer to home." Like Gollum. I owe him an email. Good thing I figured out how to invade the innards of a computer.

"As long as you don't endanger yourself and therefore us." She sighs in resignation.

"Hang on tight, babe. We're going to ride the crystal ball home, the same way we came in."

I close my eyes, grab hold of an imaginary trail of swirling minerals, and slide down a sunbeam right into the driver's seat of Tess' car.

"Whew, what a ride." I wipe imaginary sweat off my brow.

"Yeah. Quite a ride. I'm exhausted. Let's go home." She turns the key in the ignition and engages the clutch.

"Remember, you promised a stop at the mall," I whine.

"One stop. And only one stop. You may buy one feather boa and nothing else."

"You're no fun."

"I work at it."

Chapter 20

Mills End Park in Portland is two feet square and was created for leprechauns to hold snail races on St. Patrick's Day. Keep Portland Weird!

"FORGIVE ME, TESS, but I have to cut our date short tonight," Dr. Sean Connolly says as he escorts my babe to his car in the guest slot of our building's lot.

He wears a nice gray suit with a subdued silvery tie and a shirt a shade lighter than the suit. This man knows how to dress to impress. I couldn't have selected better myself. With his dark hair, fair skin, and ice blue eyes, he looks good enough to eat.

Too bad he's straight, and mundane. I can't approve of him for my dahling Tess no matter how delicious.

He's not Gollum.

I'm glad I dug out Tess' little black dress that goes with everything; add Mom's pearls and it fits any occasion. Only it isn't black—Tess hates black and it drains the color from her face—it's midnight blue. I picked it out of course. I wish she'd worn the glittery sandals with two-inch heels. They fit the dress perfectly. But no, she says. She can't afford to limp in front of the good doctor. She wears the comfortable navy flats.

"Oh?" Tess replies to Dr. Sean.

I hope she at least gets dinner after all my hard work dressing her properly. If you only knew how much trouble I have talking her out of red undies. She always wears red "cause the Sisterhood of the Celestial Blade wear only red to remind them of the blood their Sisters shed in the good fight against demons."

But red under the midnight blue? Honestly, she'd look like an American Flag. We celebrated the Fourth of July over four months ago. This is October, approaching Halloween. If she's going seasonal we'll go for gold and green.

"I'm on call at the ER from ten o'clock on." Dr. Sean looks a bit sheepish, but proud too. "It's the weekend and coming up on a full moon near Halloween. I'm expecting a full night."

Tess shivers a bit in the chill wind off the river laden with drizzle. Typical of the season. Great weather for growing mold.

"That's okay." Tess flashes a brief smile. "My leg is tired and I'll want to get it elevated in a comfy chair sooner rather than later."

"Not doing too much are you?" He looks concerned as he hands her into his dark blue BMW. A really nice car but not as flashy as Donovan's Mercedes.

I prefer Gollum's rattletrap van. Mold hides in the rusting nooks and crannies.

"I drove my stick shift out to Gresham to visit my former sister-in-law." The truth, just not the whole truth. "Working the clutch was a bit much for me."

"Former sister-in-law?" Now he looks afraid.

"My husband, her brother, died about four years ago." Four years, eight months, and three days ago. I remember 'cause that's when my Tess caught the imp flu.

Only when she'd stumbled into the Citadel with raging fever and delirium and had the interdimensional infection lanced—leaving that beautiful scar on her face only imps and our companions can see—could she and I bond to become Warriors of the Celestial Blade.

"Sorry to hear that."

"I'm getting over it. Grief never totally goes away, but we do learn to cope."

We'd learned that the hard way.

"Nice to see you are moving on, dating again." His grin brightened his entire posture. He must have used a professional whitener on those dazzling teeth. And yet his left eye tooth is slightly twisted. It gives him a wonderful puckish demeanor.

"Yeah, it's good to be out and about again. I've had cabin fever really bad with that cast."

"Let's see what we can do about that." He drove downtown

to a cozy brew pub on the riverfront with a Celtic theme. Kelly's, our favorite. Bright music spills out every time the door opens.

"I come here often," Tess says brightly. "For the music."

She certainly didn't come for the food; she hasn't eaten enough to keep a rabbit alive since Mom died, until recently that is. Almost as soon as she hooked up with her family again her appetite and her zest returned.

Time to clear out the mold behind the beer kegs. We haven't been here for a while; the garden of my dreams should be ripe.

When I've eaten my fill, I'll double-check our hiding place for the crystal ball. The Nörglein won't find it so easily this time.

I think I know what they want with it. Can't let them have it. Not ever. The ball came to Tess for a reason. She's the guardian of that new dimension. She and me.

I take my responsibilities seriously.

Well most of the time anyway.

"Who's playing tonight?" I asked as we made our way through the standing room only crowd to a table right by the stage. The waiter whisked off a reserved sign as Sean held my chair.

"Someone new," he replied a bit sheepishly. "I've never heard Holly Shannon play, but all the music here is good. I figured we couldn't go wrong."

I couldn't help the light laughter that trickled out of me. "You are in for a treat. Holly is the best Celtic harpist on the west coast. Not a bad soprano either."

"I'm glad you won't be disappointed." He covered my hand with his own on the tabletop. Our gazes met and locked.

This could get very interesting.

The waiter interrupted us, impatiently tapping his order pad with a leaky pen. We hadn't even looked at the menu.

"What's the special?" Sean stalled while we hastily scanned the single sheet of computer print out, Kelly green ink on heavy white paper.

"Give us a minute, Ian," I said with a smile.

"Oh, hi, Tess. Sorry I didn't notice you. As you can see we're swamped tonight. Holly's premiering a new CD. Let me get you drinks while you decide on the menu. The corned beef platter is the special, but we also have a salmon Caesar salad with fresh bread."

"River Dance pale ale," I replied without thinking.

"Do you have a nonalcoholic beer? I'm working tonight." Sean blushed slightly. "And I'd like the corned beef platter."

"Make that two, Ian."

"Sure thing. We've got three NAs, including a version of River Dance."

"I'll try it." Sean smiled.

"Should I tell the boss you're here?" Ian asked.

"As long as he doesn't make me sing. I'm on a date."

"Gotcha." Ian tipped his finger to his forehead in a salute and backed off.

"You come here often?" Sean quirked an eyebrow.

"I guess." I shrugged.

Our smiles and gazes locked again.

"So do I, but I've never been treated with such familiarity. How come I've never seen you in here?"

"Because you work crazy shifts and I usually avoid quiet times when I have time and peace to contemplate my sins."

"They can't be many. Your sins, I mean." He took both my hands and held them across the small table.

"You'd be surprised." I closed my eyes so that he couldn't see any secrets in their depths.

"Tess!" a squeal from across the room. Three twenty something girls sped across the room, elbowing aside anyone in their way. "When's the next book coming out?" Janni asked.

Her two clone companions, Jen and Josie, nodded in wide-eyed agreement. They dressed alike, scooped their blonde curls (only one natural) back with similar clips, and wore the same shade of lipstick. I'd learned to separate them only after a full year of association at cons and pub crawls.

"Are you singing tonight?" Jen asked breathlessly.

"No date on the next book yet." I had to finish the damn thing and turn it in to get it scheduled by the publisher. "And no, I'm not singing tonight. It's Holly's concert. You won't want to bother with me once she starts."

The girls faded away in disappointment.

"I guess you come here often," Sean said, his brow crinkling in puzzlement. "I had no idea you were so famous."

"Not really. Only in the science fiction and fantasy crowd. There's a lot of spillover between the Celtic music scene and the cons." Then I had to explain cons which can't really be explained. They have to be experienced.

Ian brought our drinks and set cutlery and Kelly green napkins before us.

"To an enchanted evening." Sean lifted his glass in toast.

I mimicked him. We took our first sips together.

Our conversation drifted from the smoothness of the ale to anticipation of the real music, not just the recorded instrumental being mangled by the sound system and the crowd noise fast becoming a wall of sound that separated us from normal pub activity.

"I remembered a conversation after the bruised bone in your right forearm from an over-vigorous fencing match. You bemoaned missing a concert by a local fiddler," he said when half his ale was gone.

"You've been memorizing information about me for a long time." That trip to the emergency room had been six months ago. "Should I be flattered or are you a stalker?" Only half a joke.

"Flattered, I hope. You've intrigued me for a long time. I've wondered what your life was like that you ended up in my ER so often."

"Been curious enough to read any of my books?"

"Sorry." He looked abashed. "I don't have a lot of time for reading fiction. Or anything else other than medical journals. But I did buy one of your books after your friend Allie suggested it. It's on my nightstand. I just haven't gotten around to it yet."

"Don't flinch, but you are about to see more of my life than you want." I leaned forward conspiratorially. Then I righted myself and plastered on a smile at the next woman to approach our table.

"Tess," Squishy said as she pumped my hand with genuine warmth and enthusiasm. "I don't want to intrude." She looked embarrassed as her gaze flicked from me to my date.

"Not to worry. Any more . . . um . . . woodland adventures?"

She shook her head. "No full moons to bring out the

craziness since we talked at the con. But I did get another short story published. On-line, but professional rates."

"Congratulations. Send me the details and I'll look it up." About time I read something of hers.

She and Sean exchanged looks again. "I know you," they said in unison.

"Mercy Hospital ER two months ago. We delivered a slash and grab baby," he said cautiously. "Patricia—Newman, isn't it? I was mighty glad psych released you long enough to help."

Uh oh. Maybe Sean did have an idea of how crazy my life could be.

"The weird one?" I mouthed my question to Squishy.

She nodded.

Then something else clicked in my brain. Patricia. Pat. Psych ward. Surely she couldn't be the nurse who helped Gollum and his wife, Julia.

I don't believe in coincidences. Too often the concentric circles in my life tilt in their orbits and collide. Like Sean delivering that woodland elf baby.

"Look, I'm here on a first date and don't want to leave her too long, she's very shy and . . . not really out of the closet yet, even if she had a few flirtations with . . . friends back east. We started getting together at High Desert Con." Squishy tilted her head toward a tall, elegant woman with shoulder length brown hair that flowed in a gentle curtain; the product of the most talented of hairdressers. My mop of dishwater blonde curls always looked the same sloppy mess even when I chanced upon a really good cut. That woman would never have to worry about how her hair looked. It always looked great.

I resented her instantly.

She tucked that perfect hair behind her ear with long tapered fingers that had been professionally manicured on a regular basis. I noticed the flash of a simple gold wedding band on the hand.

"Um . . . does her husband know?" My gut sank and soared with hope and a wild roller coaster ride. Squishy's date couldn't be Julia. Not Gollum's Julia. The Squishy I knew wouldn't be so unprofessional and unethical as to date a vulnerable patient. Too easy to manipulate emotions. Too easy to take advantage.

"I've got to go." Squishy faded into the crowd as if she'd read my doubts on my face.

"The husband is always the last to know," Sean sighed.

"You okay with alternative lifestyles?" Better to know right here and now and end our friendship before we got serious if he couldn't accept some of my friends.

"Yeah. I just feel sorry for the poor sucker who married that gorgeous woman and is now going to lose her to another woman. That's got to hurt."

It might damage him emotionally. Irreparably, I thought. My gut sank again.

I forced myself to ignore it and concentrate on Sean. After all, I had no proof that Squishy was dating Gollum's emotionally fragile wife.

Our food arrived. We reached for the spicy brown mustard together and laughed away any awkwardness.

"This is really good," I said after the third mouthful of corned beef so tender it fell apart with the touch of a fork, new potatoes dripping in butter and parsley, carrots, and cabbage.

"They really know how to cook it right. My grandmother doesn't do it any better," he replied.

"Your family is Irish?"

"Second generation. Dad was born in County Cork but the family emigrated when he was two," he worked his words around bites of food.

We talked about immigrant families. Mine had moved from Quebec to Massachusetts. His had come straight to Oregon.

Acquaintances waved to me but had the manners not to intrude.

We had just finished eating and settled in with coffee and bread pudding rich with raisins and cinnamon when Holly set up her harp on the tiny stage, two steps up from the main dining floor. Wide windows behind her looked out upon the river. Who could spare a glance for mere water and sparkling lights with Holly on stage?

She tossed her flame red hair behind her shoulders, spread her embroidered linen skirt, and sat on a stool with a lap harp, carved and painted with elaborate Celtic knots.

The strings had also been painted so a side view showed a St. Brigid cross in bright colors, to match the one on her tambourine. But it was more than decoration. The design had proved an effective protection for Holly when we had a small adventure together with a Pookah. The poor creature was lost. With no way to get home, he hung around the music and fed on other people's life energy—almost to the point of death for one of them. Holly now used a St. Brigid Cross on all her instruments as a protective ward.

I helped the lost soul find a way home. In return, he gave me a prophecy.

"By the light of the moon trailing a silver path along the river you shall find an end and a beginning."

I looked beyond the low stage to the river. No moon tonight.

The room hushed in anticipation.

Without introduction, Holly began a lively jig, her fingers dancing over the strings as light and lovely as a faery drunk on pollen.

Trust me, I've seen faeries dance. Sometimes I think Holly is one of them, loaned briefly to humans to impart a little joy.

The jig morphed into a poignant ballad. Her clear soprano sent knife blades of emotion to the heart. More than one cynical eye teared up. Mine always did and I never bothered to hide it.

About the time the audience needed to sniff, the ballad gave way to a whimsical story song, and then another lively tune. We sang along on the chorus. The bolder among the listeners began free-form dancing between the dining tables.

I smiled that Sean felt comfortable enough in the raucous party atmosphere, and with me, to clap along, and even lend his shouts of enthusiasm to the revelers. He didn't sing though.

Holly brought the set to a close by the simple expedient of stilling her harp strings with the flat of her hands.

Applause filled the room along with wild stomps and hoots of approval.

The harpist ran her gaze around the room, picking out new and familiar faces. She flicked past me, then back again. I tried to look away as she nodded to me with a wicked grin. Knowing what was to come, I took a sip of water.

"How about we give my vocal chords a break, folks.

Some of you know my good friend, Tess Noncoiré. Join me, Tess." She held out her hand in invitation.

"Do you mind?" I asked Sean, still rooted to my chair.

"Of course not!" He avidly joined the applause.

How could I turn down that kind of response?

Holly handed me a mike as I came abreast of her. We bent our heads in a moment of consultation. Then she threw back her head and laughed long and loud.

The audience quieted in anticipation.

I hummed the first note coming from the harp to make sure I matched it. Then I caressed the microphone with my voice in the sexy foreplay of a torch song. Only the tune was an old folk ballad, "Blowin' in the Wind."

Where are all the aliens,
Long time missing.
Where are all the aliens,
Gone to Roswell every one.
When will they ever learn?
When will they ever learn?

More laughter as the audience crooned along.

At least Sean got the jokes. Not a bad first date. This one might be a keeper.

After we talked about that woodland elf baby.

Have I ever said I don't believe in coincidences?

Chapter 21

In John Day, Oregon, the Kam Wah Chung State Heritage Site Museum is dedicated to a local Chinese doctor who treated local miners in the 1860s.

"THANK YOU FOR THE CD," I said on my doorstep, clutching Holly's newest recording against my chest like a teenager in lust. Sean had his own autographed copy in his coat pocket.

I didn't want to burst his bubble by telling him I already had a contributor copy. This one was special.

"My pleasure. I'd have bought it even if I didn't know you sang backup on two numbers." He grinned widely while surreptitiously checking his watch.

Nine-thirty. He had plenty of time to drive the three miles to the hospital for his shift in the ER.

"We had fun tonight. I'd like to see you again, Tess," he said softly, taking one of my hands.

His warmth and sincerity spread from his touch to the coldest part of my heart.

"I'd like that." I bit my lip in indecision about something else.

"I have Wednesday off."

"Yes."

"But? You sound hesitant."

"Sean, I haven't had a lot of luck in my romantic choices. I need to go slow this time. I need to know that you will support me in the craziness and chaos I call a career, as much as I understand and support yours. If you truly want to continue dating, there's something . . ."

"There's someone else." His face fell from joy to crushing disappointment.

Yes, there is!

"No, there's no one else." No one available anyway.

"But? There's always a but."

"Squishy . . . I mean Pat Newman confided in me a few weeks ago about a strangely deformed baby she helped you deliver."

"A trick of the light."

"Just think about it a moment. Then consider that one of the reasons I end up in your ER so often is because I'm working to keep other babies like that from being conceived."

"Are you a geneticist in secret?"

"No."

Quickly, before I lost my courage, I reached up and kissed his cheek. "I'm not insane. Read my books. Then think about it. Call me if you still want to do something on Wednesday. I'll clear the day for you."

I darted inside and closed the door. I leaned against it, waiting and listening.

He stood outside, silent for many long moments before I heard his footsteps retreat down the steps.

The crystal ball is all tucked up safe and sound where it should be. I've arranged artifacts of power around it so no demon or witch or Powers That Be can sniff it out. A LARPER might stumble upon it if they went looking in the wrong place, but they have no business playing their games behind that particular locked door.

While I was playing hide and seek, I also retrieved a certain hair comb my Tess adores. I found it in Mum's front yard a couple of years ago.

Like a lot of the detritus that finds its way into Imp Haven, the comb has magic. When my babe wears the comb she can see the truth in a person's aura. We both need to know who and what this doctor is.

I don't trust him. He's not one of us.

He's not Gollum.

Tuesday afternoon I shifted impatiently around my office, pretending to work. I moved from the desk to the bookcase. I opened and closed book after book, searching for . . . I don't know what.

Actually, I was hoping Sean would call.

Which felt stupid; like I was fourteen obsessing about my first crush.

Come to think on it, I hadn't had a real date with a man who didn't have an arcane agenda since back before I met Dill. Saturday night felt like my very first date.

The phone rang. I grabbed it on the first ring.

"Tess, have you seen Doreen?" Donovan asked. I heard a tenseness in his voice beneath his usual charming smoothness.

"Why would I have seen Doreen?" I tapped my foot impatiently, wanting to keep the line free for Sean. But something in his voice sent a frisson of alarm along my spine. I'd left with the crystal ball just as the Nörglein and his minions invaded the back office. Violently.

"She said you'd been by the store. I thought the two of you might be becoming friends." Donovan sounded disappointed.

"I haven't heard from her since she ordered me out of the store."

"Oh."

"Anything else, Donovan? Should I be worried that you can't find your girlfriend?"

"No." He hung up abruptly.

Frustrated and a little worried, I stretched and rotated my left ankle and knee until the muscles turned to pudding, desperate to rebuild my strength and limberness. Desperate to fill the hours.

An hour later, the phone rang again.

"Found her," Donovan said. "No need to worry about us." Then he hung up just as sharply as before.

What was that all about?

A timid knock came at the front door. I slid down the

hall on stockinged feet. The slick wax on the hardwood floor sped me along the way before Allie could react from her nest in the living room surrounded with bride magazines and home décor books, along with her laptop and lesson plans. She's always been better at multitasking than me. I obsess on one topic too much.

At the moment all I could think about was Sean's reaction to the finale of our first date.

As fast as I moved, Scrap appeared out of nowhere and beat me to my destination. He clung with his toes, upside down, like a bat, peering through the wood panels.

I wished he wouldn't do that. I hate bats. I hate any reminder of bats.

Donovan's tribe of Damiri demons take a bat form in their natural state.

At the door, I paused long enough to breathe, smiled brightly, opened the door, and . . .

My face stiffened into a stern frown. "Do I know you?" I asked two adolescent girls shifting from foot to foot and looking about anxiously.

Of course you do, Scrap said and blew cigar smoke into their faces.

"Um . . . Oak sent us," the one on the left, the older of the two, said shyly. She had dark shaggy hair that curled in odd wisps. Tall and sinewy, she towered over me and her sister.

"She's Blackberry. I'm Salal," said the younger sister. Closer to my height, she was painfully thin but not emaciated. I guessed she was very supple.

If they mimicked their namesake plants, Blackberry should be bold, thrusting her personality on one and all. Salal should be shier, hiding under things, seeking dark, damp places. But then Blackberry seemed to be in the midst of changing from little girl to woman. Her human hormones should be raging, making her extremely uncomfortable in her own body. Who knew how long puberty lasted in Kajiri demons with extended life-spans.

Lady Lucia's Damiri blood was so dilute she was unaware of it until she took thirty years to mature between eighteen and twenty-five. Even now, at the age of two hundred and four, she looked perhaps forty-five, maybe fifty.

These girls were a full half Nörglein. From newspaper

reports of missing hikers in the local forest about fifty years ago, I suspected they were part of that batch of ill-conceived children.

"Why did your brother think I would talk to you?" I hedged, blocking the doorway.

Scrap moved to my shoulder. He stayed his normal gray-green translucence. Nothing threatening about these girls. Yet.

"Oak said you kind of understood us. That maybe you could help us . . . um . . . figure out some things," Blackberry replied. She kept her gaze on the ground.

"Things like why your body is changing?" I'd spent a few years, early in my writing career, substitute teaching to help make ends meet. Adolescent girls didn't scare me as much as they scared themselves.

Both girls blushed.

"Are you willing to part with some information too?" I asked.

"Like . . . ?" Blackberry asked, finally looking up with the boldness that fit her namesake plant.

"Like why your family invaded the back room at Cooper's?" I wasn't about to mention the crystal ball, just in case that hadn't been the object of their quest.

Yeah, right.

"That's family," Blackberry said. She set her chin and clamped her mouth shut.

I made to close the door.

"They were looking for something to help heal Father," Salal interjected. She rammed her delicate foot in front of the door.

Try as I might, I couldn't close it, even if I was determined to crush her foot.

Demons have more strength than the average human. A lot more strength. I'd seen a Sasquatch teen, in human form, shoulder three of his fallen comrades and sprint a hundred yards without breathing hard.

Ever try to break a salal vine? The fibers will shred your hands first. Blackberries are worse with thorns that slide under fingernails and imbed deep into tender joint tissue.

"Something special that you wouldn't know about," Blackberry added.

Oh yeah? Scrap sneered.

Both girls looked at him, then away quickly, as if remembering they weren't supposed to see him.

"Were your brothers the ones who beat up my friend, Starshine, trying to get her to part with that something special?"

"Um . . ." Blackberry drew an intricate design on the floor with her bare toe. It absorbed all of her attention.

"Did you have any part in that?" I asked. My feet shifted to *en garde* and I held my hand out, palm up, ready for Scrap to transform.

But he didn't. He rose up and fluttered around the girls' heads, sticking his forked tongue out at them and lashing their hair with his tail.

"That was our brother, Cedar, and some of our father's helpers," Salal insisted. "We offered to go, but they wouldn't let us. Cedar said it was men's work. What makes one thing a man's work and the next a woman's?"

She tilted her head and stared at me in honest puzzlement.

"I think you girls should come in. I'll make tea and we'll talk," Allie said from behind me. She'd moved up silently, ready to guard my back if needed.

I opened the door and stepped out of their way. The two girls made their way to the barstools, cautiously looking over their shoulders at me with each step.

We settled around the counter that separated the kitchen from the great room. Allie and I kept to the kitchen side. I wanted the girls to feel they could leave at any time without having to go through us. Possibly violently.

Ooooh, girl talk, Scrap crooned taking a perch on the wine glass rack.

"Does he have to be here?" Blackberry asked, pointing at my imp. We all knew that the girls could see Scrap. No sense in pretending anymore.

"He's gay, no need to be embarrassed."

"We don't care if he's happy. He is male," Salal said also looking askance at Scrap's antics. But her eyes didn't truly focus on him, just tracked his general movements.

"In today's slang, gay means that he likes boys. Homosexual," Allie explained.

Our two guests stared at each other in some long unspoken communication. "Fir," they whispered.

"We'd still like this to be private," Blackberry mumbled.

"Can you take a powder, pal?" I asked. "Go find some mold to gorge on in the basement. I'll call if I need you."

Ah, you're no fun, he pouted.

Women who pout to get their own way drive me crazy. I've known too many of them—including my own mother—to put up with their practiced manipulation.

But on Scrap, the expression looked more ridiculous.

Swallowing my mirth I banished him with a gesture. I sensed he only went as far as my office and eavesdropped shamelessly.

"What do you need to know?" Allie asked, forthright and no nonsense.

"Why do I bleed?" Blackberry asked, equally forthright.

I got out a blank notebook and colored pencils. The discussion went downhill from there. I'd never had to teach sex education before but I knew how, part of my general education degree.

"In our culture, women don't have to have babies just because the men want them to," I finished.

Blackberry opened and closed her mouth a couple of times.

"Spit it out," I said gently.

"We . . . we spend a lot of time in Old Town." Blackberry traced an arcane pattern on the counter with her fingertip.

"And?"

"And I've made friends with an old woman at the Asian pharmacy."

Portland has a small but thriving Chinatown and a large Asian population, Chinese, Japanese, Vietnamese, the whole range of Oriental cultures.

"And . . ."

"She's been giving me black cohosh once a month since I started, you know . . ." She tapped the drawings we'd made in the notebook.

"To keep you from getting pregnant."

"I guess." She shrugged and turned her back to us, studying the river through the broad windows.

"Okay. But a girl your age shouldn't need it. You shouldn't have to have sex unless you want it. Even then I think you are too young to fully understand a deep relationship." Gee, I sounded preachy. But I think Blackberry needed to hear that.

She shrugged again, without looking at me.

"A woman gets to choose who she has sex with and when. For the man to force her is a heinous crime," Allie expanded my statement.

"Sex is best when shared by a couple with deep affection. It is the ultimate in communication; communication that goes beyond words. Sex should be an extension of true and abiding intimacy, not just to make babies," I added.

We walked all around the issue of their father being a scumbag who needed to be wiped out, the sooner the better.

I hoped the lingering wound I gave him from the Celestial Blade festered and caused him a great deal of hideous pain.

Salal's jaw dropped as the idea behind the words penetrated her mind first.

"How does your father feel about you having sex?"

"He has never mentioned it. He doesn't talk to us about his women and the new babies that will come to him." she whispered.

Blackberry looked off into a corner, clamping her jaw shut. I saw the muscles around her mouth twitch, as if she was grinding her teeth.

"He only talks to us about our mission to nurture the forest. Keeping out the invasive nonnative plants is a never-ending job. It's a sacred duty," Blackberry added, obviously more comfortable talking about work than life. Like most people.

Then again, a lot of people mistook their work for life. Like me.

Allie seemed to recently have made the distinction and chose the better alternative.

"What does your father do when he traps a woman and takes her home?" I asked. The girls weren't ready for the idea that their father was a nonnative invasive plant. If he didn't belong in this ecology, then they didn't either.

"Trap? He doesn't trap them. Traps are for vicious animals that go rogue," Blackberry insisted.

"He changes the paths so a woman gets lost. Then he offers her a return to safety in exchange for sex. That's a trap, coercion. And I call it rape," Allie returned equally forceful.

"What about when he traps a man, then shape-changes and spends the night with that man's wife?" I pressed on. "That's trickery of the worst kind."

"Wh . . . what do you call it when he gives me to our brothers, or his helpers to practice on?" Blackberry studied her tea mug as if the depths of the liquid held the answer. The whirlpool in her cup betrayed her agitation and shaking hands.

"That's abuse of the worse kind. You don't have to put up with it," I said, horror-struck.

"You don't have to go back to it," Allie added.

Chapter 22

1850-1941 Portland was known as the Shanghai Capital of the world. A network of tunnels beneath the city's waterfront connected pool halls, saloons, restaurants, brothels, gambling parlors, and opium dens. Up to 1,500 men and women a year were kidnapped and sold to ship captains and brothels.

"FATHER RESPECTS HIS WOMEN enough to put them in a trance so they enjoy the experience and do not remember him until after his child is born. He makes himself look very handsome for them. He also takes them into a back room in our home so that they have privacy." Blackberry didn't sound as convinced as she wanted to be.

She also completely ignored her own situation.

"More trickery," Allie snorted.

"Let's talk about your home. What does it look like?" If I could find the dark elf's lair, I could take him out. Once he was gone, the new forest babies could learn to let their human half dominate. Gradually, the woodland genes would fade into dormancy.

What would happen to the five teens? I had to get the girls out. Now. The boys?

Later. I'd make that decision later. Or they would. They were almost adults, ready to take responsibility for their own lives. But they couldn't be allowed to continue their father's ways.

No way. No how.

Something the girls had said wiggled and slid around the edges of my mind. Something about invasive nonnative species. Their father was out of his native environment and therefore a noxious weed.

I knew that keeping English Ivy from strangling native trees was an ongoing battle with the parks department. The butterfly bush had just been added to the list of pesky plants. A native of China, too many of the fragrant shrubs had escaped planned landscapes to take over creek banks, crowding out helpful natives.

The girls said that keeping those plants under control was part of their work.

Could the parks department and their volunteers manage without the additional help of a family of forest elves? Volunteer groups. They were around but how did I find them? How effective were they?

Goddess, I was digging myself deeper with every thought twist. I needed to concentrate on one thing at a time.

"What about our home?" Blackberry asked suspiciously.

If I remembered correctly, one species of blackberry, the big one with huge berries was also an invasive nonnative species too. Maybe she was named after the smaller and less aggressive local plant. The one with tiny thorns designed to hook into the delicate flesh of a bear's mouth to keep the animals from stripping the plant of greenery just to get to the berries.

"How big is your home? Forest Park is huge. There are large stretches where a small hut could blend into the background and stay hidden. But a big modern construction with lots of glass wouldn't." I needed a map.

"Not hard to hide something that's mostly underground," Salal said on a shrug. She too avoided her sister's horrible confession.

"Caves? I didn't know the geology of the hills was conducive to extensive cave systems." I'd absorbed bits and pieces of information about rocks and plate tectonics and such from my deceased husband. Dill had a Ph.D. in geology and spent a lot of our three-month marriage crawling around the high desert plateau of Central Oregon and Washington. I'd shipped his rock collection back to his parents, postage due, after they tried to stiff me on Dill's life insurance and inheritance of the house.

"She didn't say caves," Blackberry snorted. She didn't want to part with information her father wanted to remain secret, but as a teen she needed to let me know that her knowledge was superior to mine.

"If not natural caves . . ." I mused.

"Then unnatural tunnels," Allie offered.

"The Shanghai Tunnels!" I whispered. I'd seen a program on TV about what lies beneath major cities. Often whole underworlds. Portland had a sordid history of subterranean opium dens, brothels, and cells for unwilling recruits to the maritime industry. Not all of them had been fully explored. Local rumor claimed that some of them went all the way into the West Hills.

Forest Park covered a huge tract of those hills. Why couldn't some, or just one of those tunnels lead to an elven home?

"How did you get here?" I jumped topics on the girls.

Gollum had a bad habit of expecting others to follow his rapid transitions. His mind had already made logical leaps. Unfortunately, not everyone had his intelligence and extensive knowledge of seemingly unrelated subject matter.

"We took the bus." Salal shrugged just like her sister, ducking her head into her shoulders.

Okay. They'd already admitted to ranging around Old Town and Chinatown.

"How'd you get to the bus?" I pressed them.

The girls looked at their hands folded around tea mugs.

"You don't have to tell me. I'm guessing you walked a tunnel into Old Town and came up in a back alley right near a bus stop."

Salal half nodded. "It's beside a parking lot where Father keeps his car. But Oak is the only one of us with a driver's license, other than Father, that is."

"What's his connection to the Coopers?"

"How'd you know about that?" Blackberry looked up sharply.

"Scrap smelled him there a few weeks ago. His minions and your brothers invaded the office looking for something precious."

"Oh," she said flatly. "Father works there. We all help out sometimes when they have a new shipment of antiques. The boys have learned to use the computer there."

"I want to go back to the women your father attacks," Allie insisted. "And what he makes your brothers do to you. How has he gotten away with it for so long?" Her shoulders hunched and her hands reached for the gun that no longer hung on her belt. Her new revolver was locked up in the bedroom.

"Why do you say attack? He uses no violence," Salal insisted.

Blackberry didn't look so sure.

"Does your father ask their permission? Does he court them? Does he follow up with offers of a relationship?" Allie pressed.

"N . . . no."

"Then he coerces them, tricks them. He doesn't get their permission. That's rape."

"Would you like it if some man did that to you?" I brought home the concept.

"Our brothers and the helpers haven't practiced on me yet, though Father wants them to," Salal defended the nasty little man.

"Um. . . ." Blackberry hedged.

"How does your father expect you to behave when confronted with men? Do you strip off and open your legs to every man who looks at you—like a prostitute? Will you do it for your brothers when they can no longer resist his prodding?" Crude, but they didn't seem to understand subtle. "Or will you have sex with the lost travelers your father brings home just to produce more babies?"

"Yes," Blackberry whispered. "That's what he wants. That's why he insists we practice. That's why I need the black cohosh."

"He's using you like breeding cattle." Allie swallowed deeply and turned her back. She was having trouble containing her outrage.

So was I.

"Why?" I asked. "Loss of habitat and urban crowding drove him here from the Italian Alps. He doesn't belong here. Why is he so bent on rebuilding the Nörglein when there isn't enough wild land left for them all?"

"I don't know!" Blackberry shouted. She stood up, angrily pushing back her stool so that it clattered against the wood floor. Without another word she headed for the front door.

I couldn't stop her. The next decision had to be her own.

"We'd better get home," Salal said flatly. She rose more slowly, pushing her stool up next to the bar politely. She stalled by righting the fallen chair. She kept her gaze firmly on her task, never engaging me or her sister. "Thank you for the lesson on female biology. Thank you for the tea."

"You don't have to go back," I reminded them quietly.

Both girls stilled. Not even their eyelids twitched. A useful skill when hiding in the forest.

"Father will be very angry if we are late," Blackberry said after several long moments of silence.

"What will he do if you don't go back?" Allie asked. I could see ideas spinning in her head.

"He'll punish us."

"How?" I asked.

"He'll . . . he'll command our brothers to whip us with the vines of the other blackberry. The big ones."

I cringed in sympathy. The Himalayan variety had thorns big enough to penetrate the hide of a Yeti.

An odd thought. Bullets from an automatic weapon couldn't penetrate the hide of a Sasquatch—the North American version of the Yeti—because they were manmade. The blackberry, being natural, probably could. Something to keep in mind.

"Interesting that the coward will command your brothers to do his dirty work, but can't stomach it himself."

"We'll protect you," Allie insisted.

"You are awfully generous in that 'we,'" I grumbled.

"You don't ever have to go back," Allie continued as if she hadn't heard me. "You can be like normal girls, go to school, and have friends. Learn to use a computer. Date boys and make your own decisions who you have sex with and when, preferably when you have a lot more experience of life and know what you really want in a partner, a long-term partner."

Blackberry retreated one step away from the door. Salal looked up with interest.

"You can protect us?" Blackberry asked, hopefully.

"Scrap, you on alert?"

Yeah, babe. I got your back. All clear so far. Don't think the old man has noticed the girls are missing. Yet.

"Where will you hide us?" Salal asked.

"Right here," Allie replied.

"You giving up the bed to them?" I returned.

"We'll work something out." She smiled.

"I wish I could call Donovan, he's got experience in integrating Kajiri into society." He'd reached out to me in his worry over Doreen. "I don't trust him. Gollum could help. I think I have to call him."

But first I needed a double shot of single malt Scotch. The good stuff.

Oh, boy, this could get interesting. Very interesting indeed. Too bad we can't extend this apartment into the chat room and give us more space without really adding to the building in this dimension.

Nope. That wouldn't work even if I could figure out how to do it. We don't want those girls exposed to the energies of the chat room that would bring out their elven heritage even more. We want to tamp down on those characteristics.

So who's going to sleep where? Maybe we can do it in shifts.

At least my babe is calling Gollum.

Uh oh, the phone is ringing. It's Dr. Sean. He's going to distract my babe and keep her from calling the only man she can trust to help her.

What to do? What to do?

I know, I'll send Gollum an email. Hmm, if I invade his home computer monitor I can make the screen show my message.

It's going to take some work and a whole lot of energy. Best I load up on mold first. Then I'll hit his computer just about the time he gets home from teaching.

That's the trick. Show him the message once and then make it fade like an automatic delete. He'll never know it's me and not Tess calling for help.

Chapter 23

Portland, Oregon, is the only city in the US with a volcano within the city limits—three of them—Mt. Tabor, Powell Butte, and Rocky Butte; all extinct.

MUCH THOUGHT AND CALCULATION LATER, I decided it would be better to work with the devil I knew than the angel who could break my heart again.

"Who's the better computer hacker, Steve or Donovan?" I asked Allie.

Our two new guests had retired to the bedroom to discuss their decision to stay with me. If I was about to become their guardian, I didn't necessarily want them to know how I made it look legal.

"That's a toss-up." Allie hitched up the belt of her jeans as she would the utility belt she no longer wore. She used to do that as a subtle reminder to bullies and speed offenders that she had the firepower and the will to enforce the law. Her habits as a cop were going to be hard for her to drop. Those habits would add authenticity to her classes at the community college.

"This isn't going to be exactly legal. I don't want to involve Steve," I said as I punched number six on my speed dial.

"Halfling Gaming Systems, how may I direct your call?" A sultry female voice came on the line. Donovan's newest secretary I guessed. I wondered why Quentin wasn't the gatekeeper today. Maybe he was out planning a hit on someone. The big man who looked like he carried more Indian blood than demon had been Donovan's right hand for as long as I'd known him. He was also high on my list of suspects for the role of assistant to Donovan's foster father, Darren, on the night my husband died in an arson fire set outside our motel room.

That is if Donovan could be believed and he didn't have a hand in that murder.

"Tell Donovan that Tess is on the line and it's urgent," I said a little less politely than my mother had taught me.

"One moment please, I'll see if Mr. Estevez is available."

Barely ten seconds passed. "Now what?" he snarled less politely than I had. "I told you not to worry about Doreen."

"I have just taken guardianship of two Kajiri girls who look twelve and fourteen. I need to make it look legal."

"What am I supposed to do about it?" He sounded interested but still cautious.

"You've done it before for others. Someone did it for you. You know what to do and how to do it."

"You'll need birth certificates."

"Can you do it?"

"Only if I put my name on them as their father."

My stomach lurched.

"If your name is on the certificate, then you'll sue for custody." And he'd raise them with constant reminders of their dark origins.

"Not if your name is listed as their mother. But then you are a firm believer in family, in two parent families. You'd have to marry me then."

I hung up on him. So much for his relationship with Doreen. It didn't stand the chance of a snowflake inside a lava flow of succeeding.

"That was short," Allie said cautiously.

"I don't even know why I bother asking him for help. He always attaches conditions that cost too much."

"He proposed again."

"Barely."

"And you refused again."

"If he'll believe hanging up on him is a refusal. But he did give me an idea."

"Such as?"

"I don't have to go through social services and getting

certified as a foster parent if I'm their mother and they've been back east growing up with my relatives. Home schooled, therefore no records. Medical records lost in an office fire."

"Tess, you're only thirty. You'd have been sixteen when Blackberry was born."

"Not all that unusual these days. So, do you think Steve can forge the birth certificates?"

"I hate to ask him. I hate that we are doing something so illegal."

"You got a better idea?"

"Gollum."

Right on cue the phone rang. The landline, not my cell phone. Gollum would call the cell.

Gollum just sits there staring at my message. I blink and flash.

Ouch that hurts my head. My babe had better appreciate what I go through for her. This is going to require a big dose of beer and OJ to cure the headache.

And still Gollum sits there.

"Hey! Professor Van der Hoyden-Smythe, wake up. The love of your life needs you."

At last I think I'm getting through those thick glasses. He lets them slide down his long nose until they almost fall off. Then he caresses the words on the screen with a delicate fingertip, tracing the shape of the italic capitals as if they were the scar on my dahling Tess' face. The interdimensional scar that should be invisible to him, but isn't.

That's how I know he is the only man for Tess. He can see the scar. Donovan can feel it, but he can't see it.

Pansy Sean can't see it or feel it.

At last Gollum blinks rapidly and shakes his head as if clearing it.

Then he pushes his glasses back firmly onto the bridge of his nose and deletes my message!

Stupid idiot.

He starts scrolling through the rest of his email, replying here, saving there.

As tired as I am, I force a few phosphors to rearrange themselves.

THIS IS IMPORTANT YOU DUMB ASS. CALL TESS BEFORE SHE MAKES A HUGE MISTAKE. SHE NEEDS YOUR HELP.

Then I push myself halfway through the screen so he can see me.

Of course to his semi mundane brain I look like a rough squiggle of a cartoon, but he should get the message.

On the fourth ring I answered the phone, just before it went to voice mail. The caller ID said private name and number.

I don't usually answer calls I can't identify. Something in my gut said I needed to talk to this person. Too much was happening. Too many coincidences had fallen into place.

"Tess, don't hang up on me," Sean said hurriedly.

"Do I have a reason to hang up on you, Sean?"

Allie made an "Oh" with her mouth and withdrew, closing the office door on her way out.

"I hope not."

Should I tell him right away that tomorrow looked impossible to see him?

No. Better to play it safe and find out if he wanted to continue seeing me before I sent the message that I was having second thoughts, when I wasn't.

"Have you thought about our last conversation?" I asked instead.

"Yes." He sounded cautious. "I did some research too."

"Oh?" What could he find about me and the Warriors of the Celestial Blade? Not much. We were pledged to secrecy. But as more and more rogue portals opened between worlds and more and more demons infiltrated our society, we had to move out of the Citadels and into everyday life, thus exposing ourselves to possible discovery every time we invoked the Celestial Blade.

"Actually, I talked to Nurse Newman."

I breathed a sigh of relief. "What did Squishy tell you?"

"Odd nickname for a woman so solidly built and strong . . . But that's another topic for another day. She too told me to read your books, that the protagonist is you even if the setting is different."

Gulp.

"And . . ."

"And it's a little hard to swallow."

"Okay. You're skeptical. What does that mean for us?"

"I think we need to talk. I delivered another strange baby Saturday night, Sunday morning actually, right at the set of the full moon. I called in Nurse Newman to consult. The mother is fine and has the number to call for the support group you set up. I really think I need to talk to you about this. Can I see you tomorrow?"

"Actually, are you working tonight?"

"Until nine. I'm on a coffee break right now. What did you have in mind?"

I looked at the clock, almost five.

"I'd like to introduce you to two of those woodland babies grown up a bit."

He whistled long and low.

"How about I bring Chinese for four."

"Sounds wonderful. Um. . . ."

"Um what?"

"There'll be five of us. My brother's fiancée is staying with me for a while—she's my best friend actually, we've known each other since kindergarten. It's a little crowded here. I don't suppose you have a spare camp cot or air mattress hanging around?"

"As a matter of fact I do. I have a full camping set up for when my dad and I go fishing every spring," he said on a chuckle.

I heard a page in the background.

"I've got to go. I'll see you about nine-thirty."

Chapter 24

Portland's Classical Chinese Garden is the largest urban Suzhou-style garden outside China.

I WASTED A LOT OF TIME pacing my office. I schemed and plotted, discarded all my thoughts and started over again.

Allie finally knocked on the door with two mugs of coffee in her hands. "I threw together a vegetarian pot pie. It's hot. I wasn't sure what the girls would eat."

"Besides greasy pizza?" I drank deeply of the coffee, grateful for the caffeine hit, hoping it would clear the increasing number of cobwebs in my brain.

"Yeah. I figured we should start introducing them to normal food and clothes. Oh, Tess, they have nothing. Not even toothbrushes."

"I guess we need to raid the nearest discount store. As soon as we've eaten." I stepped toward the doorway.

Can we go to the mall? Scrap popped in right in front of me. *After beer and OJ.*

"You do look a little peckish. What have you been up to?" I eyed him suspiciously. His transparent green had faded to fairly ugly khaki and he had none of the glow he usually carried after a visit to Gingko.

You'll find out soon. Can we eat now?

We settled at the kitchen bar. I didn't want the girls to

get in the habit of carrying their plates into the far corners of the condo. I was bad enough about that.

"Card table and chairs are on the list," Allie hissed at me as we dug into the casserole. Allie knew how to cook hearty for New England winters. Rich in turnip and barley, along with tomatoes and cauliflower, she'd topped the dish with two inches of mashed potatoes and a garnish of sharp cheddar cheese.

Salal and Blackberry practically inhaled it—after some basic instruction on how to use a fork and a napkin instead of fingers and tongues.

"I cooked, you clean up, share the chores," Allie insisted as the girls pushed their plates aside.

"Of course. Father always insisted on chores before fun. May we watch TV?" They looked too eager.

I eyed the last portion of pot pie. I didn't really need it, no matter how good it tasted. It would make a nice lunch for one person.

"We need to take you shopping," I said instead. "Clothes and toiletries before TV. We should get going if we're going to be back before Dr. Connolly gets here."

"Doctor?" Blackberry reared back, suddenly suspicious.

"Yes. My friend is a physician."

"We don't need a physician." Blackberry backed up, hands in front of her as if warding off something unpleasant.

"He's a friend. This is not a professional visit." I glared back at both girls. "Why do you fear doctors?"

"Nothing." They shrugged and took the dirty plates and cutlery to the sink.

Another sticky topic to be approached carefully. Slowly. After we'd built some emotional trust.

"Father says that physicians are money sucking leeches who don't know anything," Salal whispered on her way past me.

I arched my back and scanned the room, assessing what we needed to make the place habitable for two extra people. Bed, eating table and chairs, more seating in the living room. Everything!

A tentative knock on the door sent my heart into my throat. It couldn't be Sean. Not three hours early!

If anything, I'd expect a doctor to be late.

Go ahead and answer it, dahling, Scrap commanded. His dinner of beer and OJ had revived him enough to send him bouncing from wine rack to TV to coatrack to top of the fridge and back again. *This is a good one. It really, really is. I promise. You'll thank me later.*

That made me stop short with my hand almost on the doorknob. "Why don't I believe you, Scrap?"

Ah, come on, babe. When have I ever steered you wrong?

"There was the time you forgot to tell me about Donovan being a gargoyle. There was the time you spent so much time painting iodine on your cat scratches that you forgot to follow WindScribe . . ."

Okay, okay, I've slipped up in the past. But this one is really, really good.

"If you say so." For the first time in a year and a half I regretted not moving the spy hole from six feet up to my eye level. With Scrap around I didn't need it. Until now.

"You'd better be right, Scrap, or you are toast. Remember who buys your beer and OJ." With that I yanked the door open and moved into a defensive stance.

All the blood rushed from my head and feet to my heart. Blackness crowded my vision.

Gollum stood there holding a single red rose and looking extremely sheepish.

"Don't pass out on me, Tess," he said, grabbing me around the waist, while managing to keep the rose undamaged.

"Um . . ." Not the most intelligent thing to say. It was all I could manage.

"Okay, girls, you and I are going shopping," Allie sang out.

"But the dishes . . ." Salal protested.

". . . Will still be there when we get back." Allie herded them out the door.

"Is that her boyfriend?" Salal whispered as she passed us.

"Will they have sex?" Blackberry continued in the same tone of voice.

I didn't hear Allie's reply over the rushing of blood in my ears that accompanied my blush.

"What was that about?" Gollum finally asked as he set me firmly on my own two feet, balanced and semi-coherent. "Did your email refer to those girls?"

"What email?" I moved back, putting distance and safety between us. The strength of his arm holding me up had felt so good, so right, like the other half of me had come home. I couldn't allow that.

"Ah, I suspect Scrap had a hand in that communication."

See ya, babe. I'm off to the mall with the girls. Think I can get a new boa, or maybe a hat with a veil out of this? He popped out with an audible displacement of air.

I stepped into the kitchen and tackled the few dirty dishes left. The girls had done a good job of cleaning up, unlike most teenagers I'd known.

Gollum, being Gollum, picked up the dish towel and began drying the clean pieces.

"So, why did I get a rather imperative summons from your imp?" he finally asked when the silence between us ceased to be companionable and grew uncomfortable.

"I'm adopting the two Nörglein girls."

"Have you thought through the consequences?"

"Not entirely. But I have to get them away from their father. He's abusive, both physically and emotionally, and . . . and sexually exploiting them, turning them into little more than prostitutes just to get more Kajiri babies," I blurted out.

"Okay. What do we need to do?"

"Too much. Everything. I need to make it look legal. Probably forge some birth certificates to begin with. I presume Allie will help them select a few clothes and toiletries."

"What else? Schools? Money?"

"A bigger house real soon. And the housing market has gone belly up. I can't afford to buy something new until I sell this place, probably for a lot less than I bought it for. I can't afford to move!"

"Slow down and breathe. We'll make lists, prioritize. What else?"

"I need to assess their schooling so I know how much intensive tutoring they need before I can put them in public school."

"Home schooling is a viable option. I can get you curriculums and study aids."

"I can't seem to get the damn book written so I can have the money to do all this."

Suddenly, the enormity of it all overwhelmed me. I just

stood there at the sink with my hands in rapidly cooling soapy water. More than a few tears fell.

"You aren't alone, Tess. Allie is helping. I'll do what I can. You don't have to do it alone. You never did, but you are so stubborn you can't see that."

"What can you do?" Suddenly I wanted to shove all of my problems onto his shoulders. I didn't want to live my life without him, or his help.

But I had to.

"I'll call Donovan if you like. Surely he has experience in integrating barely civilized Kajiri into the system."

"I already tried. His price is too high." Memory of his demands sent my blood boiling. Anger gave me strength to wipe my tears, and dump the dishwater.

"Okay. What's the first chore?"

"Birth certificates. Forged. With me listed as birth mother, father unknown."

He cocked an eyebrow at me.

"It's the only way, Gollum. Otherwise, I'd have to involve social services and formal adoption procedures. It could take years just to get me certified as a foster parent before actually beginning legal paperwork." I yanked the towel away from him to dry my hands. Then I avoided more words—and looking at him—by folding it neatly and draping it over the oven handle.

"Okay. Where's your computer and printer? Got a fax machine?"

"In there." I pointed toward the office. "Why the fax?"

"To make it look like the real birth certificates, which will be my creation, were faxed to you while the originals are still on file somewhere else." He grinned oddly. "Do you want to be a part of this, or would you rather not know how I manage?"

"I think I'll leave it to you. Can you do it and be out of here by nine?" I checked the clock on the microwave with a little trepidation. Six-thirty.

His glasses slid down and he peered at me over the tops.

"I have a date," I said firmly.

Even though Sean looked pale and ordinary in comparison.

"That's fair. I should get home in an hour or so anyway. Pat will be going to work about then."

Without another word, or argument, or condemnation, or hint of jealousy, he set about doing what he had to do.

"Oh, and can I access your bank account from here?"

"What!"

"I need to transfer some money from the trust fund to you. I think taking two children away from an abusive dark elf counts as Warrior business. I'll set it up as a monthly allowance. If the IRS asks, it's child support from the unnamed father who really doesn't want the world to know he got a sixteen-year-old girl pregnant." Again, that quirky grin.

"Thank you. Don't make it too extravagant. I intend to take care of my girls on my own as soon as I finish the book and get back on my feet financially."

"Understood." He bent his head over my computer and logged on to the Internet.

I scooped up my laptop and retired to the living room with my flash drive, oddly content and ready to work.

Chapter 25

Tabitha Moffat Brown is called the "Mother of Oregon" for the orphanage she founded in 1846.

ALLIE'S WISDOM PREVAILS. She drives the girls to the nearest all-in-one-discount store. Of course, in Portland that requires crossing a bridge over the Willamette River and driving east quite a way to 82nd Avenue and then north to the blaring lights of the parking lots and the thumping ear buster stereo systems in the cars parked there. A lot of teens who can't afford to shop the mall hang out here.

Blackberry spends the half hour drive fiddling with the radio, examining the clutch pedal, prowling through the glove box, whatever piques her curiosity.

I follow her every movement, equally eager to explore new things, but also cautious of my babe's privacy. Tess knows better than to leave anything totally personal in the car, other than necessary registration and insurance stuff. Boring.

But then there's the hairbrush in the door pocket, receipts for gas, dirty tissues, fast food wrappers, mostly empty coffee cups.

Ooooh, stale coffee with mold growing in the bottom. I slurp those up in a hurry, before the two forest girls can steal them.

"Did anyone ever tell Tess that she's as big a slob as Blackberry?" Salal snorts with disgust. She picks up some of the debris in the backseat between her fingernails and stuffs it in a makeshift litter bag that once held a hamburger and fries.

"I am not a slob. I need to sprawl. I need space to thrive," Blackberry retorts.

"Here's a notebook and paper. Start making a list of things you need," Allie jumps in, digging said notebook and paper out of her neat little purse. The purse isn't big enough to hold her gun, so she has it holstered on her left hip, hidden beneath her baggy sweatshirt. She's so organized she's no fun at all. I didn't think to remind her to bring THE gun. If Tess were here we wouldn't need it. Evah.

If I had to live with Allie I'd die of boredom inside a week, nothing to clean up after her, nothing to color coordinate. Sheesh, how come she and Tess are such BFFs? They are complete opposites.

But I digress. The issue at hand is how the two girls react to life outside a cave in the forest.

"Um . . ." Blackberry hides her hands in her armpits.

Salal looks out the window and points to a big Halloween display in front of a donut shop. There's inflatable ghosts and pumpkins, a scarecrow with crows on its outstretched arms, an ugly witch flying off the roof on a broomstick, the whole shebang.

"What is that?" she asks, seemingly quite innocent.

"Tomorrow night is Halloween," Allie says. She sounds puzzled. By the lack of awareness of the funnest holiday on the calendar, or by the avoidance of making a list.

"What's Halloween?" Blackberry asks. She relaxes her hands and returns to fiddling with the window handle—Tess' car is a bit old and stripped down. She has rolling handles for the windows rather than electronic buttons. She also has manual locks.

She says it's for safety, in case she gets into a mess and doesn't have her keys or the engine dies and she can't get out of the car. Or into it. Or something. I'm not exactly sure.

"Halloween is a contraction of All Hallows Eve. Sort of a day of the dead celebration, but it's now about parties and candy and spooky things that go bump in the night," Allie explains.

"Oh." Blackberry shrugs.

"Sounds like fun," Salal says. "I think that's the day the boys get to explore other dimensions 'cause the portals get real weird and easier to find."

"It can be fun," Allie hedges. She bites her lip, clearly thinking multiple trains of thought. "It's also a night when some people think they have a license to play mean tricks on others and tear up property."

"You . . . you mean . . . rip out grass and break shrubs and strip a ring of tree bark so the tree will die?" Blackberry asks. She sounds truly appalled and frightened.

"Been known to happen, yeah," Allie replies. "Worse than that, children, and even adults can get hurt by poisons and sharp objects hidden in treats. Or by fires that start small but get out of hand."

"But they actually kill green things!" Salal is as upset as Blackberry.

"You sound like you've had to clean up after a few pranks," Allie says.

"Yes," the girls say in unison. They don't sound happy at all.

"Father is going to need help the morning after," Blackberry says.

"He's going to be very upset if we aren't there to do the heavy work for him," Salal continues. "The boys are always useless after a night prowling other lands. They get to do all the neat things while we get stuck with the work."

"It doesn't matter if your father is upset, girls. Tess and I will protect you from him. You don't ever have to go back to him."

"But who will replant the grass and stomp out the fires and properly prune the broken shrubs?"

"Why can't your father do it? Or your brothers?" Allie is starting to get mad. She doesn't believe there is any difference between men's work and women's work. It's all work, and should be done by the person most qualified. "The parks department has trained arborists and a lot of volunteers to help too."

"Father says they're useless. And he can't do the work because he's sick. Tess hurt him bad," Blackberry protests.

"Did she truly hurt him or is he using the wound as an excuse to get out of his responsibilities?" Allie asks. "Lazy, manipulative bastard," she adds sotto voce.

Both girls have to stop and think about that.

Allie pulls into the parking lot. I see her scan the clumps of teenage boys gathering around tricked out pickups and low-slung ancient sedans. She circles until she finds a spot beneath a streetlight with a direct path to the store that doesn't intersect any of the potential gangs.

"Who are they?" Blackberry asks with extreme interest. She begins pumping out pheromones.

I'm not sure if she's just being a young teen or if she's reacting to her father's training. Either way, I see trouble looming.

The tips of my wings start to turn pink. I smell a great deal of predatory anger on one group of boys. They want to hurt people. They think that's the only way to prove to the world that they control everything within their circle.

I got news for those guys. Allie's still a cop in her heart. She's also nearly six feet tall, fit, and solidly built. She'll take them down in a heartbeat without breaking a sweat.

A lady after my own heart. She'd make a great Warrior of the Celestial Blade.

Then I spot the tattoos on the inside wrists of the boys. The black ink of a skull within a pentagram glows through multiple dimensions. They have otherworldly protection.

If they are still hanging out when Allie and my girls exit, I'll fetch Tess.

After fifteen pages and eight points of needed research noted, I roused from my self-imposed stupor to find Gollum standing in front of me holding two official looking documents.

"Are you finished already?" I asked, holding out my hand for the papers.

"It's been nearly three hours," he said. His glasses slid down his nose, revealing his pale blue eyes. Tired lines made them look heavy.

And sexy as hell.

I think I gazed longingly into his soul a little too deeply. He sat next to me and drew me close.

My head automatically drifted to rest upon his shoulder.

My eyes were just about to close in guilty contentment when something on the papers caught my gaze.

"What in the hell . . . ?" I jerked upright. "You listed yourself as the girl's father! I told you to put unknown." I was on my feet shaking the papers at him.

Actually, I was shaking all over, my tummy doing somersaults. My deepest desire was to live my life with this man and bear his children. And now . . . now . . .

"Calm down, Tess. It makes sense. If you look at the dates it makes sense. Blackberry's birthday is the day before Julia's first suicide attempt. Salal would have been conceived the night before I left for Africa as a mercenary. It explains the blind trust fund set up by my mother to avoid scandal, to avoid hurting Julia's mother who is her best friend."

"But . . . but how does it explain why no one knows about the girls, or how we met, or why you, the most honorable man I've ever met, seduced a teenager?"

Dammit, it did make sense. And it made the idea of seeing him more often plausible.

"So where have the girls been while I was in college and becoming a writer?"

"With MoonFeather. She's had numerous foster children as well as her own two, and stray students in and out of her house for years. Why not your two?" He cocked his head and gave me one of his endearing smiles, the kind that made me want to throw my arms around him and hold him so close we merged our souls and our lives.

Okay, just about anything made me want to do that. But that smile drove a stake of enduring love and guilt and loneliness deep into my heart.

"You'd better give your aunt a heads-up in case there are official questions. I showed her as the midwife in attendance at both births."

"Gollum, is this really going to work?" Butterflies erupted into flight in my gut. Thousands of them. All at once. I wanted to shake with chilled nerves. I didn't dare.

"I think so. If we're careful. I'm anxious to get to know our daughters. They should be back by now . . ."

Trouble! Scrap screamed. He burst into view bright red and flapping his wings double time.

The doorbell rang.

"Who, Scrap?"

Not him. That's just Sean. Allie and the girls need you. Now."

"Where are they?" I grabbed a pair of shoes from under the sofa, grateful they were sturdy walking shoes with good traction. I've had to fight in bad shoes before and gotten hurt.

Too far away. Too far to get you there in time. I've messed up the timing as it is. I should have come when I first noticed the bad guys. But no, I waited until Allie and the girls had finished shopping, hoping the gang bangers with demon protection tattoos had gotten bored and went away. But they didn't. They recognized the girls. Allie can't handle them alone. Hell, the police can't handle them alone.

Apparently, Gollum answered the door, keeping one eye on me, the other on my date.

"What's going on, Tess?" Sean asked. He offered me an arm for balance as I hopped around trying to put on the shoes and get out the door at the same time.

"You wanted to know about my life, Sean? You just got dumped into the middle of it. Scrap, can we go through the chat room?" Without me knowing quite how, Gollum had herded me and Sean out the door and down the steps. He had the keys to his car out and the lock button working remotely as I hit the pavement running.

Um, this could be tricky.

"Scrap, you've got to take me to Allie and the girls, now." I had one foot inside Gollum's new hybrid SUV. A red one, I noted. Sean's BMW was parked right beside it.

My heart plummeted into my stomach. "We'll never get there in one piece if you drive," I sighed to Gollum.

"What do you mean? I'm a good driver. I've never had an accident."

"Luck. Sheer luck."

"We can take my car," Sean offered.

Gotcha, hang onto your hats.

The world tilted slightly right. Light shifted slightly left. A swirl of mind numbing brightness, endless unbroken light and . . .

I stumbled out of the SUV into a different parking lot. Light and reality snapped back into normal alignment. I held my right hand out for Scrap. Brilliant vermilion spread from his wing tips to his core. He stretched into impossible lengths and thinness.

I clamped both hands around the center of the shaft he'd become and twirled. He used the centrifugal force to curve his ears into a quarter moon sickle. At the same time his legs and tail arched into a mirror twin blade.

While he did his thing, sharpening on the inside curve, extruding tines on the outside, I scouted the battle zone.

Allie planted her left foot in the throat of a dark-skinned youth nearly as tall as she. At the same time her right fist connected with the jaw of a shorter blond boy.

What did she need me for?

The six others who ringed her. As I watched they all shook switchblades, chains, and guns out of their sleeves.

She pulled her gun from its holster.

Chapter 26

Oregon is the only state where the term "Civil War" refers to a game involving Beavers (Oregon State University), Ducks (University of Oregon), four quarters, and a football.

ONE SHOT REVERBERATED around the parking lot. Allie shot into the air, a deliberate miss and a warning.

"That the best you can do, lady?" one of the gang bangers sneered. He swung his barbed chain insolently.

"Go, Tess. Go! I've got the girls," Gollum shouted behind me.

"How'd he get here?"

The magic of the chat room. Your boyfriends got caught up in the swirl, Scrap replied. He sounded tired already and he hadn't even tasted blood.

Without thinking further than taking down the guy with the lethal chain, I launched forward in a flying leap.

I landed less than gracefully in the middle of a gang of three. We all went down like I'd bowled a strike.

But I was on top.

I came up swinging the blade, right, left, low, high. Twist and spin, catch a swinging chain on the tines. Wind them tight and pull. The dark-haired boy didn't want to let go.

I twisted out of reach as I spun him past me, face first into the blacktop. Another raised his gun, a stubby little thing with a huge magazine of bullets.

Oops.

Allie chopped his wrist with the grip of her weapon. He dropped it. Then she grabbed and twisted his arm up behind him.

She was fully occupied holding his writhing body, keeping him out of the action. Why had she even bothered with her gun?

Another boy with a knife slid up behind her. He caught my blade between the shoulders. He slumped to the ground in a pool of his own blood.

The tattoo on his wrist pulsed red with black undertones.

"That important?" I asked as I removed the tines of the Celestial Blade from his rib cage.

Demon protection, Scrap gasped. Or was that a slurp as he tasted the blood. He'd earn a wart or two from this encounter.

The boy writhed. His wound closed. The bleeding stopped. He dragged himself to his knees sluggishly. He stalled there waiting to regain enough strength to heave himself upward. He waited a long time.

"But they aren't demons themselves. Therefore, they are vulnerable!" I whacked another gang member behind the knees and kicked the butt of the crouching boy. He hit the pavement nose first.

Blood spurted.

He screamed.

The boys paused.

We were no longer easy prey.

As I watched them watch me, a blackberry vine full of nasty little thorns snaked out of nowhere and wound around the ankles of the boy farthest back in the pack. Then it tightened.

His yowl as he tumbled to the ground sent the rest of them scurrying for cover. Any cover.

But there wasn't any in the nearly deserted parking lot. Flashing blue and red lights followed by wailing sirens caught them at the corner.

Six officers bailed out, weapons drawn, menace filling their posture.

"I think there's Chinese food in Sean's car. Full of MSG," I whispered to Scrap. "Disappear and gorge yourself."

He left the bags inside your front door.

In an eye blink, my weapon collapsed in on itself and faded to invisibility, leaving me to answer a lot of questions from authorities who didn't understand the true meaning of demons on the loose.

Goddess, how my leg hurt from the ill-planned leap into the fray. No more adrenaline. No more strength.

I sank to the curb, head propped on my hands, and waited.

"Tess," Gollum gently prodded me with his voice.

"Hm?" I looked up through a fog of weariness. The activity around me didn't keep my attention. For such a short fight, I shouldn't be this tired.

My leg ached terribly. I don't think I could stand up if I tried.

Gollum came down to my level, sitting beside me, stretching his long legs straight out in front of him. "I've got to take the girls home. They've talked to the police, all innocence, and told them, 'These guys just attacked us out of nowhere, tried to grab our packages.' That's all they know and they are sticking to it. I think they've done this before."

"Oh."

"I'm taking our daughters back to your place. I'll show them how to lock the door and dead bolt it, how to call you in an emergency. Then I have to get back to Julia. Sean and Allie are still here. They'll see you get home."

"Okay." I roused a little. The reminder of his *wife* felt like a slap in the face. "Thank you, Gollum. Thanks for everything." I dismissed him. I had to or I'd begin the self-destructive grief all over again.

"You too." He kissed the top of my head, squeezed my shoulders, and stood up.

I wrapped my arms around myself, instantly chilled by his absence. "Slow down and drive careful," I called after him.

"Of course. I have precious cargo."

He passed beyond my focus distance.

Allie replaced him on the curb beside me. "How do you want to explain the knife wounds?" she asked very quietly.

"They had knives. I took one away from them and used

it to defend my daughters and their godmother?" I flashed her a grin, a little energy and enthusiasm banishing the fog.

"Is that how we're playing this?"

"Got the birth certificates to prove it."

"Okay." She sounded skeptical.

And then a policeman with a notebook in hand was in front of us, looming and trying to intimidate us both.

Allie flashed him her ID—her resignation from the force wasn't official for another two weeks—and stood up. Cop to cop. Cut us some slack as a professional courtesy.

"Those gang tattoos are new. You seen them back east?" the officer asked her when he'd finished taking our statements.

"They consider themselves demon protected," I piped up. "I don't know an official name for them."

"Multiracial and multi ethnic. Unusual." The cop shook his head. "They got enough marijuana on them and in their vehicle to put them away for a long time without the added charges of assault and battery, attempted robbery, and possession of illegal weapons." He shook his head and made a few more notes.

"I've never seen any of these guys before. I thought I knew all the gangs in the area. You hurt them bad. Maybe they'll think twice about staking out territory in this town." He wandered off to supervise the loading of two lightly injured and one nearly dead into appropriate vehicles. The uninjured had been bundled off to jail sometime ago.

I noticed Sean handling IVs for the guy who fell to a blackberry vine and broke his nose.

Once the ambulance doors closed, he joined Allie and me on the curb. "Is this why you end up in my ER so often?" he asked casually.

I had to think a moment.

"Unlikely," Allie snorted.

"Oh?" Sean cocked an eyebrow.

"You saw how she tackled those guys with a weak leg. She's graceful and self-assured. She only gets hurt by mundane things."

"Oh?" This time I questioned the statement. "I didn't feel graceful when I landed on top of the pig pile." My hand massaged my aching calf absently. Sean stripped off his bloody surgical gloves and took over the job. He did a better job.

"The point is, you landed on top and knocked three guys out of the action in one blow," Allie insisted.

"Actually, she's only mostly right," I sighed. "I've been almost self-destructive in the last year, trying to kill my grief with action, getting overtired and careless. But the last time was in pursuit of a demon."

"From what I read in your book, the Celestial Blade only manifests in the presence of a demon or tremendous evil. Which were these gang bangers?" Sean asked. He wadded up the soiled gloves and tossed them into a nearby trash can basketball style. Then he resumed his massage.

"Both. The tats on their wrists didn't originate in this world," I said cautiously.

"That explains some things," he mused.

"Like?"

"Like some victims I've seen in the ER screaming about black tattoos on their attackers that glowed red with the fires of hell."

"The otherworlds are bleeding into this one, more and more. I'm surprised everyone hasn't figured out that demons walk among us on a daily basis," Allie said. "God, I want to go home and have this day be over." She lay back on the sidewalk.

The store had closed and only security lights cast baleful shadows on her face.

"The populace at large is very good at denying the obvious," Sean said. He stood up and offered me a hand. "I think I've still got Chinese food back at your condo. You up for a mundane drive home?"

I laughed. "What? You didn't enjoy a trip through purgatory?" I let him pull me to my feet, bringing me very close to him. Allie got up on her own, dusting off her jeans.

"Is that what you call it?" Sean let his hand linger on my back as he escorted us toward my little hybrid car, the only civilian vehicle left in the parking lot. I leaned into him, just a little. Time to move on. Time to give up on my fantasies of a life with Gollum. He'd always have to go home to take care of his wife.

"Scrap calls it the chat room," Allie added fishing for her

set of keys. "Hey, what happened to all the stuff we bought?" She looked around for signs of plastic bags, full or empty.

"Gollum took them with the girls," I said.

"So, how often do you have to do this?" Sean asked on a smile.

"Not as often as you might think," I hedged. "Depends on who's in town and how aggressive they are." I eyed him cautiously. This could be the beginning of something special or the end before we got started.

"I can see life with you wouldn't be boring."

"Most of the time it is. I hole up in my office for days writing and thinking and researching and thinking."

"Well, I have to say, that after the initial disorientation I had fun. When do we go after the bad guys again? And I really should do a full work-up on the girls so I have a base line if they ever get sick or hurt. And has anyone done an MRI on your brain since you had the imp flu? And . . ."

I shut him up by pulling his face down to my level and planting my mouth firmly on his.

He stilled in surprise, then drew me tight within the circle of his arms. A little thrill curled my toes. His mouth softened on mine, became more mobile.

We deepened the kiss, relishing the tingles and pressure and the joy of beginning something new and wonderful.

Even if I was settling for second best, I'd never let him know that.

Chapter 27

First name of Portland: The Clearing. A convenient stopping place on the river route from Ft. Vancouver to Oregon City.

I SHOULD HANG OUT WITH Blackberry and Salal. They hardly know how to brush their teeth or use the microwave, or anything.

At least their time at High Desert Con taught them the necessity of toilets. Otherwise, I think they'd just go squat behind a bush outside.

It's getting kind of cold and damp for that to be comfortable. I've sworn off cold ever since Mum kicked me out of the freeze-dried garbage dump of the Universe.

I left the Chinese food for Tess when she gets home. MSG works wonders to counter my lactose intolerance, but when I've had a fight and tasted blood, I need mold, mold, mold, and more mold. A little beer and OJ doesn't hurt either.

So, now that I've restored myself with the mold in the air-conditioning unit on the roof of the café down the street, (there is never a lack of mold in the Pacific Northwet) I grab my black and silver boa—evening wear don't ya know—and insert myself on the dash of Gollum's new car. I suppose his rattletrap van had to die sometime, or he needed something classier and more reliable now that he has the infamous Julia to drive around, but it was a glorious source of mold and mildew.

For the first time in like evah, dahling, Gollum drives slowly. He's lost in thought, looking deep inside himself.

What is this? He observes stop signs even when there isn't another car in sight. He stays below the speed limit and uses his turn signals. Not once does he drift out of his lane.

I hope he's not sick.

Just after he crosses the Sellwood Bridge, he pulls off into the parking lot of a convenience store and calls home on his cell phone.

"Sorry I'm late, hon. Hope everything is okay and you're just asleep. You probably took a pill, right? Call me if you get this message before I get home. See you in about fifteen minutes."

Isn't voice mail wonderful?

Now he's worried. He speeds up a bit, but he still drives carefully.

How boring. Maybe my babe is right in moving on. I never thought I'd say that suddenly Sean looks like a better partner for her. At least he can patch her up after she tumbles.

But can he heal her heart?

Blackberry and Salal seemed strangely subdued compared to Sean's manic euphoria. I guessed he'd never witnessed a fight before. Certainly he'd patched up the wounded afterward, but never been close to the chaos and mayhem. He reminded me of a first grader who'd just had the light bulb turn on inside his head when patterns of letters became words became sentences and paragraphs and suddenly made sense.

I let him carry the conversation while keeping an eye on *my* girls.

My daughters. I still couldn't believe I'd pulled off adopting them and getting them out of their father's violent environment. My heart swelled with dozens of emotions every time I contemplated them.

The girls succumbed first to full tummies and the listlessness of adrenaline depletion.

At around midnight, I guided them through showers and teeth brushing and the necessity of wearing pajamas or nightgowns. They got the queen-sized bed in the bedroom.

Then I pulled out the single malt.

We sat on the sofa, Allie and Sean on the ends, me in the

middle pressed up close to Sean with his arm around my shoulders.

I watched Sean as he gently sniffed the heady brew. With eyes closed he took a small sip, rolling it around his mouth. His Adam's apple bobbed as he swallowed and let out a contented sigh. "*Uisge beatha,* whiskey, the water of life. The only English word acknowledged to have come from the Gaelic."

"I could learn to love a man who knows how to appreciate the good stuff," I said and repeated the ritual. Sweet flowers and bitter heat burst upon my tongue and warmed me all the way down to my stomach. Well-being spread outward. Muscles I didn't know had tensed unknotted and relaxed. The fist of God wrapped in velvet. "And I know about the origin of *uisge beatha* and whiskey and English. But I'm holding out for quaff as a derivative of the Gaelic as well."

Allie stared at her glass of amber whiskey. "Never learned to appreciate the hard stuff. And I don't want to argue word origins with you two. You two can share this, I'll settle for wine. Did you leave any of the Riesling?" She set her tumbler on the coffee table and ambled back toward the kitchen.

"I've been thinking it might be a good idea to look for ways to totally separate the girls from their origins," Sean said, keeping his eyes on the magic elixir in his glass.

"I'd just as soon they forget their upbringing," I agreed.

"We could start with changing their names," Allie said plunking down beside me. She gulped half a glass of white wine and laid her head on the sofa back. "I see it in kids adopted out of abusive situations all the time. First thing they ask for is a new name."

"Blackberry and Salal do sound rather like they've been living in a hippie commune," Sean said on a half laugh as he took a bigger sip of scotch.

"My Aunt MoonFeather would give them names like that until they grew into their personalities and they selected something that fit them better." I couldn't remember the rather mundane name my father's sister had rejected when she joined Wicca and took a craft name. I'd seen her dance nude, as light as a feather graced by moonlight on the night of the summer solstice. She had selected her new name appropriately.

Allie giggled as she downed the rest of her drink. "When I think Blackberry, all I can see is a fancy cell phone."

We all laughed at that.

"Blackberry. Cell phone . . ." I played with the sounds of the words. "Phonetia!"

"Good one." Allie and I high-fived.

I took another swallow of scotch. The top of my head felt a little separate from the rest of me. A gale of giggles erupted from my toes, running upward in waves of good feelings. "Kids today seem to have their phones surgically implanted. Texting their friends is like breathing."

"Remove a teen from her phone and she feels like her arm's been cut off. But they rarely phone home," Allie added.

Sean nearly doubled over with laughter. "Phone home. *Phone home!*"

"Huh?"

"Didn't you see the movie *E.T.?*" he asked incredulously.

"E.T. phone home," I replied, my mouth threatening to gape. "Of course, Phonetia and E.T.! That's what we call my girls."

"What does E.T. stand for?" Allie asked, a little more sober than either Sean or I.

"Anything she wants."

Shortly thereafter, I kissed Sean good night and sent him on his way in a cab. We'd all had too much to drink to trust him driving. We'd worry about his car in the morning.

Allie took the sofa, and I stretched out on the cot in the office.

I promised myself this overcrowding would only last a short time. Allie was due to fly back to Cape Cod next week to wind up her duties with the police force and finalize plans for her wedding. Maybe I should just set up a real bed in the office and consolidate the computer desk and bookcases to make room for a dresser. The file cabinet in the closet could go into the dining area.

Or I should make the living and dining area one big office and schoolroom and give the office over to the girls so I could take back my bedroom.

"This could work, Scrap."

Buy you some time until the financial markets improve.

"My, aren't you erudite and succinct. What's the matter?" I looked up from massaging moisturizer into my feet.

I don't like the tattoos on the gang bangers. We don't know who authorized the protection. Takes some big bucks, some sneaky runarounds, or clout with the Powers That Be to put those tats on mundanes. He sat on the desk fading in and out of the monitor.

I shuddered. "Don't remind me of the Powers That Be. I can't imagine anyone voluntarily asking them for favors."

You did.

"Out of desperation." Unconsciously I rubbed my scar. "I needed protection for Dad and Bill. No one else could guarantee it." The scar burned and pulsed, almost as if there was a demon in the room.

There wasn't. It was just nerve memory of the deal I'd made and signed in my own blood. The onyx pen stained with my blood lay buried in the back of the side drawer on the desk.

"Could Donovan have done it?" I asked.

Why would he?

"I don't know. But then I don't truly know why he wants to create a home world for Kajiri demons. I don't understand his obsession with me. I don't understand . . ."

A tentative knock on the closed door almost slid beneath my awareness.

"Come in," I said, almost as hesitant as the knock.

The door crept open a few inches. I saw a single green-brown eye peek in.

"Come in, Blackberry."

"How'd you know it was me?" She pushed open the door another few inches and slid in, closing it behind her.

"You're taller than your sister and Allie's eyes are brown. What do you need? You should be asleep."

"I . . . Are we really supposed to call you 'Mom' now?"

I gulped. Mom. I'd begun to think I'd never have the privilege of hearing another person call me that.

"I'd like that if you are comfortable with it."

"Gollum . . . I mean Dad said we should. It shows respect. What's respect?"

Oh, boy, was I in trouble. I had to start at square one with a teenager. The dictionary definition would probably go over her head.

Tomorrow. Or rather later today. I'd deal with their education in the morning.

"Respect is an attitude of careful listening and going along with their suggestions because you've learned they are usually right. It's treating that person as if you value them."

"Oh." She looked puzzled. Then her eyes brightened. "Oh!"

I patted the place beside me on the cot, urging her to sit, get comfortable; put her in a sharing mood.

She sat slowly, careful not to touch me directly.

"And because I respect you, I'm going to ask your approval for changing your name." Part of me wanted to drape my arm around her shoulders. I needed to respect her need to avoid physical contact. "I'd like to call you Phonetia." I explained about the mobile phone that carried her real name.

"That sounds good. I like that. Can I have one of those phones?" She flashed me a huge smile that nearly melted my heart.

"We'll talk about that when you've earned the responsibility of an expensive phone."

"Oh. What about Salal?"

"We thought E.T. would be a good name. But that's more a joke than a name." I explained the line in the movie.

"I like that. I think she will too. We can think up new words to fit the initials for each occasion."

That sounded like mischief in the making. At least these two troubled girls could find something to laugh about.

"So what can I do for you this late at night?"

"I . . . uh . . . Salal—We should have said something earlier. We know the guys with the tattoos." She hung her head.

"You do?" Did I ever say that I don't believe in coincidences?

"We don't really know them. I mean we've never talked to them. And I don't know if they recognized us, they only ever saw me in the dark when Father sent them to my bed. But they do business with Father . . . with that man . . . with . . ."

Cold invaded my bones.

Phonetia shuddered too. I put my arm around her shoulder and drew her close. A morsel of warm steadiness grew between us.

"I know who you mean. And he is your father, biologically. Let's just call him the dark elf for now. What kind of business?"

"They grow something strange. Fa—the dark elf lets them use certain clearings in our forest, and he blurs the paths so the . . . the law won't find the plants and destroy them."

"Marijuana?"

"I think that's what they call it. It's not native to us. It doesn't belong in our forest. Our duty is to keep the forests healthy. Nonnative invasive plants need to be cut out and burned, not carefully cultivated and protected."

"You are right. Marijuana is a dangerous plant. So is the dark elf. He hails from a different land, a different environment. He's as invasive as the marijuana. But you and E.T. and your brothers are all native. You belong here."

She mulled over the new and frightening idea. But one that might save her sanity.

Last month three hikers on Mt. Jefferson had been shot at and chased mercilessly for days until they found their car and raced away; all for stumbling off the trail into a ten-acre marijuana patch. A SWAT team went in and cleared out the patch. They lost two members to the growers' booby traps. Hidden pits filled with poisoned stakes. Tactics straight out of Vietnam.

Big money came from those marijuana farms.

"What does the dark elf get from the growers in return for land and protection?" I asked.

"I . . . I don't know for sure what Fa . . . the dark elf gains." She looked at her hands.

"Did your father demonize the tattoos?"

"Is that what you call it?"

"I guess. I've never run into it before. Scrap gave me hints. I watched them glow. Not just anyone can do it. He'd have to have help, or permission, or something."

"He never talked to Salal—E.T. and me about his business. He talked to the boys. We only know what we overheard."

"Your brothers got the names of majestic trees. He named you two for lowly vines that need to be curbed and heavily pruned to control them."

"He doesn't respect us."

"No, he doesn't. I think you both have a lot of reasons to respect yourselves though. It's my job to help you do that."

"I don't know that anyone can do that." She stood up and made as if to go—reluctantly.

"I have to try."

"I respect you for the trying."

I knew she wasn't telling me everything. She might respect me, but she didn't trust me yet.

I reached for the phone on the desk. I knew someone who might fill in some of the blank spots. It wasn't too late to call Las Vegas. Lady Lucia kept vampire hours. I owed her a bunch of favors.

She owed me some explanations.

A clap of thunder made us both jump. Lightning right on top of it lit the entire room as bright as noon.

"It's Father!" Phonetia screamed as she dived under the cot. "He's really pissed."

Chapter 28

Stumptown became the nickname for Portland when stumps cleared for dirt roads were painted white after cutting, then leveled with the ground to show obstacles to wheeled traffic.

KABOOM. Lightning hit a transformer. The building shook. Lights flickered and died. The ever-present hum of the refrigerator silenced.

E.T. scooted into the room without knocking. As if sensing her sister's position she joined her under the cot, covering her head with her hands.

A thunderstorm in the middle of the night? In *Portland?* We rarely get more than distant rumbles over the mountains.

A tree cracked. The splintering sounded long and angry, worse than fingernails on a blackboard. Then the thud of a tree branch crashed against the ground.

"Don't hurt me," Phonetia pleaded.

I lay down beside the girls under the cot, pulling them close. "It's okay," I whispered over and over.

We clung together. Their fingers tightened on my arms like vines twining and clinging to a cliffside, desperate to survive in the harsh environment.

Then the wind came up, howling overhead like a frustrated banshee. It competed for dominance with the near continuous thunder and the hail against the roof.

This must be akin to what drove Raquel and JJ to accept shelter from the Nörglein. If the dark elf caused the storm, why didn't he bother putting JJ into a trance and transforming himself to look like Raquel's husband?

Because he'd put all his energy into the storm. He had nothing left for his usual chicanery.

Allie crept in and joined us on the floor all huddled together.

"He can't keep it up for long," I reassured the girls as well as myself. "He's hurt and sick. This has to pass soon."

The next hour felt like an eternity. We trembled as fiercely as the building. More trees fell. Wind and rain lashed the windows as if trying to break them for easy entrance to my home.

And then as quickly as it came, the storm abated. Just like a two-year-old packing up his toys and hiding in his room after a temper tantrum. Of course he had to slam the door on his way out.

One last boom, crash, and flash, followed by a torrent of hail that lasted thirty endless seconds.

"What was that all about?" Allie asked with shaking chin and darting glances. "That one was worthy of Dorothy's trip to Oz."

"I think Father found out where we are," Phonetia said.

"That is one mean bastard," Allie grunted. "Glad we got you away from his clutches when we did."

"Did one of the gang bangers with a demon tat get away to inform him?" I asked. I crawled to my knees and dusted off my jeans. I really needed to clean in here.

Allie stared through the window, looking backward through her memory. Her fingers flexed as she counted bodies. "Tall, blond guy, maybe twenty-four, gold chains on his neck, one with a pendant to match his tattoo." She looked up again almost as if emerging from a trance.

"He . . . he's the leader of Father's minions," E.T. said quietly.

"And I bet he reported everything to the dark elf. He might have followed us home," I sighed. "You girls okay to go back to bed by yourselves? I need to make some phone calls and do some serious thinking."

"I . . . I guess," Phonetia mumbled.

"I'll tuck you in and stay with you till you fall asleep," Allie offered. "Has Tess talked to you about your new names?"

She herded them out of the office like an overprotective border collie.

I reached for my cell phone. The power surge had wiped out the landline.

I'd just drifted off to sleep when the phone rang.

I flopped awake, not sure where I was, what was happening, why my ears hurt.

The phone, babe. Answer the phone, Scrap reminded me.

His voice inside my head rattled the right synapses. I plucked the phone off the cradle, dropped it, fumbled it up again, and mumbled something into it upside down.

Lights blazed around me. The digital clock on the desk blinked red numerals showing a few minutes after twelve. The power had come back on and the phone lines had been restored only moments ago.

Then I fully opened my eyes and glimpsed the time on my cell phone beside the landline. Four in the damn morning. Who in the hell had the audacity to call now?

My heart went into overdrive. *Dad!* Something was wrong with my father.

"I was thinking about calling you. Then I returned from a party and found your voice mail," Lady Lucia chuckled. "Is this a bad time, *cara mia*?"

I flipped the phone around, the better to hear her phony Italian accent.

"I have to be up in two hours and I just got to sleep."

"Sleep is overrated. We can sleep when we are dead."

"Does that mean I get to kill you and all the Kajiri demons who cross my path?" I wasn't feeling friendly at the moment.

Lucia laughed loudly. I could just picture her throwing back her head, tossing her long blonde—artificial—tresses into the desert wind, and exposing her vulnerable neck.

A challenge.

Then I had to remind myself, she never allowed herself to become vulnerable, even if she let you think she was.

"So what were you going to call me about?" I asked on a yawn.

"I will be in Portland at the end of next month, *cara*, we must talk."

"Fine. We can meet for coffee at high noon at Waterfront Park." Lady Lucia could tolerate sunlight as well as any human, even though it didn't suit the persona she projected to intimidate friends and enemies alike.

She laughed again. This time when she spoke, she ditched the thick Italian accent. Only a hint of her southern French Alpine origins leaked through now. "Why did you call, Tess? You usually avoid me unless you are in dire trouble."

"Thank you once again for helping clean up the mess of my mother's murder," I said graciously.

"And . . .?"

"And I've just adopted two daughters of a Nörglein elf. I thought you might have some pointers . . ."

"Nörglein? Did you say Nörglein? Impossible. They are extinct. I killed the last of them myself." She sounded affronted. "The nasty elf tried to coerce me into exchanging sex for safe passage through my own forest."

"One got away." Now I wanted to laugh.

"Impossible."

"Explain that to the nasty bugger, hiding in *my* forest, who preys on women hikers or binds males while he seduces their wives in their forms."

"Don't worry about him. They breed in cycles. One child, maybe two. Then none again for a hundred years. That way people forget about him and don't hunt him down." She suppressed a yawn.

"Not this guy. We're up to six, maybe seven rapes in the last year. I've got the two girls from his previous rampage about fifty years ago. They look to be twelve and fourteen."

"Impossible." She didn't sound so sure. "Nörglein only sire sons. And if these girls look like teenagers then they are teenagers. The longevity gene doesn't kick in for half-breeds until after puberty."

"But . . . but there are no reports at all of lost hikers in Forest Park ten to fifteen years ago. If five hikers got lost in the same area in a three year period, someone would have noted it."

"They might have noted it, but did they report it? Hm? Listen, *cara*, this news troubles me greatly. Your elf's genes are breaking down. He should have one son in his care. No daughters. Only one son. You say he is raising five teens and siring half a dozen more? Something is terribly wrong. I will take the next available flight. I'll call from the airport when I get in. *Ciao.*"

She hung up without further explanation.

I had a feeling I should alert someone of her coming. Like Donovan. But I wasn't speaking to him at the moment. Maybe Gollum. No. Not yet. I needed time away from him. Time to forget how much I loved him so that I could move on with Sean.

A wicked chuckle erupted from deep inside. Sean would love to meet a vampire. Even if she was a fake.

Better dig out the hair comb, Scrap said. He sat on the edge of the desk, idly swinging his bandy legs and fluttering his wings. *You want to watch Lucy's aura when she arrives.*

"I hate wearing the thing. It turns my hair brittle and gives me a headache."

Necessary, dahling. Hey, did you notice my new warts? Two of them on my chestie. Makes me look real macho, don't ya think?

The phone rang again.

"Tess, one more thing," Lady Lucia said without preamble. "I've heard rumors of a crystal ball of pure beryllium surfacing. A special crystal ball with power. If you find it, do not under any circumstances let the elf get his hands on it."

"Why?" I asked suspiciously. I looked to Scrap to see if he could enlighten me.

The ball is safe, dahling. Believe me. Short-gnarled-and-mossy can't get it.

"Later. *Ciao.*" She hung up on me again.

"I guess if you're the vampire crime boss of Las Vegas you don't have to exercise manners."

I missed my dawn appointment with the sun on my balcony. But then so did Allie and the girls. I saluted the morning light, fresh and clean after the storm, halfheartedly with a wave of my coffee cup as I went about finding breakfast stuff.

Allie rolled over on the sofa and grumbled something about too much noise.

Would the girls eat cereal? Or did they prefer eggs and

hash browns? What about pancakes and waffles? If they didn't get up soon and give me some ideas we were all going to get toasted peanut butter and jelly.

My alarm over my dad made me wonder if I should call him. No, he'd be worried about me if I called outside my Monday morning routine.

A squeak from the bedroom roused my curiosity.

"Would you girls shut up and go to sleep!" Allie yelled. "All night they've been grunting and moaning. All night long." She pulled her pillow over her head.

The squeak came again. It sounded like tree limbs sawing against each other in a high wind.

"That's not teenage girls being brats!" I dashed down the hall to the bedroom. Why hadn't I heard this earlier?

"What?" Allie asked. She came up behind me, both hands wrapped around the grip of her revolver. Weapon carefully at her side.

"Phonetia? E.T?" I asked as I tapped on the door.

The muffled squeak came again, this time I caught a hint of desperation behind it.

"Scrap, what's happening?"

Heck if I know. The other side of the door, it doesn't like . . . exist, he slurred. Then he hiccuped.

The fine hairs along my spine stood on end and my scar pulsed. Something was definitely wrong.

"If I go charging in there will I step into another dimension?" Like the Nörglein home world?

Unknown. If this is elf guy's work, he shouldn't be able to hide from me. Not unless . . . not unless . . . Back in a moment, babe, I'm gonna check on the crystal ball. He flew off in a drunken swoop.

"What did he say?" Allie's question masked the pop of displaced air as Scrap went elsewhere.

"Proceed with extreme caution. And put that thing down before you shoot someone with it. I don't think the gun will help against a forest elf. Otherworldly hide is impervious to bullets."

Allie responded by raising the gun and aiming it over my shoulder. "Open the door very slowly," she whispered. "If I need to shoot, you hit the floor."

"Okay." I drew out the word into about five uneasy syllables.

I turned the doorknob slowly. It moved easily, unlatched. A push from one finger opened it. The hinges creaked like the sound effects of a haunted house.

Different from the weak sounds coming from within the room.

Okay. Now I knew something strange was going down. My faucets didn't drip, my drawers didn't stick, and my hinges definitely didn't squeak. I made sure of that during the long hours of writer's block, insomnia, and depression over the last year.

Thick, Stygian blackness greeted me. The air felt so gelatinous and damp I could almost push it aside. It smelled of damp earth, fecund with growing things. A sharp chill redolent of fir needles and holly berries caressed my face.

Let's explore. Scrap dove back into this reality. *Whee! This is better than Disneyland!* he chortled as he thrust the magical comb into my hair. *Come on, Tessie, nothing to fear in here. It's all just a big blank nothingness filled with worms and bats. Oops, not supposed to talk about bats around you. Sorry, dahling, but one of them is just so cute and he's playing coy with his wings. What a flirt.*

"Scrap, have you been drinking?" I planted my feet firm and solid, like a deep-rooted oak.

Drunk on life, babe.

"Imp bane," I snarled. We'd run into that nasty trick before. Seems that when mistletoe, ivy, and holly are knotted together in an arcane but very specific pattern, it blocks imps' senses and prevents them from transforming into Celestial Blades.

No wonder I hadn't known what went on in this room. With Scrap blocked, so was I.

But now that I wore the comb, I caught three separate heat signatures. One was shifting about restlessly; the other two were still and recumbent.

Gathering my courage, I thrust my hand into the inky blackness and found the light switch in the usual place to the right of the door. One flip and the room sprang to light with too vivid colors and too sharp definition to each object. I saw auras everywhere; but none so vivid as around my daughters.

My girls lay on the bed, stripped to their bark and bound hand and foot with their own pajamas.

Standing over them, wearing his traditional ensemble of green coat, buff breeches, and a green tricorn hat, a thorned whip in his hand, eyes glowing demon embers, stood their father, the last of the Nörglein elves.

He must have crept in through the French doors during the storm and hidden until we all slept.

"About time you showed up, girlie. I thought you were dead the way you clung to sleep. Now you'll learn what happens to those who steal my property."

He turned and flicked the whip into my face.

Chapter 29

The James G. Blaine Society favors blocking Oregon roads at the border and setting up immigration and customs patrols.

FIZZY, FUZZY, WHIZZY. My brain is too big for my head-zee and doesn't want to do anything but curl up and pluck slub-zees off of sweaters.

No, that doesn't scan. Only half rhymes.

Something strange going down. Down, down, down I plunge.

Oops, didn't mean to kiss the floor. What's this? Pretty knots of lacy vines. Holly, mistletoe, and ivy. What a lovely song they make. I could sing of them all night. Sing to them too.

But they don't belong in my world. Something tugs at me. Hard. Pulling me back from my delightful, lazy musings.

Don't wanna go back.

Gotta go back.

A slice of pain to my brain.

Acid boils in my stomach, followed by burning anger.

The shroud of fog lightens around my mind.

Holly, Mistletoe, and Ivy.

Mistletoe, Ivy, Holly.

Knots and knots. Twists of lacey woven green. A decidedly Italian flavor to the design.

A jolt of knowledge. The Nörglein invented that spell to make imps impotent. He and his kind have been using it for centuries to keep us at bane. Oops, at bay. Bay. Bay.

Well into the bay goes the Imp bane. Gain, main, disdain, mundane.

Not exactly the bay, but the river. Sliver, quiver, dither, Indian giver.

I grab the tendrils and pop out. Almost lose them in the chat room. Can't do that. Might trap the unwary imp. . . .

A torrent of giggles bubble out of me. There are more than a few uppity imps I'd like to trap. Starting with fifty of my siblings, a few old guys at the Citadel, and Mum.

Much as I'd like to do that, I need clear passage through the chat room whenever I want.

So blip. Pop back into reality flapping my wings like mad and drop the noxious bundles into the muddy, surging water. The currents grab them, dunk them, and whisk them away over the horizon. All that rain the dark elf spat at us last night strengthened the currents and gave them speed. Speed to separate me from my nemesis.

Now back to my babe and her elf of a dilemma.

The gun exploded in my ear. Echoing, stabbing. Hurting.

I dropped face first to the floor.

I heard the shots again and again. One shot? Or had my brain replayed it?

The thorn whip lashed my back.

I curled into a fetal ball, protecting my vulnerable neck with my hands. With a second lash I yelled in pain and outrage. I couldn't hear my own screams.

But I heard Scrap howling like a coyote under a full moon.

Crazy as a loon with all that imp bane around. I was on my own.

Another lash. I inhaled sharply.

"Stand up, lowly woman. Take your punishment as you deserve," the elf sneered. He sounded like a bad actor playing a mob boss.

Another shot.

Allie landed beside me. "Ricocheted right off him," she gasped, bewildered.

"Punishment!" I screamed at the Nörglein as I rolled closer to the bed. "Punishment? I'll show you punishment."

I grabbed a rapier from its hiding place in the bed skirt, unsheathed it in one long motion as I stood and lunged.

"Missed," he chortled. "What I would expect from a woman. You shouldn't be allowed to play with weapons you don't understand. There used to be laws that kept women in their place."

Another lunge. My aim followed true. I pushed the point deeper into his arm. The same arm I'd slashed with the Celestial Blade. The same arm that seeped black sap through the green sleeve of his short coat.

The blade quivered in my hand. A tiny jolt of electricity jumped from the wound to my arm. I pulled back and struck again, slapping the dull side of the blade across his head, taking his cap off.

"My hat!" he screamed like I'd run him through. "You can't take my hat!"

Scrap swooped in and snatched the green wool felt with his hind claws as he circled the room.

Not a tilt or waver in his flight.

"King Scazzy of the Orculli trolls had a hat too. All his honor and power came from the hat. Is that true for you too?"

This guy was about six times the size of the garden gnome with teeth. Still, they hailed from a similar region and were classed together in the reference book.

Scrap burped acid. A few drops dribbled onto the bright green fabric. They sizzled and burned. Acrid smoke rose from the half dozen holes, each the size of a dime.

"My hat!" the dark elf screamed again.

Then Scrap popped out again. Hat in hand. Or paws. Claws anyway.

"That's what you get for underestimating modern women. You and your kind need to be made extinct," I yelled at him, lunging for another thrust into his wound.

"Scrap, blade now!"

He popped back in, without the hat, and landed on my hand, bright red and stretching. He bared his teeth—six rows of thirty-six razor sharp points—and hissed maliciously even as he curved.

The troll shielded his face with his hands, howling in pain. He turned and dove out through the French doors, spreading shattered glass and splintered framing behind him.

I dashed to follow. He tucked and rolled, hitting the one small patch of green between me and the river. He disappeared into a cluster of juniper tams.

Imp spit. An antibiotic against demon tags for my babe, deadly poison for trolls, elves, gnomes, and demons, Scrap grinned and paled, as he shrank back to normal translucence.

"If you'd kept your mouth shut, I could have killed him right here and now," I complained.

"Do you truly want the girls to have to watch you execute their father?" Allie returned.

I turned my attention back to Phonetia and E.T. They stared at me, eyes wide with horror, mouths and limbs still bound with magic.

"If I kill the little bastard, will his magic dissolve?" I asked Gollum on the phone around noon. He'd been in class and faculty meetings with his phone turned off until then.

I'd called him five times just to hear him on the voice mail.

"Unknown," Gollum replied.

I could almost see him pinching the bridge of his nose beneath his glasses.

While I waited for him to call me back we'd untied the girls and covered them with a sheet and a blanket. I'd already filed police and insurance reports about a break in and potential burglar/rapist. We made the noon news. If short, gnarly, and green showed his face in the neighborhood without shape-changing, he was dog meat.

A glazier and carpenter had come to replace the shattered French doors.

"Well, do you know a spell that will undo it enough to let the girls talk? They may know something. I'm betting they watched the beast work the spell on many of his victims."

"I'll call MoonFeather. We'll come up with something."

My cell phone rang beside me. I checked the caller ID.

"Call me when you know something. I've got to go. Lady Lucia may have a few tricks up her sleeve."

"Tess, wait," Gollum said anxiously. "Are you sure you want to involve her?"

"Too late. She's already in town and involved." I hung up on him, more than just a little satisfied that for once I ended the communication.

At the same time I missed him so much my gut ached.

"*Pronto*," I answered the cell half a ring before it went to voice mail.

"Ah, *cara mia*, you learn a little Italian," Lucia's rich tones filled the airwaves. The silence in the background did not indicate airport busyness.

"That about exhausts my vocabulary," I admitted grudgingly. "Have you left Vegas yet?"

"I am in Portland, *cara*. I have checked in at the Freemont." She mentioned the exclusive private hotel downtown.

"Good. How fast can you get here?"

"What has happened?" she asked. I heard soft rustling in the background indicating she moved around the room, possibly collecting coat and purse.

I told her this morning's adventures.

"Have the children eaten anything?" she asked most anxiously.

"They sipped a little chicken bullion from a spoon. Not much." I started to pace, my own anxiety increasing as I talked.

"Continue trying. They need the salt and liquid. Give me directions. I do not trust Internet maps. I shall hire a vehicle and driver. Servants do not always know the best shortcuts if they can earn more by delays."

My favorite vampire might be over two hundred years old and enamored of Goth trappings and spooky candle holders made to look like skulls, but she embraced modern technology.

About twenty minutes later, as I was dribbling more salty broth into E.T., Allie ushered Lady Lucia into the room.

Much to my amazement Lucia carried a tiny girl, less than a year old, sucking her thumb. The little one looked up at me with wide chocolate-colored eyes. Her dark hair curled nicely around her shapely face. She grinned at me around the precious thumb, revealing her new front teeth.

"Um . . ."

"Tess, this is Sophia," Lucia said, smiling fondly at her child. She looked tired and a bit . . . frazzled. Her usually immaculate blonde hair needed a touch-up around the roots—should have been done a month ago—her tidy business suit had developed creases and lost its crispness.

"Nice to meet you, Sophia." I held out my fingers for her to grasp. She did so with her damp hand. Then shyly hid her face in her mother's shoulder.

Half a heartbeat later, she turned back toward me, holding out her arms, begging for me to hold her.

I did so, cradling her weight against my chest, letting her fill a bit of the emptiness from knowing I'd never have a baby of my own.

Sophia touched my lips and nose with exploratory fingers. Then she tucked her thumb back into her mouth and settled her head against my shoulder.

"She is tired and in need of a nap. Travel does not agree with the very young," Lucia said, caressing the child's curls.

"I'll put her on the cot in my office," I said, moving toward the door.

"I usually put her to bed myself," Lucia sighed. "The one task I do not trust to a nanny. When I can keep a nanny more than a few days."

"You work too hard at scaring the wits out of them."

"Perhaps."

Moments later we returned to the big bedroom. Sophia had slept instantly on my shoulder and not whimpered when we transferred her to a new bed. I wondered if Lucia had used some kind of demon magic on her to gain such easy compliance.

Lucia stared maliciously at the glazier. She bared her teeth like he would make a tasty meal. He ignored her as he caulked and sealed each piece of glass. "See weirder on the streets downtown every day," he muttered.

"I suppose he must stay until he finishes." Again, with the heavy sigh, as if she wearied of the world. Or had being a mother drained her of her usual vitality? "Perhaps you and I should retire to the kitchen. I must gather supplies."

"I'll stay with the girls," Allie sat in the chair I had just vacated. She took up the task of spoon-feeding E.T.

Phonetia had spat out the last tablespoonful of life-giving liquid I'd tried giving her.

"If she doesn't take something soon, I'm calling Sean."

Lucia raised her left eyebrow in query.

"My boyfriend. He's a doctor and he figured out our . . . business without me telling him."

"Useful." Without another word, Lucia led me through my own apartment, down the hall past the guest bath and office, to my galley kitchen that overlooked the dinning area and sunken living room. She directed me to the tall stool at the counter while she rummaged through my cupboards and fridge.

One by one, she placed her treasures on the counter before me. A bottle of mixed herbs, a tiny canister of expensive saffron, red wine, cups, bowls, matches, votive candles.

"You didn't tell me about the baby," I tossed out a conversational gambit.

"I told no one. Especially not the father." She continued her search without looking at me.

"Who is?"

"Need you ask?" She finally gave me a direct and searing look. The arrogant and ruthless vampire returned to her posture.

"Donovan?" I coughed. Another black mark against him on my mental chalkboard.

"Yes. I should have known better than to trust someone raised by the Damiri not to use a condom. In that, I believe, you were smarter than I am."

"Yes." What else could I say? Except "I think he's in town. If he finds out about Sophia, I would not put it past him to kidnap her."

"Which is why I listed *my* assistant as the father on the birth certificate. Which brings us back to your two girls. I presume you have taken care of the legalities?"

"Yes. I have copies of the birth certificates. Duplicates of the ones on file in my home township on Cape Cod."

"Good. Get them listed on your health insurance today. You may need it."

"You don't sound hopeful for their recovery."

"They will recover. Eventually. But the longer they remain under the influence of the spell, the harder they will find it to reclaim their humanity. I noticed the older girl begins to show signs of animosity."

"Her name was Blackberry. She is . . . um . . . prickly in the best of circumstances. But she does try. We call her Phonetia now."

"Hm. Well, I'll try." She surveyed her array of ingredients. "Send your friend out for sweet onions, pine nuts—Italian if possible—and extra virgin olive oil, first pressing."

"That's going to be expensive." The primary reason I didn't stock the last two gourmet items.

"I will pay. But then, you will pay me back as well."

"I already owe you more favors than I can count."

"When this business is finished, you will do me one last favor and then I will be in your debt forever."

Which meant I was in big trouble if I had to do a favor that huge.

Chapter 30

51.3% of Oregon, 32 million acres, is forest land. One tenth of all US forests.

"MAYBE GOLLUM HAD THE RIGHT IDEA and we should consult MoonFeather," I stalled.

"We don't have time," Lucia said, lighting a candle beneath the newly installed but not cleaned French doors. That was east.

The normal little votive in an art glass cup gave off a heady aroma reminiscent of hot dry air, salty seas, and olive trees. I followed behind Lucia sprinkling the mixed herbs in her wake. She stepped carefully, making her arc to south perfect.

Allie sat on the foot of the bed, her hands on the crossed ankles of my girls. Phonetia began to struggle at the first whiff of burning herbs mixed to provoke a cleansing of magic.

At the south end of the room, Lucia lit another candle. This one smelled of ordinary bayberry, but there was something more beneath it. She'd done something weird to my dollar store finds.

I spread more herbs around the votive. So far she set up a pretty standard ceremonial magic milieu. "MoonFeather would have done much the same," I commented.

"Your aunt would not allow me to delve into the darker side of the magic," Lucia said as she lit west. I caught snow on the wind and musky animal scents from that one.

She really had done something strange to my candles.

"I don't see a pentagram. We should draw one inside the circle before we close it." The five-pointed star inscribed inside a circle was the basis of all ceremonial magic I'd ever read about or participated in.

"Trust me, there is a pentagram." Lucia continued her ritual.

"But don't we need white magic to counter the black of the original spell?" Allie asked. She'd read all the available vampire fiction and had a passing knowledge of magical theory.

Having grown up with a witch for an aunt, and having researched magic for my writing, I too knew a lot about it. That didn't mean I believed it.

Well, sometimes I did.

"For long-term effects you may repeat the spell with white parameters. But we don't have time. We must break the elf's hold on his daughters now, before the sun sets or they will never take human form again.

Startled, I looked more closely at my girls. Sure enough, their skin had taken on a green tinge; their hair had begun to clump into the shape of overlapping leaves.

E.T.'s fingertips and toes sprouted poisonous berries. The digits themselves flattened and spread, taking on a green tinge.

Blackberry, Phonetia no longer, had thorns growing from her pores. Her eyes nearly shot venom at me.

"White magic works by undermining the core of evil, worming itself into every crack and crevice. That takes time. It is more long lasting. But it takes time. Years sometimes. My spell will be quick. And dirty. But it will salvage their souls and give your MoonFeather something to work with."

Lucia hovered over the last candle on the bookcase headboard.

I knew she waited for me to give her permission to complete the circle that would bind all of our energies inside.

"We have Earth in the herbs. We have Air in the incense. We have the Fire in the candles. I presume you will need blood for the Water to complete this."

She nodded.

"We'll use mine," I said with more determination than I'd felt a few moments ago. "I will bind myself to them as if

I were their own mother. I will become a part of them and they of me."

You sure you want to do this, babe? Scrap asked. He'd been strangely silent through the entire process. *No backing out or changing your mind once you start. If they were your biological children you could give them up to foster care if things got too hairy. With this you can't. Not even if you wanted to. Not even if your life depended upon it.*

I had to think about that a moment. One look at my girls reverting to plants, with only a tiny bit of humanity still pulsing through them, reminded me of the face of the Green Man in folklore and in dozens of pagan artifacts. Not truly human, nor truly a creature of the forest. Lost and alone . . . I knew I could not condemn my girls to that kind of wild, half-existence.

"Yes, Scrap, I'm sure. Do it, Lady Lucia. Light the candle and open my vein with the knife I know you have in your pocket."

"Very well. You are wearing the pearls?"

I touched the strand around my neck beneath my sweater as a talisman. "Of course."

"Good. You will need them." She touched her lighter to the wick. The flame flared as it caught. Then it settled to burn cheerily. The scent of fresh cut pine overwhelmed my senses. Not just any pine, but an Italian Stone Pine from the Southern Alps.

The natural form of our nasty Nörglein.

Instantly, a frisson of energy coursed through my veins, burning into my heart. New awareness opened in my brain.

For a moment I was back in the audience chamber of the Powers That Be, signing my name in blood upon the contract that would ensure no demon ever again tried to wrongly manipulate the sacred, neutral space where my father's bed and breakfast sat.

I jerked back into my own body and time with a new piece of knowledge. The crystal ball Scrap had hidden in the armory closet in the basement of Dad's house ate away at the fabric of reality to open a new portal. It would be permanent and independent of the ball.

"Scrap, get the crystal ball out of its hiding place now!" I screamed before the heady aromas of the magic building within the circle made me too dizzy and incoherent to think straight.

A stream of arcane syllables spilled from Lucia's mouth. She made the harsh, glottal sounds flow like a mountain stream struggling to get past sharp cascades. She grabbed my hand in a grip that brooked no defiance or escape.

She slashed her little knife across my palm. Blood welled up before I felt the sting.

Then she produced the missing pentagram. A silver medallion the size of my open palm, a five-pointed star within a circle of entwined leafy vines—perfect for the symbolism in the spell. She smeared my blood on the amulet, then slashed each girl's palm and added her blood to the pentagram.

Sharply, fiercely, she thrust it first onto Phonetia's forehead, then onto E.T.'s.

More ritual words invoked chills and searing heat that coursed through my veins as she smeared our commingled blood on the tops of their heads, brows, mouths, throats, heart, belly, and pubis.

The seven chakra points. When all were opened, they gave a doorway into the soul. Afterimages of the pentagram glowed red where it touched each of the girls.

Then she repeated the ritual on me. The pentagram left a searing impression. Seven times it branded me.

My limbs spasmed, convulsed, and cramped. I felt myself curling in on myself and falling, falling.

My back opened with wounds reminiscent of those inflicted by the blackberry vine whip. Again and again it lashed me through time as it had lashed my girls.

My mind tore open to admit seedlings of alien thoughts. The Nörglein sent barbed hooks into my mind, gleaning information and asserting control. Through him I accessed all the fear and humiliation he heaped upon Phonetia and E.T.

My soul ripped out of my body and fled from him in terror.

Vertigo sent my senses flying in six directions at once. I lost my orientation to up and down, north and south. I fell down, down, down. Twisting around and around in a spiral of doom. Leaking magic behind in a blazing trail so bright anyone could follow me.

All Hallows Eve, the night when the barriers between worlds thinned and became vulnerable. I punched through a whole series of them, desperate to stay ahead of the dark elf. His all-consuming avarice followed me easily.

Down I passed through the shadowy illusion of the condominium complex. Past the basement, into the dirt. Rootlets reached for me, trying to snag in my hair and penetrate my skin, make me a part of the green ecosystem. Worms and burrowing beetles peered at me in curiosity, thought about feasting on what was left of me, changed their minds, and went about their business.

I became the being I feared most for my daughters, a wild thing, so much a part of the forest that I could never be human again. And yet I yearned for human contact. Any trace of language, or the touch of a hand, or shared experiences.

Isolated. Alone.

The water table flowed around me, threatening to drown what breath I had left.

And still I drilled deep, deep, deeper into the Earth, fleeing the elf mind that sought to consume me.

Darkness crowded all my senses. I had nothing to anchor myself to, if I even knew who I was anymore. Then I became aware of the pearls blazing around my neck, lighting a path of sorts for me to follow.

"I can't fight both you, evil Nörglein, and the Earth at the same time," I whispered in my mind. Exhausted, I covered the pearls with my hand and melded with the darkness. I drifted.

Which way was up? Where was home? Who was I?

"I can't do it anymore. I give up."

"Not yet, babe." Scrap reached out a pudgy four-fingered hand and grabbed hold of me. "I'm not ready to give up yet, so you can't. If you die, I die. If I die, you die."

He manifested as tall as me, solid, and reassuring. He spread his wings to enfold me in a protective blanket.

I halted the downward spiral.

"Was this what it was like for you when you were imprisoned inside the Goblin Rock by the Guardians of the Valley of Fire?" I asked him.

"Yeah. But I was alone. You do not have to be."

"What saved you?"

"I thought about what your life would be like without me. Not alive but not dead either, powerless to fight the evil that would target you the moment you became vulnerable. So I found the right answers to save us both."

"Is that what you are doing now?"

"Sorta. Come." He took my hand and led me on a new journey. Like Peter Pan leading Wendy to Neverland.

I felt like we flew sideways. But the Earth gave way to air. Tangled roots became a tapestry of branches. Leaves flowed out of me to bind themselves to barren limbs. Shadowy trees flitted past us. Insubstantial deer and rabbits peered at us curiously then returned to their browsing. And still I shed the greenery, giving it back to the original owners. I caught glimpses of sunlight, heard echoes of birdsong.

None of it real.

Except the pearls lighting our path like a fragile glow stick in the hands of a toddler on Halloween night.

I grew cold. My teeth chattered but I couldn't hear them gnash together. The landscape grew barren, devoid of green things. A frozen wasteland.

"Imp Haven," Scrap whispered, as if afraid of rousing his mum if he spoke too loudly.

More imps joined us—tall ones, short ones, young and old. Rainbows flashed across their magnificent wings. They appeared less substantial than Scrap, more present than the icy lumps of the garbage dump.

They chittered and squealed in high-pitched conversation I couldn't understand. I knew they talked about me, scolded Scrap for bonding with me as an unworthy.

One word of their tirade penetrated my understanding. *Pearls.*

"Thank you for being my friend," I told Scrap. "You're a pain in the ass, but I love you as much as I do any of my family." I couldn't remember what my life had been like before I wandered into the Citadel in a lost ravine on the high desert plateau of the Columbia River Basin in a fever delirium. The fever had opened new pathways in my brain to allow me to see and hear Scrap.

He was just a scrap of an imp, the runt who shouldn't have survived. But he was my imp. My heart filled with love.

She'll do, the other imps whispered among themselves. *Her strengths outweigh her taints. And she is the only human who could control you, Scrap. You are the only imp who can curb her instincts.* They escorted us out of the wasteland, through the shadow forest, and back into . . .

Chapter 31

Indian legend: Crater Lake was formed in a battle between Llao of Below World and Skell of Above World. It is inhabited by dangerous beings and access is forbidden to all by Native Shamans. Americans of European stock discovered it by accident in 1853.

My head jerked upright as if I awoke from a standing doze. I opened my eyes to find little changed in my bedroom. The candlelight near blinded me.

My eyesight adapted gradually, leaving afterimages of forest and candle flame superimposed upon each other.

The only evidence that time had passed was the shortness of the burning wicks and the fading of the heady incense. Twilight filled the room. The sun had set on this strange Halloween day. Trick-or-Treaters would begin their rounds soon. They rarely came here. We had no children in my building.

Except my daughters and Sophia.

My daughters. Truly my daughters now. I knew their pain and fatigue and desire to cleanse their bodies as well as their minds.

My tummy growled in sympathy with their hunger.

Phonetia and E.T. had regained their normal pink, human skin and their hair looked normal. Lank and in need of a shampoo, but normal.

"Tess? Are you okay?" Allie caught me as I swayed.

I nodded, unable to push words around a throat that felt full of dirt. I grabbed at the pearls. They'd taken on the warmth of my skin, remained clean and pure. A lifeline and an anchor to reality.

"Your eyes look funny," Allie persisted.

"Let me see!" Lucia demanded. She grabbed me by the shoulders and swung me to face her.

"*Madre de Dio!*"

"What?" Phonetia asked. She wrapped a blanket around her body as she left the bed to stand beside me. "Oh, my," she gasped, holding one hand in front of her mouth.

"Scrap, why are they so upset?" I figured he'd tell me the truth. He had to. I always knew when he lied. I just didn't know when he lied by omission.

Um, there's something about your ancestry I neglected to tell you.

"Like?"

Sorry, dahling, I need some mold to recover from saving your ass. And I've depleted the basement supply. See you in a bit. Unless you can follow me with your glowing red demon eyes. He popped out.

"What?" I screeched.

"I am so sorry, Tess. So very sorry. I had no idea you would be this sensitive. That All Hallows Eve would thin barriers between the worlds within you as well as between dimensions," Lucia sobbed. "That the pearls would amplify every aspect of the magic, including your ancestry."

"What are you talking about?"

"I had no idea. I am so sorry."

"Calm down and spit it out, lady," Allie commanded.

"First break the circle and let the girls clean up. I need some air." I sagged against Allie's strong body.

"Exit!" Lucia commanded. She cut through the invisible boundary of the magical circle with her ornate penknife. A true athame—ritual knife—if I ever saw one. She practiced magic often enough to have one at hand.

I wondered if I should be frightened. Something about the bowing of her shoulders and the less than crisp clothing eased my disquiet. She wouldn't hurt me.

For some reason she had extended her network of protection to include me.

We sorted out who got the shower first and what the girls should wear.

Their hunger gnawed at me. Even as I silently wondered what I could find in the kitchen to feed us, E.T. spoke quietly with meek solicitation. "Can we get pizza?"

I laughed and sent Allie to order in, making sure I got one without cheese. No sense in upsetting my fragile internal balance with anything resembling dairy.

Sophia awoke and fussily took a bottle from her mother while we settled in the living room with big mugs of hot tea, awaiting food.

I chose to stand on the balcony with the door open, letting the cold air and blustery rain bathe my mind and spirit. I could hear and be heard in the conversation but I had separated myself, indulging in my own spiritual cleansing ritual.

A waning moon rose in the east. Its path was wrong to leave a trail of silver on the river.

"Spill it, Lady Lucia," I ordered, my face to the river. I watched the swift currents intensely, letting part of my inner self merge with the ever constant/ever changing flow. The constant renewal. The cleansing of the Earth.

Lucia sniffed and sobbed as she caressed her daughter's curls, damp from sleep. "When I was a child, I had a great aunt who was considered a witch. We locked her away in a tower of the family chateau."

"Donovan said something about that."

"The Damiri genes are so dilute in the family that they have become recessive. Only one person in every third or fourth generation exhibited the need to feed on blood, shape-change, and wield magic. And that was two hundred years ago. Nearly ten generations have passed since then."

"Except you, you got the long life gene and then discovered you like the taste of blood. Do you change into a bat on the night of the waxing quarter moon?" I replied with enough sarcasm to cut through her hesitance.

She dissolved into a frightening bout of tears.

"Get a hold of yourself," I commanded. "The Lady Lucia I know wheels and deals massive real estate transactions, collects protection money, threatens petty criminals who don't live up to her standards of deceit, entertains in high

Goth vampire style, and never, ever, losses her cool, not even in Las Vegas in high summer."

Lucia straightened and turned her wrathful gaze upon me. "No, I do not shape-change. Unlike those with more recent demon ancestors, I have never felt the urge. I don't even know if I can." She dabbed her eyes on a black silk hankie. In silence she shook out the elegant square—it had a black lace cutout in one corner, probably Chantilly—refolded it carefully and returned it to the breast pocket of her blood-red suit. The long, tight skirt was slit up the left side to mid-thigh.

"So what does this have to do with me? Why did Scrap say my eyes glowed demon red?"

"Well, they did. But they've faded now." Allie tried to reassure me.

"What you do not know, *cara mia*, is that the blacksmith I seduced to gain the magic ring you sent back to Faery was named Noncoiré."

"I know that. He got it from a distant ancestor who was an alchemist, named Noncoiré, unbeliever, because his science experiments made him question the existence of God." I shrugged.

"What I did not tell you or anyone, was that our tryst left me pregnant. The son I bore and pawned off as the child of Count Continelli, was your ancestor, Teresa Louise Noncoiré. You carry an even more dilute demon gene than I do. But you are still sensitive to demon magic. My spell, performed on this day of days, has awakened the Damiri within you."

I have failed my Tess once more. I have lied to her by not telling her everything I know. I do not regret this latest indiscretion. She did not need to know of her relationship to Lady Lucia. She needed to know only that the lady favored her.

Would telling my babe the truth have changed her decisions, tilted her choices, made her less self-destructive as she worked through her grief and loneliness? I cannot know.

Would the knowledge of her demon ancestors have kept her from seeking protection for Dad and Bill from the Powers That Be?

I don't know. Fortunately, the seven beings that sit in judgment over creatures across the Universe were more interested in removing a *Warrior of the Celestial Blade* from proximity to the sacred neutral land of the house on Cape Cod, than on examining her father for traces of demon leanings.

The windows in the chat room that allow me to trace the history of an artifact do not allow me to see the future. Only the Powers That Be can do that. And I'm not certain they can manipulate time threads. They are, after all, merely seven beings chosen from among the sentient and benign races. I do not believe their powers change when they don the cloak of the supreme arbitrators of Universal Justice.

I do not believe they take higher precedence than the deity, whichever name you give to Him/Her.

The sin of cowardice is something I must deal with. I could not bear to disappoint my dahling Tess again. I'm sure it will not be the last time, given who and what I am.

Her pain is my pain. When she hurts because of my misdeeds, my own aches and regrets multiply.

So I wait from the safety of the roof. I listen while Lucy tells Tess the truth.

I cringe as Tess vents her anger against one and all. I wait for her to throw a piece of pizza against the wall.

I watch neighborhood children decked out as fairy princesses and spacemen and skeletons run from door to door gleaning a year's worth of sweet treats. They giggle and shout "Boo." They glory in this night when all too many monsters can creep through the dimensions seeking prey.

But none of the children or the monsters come near our building. I can see an invisible bubble of energy protecting the cement and steel and wood.

My fellow imps have woven this net for Tess. They do not tell me why. I can only hope it comes from respect. She is a true and honorable Warrior of the Celestial Blade, no matter her ancestry. Any one of them would be proud to partner her.

I wait until Lucy has taken her baby back to the hotel.

I watch Tess and Allie help Phonetia and E.T. prepare for bed and watch the news. Their education into modern life outside the forest must begin sometime.

Finally, when all is quiet, I creep back to Tess' side. I do not wake her. Instead, I sit in silence at the top of her pillow, watching through the night, ever alert to any danger. Even if the danger is only the Nörglein trying to invade her dreams.

My fellow imps assure me he cannot penetrate their net now. I almost trust them.

I shall not fail my Warrior again with my sin of cowardice.

Chapter 32

Portland, Oregon, has more bookstores per capita than any other US city.

PHONETIA AND E.T. STARED in incomprehension at the paper in front of them. I'd put six simple arithmetic equations on the page, big numerals, bold addition and subtraction marks.

We sat at a new card table with padded folding chairs. Not ideal, but cheap and easy to move around as we renegotiated space in the condo.

I drowned my self-disgust and anxiety about being part demon in work. My own and schooling my daughters.

Allie was out doing Allie things. She was due to return to Cape Cod the next day and had lots of last minute stuff to do in setting up the purchase of a house she and Steve liked.

"It doesn't mean anything," Phonetia complained. She turned her head away and folded her arms across her chest.

I felt her confusion as a solid barrier between my mind and hers.

E.T. at least tried looking at the squiggling lines upside down.

"They do make sense if you know what to look for," I said patiently. Back to basics. First grade level math. More like kindergarten.

I looked around for inspiration. My gaze lighted upon a

bowl of apples and nuts on the counter. I grabbed it and set it in front of me at the table.

"This is one apple." I held up the red and gold Jonagold before them.

"That's obvious," Phonetia snorted, arms still wrapped around her, physically separating herself from our activities.

"Still obvious if I record it on the paper." I drew a neat one on a clean sheet of paper. Then I put a plus mark beside it. "Just as obvious if I add a second apple." I put the two pieces of fruit at the center of the table and drew a second numeral one on paper. Then I put in the equals sign.

Phonetia reached over, grabbed a pencil awkwardly, and made two randomly angled scratches to the right of the equal sign.

"Right thinking, but we have a more sophisticated method of keeping track. Two apples." I replaced her hash marks with a neat two.

"Totally illogical." Phonetia turned away.

"What if you have seventy-two apples? That's a lot of marks to count. What if I sent you to the store to buy six apples, eight nuts, five oranges, and two carrots? How would you keep track?"

"I'd remember!"

E.T. continued to peer at the problem from all angles, comparing the new sheet to the first one. "There! That's the same." She pointed to the correct equation.

"Let's back up one more step." I started over listing the numerals for one through twenty. I'd just closed the zero on the last one when the doorbell rang.

"Scrap?"

No answer. Where had he taken himself off to while I worked with the girls?

Coming. Can't a guy have one minute of privacy?

"Nope," I replied. "Who's at the door?"

Curiouser and curiouser. He popped in and out. *Go ahead and open it,* he almost chattered in excitement.

"Gollum?" I asked, almost hopeful and dreading the encounter at the same time.

Better. Open it. Open, open, open.

I left the security chain on and opened the door a minimal crack.

"Delivery for Tess Non . . . non . . . crux . . ."

"Noncoiré," I corrected the youngish man in striped overalls with Cooper's emblazoned above the breast pocket. He had curly dark hair and just a hint of a Latino accent.

"What?"

Just open the damn door and see, Scrap commanded.

I sensed the girls gathering at my back, staying close. Fear wafted off them in almost visible waves. Visible to me anyway.

"Delivery of what?" I asked, getting ready to slam the door closed.

"I need a signature before I haul it all up three flights," the man from Cooper's grumbled. He held up a clipboard for me to see a stack of carbonless receipts. He returned the clipboard under his arm before I could read it.

But I'd seen his wrists. No demon tattoos on the inside or outside of either of them.

Cautiously, I opened the door. Scrap flashed several shades of lustful green.

"Don't sign it, Tess," Donovan said, clomping up the stairs. He hefted a long narrow box under each arm.

"Why not?" I wasn't about to sign for anything I hadn't ordered. But if Donovan said no, I needed to say yes just to be perverse.

"Because any gift from Lady Lucia comes with tangled strings attached." He topped the last riser and rebalanced the boxes. The writing on them suggested they might be lamps.

"The only contract in this transaction is between me and Lucia Continelli's bank. Her credit card cleared. That's all I care about," Doreen Cooper countered as she came up behind Donovan. She carried bed pillows with comforters and sheets balanced on top of them.

"Let me see the clipboard." I reached out a hand for it.

The man in coveralls relinquished it reluctantly.

"Start bringing up the rest of it," Doreen ordered him. "I'll handle the paperwork."

"What's this about?" I asked, scanning the delivery order. Two twin beds with mattresses and linens, two nightstands with lamps, two dressers, two student desks with more lamps. One Craftsman-style, round oak table with six matching chairs.

I gasped as I flipped through the pages. No contracts, no subtext.

"Oh, and there's a note," Doreen fumbled with her awkward burden trying to fish in her pocket. Donovan reached in and retrieved an envelope of rich creamy paper, the weight and texture of a wedding invitation. A familiar crowned embossed C on a sticker closed the flap.

I reached for the note with shaking hands.

"My apologies," I read in Lucia's florid hand. "A small token to ease you through the transition." Below that, her signature took up half the page.

"Small token?" I gulped. I knew how much that table and chairs cost. The rest of the stuff on the list doubled the price. At least.

When I tried to stuff the folded note back inside the envelope it caught on something. I pulled out a second piece of paper. A check. One thousand dollars in US currency, also signed in Lucia's elegant calligraphy. On the memo line she'd neatly printed "For clothing."

"We also have orders to help you move your office into the living room, clearing that room for the new furniture," Doreen added. "That's why I brought extra muscle." She nodded toward Donovan.

There was some subtext there I was too stunned to examine closely. Not that I cared. Donovan was no longer a part of my life. And never would be again.

Still . . .

He scowled. "You didn't have to come," he complained.

"Yes, I did. Lady Lucia ordered. I obey. May we come in, Tess?"

"Yes, you may." I stepped back—almost treading on Phonetia's toes—and opened the door wide.

"What's going on here, Tess?" Donovan asked the moment he'd cleared the doorway. He totally ignored Phonetia and E.T. who had retreated to the balcony, barefoot and coatless in the chill November damp. Not unusual for them, I'd learned.

"That is between Lady Lucia and me," I replied. No way was I going to relate our adventures in demonland two days ago.

"You can't trust her, Tess."

"Again, that is between Lady Lucia and myself. None of your concern, Donovan."

"I want it to be my concern," he choked out in a tight whisper. He finally looked at the girls. After a quick but thorough assessment, he checked over his shoulder to see where Doreen was.

More subtext. I had an idea what was going on. After my last rejection he'd gone running to the nearest willing female. A typical pattern for him. But he wasn't banking on that relationship if he could crawl back into my good graces.

Doreen was welcome to him.

"Did you know that Lady Lucia has hired staff and rented office space in her hotel in downtown Portland?" Doreen asked.

"I know she has business in town."

"Doesn't look like she's leaving any time soon," Donovan added. "I need to know why."

"Not necessarily. Her agenda has nothing to do with you or your grand plans." I signed the receipts with page ripping determination and handed the clipboard back to Doreen as she prowled the rooms with a decorator's eye. She ripped off the bottom copy and handed it to me. "At least I don't have to worry about clashing with your décor. I can start from scratch."

"Excuse me?"

"Just planning on how to rearrange things. I suppose the television is necessary with teenagers in the house, but I'd rather not have to work around it."

"Just dump everything. I'll manage to put everything where I want it." Anger began to boil up from my gut.

"I have my orders. Lady Lucia said to set it all right before leaving. You aren't supposed to have to do any extra work."

"That must be one huge favor she owes you," Donovan said. He raised one eyebrow practically begging me to tell him all.

"Fine, do what you want. I expect the work to be complete when I return in one hour. Lock up when you leave. Come on, girls. Shoes and jackets. We have some errands to do. Then you can have a walk in the park."

"Can we pick up litter?" E.T. asked meekly.

Chapter 33

1863: Californians first referred to Oregonians as Webfoot due to nearly incessant rain from November to March.

"WOULD YOU LIKE TO SEE the new SciFi movie *Space Pirates of the Outer Antares III*?" Sean asked when he called me the following morning.

"I'll have to ask Allie if she'll stay with the girls. It's her last night in town."

Go out with your boyfriend, babe. I'll keep an eye on our girls. And I promise to fetch you at the least sign of trouble, Scrap urged.

"Um, have you seen the first two movies?" I asked.

"I rented them last week." He paused to listen to a page in the background. "I admit though that I found the long sequences of special effects a bit boring on the small screen," he said calmly. The page wasn't for him. The next one might be.

"And I bet you were multitasking while they played so when there was a bit of plot and character interaction you missed them."

"There's a plot?"

"Not much of a one, but, yes, there is a plot, and a love triangle," I explained.

"Could have fooled me."

"On the big screen the special effects can be a bit overwhelming. They are indeed the stars of the show."

"So do you want to go see it?" he asked hopefully.

"Of course!"

"Good. I should be free by five. We can grab some burgers and still catch the six-thirty showing."

"Or the seven, or the seven-thirty. It's playing on three different screens at different times at the neighborhood multiplex." We laughed and hung up the phones. I hummed the love theme from the movies as I returned to the girls and the never-ending quest to help them delve into the depths of simple addition.

We skipped the burgers because Sean got delayed in an emergency surgery.

But he bought me popcorn and a giant soda to complete the movie experience and fill my empty tummy with empty calories.

"The first movie was based on a short story. Very loosely based," I whispered as we took seats dead center in the theater. Midweek we had plenty of seating options.

"Have I read the short story?"

"Wouldn't make any difference if you had. Other than the basic premise of a smuggler laying low while piloting an interstellar garbage scow, there's no similarity. In the story the smuggler is old and retired. He's recycling the Universe by moving one society's throwaways to places where scraps are valuable. Making the pilot a younger man—played by the sexiest actor in Hollywood—and having him end up rescuing a gorgeous female diplomat on the run from terrorists are all new."

The lights dimmed and the usual ads and previews blasted across the screen.

"Rumor has it, Holly composed the love theme music, but I haven't seen her name in any of the official credits," I dropped my voice to a whisper.

"By changing the plot I'm guessing the producers left plenty of room for sequels, and prequels," Sean returned to the topic of the movie in hushed tones.

"Hollywood loves sequels ad nauseum. In this case they don't have to worry too much about scripts and actors, though Malcolm Levi is mighty easy on the eye and really can act. These movies launched his career. I saw him in an historical drama as Attila the Hun. He did a great job."

"So Hollywood spends most of their money on special effects. That's what people pay money for at the theater."

"Shush," the couple behind us admonished us.

We slunk down a little lower in our seats, embarrassed.

"Should we have brought the girls and Allie?" Sean asked on a whisper as the movie opened with a long shot of a boxy and beat up spaceship hauling an uglier crate four times its size that leaked bits and pieces of garbage.

"I don't think the girls are up to this yet. They're having enough trouble understanding reality. This kind of fantasy would challenge them more than I want to have to deal with."

"This isn't fantasy, it's science fiction!" the couple behind us insisted.

Sean looked as if he wanted to debate that issue. I touched his arm to quiet him. He turned his hand over to clasp mine.

We sat there like teenagers on a first date.

Sean's cell phone vibrated and buzzed before the opening credits had finished. Not an actual ring, just an audible reminder that he had to answer the damn thing.

A dozen people in widely scattered seats turned and frowned at him.

"I've got to go," Sean groaned. "Stay and watch the movie. Here's cab fare home." He reached for his wallet.

"Just drop me off at home. I've watched enough movies alone." A gaping hole threatened to open in my chest. Loneliness, rejection, depression vied for dominance.

"Okay if I call you when I'm free?" He held my hand as we exited the theater by a back route directly into the parking lot without having to wind through a crowded lobby.

"Sure. I'll be up. Most likely working, after the girls go to bed."

Ten minutes later, I stood on the sidewalk outside my condo in the rain, watching his taillights reflect like blurry demon eyes in the puddles. "Is this what my life will be like if I stay with Sean?" I asked the ether.

Probably, Scrap answered. He alighted on my shoulder and tickled my ear with his boa.

"Will I ever get used to knowing his work is more important than I am?"

No.

"Something to think about anyway."

I spent the rest of my evening surrounded by the girls helping Allie pack. I made popcorn for them and let them drink soda. We giggled and made sure Allie took her bride magazines with her.

She made a point of showing me where she'd hidden the revolver in my walk-in closet since she couldn't take it on the plane and didn't trust it in her luggage.

Eventually, we settled the girls in bed and I curled up on the sofa with the laptop while Allie channel surfed for something more interesting on the TV than travelogues.

"That was fun," I confessed while I waited for the computer to boot up.

"More fun than dinner and a movie with your boyfriend?"

I had to think about that a moment.

"Maybe not. But I've missed girl giggle fests as much as sharing a movie with a friend."

"I think you are fully mended now, Tess. I can leave you with a clear conscience. Except I worry about you alone with the girls."

"We'll manage for the few weeks until you and Steve come back. And we'll fly east for the wedding. I'll make sure you get your full share of godparent time with them."

We laughed together.

Around midnight, my phone rang. I took it in the bedroom. Alone. "Hi, Sean," I said with only a brief glance at the caller ID.

"You're still awake, good. I was afraid I'd wake you."

"I told you I'd be working. I finished another chapter."

"Did you miss me?"

Did I? Sort of, but not nearly as much as I thought I would. "Of course," I lied.

"Tess, I looked up your professor on the Internet," he said. Was that a trace of guilt in his voice?

Every nerve ending in my body froze.

"There are a lot of holes in his profile."

"I know."

"Did you know he's married?"

"Yes. He and Julia have been together since they were children, married quite young and stayed together." Sort of.

"So there's nothing between you?"

"Not anymore."

"I'm guessing he was one of your mistakes, one of the reasons you want to go slowly in our relationship."

I gathered my courage, as if preparing to face a demon in a full fight. "I'm over him."

Liar! Scrap sneered at me from somewhere else.

While Tess and the girls take Allie to the airport the next day, I scoot back to Cape Cod. I've postponed this trip longer than I should. Tess needed me close. Her psyche is fragile. Knowing that Damiri blood flows in her veins, no matter how dilute, preys upon her mind. It eats away at her sense of self. She doubts that she is the proper person to raise our daughters.

That's right, they are my daughters too. And I won't let Tess change her mind about raising them. Not that she could with that magic bond and all.

Tess needs to realign herself with her former life as a Celestial Blade Warrior. When I get back, we'll do a little meditation so that she can connect with her friends at the Citadel.

As I hightail it through the chat room, I note that the Sasquatch are back on duty. They've kinda been quarantined since that little kerfuffle with a rogue portal underneath Donovan's uncompleted casino at Half Moon Lake. Donovan lost a lot of money when we imploded his investment in order to close the portal.

He has recovered financially. I don't know if his agenda was truly damaged or not.

Speaking of which, I wonder if he knows that Tess is Lady Lucia's descendant. If he knows, that would explain his unrelenting pursuit of her as his ideal mate, the mother of the children he craves, the matriarch of his planned homeland for half-breed demons. The connection is another form of power. He thrives on power.

I land on the boundary of the two point five acres Tess used to own. She and her late husband, Dill—Doreen's brother—bought this place for many reasons. The special energies of the place are particularly inviting. Calm, peace, security.

Since time out of mind, this plot of land is where treaties were signed, alliances negotiated. All welcome without prejudice. That invitation is stronger now that Dad and Bill run a

B&B here. Actually, Bill owns it. Dad put it in his name for arcane tax reasons. And Bill has no demon blood in him, dilute or otherwise. Dad has a drop more than Tess but super recessive. He's never even heard of the Warriors of the Celestial Blade.

The land has a Neutral owner once more.

Except . . .

Something eats away at the neutrality. I can peel threads of power out of the air around me. They come from every direction, every dimension. They twine together. They twist into arrows seeking a way of penetrating the boundaries of this dimension. They burrow upward. They spiral downward. Little bits here and there, not so much as to draw attention, unless you are looking for it.

They seek the crystal ball. It is a focus. It draws diverse strands of life together from this place and that.

A whiff of something elusive crosses my nose. I follow that thread as far as I can without going into the chat room.

I have smelled that particular odor before. Sort of imp. Sort of something else. Something older and rotting with insanity. There are cracks in the diamond we sent back to Faery. Energy leaks through those cracks.

The ball is funneling energy into the new dimension from every crack and crevice that no one thinks to shield. Like from the ring. That needs to stop. Who can control it? Who should be the one to claim that new dimension and shape it?

Not the Nörglein, that's for sure.

I creep around to the sloping cellar door against the outside foundation. Overgrown shrubs hang in shielding blankets of intertwined branches over the door. The big oak crowned in mistletoe with a swing slung from the limbs in the yard shadows it. Even if the Powers That Be have set a watchdog here I do not believe they will notice me. Watchdogs get lazy if they are not challenged. The deal Tess signed in blood guarantees that unauthorized personnel cannot come here.

I'm not exactly authorized anymore. Just because I shouldn't come back here doesn't mean I can't. Tess and I lived here almost three years. I know secrets about this place outsiders will never find.

If I pop into the chat room and back inside the cellar, the transition will alert someone. I need to be sneakier.

I flit from shadow to shadow watching and sniffing for any

trace of observers. Ah, there in the oak hangs a bat, upside down with wings only partially wrapped around him. He's awake. No self-respecting bat from Earth would show his face with the sun nearing high noon. It's too small to be a Damiri. Must be someone else. Someone to be avoided.

The presence of a bat almost guarantees that Tess will stay away from here. She hates bats.

I fold the shifting light around me, circling with the wind like a fallen leaf—there are lots of those around. The bat ignores me when I land on the old slats of the door. There's a gap between two of them, just a teensy bit wider than the others.

I squeeze through into the dank and moldy cellar.

Mold! Glorious mold. It permeates the dirt walls; it hides in the corners near the floor. And it tops the discarded jars of jelly Mom put up. Clearly Bill and Dad don't clean down here like they should. They've moved the washer and dryer up to the attached apartment for convenience.

Of course the mild repulsion spell MoonFeather placed on the armory door beneath the stairs would make even the most insensitive feel prickly and uneasy.

The padlock on the door is firmly in place. As it should be. But what's a mere padlock to an imp?

I slide underneath the door into the closet that has been a priest hole, a station on the Underground Railroad, and housed Tess' collection of mundane and not so ordinary blades.

She took all the good stuff with her. Most of it's in mini storage now. But she left a few cheap replica weapons just to make it look like she doesn't have an armory elsewhere.

I stashed the crystal ball here because of the magical shielding MoonFeather added.

And there it is, sharing a shelf with a stiletto. It glows and pulses, more powerful now than before. It pulls energy into itself.

I am afraid of what I will see if I look too deeply into the swirling milky depths of the sphere.

But look I must.

First I light a cigar, one of my favorite black cherry cheroots. Three quick puffs and I feel fortified to face anything.

I expect to find spirals of malicious black sparked with red embers, something stark and barren and evil.

Much to my surprise, I find green and blue with pink and white sparkles. The entire globe is filled with The Essence of Faery. Not just the little patch Tess and I explored.

Faery lost more energy than we could account for while a smarmy producer kept twenty real faeries imprisoned in his casino in Las Vegas. Tess and I rescued the faery dancers. We thought we closed the portal that brought them to this world. Apparently, we didn't seal it tight enough. Faery is still leaking.

All that energy in the new dimension is waiting for a hand or mind to turn it to good or evil, a haven for refugees, or a hiding place for outlaws and renegades.

And the crystal ball is the only portal.

Chapter 34

1844 Oregon law forbade slavery in Oregon. It also forbade free blacks to live in Oregon as well.

UM, TESS, ARE YOU AWAKE? Scrap asked.

I looked up from scrubbing my face. Scrap showed up as a dim outline of wavy lines reflected in the bathroom mirror.

Six very long weeks of sleeping on sofas and cots, I hadn't fully adjusted to having my own room and private bath back.

No word from Lady Lucia since the furniture delivery this morning. Her guilt gift. But Scrap informed me she had hired a new nanny and was running her empire from a second suite in her hotel.

I'd made a little progress assessing what the girls could and could not do academically. A mixed bag of skills. Math went no further than the girls painfully copying the numerals in order. They read the classics beautifully but could not write, not even their own names.

"You know I'm awake, Scrap. What's wrong that you felt you had to ask?"

I fetched the crystal ball, just like you told me.

"I asked you to do that days ago. But we've been a little busy since then. What did you do with it?"

I hid it at the bottom of the river. I can get it back any time you need it.

"Will I need it?"

Probably.

"Why will I need it?"

Bargaining chip with the Powers That Be.

"Huh?"

Then he told me about the power leakage from every corner of the Universe. He held something back. He always did.

"Scrap, I'm not likely to need to get out of my bargain with the Powers That Be."

What about Sean?

"We haven't gotten that far." I wasn't going to jump into a serious relationship after the last three disasters. "How come you aren't pushing me to renew my relationship with Gollum?" My heart sank. If Scrap gave up on us, then there really was no hope.

You know that he truly loves his wife.

"Yes, I know that."

I mean more than just a need to protect his childhood girlfriend.

I sighed. "Yeah, I know. If he only needed to protect her, he'd have set up a trust fund and divorced her. She probably wouldn't know the difference while she was in the asylum."

And now she's out. And he's committed to her, come hell or high water.

"It's probably going to take both of those and then some to separate him from her. If she is Squishy's new lover, I'm not sure even that will separate them. So, do you think Sean and I might make a go of it?"

See how he reacts to the con and filking before you decide.

"Good advice. If he can't survive two days at the local con, he'll miss out on a big part of my life. He won't know what makes me tick, why I need the stimulation and support of that community. He'll already miss big chunks of my life because of his job commitment."

At least he's reading your books, and some recommended classic SF. I peeked. He's gone through almost half your list in a week.

"Is he really reading and enjoying them, or just skimming to please me?"

Scrap gave an impish shrug.

"He calls me and talks about the books as if he has a passing acquaintance. And he is cute. And sexy. And intelligent. But he keeps worse hours at work than I do. It's a little difficult to base a relationship on telephone calls."

Tess, what are we going to do about the new dimension?

"I don't know yet. Do we have to do anything?"

Yeah, I think we do. Donovan would move heaven and earth to have access to a whole new dimension for his Kajiri. The Nörglein is trying to breed an entire new tribe. He'll want a homeland for himself. The Powers That Be have the ability to back up their decrees. They know how to stop the leakage. Some of it is still coming from Faery. The big shots need to make the decision of who gets the place.

"But will they ever make that decision, or just let it ride, holding it as a carrot in front of the applicants to force them into obeying their rules?"

Unknown. You may be right.

"Phonetia suggested the forest elf might need the crystal ball to heal the wound I gave him."

Possible. But think about it. If he can claim the new dimension by right of first possession, he gets to set up the parameters. He can make it so that just stepping into his new home cures him. Like Prince Mikhail needed to go back to Faery to heal after the dynamite explosion in this dimension.

"We can't allow the Nörglein to get near it. I won't let the little bastard live to rape another woman."

What about his sons?

"I'll reserve judgment to see if they are redeemable. Are you sure they can't fish the crystal ball out of the river?"

No.

"Then move it again. Keep it moving so no one with the talent to sense it can hone in on it. What about the freeze-dried garbage dump of the Universe?"

The cold in Mum's front yard might make it inert. But I doubt it. I found the comb and the Celestial Goddess brooch there and they are less powerful than the crystal ball.

"I wish I knew someone I could entrust it to."

Lady Lucia could protect it.

"I said, someone I trust!"

Someone I trust.

I slapped my forehead then pounded it into the desktop. I'm an idiot. And then some.

As Sean so aptly pointed out, part of my depression and self-destructive tendencies stemmed from my isolation. I'd grown too used to having to work on my own, without any guidance from the source of my status as a Warrior of the Celestial Blade.

I needed to reconnect with the Citadel. Deep in a lost ravine between here and there, part of the twilight world that forms a barrier between light and dark, good and evil, I'd stumbled on the place in a fever delirium.

Sister Serena, the physician, had cut the otherworldly infection from my body, leaving sickle shaped scars from my right temple to jaw, beneath each breast, and across my belly. Because the infection originated outside current reality, the scars remained partially outside normal sight as well. Only another Warrior could see them. Or Gollum— I still hadn't figured out how he could. All Warriors bore at least some of those scars.

I needed to reconnect with my origins.

With Scrap perched on the windowsill watching for danger, I propped myself up against the headboard with extra pillows and relaxed.

Meditation requires stillness within.

Not an easy task for one as restless as me. If I'm uncomfortable in an exotic yoga pose I might as well forget even trying.

I went through a ritual of progressive muscle clenches and releases, working from brows to toes, letting the energy flow more readily. Once my body felt as if it melted into the quilted coverlet, I visualized a bright tornado of tension spiraling down from my mind to my feet and out into the world.

My subconscious took over, relaxing me to almost sleep, and brought new energy into me. I visualized it creating a bubble around me. A bubble that would transport my thoughts on a direct line north by northeast to the home of my Sisterhood.

Past midnight. The Sisters slept the sleep of the just. Their routine demanded long hours keeping the Citadel mostly self-sufficient along with harsh training in the military arts. During my year there, I had collapsed in my bed every night, too exhausted to dream.

But someone was always on watch. The Citadel sat atop a portal to a demon world. We could not allow our enemies to breach it while we slept.

"Who?" a weary mind answered my gentle probe.

I flashed an image of myself to the woman on guard. Telepathy isn't so much an actual conversation as a series of images and impressions, it's just easier to transcribe in words.

"Oh, Tess. Greetings."

"Tess, where are you?" Gayla, the senior Sister interrupted. I'd been the one to admit Gayla to an overcrowded Citadel when she burned with the imp flu. I had cut the infection from her.

She had defied the previous leadership to send me backup when I faced an entire horde of rampaging Sasquatch.

We'd been close ever since.

"Home. Why?"

"Ginkgo said that Scrap said we needed to talk. I called just a bit ago. Your line was busy."

"Huh? Scrap, who's on the phone?" I searched my tentative connection to the girls. Both slept soundly in their room.

Line's clear now. Scrap sat a little further forward, alert.

Previously, I'd have defaulted to calling Gayla, since she was obviously awake.

Having sunk deep into meditative mode, I decided to stay there. Less chance of eavesdroppers.

"I have an artifact of power that needs to disappear for a while, but still be accessible to me," I said as I showed an image of the crystal ball as I'd last seen it, resting in my hand, inviting me to gaze deeply into the swirls of milky minerals, losing myself in the power and the other worlds it tapped.

"Wow! You aren't kidding, that's an artifact of power. I'd give up my claim on the Goddess Brooch for that."

"I claim both as gifts of fate!"

Me, territorial? Just look at how long it took me to come to the practical solution of giving up my office.

"Acknowledged," Gayla said formally. "Where should I put it?"

"At the bottom of the midden. I don't care, just so long

as it doesn't get near the portal. It might totally dissolve the barriers."

"Agreed. Have Scrap drop it off to me and me only. There are a few malcontents—overachievers actually—we've recruited recently. They want to storm the portal and slay anything they can find on the other side."

"Are they candidates to go rogue?" Technically, I was rogue since I fought the forces of evil on the outside. We used to be rare. With shifting portals, changing power dynamics, and Donovan's half-breeds agitating for a home world, we needed more people on the outside than in the past six centuries.

I wondered if the crystal ball had something to do with these changing times.

It needed to go to someone powerful enough to control it. Not yet.

"Not yet," Gayla echoed my thoughts. "I don't trust these new Warriors on their own. They'd go looking for trouble without backup."

"Been there, done that." We both chuckled.

"You, I trust to have common sense eventually. These gals, I don't. So what have you been up to?"

"Too much." I uploaded the rescue of my daughters from their abusive father in a series of tableaus, carefully editing the aftermath of Lady Lucia's spell.

I hadn't come to terms with my demon ancestry enough to entrust that knowledge to even a dear friend.

Gayla whistled through her teeth. "I'd offer to train the girls and keep them isolated but they'd meet opposition right, left, and sideways."

"Which is why I didn't ask."

"Ginkgo just dumped the crystal ball in my lap. I'd better do something with it quick, while the boys are off for some quick cuddling."

We signed off with proper telepathic protocols, an image of a good-bye wave, then a gray wall that faded to black. I slowly withdrew from the meditation.

When I opened my eyes, both Phonetia and E.T. stood in my doorway staring at me with eyes wide in awe.

"We thought only Father could communicate that deeply," Phonetia whispered. "Did Lady Lucia's spell give you that power?"

"I've always been able to contact my Sisterhood this way." But never so easily or completely.

I didn't want to think about how or why.

"Practice. It just takes practice."

"We can't do it and we've practiced," Phonetia insisted. "Same with our brothers. We just have this general awareness of where you are and what your mood is. Like we used to have with Father and the boys."

"Why are your eyes glowing red?" E.T. asked.

My heart sank.

Chapter 35

In 2006, the American Podiatric Medical Association listed Portland as the #1 US city for walking.

"PHONETIA, WHAT DID I TELL YOU about wandering around the house naked?" I demanded the next morning.

"Ah, Mom," she whined. No excuses or explanations.

"You don't live in a cave in the woods anymore. There are rules of civilization. Wearing clothes is one of them."

"Clothes are dumb." She tried walking past me from her bedroom to the bath.

"You didn't think so when you and E.T. spent an entire afternoon trying on the new outfits Lady Lucia's money bought you."

"E.T. snores. Why can't I move into the big room and *you* share with her?"

"Because then I wouldn't sleep either. You really don't want to deal with me when I'm sleep deprived." Like today. After last night's easy communication with Gayla and E.T. proclaiming that my eyes glowed demon red, I hadn't slept much. When I did, my dreams were filled with strange aches in my joints and a need to fly.

No way in hell would I transform into a bat.

I couldn't suppress my atavistic shiver of fear. Bats! Anything but a bat.

Phonetia rolled her eyes like any teenager with the

weight of the world on her shoulders. Hey, it's part of the job of being a teenager.

"Get your shower and put on some clothes. Breakfast will be ready in twenty minutes."

"If you say so."

"I don't snore. You do! I don't want to share with you either," E.T. yelled from deep within the tangle of a typical teen's room. All those beautiful, expensive, new clothes and they couldn't figure out how to hang them in the closet or pick up dirty underwear. They'd shared that room only a few days and already it looked like ground zero of a force ten hurricane.

"Scrap tells me that I'm the one who snores, so you're both wrong," I proclaimed. "We've got a full day of lessons and cleaning your room today so get moving while I fix waffles."

"With strawberries?" E.T. asked. She stuck her head out the door. She at least held her nightgown in front of her, protecting my modesty if not hers.

"Strawberries are out of season and I don't like frozen. How about blueberries? They survive the freezer better. And I've got whipped cream." Girls who loved the same food I did, what more could a mom ask?

"Waffles aren't any good without bacon," Phonetia sniffed superiorly.

"Bacon I can do. Better hurry or your sister and I will eat it all."

Finally she made tracks for the bathroom, presenting her long slender back to me.

I gasped at the snaking scars showing white against her youthful skin.

"Did your father do that to you?" I stopped her with a gentle hand on her shoulder. I remembered the agony of the blackberry whip hitting me repeatedly as my blood worked to share the lives of my girls during Lady Lucia's spell. I'd barely endured. How had this child survived such abuse?

"Yeah, what of it. He said I deserved it."

"No child deserves that kind of punishment no matter what their problem."

"If you say so." She shrugged out from under my touch.

"I say so." My words got lost in the slamming of the bathroom door.

"Mom," E.T. asked hesitantly, still hiding behind her nightgown.

"What, sweetie?" I rearranged my face from stern disapproval to careful concern.

"She called Oak last night, after midnight. We thought you were already asleep. Maybe you'd just gone quiet in your meditation."

That explained the busy phone line.

Everything inside me stilled. "Why would Phonetia call your brother?"

"She's worried. The spell, the one Lady Lucia performed . . . it severed our link to our brothers as well as our father. We can't tell if he's taking out his anger on the boys."

"Is he?"

"We don't know. Oak didn't answer the pay phone on Second and Ankeny at the prearranged time."

I should have known. These kids were close. They roamed the city, knew the bus routes, spied for their father. Of course they'd have communications backup.

"Get ready for breakfast. If your lessons go well, we'll walk the river path after lunch." I squeezed her shoulder reassuringly.

"Can we go south this time? We haven't been that way and need to pick up litter."

"I think that can be arranged."

The doorbell rang as I forked the last piece of bacon from the frying pan onto paper towels to drain.

"I'll get it!" Phonetia called, sliding down the hardwood floor on stockinged feet. Her dark hair flew out behind her in a silken wave. A wisp of fresh evergreen and mown grass followed her. She curved and braked with uncanny precision right in front of the spy hole.

She'd donned new green jeans, mint polo, and a sweatshirt that splashed bright autumn leaves across the front in puffy rubber paint. No visible scars. She looked pretty, fresh, and eager, like a typical fourteen-year-old.

"It's just Dad." She flung open the door and stalked to the table.

"Who were you expecting that I'm such a disappointment?" Gollum asked from the doorway.

"Your brother, Oak?" I asked quietly.

"How'd you know?

"That bond we have, the one forged of blood and magic. I try not to pry, Phonetia, but it's dangerous to maintain contact with your brothers."

Gollum wandered by, snagging a piece of bacon.

"Do you have a reason for dropping in for breakfast unannounced?" I scraped more batter into the waffle iron.

He found his own plate and cutlery to put on the table along with the three primary settings.

"Do I need a reason to drop by to see my daughters?" His glasses slid to the end of his nose and he peered over them at me. A gentle smile lit his face.

"Yes." I turned my attention to coffee for me, milk and juice for the girls. Let him get his own damn coffee.

"Actually, Julia wanted to go to her psychiatric appointment by herself after I arranged for TAs to take my classes all day. I dropped her off. Pat will pick her up. Then they plan to hit some of the Veterans Day sales."

The girls each gave him a hug before they took their places at the table. More affection than they gave me.

"How would you like to help the girls with their lessons? I could really use some time alone with my laptop to get some work done."

"Oh, Mom, do we have to?" the girls chorused.

"Yes, you have to do schoolwork. With me or with your dad, take your pick."

They chose Gollum, thinking he'd be a gentler taskmaster. I had news for them.

Three hours later, with three chapters edited and a new one written, I peeked out of my bedroom, amazed at the happy giggles and soft murmur of voices.

"May we please go pick up litter in the park, Dad?" E.T. asked.

"If you've finished your spelling practice."

I eased into the hallway. "You know the drill, girls," I said authoritatively. "Shoes, coats, and hats. Gloves and trash bags, one for garbage, one for recycling, and one for returnable bottles and cans." They'd picked up the idea of recycling faster than they did writing and math.

"Yes, Mom." They both rolled their eyes as if my rules were the most outrageous ideas of all time. To them shoes, hats, and coats in a cold November drizzle were unnecessary.

I listened as they thumped down the concrete and steel stairs. When they jumped off the last two steps to the ground, I moved to the French door to watch them amble along the river path.

"You don't need to watch them every moment. They've been roaming the city on their own for years," Gollum said, coming up behind me. He stood too close, the warmth of his body filled me with yearning.

One and a half dates with Sean plus a lot of phone calls when he canceled on me, and I still longed for the man I couldn't have.

"I know. But I'm still new to this mothering business."

"Do you trust Scrap to keep an eye on them and alert you to any danger?"

"Of course. He's the best baby-sitter ever invented. Sometimes I think he thinks he's their mother."

We both laughed.

"Have you told Julia about your illegitimate children?" I had to ask. I had to put the psychic distance between us.

"Not yet."

"Will you?" I moved away from him, into the kitchen. I stirred a hearty beef stew that simmered in the slow cooker. (I'd discovered that the girls ate just about anything. They preferred vegetarian more from habit than choice.) Something to do. Anything to keep me from throwing myself at him.

That was dinner. What would I do for lunch, especially if Gollum hung around?

"I don't know if I'll tell Julia or not. I don't trust this new stability and happiness. She's been like this before, usually just before a major crash that sets her back years in her recovery." He bent his head as he polished his glasses on a pristine handkerchief he fished out of his pocket.

"Veterans Day is this Monday. That means the local convention happens this weekend, day after tomorrow." I checked the wall calendar to be sure. I'd gotten so caught up in the girls that I'd forgotten one of the most important weekends of the year for my career.

"I'm obligated to go." I didn't tell him that I'd given my guest membership to Sean. He was really looking forward to the costumes and nonsense, the music, the fight demonstrations, and the literary discussions.

If he didn't get called in to work.

"Maybe we should take the girls," Gollum said happily. "I'm sure they'll enjoy it."

"I know they will. They'll disappear into the gaming rooms and I won't see them for seventy-two hours. They still bug me to call someone and find out who won the interrupted game at High Desert Con last month."

"Pat thinks she should move out. Maybe this would be a good test to see if Julia can be left alone."

"Um." An image of a pale woman with exquisitely cut hair sitting in a corner of Kelly's Brew Pub while Squishy spoke to Sean and me flashed before my mind. Was that Julia?

For my sake I almost wished it were. For Gollum's, I wasn't so sure. How would he handle the news that his wife loved another woman more than him?

But if it was Julia on her first lesbian date, at least Squishy was moving toward an ethical separation from her patient.

I almost chuckled at how Sean had made a point of dismissing me as his patient before he asked me out.

"I'm close enough to commute to the con, so I won't stay at the hotel," I mused, making plans and lists in my head, half thinking out loud. "That means a little closer supervision of the girls when I bring them home at night."

"You'll miss out on some of the best filk," Gollum reminded me. "They usually don't get started until after ten. And Holly Shannon will be there."

"There is life outside of filk." As if the music on the stereo in the background was anything else but the folk music of Science Fiction-Fantasy conventions.

"There may be life after filk, but is it a con without it?"

"Barely," I acknowledged. Gollum and I had found common bonds at the filk sessions of our first con together.

Would I feel like I had to sing "Heart's Path" again?

I had to remind myself that I had moved on. I had Sean. We liked each other. We shared a lot of common interests.

Trouble, babe. Scrap popped in and out again.

"Scrap?"

"What?" Gollum asked. He'd already scooped up his jacket and headed for the door.

"Where are the girls and what is wrong, Scrap?"

Path, two blocks south. Oak, Cedar, and Fir are waiting for them.

Chapter 36

Teasel thistle seeds were brought to Oregon by Methodist missionaries to card wool in their mission mills. They escaped and became an obnoxious ditch weed.

"HOLD BACK, TESS." Gollum grabbed both my shoulders as I passed him on the paved path.

I tried to wiggle out of his grasp. "The hell I will. Those are my girls." I pointed to the two figures ahead of us, rapidly disappearing around a curve.

They bent their heads together in close sisterly discussion.

"Their brothers are waiting for them. Family. Blood kin. They need to see them," Gollum said.

"No. You don't know half of what their father has done to all of them." I slipped my jacket, leaving him standing there, holding the damp garment while I ran forward, full tilt. My left leg ached. I ignored the protest of atrophied muscles just coming to life again. Good thing I'd doubled up on my PT exercises. My therapist was nearly ready to dismiss me because I'd recovered strength and maneuverability so rapidly.

"Scrap, what's happening?" Between the mist rising from the river and the drizzle sliding into my eyes, I could barely see the two blocks to where the girls had passed beyond my sight. A fat raindrop plopped from my tangled hair into my left eye, further blurring my perception.

I cursed and shook my head like a dog shedding bathwater.

"What has the elf done?" Gollum demanded. He kept up an easy loping stride; his long legs matched my running pace.

"He's training the boys to continue his work of begetting an entire tribe of Nörglein. He wants them to practice on Phonetia and E.T. and strengthen the DNA in their children. I think he may have given Phonetia to his marijuana growing minions as a reward."

"Shit!" He increased his pace, quickly outdistancing me.

I couldn't remember ever hearing him curse. I wondered if outrage of this magnitude would push him to break his vow of nonviolence.

Better hurry, babe. I'm getting hot and thin, Scrap snarled.

A burst of adrenaline gave my feet near levitation. Blood flowed strongly through my legs, eliminating lingering traces of my injury.

"Scrap, report," I barked as the girls came into view again.

They ambled forward, oblivious to our pursuit or the danger that awaited them in the little hollow where the trail dipped and blackberries crowded close.

Demon tats in the shrubs behind the boys.

Damn.

I held out my hand as I ran, willing Scrap to land there and transform.

He obeyed.

A deadly calm replaced my panic. My stride evened out and stretched. Scrap elongated, thinned, curved. Faster than I'd ever seen him he sharpened the inner curve of the twin blades and extruded tines from the outside.

The quarter staff balanced precisely in my hand.

I bounced around the girls and skidded to a halt, blade at the ready, feet *en garde* just as Oak, Cedar, and Fir stepped onto the path.

"Oak!" Phonetia called. "You didn't answer the phone."

I brought the Celestial Blade horizontal, blocking him.

Both Phonetia and Oak took one step forward, looked at the blade, then at me, and back again to my weapon.

"I will protect the girls with my life," I announced.

Six men, late teens and early twenties, who sorely needed

showers and shaves, stepped from the concealing shrubbery. They twirled long chains with barbed links and unsheathed long knives. Their demon tats on their inside wrists pulsed red beneath the black ink.

"We can take her," the leader, a stocky, bleached blond with swarthy skin, said. He wore a silver pendant on a black thong that replicated his tattoo. He extended the length of chain, coming dangerously close to Phonetia.

E.T. wisely retreated behind Gollum.

Easy pickings, Scrap snarled to me.

None of the forest elf children or the demon-protected seemed to hear him.

Gollum came up beside me. He held his hands up, closed his eyes, and relaxed into an easy martial arts pose.

"What are you, some kind of blind Ninja?" the blond delinquent asked. He started swinging his chain.

"Something like that," I replied, not wanting to break Gollum's concentration.

Before I finished speaking I swished the blade, tangling the chain in the tines. I yanked.

This guy wisely released his weapon. I stumbled backward with the unexpected change in balance. E.T. yelped and retreated as I stepped on her toes.

Blondie's comrades flanked him, trying to ease around our backs.

Gollum pushed his hands out in front of him.

I heard air displacement. I felt the recoil as the leader flew backward and landed on his butt in a tangle of blackberry vines and jutting teasel thistle, a nasty place. He had to hurt almost as if the Nörglein thrashed him with his wicked whip.

Gollum hadn't laid a hand on him.

The five remaining men flowed into the space left vacant, advancing with weapons drawn.

The tree boys faded out of my periphery.

Duck, parry, turn, jab. I flew into action. Scrap took a long strip of skin off of one arm. Blood flowed freely. At the moment crimson drops touched the tattoo the elven minion yowled as if he'd been burned. The enchanted ink dissolved. His entire arm flushed with a serious inflammation. He rolled into the wet grass trying to extinguish the magical fire raging within him.

The men gave ground until we came abreast of where the leader pulled himself upright. He brandished a gun at me.

A little gun easily concealed inside his pant leg. A big magazine, almost as big as the gun itself hung below the barrel. He pushed the muzzle forward until his reach ended mere inches from my chest.

I froze in place. The sweat on my brow and back turned to ice.

My mind whirled, trying to figure a way to get the gun away from him. Could I block a bullet with the blade?

"We want the girl," Blondie sneered.

"You can't have her."

"Her father said we could," he laughed, an evil sound that had no humor in it.

"The Nörglein isn't her dad. I am," Gollum insisted. He shifted his feet and hands, gathering energy again.

"Please, Miss Tess, don't fight us," Oak pleaded.

"Did he hurt you?" Phonetia called from behind me.

Oak stood stalwart, off the path but still part of the action.

"He whipped you, didn't he!" Phonetia cried. She sidled toward her brother.

Before I could stop her, or protest, her broad-shouldered middle brother grabbed her arm with one hand and wrapped his other arm around her throat.

"Try to stop us and I kill her," he said.

"Cedar, no!" Oak took one step closer.

Cedar tightened his pressure on my daughter's throat.

She gargled something, struggling for air.

Cedar backed up, dragging his sister with him. "Father whipped me too, for letting the girls get away. I won't let that happen again." Anger and pain warred for dominance in his voice.

The demon tats moved between the retreating boy and me. The leader kept his gun leveled on me as I tried to follow.

I slashed at his gun hand.

The weapon exploded, near deafening me. I dove for the ground.

Ducks and geese squawked mightily, rising from the water with much awkward fluttering.

Boaters paused and reached for communications.

"Follow her!" I commanded Scrap and dropped my blade. He dissolved into the barest outline of an imp. Then he was gone.

I returned to my knees, checking to see who was hurt.

Gollum held E.T. tightly against his chest, her mouth working in protest.

"You want to fight dirty?" I asked Blondie. Nothing left to lose. Before the last syllable escaped I hit the gun with a roundhouse kick and smashed the flat of my hand against Blondie's nose.

The gun skittered across the ground until it plopped into the water.

Blondie grabbed his bleeding nose with both hands and fled.

His minions followed close on his heels.

"Scrap? Where are they taking my girl?"

A car. Shiny new Hummer, black. Peeling out of the parking lot. I'm on the roof.

"License plate?" I asked, noting Gollum had his cell phone out.

Mud encrusted. Only dirt on the vehicle. Oregon custom BAD2BNE.

I repeated the number. Gollum spat it into the phone. "Police are on the way. Amber alert in progress."

"I'm going after them."

"Without Scrap?"

"He'll be there when I catch up. Take care of E.T."

"I must help," Oak said. Fir slunk behind him. "They will hurt my sister a lot before they turn her over to my father," he added quietly. "I can't allow that."

"Your father hurt her a lot every day she lived with him," I told him, fists clenched and aching to slam them into his face.

"I know. That is why I sent the girls to you."

"Then why did you agree to bring them back?" This time I yelled loud enough to startle the geese again.

Mutely, he turned around and lifted his T-shirt.

I gasped at the bloody mess of his skin.

"The only way I could get him to stop was to promise to bring Blackberry back to him."

"We'll *all* go after them. Two cars. You take E.T., I'll take the brothers," Gollum decided for us.

Cruising up Pill Hill, back road, Scrap informed me.

The Medical School and VA Hospital connected by a sky bridge crowned a couple of hills southwest of downtown—a lot of trees, ravines, and places to get lost around and behind. The forest there melded into Forest Park, the home of the Nörglein.

"On our way!"

Phonetia struggles against the duct tape binding her. Something about the unnatural fibers keeps her from morphing into her native plant. Otherwise, she could sprout fat thorns sharp enough to slice through the tape.

The Hummer careens around a twist in the narrow road. I'm nearly flung off the car. Only my talons latched around the roof rack keep me in my observation post. The wind tries to catch beneath my wings and lift me wide and free.

We come to an abrupt halt on a gravel shoulder that overlooks the city spread out far below. A pretty city. I don't have time to admire the view. No guard rail between us and the steep cliff. The Hummer barely fits. Half of two wheels rest on the pavement. A couple of cars pass, honking at the intrusion of the wide vehicle into their space.

When the traffic passes, leaving the road open and free for a bit, the back door flies open. Blondie and Cedar jump out, dragging my Phonetia with them. They cross the road and head into the woods. The Hummer speeds away.

Cedar leads along a creek and up a narrow ravine.

I flash images of the spot to Tess. Then I fly after our fleeing quarry. Fatigue drags at my wings. Adrenaline pushes me forward.

If only I could rest a bit by perching on Phonetia's head.

Can't risk it. Cedar will be aware of me if I get too close.

Phonetia drops to her knees, dragging Blondie with her. He yanks and yanks at her arms trying to get her to stand up and follow them.

She goes limp and slides through his grasp. Good girl.

Then she thrashes around breaking sword fern fronds and snagging alder branches. A blind man could follow the path she leaves. Cedar closes his eyes and concentrates hard. I can feel the plant life flowing over the break in its growth where deer, coyote, and raccoons have beaten the ground hard. Their roots resist pushing through the narrow game trail. He's too young and inexperienced to make them obey. He's close to panic and loses his concentration before the plants complete their task. Then he has to start over.

Blondie grows impatient and drags Phonetia deeper into the woods, oblivious to signs she leaves in their wake.

Gollum will know what to look for.

If they get here in time, before we meet up with the Nörglein and he truly obscures the path.

Chapter 37

The joint Occupancy Treaty of 1815 between the US and Great Britain forbade a military presence from either nation in the Oregon Country, but settlement was open to citizens of both from California to Alaska, the Rockies to the Pacific.

"WHERE IS IT, where is it, where is it?" I murmured as I yanked the steering wheel right and left, taking the curves uphill way too fast.

Behind me, Gollum, driving his new SUV, trailed at a moderate speed. He braked and accelerated smoothly. When did he learn to drive!

"There, there, there," E.T. pointed excitedly to a widening of the shoulder on our left.

I stomped on the brake and clutch so abruptly Gollum's vehicle came within inches of rear-ending me. Thankfully, he has amazing reactions. All that Aikido and other martial arts training. We squeezed both cars into the miniscule gravel area.

"This way," E.T. called over her shoulder as she flung open the door and scooted across the road without looking for traffic.

My heart nearly stopped as a car coming downhill way too fast skidded and screeched to avoid hitting her. The middle-aged woman driving leaned out her window and yelled obscenities. But she didn't slow down much or stop to make sure E.T. was okay.

I ran after my daughter just as recklessly. Gollum and the two boys jogged along hard on my heels.

"They came through here just minutes ago," Oak said, glancing at a swath of wreckage to the underbrush.

"Scrap?"

Under log bridge. Left uphill away from the creek. He sounded breathless and anxious.

I spotted the huge Douglas fir that had uprooted and fallen across the ravine, its top branches bent and broken against the opposite hillside. We all ducked and squeezed beneath it then stopped.

If anyone had gone this way within the last century, I couldn't spot it.

Fir did. He loped upward, pulling himself along by grabbing branches, ferns, and protruding roots that formed steps across the path. Oak paralleled him, using his greater strength to kick footholds into the steep incline.

E.T. climbed as nimbly as her brothers, inserting her wiry body between branches and trunks.

Gollum and I looked to each other in puzzlement, shrugged, and followed more slowly.

We crested the slope. Nothing around us but underbrush, fallen trees, and impenetrable blackberry thickets.

The boys had disappeared. E.T. looked as confused as Gollum and I.

"Scrap, now where?"

I don't know, he wailed landing heavily on my head. *I can't do it anymore. I'm too tired. Couldn't go sharp if I had to*. He curled up and started snoring.

"I'm sorry, buddy. I shouldn't have asked so much of you, transforming, fighting, barely tasting blood, then chasing the bad guys without a break or food." I reached up and petted him.

A lump formed in my throat. Tears of frustration and despair pricked my eyes. I checked the link between me and Phonetia. A faint tendril of life glowed in my heart. Unharmed, but frightened.

"I hear something. This way." Gollum blinked rapidly behind his glasses as he held back crossing fir branches. Sure enough, another narrow pathway opened before us.

Shouts ahead drew us onward. Gollum led, breaking the way through and beneath the overgrown bush.

"Bushwhacking in Africa," he explained briefly. He didn't have his backpack filled with essential tools. But he had experience. I trusted him to get me to my daughter.

The link between Phonetia and me suddenly flared.

I surged forward, passing Gollum.

"Put the gun down, little boy, before you hurt yourself," Blondie sneered.

"Let my sister go or I'll shoot," Fir announced firmly, not a bit of a quaver in his voice.

Hope flared within me, fueled by Phonetia as much as the conversation.

"Fir, they wear Father's protection. The gun won't kill them," Oak explained calmly. Anxiety tinged his voice.

"Maybe I can't kill him. But I can hurt him."

We burst through the last thicket of alder saplings just as Fir lowered his aim from Blondie's chest to his groin.

Phonetia threw herself sideways and down. She rolled until she fetched up at Gollum's feet. He pulled her upright as he produced a pocketknife and began sawing away at the multiple layers of duct tape around her wrists. More strips covered her mouth.

He seemed absorbed with his task, but I saw his eyes flicker, keeping the boys and the marijuana farmers under close observation. "At the first opportunity you and your sister need to run. Get back to the cars and lock yourselves in," he whispered.

I nodded firmly, seconding his order. My connection to the girls surged with agreement. They were both scared enough not to fight me.

A quick scan of the miniature clearing and Blondie was the only demon tat I could see. I closed my eyes for half a second, concentrating on the tiny sounds of the forest.

Where had the others gone?

Waiting with elf daddy at the home base, Scrap murmured, half awake.

"Give me the gun, Fir," Blondie ordered, holding out his hand.

The weapon exploded. Blondie flew backward from the impact. I cringed.

"Run!" Oak commanded.

Gollum grabbed both girls and headed back the way

we'd come. Downhill. He only needed to keep going downhill and he'd hit the road sooner or later.

I stayed put. My feet took a defensive stance.

Oak and Fir closed ranks between me and Blondie. Cedar crouched over the fallen man, oblivious to the poison oak that brushed at his legs and hands.

I looked for blood. None. The bullet hadn't penetrated. I wondered if the demon tattoo protected Blondie from the toxic oils of the plant too.

"Take care of my sisters," Oak said to me. "Get out now, before Father comes to investigate."

"Come with me."

"We have to stay here to blur your path."

"He'll kill you."

"No, he won't. He'll hurt us. But he won't kill his sons."

"He values you more than his daughters," I sighed.

"Girls are only good for sex and bearing children," Cedar said. He came up from his crouch and leaped at me, hands folding into tight fists.

Oak caught him, then cast him aside as if he weighed no more than thistle down.

"Run, Miss Tess. Run quickly. You haven't much time to get free of the forest before Father finds you."

I ran. I'd never run from a fight before, but I ran from this one.

For the sake of my daughters, I ran, skidded, and slid downhill. I had to stop thinking like a Warrior and start acting like a mother.

Lady Lucia had warned me about this. She'd told me never to get involved, never let my emotions get between me and my job.

I had to. I had to protect my daughters.

Chapter 38

Portland native Matt Groening is the creator of "The Simpsons" TV show, proving to audiences one and all that life really is just a cartoon.

THURSDAY AFTERNOON, the girls huddled over registration forms I'd downloaded from the local con. Their lesson after lunch consisted of figuring out how to write the correct information in the appropriate boxes.

I'd learned to read and write at the same time. They'd only learned to read. Writing came hard.

I sat at my desk in front of the computer, adjacent to the dining table. My concentration wandered from the view out the windows, to the half-written page in front of me, to blatantly eavesdropping on their whispers. Much as I wanted to jump up and prompt them through the procedure, I knew they needed to figure out as much as possible on their own with the help of a few writing samples I'd left for them.

They seemed to have recovered from their confrontation with their brothers and the dark elf's minions the day before. I hadn't. My hands still shook when I thought about how close we'd come to losing Phonetia.

Scrap sat on the balcony railing smoking a big fat cigar. He could see all of us, the river path, and if he craned his neck, around the side of the building, the parking lot.

Interesting, he said as he flew off.

"Scrap, what's up?"

Oh, this is a good one, babe. Forget about pretending to work and answer the door. He popped back into the room and hung upside down from the wine glass rack. *E.T. needs some help here.*

"Scrap, what is going on?"

Just answer the door. Your guest has her arms full.

Her. That eliminated the Nörglein and his sons and minions.

I heard clumping on the metal stairs. A bit of anger and frustration was in those footsteps.

Then I heard a baby cry. Not the basic needs kind of cry of a tiny infant. This was the full-blown temper tantrum of a toddler. I flung open the door.

A roundly built young woman, barely out of her teens wearing loose jeans and a purple sweatshirt, trudged up to the last landing, a squirming Sophia in her arms. Lady Lucia's daughter protested as loudly as possible to the entire world that nothing was right in her Universe. Nothing. And no one could ever make it right. Ever.

The young woman looked up. A deep frown and extreme anger turned her pink and white complexion into a parody of Little Orphan Annie. Her short blonde curls no longer bounced. All her energy went into confining Sophia and lugging her diaper bag.

"Are you Tess Noncoiré?" she demanded.

"Yes." I stepped toward her and held my arms out to Sophia.

She half turned in the woman's grasp and held out her chubby little arms to me. Her chin quivered and her cries turned from angry to forlorn. Pleading with me to tilt her world back on its axis.

"Ms. Continelli said I was to come to you in an emergency." The woman practically shoved Sophia at me.

"Where is Lady Lucia?" I cradled Sophia's head against my shoulder. She sobbed and beat her fists but did not squirm.

"How the hell am I supposed to know? And she isn't any lady. At least not by my definition."

"You must be the newest nanny."

"Ex-nanny. I quit." She unslung the diaper bag and dropped it at my feet.

Phonetia scooted out of the doorway and grabbed the

bag. She and her sister stayed at my side, blatantly observing.

"What happened?" I asked. "Look, why don't you come in and have a cup of tea. We'll talk. I'll call Lucia. I have her emergency cell phone number."

"I've already called it three times. She's not answering."

"What's your name?"

"Anita Madison. I'm a licensed nanny. I graduated top of my class from the Northwest Nanny Institute. I love kids. Kids love me. But not that one." She pointed accusingly at Sophia. "I've tried everything. And she won't settle. And Ms. Continelli gives me the creeps. She keeps blood in the fridge. She decorates in skulls and swaths of black around pictures of graveyards. And those teeth! She bares her fangs all the time."

"Anita, it's all stage dressing."

"I don't care. She gives her own baby nightmares. Sophia wakes up so frightened, her muscles clenched so tight she spasms. That's not right. I'm out of here. Even without a reference. Just keep the kid safe until that . . . that vampire comes and gets her." Anita turned abruptly and stomped down three flights of stairs. "And tell her that I'm keeping the car she gave me. I'll leave the baby seat and stroller at the foot of the stairs along with that hideous black uniform she insisted I wear. Straight out of Jane Austen!"

Having exhausted herself, Sophia laid her head on my shoulder and stuffed her thumb in her mouth. Then she spat it out and began whimpering again.

"Hmm," I mused. Something about the way she worked her jaw reminded me of my sister Cecilia's youngest.

"Back to work, girls. I think I know the baby's problem."

"What?" E.T. asked, fascinated by the tiny child.

"Teeth. She's got new teeth coming in. Probably crooked. A tiny bit of scotch rubbed on her gums ought to help."

"You'd get better results putting the scotch in her bottle." Phonetia turned and stalked back into the condo. But she took the diaper bag with her. She rummaged around in it until she found a soft pink flannel blanket with a worn satin binding. She wrapped it around Sophia, making certain the little girl could clutch the edges.

The baby immediately rubbed the satin against her cheek and settled. But her mouth still hurt.

An hour later, as the sun neared setting, Lady Lucia blew in. Her pencil slim, black suit skirt that teased her ankles was slit to the top of her thigh. The short-waisted matching jacket strained to close beneath her breasts with a single jet button the size of Sophia's hand. I'd seen that red blouse before, or its twin, with silk ruffles on the deep v-neck and French cuffs.

She'd had her hair touched up since I'd last seen her. The glossy blonde length was twisted into an elegant chignon complete with antique mantilla comb scintillating with jet and rubies.

"What now?" She tapped her foot impatiently just inside my door. She rocked back and forth on her black four-inch stiletto heels. "I was in a very important meeting."

"Your latest nanny quit and left Sophia with me." I caressed the baby's dark head where she slept on my lap. "Too bad, Anita might have been a good one. She might even have figured out that your daughter hurt when she cut a new tooth if she hadn't been so spooked by your décor."

I took a good-sized sip of single malt. Sophia had only needed a few drops to numb her gums enough to get some relief from the troublesome tooth that had poked through red and swollen tissue about ten minutes before. It looked twisted. If the adult tooth followed the same path, she'd need braces in about ten years.

"What is wrong with the servant class these days?" Lady Lucia flung herself into the armchair set at an angle to the sofa. She didn't reach for her child. "Phonetia, I need a drink. Bring me some of that." She pointed toward my scotch.

Phonetia looked to me for instructions.

I shook my head slightly. My daughter went back to the problem of figuring out how to write her birth date.

"That's part of the problem," I said curtly. "Nannies aren't servants to be exploited. They are highly trained professionals to be respected. You owe her a good reference. She could have just left Sophia with a hotel maid or someone totally unsuitable."

"I paid her twice the going rate and gave her a car so that she could take Sophia with her on errands and such." She threw up her hands, completely forgetting her order for Scotch.

"You still treated Anita like she should cower before you and obey your whims without question. Society has changed since you had a nanny of your own, Lucia."

"Unfortunately, you are right."

"Anita said Sophia has nightmares. Bad ones. The kind a baby shouldn't have."

"Anita? Is that her name?"

I grunted my disgust.

"Will you please keep Sophia a little longer? I must get back to my meeting or I will lose a great deal of money and much respect from my associates."

I looked at the clock. Five-thirty. "Sophia may stay for a short time. I hate to disturb her now that she's fallen asleep. I'll feed her when she wakes. But I need you to fetch her by eight. *My* daughters and I have things to do before we go to the con tomorrow."

Lucia opened her mouth to protest my restrictions. Then closed it, thought a moment, and heaved a sigh of resignation. "Very well. I shall return at eight. I should be able to conclude my business by then." She left without so much as looking at her daughter.

And she didn't come back until nine.

"We need to talk," Lady Lucia said before Phonetia had finished opening the door for her.

"You bet we do." I entrusted a wide awake Sophia to my daughters. They seemed delighted to entertain her by stacking brightly numbered and lettered blocks together. Sophia was more interested in knocking down the teetering towers, clapping her hands as she made new patterns of the colored squares.

I heard more than a few whispers over the similarity between the numbers on the toys and on their daily math sheets.

"Five and three equal eight!" E.T. whispered excitedly. "They equal eight!" she chortled louder.

"I don't see it," Phonetia murmured.

Her embarrassment that her younger sister figured it out before she did burned on my nape.

Hmmmm . . . building blocks; back to kindergarten

again. Whatever worked to get the girls thinking in twenty-first century terms. Or even nineteenth century terms.

Lucia perched on the comfy armchair like she would a board of director's chair, or a throne. "I have been thinking for some weeks now that I am not a fit mother for Sophia," she said.

I could almost see the clipboard in front of her as she mentally ticked off items on the agenda.

"You think?" I still steamed at her offhand treatment of the child earlier. And her deliberate intimidation of her nannies.

"Therefore, I have decided that since you are my closest blood relative, you should adopt my daughter," Lucia announced. Her eyes tracked Sophia's every move. A drop of bright moisture glistened in the inside corners of her eyes.

Oh, yes. Yes, we have to do it, babe, Scrap said. He flitted about the room three times before taking up a perch on the wine glass rack where he could oversee everything.

"What about her father?" I asked, not daring to hope, not daring to breathe.

A baby! Lucia offered me this charming baby as my own. I'd never have one of my own, but, oh, how I longed for one.

Our baby, Scrap reminded me.

"Donovan is an adolescent. I do not trust him."

"Adolescent?" I choked. "He fell over fifty years ago. He was a teenager then. That's a very long adolescence."

"When Donovan fell, he was a teenager because he was barely into adolescence in gargoyle terms when he took form inside a statue. He has barely had time to mature by Damiri standards." Lucia dismissed my objection with a wave of her hand.

"I wonder if all of his faux pas are just teenage posturing?" I mused.

"Besides," she continued as if I had not spoken, "if Donovan ever obtains a home world for the Kajiri, he will take his children there and he won't allow them to know their humanity. I want my child here, in this dimension, learning her full potential."

"Lucia, you are asking a lot. As you noticed, this place is barely big enough for me and my daughters. To add a baby would complicate things beyond measure." My middle began to ache with longing.

A baby to call my own!

"Details. We can figure out the details later. Will you adopt Sophia?"

Do it, do it, do it, Scrap pleaded from his perch on the wine glass rack. He flew down beside Sophia and rubbed his cheek against her arm.

She patted him idly and went back to destroying more block towers.

"I need time to think about it. It is an honor, but a huge responsibility." I twisted my hands inside my sweatshirt to keep from reaching for Sophia and holding her close, never letting her go.

"A responsibility you are equal to."

"You are the one who told me never to take on emotional entanglements that will interfere with my work as a Warrior of the Celestial Blade."

"Perhaps I spoke prematurely. Perhaps I merely said the words you needed to hear in your moment of great loss." She shrugged.

"Of course," Phonetia whooped. "Three plus five equals eight." I almost heard the click in her brain as numbers began to make sense.

"Sophia will help Phonetia and E.T. learn more about their own humanity," Lucia reminded me. Her voice—devoid of the Italian accent she affected with strangers—sounded desperate.

"Let me get through the convention this weekend. I'll be very busy with my own schedule as well as monitoring two teenage girls. We'll talk again on Monday."

A baby! Lucia was giving me a baby. I had no doubt I'd agree to almost any terms to bring Sophia into my family.

A baby of my own. And not my firstborn, so the Powers That Be could not take her away from me.

Chapter 39

Portland is often called the City of Roses. The Grand Floral Parade during the Rose Festival in early June is the largest floral parade in the U.S. founded in 1907.

"WHAT DO YOU DO if you see one of the men with a demon protection tattoo?" I stopped E.T. and Phonetia from entering the front door of the downtown hotel where the local Science Fiction-Fantasy convention was being held.

"We call you," E.T. said brightly, holding up her new disposable phone.

"And if I don't answer?"

"Then we call Dad, after him we call Dr. Sean, and Lady Lucia as a last resort." E.T. beamed at me proudly. "I programmed all their numbers into my phone."

"I'm named after a super phone, why can't I have one?" Phonetia demanded. She placed her hands on her hips, not acknowledging her own disposable cell in a green fabric holster on her jeans' waistband. She'd shown E.T. how to program numbers.

"Because I think you should have to earn that phone by showing a great deal of responsibility." I glared back at her, more stubborn than she.

"Whatever." She shrugged. "Can we go and start gaming now?" She peered longingly over her shoulder at the lines of people in front of the con registration desk. A half smile brightened her face as she recognized someone, probably from High Desert Con.

I wasn't sure at all that we should have come. My instincts told me to sandbag the door, cover the walls in St. Brigid crosses and other wards, lay in enough food for a siege, and never emerge from the condo again.

If I did that, I'd admit that the dark elf had won and I wasn't a worthy Warrior of the Celestial Blade.

"Let's go buy your memberships, then I'll introduce you to the people in the Green Room where I'll pick up my badge and schedule. The volunteers in the Green Room are a last resort backup. There is always an adult there who can summon help. You just have to tell them you think you picked up a stalker."

"Do Oak, Cedar, and Fir count?" E.T. looked a little scared.

"The tree boys count. So does the Nörglein."

"There's Dr. Sean!" E.T. jumped up and waved both arms at the man who scurried across the parking lot.

I waited for my heart to do that silly little flip of joy. Nothing happened. I hadn't seen him since our abortive movie date.

Phone conversations on the run are okay, but they aren't a solid basis for a lasting relationship.

My mind kept darting toward Lady Lucia and her proposal. A baby to call my own. My heart was more excited about that than Sean.

He leaped over a puddle that had collected at the curb, landing neatly at my side, a wide smile on his face. His mouth met mine in a quick kiss of greeting.

I pulled back first, fully aware that my heart wasn't engaged.

I'd seen Gollum only a few days ago, talked to him twice since then. Sean was certainly more handsome, less enigmatic and frustrating, a good solid partner in the making. A possible father for my growing family?

He wasn't Gollum.

He seemed oblivious to my coolness and just draped an arm over my shoulders as he escorted me and the girls into the hotel lobby.

He doesn't smell right, Scrap grumbled.

He changed his aftershave, I replied on a tight telepathic link. *He smells like a bright crisp winter morning when the snow has snapped the pine trees. I loved that smell as a kid back home. The fir trees out here are great but not the same. We don't get the cold and snow.*

Yeah, right. I need some mold. He flew off in a wide circle, looking decidedly jealous green.

But I knew he scouted the terrain for possible enemies.

We got in line to purchase memberships for the girls. Not too bad a crowd yet. Noon on Friday before a long weekend. Most of the young people were still in school and their parents at work.

"E.T., come back here," I called as she dashed ahead of us. Three groups of people stood between me and my girl.

She skidded to a halt in front of a short boy about her own age. His ears and throat apple were too big for his narrow frame, and matched the thickness in his glasses.

"That's just Adam. She met him at High Desert," Phonetia explained, clearly bored. But she openly searched the growing crowd.

Suddenly, her eyes brightened and she waved at a stout girl a year or two older than her. "Mom, may I go talk to Barbara?" she asked politely.

Ah, some of my lessons in civilized living had penetrated. She must want something more than permission to talk to a friend. Like an expensive phone.

"Yes, you may. But come right back when we get near the front of the line."

She hastened toward her acquaintance with a little more dignity than her sister.

"Friends are important at that age," I muttered, as much to reassure myself as Sean. "Friends are a sign that they grow into normal young women."

Sean just chuckled and pulled me closer, as if the absence of the girls gave him permission to show more intimacy.

I had an idea where this was going. I should lean in to him, give him a quick kiss for reassurance.

But I couldn't. I just couldn't.

So there I stood, my heart a heavy lump in my gut as we inched forward. I had to keep my concentration on my girls, not think about my boyfriend who was absent more than present, or a new baby.

At last we were close enough to call the girls back.

"They're reviving an old version of *Dungeons and Dragons*," E.T. gushed.

"Some of the older kids are getting together to go for pizza later," Phonetia added. "May I go with them? I'll need some money." Aha. That's what dragged the politeness out of her.

"Find me just before you leave. I may want you to go for dinner with me and my friends. If not, I'll give you some extra money then. You both have your allowance for snacks and gaming pieces?" We'd eaten lunch before leaving home.

They nodded enthusiastically.

"I'll get the memberships," Sean said, easing forward, arm still draped possessively around me.

"Have you filled out the forms I downloaded for you?" I asked the girls.

E.T. bit her lip before nodding.

I held out my hand for the much folded and slightly soiled paper. Phonetia handed hers over more readily.

I scanned their block printing carefully, in case I'd missed something this morning when they weren't looking. Then I fished a pen out of my belt pack and signed on the line marked parent or guardian.

Pride filled me. These were *my* daughters. They shared my name, right down to the correct accent mark on the last e of Noncoiré.

"Your birth date, E.T.," I reminded her softly.

"I . . . don't remember . . ."

"September twenty-first," I prodded.

"Okay." She wrote that down, using the registration table to hold the paper. "But the year?"

"Can you subtract twelve from this year?"

A tear gathered at the corner of her eye.

I wrote the numbers on a corner of scrap paper and showed her. Dutifully, she copied them into the proper box and handed the paper back to me.

Then I handed it to the volunteer behind the table.

"Oh, hi, Tess," she said brightly. "Glad to see you back this year. But you're a pro, isn't your badge over in the Green Room?"

"Hi, Maggs. Yes, my badge is. But my daughters need to register. We didn't know until the last minute they'd be coming." I placed one hand on each girl's shoulder, thus shrugging off Sean's clinging attention.

Sean plopped his platinum credit card on the table for the volunteer. Maggs swiped it and recorded the information on her official forms while the mini printer spat out the double receipt for his signature. Then she half turned to a computer keyboard and began entering information faster than I could type. She paused a moment, peering at both the registration forms and her terminal.

"E.T.? Are you really an alien?"

"No. It stands for Eternally Tenebrous," E.T. said proudly.

"I don't even know what that means," Maggs muttered, shaking her head. "No doubt about it, they are your daughters, Tess."

"It means obscure. You could try Extra Troublesome," I laughed. "What did you two do? Stay up all night reading the dictionary?"

"Of course," Phonetia returned. "It's our favorite book."

"Definitely your daughters, Tess."

Something is wrong. I want to fly off and scout out the entire con, check out who's here and who's missing. I need to find stashes of mold ahead of time.

I need to mark hidey holes for both my babe and me and the girls in case of multiple attacks.

My range has decreased to a line of sight with Tess. If I turn my back on her or try to go around a corner I find myself thrown backward in a straight line toward my Warrior.

I can fly up to the top of the dome over the central courtyard and play hide and seek among the prisms arcing down when the sun peeks through the cloud cover and strikes those lovely panes of glass.

I can tweak the hair of the girls at the hotel registration and make faces at the parrot on the shoulder of one of the con members. I flick my hot pink feather boa in the face of a black pug in a harness that matches my accessory. The ugly mutt sneezes and snorts like a steam engine. No demon hiding in that body. Pugs are weird but they aren't evil.

A couple, way back at the end of the prepaid registration

line, have a fat tabby cat in a canvas-and-mesh shoulder bag. Cats are evil. I don't know which dimension spawned them, but they don't belong in this one any more than the full-blooded Windago Tess and I fought a couple of years ago. But cats are everywhere. This overweight antique shouldn't hinder my movements though.

I can do all these normal things. But I cannot pop into the chat room or get out of Tess' line of sight.

So I find a perch in a ficus tree that's trying to pretty up an overflowing trash can—some great mold in the can—and watch.

I'm good at watching and noticing things that don't fit patterns. Demons can mask themselves, but they can't hide forever. Sooner or later they will do something outside the pattern and I'll see it.

This means I can't keep an eye on E.T. and Phonetia in the gaming rooms. I can't monitor the con as a whole.

Maybe I need some help. That parrot has potential. The pug, too; she's crazy enough to chew through her leash and run around yapping at everything outside her limited experience, including demons. But I'll never enlist that damned cat to our cause.

Chapter 40

A.L. Lovejoy and Francis W. Pettygrove flipped a coin to name their land claim, known only as The Clearing, after their hometowns: Portland, Maine and Boston, Massachusetts. Pettygrove won and the city of Portland began building.

I LED MY TROUPE AROUND the domed courtyard at the center of the hotel. A paved path encircled the area, lighted by the multiple triangles of lightly tinted glass four stories above. Graveled paths wandered through small landscaped mounds with fanciful fountains and park benches. Tasteful groupings of roses dotted the gardens. Portland was known for its plentiful and award winning roses. At the very center of the lobby a bevy of volunteers set up the weapons demonstrations on a raised cement slab that could serve double duty for small concerts and filking. An array of boffer weapons, specially designed with cushy balls on the ends of arrows or padded PVC tubing in place of swords, lay stacked untidily all around.

I explained to Sean about the arena. "No one gets inside the circle without a helmet and padded gloves. The only people allowed to wield real weapons—and only if they've been foiled—are armored historical re-creationists."

"Good idea. If I wanted to spend my weekend patching up people I'd have stayed at work."

We took a side corridor to a ground floor suite with sliding glass doors that opened onto the indoor pool. Guests of the con, professional writers, costumers, and other panelists or presenters gathered in the Green Room for snacks, networking, consulting with the con volunteers on scheduling, and just a resting place away from the nonsense of the rest of the events.

We went through the drill of introductions once more. Volunteers gave me my badge and printed schedule and then had to hunt for Sean's. I'd listed him as my guest when I filled out the forms on-line. As usual, someone's badge always got lost in the melee.

While they searched, I turned away and showed the girls how to find the schedule in their pocket program, making sure they read the modern words correctly—they excelled at convoluted classical sentence structure but still struggled with modern abbreviations. And glory be, the program actually matched the duplicates on the back of my badge and on my table tent, the folded piece of card stock with my name printed in two-inch high letters. With all that duplication, you'd think that authors tended to get spacey and forget.

Well, duh. I've had idea attacks that completely removed me from reality for days on end until the story or chapter was committed to words.

The girls scampered away, eager to begin gaming again. Thank goodness I hadn't had time to show them computer games and on-line groups. They'd never surface again.

I checked my telepathic link with them and knew precisely where they'd stopped in the courtyard to study the hotel map and find the gaming room they wanted.

"Oh, Tess, I need to tell you there's a last minute addition to your three o'clock on folklore. An anthropology professor from McLoughlin College agreed to join us," the volunteer called to me. "He's going to be quite an asset on a number of panels, and he's going to do a slide show on Saturday afternoon on the anthropology of dragons."

"I've met Dr. Van der Hoyden-Smythe. He puts on quite a show." I grew hot all over. At the same time a chill began eating at my fingertips and toes.

"Let's go get a cup of coffee." Sean steered me toward the door.

"We have coffee and hot water for tea, and a few snacks," the volunteer added hopefully.

I glanced toward the buffet table at the far end of the suite. Already half a dozen authors crowded around the free food. During the early years of my con life I'd lived exclusively on the free food. The only way I could afford the con was to crash on the floor of someone else's room and stuff myself on the free snacks.

"Oh, and your daughters might like to know that the owner of Halfling Games has joined our guest list too," the volunteer added.

Now I really did need to sit down. Rather than an opportunity to reconnect with the writing and fan community, this was turning into a convention of my exes.

"Now all I need is for Lady Lucia to show up."

Don't look now, babe, but her pearl gray limo just pulled into the porte cochere. Scrap nearly chortled with glee. *And she brought the kidlet, complete with stroller and diaper bag!*

"I guess she couldn't find a new nanny. Let's go to the coffee shop, Sean. I think I'm going to need more fortification than just snacks." Then sotto voce I said, "Scrap, start loading up on mold now. You're going to need it."

Can't I play with Sophia first?

Lucy and Sophia have taken over a banquette in the back corner of the garden café. She has a name badge discreetly clipped to the waistband of her ankle-length, pencil slim, slit to the thigh, hot pink skirt. Only a long strand of black pearls adorns her tight black blouse with ruffles at neck and cuff. Her badge has a KIT sticker on it. That's Kid-In-Tow, so people know that the kidlet with a matching sticker belongs to her. Sophia's badge hangs from the hem of her frilly black skirt. Her hot pink tights and knit top are wrinkled and just a bit saggy, as if she's rearranged her clothing trying to get out of Mom's clutches.

Dr. Sean and Tess have taken a table across the café. The buffet and some more dusty ficus trees block the path between Lady Lucia and them. They don't seem to notice each other. But I can see both.

So I alight on the lady's table and waggle my boa in her face until she notices me. She pretends not to. But she has just enough demon blood in her to make me almost visible to her.

"Hey, crime boss lady, I can keep an eye on Sophia. Let her run a bit."

Lady Lucia sighs, almost in relief. "I've hired and fired three nannies in as many weeks. I don't know what I'm going to do until Tess agrees to our little arrangement."

"Let me baby-sit a bit. I'm good at it. Really, really good at it. Just ask Tess how good I keep an eye on E.T. and Pho-netia."

"Okay. But just for a minute to let Sophia stretch her legs." She lifts the toddler out of her high chair and sets her on her feet.

The little girl squeals in delight, balances briefly—I can actually see her thinking about taking a step—then plops to her bottom. She rolls to her knees and hits the floor crawling. I have my work cut out for me, herding her in circles that don't intersect Tess' line of sight. Tess needs to concentrate on whatever is hanging around the con that keeps me within her line of sight, not longing over the baby coming our way.

Sophia and I have fun!

And Lady Lucia smiles fondly at our antics.

"All that cholesterol is going to clog your arteries," Sean said with distaste as I polished off the last of my hot turkey sandwich with gravy and mashed potatoes, cranberry sauce, and steamed mixed vegetables. I'd also had a salad with Italian dressing. Now I was eyeing the dessert menu.

Out of the corner of my eye I caught a glimpse of Scrap playing hide and seek with a laughing toddler. He was doing a good job of staying between me and the little girl. But he is transparent. Sophia was probably the most beautiful child I'd ever seen.

And if I played my cards right, in a few days she'd be *mine.* I think I paid more attention to Scrap and the baby than to Sean.

As soon as I recognized Sophia, I spotted her mother in the back corner. Okay. The vampire crime boss of Las Vegas wanted to watch from the shadows, observe my lifestyle to see if she still approved of me. I'd let her. For a while. Until

I figured out why all the remnants of my Scooby gang gathered here this weekend.

Did I ever say that I don't believe in coincidences?

"I'll worry about too much fat, salt, and sugar later. The imp flu supercharged my metabolism. Let's get to the dealers' room before the big crowds show up." I pushed back from the table, my appetite barely satisfied.

"Will they all be set up?" Sean took the bill to the cash register and once more presented his credit card. On our few and too brief dates he'd paid cash. Must be close to the end of the pay period for him. I'd have thought he made enough money not to run low on cash.

"The dealers set up last night or early this morning," I replied, seeking the proper escalator to the ballrooms on the mezzanine. The one rising behind the cash register should dump us right in front of the section designated for dealers. It also passed right above Lady Lucia. I'd be able to scout her unobtrusively.

"You only have an hour and a half before your first panel," Sean said, consulting his pocket program. "*Thinking outside the Celtic Box: folklore of other lands in SF/F literature*. Sounds a bit boring."

"Just wait and see. Fans get a bit passionate about their favorites. Even the most boring topic can turn into a verbal brawl. Depends on the people on the panel." I took his arm and nearly pulled him onto the first riser on the escalator.

"You and this professor person seem to agree a lot."

"But we don't have to on a panel. He'll probably quote some obscure African myth and I'll counter with American Indian. The young adult writer will throw in something Japanese; the audience will say something about validating the cultural heritage of the majority of Americans—usually of British descent. Or Irish," I chided him. "Then we're off and running. But in the end we'll all agree that a story should hold a universal truth. That's what folklore and myth do. Sometimes I think modern SF/F writers are creating the new myths and folklore for our multicultural world that no longer anchors itself in a single past or ethnic bond."

New energy and enthusiasm countered the heaviness of my meal. I really loved a good con. Next year I could bring Sophia with me.

Three dozen dealers had opened for business. A few still

arranged stock on their tables, but they were all ready and willing to take our money.

I left Sean in front of an array of used classic SF books and movies. Starshine's crystals and minerals brightened the back corner. She'd turned on mini black lights to make some of her specimens glow.

On close inspection I could see fading bruises beneath her heavy makeup. I'd never seen her wear makeup before.

Her eyes darted about, warily searching every shadow.

"Oh, hi, Tess," she greeted me in a lackluster whisper.

"Starshine, I need you to know that a certain object is safe," I replied cryptically. "And the men who tried to take it from you are also taken care of."

Her face brightened a bit. "You're the first to know that everything on the table is half price after noon tomorrow. I could give you the discount a little early."

I raised my eyebrows in mute question.

"This is my last show. I've sold the business. Retiring."

"I'm sorry. I know you love working with the minerals. Who bought it?"

"Her." Starshine pointed to a tall woman, dressed in flowing red draperies that disguised her broad hips, striding gracefully toward us. A white streak ran from each temple the full length of her long black hair flowing down her back. No neat chignons or twists today. No business attire either.

She looked more natural, happier, and . . . beautiful.

"Doreen Cooper."

"You know each other?" Starshine asked. She slithered back behind her tables and off to one side, leaving the gap between them open for Doreen.

"Her brother was my deceased husband," I said.

"So that's why she entrusted the artifact to you," Starshine said.

"Yes. How do you two know each other?"

"We met at a flea market where we both tried to buy that artifact," Doreen said. "Starshine got to it first." She swept past me, her gaze taking inventory. I was sure she knew to the penny the exact value of each item and the total.

"Semiprecious stones and minerals are a bit out of your usual merchandise, Doreen. Dill would have loved them though."

"I got bored with furniture." She turned defiant and angry

eyes upon me. "I got tired of working for the parents rather than managing the business so they could retire. I got tired of working with the rather questionable employees they took in from . . . from homeless shelters in the forest. And their sons and friends."

I didn't flinch, much as I wanted to.

"This won't be nearly as lucrative," I hedged.

"I won't need the money. Donovan Estevez and I are getting married on Thanksgiving Day." She flashed a large but ordinary solitaire. Easily two carats in a simple setting that demanded one look at the stone and only the stone.

The antique ring Donovan had offered me, the one I'd sent back to Faery where it belonged, had a stone just as large, square cut, surrounded by an elegant filigree. That ring demanded one look at the whole and gape in awe at the beauty and power contained within. The stone and setting belonged together, were incomplete alone.

So that's why he hasn't been sniffing around lately, Scrap giggled.

Did you know about this? I asked him.

I know she's already preggers. I can smell it on her. Not far along, maybe only a week, possibly two.

A week. The night I asked him to forge birth certificates for the girls. True to form, Donovan hopped into bed with someone else the moment I rejected him.

Or he was already in bed with her.

"Get a good pre-nup from him," I warned Doreen.

"Done. I drew it up. No loopholes. He stays faithful to me or he loses half of everything. And if I die in unusual circumstances half of everything he owns goes to our children in an unbreakable trust with my surviving brother as executor. If he predeceases me, you are executor. Neither of us wants to tangle with you."

"Sounds like you don't trust him any more than I do."

"I trust him to be who he is and loyal to his own best interests. He'll grow out of his teenaged self-absorption sooner or later. He's still a good man at heart."

I saluted her. Not a bit of jealousy ate at my bones. In fact, I felt enormously relieved. Maybe now Donovan and I could be friends without the sexual tension that had brought us together in the first place. I trusted him with my life, just not my heart and soul.

"I hope Donovan is here at the con to support her and not for his own agenda," I whispered to Scrap. Donovan's agenda always revolved around finding a home world for half-breed demons, like Doreen.

Mr. Toxic's agenda includes DBC and her new business. Otherwise, she wouldn't be here.

Chapter 41

1962 Columbus Day storm, a late season Pacific hurricane, felled fifteen times more trees than the 1980 Mt. St. Helens eruption.

AT THE BOOK DEALER, I succumbed to a signed first edition of Marion Zimmer Bradley's *Mists of Avalon*. I'd read it, of course, had a trade-sized paperback of it around somewhere. But a signed first edition hardcover of this classic couldn't be left behind for someone else. It made a dent in my revived checking account, but nothing too serious.

Strangely, Sean passed up a number of out of print classics I suggested for him. I hoped his passionate reading hadn't waned.

"Do you need time to prepare for your panel?" he asked as we wound our way out of the dealers' room.

"Not really. I've presented workshops on the topic before. I have good co-panelists. We'll wing it."

"But isn't that unprofessional?"

"That's the physician in you talking. This isn't a major research presentation. Though Gollum will come prepared with reference books, illustrations, and possibly a power point presentation. A con is casual and unrehearsed. It's more about spontaneous fun than serious education. Lighten up, Sean." *And let me think about Sophia.*

"Okay," he said reluctantly. "Let's peek in on the girls. We want to make sure they are safe."

"The girls are safe. And having fun." A little bubble of mirth behind my heart told me that. "But I'd like to make sure I know where the gaming rooms are and who they are with."

Teenagers faced human predators as well as demons.

My link led me unerringly to the three connected rooms at the end of the conference wing. E.T., her new friend, Adam, and another girl slightly younger occupied stools in front of a computer terminal. Each of the kids had a game keyboard in front of them. Gone were the simple joysticks of my youth. Now they needed a full array of high-tech remotes.

Phonetia was a little more difficult to locate in the midst of an intense board game filled with multi-sided dice and arcane figures. With her head bent in concentration, she blended in with all the others.

How could she figure out complex dice combinations in moments but still be puzzled over simple numerals and addition problems?

Funny, I'd never noticed the green streaks in her hair brought out by the fluorescent lights. Or maybe her intense concentration thinned the boundaries between her human body and her native guise.

Something to remember. E.T seemed to have embraced her humanity a lot more readily than her older sister.

I wondered if Phonetia needed to maintain a bit of dark elf in her makeup to justify to herself the sexual abuse she'd endured. Elves didn't consider it wrong. Humans did. E.T. hadn't been sexually abused by the Nörglein or his tattooed minions. Yet. She approached puberty rapidly. I'd gotten her out just in time.

"Okay, time to check in to the Green Room to see if my other two panelists are there before going to the programming rooms." I dragged Sean away from a fascinated study of the gaming process.

Should I leave him there?

"I find this counterculture amazing," he said, holding my hand as we trekked back the way we had come. "To think I never knew it existed right under my nose."

"A lot like the Kajiri demon culture. It's out there in the least expected places, alive and thriving, though very few even believe it could exist and turn a blank eye when they do see it."

As we passed the garden café I noticed a familiar figure engaging Lady Lucia in conversation. Squishy, or Pat, the psych nurse. And beside them, her elegantly frail companion played peek-a-boo with Sophia.

"Um, maybe we should just go straight to the programming room. The other panelists will find us."

"What's wrong, Tess?"

Sean looked suddenly alert, scanning the knots of people for signs of trouble.

"Someone I don't want to talk to just yet."

"You sure?" He looked at me with concern and affection.

"It's okay. A personal difference of opinion that has nothing to do with my problems with the tree boys or their father."

As long as my babe takes her time wandering through the courtyard I can run interference and check in with my spies.

"Report," I demand of the parrot.

"Awk, all quiet. All quiet. Only humans. Two, tall enough to perch on. Smell like humans."

"Gotcha." I spot the pair wearing stilts. "Keep your beak looking for anyone that smells like a plant."

"Awk, lady left got roses on her skin."

I fly over to the wide female swathed in about ten yards of Gypsy red and purple with bells and beads and bangles all over her hips and head. Nothing weird in a demon way about her. Just con member normal weird. She's got a perfume that fills the air with the scent of roses in a ten-meter aura.

More than one sensitive nose explodes in cascades of sneezes as she passes.

Mine too. I'm surprised the parrot hasn't developed sinusitis.

Time to check in with the black pug wearing the lovely harness accessory. She wiggles her entire body in ripples of skin from tail to squashed nose. I wonder if she can smell the artificial roses through her wheezes and snorts.

"Report!" I bark at her.

She yips and wiggles some more.

"No one I want to widdle on," she sighs. "But I could use a

walk on that nice patch of grass around the arena. My leash won't stretch that far and my person is too interested in flirting with the Klingon showing too much cleavage to notice my needs."

"No problem, friend." While her person, a slender man wearing a shapeless and sagging stretch shirt that's supposed to look like a TV spaceman's uniform, has his eyes superglued to the alien's boobs, I untangle the hot pink leash from his belt clip. It's barely looped in a slip knot. The stupid dog stops tugging at the first point of resistance. She doesn't realize that a bit of a yank would release it.

It takes me a bit of manipulation to come into this dimension enough to wiggle the knot. Then I slap the dog's wrinkled butt. She dashes toward the grass and shrubs in their redwood tubs.

With an audible sigh of relief she squats right beside a spindly tree in a redwood tub. It's trying to imitate a Norfolk Pine but looks a lot like a grand fir sapling.

A distinctly human foot extrudes from the trunk and kicks the dog away. She yips and scoots back to her person, tail between her legs. As much as a pug with a cropped tail can drop her appendage. Her person greets her with an admonition for obedience.

The dumb dog cowers against his leg, accepting his reprimand gladly.

I flit up to Tess' shoulder and whisper in her ear.

She whirls to return to the gaming rooms.

"Not yet, babe, let them call you."

"That may be too late!"

"Let them learn to trust you a bit. Hey, where's the boyfriend?"

"Sean went back to look at books. The folklore panel doesn't really interest him."

Huh? I understand his fascination with books, the way he read through Tess' list so quickly. But not interested in folklore? Half of what SF/F is about is folklore.

"Let me circle about and see what's up." I hadn't told her that for a while I had to keep her in sight.

Now it seems I can fly into dark rooms and down halls. I peek in on the girls. They are still obsessed with their games. Not a plant in sight.

Back in the dealers' room I find the book dealer wrapping

up a stack of books for Squishy and her lady. No sign of the good doctor.

I sniff for his Winter Pine aftershave and find him in the hospitality suite checking out the box of donuts with a large can of cola in his hand.

Double huh. I did not expect this.

I should have expected Gollum to arrive at the panel early with a stack of reference texts and a power point multimedia projector.

"Why should I even bother sitting on the panel?" I slumped against the doorjamb, arms crossed. I had to bite my cheeks to suppress the wave of joy that swamped me.

I kept trying to tell myself I had moved on with Sean. I wanted a real life, not the depressed pining I'd endured for a year and a half.

Just thinking about Gollum made my heart flip. The sight of him and his inevitable laptop took my breath away.

He pushed his glasses up to the bridge of his nose and peered at me across the room, a gentle smile softened the worry lines radiating out from his eyes and mouth.

I needed to smooth those lines away.

Before I could act on my impulse a half dozen people pressed behind me, eager to weigh in with their own opinions on the discussion.

I flowed forward with the surge, letting their momentum carry me toward the long table at the front of the room. To mask my emotions, I fussed with pouring myself a glass of ice water from the carafe, setting up my table tent and a small display of book covers and bookmarks.

We started a little late. The sparse audience remained sparse—it was early on the first day of the con.

"*Star Wars* is a retelling of the Arthurian legends in a milieu that speaks to modern audiences," I said about twenty minutes later in the midst of a discussion on the value of ancient legends to a diverse and multicultural society.

"No way!" Gollum protested. "Light Sabers are Samurai Swords. Look at the two-handed fighting stance . . ."

"The story is about more than your fascination with

swords," I returned. "We have to look at the story and the moral lessons imparted."

A fluster of movement in the back of the room captured my attention. A bigger audience maybe?

Squishy and her lady took seats in the back row. They held hands and leaned their heads close. A sense of intimacy isolated them from the rest of the room.

Gollum froze, mouth half open, his retort swallowed.

I had no more reason to wonder if Squishy's lady was Julia. I knew.

I opened the discussion to the audience, letting Gollum retreat into unnatural silence, power point presentation forgotten.

Chapter 42

Oregon has twenty-one active volcanoes, the most in the U.S.: Among them, Mt. Hood, Mt. Bachelor, Mt. Jefferson, Mt. Mazama (Crater Lake), South Sister (Charity), and Newberry Crater.

"SORRY I FLAKED OUT ON YOU, TESS," Gollum said quietly as I dismissed the audience five minutes before the hour. I'd have gladly let them go half an hour before.

"No problem." The other author on the panel flashed me a grin. Somewhat shy about butting into a discussion, she'd managed to insert more of her opinions than usual with only me sharing time with her.

"Tess, I owe you an explanation." Gollum stopped me with a hand on my arm from clearing my nice display.

A couple from the audience dashed forward and snatched some bookmarks before I could put them away.

"No, you don't, Gollum. She owes you an explanation. I think the three of you need to go find someplace private and talk. Don't let either of them dance around the issues."

"You knew?"

"I suspected when I saw them at Holly's concert a few weeks ago. And I don't know that Pat is Julia's first flirtation. Now go talk to them and let me continue with the con. I'll cover your next panel with the power point if you want."

"Thanks. But the panel on dragon evolution isn't until tomorrow afternoon. If you could stash this stuff in the

Green Room I'd appreciate it. And I'll let you know if I can't get back." Awkwardly, he moved behind me and used his long legs to eat the distance between him and his wife and her lover where they lingered in the back corner. They left with a minimum of discourse. All three walked as if treading on dragon scales, not wanting to awaken the beast.

I occupied my curious mind and imagination with packing up the power point stuff rather than speculating on the conversation taking place elsewhere. Then I could always think about Sophia and my girls. There was plenty to occupy my thoughts without speculation about Gollum and the ladies.

"Scrap, how are the girls?" I whispered.

Still okay and still no sign of plants. He darted out of the room and back again in an eye blink. *Heads up, babe. New crop of demon tats filling the doorway.*

"Shit. Where's the Nörglein getting them?" Five young men in their late teens blocked the entrance. They all wore expensive leather jackets and ragged jeans. Their grimy T-shirts smelled of compost, heavy on the manure.

No sign of Blondie with his pendant to match his tattoo.

What grabbed my attention about the new group were new tattoos of a pentagram around a skull. The placement on the insides of their wrists had to hurt more than inserting the ink on the back of their arms. To my eye, the ink pulsed red around the black lines. That was raw infection from the recent and inexpert application. I couldn't see any sign of other dimensional origins to the ink.

Druggies looking for easy money growing a secure crop of weed.

"Pay back time, lady," the first one through the door growled. His buddies made an impenetrable phalanx behind him, crowding out the surge of con members trying to get in for the next panel.

"Scrap, get to the girls. Don't let Tree Daddy near them while I'm distracted."

Um, dahling, I'm turning a lovely shade of red. You are in danger. I can't leave you.

"Just a little pink around the edges. Get your ass over to my daughters. I can handle these guys." To prove it, I took an *en garde* stance and looked for a mundane weapon.

"Hey, Tess." A semi-familiar voiced piped up from the

doorway. "Use this!" A fan I recognized from last year's con tossed me an unsharpened broadsword from his Conan costume. It had a plastic band around the grip indicating his "Peace Bond" or promise not to draw the weapon while at the con.

I plucked the sword out of the air by the grip, flipped it expertly, and readied to fight my way out of this mess.

"Call security!" I called to anyone listening.

"On their way. These guys have fake badges."

"Ghosts as well as bad ass and ugly," I sneered.

"We ain't dead yet." The leader advanced one step.

I whopped him upside the head with the flat of the blade. "Ghosts are scumbags who don't bother to pay for their memberships," I explained whirling to catch the next two with a side kick to the groin and an elbow to the nose.

"The attitude and the smell I could cope with. Forging a con badge? That's unforgivable."

My combatants staggered into the audience and got shoved back and forth for their trouble. Off-balance and confused, the leader dropped to his knees right in front of the chain mail clad giant who wore a bright red ribbon on his badge that proclaimed to the world "Security."

He hauled that one up by the collar of his pricey leather jacket, caught another by his belt, and marched them out. My friend, Conan, grabbed another one and followed.

The other two, the ones I hadn't engaged in combat, fled.

"Incompetent newbies," I muttered. "You'd think Tree Daddy would give them a bit of training before turning them loose. Demon tats don't protect minions like they used to."

Or maybe Tree Daddy had run out of goodwill with the higher ups and had to use his own dwindling magic to demonize the tattoos. The bespelled ink wasn't as strong or as effective as the real thing.

Scrap had destroyed his hat, taking with it a power reserve.

If that were the case, he'd be getting desperate to get his girls back and begin inbreeding to strengthen the elf DNA.

I dashed to catch up to Conan and return the sword. "No one saw me draw this, right?" I called back to the room at large.

"What sword?" someone yelled.

"Could someone get the power point stuff back to the Green Room for me?"

"Sure thing, Tess."

"Anything for our Tess!"

Goddess, I love a con. Where else could I trust strangers to provide me with a weapon, and return expensive audio visual equipment to a secure location? Strangers in wild costumes. But then the costumed ones are loyal, come back every year, and thrive on the con culture. At a con everyone is your new best friend, especially when crowding into an elevator drives us to more intimate than casual contact.

And I had to get down to the gaming rooms to make sure nothing terrible happened to my daughters that would close down the con prematurely. I didn't want two thousand fans angry at me.

"Scrap, report!"

"About time you showed up," I squawk to Tess as she dashes down the winding steps to the garden café, makes a screeching turn past Lady Lucia, scanning briefly to make sure Sophia was still there, and into the suddenly murky corridor.

"Fuck!" she screams as she barks her shin against an abandoned redwood tub. Rich soil spills out of it. I smell dirt filling the air, clouding the lights, making the place inhospitable to all but the most determined.

In short, it smells of Nörglein.

I can see traces of a masculine footprint tracking dirt on the vinyl flooring. A bare foot, no shoes.

"Had to have been Fir," I tell Tess. "He was masquerading as a Norfolk Pine but he looked more like a grand fir to me." My voice comes out an octave higher as my body stretches.

Hot blood quickens in my veins. My wing tips are near scorching. My tail gives off a pulsing red glow.

I fly just ahead of Tess, guiding her to the gaming rooms.

"Oh, hi, Cedar," Phonetia says blithely, as if we didn't know that the tree boys have become her enemies. "Pull up a chair. I think we can roll you into the scene in about three moves."

The stocky—or is that stalky—boy bites his lips, eyeing the game board avariciously.

Fir stretches tall and peeks over his brother's shoulders.

"Can I play too? I think I can pick up where I left off at High Desert Con."

An addiction in action. Is it stronger than the compulsion their father laid upon them?

Some of the heat bleeds off my extremities. I'm still ready to taste blood, if only my babe will command me.

But we are in a public place. Not good to reveal ourselves just yet.

This is a con. Who'd notice anything out of the ordinary? I've already seen three Celestial Blade replicas in honor of characters in Tess' books.

"Scrap, stay close and ready. I'm going to see if I can get the boys away from Phonetia," Tess whispers as she edges up behind the two boys.

"No need, Lady Tess," Oak says, skidding to a halt beside her. "I will contain my brothers."

Huh? both Tess and I grunt.

"I want my sisters to be safe from *all* harm. Even that inflicted by the family."

"Believe him, babe. He smells human. I can't find a trace of elf, dark or light, or otherworld on him, except that he brings in a breath or two of fresh air hinting at rain washed forest."

"Are you sure, Oak?" Tess asks him, almost as concerned for him as the girls.

That's my Tess. She does love kids. Too bad she's not likely to ever have any of her own. Even if Gollum does work out his problem with the elegant and fragile Julia so he can return to Tess.

We'll have to settle for Sophia. Though she's pure joy; not settling for less.

"I am sure." Oak looks grim and sad. He knows what's coming.

"You know what I have to do, Oak?" Tess clasps his shoulder and squeezes reassurance.

"I know. And though I cannot bring myself to do the deed, I trust another to do what they must to keep my sisters safe. Now I will remove Cedar from the premises. He is still confused about his loyalties. Fir is young enough and innocent enough to learn new ways. I entrust him to you, my lady."

With that, the boy verging on manhood gives Tess a little bow of respect. Then he grabs Cedar by the collar and retreats out the fire exit onto the rain-slick streets of the city. No longer part of the con.

"Scrap, check Fir's badge, see if it's real or a forgery," Tess says quietly.

"It looks real and smells of the people at the registration desk."

"Then we'll leave him to the game. Now let's make sure E.T. is okay."

"Hi, Sean," I greeted my date.

He jerked his head back as if startled. "Oh, um, hi, Tess." He paused in his inching progress through the computer room. "Do you see what's on those computer screens? This is all very strange."

"Agreed," I chuckled, taking in realistic action figures jumping and shooting and diving through some arcane adventure. "I'm free until Opening Ceremonies at seven, then we have our choice of filk or Pictionary at eight."

"Are the girls okay here by themselves for so long?"

"I believe they are." I checked my link. As far as E.T. and Phonetia were concerned nothing existed beyond their games. Nothing alarmed them, except Fir's next unorthodox move in the tabletop game.

"What about . . . you know, the forest folk?"

"I can account for the boys. They'll be no trouble for a while. Scrap will tell me if Tree Daddy enters the premises." I took Sean's arm, companionably. "Come on, let's do the art show before it gets crowded or I get too busy. Or if you'd rather, I think we can just sit and talk to my friend Lucia where she has set up camp in the garden café." *And I can hold the baby*.

Sean looked around him nervously. "The art show sounds fun. I'd like to see some of the paintings that became book covers."

We nearly skipped back down the newly bright corridor. The redwood tub still rolled on its side, spilling dirt, but the air had cleared. I smelled a new freshness instead of the usual hotel cleansers and recycled air.

Sean chose the path that took us around the central

garden—on the opposite side to the café—and upstairs to the ballroom adjacent to the dealers' room.

My heart didn't even twinge when I spotted Donovan and Doreen, arm in arm, heads bent together entering the gallery ahead of us.

Chapter 43

Douglas firs reach an average of 200 feet and grow up to 325 feet. The wood is claimed to be stronger than concrete.

"AS OF THIS MOMENT, your name is Doug," I told Fir as I led him and the girls out to my car at eleven o'clock that night.

I sang my lungs out in filk, with Sean sitting quietly off to the side. And I had sung "Heart's Path." I was still working out what I would do if Gollum and Julia resolved their differences and stayed together.

I didn't dare hope. So I buried my emotions in the problems of my growing household.

And then there was Sophia. Lady Lucia continued to hold court in the café with the tired and cranky baby. I needed to take that child home, give her a bath and a good supper, and put her to bed for about twelve hours.

Sean barely brushed the surface of my consciousness.

"Cool," Doug said, scouting the parking lot. "Oak said I need to stay with you now. I'm not really a fir anyway. I'm more of a filbert." He shrugged.

We call hazelnuts filberts in Oregon. And we grow a goodly portion of the world's supply in the Willamette Valley.

Then he spotted my little hybrid car. "Can I drive?"

"No."

"But I drive Father's car. It's a real tank. A 1974 Buick

Riviera. Forest green. V-8. Automatic." He proceeded to give me statistics on the engine and gear ratio that meant nothing to me.

"That car probably only gets fourteen miles to the gallon. It's hypocritical for him to drive a gas hog like that when he claims to be the guardian of the forest trying to correct pollution and global warming."

"That describes the old man perfectly," Phonetia snorted as she claimed the shotgun position, relegating the backseat to Doug and E.T. He grumbled a bit about male superiority.

"But you're gay, so you aren't truly male," E.T. objected.

"Just try convincing Father of that." His buoyancy evaporated.

"The Nörglein and his opinions don't matter anymore as far as you three are concerned. He no longer has authority over you," I replied. "My imp is gay. So I have no problem with you preferring boys, Doug. I have no expectations from any of you on that front."

Silence reigned on the short drive back to the condo. We were suddenly overcrowded again, lacking bed space, and three teens sharing one small bathroom guaranteed squabbles. Where would I put a crib? In my room. The only place left that wasn't occupied.

I might have to sell at a loss to get into a bigger place sooner rather than later.

I'd worry about that next week, after the con. In the meantime, I had to come up with another cover story to explain the sudden addition of Doug into the family. No way could I pass the tall gangly youth as my own. I'd already stretched that lie to near the breaking point.

Time to consult Gollum, Scrap suggested.

"I don't dare call him tonight. We'll talk tomorrow." I had no idea how he fared with his own family issues.

Tomorrow. I'd deal with that tomorrow.

"Scrap, can you keep watch tonight? I really need some sleep."

Can do, babe. Doug wants to watch TV since he's sleeping on the sofa. I'll make sure he doesn't find the porn stations.

"I don't subscribe to any porn stations. They're boring."

Hee hee hee, that's what you think. Doug needs an education. And I'm just the imp to give it to him. But not tonight.

"But he can't see you. Can he?"

Nope. The girls can't either, but they can sense my presence. That's enough for now. Your family is my family.

"Does that mean your family is my family?" I'd really like to meet his harridan of a mum.

No way, babe. No freakin' way would I wish any of my family on you. Be content with what you can get since there won't be any of your own, even if Gollum frees himself from Julia. I bet you won't even mind changing diapers for a baby as cute as Sophia.

"You're right," I sighed in regret. I had always wanted children of my own, lots of them.

"What am I going to do, Allie?" I wailed into the telephone at six the next morning.

I could hear the children stirring. They'd want breakfast and an early start at the con. Soon I'd have to settle squabbles over who got the shower first and fix them something to eat. Maybe they'd settle for cold cereal.

"About the dark elf?" Allie asked. She sounded bright and chipper, but then she was three hours ahead of me and had probably slept the night through.

"That and Gollum. What if he and Julia make up their differences and stay together?"

"You'll go on as you have been. How are things with Dr. Sean?"

"Okay." I couldn't drag any enthusiasm out of my tired mind.

"Concentrate on him until you know any different," she advised solemnly.

"I know. But I don't love Sean. Gollum's the only man I truly want."

"What did Lady Lucia tell you about family and relationships? They don't fit with the life of a Warrior."

I laughed at that. I hadn't told her about the baby. Not until I knew for sure. "But now I've got the girls, and Doug. I have children," I hedged.

"Teens. You have teens, not infants. Teens can be left alone occasionally. Teens can actually help you; act as spies and such. Teach them to be your allies." The last sentence faded and veered off, as if she got distracted.

"Did I call at a bad time?" Dammit, she was my friend. She should be there when I wanted to talk about my problems.

"Steve's in town for the weekend. We're getting ready to go talk to the priest about the wedding," she replied. "Look, I know you need a friend right now. But I've got to go. Call me tonight and we'll hash it all out. There's nothing you can do about Gollum until you actually talk to him."

"What about the Nörglein and the kids?"

"Take that one step at a time. That's what motherhood is all about. Live from one minute to the next. Deal with each crisis as it comes."

"When did you get so smart?"

"Since your brother and I decided to get married and I started thinking about having children of my own. Wasn't sure I could handle them while I was a cop. Now I'm not a cop and I really, really want babies. Lots of them."

"So do I." But I'd never get my own children. Just the strays that fell into my lap.

The Powers That Be had made sure of that. Unless . . .

What had Scrap called the crystal ball? A bargaining chip?

"Bye, Tess. I've really got to go. Call me tonight. Even if it's the middle of the night." She rang off, leaving me alone with my problems.

As alone as I'd ever been.

"You got first shower yesterday. It's my turn!" E.T. yelled.

"What about me? I haven't had a real shower in ages," Doug chimed in.

Except now, I had to deal with three teens on my own.

"Andiamo, cara mia Tess," Lady Lucia gushed a few hours later as I passed her in the garden café. If she hadn't changed clothes to black slacks, red silk blouse, and simple gold necklace and hoop earrings, I'd think she'd spent the night in the corner with Sophia.

I held out my arms to the little girl and she toddled two steps to hug me about the knees.

"Oh, my, her first steps!" Lucia looked as if she might cry.

"I'm honored, Sophia, that you chose to walk to me for those first steps." I picked her up and hugged her close.

She tugged on my dangling dragon earrings with her right hand while sucking the middle two fingers of her left.

Gently I extricated her sticky fingers from the pewter jewelry. "Maybe she just wanted to investigate rather than honor me," I laughed, taking a seat beside Lucia, the baby still in my arms.

This is what it would be like if I accepted Lucia's offer. Sophia in my lap by right and preference.

"I believe you should have this," Lucia said, pasting a KIT sticker on my con badge that matched hers and Sophia's. "I ordered an extra just in case you needed it."

"I'm not . . ."

She held up a hand, blocking my protest. "In case of emergency, you may stay with my daughter without questions." Then she signaled the waitress for a new carafe of coffee and an extra cup for me.

"I never needed coffee until Sophia was born. Now I cannot live without it," she said, almost apologetically. "More refreshing than blood."

I almost gagged, but smiled squeamishly instead. I knew she had killed a man by draining his blood. Gary Gregbaum was a scumbag of a white slaver who had upset forever the balance of Faery to the other dimensions. He needed to be taken out. But that way? I honestly didn't know if Lucia had served justice or not.

"I will host a party in my suite next week. I'd invite you to share my volunteers, but I need you to keep Sophia. She should not be exposed to my life . . . style." She added the last word almost as an afterthought.

"Nothing is fully decided yet. I have to check my calendar. I have *three* teens to consider now."

"If you must. I trust you with my daughter more than any of the nannies I have hired. They all quit after only a few days."

"You scared them away."

I covered my unease with a sip of very good coffee. "Bless you. I barely had time for a single cup with breakfast before my girls and their brother dragged me out this morning. They couldn't wait to get back to their games. I hope they aren't disappointed that their friends might not be here yet."

"Very interesting, this convention of yours. In some ways it reminds me of the market fairs in my youth."

"Not terribly different from Renaissance Faires and Highland Games. A gathering of people who want to celebrate a certain aspect of their hobby or culture," I replied.

"I do not fully understand the source of this con culture."

"Then you haven't read much science fiction or fantasy."

"No. But I have seen this 'Star Trek' as part of the exhibit and rides in Las Vegas."

"There are Trekkers here too."

"I saw the costumes. Some are very good. Some not so."

"People do what they can within their budgets and sewing talents. The idea is that they help re-create their favorite part of the genre."

"Ah. And the vampires?"

"That's part of the genre too. Though I don't think many of them will take it as far as you have."

She grinned, baring her fangs. Very good implants to complete her persona. "Perhaps I can find new recruits . . ."

"Leave it alone, Lucia. These people are mostly innocent. The hard-core Camarilla followers hang out in different venues. You've found them already if you're hosting a party next week."

"Ah, wishful thinking. I need a dose of my reality." She sighed and shrugged her shoulders. "Since Sophia came to me I have not the taste for innocent blood that I used to. Most of my party guests are flying in as . . . um . . . escorts to business people I need to entertain in high Goth style."

"You mean intimidate them into signing one-sided contracts."

"Of course."

Sophia climbed over me to return to her mother. Then she slid down beneath the table and crawled out to the opposite side where she pulled herself up by the chair. Carefully she eyed each potential handhold and how many exciting steps she'd need to take to get there.

"No holding her back now!" I said. Since I was closest to her, I stood and hovered over the little girl to make sure she didn't get into trouble.

Lucia looked relieved that she didn't have to move.

"Can I leave Sophia with you for a brief time? I need to . . . um . . ."

"Sure. The ladies room is in the corridor to our left." Idly I followed Sophia a whole three steps before she wobbled and plunked onto her bottom with a wail. I picked her up, comforting her. She cried from disappointment more than any hurt. Her bottom was very well padded with diaper and frilly panties.

I put her back into her high chair and offered her some breakfast. She nibbled a triangle of toast, getting more grape jelly on her face than in her mouth while I savored the very good coffee. Fortunately, her frilly dress was royal purple. The jelly stains wouldn't show, much. If . . . when . . . the child was mine, I'd have her in sturdy, washable rompers.

Lucia returned. She'd freshened her makeup and brushed her lustrous hair. She looked less weary and worried. I wondered if she had a flask of blood secreted in her bag.

Sophia ignored her. Finding more interest in my dragon earrings than her mother.

"You two look well together, *cara mia* Tess. Like you belong together," she said, resuming her place on the corner banquette as if sinking onto a throne. Her regal bearing invited lesser folk to approach but not to get too close. "Fitting, that you are my only living relative. Of sorts."

"I have a brother and sister, nieces and nephews. My father is a Noncoiré too. He has brothers and sisters. One of them, MoonFeather, is a witch."

"But they have not your special talents. Nor do they have an imp companion to bridge the gaps between this world and the next." She gestured vaguely to where Scrap dangled from a tree in the garden area, seemingly conversing with a pet parrot and a pug wheezing on the ground.

"Can you see him?" I asked, remembering Scrap's comments from the night before.

"Not really. Just an awareness that he is somewhere close, in that direction. If we both concentrate we can communicate."

That was a relief. Lady Lucia wasn't really as spooky as I first thought. Most of her violence and bloodlust was an act to intimidate enemies, business associates, and district attorneys.

"I have decided. Tomorrow morning we will go to early Mass together. You will stand as godmother to my baby." An order, not a request. "A prelude to your adoption of my child."

"I'm honored . . . Are you sure? Can you step onto sacred ground?" Vampires couldn't, if you believed the literature. Fiction and legend weren't so detailed about very dilute demon blood. I had no trouble in churches. But Lucia was almost two hundred years closer to the source than I.

"I would not ask if I were indecisive. And I have been baptized. I attended Mass most every day of my life until I escaped from Count Continelli. Since then?" She shrugged as if not interested. "You are the only one I trust with my daughter's soul, and her upbringing. I have already changed my will, regardless of your decision to adopt my baby or not."

"Then I'll see you at St. Mary's at six." Before dawn, in keeping with her persona. I felt honored by her trust. But I was also a little afraid of the heavy portent in her words. Life wasn't going to be easy anytime soon.

"You are wearing the pearls?"

"Almost always." I fingered the strand hanging beneath my bulky Aran Isle sweater.

"Good. You never know when you'll need them."

What did that mean?

She turned her focus onto Sophia, pulling a wet wipe out of the diaper bag and cleaning jelly off her face, hands, knees, dress front . . .

"Thank you for the coffee, Lady Lucia." Somehow her manner indicated she required the title now rather than the more familiar form. "I need to talk to some people in the Green Room before my ten o'clock panel."

"I can spare you. But first, tell me where is the charming physician who escorted you yesterday?"

"Sean should be here anytime. Unless he got called to work on an emergency. He's supposed to have two full days off, but that doesn't always happen."

"I understand. And was that Donovan Estevez I saw with Doreen Cooper yesterday?"

"Sure was. They're engaged."

"Ah, that is good. He will have less need to take interest in me and my child. The Cooper woman will be a steadying influence on him. He will be an impressive man when he matures into his responsibilities."

"Still might be a good idea to stay out of his way."

"Agreed. Now off with you to your appointment. I have things to prepare for the baptism. White lace gowns in the appropriate size are very difficult to find."

"Harder to keep clean."

Chapter 44

The World Forestry Center next to the Oregon Zoo has 20,000 square feet of exhibits and two working forests to teach about world trees and their importance to all life on the planet.

DOREEN WAITS FOR MY DAHLING TESS in the Green Room. She cradles a cup of very fragrant coffee between her lush breasts. Her eyes are half closed and her thoughts turn inward. I think she knows that new life has begun inside her. She marvels at the idea. And yet I smell a touch of sadness in her.

"Tess." She nods succinctly.

"Doreen. I got your email. What's up?" Tess fills a plain black ceramic mug of generic coffee from the carafe on the side table. Only a brief wince betrays the staleness of the brew. It's not the good stuff Doreen sips.

"Not here." Doreen looks around warily. A dozen or more pro writers, artists, and other guests of the con mingle, fixing bowls of cereal, nibbling on toasted bagels, and chatting amiably about everything from politics to the business of writing, to their next panel topic.

"This sounds ominous, babe. Let's decamp to the back of the dealers' room. They don't open for another hour and it's nearly deserted," I suggest to Tess.

She and Doreen come to an agreement. I flit off to check on the kids. They need me more than the ladies do.

Doreen waited until we were tucked behind her sales table in the back of the dealers' room. Then she turned on me with impossible quickness. "Is the crystal ball safe?"

"Yes." I sent a quick query to Scrap.

Of course, dahling.

"Do you know how to use it?"

"Not really."

"Will it . . . will it help you find someone?"

"Possibly."

Donovan would kill me or anyone else who stood between him and that crystal ball if he knew what it could do.

Doreen was engaged to Donovan.

The Nörglein wanted it too. For his own purposes.

He worked for Doreen's parents.

Too many connections. Best say as little as possible.

"Can we make a date to try it?"

"Later. After the con."

She nodded in mute understanding. "I saw you with two girls yesterday. I recognized them."

"They are my daughters now. I have the paperwork to prove it and . . . and a magic link to them stronger than any birth mother's . . ."

"Are you sure it's a stronger link than a true mother to her baby?"

"I don't know that for sure since I've never had a child of my own."

"But you believe in that link."

I thought of my own mother and how often she'd sensed my moods and problems before I did. I still missed her terribly. "Yes, I believe in a mother's link to her children."

"Will you use the crystal ball to help me find my son?"

I paused a moment in puzzlement. "I didn't know . . .

"The Nörglein used me—at my parents' prompting but without me agreeing—"

"He raped you."

She nodded silently. "Sixteen years ago. Then when I wouldn't turn over my baby to him, my parents gave my son to the monster."

"That's awful. I'm surprised you waited so long to go out on your own."

"I tried. Desperately. Fourteen times I packed a suitcase and went looking for my son. My parents always found me and dragged me back home. They've bound me with magic so many times I know the ritual backward and forward. But not how to break it. Only how to let it wear off over time. This time I have Donovan to protect me. They approve of Donovan."

"Of course they do. Do they know he's fully human now, even though his sympathies lie with the Kajiri?"

"Yes. They have blinders on when it comes to the grand scheme of a Kajiri home world. They hate their human connections. They hate the restrictions of living in secret among humans."

"They certainly had no use for me as a daughter-in-law."

"I can not know for certain, but they may have agreed to Dill's murder. Since he embraced his humanity and a human wife, they had no more use for him."

My breath caught in my throat. My heart froze and threatened to shatter. Again. "I have evidence that Dill planned to betray the 'great plan' to a human. To my archivist."

"I helped him find Professor Van der Hoyden-Smythe. Neither my parents, nor Darren Estevez could allow Dill to live after that. I've thought about who Darren might have used as an accomplice. Quentin is loyal to Donovan, despite his love of money and lack of concern how he gets it. I think the Nörglein may have been a little too eager to help."

We mourned together a moment for the man we'd both loved.

"Is your son Oak, Cedar, or Doug . . . I mean Fir?"

"I don't know." A long moment of silence as she mastered her breathing and blinked back tears. "I named my child Dillwyn, after my brother. I loved my brother very much. I wanted him to be happy. I loved my baby too."

"Does Donovan know about the boy?"

"Yes. He promised to help me find him. We started talking at Dill's funeral, reminiscing about Dill and the time Donovan stayed with us before he was sent to Estevez. Then one thing led to another and another. Now we're in love. Or at least compatible with a similar agenda."

"How will he know which boy is yours if you can't tell?"

"I don't know. All three boys are very close in age. All

three have medium brown hair and hazel eyes. I can't find a Damiri trait among them and I have studied them carefully. The Nörglein—we call him Pete by the way—brings them to work sometimes to help with moving merchandise and such. I've talked to all of them. Searched their faces. Nothing. The magic my parents bind me with is Pete's spell. It keeps me from asking the boys if they want to come to me."

"Pete? I suppose that could be a shortening of *Purzinigele*, his real name," I said quietly. "Professor Van der Hoyden-Smythe gave me a file full of information. The name was in there. If I speak his real name out loud, in his hearing, he'll be forced to leave the region. But he'd just set up shop elsewhere. Become someone else's problem. I need him dead, or permanently exiled to another dimension under lock and key."

"Unfortunately, King Scazzamurieddu of the Orculli can't lock him up in the pandimensional prison for rape. Only for endangering the balance among the Universes," Doreen agreed. The foreign words tripped from her tongue as if part of her native language.

"If he stole the crystal ball I could turn him in. But he'd have to steal it. I can't arrange for him to 'find' it."

"Damn."

"Fir is the youngest," I mused. "He came into my family last night. We call him Doug. He looks like he'll be the tallest, slender too."

"Is he truly the youngest, or the least mature? The men in my family are slow to go through puberty."

I shrugged. "Cedar appears to be the middle child, he'll be broader in the shoulder than Doug, maybe not as tall. Oak is the oldest. Not as tall, but he has heavier bones and muscles. He acts the oldest, taking responsibility for the younger ones, doing what he can to protect the girls and Doug, who has decided to be gay."

"I doubt that Doug is mine. Damiri are never gay."

"Okay." I thought a moment. "Scrap, get your ass back here. Now."

But E.T. is about to make a power play.

"E.T. will tell you all about it later. I need you now."

What's so fraggin' urgent? he snarled, landing on my shoulder, blowing cigar smoke in my face.

I grabbed the noxious weed away from him and stubbed

it out in my coffee cup. The coffee wasn't worth drinking anyway. "No smoking inside. That's the law."

Stupid law, he sulked.

"Scrap, I need you to concentrate. Is there a way to tell if Doreen is the mother of any of the tree boys?"

Oooh, now that's a piece of gossip. Do tell all!

"Later, brat. We need to know now. Is there a way to tell, short of a blood test?" Which would take two weeks once it cleared the backup and paperwork. Possibly a year or two.

Maybe. I'd have to take them both into the chat room to be sure.

"What about the crystal ball?"

Scrap's eyes turned red with an inner glow of excitement. *That's a good idea. Want me to go get it?*

"Not yet. I think we should wait until after the con. I have this nagging feeling that I'm missing something. Before we do anything, I want the Nörglein out of the way, permanently."

"Good luck," Doreen said skeptically. "I've tried killing him at least a dozen times. He's always one step ahead of me. Smarter and faster. He lies, and cheats. Anything to get his way."

"He is truly evil," I agreed.

"But without him the forest will die. Are you willing to take on that responsibility?" Doreen reminded me. "I will take the responsibility, but I don't know how to cut out invasive plants, balance destructive and helpful insects, deter people from damaging it beyond repair."

"Let me think about that." My aunt MoonFeather came immediately to mind. And so did the World Forestry Center and their army of volunteers and educational programs.

No one person should have to protect the forest on his own, like I had tried fighting demons on my own. And failed.

I had backup now. I had family and friends.

Lunch came and went with no sign of Sean or Gollum. I checked my cell phone for about the sixth time to see if I'd missed a call from either of them. I had a lot to think about between times.

I wondered if Donovan and Doreen would take both Cedar and Oak. A good resolution as long as I got "Pete" out of the way. Deprived of all three of his sons, he just might go berserk, raping even more women.

"Have you seen Squishy?" a Green Room volunteer asked while I checked out the power point equipment and slides. Evolution of Dragons. I could do this. Mostly Gollum had assembled pictures of early artwork depicting dragons. The Egyptian stuff was new to me but flowed naturally into the classical Greek. The middle ages, and modern fantasy book covers grew out of that. The section on Oriental dragons felt strange and wonderful and awesome. I could probably wing it.

"Um, no I haven't," I replied. "She was here yesterday."

"And she left in a hurry, blowing off her five o'clock panel on field treatment of sword wounds. Then she missed her eleven o'clock this morning on electronic publishing of short fiction," the volunteer grumbled.

"I heard that she might be moving soon. Maybe something came up and she had to move out sooner than expected," I hedged. I hoped she had a new roommate moving in with her too.

"Maybe so. But it's not like her to not say something, or apologize, or *something*."

"Yeah, you're right." Maybe bad news for me. I didn't dare hope for good news.

Sean hurried into the suite. He paused for only half a breath until he spotted me on the sofa beneath a window at the far end. Then he zeroed in on me with a big smile and flattering haste.

"I am so sorry I'm late," he said on a gush. "I got tied up at . . . work." He plunked down beside me and took my hand in both of his—the one I was using to fiddle with a setting on Gollum's laptop. Gently he kissed the back of my hand, then turned it over and flicked his tongue along the pulse point of my wrist.

Tingles flashed up my arm, robbing me of balance for a heartbeat. Oh, boy, this could get interesting.

At least I had someone to turn to if Gollum and Julia got back together.

"I don't suppose you have a few hours free this evening. We could slip away to my place for some privacy. Blackberry and Salal are so engrossed in their game they won't notice." He continued pushing up the sleeve of my sweater to kiss the inside of my elbow.

My bones began melting.

Not a good idea, dahling. Scrap swooped in and landed on my head. His talons tangled in my hair. Just enough pressure to jerk me back to reality.

"Um . . . Sean, don't you remember, we changed the girls' names? You came up with E.T. 'Phone home.'"

"Of course. I'm just flushed from my hurry to get here. Phonetia and E.T."

The children are getting restless, Donovan is zeroing in on Lucy, and Gollum has entered the building.

My breath caught in my throat.

"The imp will leave us alone, won't he?" Sean continued, taking responsibility for my breathlessness.

I had to remind myself he couldn't see or hear Scrap.

"Can I have a rain check, Sean?" I asked. I had to breathe to speak. I had to breathe for my heart to continue beating.

My skin twitched with uneasiness.

Gollum was in the building. I'd know soon if we had a chance of a future together.

Awkwardly, I rose from the deep sofa cushions and extricated my hand from Sean's grasp. "Later. I have an appointment," I lied.

It took all of my willpower not to run out the door in search of Gollum.

I'd no sooner cleared the doorway and veered right when someone caught my elbow and steered me left.

Two sharp breaths later Gollum pressed me into the alcove by the service elevator. I opened my mouth to ask the most important question of the moment.

But he stopped me with his mouth planted firmly atop mine. My arms crept about his neck. He deepened the kiss and pulled me tight against his chest.

The world fell away. We had only each other, this moment, the glorious blending of two people into one.

Satisfaction, well-being, a sense of belonging right here and nowhere else settled all of my nerves.

Our tongues found each other in a questing dance filled with life and love. My body molded to his along with my soul.

When we finally came up for air he lifted me off the ground and swung me around in joy.

"Don't suppose you could put me up for a few days while Julia and Pat move elsewhere?" he asked softly, still holding me aloft, pressed against his long length, held in place by his incredibly strong arms. "I talked to my lawyer last night. The divorce is in the works, papers to be filed at eight am Monday."

I gulped air praying for strength and common sense. "You can move in the day your divorce is final."

"I plan on walking you and our daughters down the aisle the day after the divorce is final. If you'll still have me."

"All you have to do is ask. And give me details," I laughed. "What happened last night?"

"Julia has done what a lot of victims of abuse do. She found a sense of safety in a homosexual relationship with a woman her own age. She started with other patients in the asylum who were hungry for any kind of peer relationships. Then she latched onto a health care professional. Typical pattern. She'll never truly feel safe with me because I'm the one who abandoned her to the asylum where her mother could come and go at will. Nurses and aides were the only ones who ever put a buffer between Julia and Bridget. The fact that she interprets that sense of safety as love is not necessarily correct, but she took a risk, made a decision on her own. *She* approached Pat. She made a choice that wasn't me. I'm free! Free to marry you."

"I will."

"You know what the funnest part of last night was?"

I shook my head, too happy to speak coherently.

"I got to tell Bridget! She sputtered and snarled and threatened to cut off Julia's trust fund, but I reminded her I'm a professional researcher. I know things about her and her family tree she doesn't want known."

"Then I don't have to send Lady Lucia to have a talk with her?"

He laughed long and loud. "One bloodsucker to another. I love it. Later, when things are a bit more settled I'll get down on bended knee with the biggest diamond I can find and propose properly." He kissed me again and set me on the ground. We clung together, neither of us certain we could stand upright on our own. "Consider this a promise.

But right now I'm obligated to lead a discussion about the evolution of dragons."

"And I should go see about slaying one."

He quirked an eyebrow.

In short and choppy sentences I related the latest developments. "Pete's desperate, Gollum. He's lost three of his children, his ability to demand demon protection on his pot-growing minions, and his hat. That's a lot of power gone in a short period of time. I have a feeling he's up to something. I just don't know what yet. I've got to stay close to the kids today. Even if it means dragging them out of their game to sit with me on panels."

"Meet me back in the Green Room at five. We'll take them out for pizza and see if they can come up with some ideas. No one knows the Nörglein better than they do."

"Pete might have confided in, or bragged to Doug," I continued his thought. "What are we going to do about legitimatizing him?"

"Don't you have any ideas?" he asked.

"Fresh out. Do you have any relatives who might have orphaned him? He says he's gay by the way." I let my fingers brush the fine hair on the back of his head, cherishing the silky texture.

"Hmmm. Let me think a moment."

"None of my family knows your family. Could he be your nephew sent to us because his parents can't deal with him?" I speculated.

"Yeah." He paused in thought. "First cousin and his wife on Dad's side—Mom doesn't speak to them and I haven't seen them since Dad's funeral—are frothing at the mouth conservatives and really hate gays. They'd throw a kid out very quickly at the first hint of alternative sexuality. I'll do the paperwork tonight. And take him home with me. He can have Pat's old room since she's sleeping with Julia these days."

One more quick kiss and we parted to our mutual con obligations. I couldn't help smiling and barely noticed Sean's frown when he joined me.

Chapter 45

Boring, Oregon was named for W.H. Boring, not a comment on the social climate.

MY NOSE TWITCHES. Something is wrong. Very, very wrong. Time to check on the kidlets. I fly ahead of Tess.

And slam into a force field. It's as thick and as hard as anything Donovan used to emit. Maybe he still has enough gargoyle left in him to set up the same kind of barrier. But I've overcome the darkness in my soul so he doesn't repel me anymore.

My nose hurts. I wiggle it to make sure it's all in one piece.

Hey! I've got a new wart there. All this protecting our girls from their blood relations has its rewards. Gingko is going to think me more beautiful than evah.

Flapping my wings rapidly and awkwardly to regain my balance, I return to Tess' shoulder, my tail around her neck and my talons clutching her cable knit sweater—a really drab cream color but it doesn't clash with her brown slacks and gold blouse. She even put on amber beads and earrings. The pearls, as always, are next to her skin, covered with clothing. We were so busy this morning I didn't have time to choose her outfit. How did she manage to color coordinate anything without me? Maybe some of my good taste is rubbing off on her.

Good. That will give me more time to work with our girls on their hair and wardrobe.

Anyway, we pass the spot that stopped me. Not something ahead of us keeping me out.

I fly behind us. This time I'm more cautious and see a faint shimmer in the air moving forward.

Something dangerous is keeping me close to my babe.

So I park my cute behind on top of her head, tuning my ears to every sound, tasting the air with my tongue as well as my newly adorned nose.

Sean's musky pine aftershave gets in the way of smelling anything untoward.

I know something is wrong I just can't figure out what it is yet.

"Tessie, babe, swing by the gaming room," I advise. "Something isn't right."

As Scrap tangled my hair in his talons and yanked, I pulled out of my euphoria long enough to notice Sean scowling and Lady Lucia approaching with a fussy Sophia sucking her fingers while strapped into her stroller.

I crouched down in front of Sophia noting her tear-streaked face. "What's the problem, little one?"

She held out her arms to me and bounced in the stroller, clearly not happy confined.

"It is time for her nap, but there is too much activity in the garden. She will not go to sleep and she will not stop crying," Lucia complained. She sounded like any other frustrated mother. "She needs your special touch."

"I'll run a quick check on the girls in the gaming room," Sean said. He didn't look too happy at my delay. "Meet me there."

Without asking, I removed the straps from around Sophia and picked her up, blankie and all. She instantly returned her fingers to her mouth, dropped her head on my shoulder, and fell asleep.

Her warmth and absolute trust filled me with longing. I cherished these few moments with my godchild.

Relief warred with jealousy on Lucia's face. "You will be a wonderful godmother and mother," she finally said. "Tomorrow morning, six o'clock Mass." She turned and started to leave, without the stroller, diaper bag, or her daughter.

"Aren't you forgetting something?"

"She will awaken if you remove her from your shoulder."

"Not now." Carefully, I shifted Sophia back into the stroller, tucking her blankie beneath her head when it lolled sideways. She whimpered briefly but fell back to sleep. "See? Now she just needs quiet for a few moments more. Then she'll be out cold for at least an hour."

I pushed the stroller beside Lucia as we returned to the central garden area. Holly was on the stage testing sound equipment and tuning her harp. She wore a full long skirt made of patchwork velvet and a white velour peasant blouse embroidered with Celtic knots and St. Brigid crosses at neck and cuff. The costume was new, her absorption in her task typical.

"I heard you sing last night." Lucia paused at the edge of the open area.

Late afternoon, more and more people congregated here, getting the parties started. Many wore costumes in preparation for the masquerade competition scheduled right after Holly's concert.

A man and a woman, both in chain mail, helmets and surcoats, bashed each other with broadswords made of PVC pipe and foam rubber. They wove around the arena below the stage in the intricate dance of dueling.

Utter chaos. And I loved it all.

"I enjoy singing filk," I replied to Lucia.

"You inherited your talent from your mother."

I swallowed a moment of sadness that Mom had just found a new life as a chanteuse in Vegas when she was murdered.

"I'm not nearly as good a singer as my mother," I replied around the lump in my throat.

"Do not be so sure of that. You have the pearls to amplify your talent. They are special pearls. The seed they are cultured around is a fragment of a goddess' bones. No one remembers which one, something Greek I believe."

"What!" I stopped dead in my tracks.

"Didn't I tell you that already?" A quirk of mischief entered her eyes. Her posture flowed from frustrated and exhausted mother to Goth manipulator, dribbling secrets on her own schedule.

"No. You told me nothing about the pearls other than that I should wear them always because I'd never know when I'd need them." I narrowed my gaze to concentrate on her. "Doreen has a similar set."

"Yes."

Scrap mumbled something anxious in the back of my mind. But the girls were quiet and content. I had a few moments to explore this new bit of information.

"I had forgotten how much I miss music in my everyday life," Lucia's voice drifted off into nostalgia.

"Tell me more about the pearls," I demanded, before she could veer off topic in her maddening way.

"They were mine once. Given to me by my great-grandmother on my wedding day. She was one of the ones we thought were witches but really just displayed her demon origins. She said the pearls always go to the one who needs them. I left them with my son in France with his Noncoiré grandparents. They passed from generation to generation in a not very straight line until your mother received them on her wedding day from your grandmother. Strangely, she didn't really need them. She was just a conduit to get them to you."

"My mother's ability to hold an audience captive with a song . . ."

"Her own talent. She didn't know how to invoke the pearls. She didn't need to."

"But what about the seed being a bone fragment from a goddess?"

She shrugged and started walking away. "I know nothing more about them. Have you, by chance, recorded music? I should like to take your voice back to Las Vegas."

"I did some back up for Holly's latest CD. Along with some other people. That's the best I can offer. I'm not a pro and don't pretend to be."

"Then you will join Miss Holly in her concert tonight?"

"Maybe. If she asks."

On the stage, Holly whipped her cell phone out of her skirt pocket. She spoke quietly for a moment and smiled. Then she closed the phone decisively and marched toward the front entrance.

I thrust the stroller back toward Lady Lucia. "I've got to check on my own daughters now." Before she had a chance to offload Sophia onto me, again, before I was ready to take her full time, I made my exit, wondering who Holly had comped for her concert. She was always giving away tickets—or in this case a con membership—to some special fan. Many of them celebrities.

A hush fell over the crowd.

I swiveled my attention back to Holly's mop of red curls by the revolving door. A tall man with flowing blond hair stepped free of the rotating glass panels.

Malcolm Levi, star of *Space Pirates of the Outer Antares.*

Every woman in the lobby gasped at one of the most beautiful men in the film industry. One of the finest actors of this generation and he'd come to the con as Holly's guest. I wondered if he was just a fan or something more. The hug she gave him could be interpreted as anything from deep gratitude to close friend to lasting lover.

Then I remembered a cryptic acknowledgement on the CD to the sweet tenor voice on a love ballad sandwiched between two rollicking fun cuts. The tenor was listed as M. Levinski—Malcolm Levi?

Oh ho. So there was something special between them.

Sixty-five cell phones appeared in hands as if by magic. Thumbs worked furiously texting and tweeting news at the speed of sound.

People all over the hotel began streaming out of side corridors and converging on the lobby to gape in wonder at the celebrity in our midst. Lucia pushed forward to the command position three feet to the left of Holly. An aggressive teen with a cell phone camera shoved her aside. The vampire crime boss of Las Vegas bared her fake fangs. The teen bared her longer fake fangs and continued taking pictures.

The railing on the mezzanine was pressed hard to hold back the eager viewers. Front and center Doreen stood tall and Junoesque with short and dumpy Starshine right beside her. I think they both drooled a bit. Malcolm Levi was as beautiful in his own way as Donovan.

Either man could set a woman's hormones jumping.

Gollum peered over the tops of several heads at the commotion. His presentation must have ended abruptly when the room emptied upon the news.

I smiled and waved at him. He waved back.

My heart flipped with joy and my interest in Malcolm Levi faded—looks and fame aren't everything.

The kids deserting the gaming rooms drew my attention back to my mission. I needed to check on my daughters. Our link told me only that they were a bit confused by the excitement.

They had no way of knowing about the famous man who smiled so endearingly at Holly.

"What's going on, Tess? A whole roomful of gamers just deserted my presentation," Donovan said emerging from a big room on my left.

"Malcolm Levi just showed up to attend Holly's concert. Even you and Halfling Games can't compete with the star of *Space Pirates of Outer Antares*." Hence Holly's new costume, reminiscent of the one worn by Malcolm Levi's love interest in the movie. I chuckled and moved on.

Donovan followed his audience.

I continued on to the gaming center. The computer room where E.T. should be was empty. And it looked as if someone had turned out the lights but left the computers running.

The corridor had grown dim as well. Moisture lay heavy in the air, almost visible. I smelled wet earth, musky rotting leaves, and heavy evergreens.

A Pacific Northwest rain forest. The Nörglein's preferred environment.

The hair on my nape stood on end.

"Scrap, we've been through this dirty air before."

Yeah, babe. I still can't smell what's wrong though. Sean's aftershave keeps blocking up my nose. And I haven't turned even a blush pink yet.

Odd memories of sentence fragments and ideas began to coalesce. I didn't like where my thoughts took me.

I stepped cautiously through the open accordion door separating the rooms, holding my right hand out for Scrap.

A bit brighter in here. E.T., Phonetia, and Doug sat hunched over a gaming board, gazes firmly fixed on their twenty-sided dice and fantasy figures. Sean faced them, anger stiffening his shoulders.

"Blackberry, Salal, Tess says you are to come with me now." A swirl of humid murk kept me from seeing fine details of his form.

"Sean, why did you just call the girls by their former names? This is the second time you've done it." Once a slip. Twice a problem. Another memory slipped into place: The Nörglein's victims complaining about his *pine* aftershave.

I took a defensive stance and held out my hand for Scrap.

Sean turned confused eyes on me, keeping his body half facing the children, so that they never got totally out of his line of sight. "Tess, sweetheart, when they didn't agree to come the first time, I had to try something more drastic."

Phonetia shook her head slightly.

He was lying.

Scrap flushed red all over.

I smell fear, babe. The kids are desperately afraid of Sean who isn't Sean. All three of them.

"You called them by the old names because you're not Sean, you slimy bastard. Show your real self, shape-changer!"

This was why he'd tried to lead me back to Sean's home to seduce me. I was to be his next victim. Some fast math in my head told me I was fertile and vulnerable.

"I got news for you, elf, my firstborn is already promised to the Powers That Be. You'll never get your hands on me or my children."

"Your bargain with the Powers That Be is less than my need. Your demon blessed DNA is a triumphant bonus."

"How did you know?"

"All Warriors of the Celestial Blade have a drop or two of demon in their genes. That's the only way the imp flu can infect you. That's the only way you can find the Citadels halfway between dimensions. But I don't truly need a child from you. I want the crystal ball."

"You can't have it."

"I'll find it eventually."

"Not bloody likely." Scrap had stretched and curved, halfway to ready. "You won't run away from me this time, Nörglein." I slashed at him with the still dull blade.

"This time I came prepared." The words were barely out of his mouth when he shrank and broadened. His face took on the color and texture of mellow yellow pine as his nose and chin elongated, reaching toward each other. Modern jeans and polo shirt melted into a short green coat and tricorn hat over buff breeches and shirt. The hat was brand-new and lacked the luster of power in his real one. Large, hairy feet replaced the athletic shoes.

And he drew a long, wickedly sharp sword from a fine leather sheath on his belt. This was no foiled weapon legal at the con. This was a deadly serious blade meant for a duel to the death.

Chapter 46

Oregon Shakespeare Festival in Ashland was founded in 1935. It is the largest repertory theater in the US. Supposedly, the ghost of Charles Laughton haunts the place in his King Lear *costume, though he died before he could actually perform there.*

"I HAVE REMOVED THESE CHILDREN from their mothers, I will take them from you more easily," the Nörglein snarled. His sword lashed out in a neat swipe across my middle.

I ducked and backed up. Scrap was still curving and sharpening.

The elf lunged with a circle down.

No polite chitchat while I got ready to fight. No salute or referee. No confines of a fencing strip set to tournament regulations.

No rules or honor either.

I retreated to the corridor, twirling Scrap to help him finish transforming. We were alone.

Another cut and stab.

This guy was good. He handled his weapon like he'd studied with the best Italian masters.

He probably had.

"Phonetia, get your brother and sister to Gollum or Lady Lucia. Now." I didn't want them to have to watch one of us die.

"You stole us?" Phonetia screamed. "You stole us from

our mothers? Then you raped me from the time I started bleeding. You freaking pervert! We could have been raised with love, gone to school, seen movies. We could be normal. Not your fucking slaves and brood mares."

"Such language, Blackberry. You never learned those words from me. A sure sign I should be the one to raise you," the elf said, almost congenially. He used his bland demeanor to cover his next vicious attack.

I blocked his thrust with the shaft, twisted and set the outer tines to scrape his torso.

Scrap tasted blood and chortled.

"Phonetia, get out. Protect Doug and E.T. That's an order," I said with more calm than I felt.

Tree Daddy slashed again. I backed up, not sure where I was going.

I heard my kids scramble toward a sliding glass door that led to the domed pool area. From there they could easily get to the Green Room.

The tip of one half moon blade scraped the corridor wall on my next slash, throwing off my timing and my aim. Not a lot of room. Better than the water slick floor of the pool deck.

I continued backing up, searching for an opening.

The dark elf only stood four feet tall but he had extraordinarily long arms that seemed to stretch and withdraw with each movement.

I shifted my grip to one end of the Celestial Blade, grabbing the shaft two-handed, like a broadsword.

Duck and lunge. Parry and riposte. My long hours in the fencing salle came back to me, thought became instinct.

The Nörglein twisted his blade in a neat circular parry and riposte. I caught the tip on my left arm. Barely a pinprick of pain as adrenaline countered the nerve reaction. Then a hot trickle of blood. My arm felt as if he'd stabbed deep and long. The muscle spasmed.

Damn, this elf knew his business.

I cut over and jabbed at his lower left. He yelped and skipped back. But not for long.

Before I recovered to *en garde* he was on me, fast and furious.

I kept backing up, chancing quick looks over my shoulder to make sure I didn't trip.

A roar of applause and the squeal of microphone feedback erupted behind me. Close. We were too close to the lobby. Innocents could get drawn in.

But then so could my backup. I couldn't count on them. A rogue Warrior of the Celestial Blade worked alone.

Not anymore. I had family and backup.

The noise invigorated the elf's smile. He showed a lot of pointed teeth, black around the edges.

"Forget to floss?" What can I say? I get sarcastic when I'm scared.

Come to think on it, his toes and fingertips looked like they were crumbling back to dirt. This guy was old and rotting.

And therefore, more desperate than I thought. Well-armed, trained, and still strong. I had to come up with a plan. I had to become more devious than he.

He forced me back. One step. Then two more. I lunged under his blade. He retreated just enough to evade. Then pressed me harder.

My breath caught in my lungs, sharp and short. My legs grew heavy with fatigue. Scrap looked a little dull. We flagged, in serious danger of getting hurt from carelessness.

Don't say his name. We can still take him. Scrap sounded breathless and far away.

My muscles grew heavy. His name rose to my lips.

I clamped them shut.

I had one chance and one only. The lights behind me grew brighter as we cleared the forest murk the Nörglein had raised. He blinked rapidly.

I skipped back into the light.

Three people hopped out of my way. "Ooh, a new demo," a large woman swathed in Gypsy red and purple silk scarves with lots of dangling jewelry crooned. She smelled strongly of roses. Artificial roses.

The Nörglein sneezed and lost his attack posture.

"Clear the way!" I shouted, dashing for the open arena around the stage.

Tree Daddy followed me, eyes and nose clearing.

"Fight, fight, fight," the crowd chanted.

I spotted Squishy physically holding people away from my path. Cameras flashed and thumbs sped over cell phone keypads.

We danced around the arena twice, blades flashing in the bright lights before I could catch my breath.

"What have you done with Sean?" I demanded as I pressed my foe closer to the stage. Gollum leaped up onto the raised platform from the other side. He grabbed a length of sound cable ready to loop into a noose.

"You will never find your boyfriend," the dark elf chortled. I have destroyed the paths."

"He's an innocent in this. He deserves to be rescued."

"But not by you. I will set him free when I am done with you. As I have honorably done to all the men who loaned me their wives."

"That's rape. None of them were willing participants in your scheme to repopulate this world with your get."

"You know nothing. I have the right to protect my race from extinction. Now, where is the crystal ball?" He slashed again.

I parried half a heartbeat too late. Blood poured down my left arm, making my grip on the staff slick and uneven.

I could say his name.

Desperate to end this, I lunged again. Scrap sharpened enough to slice Pete's old-fashioned shirt from left shoulder to right hip. Somewhere in there we got a piece of skin. Green-black blood stained the creamy linen.

The lights, the noise, fatigue, and blood loss took their toll. My lunge skewed my balance. I tilted too far forward. My right knee gave up trying to support my weight, followed by the collapse of my left.

My left shoulder hit the floor first sending long lances of pain down my back and up into my skull.

I lost my grip on my blade.

The Nörglein didn't wait to gloat. He raised his sword in both hands, ready to plunge it into my heart.

"Purz . . ."

I rolled, expecting the fatal blow in my back. The end of his name got garbled in the tangle of plants that caught me.

Nothing.

I rolled farther away.

"Drop the weapon," Donovan said very slowly and precisely.

No sign of Gollum on the stage.

A quick glance over my shoulder showed my rescuer holding a plastic ray gun to the Nörglein's neck.

"Mundane weapons cannot hurt me." The troll raised his blade another fraction, shifting his aim.

"Who said this is an ordinary weapon?" Donovan asked. Still no emotion in his voice.

Then Gollum was at my side, wrapping his handkerchief around the slice on my arm, reaching to help me up, handing me my blade. My girls clung to his belt behind him.

The Nörglein hesitated, weighing possibilities.

Donovan eased the pressure on the Nörglein's neck.

Pete shifted his feet and his grip, engaging my blade once more.

I tangled his sword in the tines. We stared at each other, frozen in impasse.

Phonetia's arm morphed into blackberry vines, shooting out from her sweatshirt sleeve faster than Spiderman's web. Vicious thorns bit into the elf's woody hide at ankle and calf. The plant fiber looped and doubled back on itself. She tightened the vine around the elf's feet and yanked.

He fell forward onto his ugly nose, yowling in pain and outrage. "How dare you defy me!"

Gollum, the eternal Eagle Scout produced plastic zip strips from his pocket and snapped them in place around thick troll ankles and wrists.

The Nörglein fought his mundane restraints.

"Artificial. He can't manipulate the fibers," Gollum said, pushing his glasses higher on his nose. He looked ready to lecture the audience.

"You can't do this to me!" The Nörglein wiggled.

Donovan placed his heavy foot in the middle of his chest.

Phonetia withdrew her vines.

I lifted my blade for the coup de grace.

"Before you send this heap of garbage off to hell, I need to know something," Doreen demanded. She stayed my blow with a brief touch of her hand. "Which of the boys is my son?"

"How am I supposed to remember that?" the Nörglein replied. "They're all alike."

"But you stole my baby from me! Surely you remember that."

"Why should I?"

Anger at the elf's total lack of care for his children sent waves of fire through my blood. I raised the blade.

Loud applause stopped me. The con populace really didn't need to see the execution of this guy. We weren't play acting. My girls didn't need to watch me murder the being who had raised them, even if he had abused them.

"We'll do this." Oak appeared at the edge of the crowd, Cedar close beside him.

"No. I will. This has been a long time coming." Donovan hauled the bound Nörglein to his feet and slung him over his shoulder.

"Allow me." Lady Lucia bared her fangs. "I thought I killed you once, you disgrace to decent timber. This time I will make sure. This time we dump the body in the river so you cannot regenerate in the soil. Tess, watch the baby."

Before they could take two steps toward the rapidly clearing corridor to the gaming rooms, the Nörglein shuddered and spasmed.

Donovan dropped him unceremoniously. He landed with only a light wisp of sound. Smoke streamed upward from where the plastic strips bound his wrists and ankles. It smelled sweet, like burning pine, but with a bitterness of old and rotten wood beneath it.

The dark elf screamed, high and piercing.

"God, I'm sorry. I had no idea the plastic would do that to him." Gollum bent to remove the lethal restraints.

Cedar beat him to it. The boy bit his lip and tears moistened his eyes.

"No." Oak stayed his brother with a firm grip on his arm. "What will be, will be. We agreed. He's no longer fit to maintain the forest. He needs to be culled."

"If my forest dies, let it be on your head, Tess Noncoiré. You are responsible for the death of all the trees and the living things that depend upon them!" The dark elf fixed an angry, defiant gaze upon me. Smoke poured from his mouth.

His eyes remained open, accusing me as his body convulsed once more and lay still.

My girls fell on me, hugging me tightly, crying and shaking.

I wasn't too steady myself. Gollum joined the family with Doug close on his heels. He pulled another handkerchief and a wet wipe from somewhere, taking care of my wounds even as he joined the family embrace.

Through the shimmering veil of my own tears of relief, I noted Doreen approaching Cedar and Oak with a tentative offer of her own embrace. As tall as she, the boys clung to her, silently burying their faces in her shoulders.

Donovan and Lucia made off with the smoldering body. "The river," Lucia said quietly. "It's the only way. Too bad he's already dead. I looked forward to a long, slow, tortuous feed."

Scrap dissolved and crept off to reçover. I knew he'd find ample mold in the basement levels. But I'd make sure I provided him with beer and OJ in the café.

"Pretty good skit. The smoke was a nice touch. But the blood was too dark, not green enough," Malcolm Levi laughed over the noise of the clapping crowd.

Chapter 47

Between 1870 and 1930, seventy miles of tunnels beneath Pendleton, Oregon, housed entire businesses from butcher shops to opium dens.

"WE NEED TO FIND SEAN," E.T. whispered, still clinging to me.

"The binding will wear off . . ." I said hopefully.

"If Pete doesn't return by midnight, the minions with demon tats will kill the man," Doreen said. She and the boys joined our group. Cedar and Oak had withdrawn from her, mastering their emotions in stoic acceptance. She looked disappointed and lonely.

Gollum continued to fuss over my already healing wounds.

"A little imp spit would work faster than those wet wipes, but Scrap's not around," I whispered. My love for him grew and blossomed, threatening to choke me.

"The paths have been destroyed," Oak said. "I don't think either Cedar or I could find our way home again."

"Is there a back door?" Gollum chimed in. He accepted a gold silk scarf from a fan's costume to tie his makeshift bandage in place.

"Back door?" Oak's face went blank.

"There is always a back door. Only a fool builds a secret lair with only one entrance," Gollum replied. "First law of super villains."

"The tunnels," Phonetia said barely above a whisper.

"The what?" Cedar shot her a wicked glare.

"I don't have to keep the old man's secrets anymore," she returned haughtily.

"I know an entrance three blocks from here," E.T. said quietly. "It's nearly blocked in places between there and the main passage. Hard going. But it's not as heavily trafficked around the entrance. And it's raining hard out. We'd get soaked before we found the trapdoor."

"A rainy Saturday night in Old Town, the parking will be difficult at best. We'll probably have to walk half a mile. Might as well take the more difficult but closer tunnel," Gollum added.

"Let's go." I stepped back and nearly tripped over Sophia's stroller. She woke up and wailed.

My heart flipped with the need to hold and comfort her. At the same time I sank within myself, knowing I'd have to wait for Lucia to return before I could go find Sean. At this point every moment of delay endangered him from the latest batch of men with demon tattoos.

More incompetents or had Pete held back the best of his minions?

I was betting on the latter and Scrap was in no condition to help.

"I'll watch the baby for Lucia," Doreen offered.

"Can I trust you to return Sophia to her mother, and only her mother? If Donovan comes back first . . .?" With her Damiri black hair, he might assume the obvious and claim her as his own.

I looked around at the assembly. Most of the crowd drifted off, or found seats in front of the stage waiting for Holly to begin her concert.

I needed my girls and their brothers with me, leading me through the tunnels. I wanted Gollum at my side.

Solemnly, I approached Squishy and Julia, hovering indecisively in the background. "Hi, I'm Tess," I introduced myself to Julia. "I saw you playing with Sophia yesterday. Could I trouble you to watch her for a little while until her mother returns?"

"You trust me with her?"

"I trusted you with Gollum's heart. Nothing is more precious to me. You gave that back to me. I trust you with my goddaughter as well."

"Thank you," she said graciously. "I never meant to hurt him."

"I know. We're all happier this way. And I know we all have to get along. So why not start now. Can you watch Sophia?"

"Yes. I'd be honored," she said enthusiastically reaching for the little girl.

Sophia willingly went into her arms and immediately began playing with her expensive golden knot earrings.

I transferred the KIT sticker from my badge to hers.

"Well done, Tess," Gollum said, kissing my temple. "I think we need to get a move on though. Phonetia says it will take us a least an hour to hike up to the hills."

"Let's get moving. Maybe Scrap will recover enough to help by then."

Don't bet on it, I heard a disgruntled mumble in the back of my head.

"Squishy, why don't you and Julia take Sophia to the café? Order a beer and an orange juice. Don't be surprised if it disappears on its own."

"Draft or bottle?" Squishy called back.

"Doesn't matter." A new thought wiggled forward in my mind. I fished my cell phone out of my fanny pack and tossed it to Squishy. "Call Raquel and JJ Jones. Tell them they can keep their baby! Spread the word to the entire support group."

Squishy is a good baby-sitter for me. Julia is an attentive baby-sitter for Sophia. The two women make an interesting couple. Physical opposites. Emotional opposites. They're kinda cute together. Maybe they really are in love.

They coo and fuss over Sophia with poignant joy, knowing they will never have a child together, but delighting in this little bundle of energy.

Sophia has decided a bottle is too tame. She wants a cup. And she wants it now. She makes a mess of the peanut butter and jelly sandwich Julia orders for her. But amazingly most of it ends up in her tummy.

Squishy takes a few moments to make the requested phone call. She's smiling by the end of it. I can hear Raquel's joyful tears through the tiny speaker.

I watch from the safety of the bank of ferns in a raised bed behind their table. The moment the beer and OJ arrive I creep out from my safe observatory and take a few sips. Then I creep back and wait a few minutes for the waters of life to work their magic. Another few sips and I'm up to making faces at Sophia.

She blinks at me, not certain she sees me. Then she sticks out her tongue, aping me. She's so cute. I waggle my wart enhanced bum at her.

She stands in her high chair and flashes her ruffled panties at me.

Squishy coaxes her back to sitting with more PB&J.

Doreen joins us, gazing at Sophia with intense longing. Movement in her peripheral vision draws her attention to the side passage. She's impatient for Donovan to return. At the same time, she wants to enjoy the baby as long as possible.

A couple more sips of beer and I can almost work up the energy to go find some mold.

You okay, Scrap? Tess asks from someplace dark and dank. Oh, I bet she's got good mold all around her.

Working on it, I flash back to her. *Where are you?* I could find out if I just thought about her for a moment. But I don't have the energy yet.

Deep in the tunnels. E.T. says we're about a hundred yards from the main passage.

Careful. I think there's a rockfall just ahead of you.

I see it. Gollum has the most amazing flashlight.

Of course he does. He's Gollum.

And his backpack, of course.

He's always prepared.

Lucia returned from her errand yet?

Nope.

Scrap, hurry and get your strength back. This place is really, really creepy. I feel like I'm being watched by a thousand ghosts and none of them want me here.

Working on it. Stay close to Gollum. Keep the girls from straying. I'll be there as soon as I can.

She fades from my consciousness and I finish my beer and OJ. My skin glows a bit orange and my tummy bulges. Time for dessert.

Sophia reaches for my tail as I prepare to fly off. Oops, can't allow that. There's this special grip that only Tess is supposed to know about. When she tangles her fingers just above the barb, I can't get away, even though I'm only partly in this dimension and should be able to slip through anything. This little lady is looking to learn the grip quite by accident. And she's not yet a year old.

I sense a Warrior in the making. I'll keep a look out for a likely imp to bond with her. Can't let just anybody infect my Sophia with the imp flu.

Chapter 48

The largest gold nugget found in Oregon weighed seventeen pounds.

"WHAT WAS THAT ABOUT YOU having demon blood in you?" Gollum asked quietly as he helped me negotiate a pile of cave debris that nearly blocked the passage.

I didn't really need the help, but it felt good to let his strength and height aid me.

I took comfort that I wasn't alone in these tunnels. There was a malevolent presence here. Resentment. Fear. Greed.

"Um . . ."

"We didn't tell anyone," Phonetia said. "The Nörglein figured that out on his own."

So I told my Gollum how Pete had bound the girls and how Lucia and I had broken the spell. Then I slowly and carefully told him about Lucia and my Noncoiré ancestor; sounding out my own emotions as I spoke. He had a right to know.

"In a weird way that makes sense," Gollum said. Then he grew silent.

"What? No lecture? No dissertation?"

I sensed his shrug more than saw it. I had to watch where I put my feet on the uneven ground in the limited light.

"I can see the safety lights in the main tunnel," E.T. announced.

"Thank God," I muttered.

Help me! A faint cry in the distance froze me to the bone.

"Did you hear that?" I started shaking. My feet refused to take the next three steps, even though the way was clear.

"Hear what?" Phonetia asked. She stopped too, turning her head right and left.

Get out! a different voice said; closer this time.

"I don't hear anything," Gollum said. He pushed his glasses higher on his nose, as if that enhanced his hearing.

Despair threatened to overwhelm me. Tears burned in my eyes. No hope. No way. out. Nothing but this endless darkness, pain, thirst, hunger. Fear. Alone.

I was going to die alone in this god-awful place.

My legs turned to jelly. I sank to my knees weeping. My shoulders felt too heavy to remain upright. I curled in on myself, resting my forehead on the cold earth, not caring that a sharp rock pressed against sensitive flesh.

Gollum knelt beside me, cradling my body against his.

No help. No use.

"Maybe it's the ghosts," E.T. whispered.

"They don't bother with us much," Phonetia added.

"Father never cleared them out," Oak added. "He said they kept mundanes from penetrating the tunnels far enough to know just how deep they go."

"Greed from the gold rush eras intensifies all the emotion of the spirits that refuse to leave," Doug added. He spun in place, arms extended, palms up, absorbing the psychic emotions.

"Is it true that Doreen is the mother of one of us?" Cedar spoke for the first time.

"Yes," I said, clinging to the ordinary world of words, questions, and answers.

The heavy ache of despair lifted a little. I was able to pull myself up a bit.

"You're more sensitive than most to otherworldly creatures," Gollum said. "We already know you're a projecting empath. Probably a receiver too. You've got to blank your mind to the echoes of the past. They are long dead. They cannot hurt you. There is nothing you can do to help them."

"I can get a priest down here tomorrow morning and exorcise them," I replied firmly. Determination returned. I stumbled to my feet. Gollum rose up with me, taking my hand in his.

That little bit of connection to a living human helped banish the weight of the dead. I wasn't alone.

We moved on, clambering over the last obstacles to the clear passage that rose gradually. Brick archways led to side tunnels; each one the subbasement of a different building. Wooden walls closed off holding cells for the Shanghai shipmasters, and the white slavers.

I guessed we turned west, uphill and away from the river.

I heard footsteps, loud and clear from the northeast. I started shaking again.

Gollum thumbed off his light.

"They're real this time," Phonetia whispered. She and her sister melted against a smoothly carved dirt wall, blending with the earth. Becoming invisible. I followed their example, finding worn bricks and crumbling mortar behind me. At times I can become a chameleon. A shift of posture, rearrangement of hair and costume and I blend in, sending questing eyes everywhere but at me.

All three boys did their own disappearing act in a shadowed alcove fitted out with stacks of bunk bed frames, four up on each of three walls with barely three feet walking space in the center. An opium den.

"Probably just a caretaker," Gollum whispered, drawing me closer with an arm around my shoulders.

"Tess? I know you're down here somewhere," Donovan called.

Gollum turned on his light again, aiming it directly into the newcomer's eyes.

Donovan shaded his brow with one hand as he walked hesitantly out of a side corridor.

"Where'd you come from?" I asked, pushing Gollum's hand down so Donovan wasn't blinded by the flashlight.

"I own the building that used to house a saloon with a Shanghai trapdoor. The trapdoor is still there if you know how to find it. But it's easier to come down the cellar stairs into the basement." He flashed a grin.

"Shanghai trapdoor?" I mused. "That explains the ghosts."

Donovan blanched, then recovered his normal aplomb.

"You hear them too, don't you," I commented, stepping out from behind the light so Donovan could find me.

"The passage is clear and easy going for about a half mile, then it gets rough, narrow and steep. You up to it?" Donovan avoided the subject of ghosts. He'd probably lived with them every day during the eight hundred years he inhabited a gargoyle statue.

"Did you complete . . . your . . . errand?" Gollum asked. He kept a wary eye on all five of the children.

Donovan nodded mutely. "The old bastard won't rape any more women, or bind any more men. Lady Lucia made sure of that before we weighted the body with plastic bottles filled with stones and dumped it into the river." He turned his head away and swallowed heavily.

"I bet that Lucia's handling of the body wasn't pretty."

We all nodded in mute agreement. I swallowed my gag reflex. Motherhood had mellowed Lady Lucia, but only when it suited her. I briefly worried about Sophia's upbringing with a bloodthirsty demon mother. Lucia was right to give her to me.

Suddenly, I didn't want that sweet and innocent child growing up like her mother. I'd made my decision and wouldn't postpone our discussion any longer. We'd figure out the details tomorrow. My feet really wanted to retreat and protect the child.

But I owed Sean a rescue first.

Determinedly, I set a brisk pace through the tunnel. I didn't look right or left. I didn't want to know the horrors that had taken place down here when Portland was an ungoverned seaport. Gold in California, gold in eastern Oregon, gold in the Black Hills. All that greed had prompted men and women to behave as badly as any demon.

"Is it true, Mr. Donovan?" Oak asked quietly as we trudged along.

"Is what true?"

"That the Cooper woman is mother to one of us." Like the boys didn't believe me.

"Yes."

"Which one?"

"We don't know. But when I marry Doreen in two weeks, I will adopt both of you."

Good for him.

"Unless Tess agrees to marry me first. Then I'll adopt all five of you." Donovan flashed me a bright grin. His teeth nearly glowed in the beam of the flashlight. "I'll give you the saloon as a wedding present and you can turn the tunnels into an amusement park."

I groaned. "Not a chance, Donovan. I'm spoken for." I slipped my hand into Gollum's.

"Isn't he taken?" Donovan protested.

"Not any more," Gollum replied. Then he stopped abruptly, playing the light over a seemingly blank brick wall with a pile of dirt and building debris at its base. "End of the road. We'll have to turn back. Maybe one of the side tunnels," he said.

The ones filled with ghosts.

"No, it's not the end of the road," E.T. said. She surged from behind and grabbed the light from Gollum. "See this crack between dirt and brick?"

Before we could reply she twisted sideways and slithered through. She shone the light backward, illuminating the impassible path.

"It's easy," Phonetia echoed. She too slid inward.

"Maybe for you two. You're vine skinny," I complained.

"So are you, love." Gollum pushed me forward. Sure enough the crack was wider than it looked. Rough rock and dirt scraped my sweater, reopening the mostly forgotten sword wound as I inched my way through. Then I popped out into a wider room. I could just barely see steps cut into the rocky slope that formed the back wall.

"Not far now," Oak said as he too came through the barrier.

"I don't want to be adopted. Not by you. Not by anyone even if the Cooper woman gave birth to me," Cedar said defiantly. He blocked Donovan and Gollum from entering the crack.

"Cedar, we talked about this," Oak said. He sounded worried.

"Who will guard the forest if we give in to these people? Who will tend it with the love and care it needs to protect it from casual bits of harm and major influxes of danger?"

We all stopped and thought about that.

"Cedar, you don't have to do it all alone. It's time to let

humans help you," I reassured him. That was a lesson I'd found hard to learn.

"Father says . . . said that humans are incompetent, and more dangerous than fire during a drought." He stood solid and strong in the wind of my argument.

"The Nörglein never grew with the times. He knew humans with the medieval belief that the forest was a dark and dangerous place to be destroyed or avoided. Because he kept it that way."

I let that sink in a moment before continuing. "Because of the Nörglein and creatures who didn't really belong there, the forest *was* a place to be exploited and eliminated for the protection of people and their families. Humanity has learned a lot about the value of the forest. We're working hard to preserve what we have and restore some of what we've lost."

"You've lost too much! The forest we have is barely enough!" Cedar cried. Moisture gathered in his eyes. He truly loved his patch of wilderness.

"I know someone who has trained volunteers to help a forest grow and thrive," I said quietly. "My aunt, MoonFeather, is a special person. She has an affinity with the natural world. She'll know how to keep you involved with the volunteers while you lead a more human life in a family. In case you haven't noticed, Portland . . . the entire state has spearheaded conservation. With your help we can do even more."

Cedar bit the insides of his cheeks. "I'll help you tonight because I do not like the minions with tattoos growing marijuana in *my* forest." He pushed himself through the crack with some difficulty, his barrel chest scraping the dirt hard. "But I will not leave with any of you when you remove the Sean person from my home."

Donovan reached an arm through and grabbed the boy's shirt.

"Easy. Don't force the issue," Gollum said.

"He only knows threats and violence. He won't respond to anything else," Donovan protested.

"All the more reason to break the cycle of threats and violence. Give him a chance to get used to the idea of regular meals, a comfortable home, and family to keep loneliness at bay. There will also be friends, books, TV and movies, more cons and gaming for him to adjust to. Let him think."

My Gollum knew what he was doing. He planted the seeds of ideas. Only time would tell if they fell on fertile ground.

"We'll talk later," Donovan promised.

We pushed upward in silence.

My calves burned from the steep climb. Too often I felt Gollum push my back upward and welcomed the boost.

E.T. and her sister bounced up the steps as if they danced on the flat. I thought I was fit. They put me to shame.

A whiny tenor voice drifted downward:

We wuz made to pump all night an' day.
Leave her, Johnny, leave her!
An' we half-dead and bugger-all to say
An it's time for us to leave her!

I recognized the old Irish drinking song about a ship. Taken out of context, as it usually was, it could mean a whole lot of bawdy things.

The girls rolled their eyes and pressed on.

"What?" I mouthed more than whispered.

"Shush. We're close. They'll hear us," Phonetia admonished. "Sound carries strangely here."

We'll leave her tight an' we'll leave her trim,
Leave her, Johnny, Leave her!
We'll heave the hungry bastard in.
An' it's time for us to leave her!

I finally recognized Sean as the off-key vocalist. He wandered around several high notes before finding one he could settle on. Not the one meant for the song.

I can sing better than that, Scrap said on a yawn as he popped out of nothing and onto my shoulder with precision I hadn't seen in him before.

Oh, sing that we boys will never be
Leave her, Johnny, leave her!
In a hungry bitch the like o' she.
An' it's time for us to leave her!

"Pinpoint landing, Scrap. Good one." I relaxed a bit knowing my friend and ally had come back.

Tight quarters, babe. Tight time line.

Uh, oh. Scrap had lingered in his recovery too long and had to use a bit of time travel to get back to me before disaster struck.

He wouldn't have risked slipping up on the tricky maneuver if disaster weren't about to close in on us.

A dozen demon tats armed with Uzis and ropes of ammo. Straight out of a Mexican Bandito movie.

Chapter 49

Hells Canyon, between Oregon and Idaho along the Snake River, is the deepest river cut gorge in North America. At one point, it's 8043 feet deep, 1/3 mile deeper than the Grand Canyon.

"WE'RE MARCHING INTO HELL. Again," Tess says.

I feel her wilt beneath my talons.

"I'm tired of killing," she whispers. Her hands go to her mother's pearls. She ratchets them around and around her neck. She's favoring her left arm, the one the Nörglein stabbed.

"Wrong answer, babe," I reply. "These guys are mean. They're territorial, and you've just taken out their protector and mentor."

"But the Nörglein was old and rotten to the core, a being from another dimension that didn't belong here. These are men. Humans, no matter how warped and murderous. They need to go to the law."

The pearls increase their speed around her neck, then stop suddenly as she stares at them.

I can see ideas forming behind her eyes. She quirks a half smile.

"Not enough, dahling. You can't be sure this plan will—like—work."

"I calmed a plane full of panicking passengers on the verge of a riot," she says. "I kept them from opening the hatch of a pressurized cabin at twenty thousand feet. And I didn't have the pearls to help."

"These guys aren't panicking."

"No, but they are nervous and vulnerable. Sean's off-key singing has set their nerves on edge. All I have to do is tip them over the edge to hopelessness and despair. Like the ghosts down below did to me."

She turns to her crew with bright eyes and a jaunty set to her shoulders.

I really don't like this plan. I don't trust it. But I'm tired enough, I hope it works. At best it will give me a few extra moments of rest before transforming again.

"Donovan, follow me in with your famous smile," I ordered as I fingered the latch on the back door to the Nörglein's lair.

"And which smile would that be?" he asked, flashing me the one that used to seduce me.

"The one you use to lull a crowd into agreeing with you no matter how outrageous your words." If that wasn't seduction, I'd eat Scrap's boa.

"Oh, that smile." Donovan showed his teeth. They shone nearly as brightly as Gollum's flashlight.

We didn't need to worry about being heard. Sean had ramped up the volume of his drinking song more than a notch. His wavering tenor kept sliding just far enough out of tune that he made my teeth hurt.

I don't think I could ever be truly happy with a man who couldn't filk with me. Good thing Gollum had come back. I liked the way he fit his light baritone in a neat harmony with my soprano.

But I had to remember acutely the eighteen months of loneliness while my one true love lived with another woman.

"Gollum, got any more of those zip strips?"

"Of course." He drew a whole wad of them out of his backpack.

"Boys, stay behind Gollum and help him restrain the bad guys the best you can. Girls, collect weapons and ammo and stash it out of reach. But don't leave any fingerprints. We want the law to find them in the marijuana patch. We'll get them on illegal weapons charges as well as drug production."

I took a deep breath and touched the pearls one more time for luck, and for insight. I needed to channel my mother's talent and invoke the goddess within.

You have your own talent, dear, I heard her sultry voice in the back of my mind.

I opened the door and peeked into the candlelit bedroom. A massive four-poster bed sat dead center, with rich green on green damask coverlet, curtains, and canopy. A matching wardrobe stood against the far wall with padded damask insets in the doors. They belonged in a seventeenth century Italian villa.

Very modern wing back chairs in the same upholstery and stark end tables sat in a grouping in the far corner. I'd seen almost identical chairs and tables at Cooper's. Four bored banditos slumped in the chairs, weapons across their laps; deceptively small guns that could hide inside a jacket or down the leg of baggy pants. The young men supported their heads in their hands, rubbing temples as if to relieve a headache.

A headache caused by Sean. He stood stark naked—and a very nice body he had—at the foot of the bed, singing at the top of his lungs, swilling something dark and thick from a glass mug.

Leave her, Johnny, leave her.

An we half-dead and bugger-all to say

The air reeked of burning marijuana and other herbs.

The Nörglein didn't need magic to bind a victim with that heady mixture. His magic had grown dim and he didn't waste it when he had drugs that did the same thing.

I opened my mouth and let the first notes of "Heart's Path" slide under and around Sean's bawdy ditty.

He paused and stared at me through bloodshot eyes that didn't focus or track well.

I raised my voice and poured all of my loneliness and pain into the words. With eyes closed and chin trembling I let all of my pent-up emotions, the sense of betrayal and desertion, the grief, the aching emptiness that had built into a year and a half of depression, bleed through the music.

I have watched you go; I have seen the change
Though my pledge to your side I will keep
It is not enough to be who I am
And to savor your smiles in my sleep

I opened the ache of all the nights I'd tossed restlessly, reaching out to the emptiness beside me in the bed. I relived the horrible heaviness in my heart as I watched Gollum walk away. I cried all the tears I had bottled up for eighteen months.

He will tell you now that three is a crowd
And you know that I leave with my heart
It is not enough to just take what is left
So I'll love you and serve you apart
Follow your heart's path, in Valen's name
Now it leads me away to defend.
I will fight, I will die, I will be what you wish
And my love for you will never end.

I repeated the last two lines with emphasis on "I will die."

I heard a sniffle behind me. Phonetia dashed tears away with the back of her hand. E.T. cried openly.

The guys in the corner stared at me dumbly, not moving, not raising their weapons.

So I stepped closer, aiming my voice at them and sang the song again. This time I held the pearls, twisting them around and around my neck, as I'd needed to twist the faery ring to activate it.

"Ah, Tessie, 'tis a mournful day the Irish left the Emerald Isle behind," Sean slurred. He took one step toward me and tumbled onto the bed, snoring.

One of the bad guys looked up, blinking rapidly. "Who . . . who are you?" he asked, swallowing several times.

I felt the lump in his throat and the trembling in his chin.

"I am the avenging angel who is going to end your tyranny over the forest," I sang, keeping the song, and the agony alive in conversation. I projected as much fear as I had ever felt into the statement.

All four of them fell to their knees, holding their heads. Three of them bent double, sobbing uncontrollably.

Then I sang an Irish lullaby. *Tura lura, lura.* Those three men fell asleep, sniffling and sobbing in their twisted dreams. Still, the one who spoke resisted me.

So I found in my memory the tune of a Scottish dirge, usually played on the bagpipes, and gave him all of the anguish I felt when I'd held my mother in my arms as she died; the last words on her lips, "I love you."

By the time I breathed before the third phrase, all four men had zip strips on wrists and ankles. The girls stashed the weapons and ammunition in the wardrobe.

Then E.T. shoved tiny toxic berries from her fingertips into their mouths. "Just enough to make them sick," she said on a grimace. "Not enough poison to really hurt them."

Four down, eight to go in the outer rooms, Scrap reminded me.

He turned bright pink as the door crashed to the floor and those eight men flooded in. I heard eight safeties click off as I stared down the muzzles of eight very nasty guns.

Chapter 50

The largest meteorite found in the US, 16th largest in the world, was dug up in West Linn, Oregon, in 1902. 32,000 lbs, 10' tall, 6'6" wide and 4'3" deep. It is now in the American Museum of Natural History in New York. Negotiations to return it to Oregon continue.

DONOVAN STEPPED IN FRONT OF ME, putting a solid barrier between the bad guys and the rest of us.

"You don't really want to do that," he said calmly.

"Wanna make a bet?" Blondie sneered in reply. Then he spoiled his menacing attitude by scratching his ass. Poison oak had breached his protections. Or was that *breeched?*

I caught my giggle in mid-throat, nearly choking.

"The demon tattoos are protecting them from your smile, Donovan," I whispered.

"Shouldn't make a difference," Donovan replied, clearly puzzled, though he kept the smile in place.

In my peripheral vision I saw all five children sidling along the walls, converging on the crowded doorway.

"Tura lura lura," Sean sang into the damask bed covering, still mostly unconscious in his drunken stupor.

"Huh?" Blondie said.

Donovan backed up a bit, pushing me deeper into the room.

I planted my feet, ready to resist, when I saw Phonetia

lighting a smudge pot. The sweet aroma of burning marijuana filled my senses. My vision reeled.

Careful, babe. Breathe short and shallow.

On the other side of the room, Doug carried another smudge pot. This one reeked of something else.

Blondie raised his weapon.

Scrap flashed bright red and stretched. From one eye blink to the next he changed from cute little imp to lethal weapon.

Even before he finished sharpening, I lashed out from behind Donovan, whacking three weapons out of slack hands.

Phonetia loosed her sharp blackberry arms, grabbing another rifle.

Oak and Cedar launched into a flying tackle that tumbled the entire bunch of startled men into a tangled heap.

I reversed my blade, scraping each demon tat with the tines, drawing blood. They writhed with inner fire of magic foiled. Or was that fouled?

Somehow Scrap managed to emerge from the blade just enough to spit into each of the wounds.

Imp spit.

A powerful antibiotic against a demon tag. Poison to all else. *Borrowed the idea from E.T.*

Wild screeches and howls pierced the drug haze swirling around the room.

The demon tats no longer protected them.

Gollum whipped out plastic zip strips. The boys snapped them in place.

And it was over before I had time to breathe.

I didn't have to kill anyone and I didn't have to bring down a band of criminals alone.

My Tess sort of wilts. Working magic takes a lot of energy and she just loosed some pretty powerful juju.

I'm tired for her, but in better shape for all the ambrosia I ate. The food, not that awful ink tainted blood on the wrists of the bad guys. Humans don't taste all that great at the best of times. Lightly spiced with demon makes it worse.

I'm still spitting out the acrid bile of it while Oak, Cedar, and Doug haul the bad guys off in the wooden wheel barrel to their little drug farm. Donovan helps with the heavy lifting—keeping an eye on the boys, watching for signs of Doreen in any of them.

Teams of bad guys have beaten a pretty heavy and careless path to their marijuana patch. Seems that now the dark elf is dead and his magic negated, the natural paths in the forest have opened on their own. The stupid minions trusted the Nörglein's magic too much.

Don't they know that super villains always either get killed at the end of the movie, or they betray and sacrifice their employees? If the minions had half an ounce of the wits they were born with, they'd have a backup plan.

Donovan pauses in the work long enough to call in a report to the police about the marijuana patch and how to find it.

The girls find Sean's clothes in the wardrobe and pour him into them. He's still singing, but quieter now, more maudlin and keeping closer to in tune.

I said closer, not all the way there yet.

Then the girls open both the front and back doors wide and prop them open. The air starts to clear of the heady mixture of drugs.

They've done this before.

Meanwhile, Tess wraps an arm around one of the tree trunk sized bedposts and concentrates on staying upright. She pretends she's supervising. Mostly she's just watching the others do what has to be done. They don't need her direction anymore.

Feeling useless is preying on her energy as much as the huge expenditure of magic.

Then Gollum creeps up to her and falls to his knees. "Oh, God, Tess, I had no idea I hurt you so badly. I am so very sorry. How can you forgive me?" He hangs his head.

Tess tangles her fingers in his fine, silver gilt hair and whispers, "Because I love you."

We returned to the con en masse. I wasn't much interested in the crowds and party atmosphere, but Gollum convinced me I should stop in for a few moments on the way to my car, at least to catch the last of Holly's concert. I revived a little

while we trekked back through the tunnels toward civilization. The farther away I got from the drugs and the Nörglein's lair the better I felt.

Even Sean stumbled along with us, growing more sober with each step, but still strung out.

Someone had to drive him home. Not me. Maybe Squishy and Julia could do that.

The rain had stopped by the time we emerged from the tunnels through the basement of an old department store that filled an entire block. Fitful clouds allowed a waning sliver of a moon to peek through. I glanced toward the river. A slender trail of silver snaked along the black water.

"An end and a beginning," I whispered, reaching for Gollum's hand. "The prophecy fulfilled."

As we all trooped into the hotel by one of the back doors I heard Cedar speak behind me. "I'll go with you tonight, Oak. I'll stay a short while only. You promised that if I helped you remove Father, the forest would be mine."

"I'll abide by my promise," Oak replied. He sounded very adult and honorable. "Explore the possibilities of help before you cut all ties to humans."

Donovan stopped short and turned toward the boys. One side of his mouth tugged upward. "That's Doreen's boy. Oak. I know it," he whispered to me.

"Don't bet on it. Mr. Surly and Selfish better fits the definition of a Damiri, if you ask me," I replied.

Donovan acted as if he didn't hear me.

"I don't see why we can't all continue living in the cave as a family. Our own family," Cedar continued to whine. "The girls are safe from Father now."

"But are they safe from you?" Doug asked so quietly I had to strain to hear him.

Cedar shut up.

"You know I just pretended to be gay to make the dark elf mad," Doug said on a laugh. Then he sobered. "And so I wouldn't have to fulfill his expectations of me." His glance lingered lovingly on his sisters. "I'd never hurt them. Ever. You should have shown more courage and creativity to defy the old bastard, Cedar."

Lights and noise and crowds assailed my eyes and ears the moment we stepped from the quiet corridor into the lobby.

"I thought it was later," I said, suddenly tired again. "I expected all the excitement to have died down."

"It's only seven-thirty. We've been gone about two hours," Gollum replied. He'd kept his arm about my waist most of the trip, letting me lean on him until I had enough strength to manage on my own. He's good about that sort of thing.

The noise that had blindsided me turned out to be applause for Holly. Seven-thirty. She'd only been singing for half an hour.

As I watched, she signaled for Malcolm Levi to join her on stage. He bounded up the three steps and took her hand in both of his. The audience went wild. I winced at the noise.

Then Holly crooned a low note filled with longing and promise. I recognized the chords she plucked from her lap harp. She sang sweetly of new love, innocent love. Malcolm picked up the chorus. Together they sang the ballad from the CD.

Haunting chords echoed but did not match the love theme from his movie. I knew Holly had composed that song. For him.

The entire audience sighed with content.

Holly had my mother's talent. Her voice became more than a memory. She made the music a fully shared experience.

Donovan led us all toward the garden café, ordering coffee and sandwiches all around. The girls amended that to herbal tea for them.

I sank gratefully into the chair Gollum held out for me. With the special emotions of the song filling the high domed area, I found myself leaning into him, cherishing his warmth and treasuring the affection that surged between us.

Squishy and Julia with Sophia and then Doreen joined us, adding a second table to our crowded group. Sophia raised her arms to me from the confines of her high chair. She looked tired, verging on cranky, upset that her mother had left her for so long with strangers.

I brought her into my lap and let her suck her fingers while clinging to her blankie as I stroked her dark hair.

The ballad came to an end and our coffee arrived. I drank greedily. Squishy plied cup after cup into Sean. But he fell asleep with his head on crossed arms on the table halfway through the third cup. Scrap made another beer and orange juice disappear in short order.

Julia shook her head in amazement. "Pat says I have to read your book to understand this," she said.

We all laughed a little nervously. At this rate, Scrap wouldn't remain a secret much longer. I needed to do something about that, but my brain was too tired to know what.

"Um, Pat, where did the nickname Squishy come from?" I asked, just to have something else to think about.

"My brothers," she replied. "Patricia became Pasquisha when they wanted to make me mad. That morphed into Squishy. It's a useful on-line and con handle." She shrugged and added sugar to Julia's coffee.

"Mr. Levi and I will be available for autographs here on stage at the conclusion of the masquerade, coming up next," Holly said into her microphone. Before the audience could react she launched into a rousing piece that nearly required rhythmic clapping and stomping feet from everyone within earshot.

"You have a way with my daughter," Lucia said, coming up behind me.

I started, then forced my nerves back into calm order.

"She misses you," I replied. I knew I should relinquish her to her mother one last time, but the precious weight of her against my arms felt more natural than I wanted to admit. I needed to hold on to each moment like this as long as possible. I'd never have a baby of my own. Not if I had to give it up to the Powers That Be, much as the Nörglein's victims had their babies stolen from them.

Sophia whimpered and I stuck a bottle into her mouth. Instantly she settled.

"I have decided. You need to sign these papers now. Not tomorrow after the baptism as I planned. Now." Lucia threw a fat manila envelope on the table in front of me.

"What is that?"

"Sign it. You may read it later."

"No way. I know how you put traps and clauses subject to misinterpretation into legal shenanigans." I tried to reach for the envelope but found my hands full of Sophia.

Gollum, bless him, withdrew a stack of legal size documents, several stapled together.

"This first one is the formal adoption of Sophia Maria

Teresa Continelli by Teresa Louise Noncoiré," he read, peering over his glasses at the fine print.

"Agreed," I sighed. Tonight. In a few moments, as soon as I put my signature on that paper, she'd be mine.

Sophia popped the bottle out of her mouth and fussed.

I jammed the nipple back between her teeth before her protests became a wail louder than the crowd.

"It is for the best, Tess," Lucia said, pulling another chair up to our table. "I like my life in Las Vegas. I like midnight hours and Goth parties. I like the taste of blood. That is no way to raise a child. She has never tasted blood. She has never tasted meat. I want a real family for her. You are the closest I have to a relative. I want you to raise my daughter and never tell her about who and what I am until I deem fit." She produced an onyx fountain pen, unscrewed the top and handed it to me. It looked an awful lot like the pens used by the Powers That Be when they needed a signature in blood. "Sign and the child is safe with you."

I inspected the pen for traces of blood on the nib. Sure enough, a bit of rusty brown clung to the point. If I signed, with or without my own blood, Lucia was bound to keep the agreement. If she backed out or broke it in any way, her blood would boil and she'd end up facing the Powers That Be.

"Lucia, you were the one who told me, practically ordered me, to remain alone, focused and angry enough to complete the jobs the Universe hands me."

"Si," she sighed. "But now the Universe hands you a new task. You proved tonight that you can quell demons without violence. You can protect your children and still care for them. A new path opens for you, Warrior of the Celestial Blade."

"We'll see." I nodded for Gollum to read the next clump of documents.

"This establishes a rather substantial trust fund for Sophia naming you as trustee." He read the pages rapidly. "Fairly standard setup. Interest to be used for normal household expenses and education—including extra artistic endeavors like ballet and horseback riding. Fairly liberal wording. This one is safe to sign. If you choose."

"If *we* choose to adopt Sophia." Though how I could give

her up at this point, I didn't know. "What's the last set of pages?"

"That's the deed to a house!" Donovan proclaimed, reading upside down. "I don't have to read the particulars to recognize the format."

"Donovan is correct," Lucia said, still holding the pen out. "I had to foreclose on the dwelling and repair large sections of it. That is what brought me to Portland originally."

"Foreclose?" I asked hesitantly, wondering what the family who had lived there was doing for shelter without it.

"I took the house as collateral on a *legitimate* business loan. A trusted employee franchised certain aspects of my, um, enterprises. Unfortunately, the economic climate in Portland is different from Las Vegas. He did not succeed. I gave him a year longer than I should. Do not worry that I have evicted children. The man is single, and I suspect guilty of embezzlement. No one steals from me and goes unscathed. I have sent his accounts—both sets of them—to the DA and the IRS."

"I know that address, Tess," Gollum said under his breath. He swallowed heavily. "The president of my college lives on that cul de sac. The house is huge, mock Tudor brick with a three-car garage. Two acres is the standard lot in that neighborhood. This one is bigger."

"And a guest house you can use as an office to get away from the children while you work, Tess," Lucia prompted.

"I can't . . . it's too generous."

Sophia yawned and snuggled down for a much needed nap. I held her close.

"The house is in trust for Sophia," Lucia said. "I'm not abandoning my child."

"Let me see those. I'll tell you if it's safe to sign." Donovan grabbed the entire stack. He and Doreen bent their heads over them.

"She's really smart about papers and stuff," Doug said around a mouthful of a veggie and cheese sandwich. He'd taken out the ham and packed half his salad between slices of bread. The girls had done the same. No problem getting them to eat their vegetables.

I bet Doreen knew her way around legal documents if

she drew up the prenuptial agreement she'd forced on Donovan. A vague memory of my husband, Dill, came to mind, of him explaining to me that while he'd pursued his doctorate in geology, his sister had gone to law school. But she hadn't bothered to take the Bar.

Her parents probably put a stop to that just to keep her close.

"The documents are amazingly straightforward, without hidden provisions or sleeper clauses. Not one vague word subject to misinterpretation in them," Doreen pronounced. "I'd say it's safe to sign, if you want to adopt the child." She touched her own belly possessively.

"Gollum, if *we* do this, we'll start our life together with four children. They've been seriously abused. They'll need counseling, special schooling, and all the unconditional love we can pour into them. Do you truly want that? Can you do that?" I would. Gladly. Oh, yes, I wanted them all with every molecule in my being.

"Yes, Tess. That is what I want." Gollum rested his hand over mine and fixed his gaze on me, glasses halfway down his nose so I could see his eyes clearly and know his sincerity. "And I look forward to adding a couple of our own children to the family. I want all our children to be close to Cedar and Oak too. I don't mind if Pat and Julia wander in and out at odd hours. I want our lives overflowing with children, with family, and laughter and love."

I took a deep breath and shot a silent query to Scrap.

The more the merrier. Remember that empty kitchen table in Cape Cod? Remember how often you regretted you hadn't a chance to fill it with children? Now's your chance, babe. Grab it!

"We'll baby-sit during your honeymoon, if you'll watch the boys during ours," Doreen offered. "Both Cedar and Oak are coming home with us tonight."

"Okay. We'll do it."

The entire table loosed a collective sigh of relief.

I grabbed the pen from Lucia and affixed my name (ink only, I didn't need blood to bind me to this) in a dozen places, then passed each paper to Gollum so that he could add his name and signature and become part of the legal process. Then Donovan witnessed each page. So did Pat.

"Now there is one chore left," I sighed.

No, Tess. No way. You can't do that. This is the worst plan ever. Worse than . . . worse than . . . you know what it's worse than.

I ignored Scrap. He'd go along with me. Because it was the only way I could find the happily ever after Holly promised in her love ballad.

Chapter 51

Oregon was the first state to levy a gas tax to take advantage of tourist dollars.

"I CAN'T BELIEVE YOU TALKED ME into this," Donovan whispered as he surveyed the vast emptiness of the chat room.

"I can't believe you finally convinced me the Kajiri demons need a home world," I replied, barely breathing. As often as Scrap had dragged me through here, I never quite got used to the lack of sensory input. All white, no direction, no dimension, no sound other than my heartbeat and our quiet words that seemed to bounce and magnify.

The lump of beryllium in my pocket weighed three times as much here as it did back home.

"That's just it, I didn't convince you. The kids did. You see in them the need for an occasional time out, away from the pressures of humanity."

"I hope the kids are safe while we're here." I chewed my lower lip, wondering how Gollum and Doreen were managing with six children in my tiny condo.

"Don't worry. Gollum and Doreen are sensible and smart. They'll be okay, even if you and I don't make it back alive."

And if we didn't make it back? I couldn't, wouldn't believe such a thing was possible.

But I'd made contingency plans and updated my will at the last moment.

"Will you guys shut up!" Scrap ground out.

Another thing I never got used to, Scrap bigger than me, and solid, with a deep voice. A new array of warts adorned his wing joints. I spotted a special one on his pug nose and another on the tip of his tail—highly prized locations for Imps.

I'd worked him hard these last few weeks.

"There's a Cthulu demon on guard today," Scrap added. "You really don't want to get on his bad side."

"Don't the demon guards always work in pairs?" I asked.

"Cthulus don't need a partner. They're mean enough on their own."

We tiptoed past the sort-of-squid shape with more head and arms than the ocean-bound critters I'd seen on TV. It kept its eyes closed, supposedly sleeping on duty.

I didn't trust it. It probably had six or more layers of eyelids and could look asleep while still having four more steps to go to blot out the flat light.

He, or his kind, had let me pass before. I bowed politely to it. "We're going to the Powers That Be. That's allowed," I said.

An extra eyelid winked at me. *Allowed. Not recommended.*

"You know, of course, that very few people who get called before the Powers That Be survive the encounter," Donovan reminded.

"You did."

"Barely."

"I did, once before. But then I sought them out, they didn't drag me in to face justice."

"They don't like their privacy disturbed."

"Maybe. Maybe not. Ever think they might get lonely trapped in their courtroom for aeons at a time?"

"Impossible."

I shrugged.

Scrap planted himself in front of the ornate door with the huge brass knocker. "You can still back out, babe. I'll cover your ass."

I centered myself to find my courage. "I have to do

this." Then I lifted the ring above the lion's head and let it fall.

The brass bonged loudly, bouncing back for a second clang and then a third. The noise echoed through the vast white space, reverberating down all the hidden corridors and through all the closed doors to other dimensions.

"No privacy when you call on the Powers That Be," Donovan quipped.

The door swung inward slowly, silently, revealing a dim room, lit by unseen fixtures with a reddish hue. Spooky. Alarming to the uninitiated.

Stage dressing.

I gathered my determination, firmed my chin, and marched forward until I stood before the long judicial bench that looked like a solid ten-foot mahogany wall.

Scrap cowered beside the door. Today, he was only my escort, not willing to be a part of these proceedings.

"Anybody home?" I called up to the seven empty seats.

"Not so loud!" Donovan admonished. "They might hear you."

"That's the idea. I think they're more afraid of us than we of them."

"Not very likely."

I raised my eyebrows at him in a parody of his sardonic cocking of one brow.

"Who dares approach these hallowed halls?" a deep voice boomed from above us.

"If you don't know then you aren't very observant or don't have a good memory."

"Tess, careful. You need to be respectful."

"No, I don't. I have something they want very badly. And they are going to have to bargain hard for it." I fingered the cool ball of beryllium in my pocket.

I heard a group gasp above my head.

The judicial bench sank back to normal size, about level with my shoulder. All seven of the Powers That Be arranged themselves behind, including a larger version of the Cthulu on guard in the chat room. This guy looked as big as the glacier on top of Mt. Rainier, the first place I'd spotted him.

Maybe he was a god and not a demon. What's the difference if he's from a different dimension preying on innocents in mine?

"Why have you come?" asked a heavily cloaked figure from deep within its cowl.

I just made out burning embers where the eyes should be.

"The last time I was here, you made me sign in blood that I would give up my firstborn child to you in return for the safety of my father and end the ownership dispute over the piece of neutral ground where his home now sits." The home that had once been mine.

"Yes," intoned another voice. This one almost feminine.

A piece of parchment fluttered out of the air to land on the desk. I recognized my signature in rusty brown dried blood.

Beside me, Donovan shuddered. He tried to slink behind me. He'd signed one of those documents too, promising never to reveal his origins. He hadn't told me he'd fallen from being a gargoyle. I figured that out on my own.

"You signed in blood. You cannot reverse the agreement," a third voice said. This one was high and reedy. Impossible to discern gender or species.

"I don't want to reverse it. I still need protection for my father from rogue demons who will seek to use the neutral energies of that land to open a new portal that bypasses the chat room. I want to exchange the price of that protection."

"Impossible," a group denial.

"You have nothing we want more than your firstborn," that was the first deep voice.

"Oh?" I held up the crystal ball. The milky swirls deep inside the mineral matrix caught the red hues of the lights, swished them around and turned them into sparkling faery dust.

The scintillating pinpricks of light shifted and formed the image of a gateway arch framed in bright flowers.

"What is that?" asked the feminine voice. She pushed back her hood and leaned over the bench for a better look. Her head remained in shadow. Impossible to tell her true form, but I thought she might have been a faery originally.

"A portal," I replied.

"We have many portals available to us," said the reedy voice.

I caught a whiff of fish from his breath. Did he eat fish, or did he have fins?

"Not like this one. The crystal ball opens a doorway that doesn't exist anywhere else."

"Impossible."

"Ever wonder what happened to all the energy that drained out of Faery until I returned the kidnapped dancers where they belonged and sealed that portal?" I stared longingly into the crystal ball a moment longer, then reluctantly made to return it to my pocket; taking it off the bargaining table. Or at least threatening to.

"Wait, please," the former faery pleaded. She reached a long-fingered, elegant hand out for the treasure.

I kept the ball firmly in my own hand.

"A new dimension?" asked the androgynous voice.

"Yes," I replied. "A new dimension that only the possessor of this crystal ball can gain access to. A new dimension ready to be shaped by a single mind."

Donovan shifted from foot to foot. I touched his arm, trying to convey the need for a solid, confident front. We had to let these pettifogging bureaucrats know that we could walk away from this deal without changing a thing.

"The crystal ball belongs to us," the deep voice announced.

The squid reached a long tentacle across the bench, ready to pluck the thing from my hand.

I closed my fingers around it and pocketed it for real this time. They'd only get it by stealing it. Wouldn't put that past them.

"Not yet it doesn't." I turned on my heel and headed toward the door, dragging Donovan with me.

"What do you want for the ball?" the faery asked.

"I want the dimension opened to the Kajiri as a home world. A place where they can retreat when the demands of their half-breed status grow too heavy. A place where they can be either human or demon, they can succumb to their instincts and not hurt innocents."

"We agree," a new voice interjected. This one sounded old and wavery, like the oldest person in the Universe weighed in.

I fingered the ball in my pocket, thinking.

"What else?" asked the old one. He (she?) sounded almost human in tonal quality.

"If I entrust this ball into your keeping, I want to exchange possession of it for my firstborn child."

Donovan gasped at my audacity. "It's true?" he whispered.

"Of course it's true."

"How could you make such a bargain?"

"I had nothing to lose. At the time I knew I'd never marry you and Gollum had gone back to his wife. I didn't think I'd have the opportunity to bear a child, except by artificial insemination and I'm a bit too Catholic to do that."

"Oh." He sounded deflated. "I never had a prayer of winning you, did I?"

"Nope."

He heaved a sigh of resignation. Then he turned back to the Powers That Be, squared his shoulders and approached the bench with pride and dignity. This was the man I'd longed for him to grow into. But he didn't value *me* enough for him to become honorable for me. He remained a manipulative, lying cheat.

Or was that a teenager in an adult body?

"Your honors, I have worked long and hard to find a home world for Kajiri, half human, half demon, belonging in neither world. I respectfully request the duty of administering this new dimension."

"Granted," the faery agreed hastily, before the others had a chance to argue for the sake of arguing.

"Possession of the ball must come to us first," fish breath demanded.

"How will I access this new dimension if you possess the ball?" Donovan asked. Back to Mr. Manipulation.

Seven heads bent in hooded consultation.

"We will send a representative there who will open a new portal and give you the key. That key may be revoked and the portal closed at any time for any reason," deep voice pronounced. "We keep the ball."

"You'll need to close the energy leaks from all over the Universe," I reminded them. "One of those leaks is from the cracks in the faery ring that took Prince Mikhail home."

"The ring that entombs a live imp inside a diamond?" the former faery asked.

"Yes. Seems that every time it changes ownership, the

diamond cracks a tiny bit, allowing the black imp to foully manipulate the wearer of the ring."

"Done!" the old one announced.

"What about my father's safety?" I demanded, ignoring the squid's twitching tentacle tip.

Another longer consultation among the shadowy hoods.

"In return for the ball, we grant your request. New agreements must be signed, one for each of you."

"I don't suppose we can use regular ink?"

"No."

Epilogue

The town of Bridal Veil is now home only to the waterfall that once powered a lumber mill and gave the town its name, a community church, a cemetery, and a post office. The number of wedding invitations sent there for postmarking each year more than pay the postmaster's salary and support the post office.

"CAN WE GET A DOG, MOM?" E.T. asked. She bounded out of Gollum's old van—the only vehicle between us with enough room for two adults, three teens, and a baby in an unwieldy car seat—without waiting for an answer. She carried Gandalf, Gollum's ancient long-haired, white cat, over her shoulder.

Better a dog than that evil cat. I won't share digs with a cat! Scrap insisted from his perch on the dashboard. He sneezed for emphasis, reminding me of his allergies.

Since I'd inherited his lactose intolerance, I too might become allergic to the white lump of fur Gollum held so dear to his heart.

I ignored Scrap's complaints, just sitting and staring out the window at the house. Three stories and a basement, interesting windows, protrusions and nooks at every turn, gables, crosshatched brickwork, everything I wanted in a home.

And big. Six bedrooms, three baths, formal dining room and parlor, family room upstairs and in the finished basement. Plenty of room for three teens, a toddler, and however many children Gollum and I wanted to have together.

Phonetia followed her sister out of the car and headed right for the rose garden on the far side of the driveway. She started deadheading the soggy and spent blossoms, piling the debris neatly at the edge of the circular garden space. She swept the stone bench clear of leaf litter, then leaned over the edge of a small fountain, peering into the dirty water.

"At least we won't have to hire a gardener to tame two point eight seven acres," Gollum muttered.

Doug piled out next, but he took the time to release Sophia from her car seat and carry her along the brick pathway toward the front door. When she fussed to get down, he let her wrap her tiny fists around his fingers for support so she could "walk."

Scrap hovered nearby, anxious that the toddler might fall and scrape her knees. Less likely in her pink corduroy rompers than the frilly dresses Lucia had insisted upon.

At moments like this, I thought Scrap loved the children as much as I did. But he hated Gollum's cat.

"Have you noticed how much the kids enjoyed the music at the con?" Gollum asked.

"How could I avoid noticing? They sang Holly's music all day yesterday, adding their own harmonies and bizarre rhythms," I groaned.

"Maybe we should help them form a garage band. All five of them. It will give them focus, and a creative outlet for the anger and frustration they are bound to feel over and above normal teenage angst."

"Good idea. Later. I'm too tired to deal with it today."

"You have the keys?" Gollum asked. He didn't seem in a hurry to leave the quiet car.

I held up the key ring shaped like a faery in flight with four shiny new keys. I knew they'd all fit into the pristine locks. A huge yawn escaped my mouth rather than words.

After twelve hours of sleep Saturday night, I'd shuffled through Sunday's baptism ritual and the wind down of the con, barely aware of what I was doing. Another twelve hours of sleep last night and I thought I might begin functioning again.

I could use another thermos of coffee.

"We've only got an hour to explore before we leave to meet Steve and Allie at the title company. Their flight is on time," Gollum said consulting his phone-that-did-everything.

"It's just . . . just surreal, everything falling into place like it did."

"I know. My divorce papers got filed this morning and my lawyer said that since there's no contest, the house belongs to the college, we each have our own money, nothing to split, it should only take a couple of weeks to get an appointment with a judge. Then you and I can get married and live here with *our* children."

"Valentine's Day?" Three months away; plenty of time for inevitable legal delays. Hope brightened my mind and banished the last of the cobwebs. "April Fools Day might be more appropriate considering how we live our lives."

"Whatever you want. Put together the wedding you've always dreamed of. Invite everyone you've ever met. I don't care. I just want to be with you. Forever." He kissed me long and lingering.

I didn't want to let go of him long enough to breathe. Sophia's squeals of delight dragged my attention away from how he nibbled my lower lip.

"Let's go see what kind of kitchen I'm going to have. MoonFeather and Lilly are coming for Thanksgiving. I want to put on the biggest and best holiday feast for the whole west coast clan."

Holding hands we ambled up the path toward the front door. Morning sunshine broke through the scattering clouds, turning the last of the raindrops trapped on the grass and in the cups of dying flowers to crystal prisms.

"Faery dust," I gasped.

"Not quite," a strangely accented male voice said from the region of my elbow.

I whirled, ready to fight. I hadn't done much else for the last three months. "Mickey!" Tension and anxiety fell away as I threw my arms around the crown prince of Faery.

The silver circlet around his brow had turned into three gold strands twisted and knotted intricately.

"Mom, who's he? I thought the con was over?" E.T. asked, returning to my side. No cat on her shoulder. A lump of long white hair on the flagstone porch must be the geriatric beast. "People aren't supposed to wear costumes out in public."

I'd drilled that one into the girls yesterday when they fell in love with space pirate uniforms.

"Costume?" Mickey's eyes twinkled. He gazed in mock puzzlement at his gold tights and white on gold brocade tunic. Even his blue butterfly wings had shifted to gold with just a hint of blue and white sparkles on the edges. "This is no costume. This is what I wear to work," he laughed.

"Huh?" Phonetia chimed in. She left her work with the roses to join us.

Doug returned from the covered porch with Sophia in his arms. "He wasn't at the con. I'd remember those wings. They're cool. How do they attach? And those ears. Those aren't gelatin attachments."

"No, they're the real thing," I told the children. "Prince Mikhail of Faery, meet the children."

Mickey bowed formally. The kids mimicked him. Sort of.

Hey, Mickey, what's with all the gold tarting up your outfit? Scrap flitted from the top of my head to Mickey's shoulder and back again.

"I'm afraid I have been promoted to King of Faery," Mickey sighed as if shouldering a great burden. "After rescuing the kidnapped dancers—with your help of course, Lady Tess and Professor Gollum—my people decided I was better suited for the job than my stepmother who allowed the kidnapping to take place."

"I think your people chose wisely," I said. "Thank you for telling us the news in person. But that is not why you came, I think." I nodded my head in respect.

"May we have a moment of privacy? You and Professor Gollum, Lady Tess?" Mickey asked.

"Certainly. Phonetia, take the keys, you and the others can go choose your own bedrooms. But wipe your feet on the mat. There's new carpet and tile so take your shoes off before you go beyond the entrance."

"Shoes should always be left outside," E.T. replied. She grabbed the keys out of my hand and ran to the door with them.

Doug and Sophia followed.

"I'd rather finish grooming the roses," Phonetia said, looking back to her project.

"A fine idea, Miss Phonetia. I will walk with Lady Tess and the Professor to the gazebo in the back. This should not take long." Mickey bowed again and gestured for Gollum and me to lead the way around the house on a different brick path.

"We have a gazebo?" Would wonders never cease? I'd always wanted a gazebo. With roses climbing the arched entrance.

What's the latest gossip out of Faery? Scrap demanded to fill an awkward silence as we progressed past French doors and a wide side patio to a scraggly herb garden and then emerged into an expanse of overgrown lawn extending beyond another flagstone patio, complete with gas grill and sagging and saturated lawn furniture.

I could just see the roofline of the guest cottage beyond a blackberry thicket.

Gollum's eyes lit with excitement as he tried to veer toward the grill.

But it was the gazebo that captured my attention. It sat off to the side next to a deep goldfish pond. White paint flaked from the slats, but it looked sound, cozy, and inviting.

"Faery heals," Mickey said at last. He seemed weighed down with sadness. Worry added lines around his eyes and dimmed their sparkle. "Slowly. But we heal. The loss of energy from the previous crises caused much more damage than I thought possible."

"I'm sorry. Is there anything we can do to help?" I touched his hand in sympathy.

"You have done more than could be expected of any human, Lady Tess." He mounted the three steps to the gazebo and sank onto a bench to the left of the entrance. Two-person benches circled a gas fueled fire pit made of more flagstones. I fell in love with the place. Dreams of sitting out here with my laptop on hot summer afternoons, or sharing a glass of scotch with Gollum on brisk autumn evenings with the fire going, almost took me away from dowdy reality.

"How long will the healing take?" I knew we couldn't replace the energy that had built a new dimension.

"Longer than I want to admit. I need to close Faery," Mickey said.

"I'm sorry," Gollum added. "Faery has always loaned brightness and joy to the other dimensions. Your loss is a huge loss to the Universe."

"The Powers That Be have removed the three demon ghettos from my dimension and housed them elsewhere. I don't know where. That has stopped a huge drain on our resources. They have healed the cracks in the imp diamond as well. But it isn't enough."

"What more can you do?" I asked. "I can give a few faeries space in my garden if they need it."

"That is not the problem, Lady Tess," Mickey flashed me a grin, reminding me of the lighthearted taxi driver who befriended me in Las Vegas. "I thank you for the offer but the solution is the opposite. We need to keep all of the faeries in Faery."

"That might be hard, since they are used to popping in and out at will," Gollum mused.

"Yes. And so I have closed the portals into and out of Faery. All except one." He twisted a ring around his finger idly, as if a long habit.

Everything in me stilled. He didn't twist the ring in agitation.

He can use the ring to open a portal! Scrap chortled. *I knew I smelled imp. The black imp is still imprisoned in the diamond.*

"An imp can go anywhere, anywhen," I said.

"This ring is a great temptation to my people. And to me," Mickey removed his fingers from the diamond that glittered more brightly than sunshine on raindrops. "I would enjoy visiting with you more often and longer, but I owe the entire realm of Faery my duty to remain there as long as it takes to heal the damage."

"What do you have in mind, King Mikhail?" Gollum asked solemnly. "That ring is an artifact of power. It requires protection. It also needs to be kept secret from the Universe at large, or many who would not use it wisely will covet it."

"I know. That is why I offer the ring to you, Lady Tess and Professor Gollum. I know of no one else who could protect it as it must be. You can hide it where no one will expect to find it."

Hey, with the ring we can whisk any bad guys off to Donovan's new dimension for a time out before they have a chance to threaten the kids. You can almost retire and I can baby-sit.

"And where would I hide this ring?" I asked almost fearfully. Power pulsed from the intricate gold work and large diamond like a huge magnetic field.

"In plain sight."

"Huh? I was thinking along the lines of Scrap's mum and the freeze-dried garbage dump of the Universe. The cold and the other powerful artifacts will mask it."

Nope, nothing can mask that kind of power. And a black imp in Imp Haven is just asking for trouble. He'll get more powerful in his home dimension. The ring needs subtle magic to make it look like it belongs where it is, Scrap lectured. He sounded like Gollum when he got wound up on a favorite topic.

"The most powerful of the subtle magics Scrap speaks of is love." Mickey looked from Gollum to me, the twinkle back in his eyes. "I freely gift this ring to both of you as an engagement token. Anyone looking for the ring will sense the power and assume it is you, Lady Tess and the love you share with the professor, not an artifact."

Before I could object he ripped the ring from his finger and placed it in Gollum's hand, gently closing his fingers around it.

"Now if Scrap will return me to my home, we will give you two a moment alone." Mickey rose to his majestic height.

Scrap landed on his shoulder. *Much as I'd like to stick around and eavesdrop, I think Mickey has the right idea. You ready, Mr. King?*

"Yes, Mr. Imp."

They disappeared in a showy blanket of scintillating mist. I thought I caught a glimpse of Scrap's face lingering in the swirling lights.

"Tess." Gollum got down on one knee in front of me and took my left hand in both of his. "I promised to do this. The time seems most appropriate. Tess, beloved, will you marry me?"

I had to swallow twice to get rid of the lump in my throat. "Yes," I whispered. "Yes!" I said louder. "Yes," I shouted loudly enough to draw children's faces to the windows above us and from around the corner to the rose garden.

"Yes!" I shouted with glee.

Then *my* Gollum gently slipped the ring on my finger. It snuggled behind the knuckle as if made for me.

Irene Radford

The Pixie Chronicles

Dusty Carrick lived in the small town of Skene Falls, Oregon, her entire life. And, like many of the local children, she played with "imaginary" Pixie friends in Ten Acre Woods.

But the Pixies are not imaginary at all, and Ten Acre Woods is their home. Now, the woods are in danger, and if it falls, the Pixies too will die. Only Thistle Down, exiled from her tribe and trapped inside a mortal woman's body, can save her people-as long as she can convince Dusty Carrick to help her before it's too late.

THISTLE DOWN
978-0-7564-0670-7

CHICORY UP
978-0-7564-0724-7

"Enjoyable romantic urban fantasy." —*Alternative Worlds*

To Order Call: 1-800-788-6262
www.dawbooks.com

DAW 208